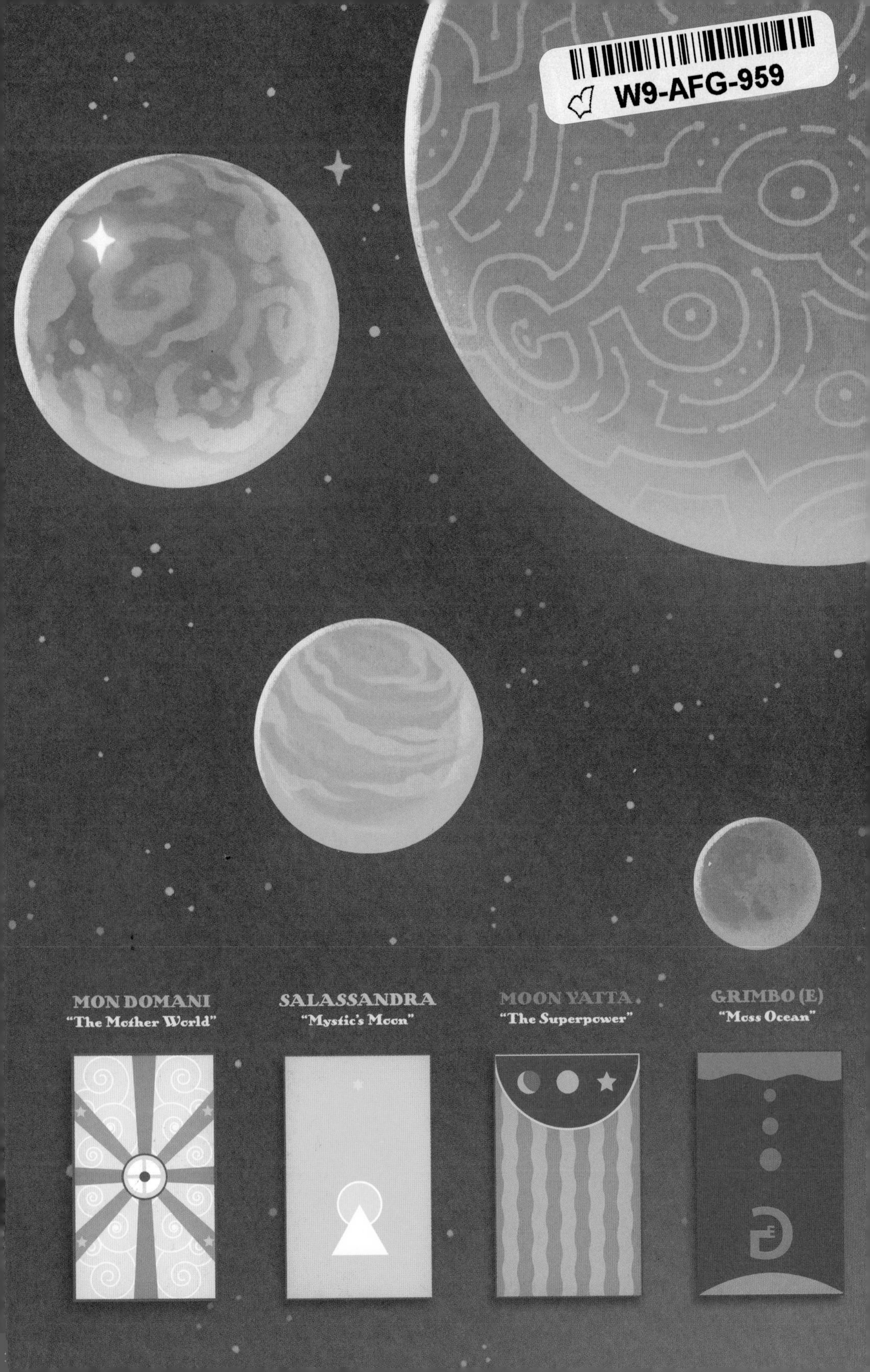
MON DOMANI
"The Mother World"
SALASSANDRA
"Mystic's Moon"
MOON YATTA
"The Superpower"
GRIMBO (E)
"Moss Ocean"

The Praise for 5Worlds Is Out of This World!

A New York Public Library Top Ten Best Books for Kids Selection

A *Publishers Weekly* Best Summer Book

A Junior Library Guild Selection

"A bang-zoom start to a series
that promises to be epic in both the classical
and internet senses of the word."
—*The New York Times Book Review*

★ "Sensitive writing, gorgeous artwork, and riveting plot."
—*Booklist*, **Starred Review**

★ "A dazzling interplanetary fantasy . . . that will easily appeal to
fans of *Naruto* or *Avatar: The Last Airbender*."
—*Publishers Weekly*, **Starred Review**

"Exquisitely imagined. . . . For kids who love fantasy and other-world adventures,
and for any fans of graphic novels, this book is a must-read."
—R. J. Palacio, #1 *New York Times* **bestselling author of** *Wonder*

"Epic action, adventure, and mystery will draw you in,
but the heartfelt characters and their seemingly impossible journey
will keep you turning the pages."
—Lisa Yee, **author of the DC Super Hero Girls™ series**

"This stellar team has created a gorgeous and entrancing world like no other!"
—Noelle Stevenson, *New York Times*
bestselling author of *Nimona*

"The beautiful illustrations will have
young readers flying through the pages."
—*Deseret News*

"A rare adventure."
—*Kirkus Reviews*

"Ends triumphantly and tantalizingly."
—*The Horn Book Magazine*

"Distinctly unique . . . it oozes with imagination and creativity."
—*Bam! Smack! Pow!*

"An intriguing beginning to what is sure to be a fascinating series."
—*BookRiot*

"I dare you not to get immediately caught up in Oona's epic tale!"
—*MuggleNet*

"Beautiful, with a vast array of characters and
creatures from the various worlds."
—*GeekDad*

"A magical adventure full of wisdom, humor, and enough girl power
to make you root for Oona in her quest to light the beacon."
—**Abigail, age 10**

"This book is great! I usually don't like graphic novels,
but this book changed my mind."
—**Lucius, age 9**

5 Worlds

BOOK 2

THE COBALT PRINCE

Mark
SIEGEL

Alexis
SIEGEL

Xanthe
BOUMA

Boya
SUN

Matt
ROCKEFELLER

Random House 🏠 New York

"Moons become wet and grow into planets.
Planets become bright and grow into suns.
Suns give and give and join the stars.
And stars . . . what are stars?"

—FROM MASTER ZELLE'S *THE BALLAD OF THE FIVE BEACONS*

PROLOGUE

SISTERS ARE FOREVER

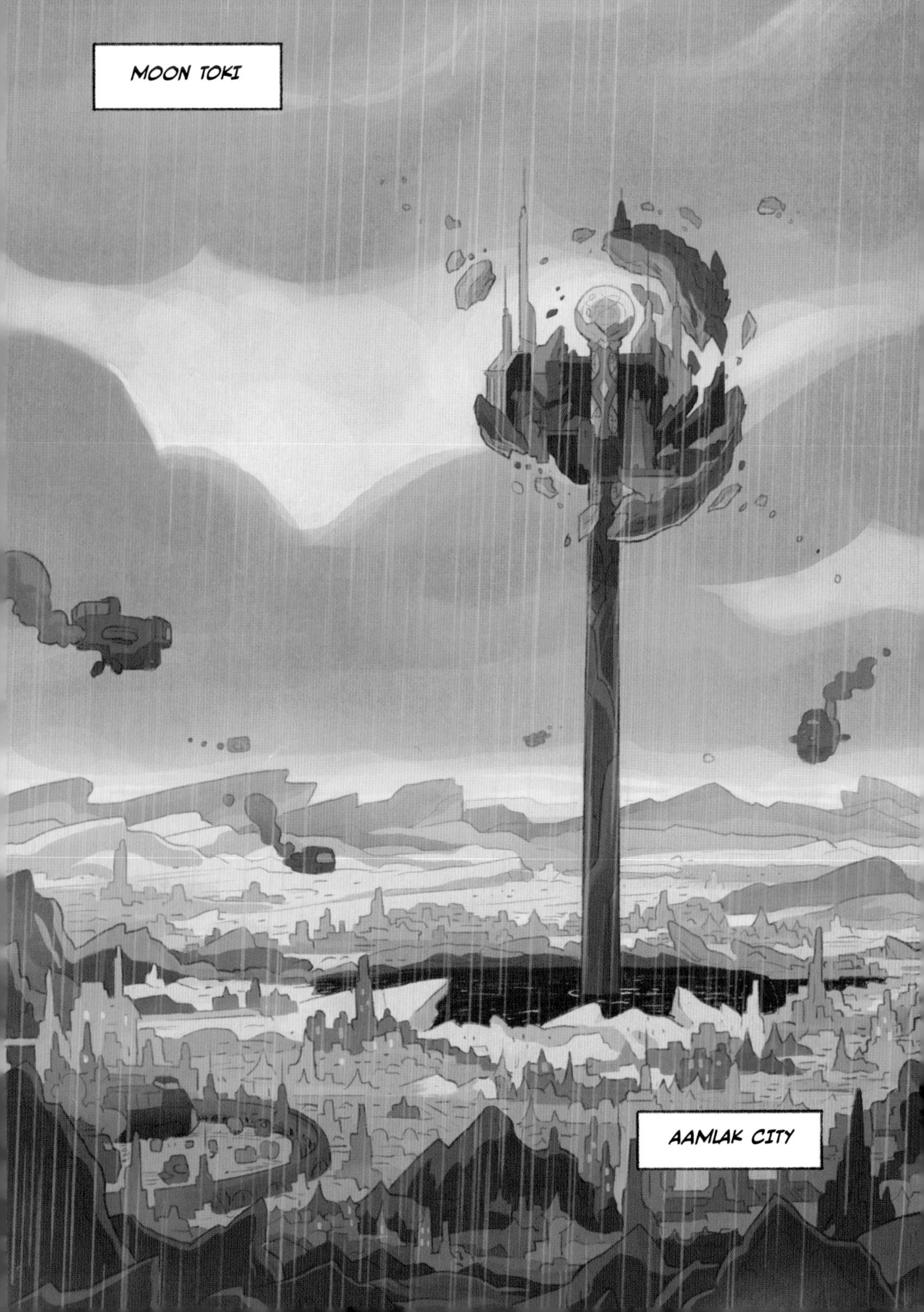
MOON TOKI
AAMLAK CITY

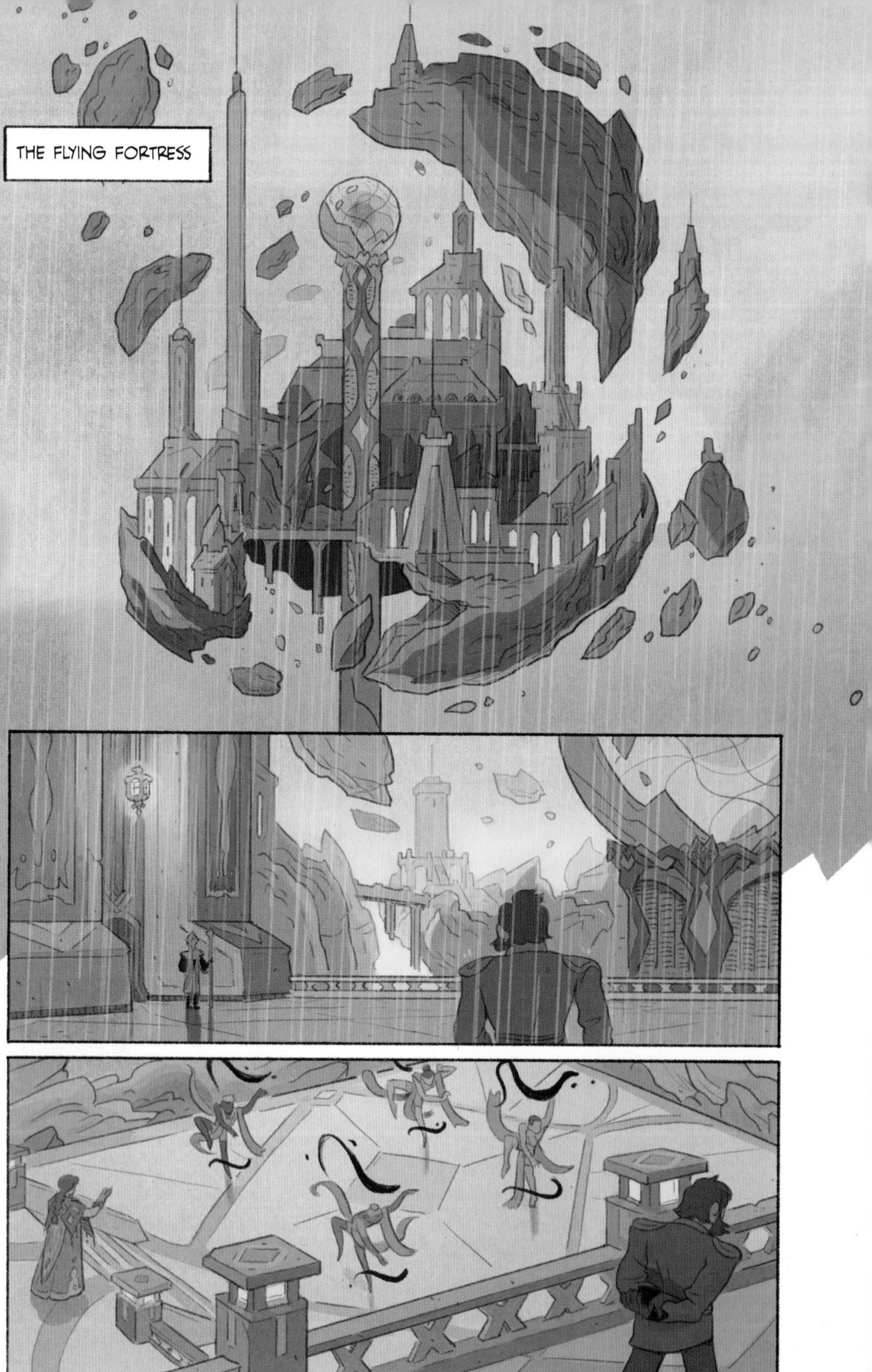
THE FLYING FORTRESS

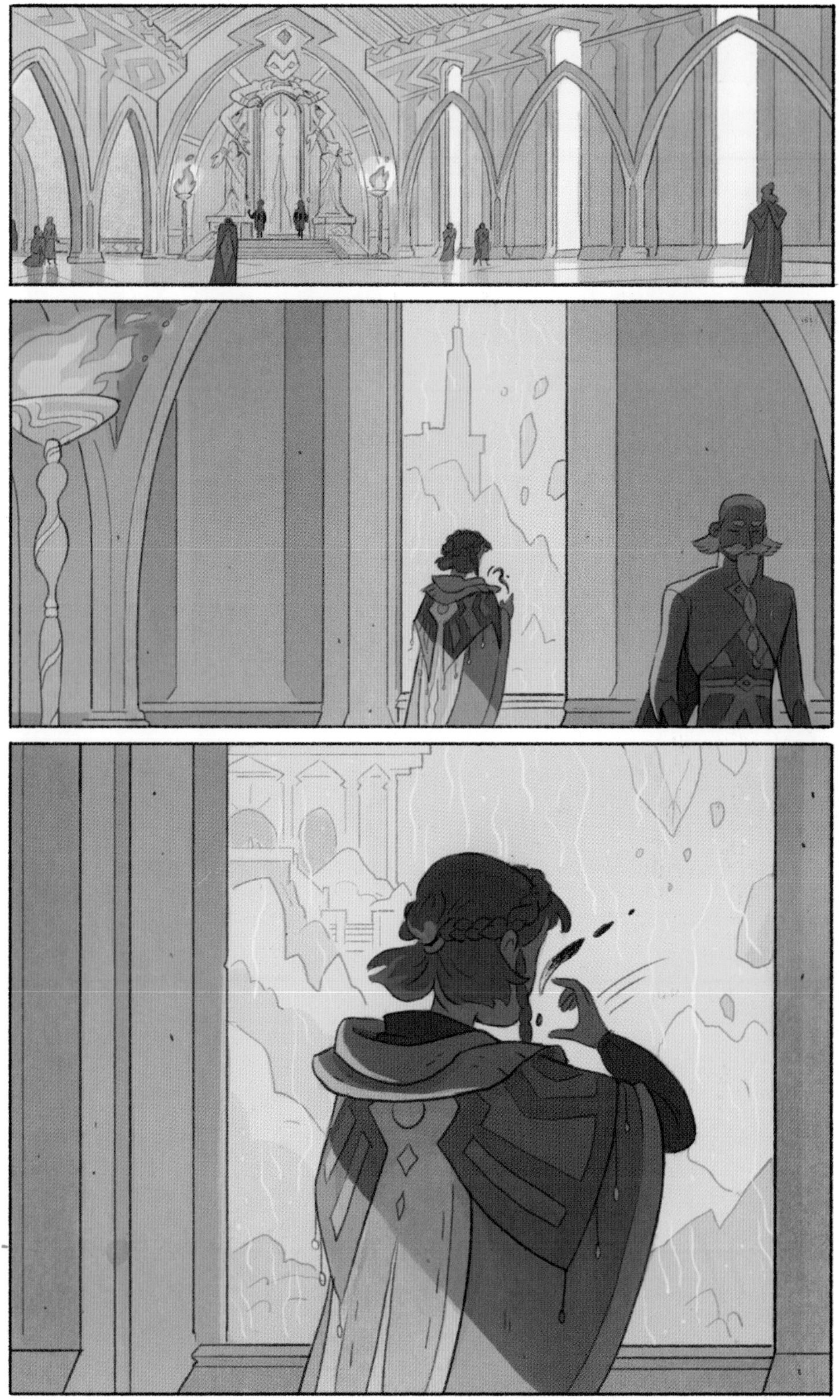

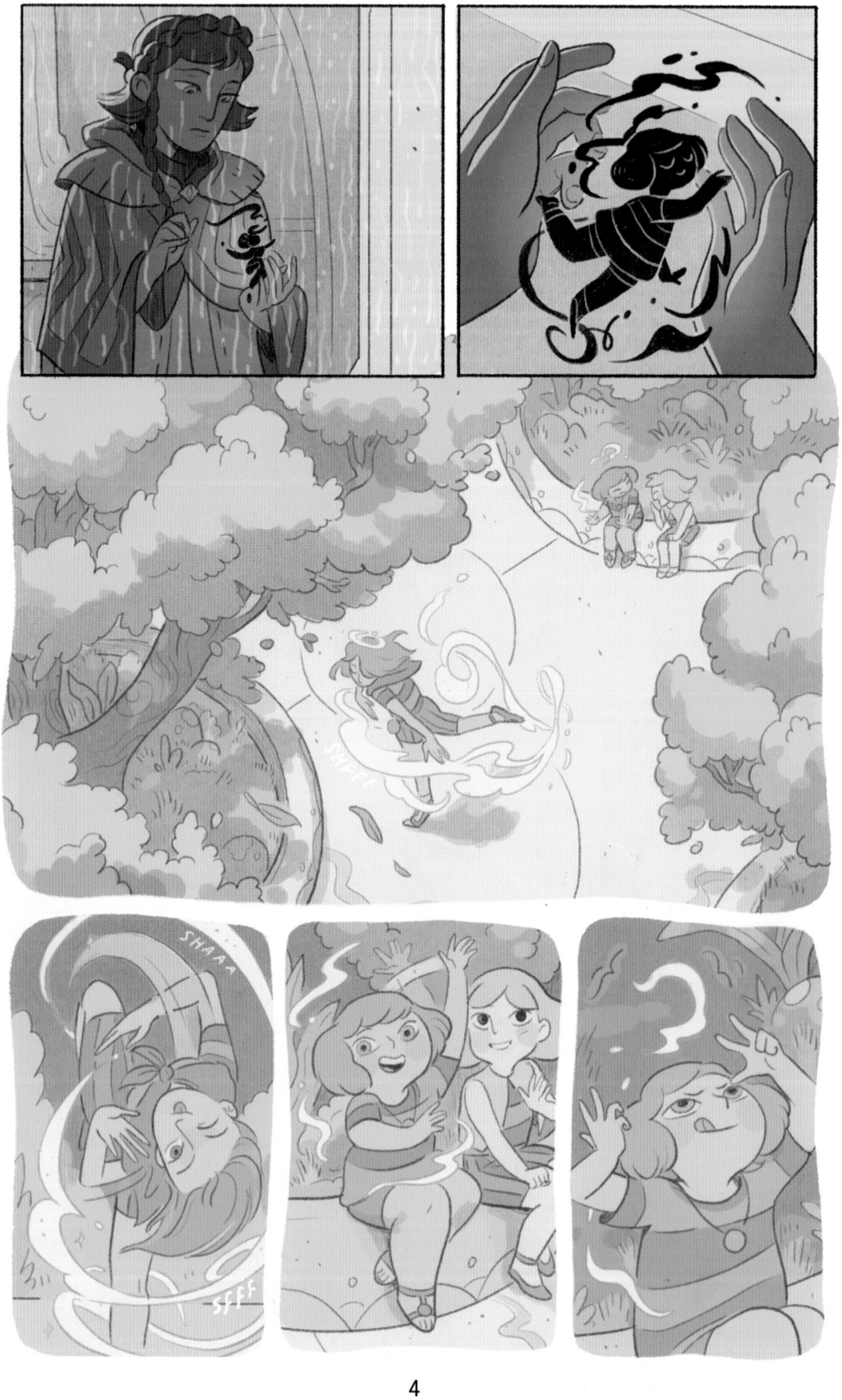
SHFFF
SHAAA
SFFF

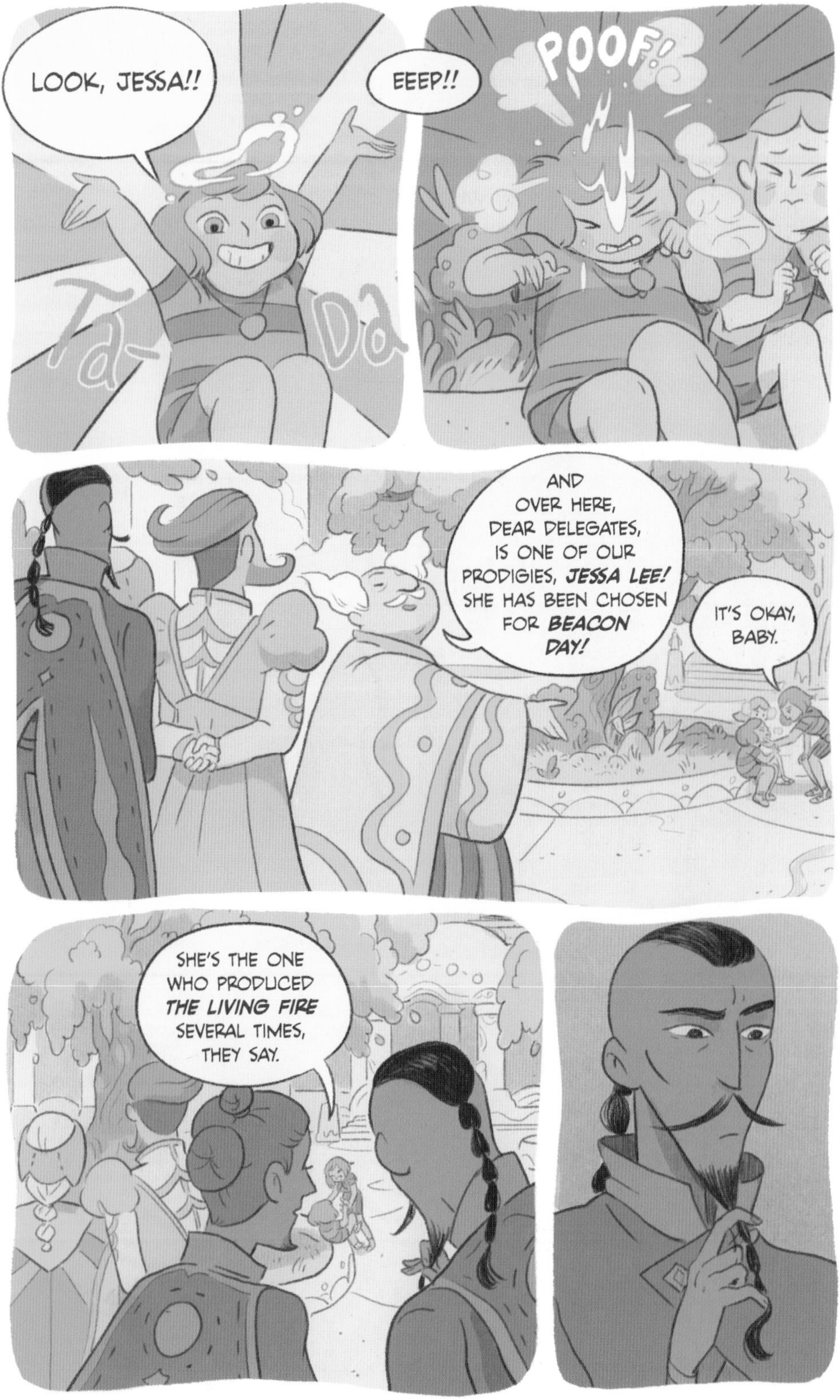
LOOK, JESSA!!
Ta-Da
EEEP!!
POOF!
AND OVER HERE, DEAR DELEGATES, IS ONE OF OUR PRODIGIES, JESSA LEE! SHE HAS BEEN CHOSEN FOR BEACON DAY!
IT'S OKAY, BABY.
SHE'S THE ONE WHO PRODUCED THE LIVING FIRE SEVERAL TIMES, THEY SAY.

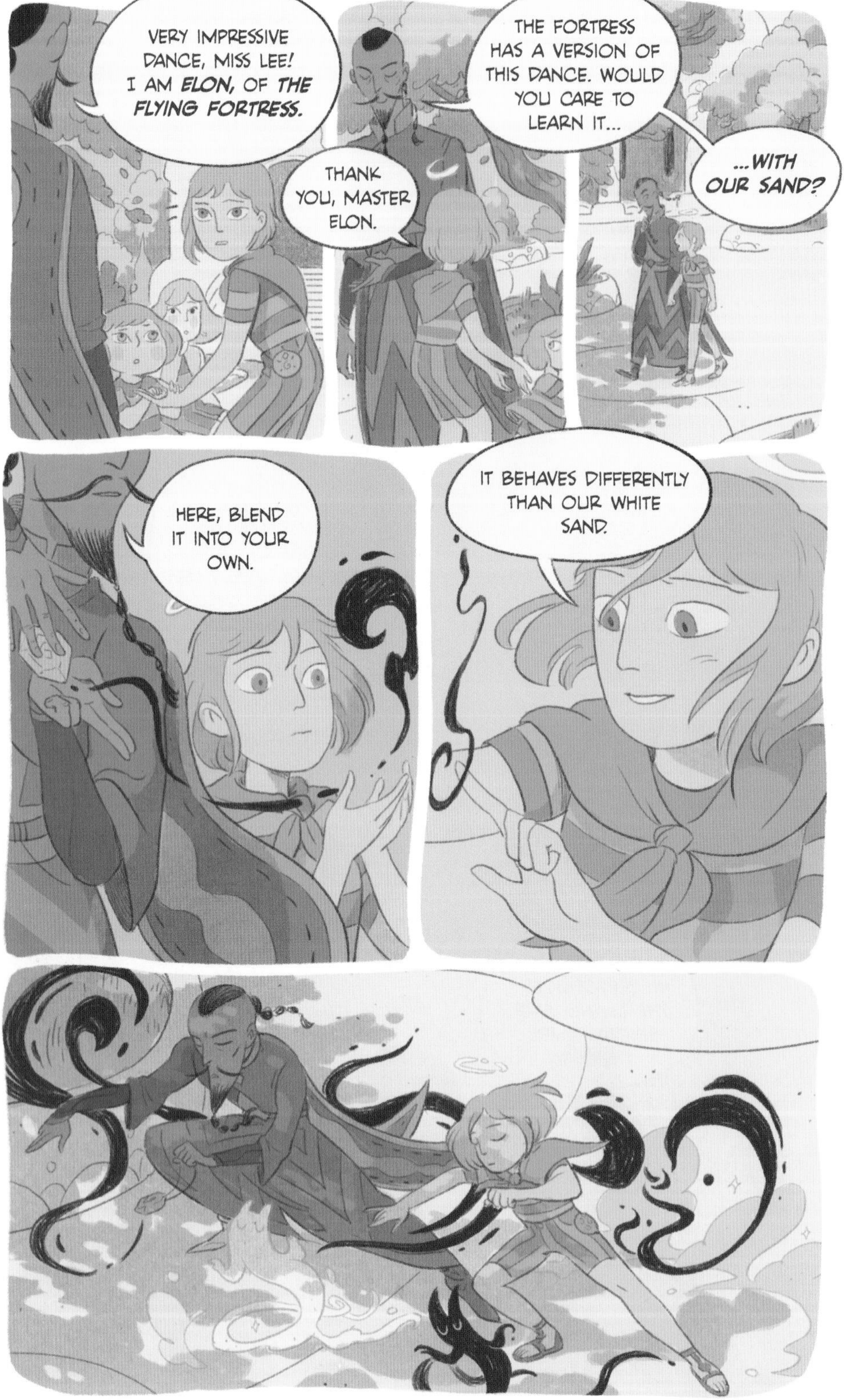
VERY IMPRESSIVE DANCE, MISS LEE! I AM ELON, OF THE FLYING FORTRESS.
THANK YOU, MASTER ELON.
THE FORTRESS HAS A VERSION OF THIS DANCE. WOULD YOU CARE TO LEARN IT...
...WITH OUR SAND?
HERE, BLEND IT INTO YOUR OWN.
IT BEHAVES DIFFERENTLY THAN OUR WHITE SAND.

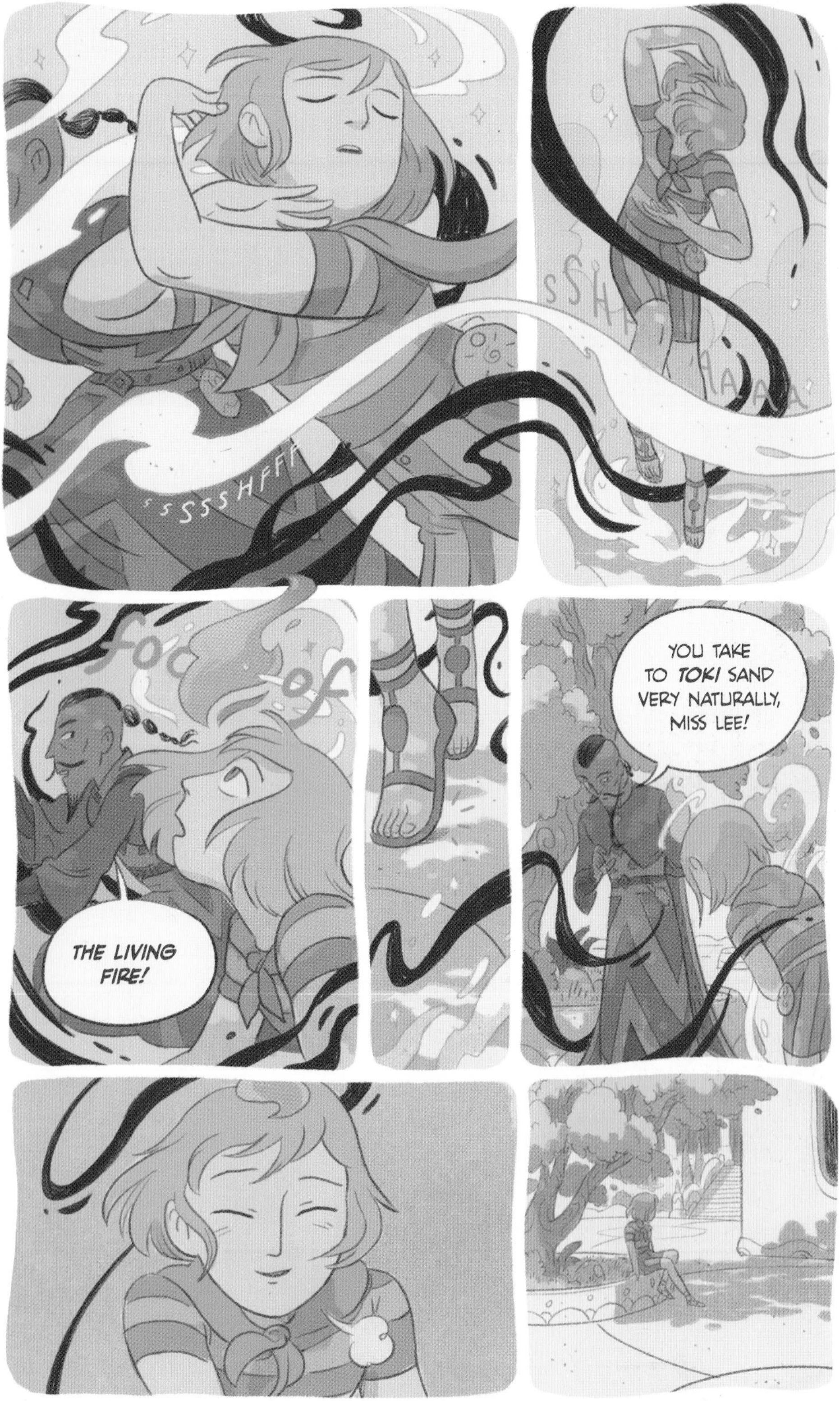

sSSSSHFFF
SSHH
HAAA
foof
THE LIVING FIRE!
YOU TAKE TO TOKI SAND VERY NATURALLY, MISS LEE!

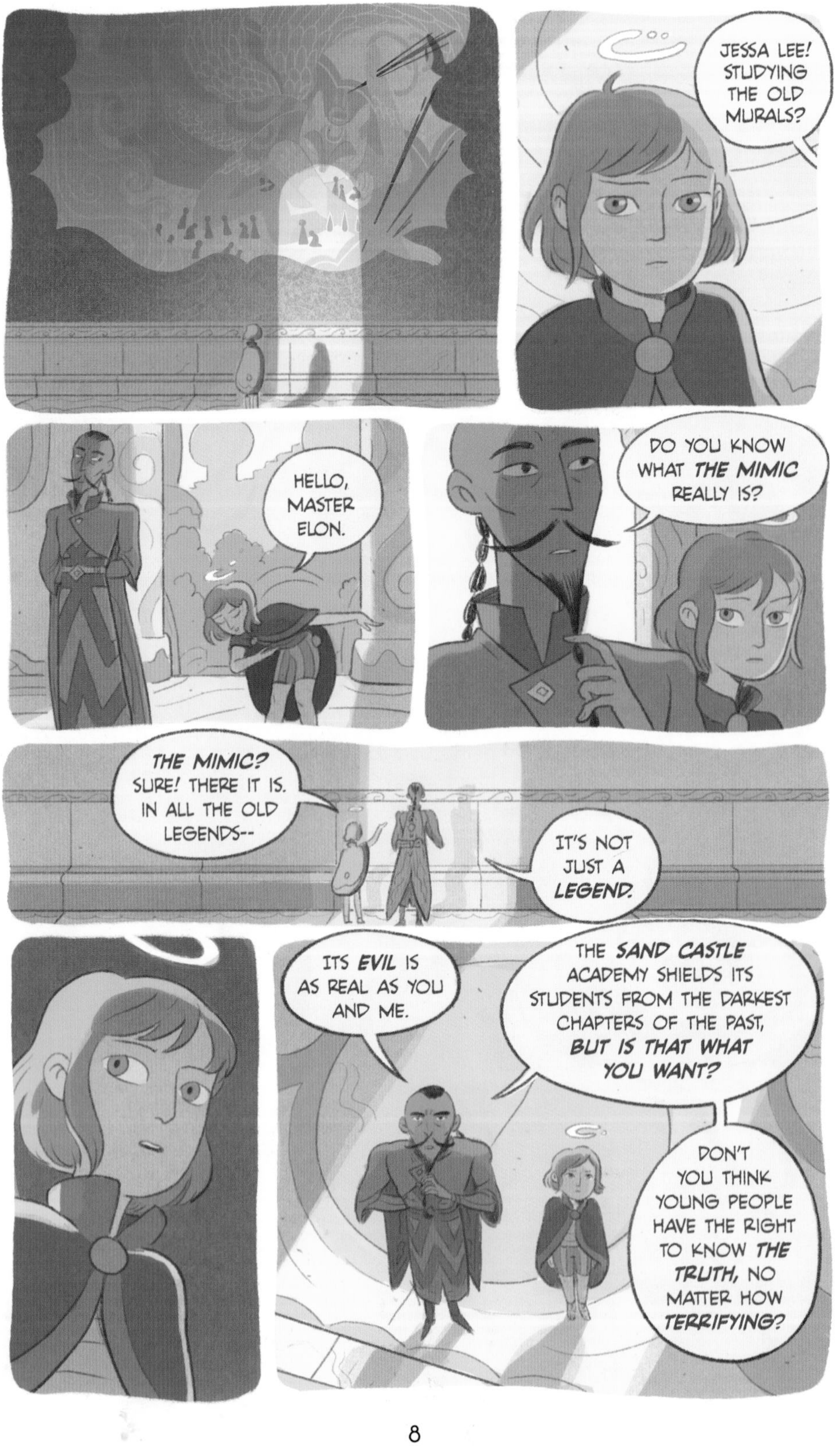
JESSA LEE! STUDYING THE OLD MURALS?
HELLO, MASTER ELON.
DO YOU KNOW WHAT *THE MIMIC* REALLY IS?
THE MIMIC? SURE! THERE IT IS. IN ALL THE OLD LEGENDS--
IT'S NOT JUST A *LEGEND.*
ITS *EVIL* IS AS REAL AS YOU AND ME.
THE *SAND CASTLE* ACADEMY SHIELDS ITS STUDENTS FROM THE DARKEST CHAPTERS OF THE PAST, *BUT IS THAT WHAT YOU WANT?*
DON'T YOU THINK YOUNG PEOPLE HAVE THE RIGHT TO KNOW *THE TRUTH,* NO MATTER HOW *TERRIFYING?*

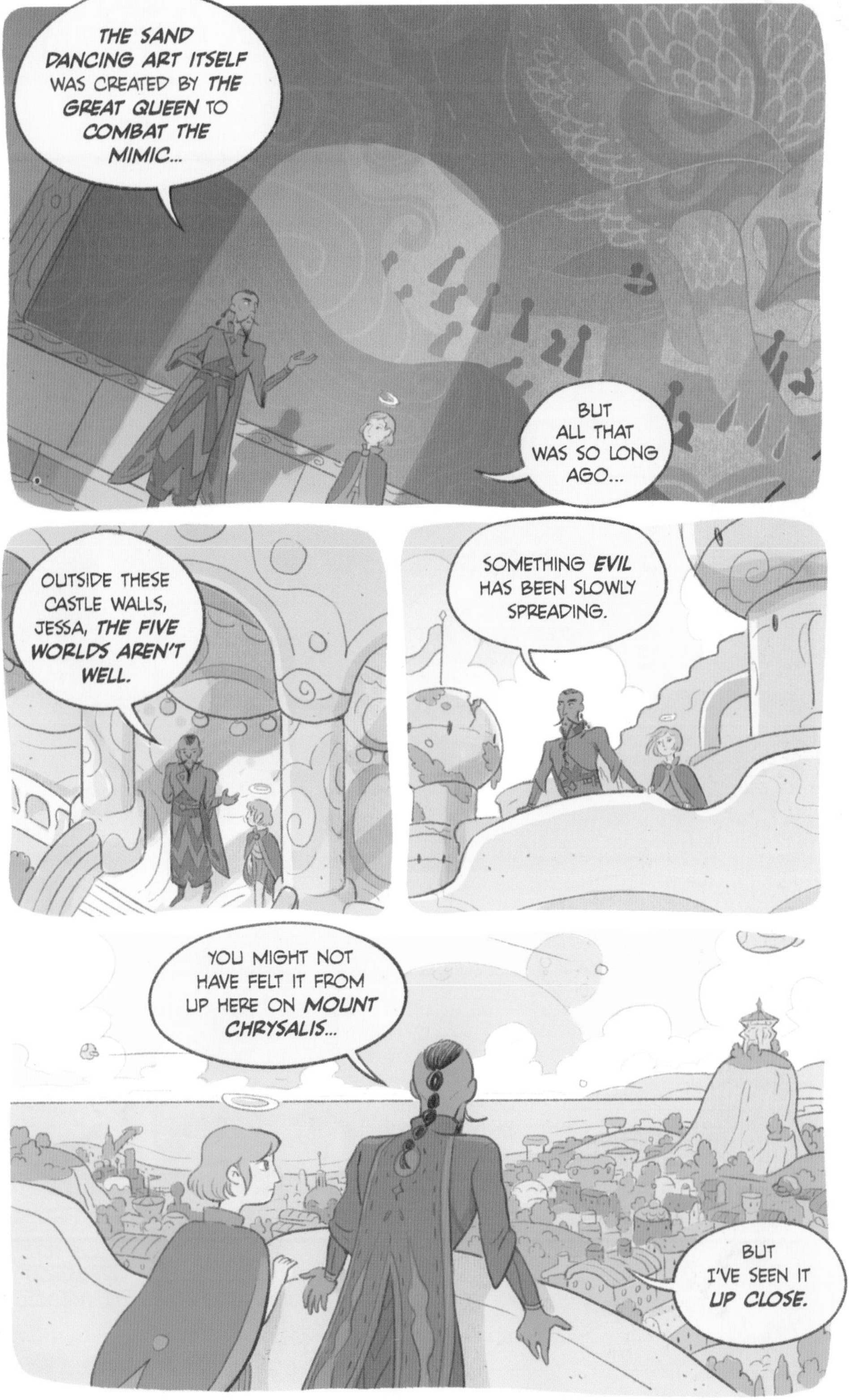
THE SAND DANCING ART ITSELF WAS CREATED BY THE GREAT QUEEN TO COMBAT THE MIMIC...
BUT ALL THAT WAS SO LONG AGO...
OUTSIDE THESE CASTLE WALLS, JESSA, THE FIVE WORLDS AREN'T WELL.
SOMETHING EVIL HAS BEEN SLOWLY SPREADING.
YOU MIGHT NOT HAVE FELT IT FROM UP HERE ON MOUNT CHRYSALIS...
BUT I'VE SEEN IT UP CLOSE.

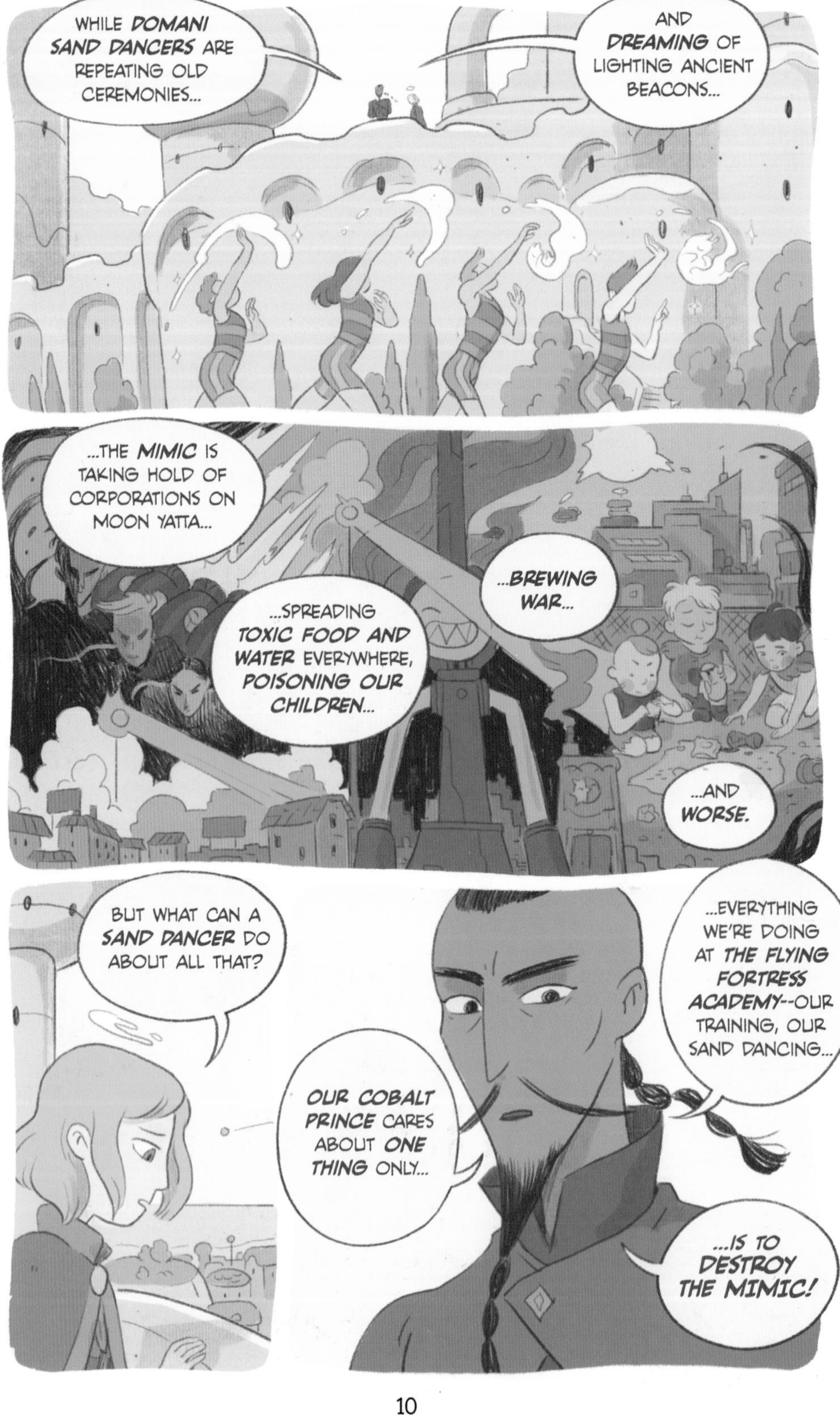
WHILE DOMANI SAND DANCERS ARE REPEATING OLD CEREMONIES...
AND DREAMING OF LIGHTING ANCIENT BEACONS...
...THE MIMIC IS TAKING HOLD OF CORPORATIONS ON MOON YATTA...
...SPREADING TOXIC FOOD AND WATER EVERYWHERE, POISONING OUR CHILDREN...
...BREWING WAR...
...AND WORSE.
BUT WHAT CAN A SAND DANCER DO ABOUT ALL THAT?
...EVERYTHING WE'RE DOING AT THE FLYING FORTRESS ACADEMY--OUR TRAINING, OUR SAND DANCING...
OUR COBALT PRINCE CARES ABOUT ONE THING ONLY...
...IS TO DESTROY THE MIMIC!

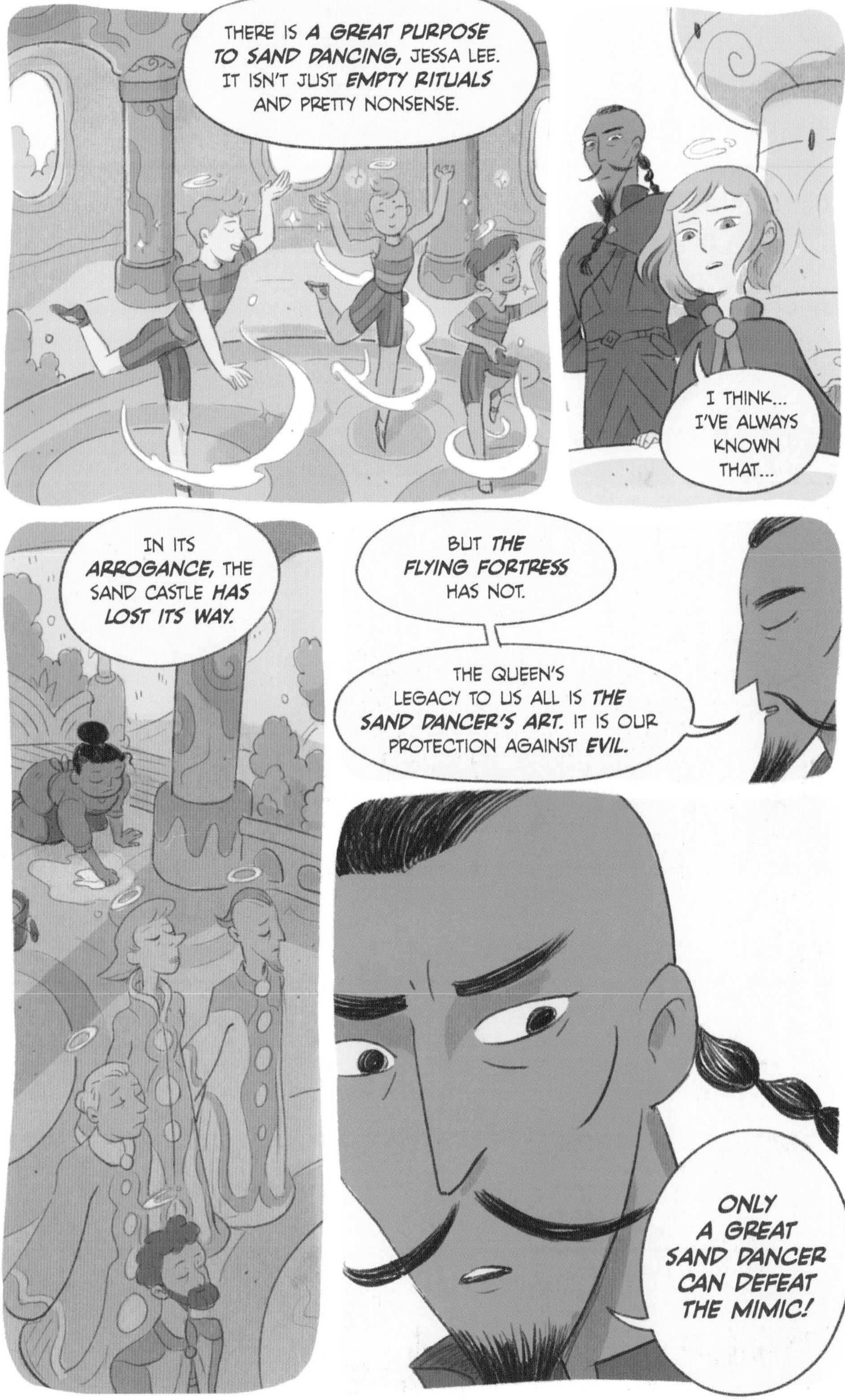
THERE IS A GREAT PURPOSE TO SAND DANCING, JESSA LEE. IT ISN'T JUST EMPTY RITUALS AND PRETTY NONSENSE.
I THINK... I'VE ALWAYS KNOWN THAT...
IN ITS ARROGANCE, THE SAND CASTLE HAS LOST ITS WAY.
BUT THE FLYING FORTRESS HAS NOT.
THE QUEEN'S LEGACY TO US ALL IS THE SAND DANCER'S ART. IT IS OUR PROTECTION AGAINST EVIL.
ONLY A GREAT SAND DANCER CAN DEFEAT THE MIMIC!

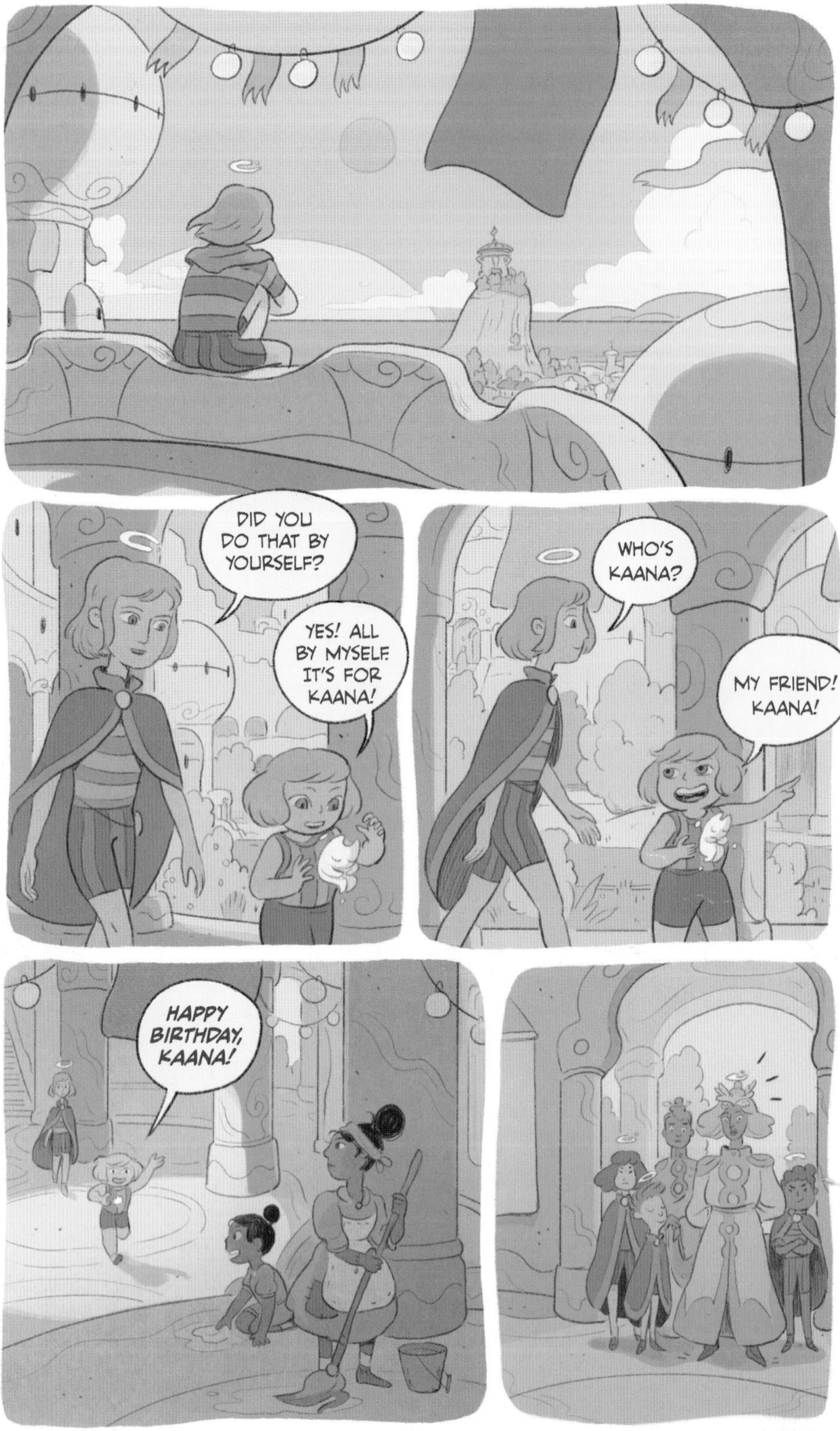
DID YOU DO THAT BY YOURSELF?
YES! ALL BY MYSELF. IT'S FOR KAANA!
WHO'S KAANA?
MY FRIEND! KAANA!
HAPPY BIRTHDAY, KAANA!

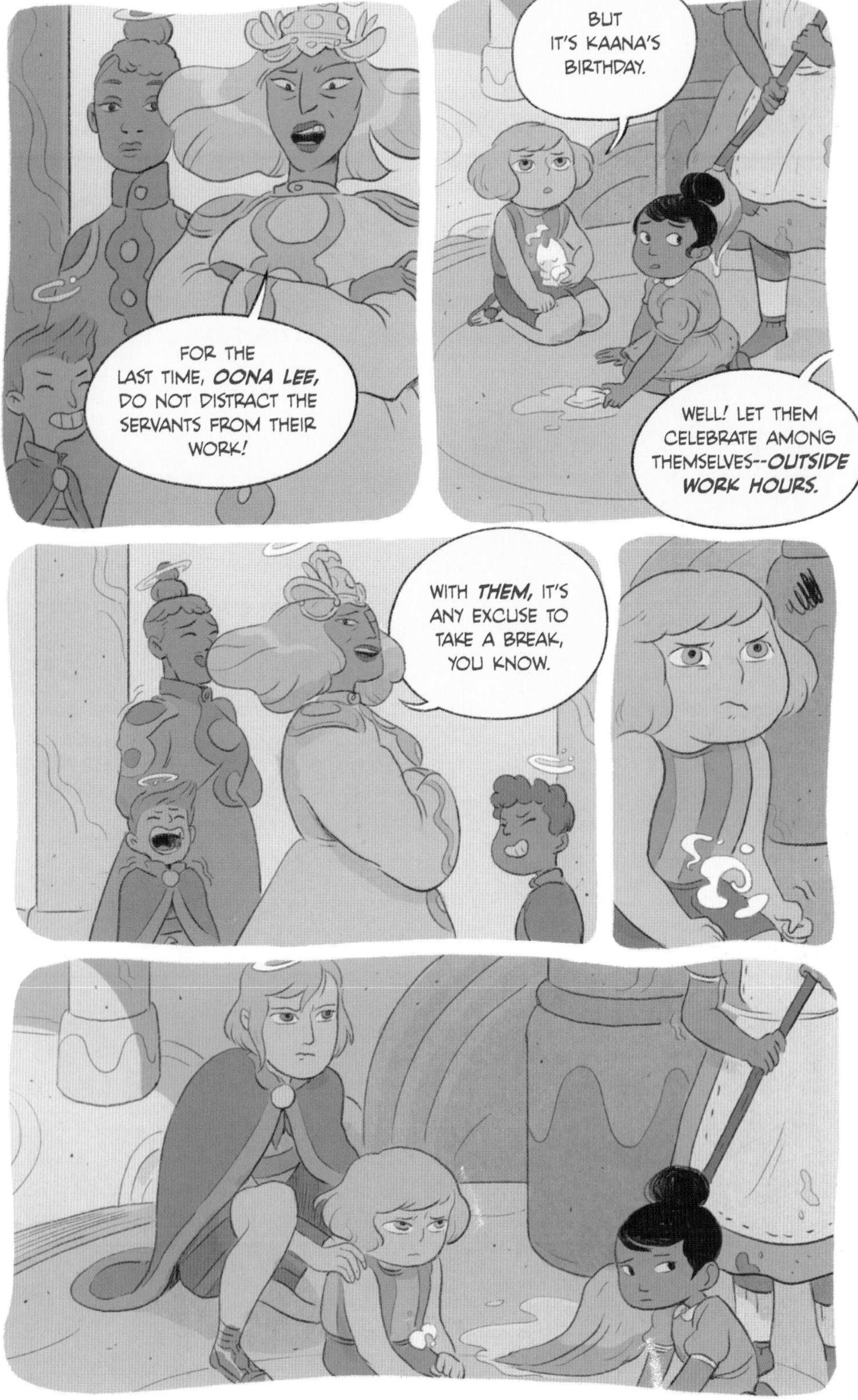
FOR THE LAST TIME, OONA LEE, DO NOT DISTRACT THE SERVANTS FROM THEIR WORK!
BUT IT'S KAANA'S BIRTHDAY.
WELL! LET THEM CELEBRATE AMONG THEMSELVES--OUTSIDE WORK HOURS.
WITH THEM, IT'S ANY EXCUSE TO TAKE A BREAK, YOU KNOW.

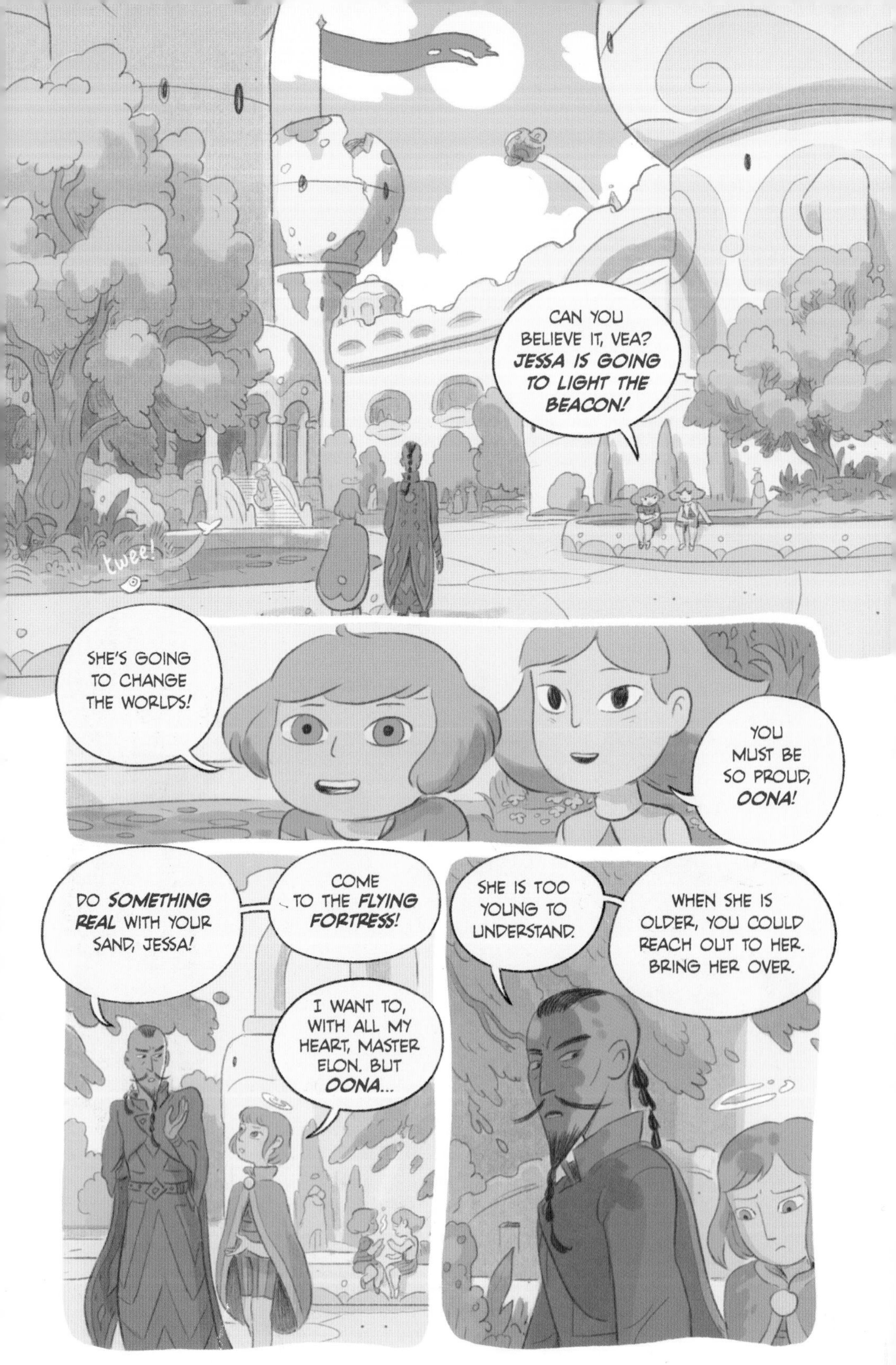
CAN YOU BELIEVE IT, VEA? JESSA IS GOING TO LIGHT THE BEACON!
tweee!
SHE'S GOING TO CHANGE THE WORLDS!
YOU MUST BE SO PROUD, OONA!
DO SOMETHING REAL WITH YOUR SAND, JESSA!
COME TO THE FLYING FORTRESS!
I WANT TO, WITH ALL MY HEART, MASTER ELON. BUT OONA...
SHE IS TOO YOUNG TO UNDERSTAND.
WHEN SHE IS OLDER, YOU COULD REACH OUT TO HER. BRING HER OVER.

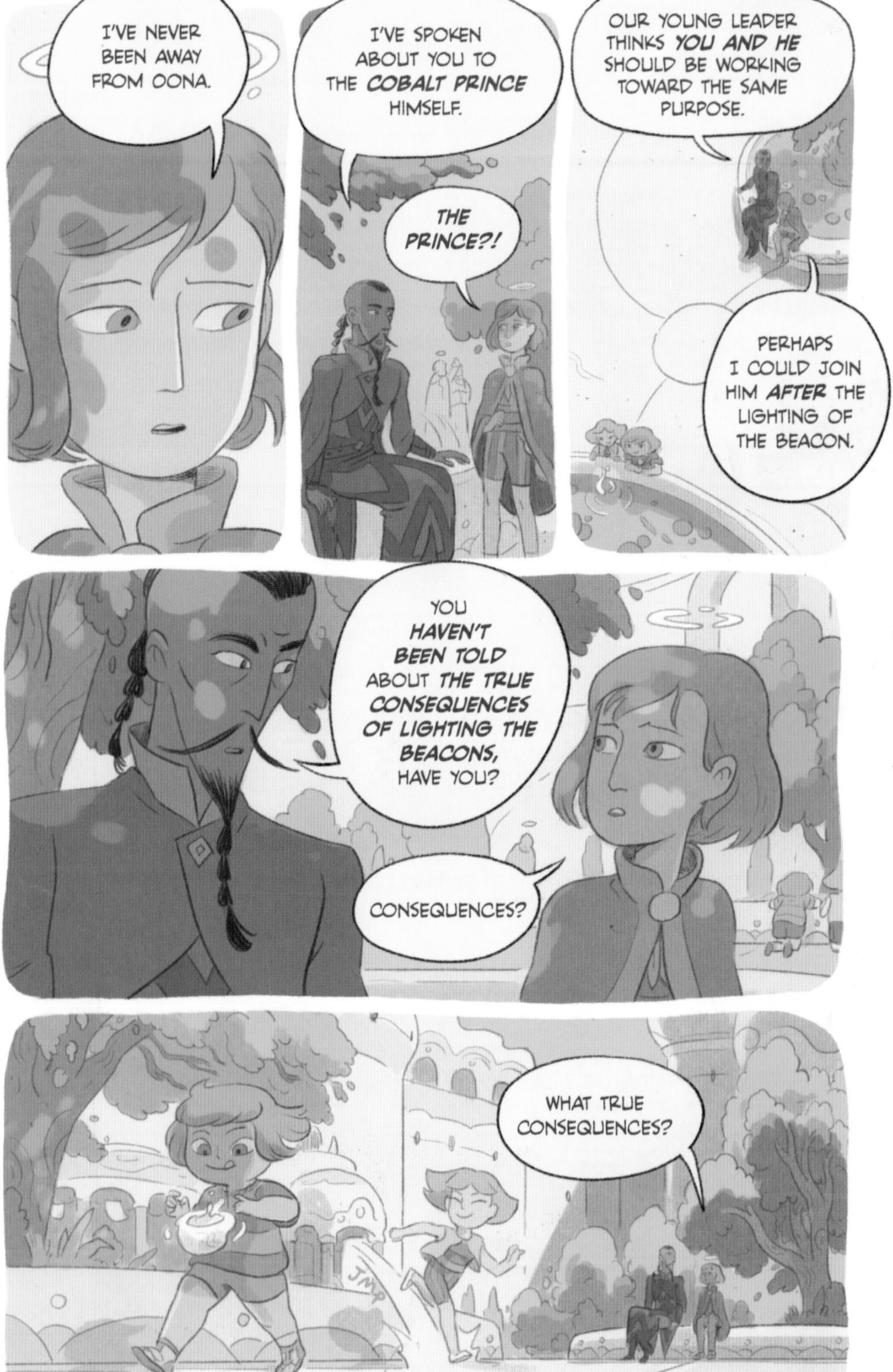
I'VE NEVER BEEN AWAY FROM OONA.
I'VE SPOKEN ABOUT YOU TO THE *COBALT PRINCE* HIMSELF.
THE PRINCE?!
OUR YOUNG LEADER THINKS *YOU AND HE* SHOULD BE WORKING TOWARD THE SAME PURPOSE.
PERHAPS I COULD JOIN HIM *AFTER* THE LIGHTING OF THE BEACON.
YOU *HAVEN'T BEEN TOLD* ABOUT *THE TRUE CONSEQUENCES OF LIGHTING THE BEACONS,* HAVE YOU?
CONSEQUENCES?
WHAT TRUE CONSEQUENCES?

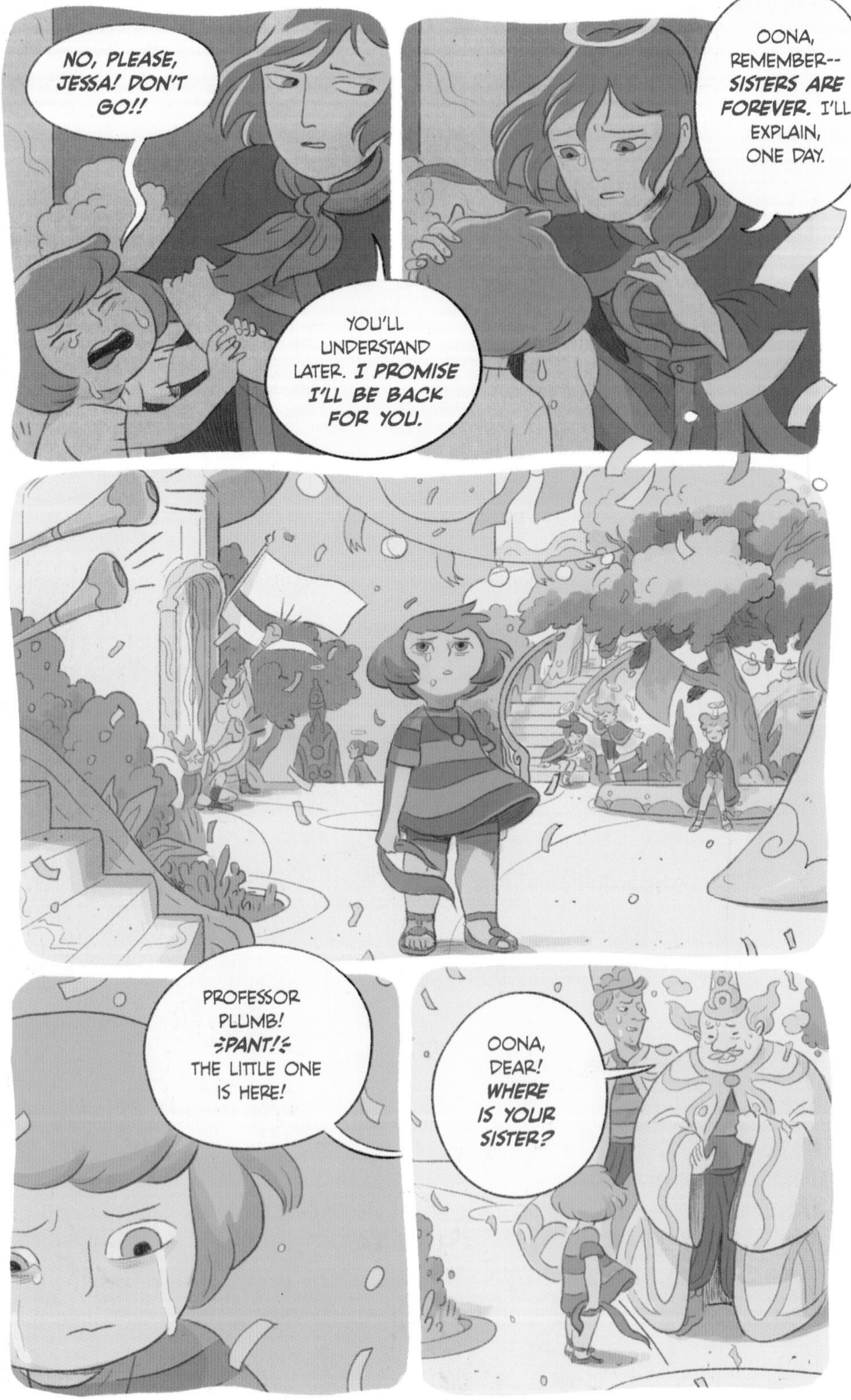
NO, PLEASE, JESSA! DON'T GO!!
YOU'LL UNDERSTAND LATER. I PROMISE I'LL BE BACK FOR YOU.
OONA, REMEMBER-- SISTERS ARE FOREVER. I'LL EXPLAIN, ONE DAY.
PROFESSOR PLUMB! PANT! THE LITTLE ONE IS HERE!
OONA, DEAR! WHERE IS YOUR SISTER?

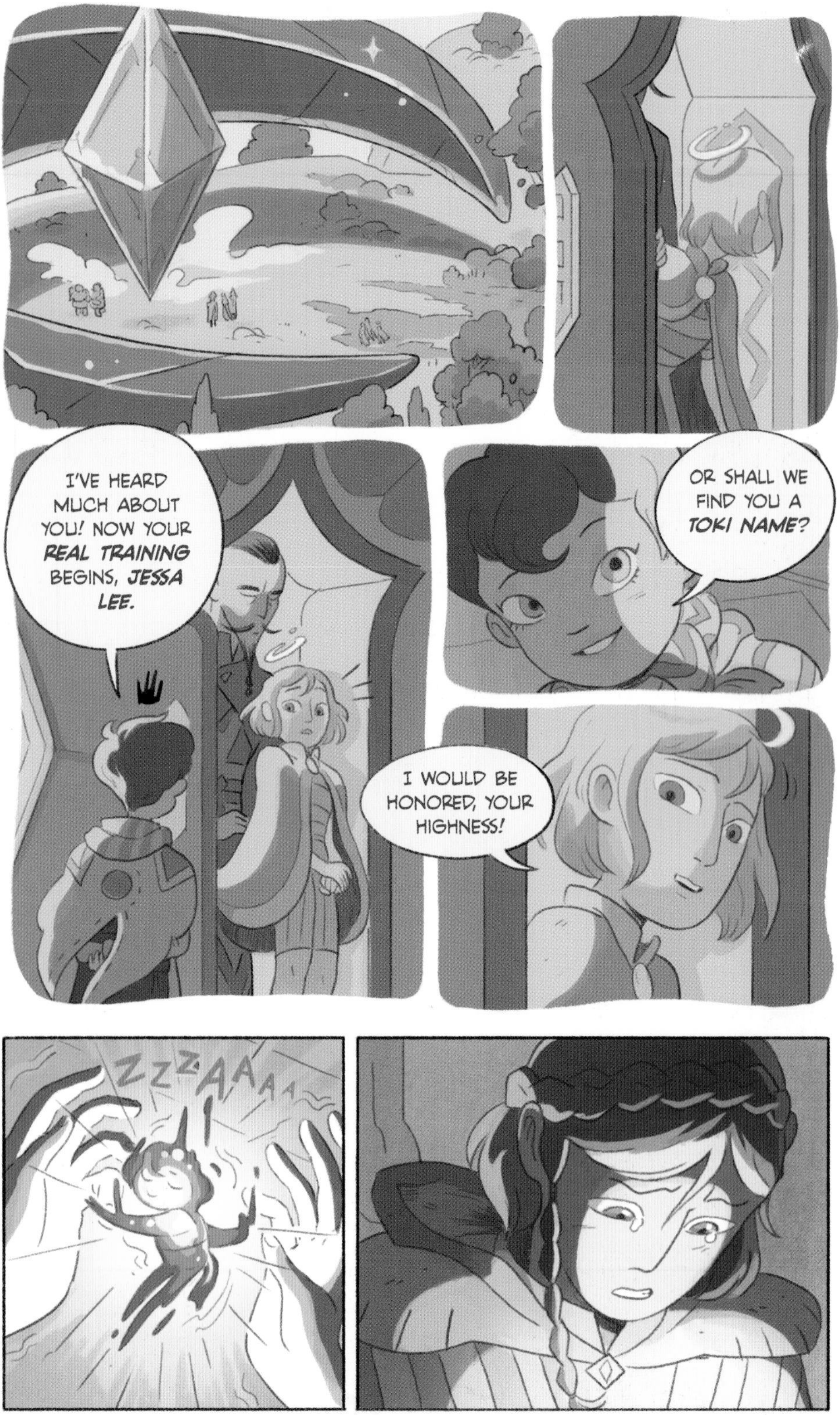
I'VE HEARD MUCH ABOUT YOU! NOW YOUR REAL TRAINING BEGINS, JESSA LEE.
OR SHALL WE FIND YOU A TOKI NAME?
I WOULD BE HONORED, YOUR HIGHNESS!
ZZZAAAAA

CHAPTER 1

THE COBALT KEY

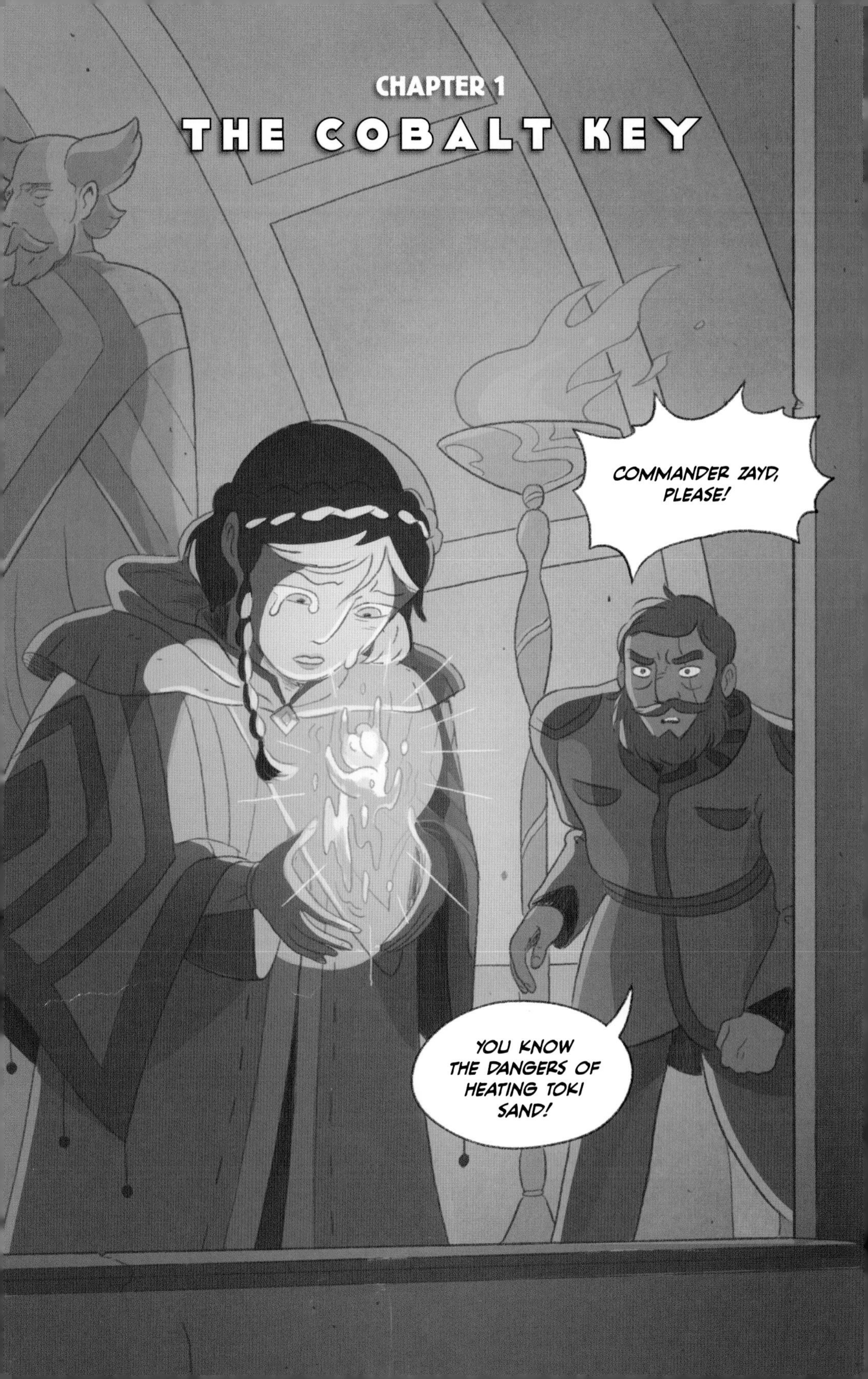

THE COUNCIL IS READY TO SEE YOU... DO BE PATIENT AND RESPECTFUL IN YOUR ANSWERS.

I *HAVE* BEEN PATIENT, *RONAK!*

WHY AM I STILL HERE? AREN'T THEY SENDING ME BACK TO *MON DOMANI?*

I'M AS PUZZLED AS YOU ARE.

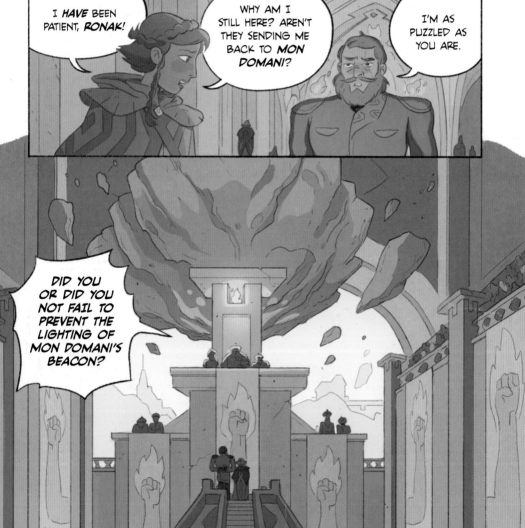

DID YOU OR DID YOU NOT FAIL TO PREVENT THE LIGHTING OF MON DOMANI'S BEACON?

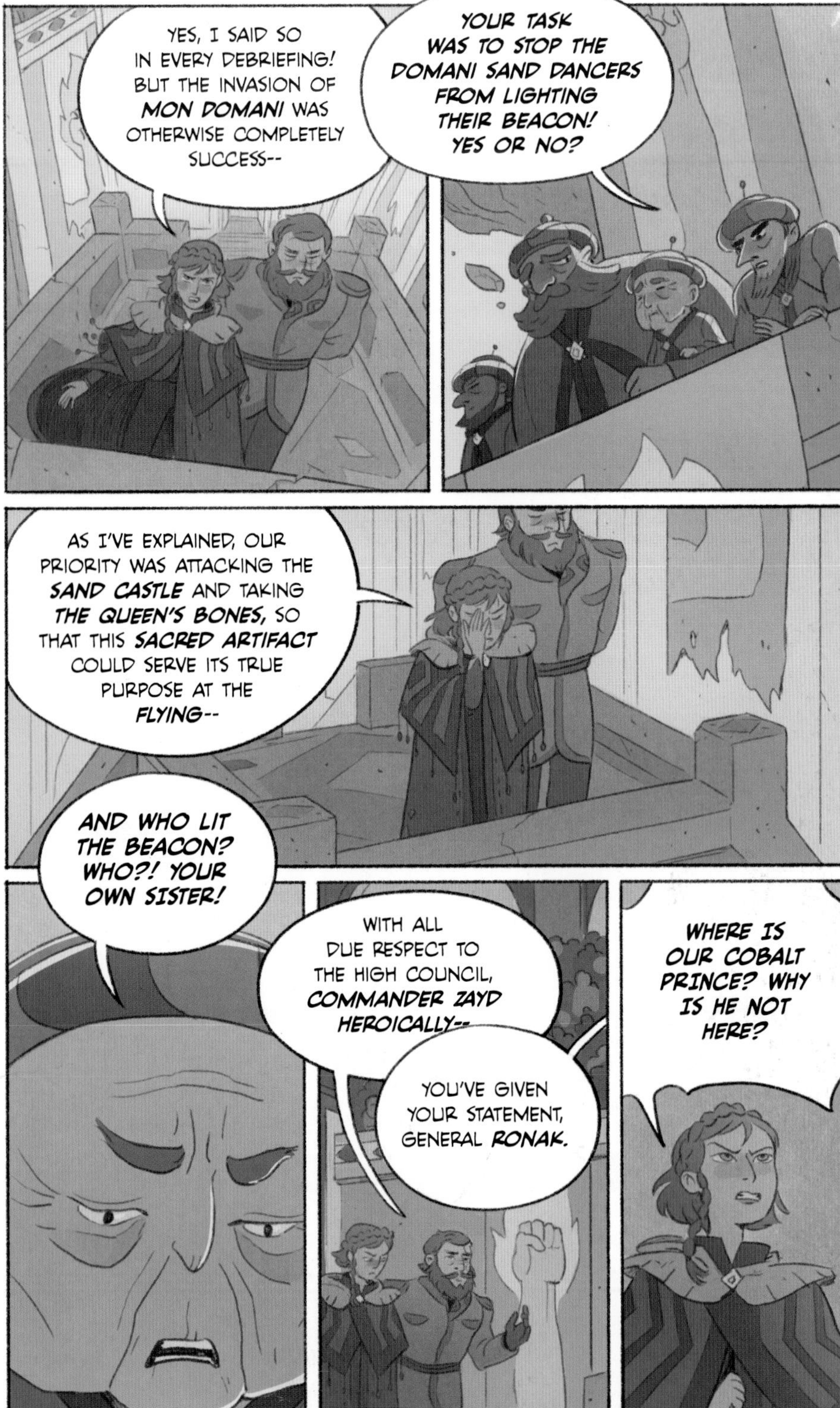
YES, I SAID SO IN EVERY DEBRIEFING! BUT THE INVASION OF MON DOMANI WAS OTHERWISE COMPLETELY SUCCESS--
YOUR TASK WAS TO STOP THE DOMANI SAND DANCERS FROM LIGHTING THEIR BEACON! YES OR NO?
AS I'VE EXPLAINED, OUR PRIORITY WAS ATTACKING THE SAND CASTLE AND TAKING THE QUEEN'S BONES, SO THAT THIS SACRED ARTIFACT COULD SERVE ITS TRUE PURPOSE AT THE FLYING--
AND WHO LIT THE BEACON? WHO?! YOUR OWN SISTER!
WITH ALL DUE RESPECT TO THE HIGH COUNCIL, COMMANDER ZAYD HEROICALLY--
YOU'VE GIVEN YOUR STATEMENT, GENERAL RONAK.
WHERE IS OUR COBALT PRINCE? WHY IS HE NOT HERE?

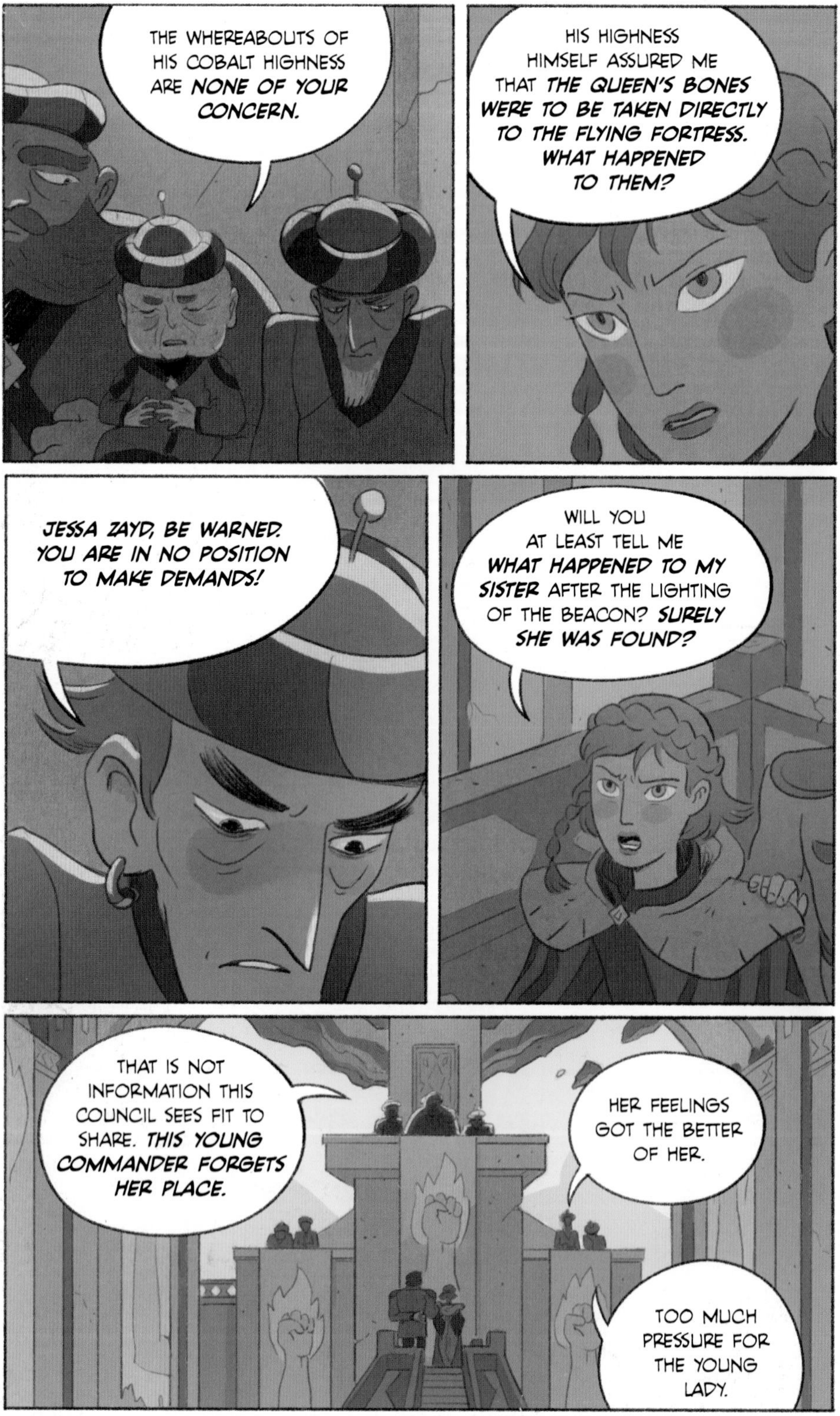
THE WHEREABOUTS OF HIS COBALT HIGHNESS ARE NONE OF YOUR CONCERN.
HIS HIGHNESS HIMSELF ASSURED ME THAT THE QUEEN'S BONES WERE TO BE TAKEN DIRECTLY TO THE FLYING FORTRESS. WHAT HAPPENED TO THEM?
JESSA ZAYD, BE WARNED. YOU ARE IN NO POSITION TO MAKE DEMANDS!
WILL YOU AT LEAST TELL ME WHAT HAPPENED TO MY SISTER AFTER THE LIGHTING OF THE BEACON? SURELY SHE WAS FOUND?
THAT IS NOT INFORMATION THIS COUNCIL SEES FIT TO SHARE. THIS YOUNG COMMANDER FORGETS HER PLACE.
HER FEELINGS GOT THE BETTER OF HER.
TOO MUCH PRESSURE FOR THE YOUNG LADY.

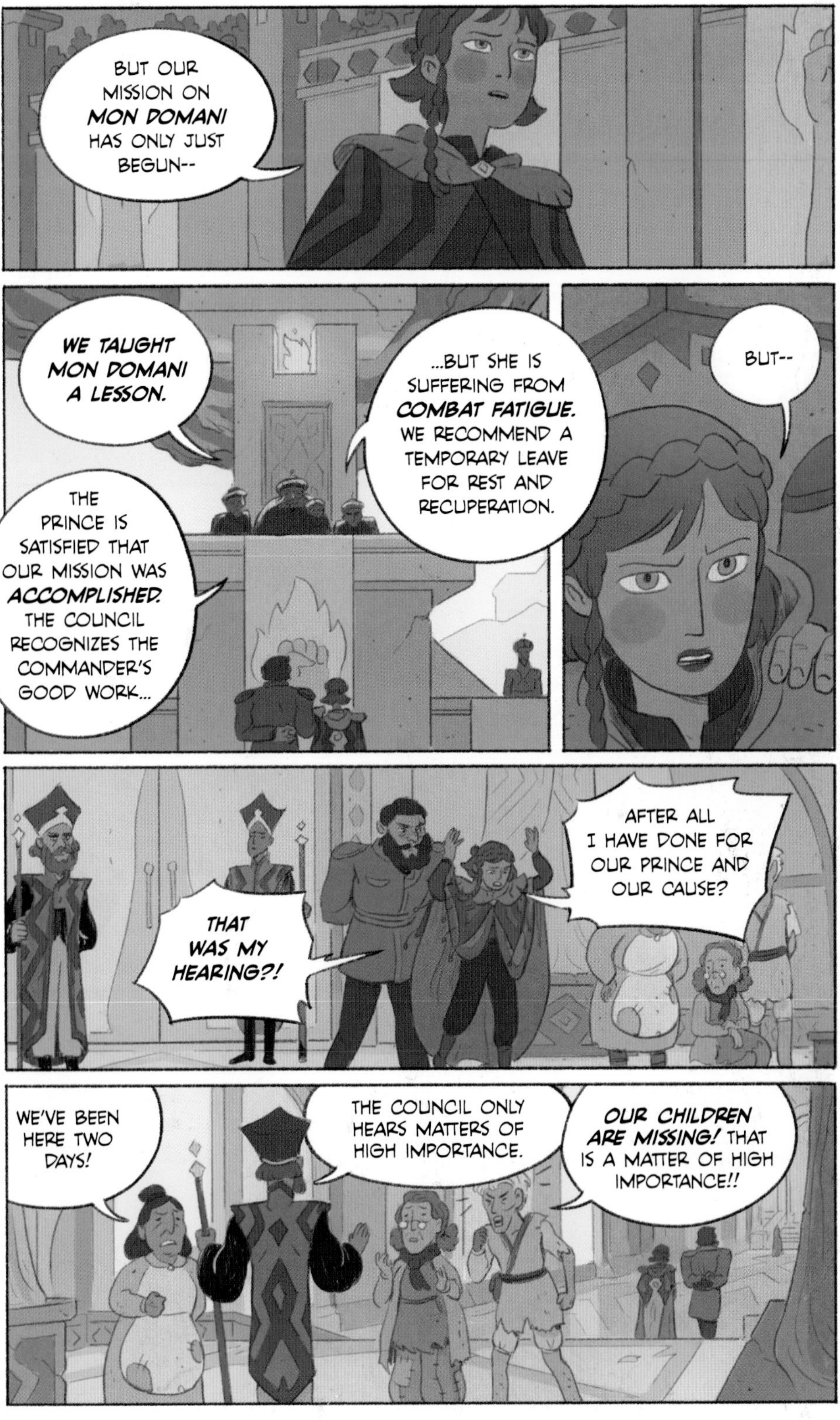
BUT OUR MISSION ON MON DOMANI HAS ONLY JUST BEGUN--
WE TAUGHT MON DOMANI A LESSON.
THE PRINCE IS SATISFIED THAT OUR MISSION WAS ACCOMPLISHED. THE COUNCIL RECOGNIZES THE COMMANDER'S GOOD WORK...
...BUT SHE IS SUFFERING FROM COMBAT FATIGUE. WE RECOMMEND A TEMPORARY LEAVE FOR REST AND RECUPERATION.
BUT--
THAT WAS MY HEARING?!
AFTER ALL I HAVE DONE FOR OUR PRINCE AND OUR CAUSE?
WE'VE BEEN HERE TWO DAYS!
THE COUNCIL ONLY HEARS MATTERS OF HIGH IMPORTANCE.
OUR CHILDREN ARE MISSING! THAT IS A MATTER OF HIGH IMPORTANCE!!

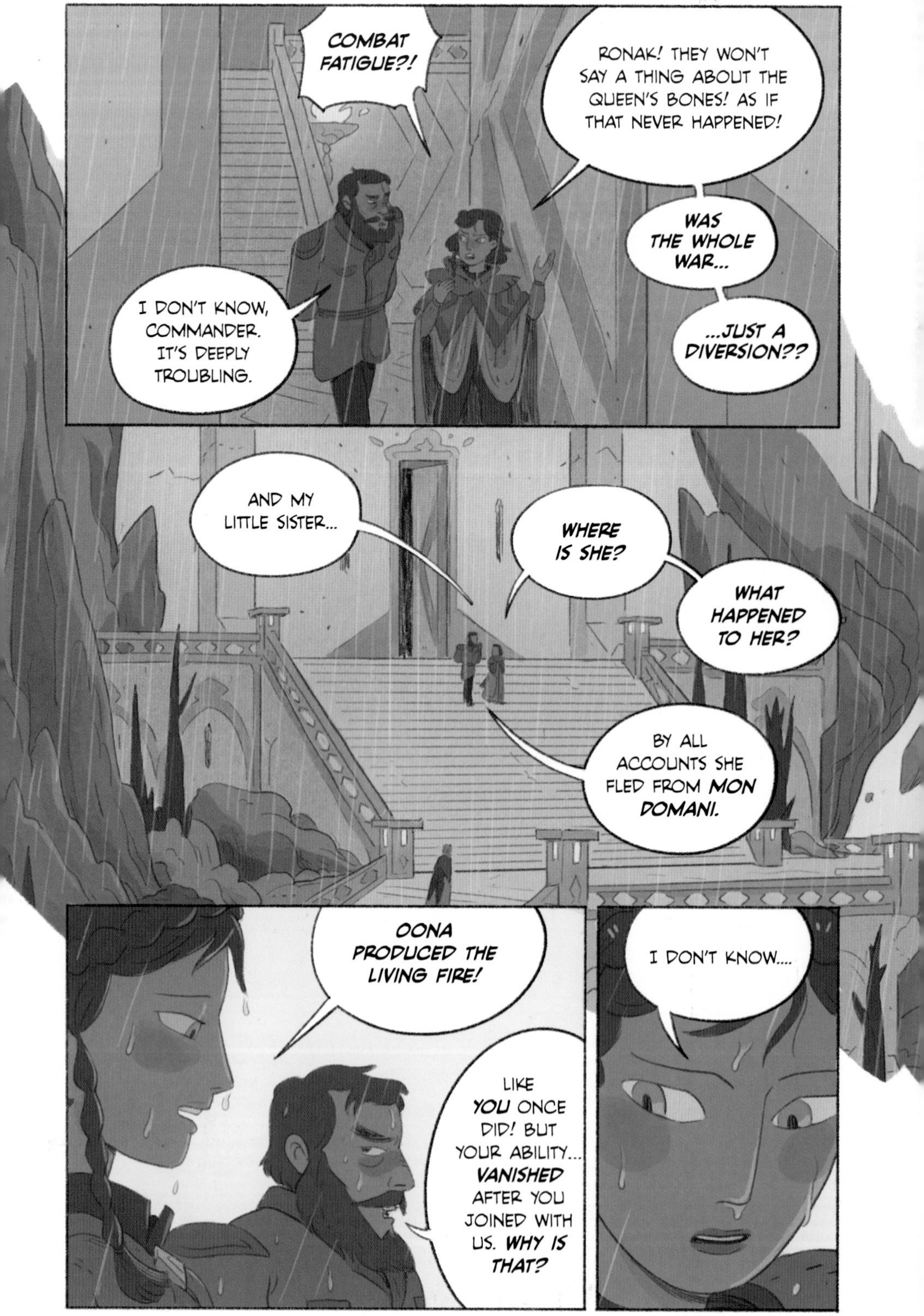
COMBAT FATIGUE?!
RONAK! THEY WON'T SAY A THING ABOUT THE QUEEN'S BONES! AS IF THAT NEVER HAPPENED!
WAS THE WHOLE WAR...
...JUST A DIVERSION??
I DON'T KNOW, COMMANDER. IT'S DEEPLY TROUBLING.
AND MY LITTLE SISTER...
WHERE IS SHE?
WHAT HAPPENED TO HER?
BY ALL ACCOUNTS SHE FLED FROM MON DOMANI.
OONA PRODUCED THE LIVING FIRE!
LIKE YOU ONCE DID! BUT YOUR ABILITY... VANISHED AFTER YOU JOINED WITH US. WHY IS THAT?
I DON'T KNOW....

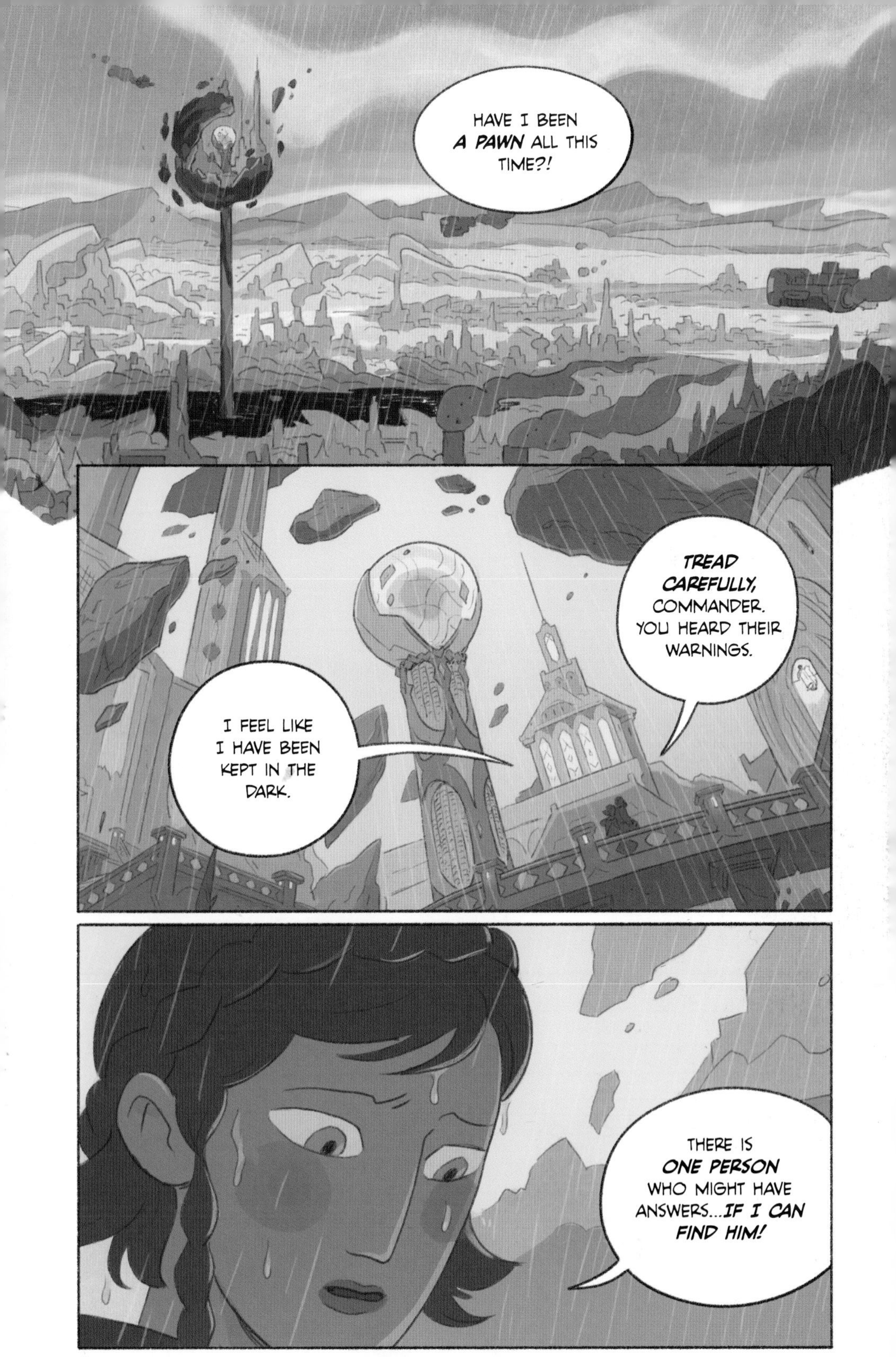
HAVE I BEEN A PAWN ALL THIS TIME?!
I FEEL LIKE I HAVE BEEN KEPT IN THE DARK.
TREAD CAREFULLY, COMMANDER. YOU HEARD THEIR WARNINGS.
THERE IS ONE PERSON WHO MIGHT HAVE ANSWERS...IF I CAN FIND HIM!

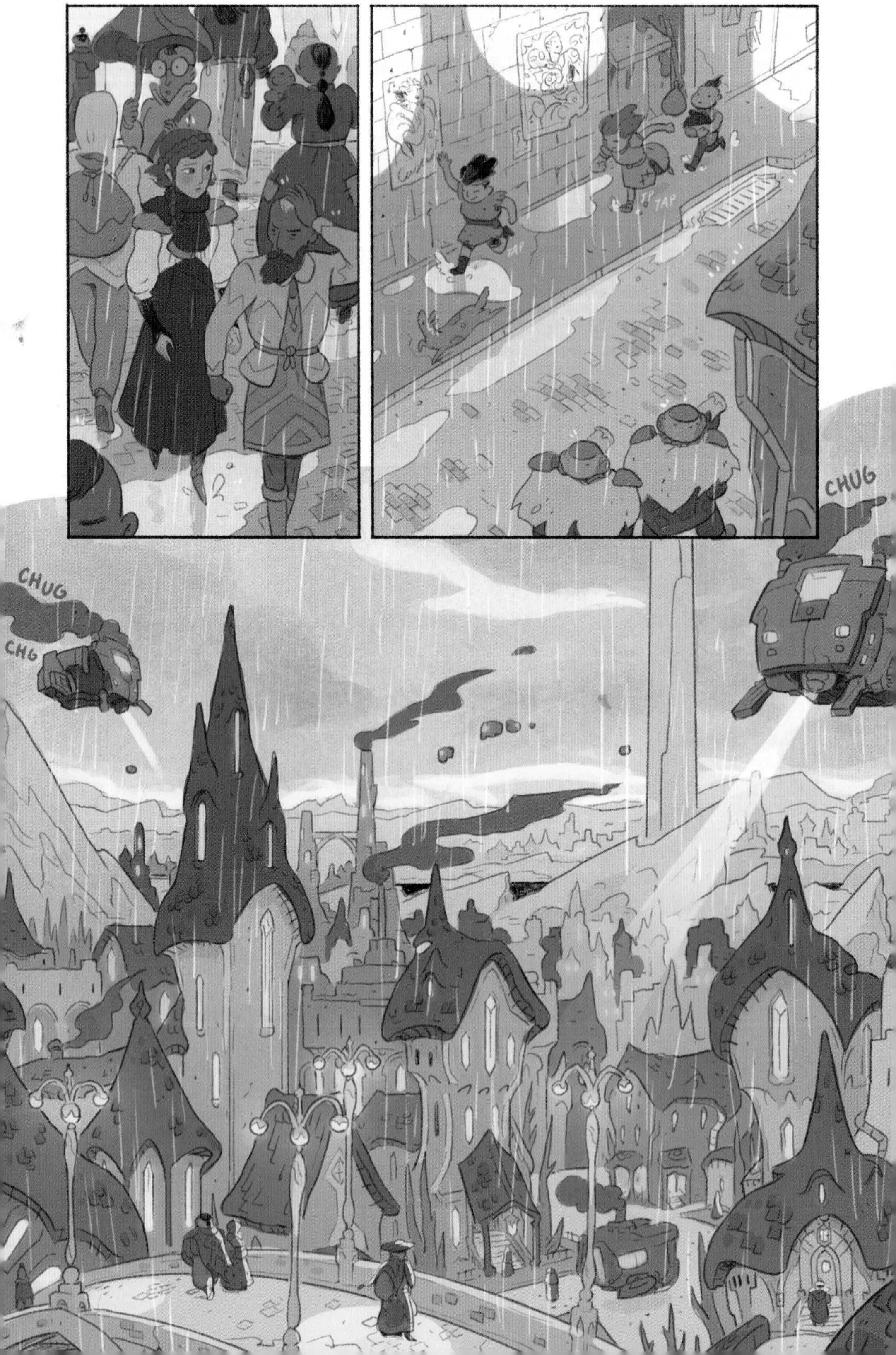
TAP
TP TAP
CHUG
CHUG
CHG

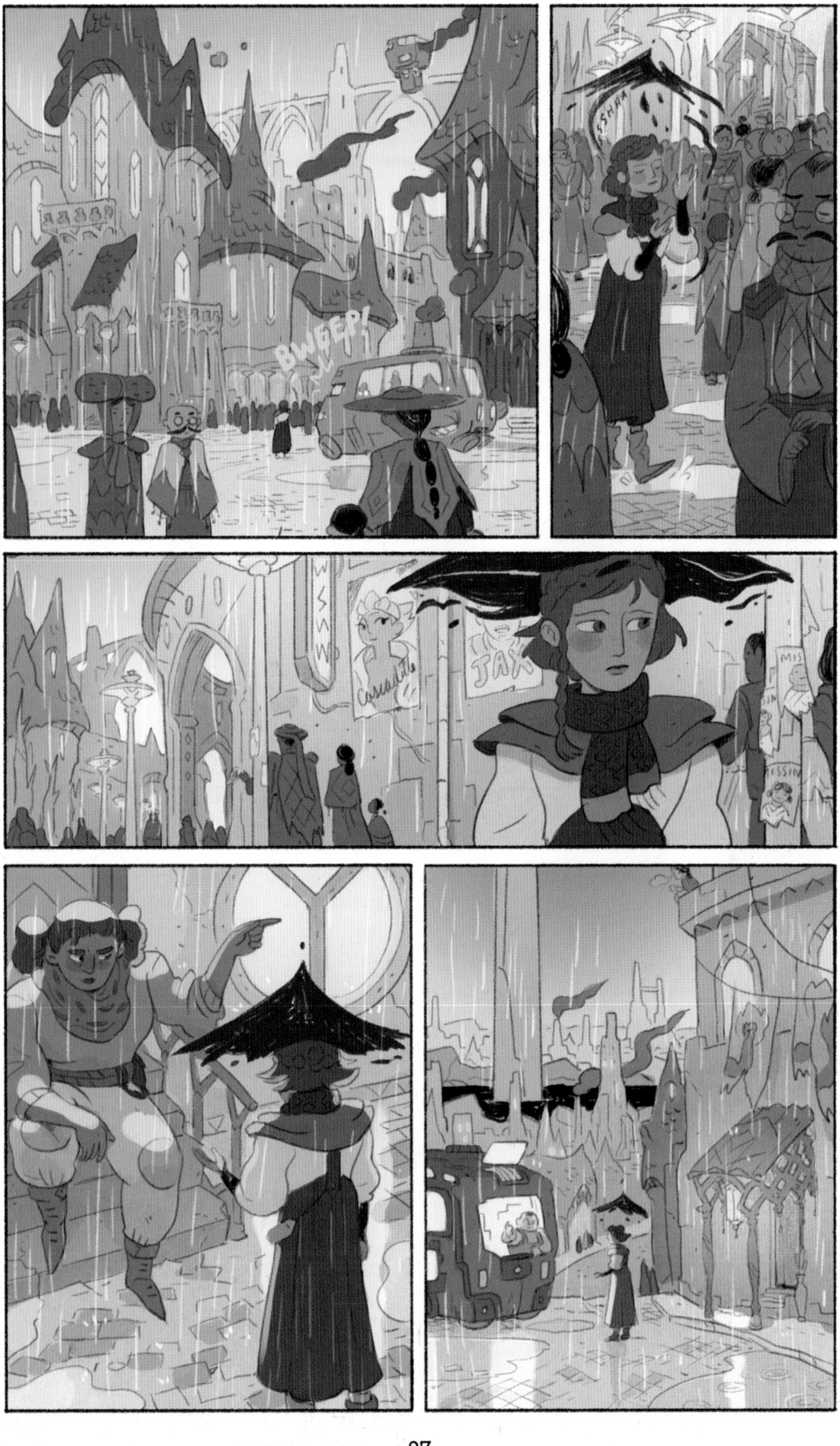
BWEEP!
SSHAA
JAX

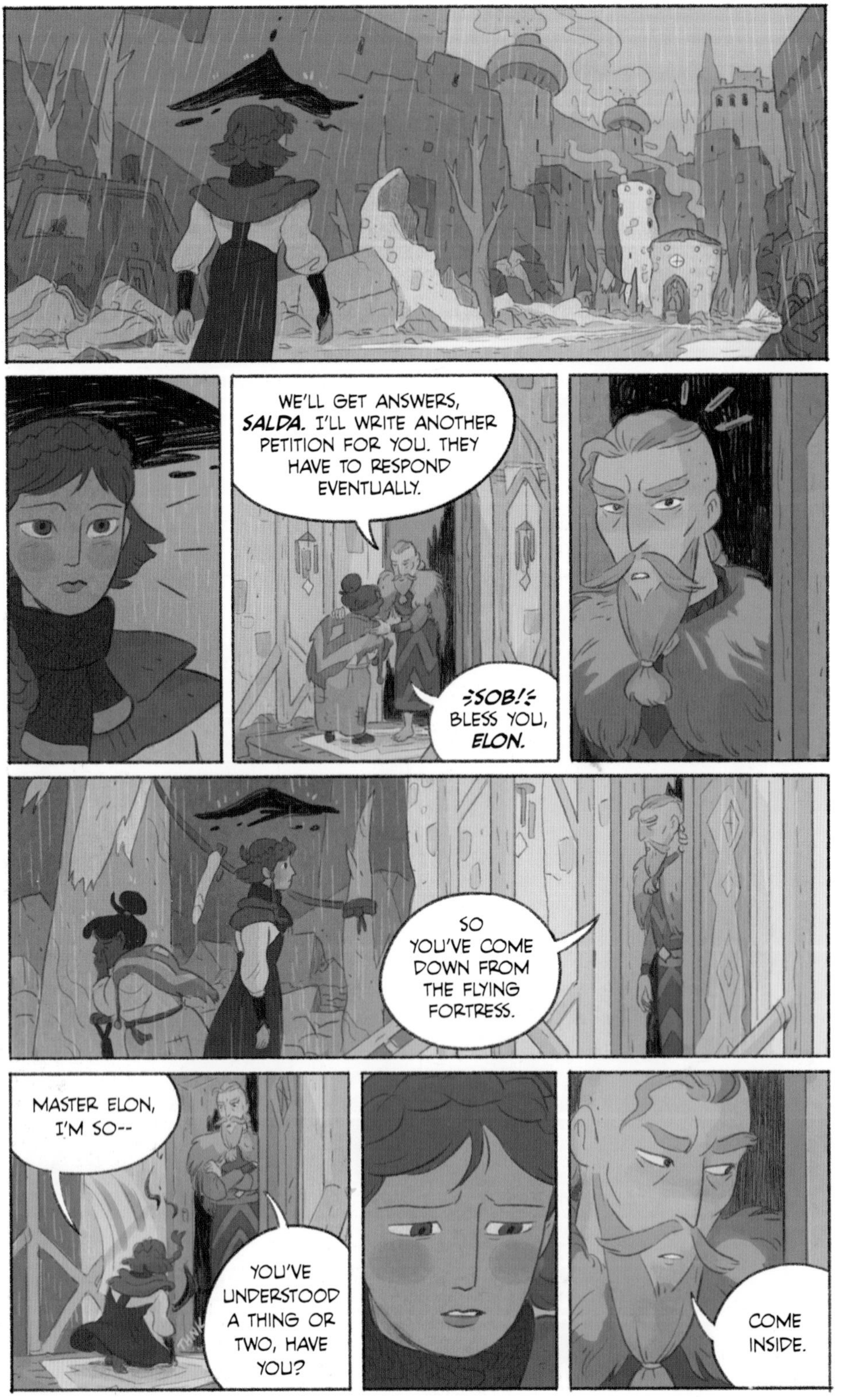
WE'LL GET ANSWERS, SALDA. I'LL WRITE ANOTHER PETITION FOR YOU. THEY HAVE TO RESPOND EVENTUALLY.
SOB! BLESS YOU, ELON.
SO YOU'VE COME DOWN FROM THE FLYING FORTRESS.
MASTER ELON, I'M SO--
YOU'VE UNDERSTOOD A THING OR TWO, HAVE YOU?
COME INSIDE.

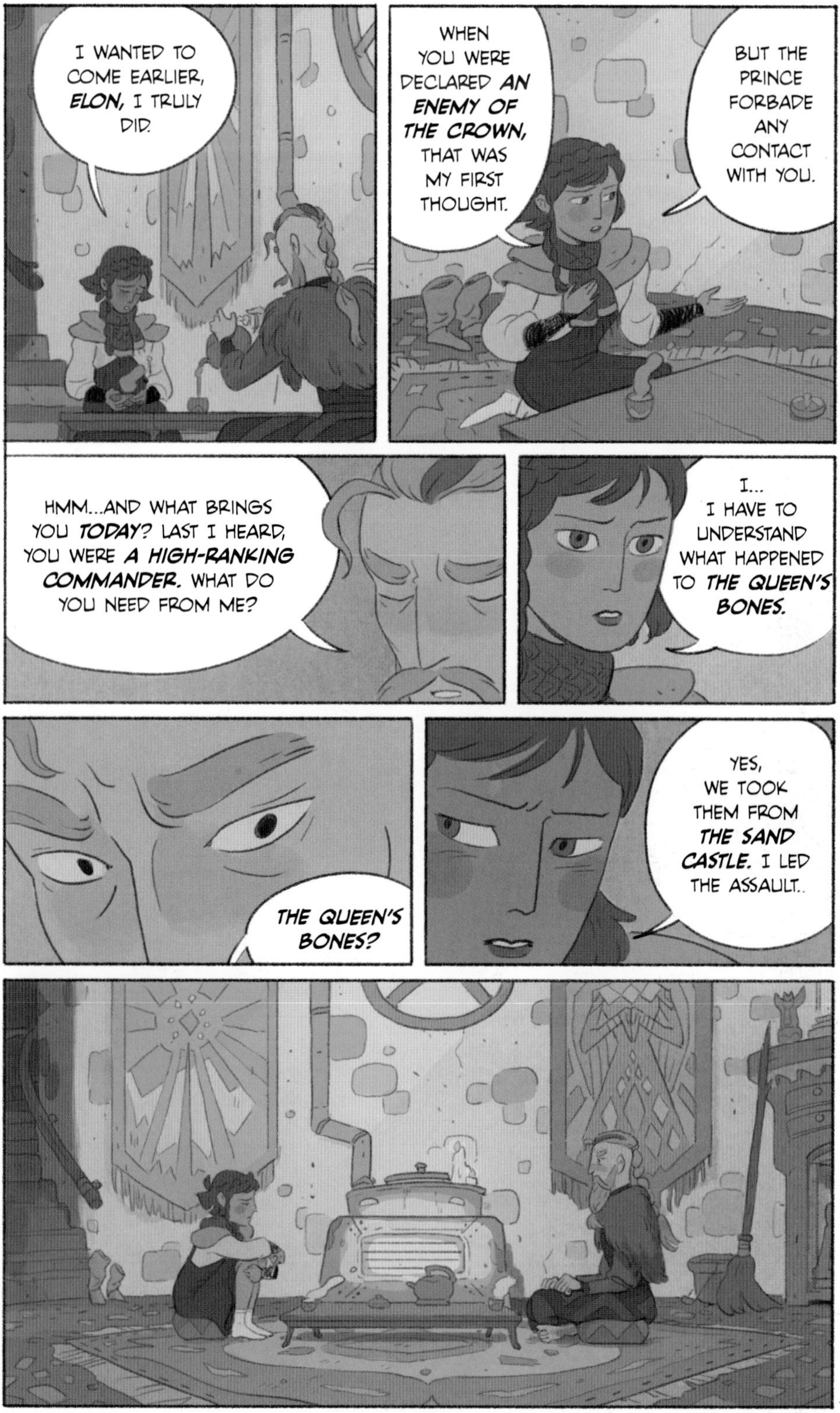
I WANTED TO COME EARLIER, *ELON,* I TRULY DID.
WHEN YOU WERE DECLARED ***AN ENEMY OF THE CROWN,*** THAT WAS MY FIRST THOUGHT.
BUT THE PRINCE FORBADE ANY CONTACT WITH YOU.
HMM...AND WHAT BRINGS YOU ***TODAY?*** LAST I HEARD, YOU WERE ***A HIGH-RANKING COMMANDER.*** WHAT DO YOU NEED FROM ME?
I... I HAVE TO UNDERSTAND WHAT HAPPENED TO ***THE QUEEN'S BONES.***
THE QUEEN'S BONES?
YES, WE TOOK THEM FROM ***THE SAND CASTLE.*** I LED THE ASSAULT..

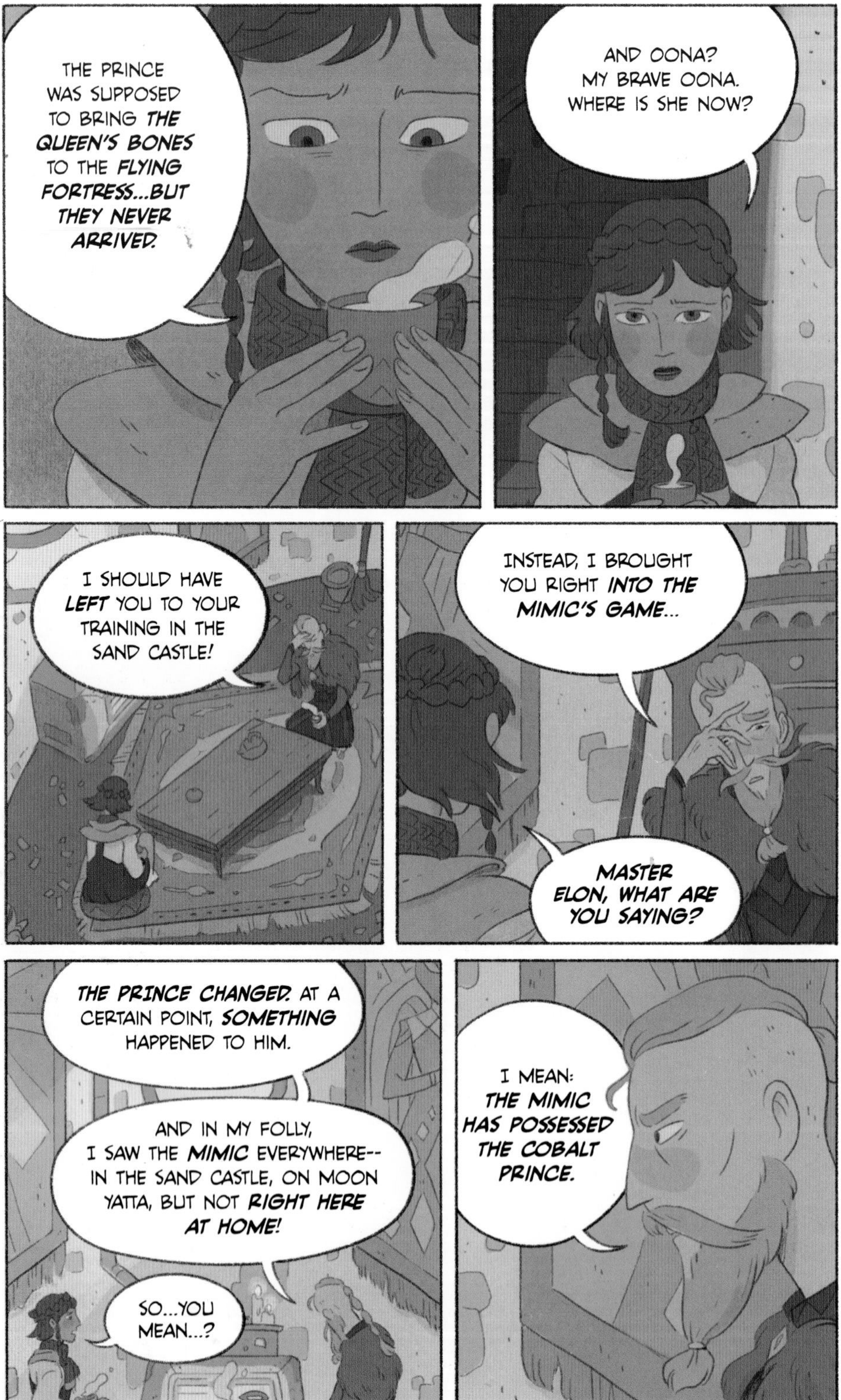
THE PRINCE WAS SUPPOSED TO BRING THE QUEEN'S BONES TO THE FLYING FORTRESS...BUT THEY NEVER ARRIVED.
AND OONA? MY BRAVE OONA. WHERE IS SHE NOW?
I SHOULD HAVE LEFT YOU TO YOUR TRAINING IN THE SAND CASTLE!
INSTEAD, I BROUGHT YOU RIGHT INTO THE MIMIC'S GAME...
MASTER ELON, WHAT ARE YOU SAYING?
THE PRINCE CHANGED. AT A CERTAIN POINT, SOMETHING HAPPENED TO HIM.
AND IN MY FOLLY, I SAW THE MIMIC EVERYWHERE-- IN THE SAND CASTLE, ON MOON YATTA, BUT NOT RIGHT HERE AT HOME!
SO...YOU MEAN...?
I MEAN: THE MIMIC HAS POSSESSED THE COBALT PRINCE.

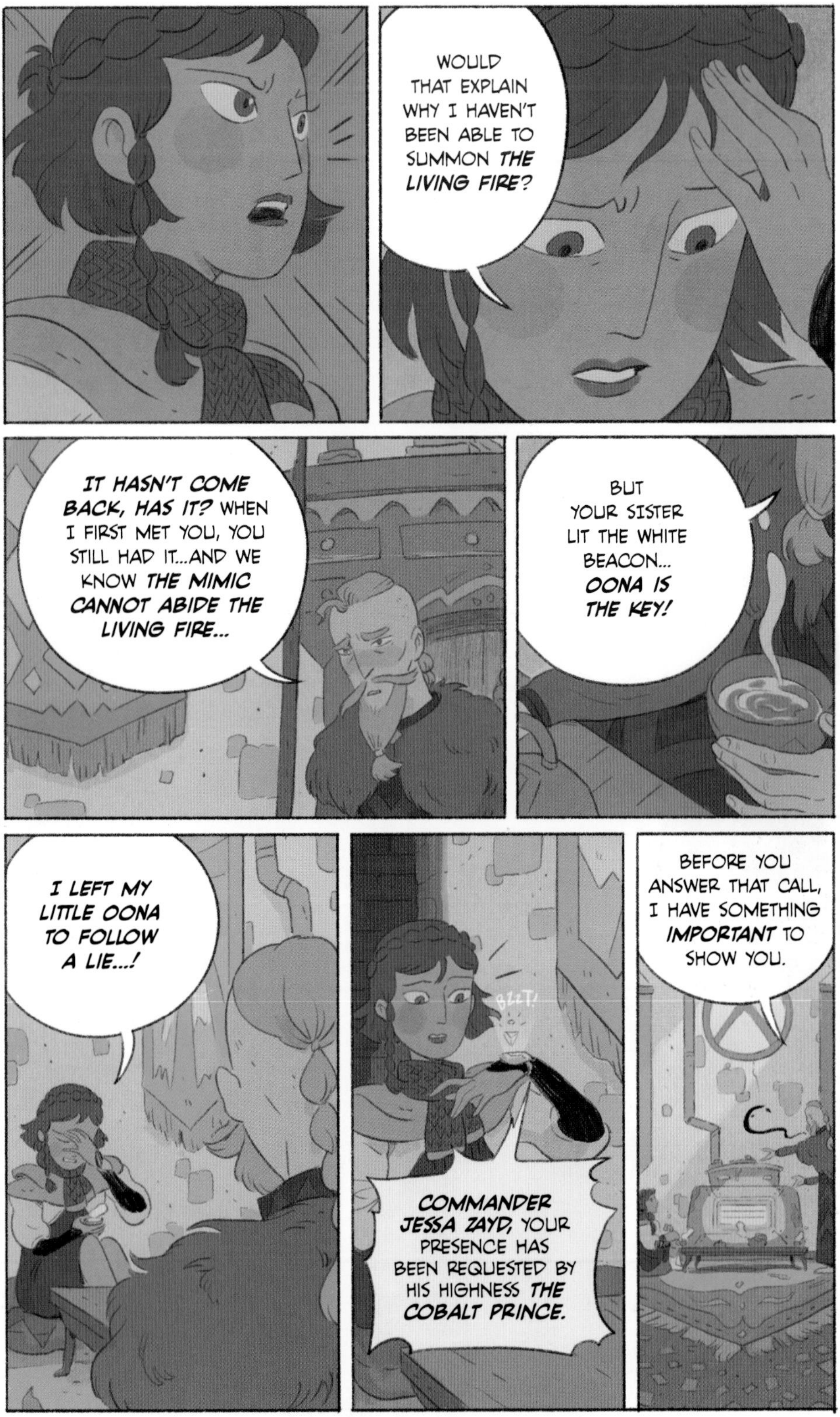
WOULD THAT EXPLAIN WHY I HAVEN'T BEEN ABLE TO SUMMON *THE LIVING FIRE*?
IT HASN'T COME BACK, HAS IT? WHEN I FIRST MET YOU, YOU STILL HAD IT...AND WE KNOW *THE MIMIC CANNOT ABIDE THE LIVING FIRE...*
BUT YOUR SISTER LIT THE WHITE BEACON... *OONA IS THE KEY!*
I LEFT MY LITTLE OONA TO FOLLOW A LIE...!
BZZT!
COMMANDER JESSA ZAYD, YOUR PRESENCE HAS BEEN REQUESTED BY HIS HIGHNESS *THE COBALT PRINCE.*
BEFORE YOU ANSWER THAT CALL, I HAVE SOMETHING *IMPORTANT* TO SHOW YOU.

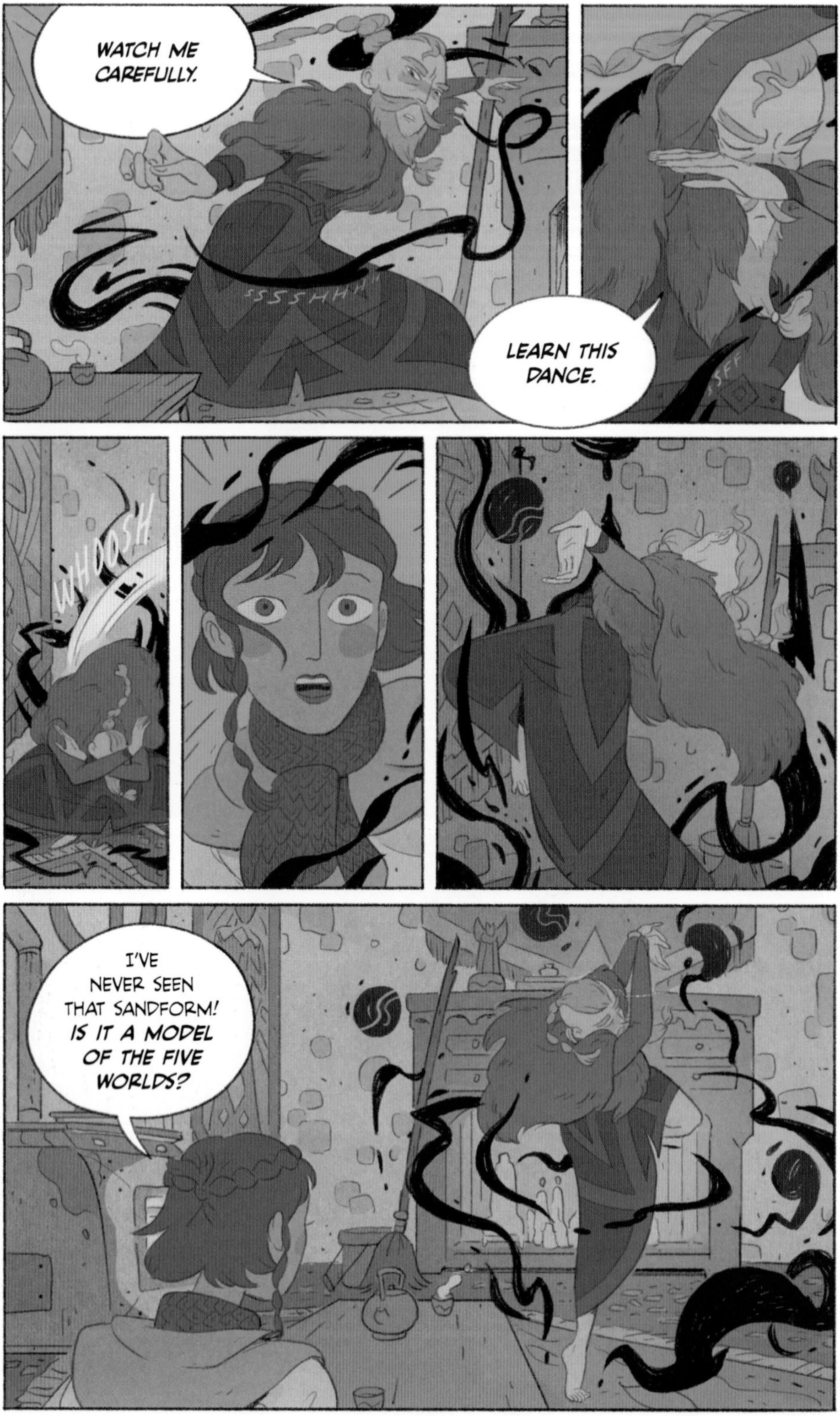
WATCH ME CAREFULLY.
SSSSHHH
LEARN THIS DANCE.
SFF
WHOOSH
I'VE NEVER SEEN THAT SANDFORM! IS IT A MODEL OF THE FIVE WORLDS?

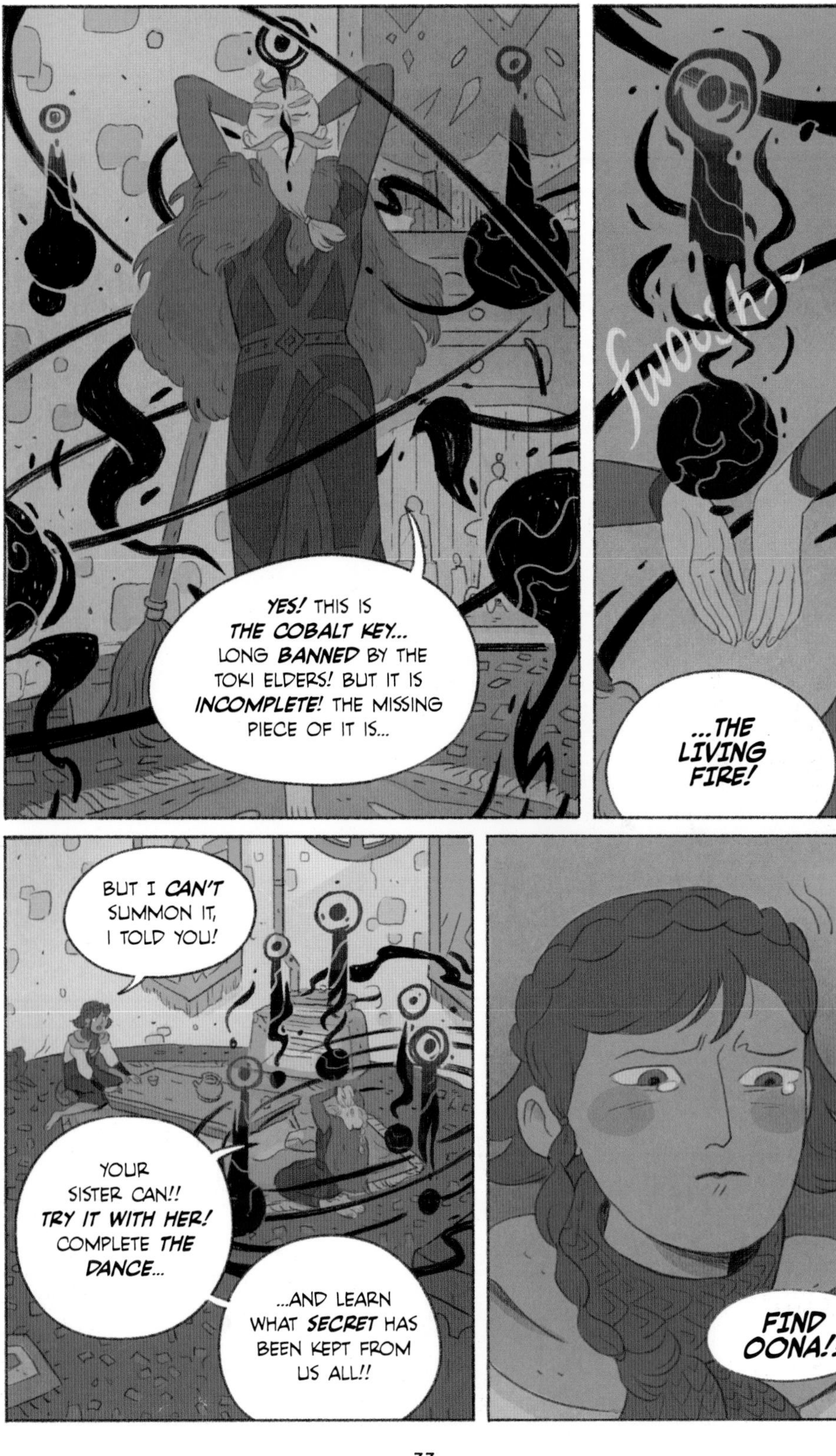
YES! THIS IS THE COBALT KEY... LONG BANNED BY THE TOKI ELDERS! BUT IT IS INCOMPLETE! THE MISSING PIECE OF IT IS...
fwoosh
...THE LIVING FIRE!
BUT I CAN'T SUMMON IT, I TOLD YOU!
YOUR SISTER CAN!! TRY IT WITH HER! COMPLETE THE DANCE...
...AND LEARN WHAT SECRET HAS BEEN KEPT FROM US ALL!!
FIND OONA!!

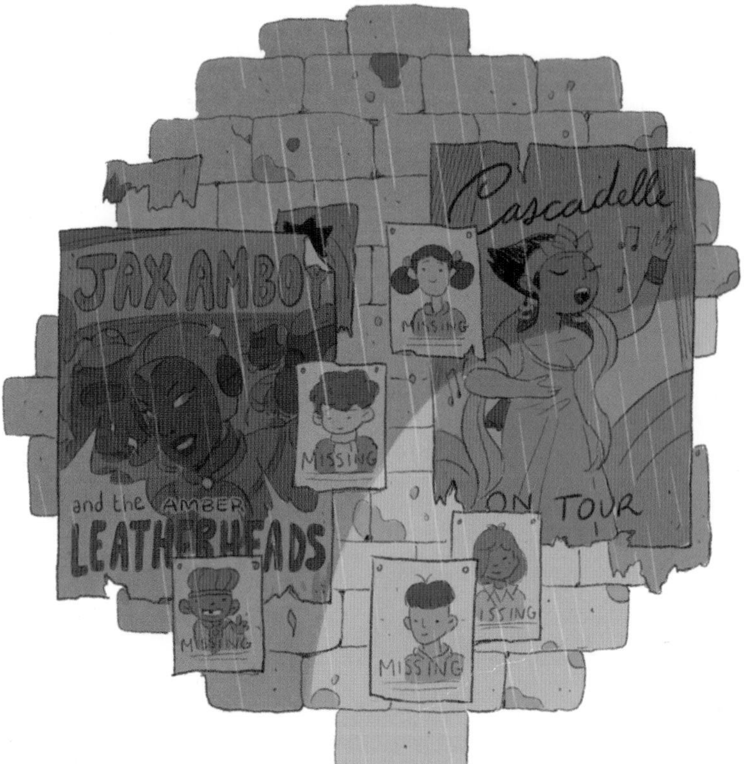
JAX AMBOY
and the AMBER
LEATHERHEADS
Cascadelle
ON TOUR
MISSING
MISSING
MISSING
MISSING
ISSING

Chapter 2
SALASSANDRA

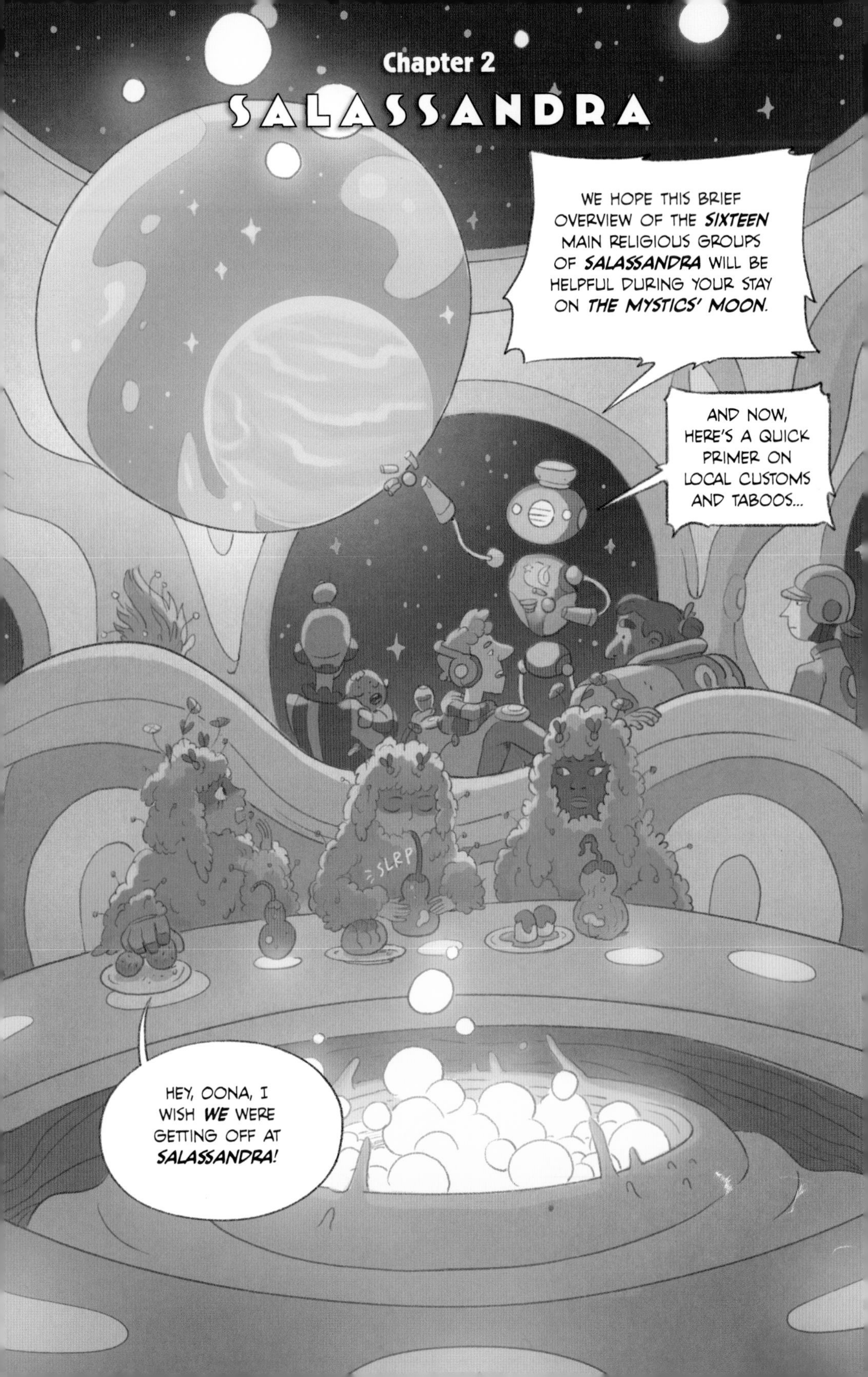
WE HOPE THIS BRIEF OVERVIEW OF THE *SIXTEEN* MAIN RELIGIOUS GROUPS OF *SALASSANDRA* WILL BE HELPFUL DURING YOUR STAY ON *THE MYSTICS' MOON.*
AND NOW, HERE'S A QUICK PRIMER ON LOCAL CUSTOMS AND TABOOS...
SLRP
HEY, OONA, I WISH *WE* WERE GETTING OFF AT *SALASSANDRA!*

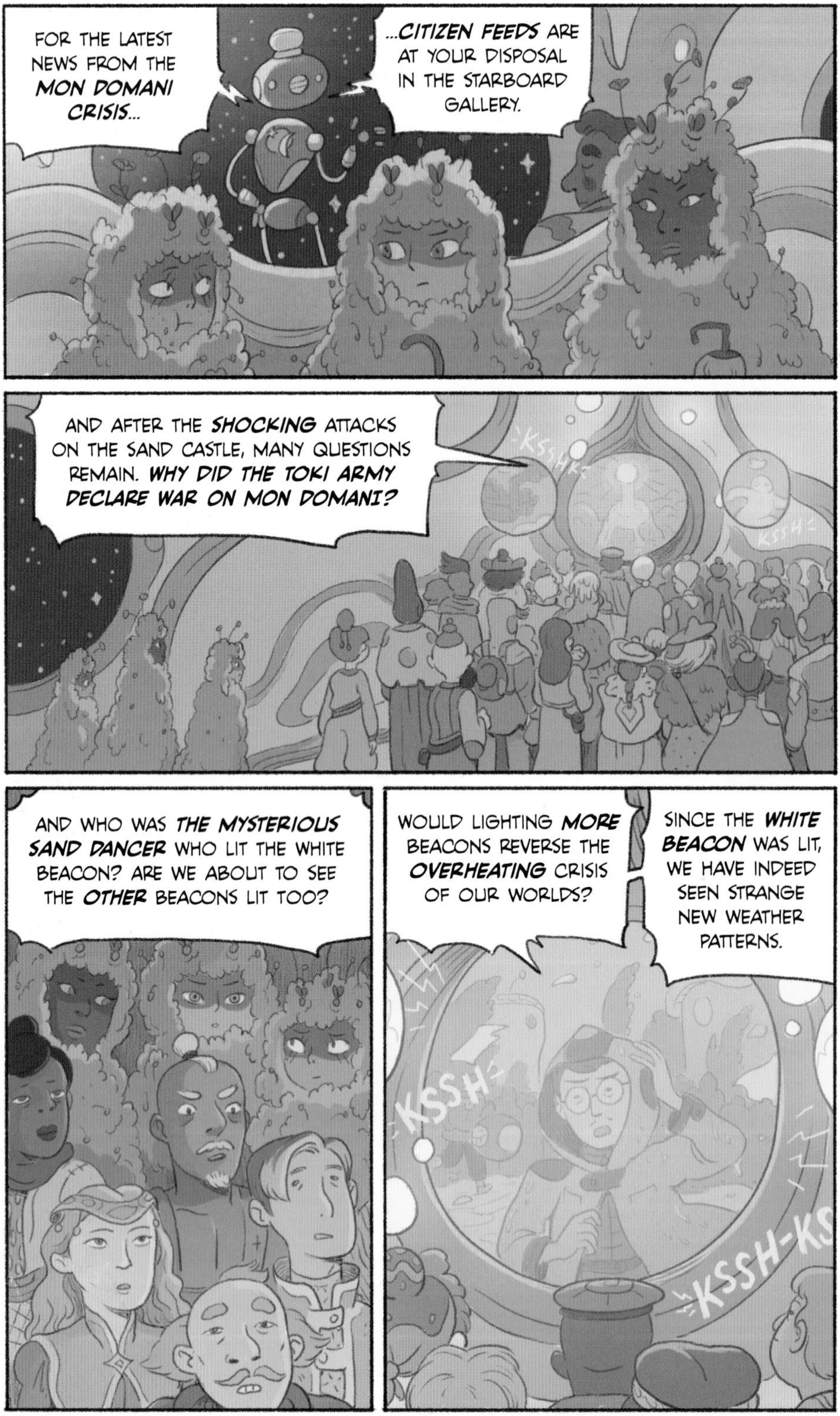
FOR THE LATEST NEWS FROM THE MON DOMANI CRISIS...
...CITIZEN FEEDS ARE AT YOUR DISPOSAL IN THE STARBOARD GALLERY.
AND AFTER THE SHOCKING ATTACKS ON THE SAND CASTLE, MANY QUESTIONS REMAIN. WHY DID THE TOKI ARMY DECLARE WAR ON MON DOMANI?
KSSHKS
KSSH
AND WHO WAS THE MYSTERIOUS SAND DANCER WHO LIT THE WHITE BEACON? ARE WE ABOUT TO SEE THE OTHER BEACONS LIT TOO?
WOULD LIGHTING MORE BEACONS REVERSE THE OVERHEATING CRISIS OF OUR WORLDS?
SINCE THE WHITE BEACON WAS LIT, WE HAVE INDEED SEEN STRANGE NEW WEATHER PATTERNS.
KSSH
KSSH-KS

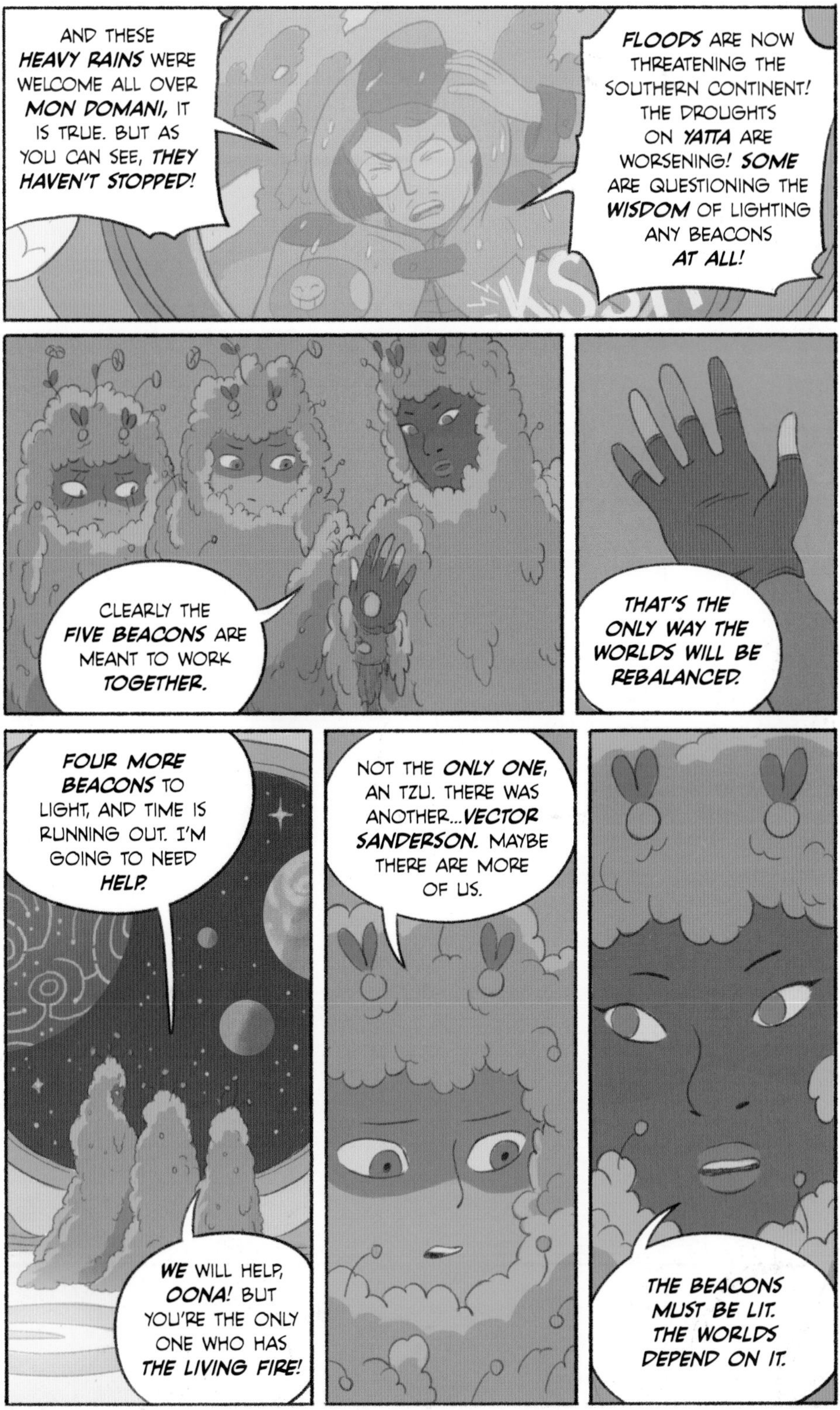
AND THESE HEAVY RAINS WERE WELCOME ALL OVER MON DOMANI, IT IS TRUE. BUT AS YOU CAN SEE, THEY HAVEN'T STOPPED!
FLOODS ARE NOW THREATENING THE SOUTHERN CONTINENT! THE DROUGHTS ON YATTA ARE WORSENING! SOME ARE QUESTIONING THE WISDOM OF LIGHTING ANY BEACONS AT ALL!
KSSH
CLEARLY THE FIVE BEACONS ARE MEANT TO WORK TOGETHER.
THAT'S THE ONLY WAY THE WORLDS WILL BE REBALANCED.
FOUR MORE BEACONS TO LIGHT, AND TIME IS RUNNING OUT. I'M GOING TO NEED HELP.
WE WILL HELP, OONA! BUT YOU'RE THE ONLY ONE WHO HAS THE LIVING FIRE!
NOT THE ONLY ONE, AN TZU. THERE WAS ANOTHER...VECTOR SANDERSON. MAYBE THERE ARE MORE OF US.
THE BEACONS MUST BE LIT. THE WORLDS DEPEND ON IT.

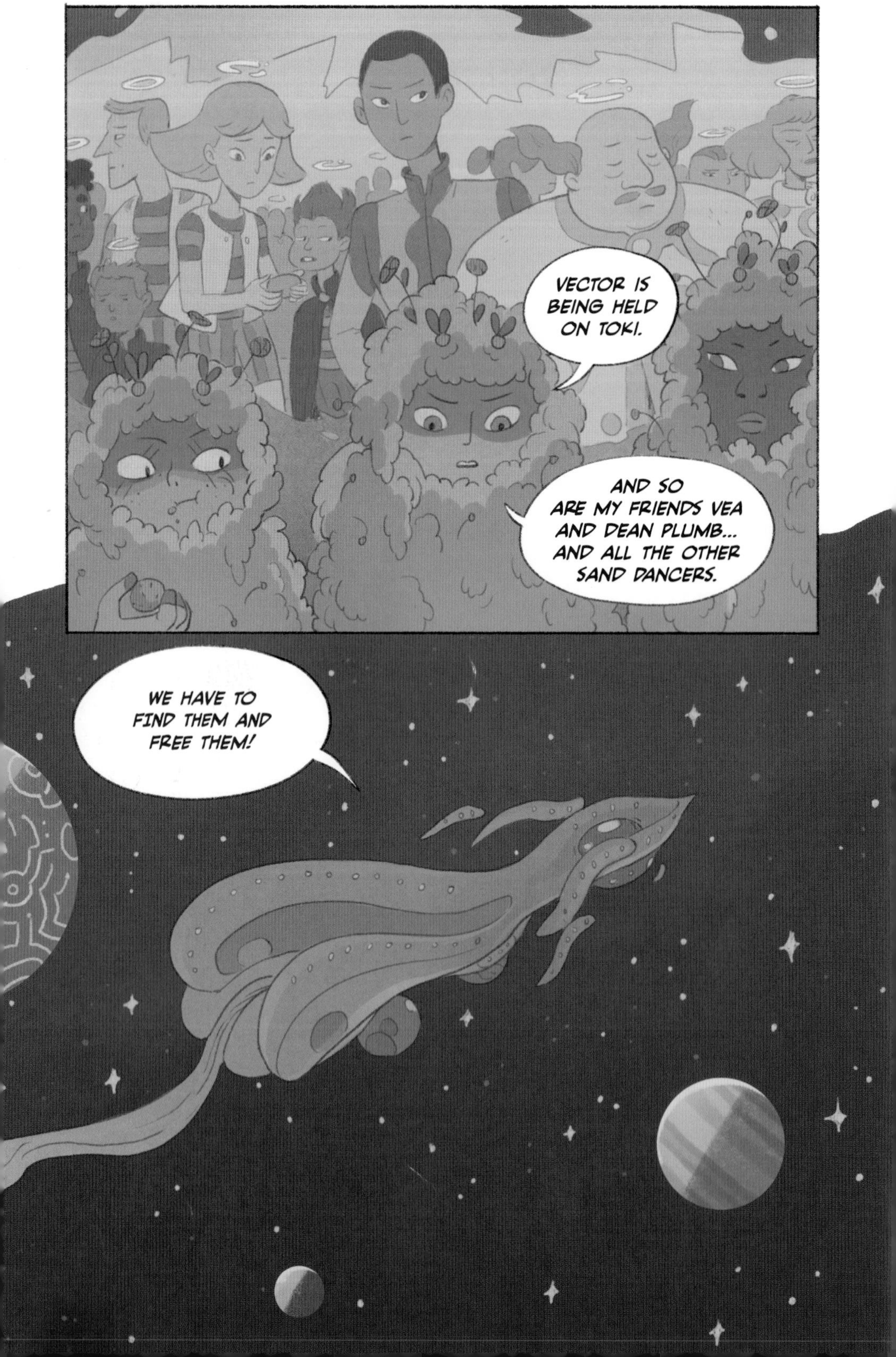
VECTOR IS BEING HELD ON TOKI.
AND SO ARE MY FRIENDS VEA AND DEAN PLUMB... AND ALL THE OTHER SAND DANCERS.
WE HAVE TO FIND THEM AND FREE THEM!

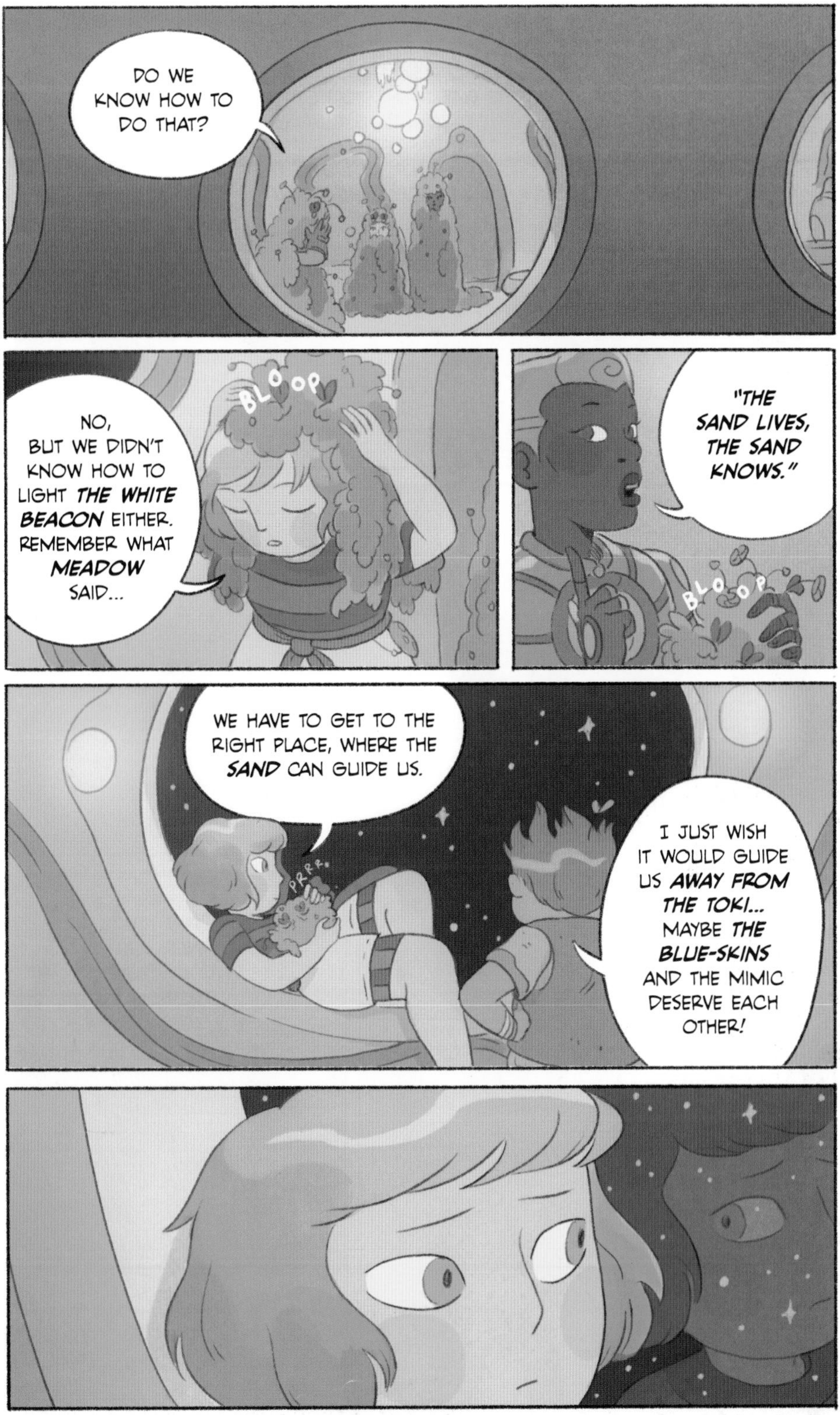
DO WE KNOW HOW TO DO THAT?
NO, BUT WE DIDN'T KNOW HOW TO LIGHT THE WHITE BEACON EITHER. REMEMBER WHAT MEADOW SAID...
BLOOP
"THE SAND LIVES, THE SAND KNOWS."
BLOOP
WE HAVE TO GET TO THE RIGHT PLACE, WHERE THE SAND CAN GUIDE US.
PRRR
I JUST WISH IT WOULD GUIDE US AWAY FROM THE TOKI... MAYBE THE BLUE-SKINS AND THE MIMIC DESERVE EACH OTHER!

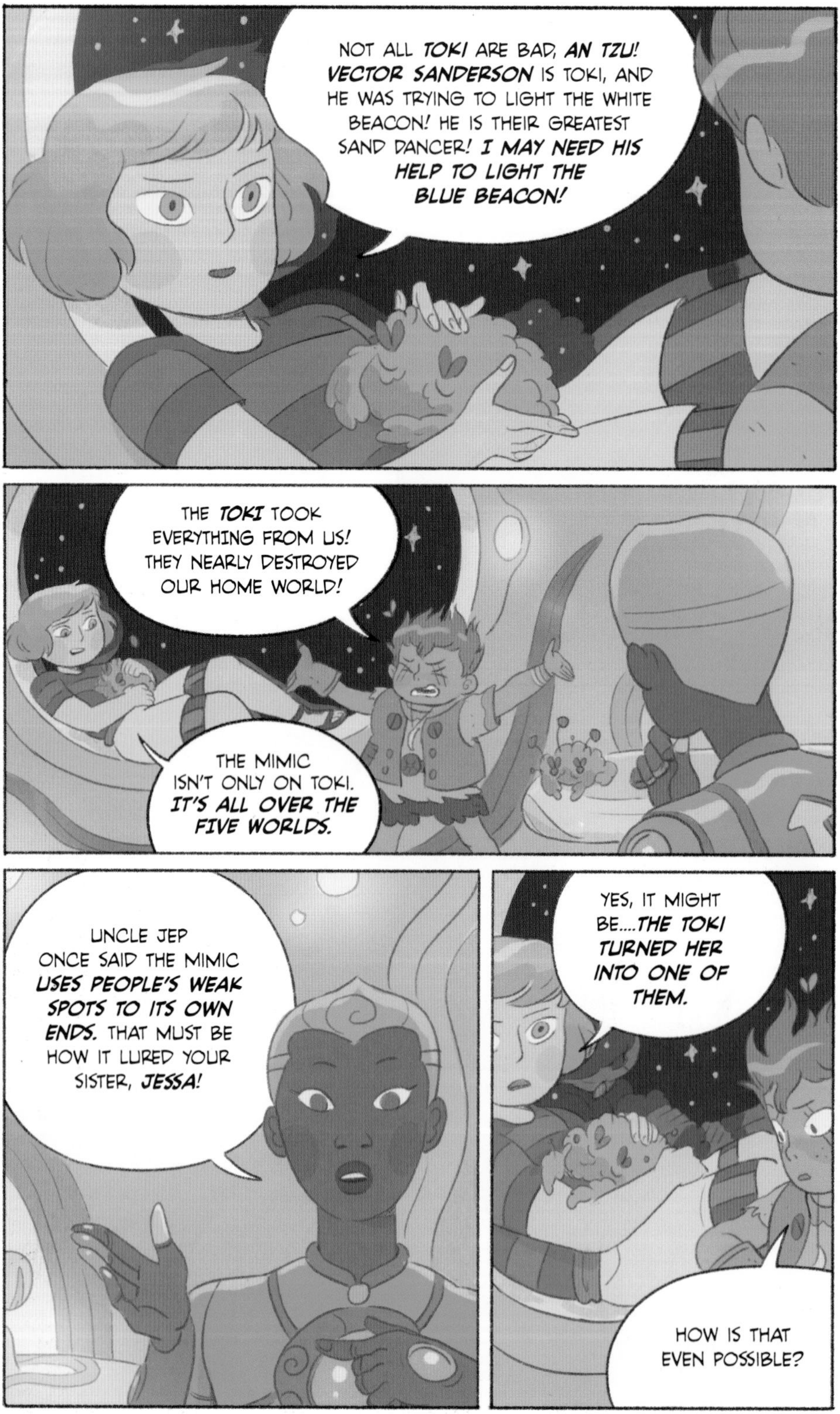
NOT ALL TOKI ARE BAD, AN TZU! VECTOR SANDERSON IS TOKI, AND HE WAS TRYING TO LIGHT THE WHITE BEACON! HE IS THEIR GREATEST SAND DANCER! I MAY NEED HIS HELP TO LIGHT THE BLUE BEACON!
THE TOKI TOOK EVERYTHING FROM US! THEY NEARLY DESTROYED OUR HOME WORLD!
THE MIMIC ISN'T ONLY ON TOKI. IT'S ALL OVER THE FIVE WORLDS.
UNCLE JEP ONCE SAID THE MIMIC USES PEOPLE'S WEAK SPOTS TO ITS OWN ENDS. THAT MUST BE HOW IT LURED YOUR SISTER, JESSA!
YES, IT MIGHT BE....THE TOKI TURNED HER INTO ONE OF THEM.
HOW IS THAT EVEN POSSIBLE?

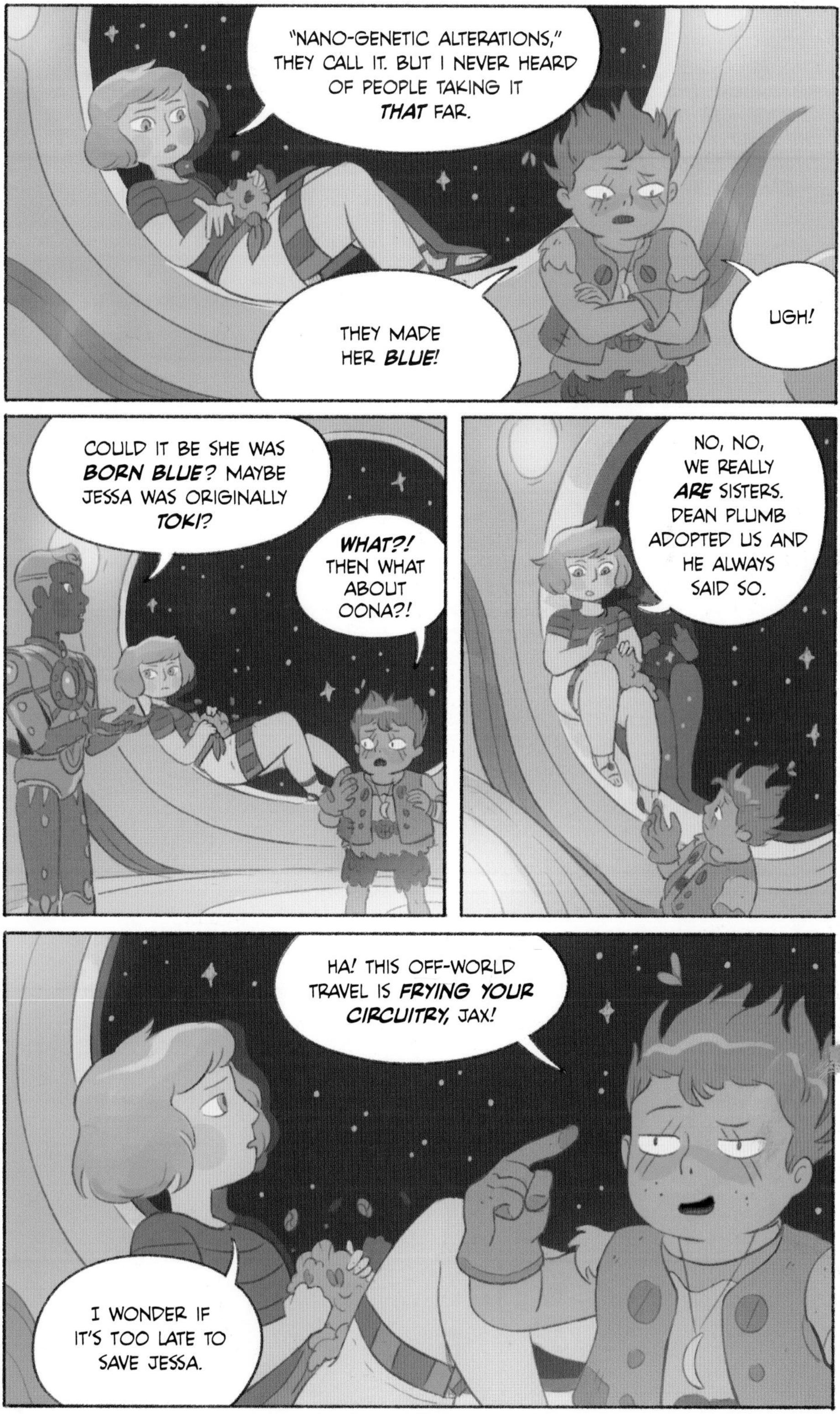
"NANO-GENETIC ALTERATIONS," THEY CALL IT. BUT I NEVER HEARD OF PEOPLE TAKING IT *THAT* FAR.
THEY MADE HER *BLUE!*
UGH!
COULD IT BE SHE WAS *BORN BLUE*? MAYBE JESSA WAS ORIGINALLY *TOKI*?
WHAT?! THEN WHAT ABOUT OONA?!
NO, NO, WE REALLY *ARE* SISTERS. DEAN PLUMB ADOPTED US AND HE ALWAYS SAID SO.
HA! THIS OFF-WORLD TRAVEL IS *FRYING YOUR CIRCUITRY,* JAX!
I WONDER IF IT'S TOO LATE TO SAVE JESSA.

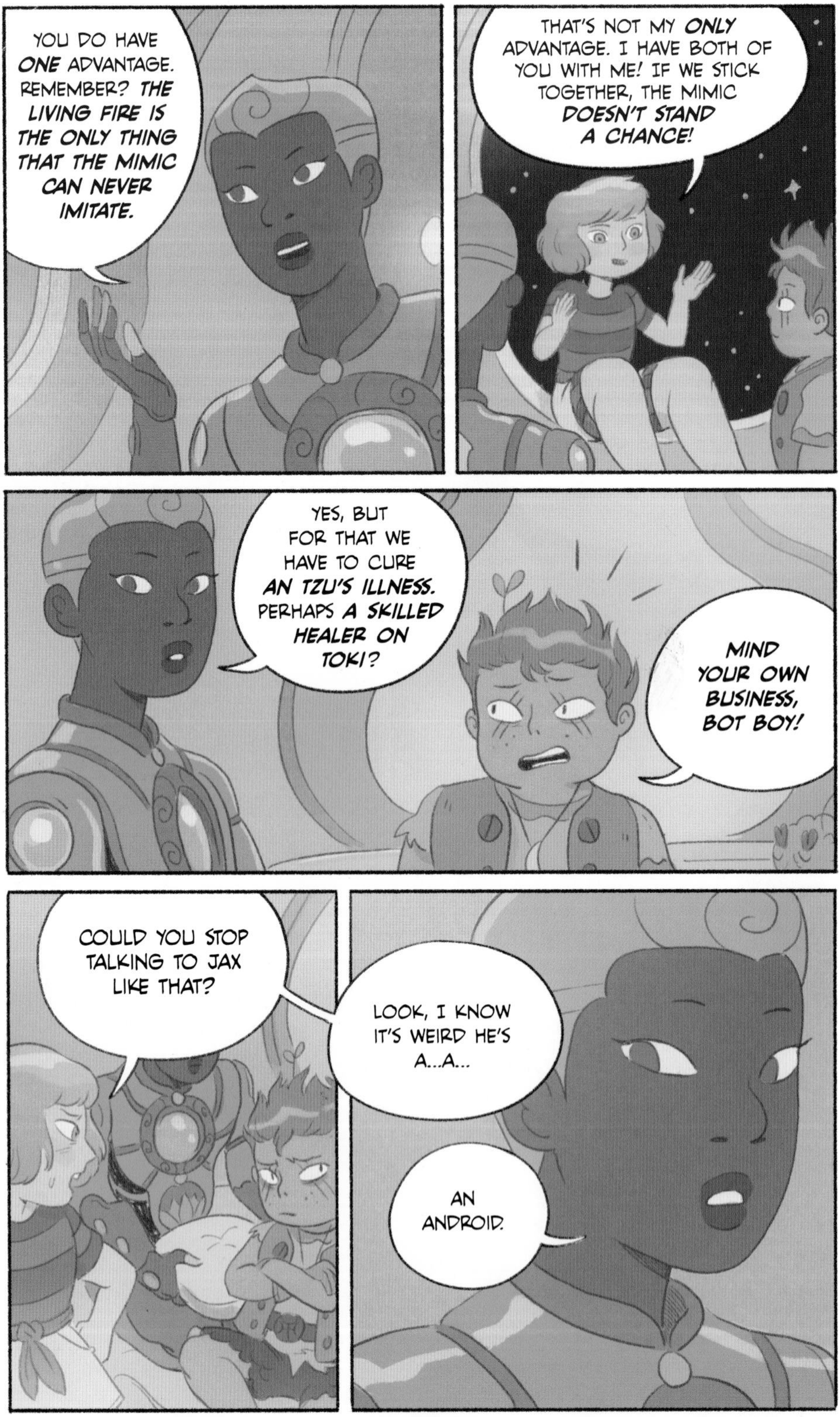
YOU DO HAVE ONE ADVANTAGE. REMEMBER? THE LIVING FIRE IS THE ONLY THING THAT THE MIMIC CAN NEVER IMITATE.
THAT'S NOT MY ONLY ADVANTAGE. I HAVE BOTH OF YOU WITH ME! IF WE STICK TOGETHER, THE MIMIC DOESN'T STAND A CHANCE!
YES, BUT FOR THAT WE HAVE TO CURE AN TZU'S ILLNESS. PERHAPS A SKILLED HEALER ON TOKI?
MIND YOUR OWN BUSINESS, BOT BOY!
COULD YOU STOP TALKING TO JAX LIKE THAT?
LOOK, I KNOW IT'S WEIRD HE'S A...A...
AN ANDROID.

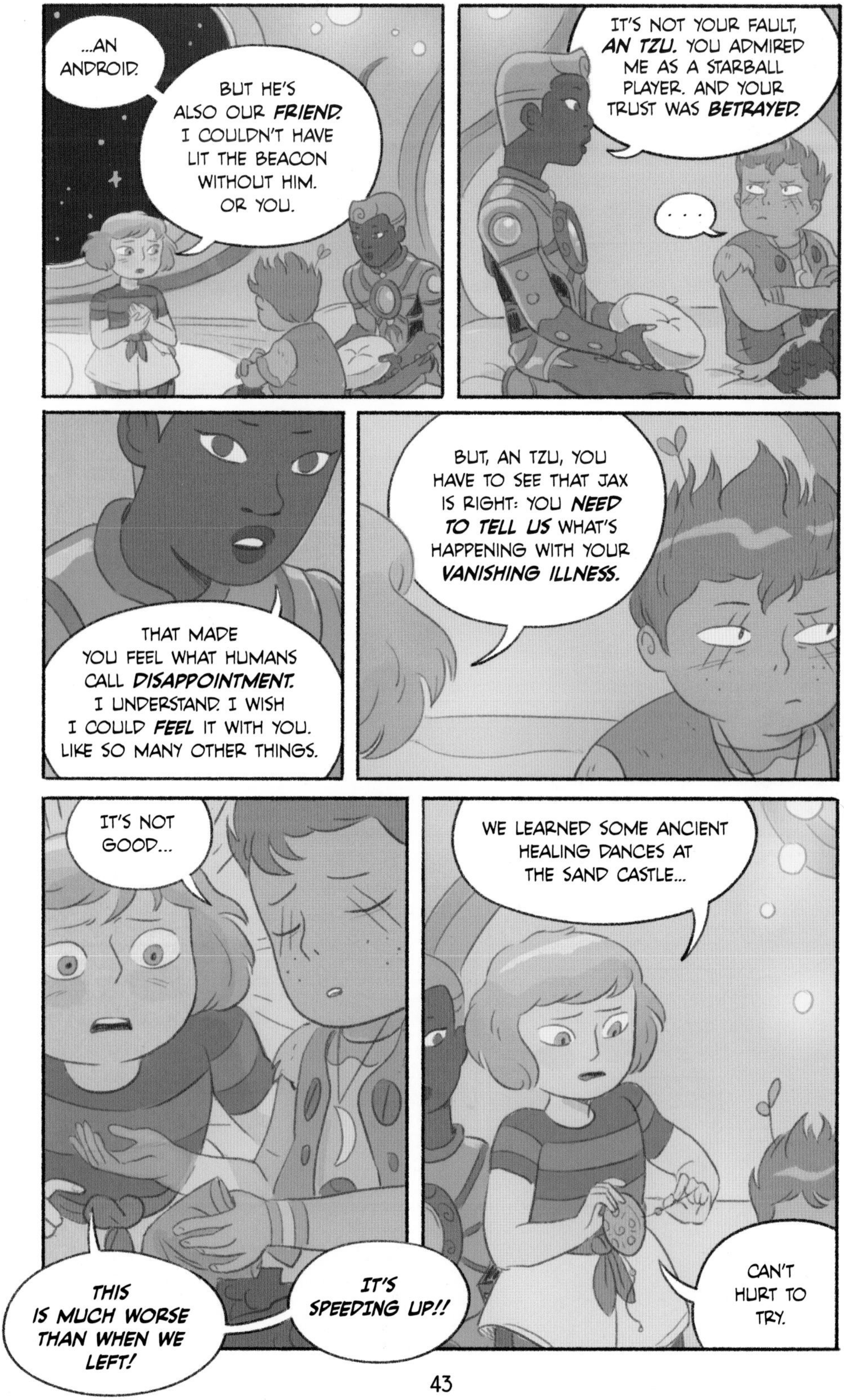
...AN ANDROID.
BUT HE'S ALSO OUR FRIEND. I COULDN'T HAVE LIT THE BEACON WITHOUT HIM. OR YOU.
IT'S NOT YOUR FAULT, AN TZU. YOU ADMIRED ME AS A STARBALL PLAYER. AND YOUR TRUST WAS BETRAYED.
. . .
THAT MADE YOU FEEL WHAT HUMANS CALL DISAPPOINTMENT. I UNDERSTAND. I WISH I COULD FEEL IT WITH YOU. LIKE SO MANY OTHER THINGS.
BUT, AN TZU, YOU HAVE TO SEE THAT JAX IS RIGHT: YOU NEED TO TELL US WHAT'S HAPPENING WITH YOUR VANISHING ILLNESS.
IT'S NOT GOOD...
THIS IS MUCH WORSE THAN WHEN WE LEFT!
IT'S SPEEDING UP!!
WE LEARNED SOME ANCIENT HEALING DANCES AT THE SAND CASTLE...
CAN'T HURT TO TRY.

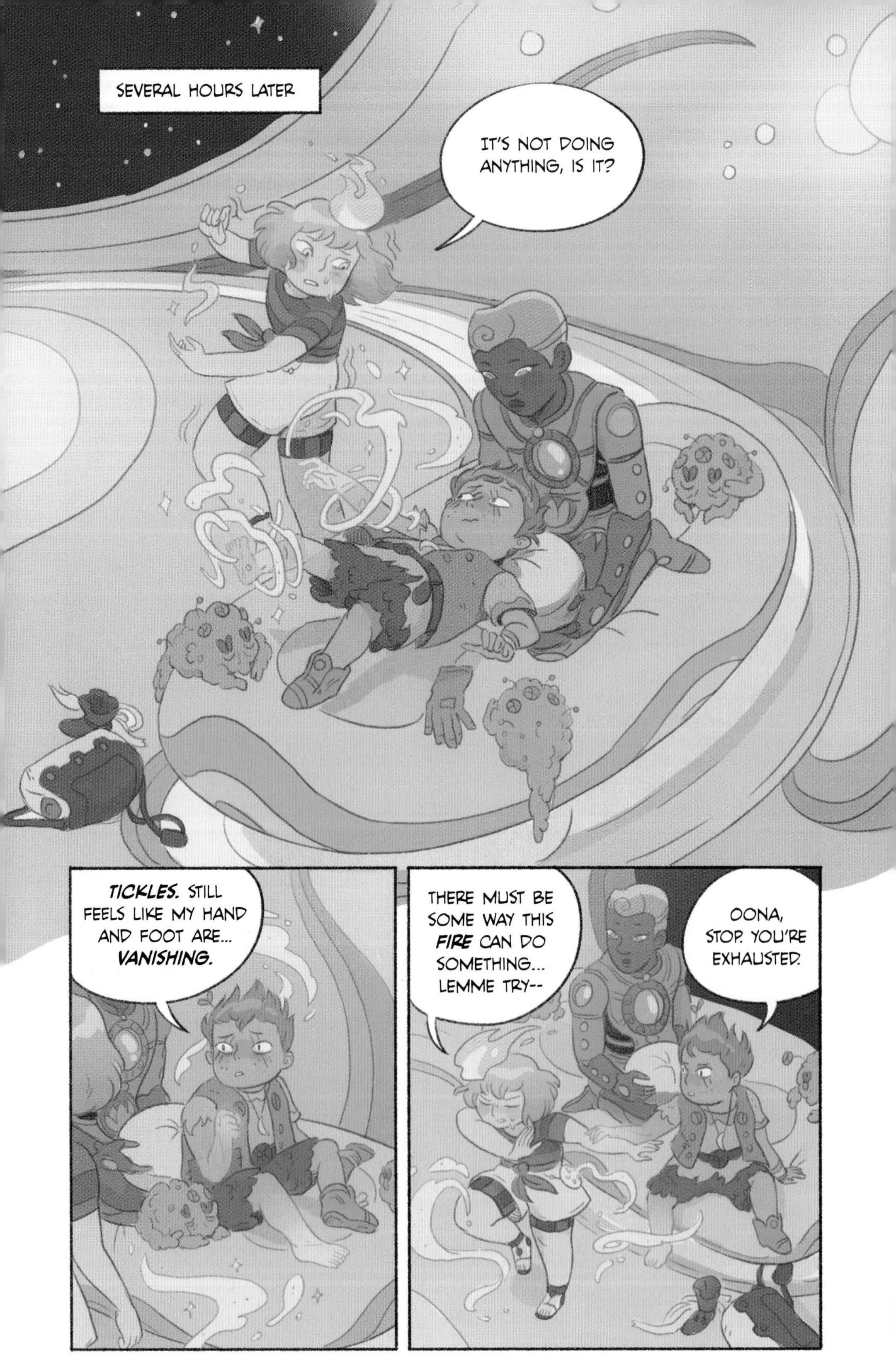
SEVERAL HOURS LATER
IT'S NOT DOING ANYTHING, IS IT?
TICKLES. STILL FEELS LIKE MY HAND AND FOOT ARE... *VANISHING.*
THERE MUST BE SOME WAY THIS *FIRE* CAN DO SOMETHING... LEMME TRY--
OONA, STOP. YOU'RE EXHAUSTED.

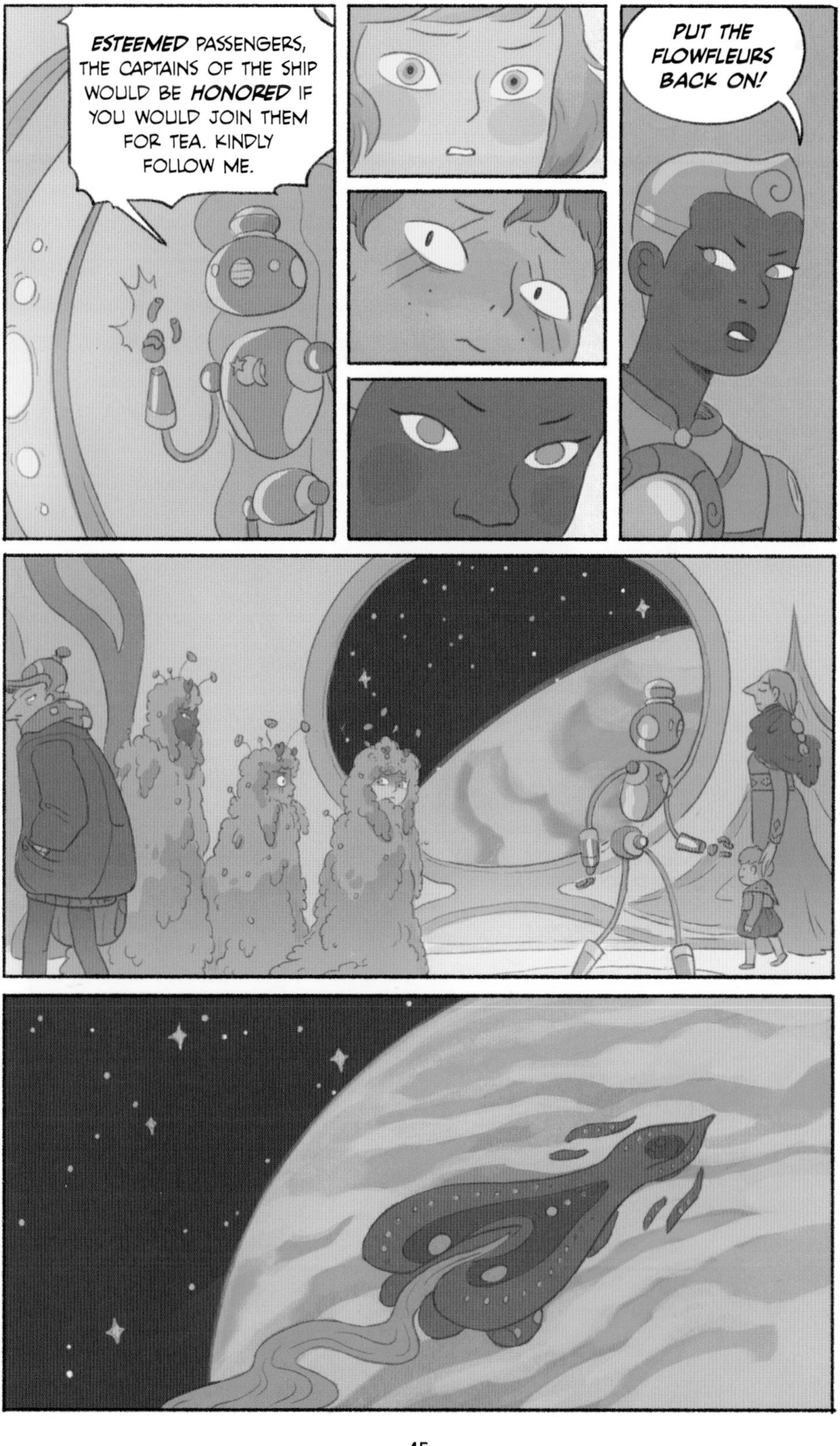
ESTEEMED PASSENGERS, THE CAPTAINS OF THE SHIP WOULD BE HONORED IF YOU WOULD JOIN THEM FOR TEA. KINDLY FOLLOW ME.
PUT THE FLOWFLEURS BACK ON!

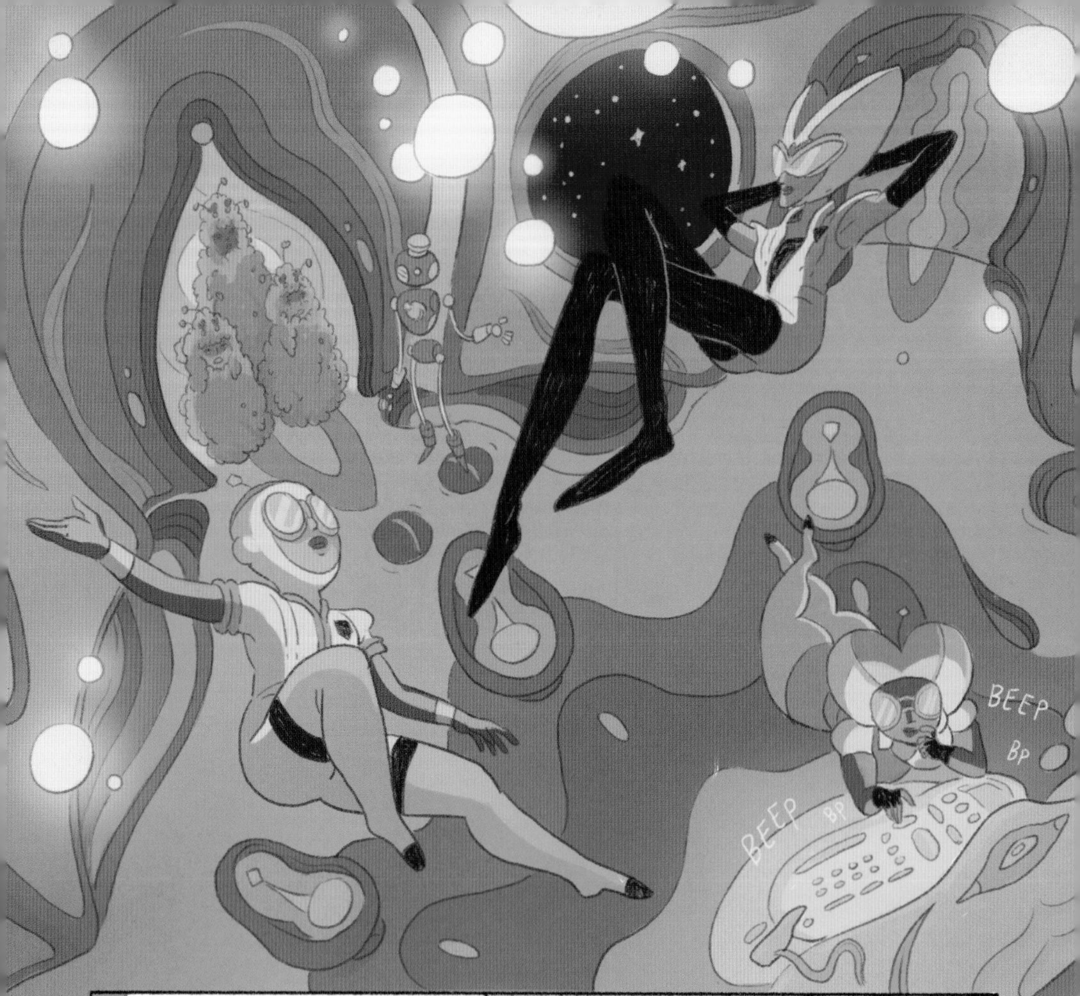
BEEP
Bp
BEEP
BP

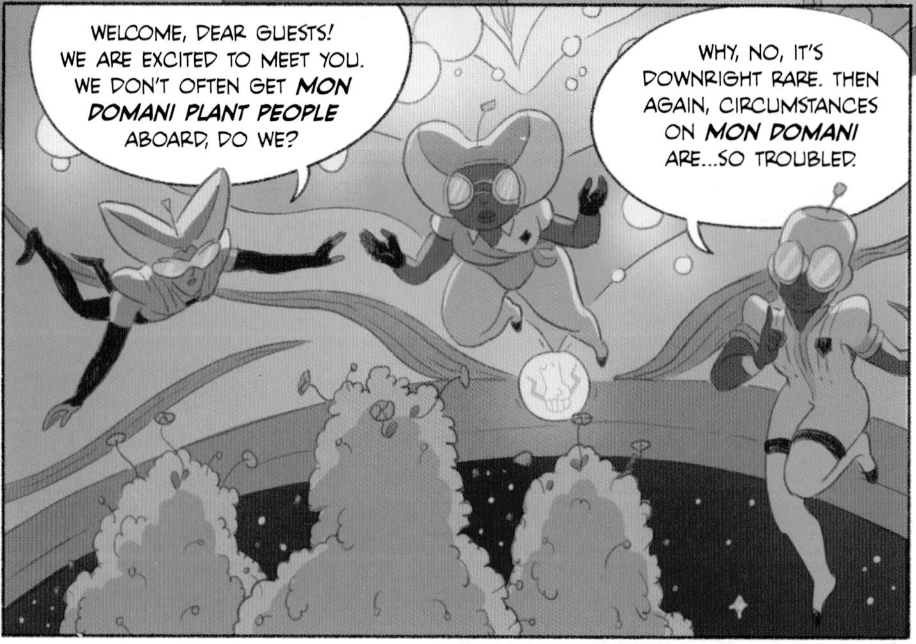
WELCOME, DEAR GUESTS! WE ARE EXCITED TO MEET YOU. WE DON'T OFTEN GET ***MON DOMANI PLANT PEOPLE*** ABOARD, DO WE?
WHY, NO, IT'S DOWNRIGHT RARE. THEN AGAIN, CIRCUMSTANCES ON ***MON DOMANI*** ARE...SO TROUBLED.

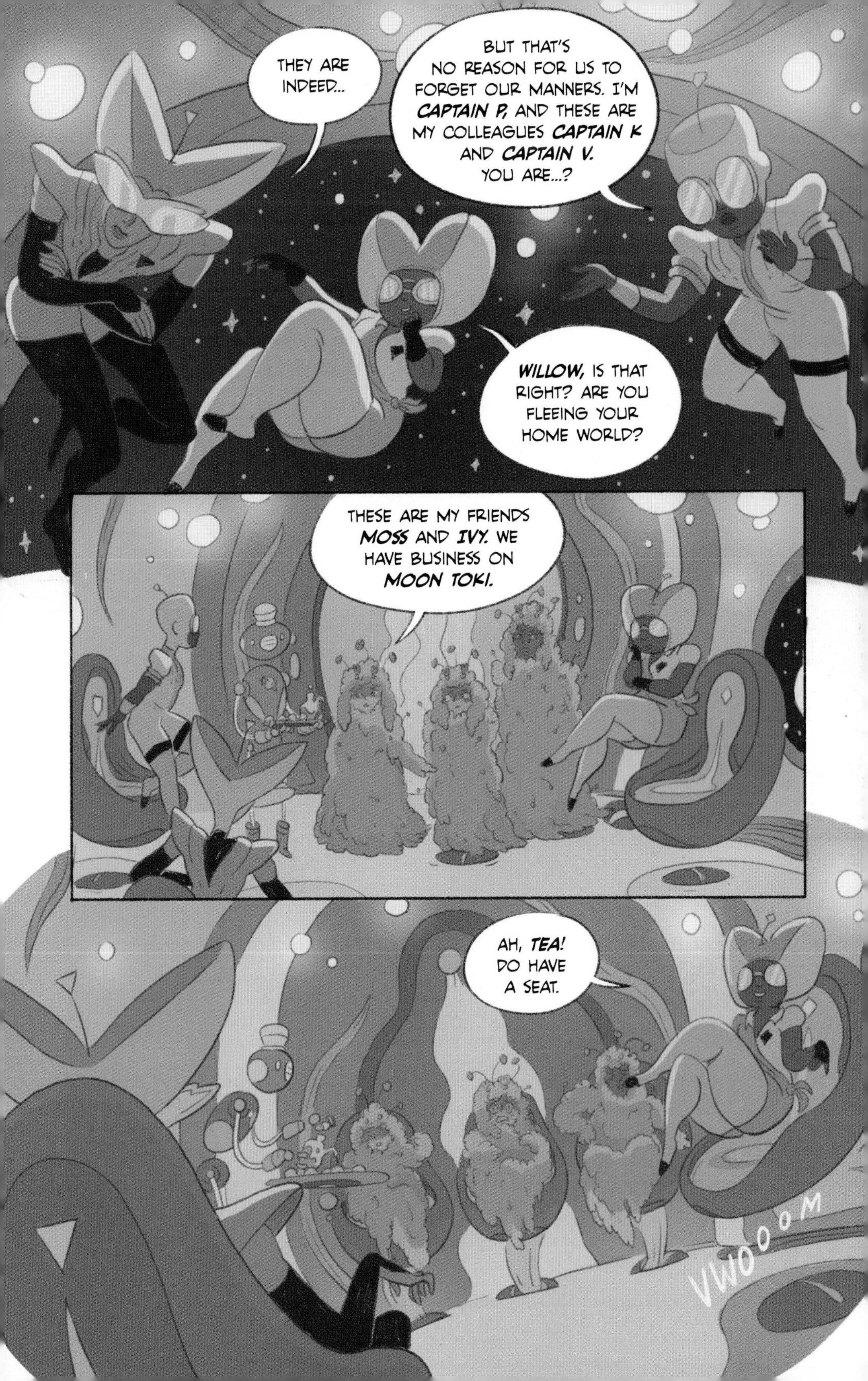
THEY ARE INDEED...
BUT THAT'S NO REASON FOR US TO FORGET OUR MANNERS. I'M CAPTAIN P, AND THESE ARE MY COLLEAGUES CAPTAIN K AND CAPTAIN V. YOU ARE...?
WILLOW, IS THAT RIGHT? ARE YOU FLEEING YOUR HOME WORLD?
THESE ARE MY FRIENDS MOSS AND IVY. WE HAVE BUSINESS ON MOON TOKI.
AH, TEA! DO HAVE A SEAT.
VWOOOOM

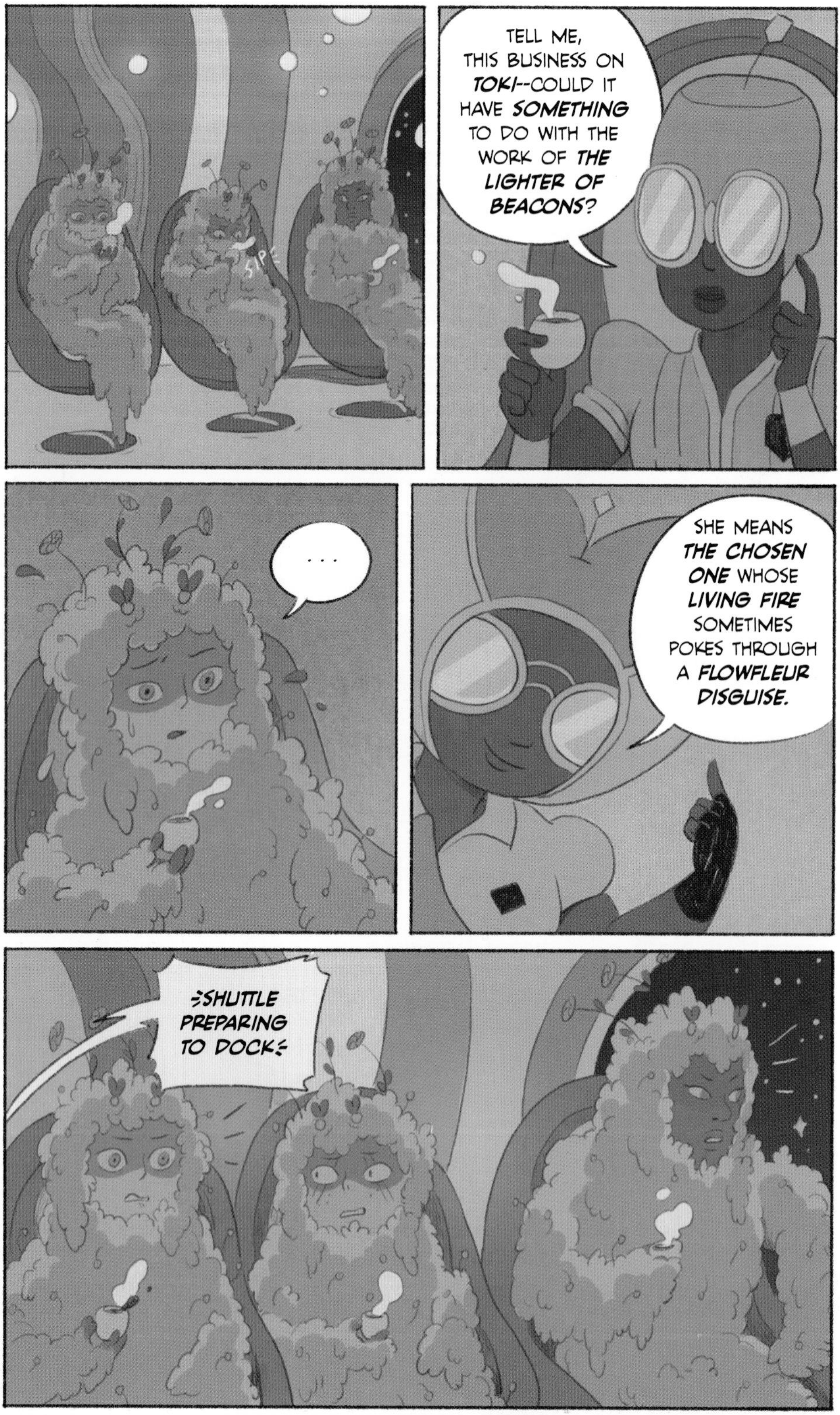
SIP
TELL ME, THIS BUSINESS ON TOKI--COULD IT HAVE SOMETHING TO DO WITH THE WORK OF THE LIGHTER OF BEACONS?
. . .
SHE MEANS THE CHOSEN ONE WHOSE LIVING FIRE SOMETIMES POKES THROUGH A FLOWFLEUR DISGUISE.
SHUTTLE PREPARING TO DOCK

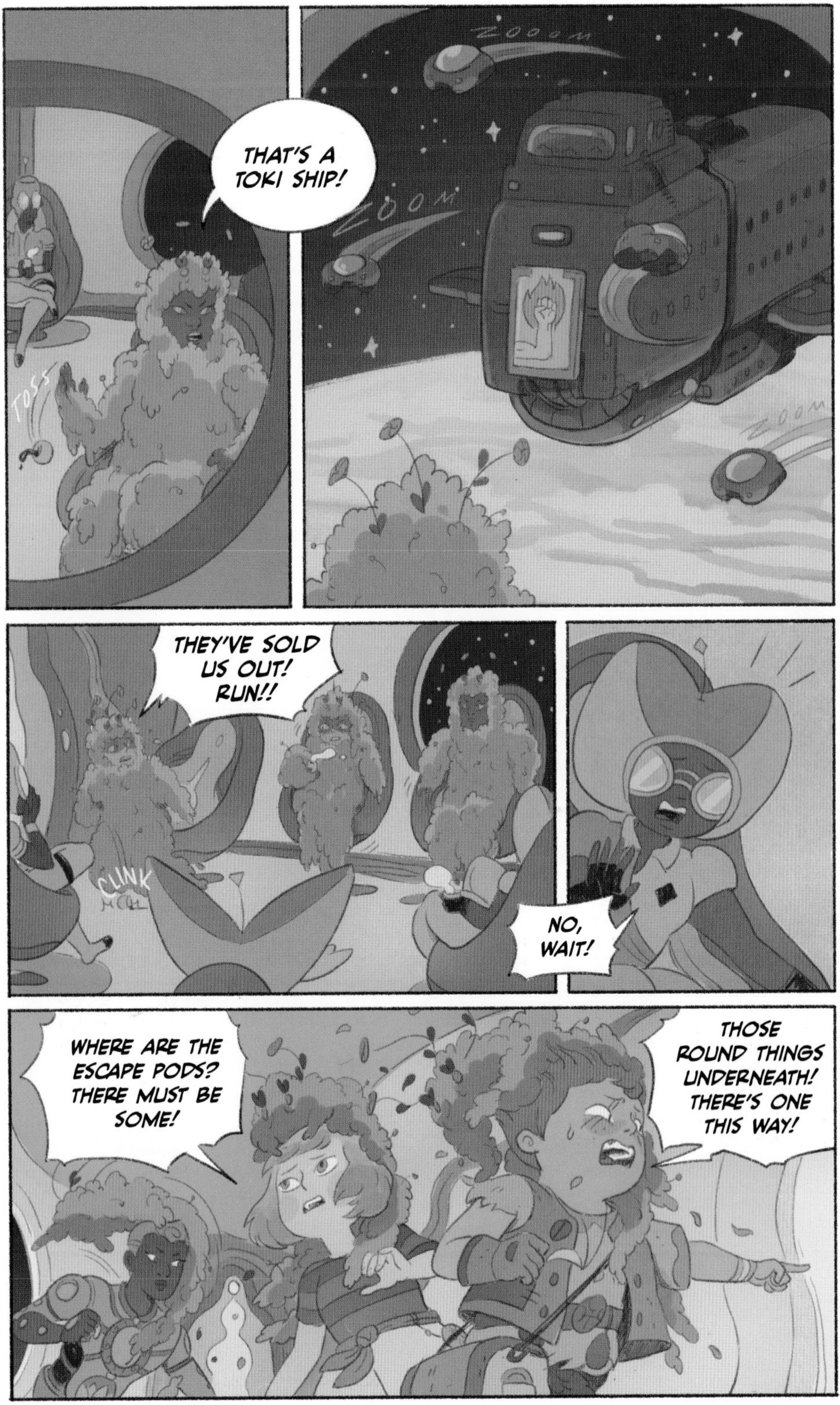
THAT'S A TOKI SHIP!
TOSS
ZOOOM
ZOOM
ZOOM
THEY'VE SOLD US OUT! RUN!!
CLINK
NO, WAIT!
WHERE ARE THE ESCAPE PODS? THERE MUST BE SOME!
THOSE ROUND THINGS UNDERNEATH! THERE'S ONE THIS WAY!

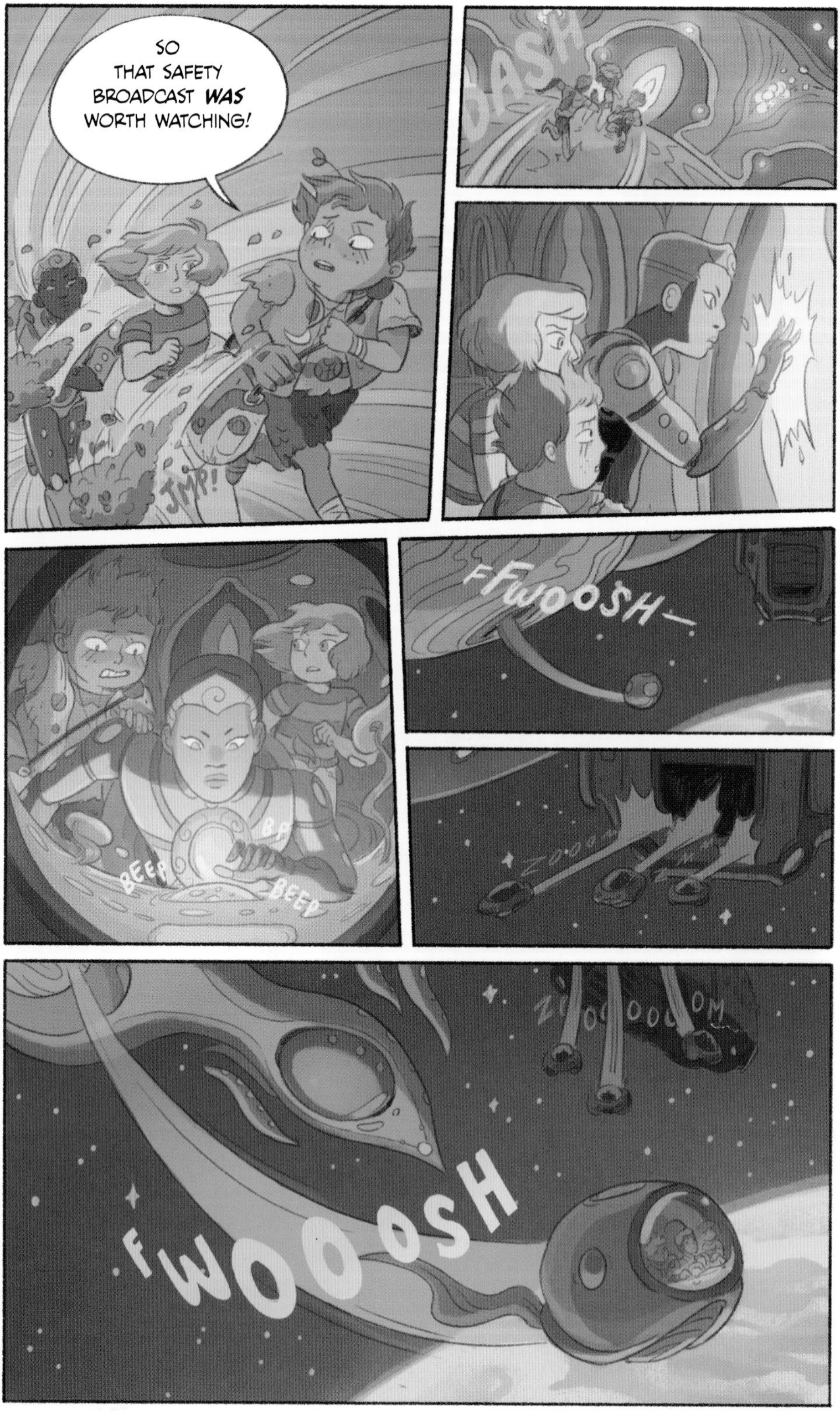
SO THAT SAFETY BROADCAST **WAS** WORTH WATCHING!
JMP!
DASH
FFWOOSH—
BEEP
BEEP
BEEP
ZOOOOM
ZOOOOOOOM
FWOOOSH

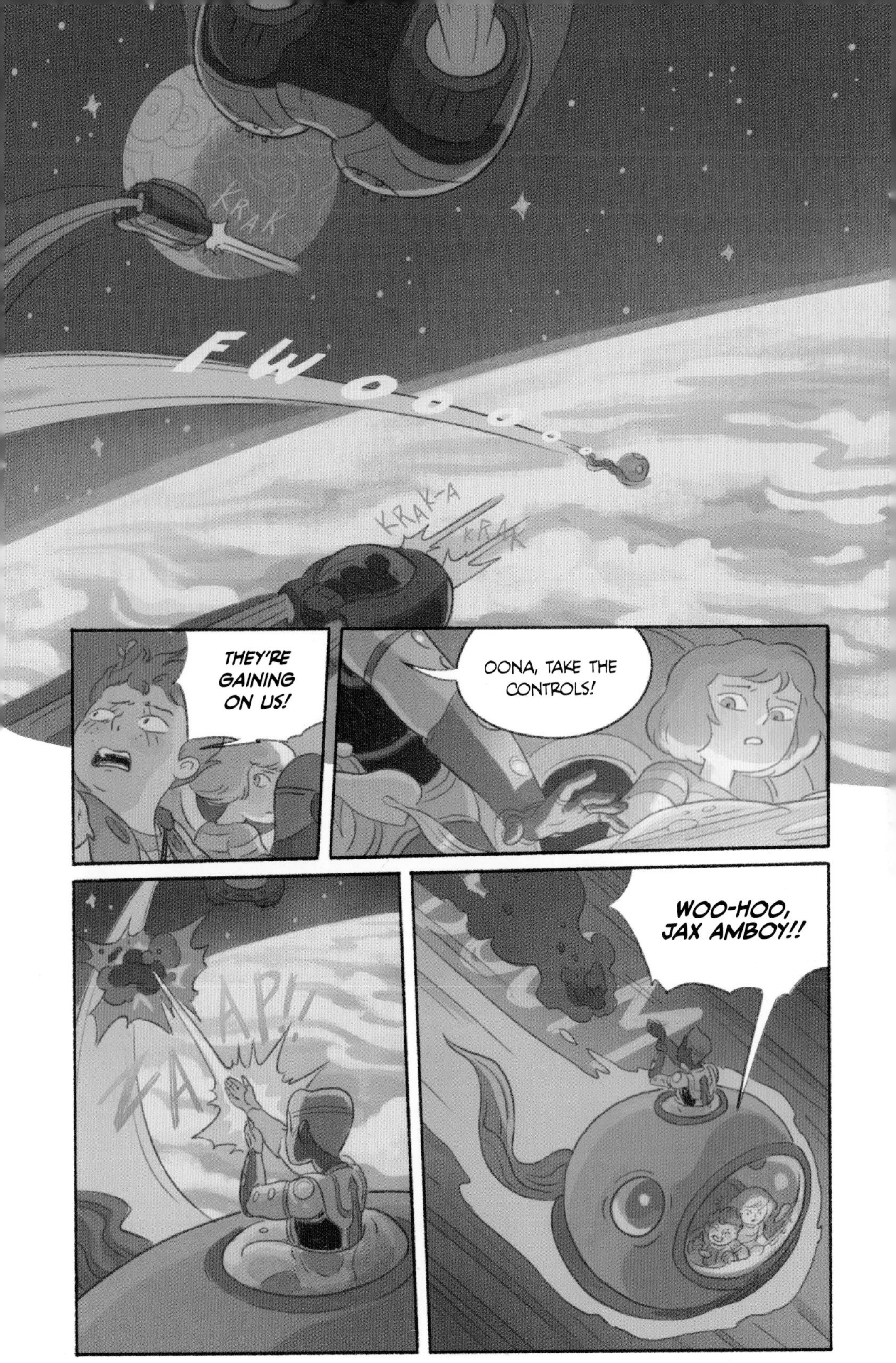
KRAK
FWOOOOO...
KRAK-A KRAK
THEY'RE GAINING ON US!
OONA, TAKE THE CONTROLS!
ZAP!!
WOO-HOO, JAX AMBOY!!

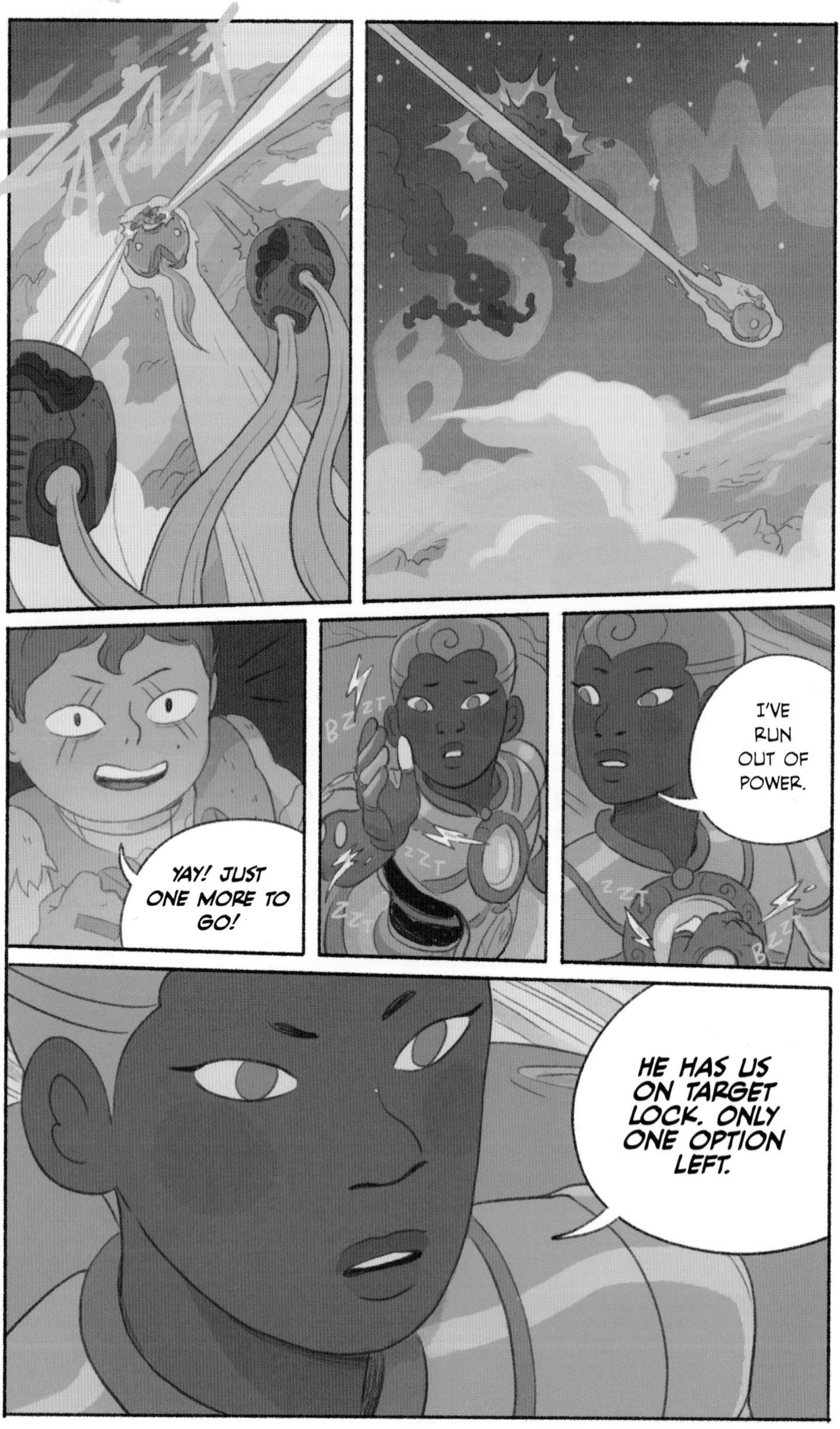
ZAPZZZT
BOOM
YAY! JUST ONE MORE TO GO!
BZZT
ZZT
ZZT
I'VE RUN OUT OF POWER.
ZZT
BZZT
HE HAS US ON TARGET LOCK. ONLY ONE OPTION LEFT.

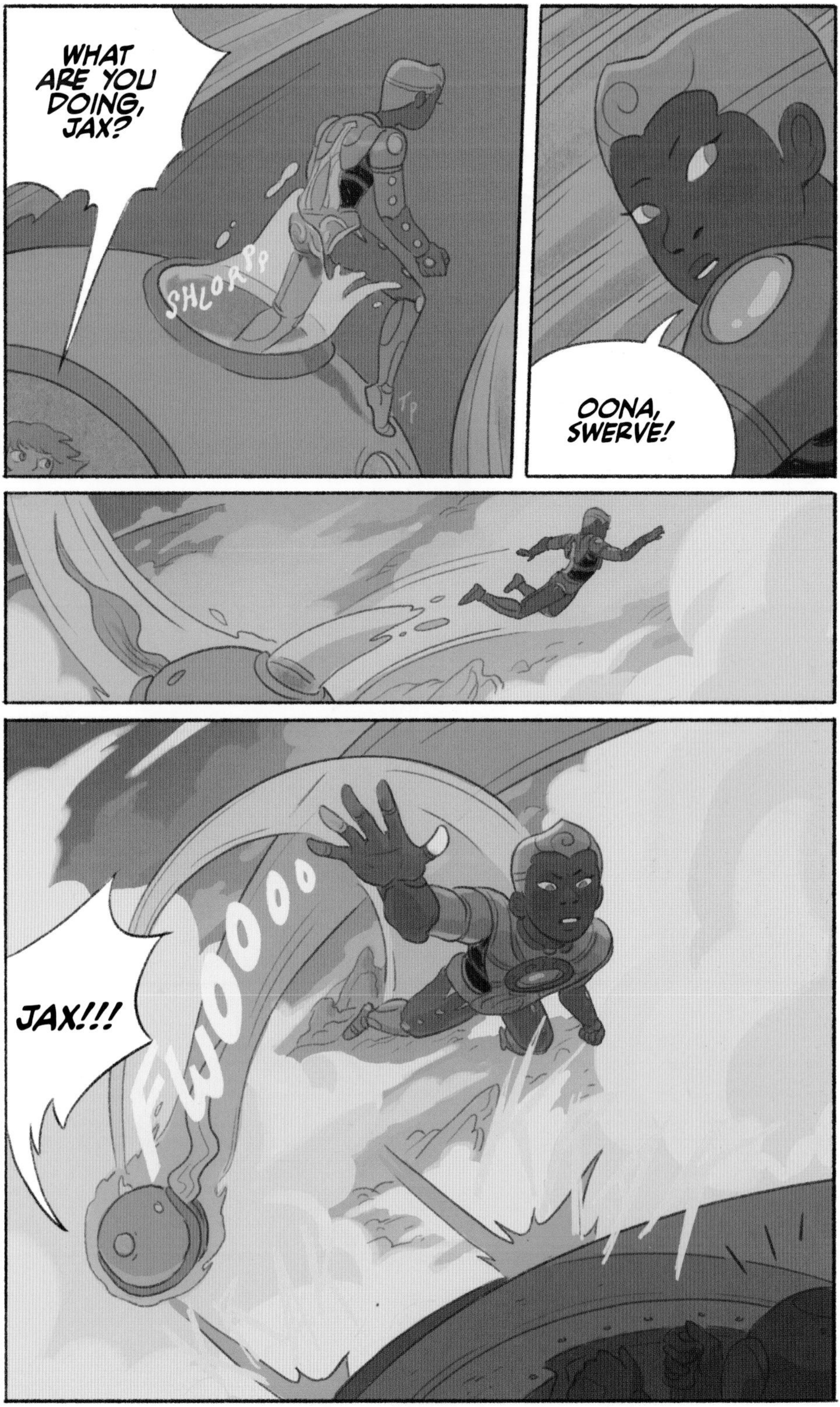
WHAT ARE YOU DOING, JAX?
SHLORPP
TP
OONA, SWERVE!
JAX!!!
FWOOOO

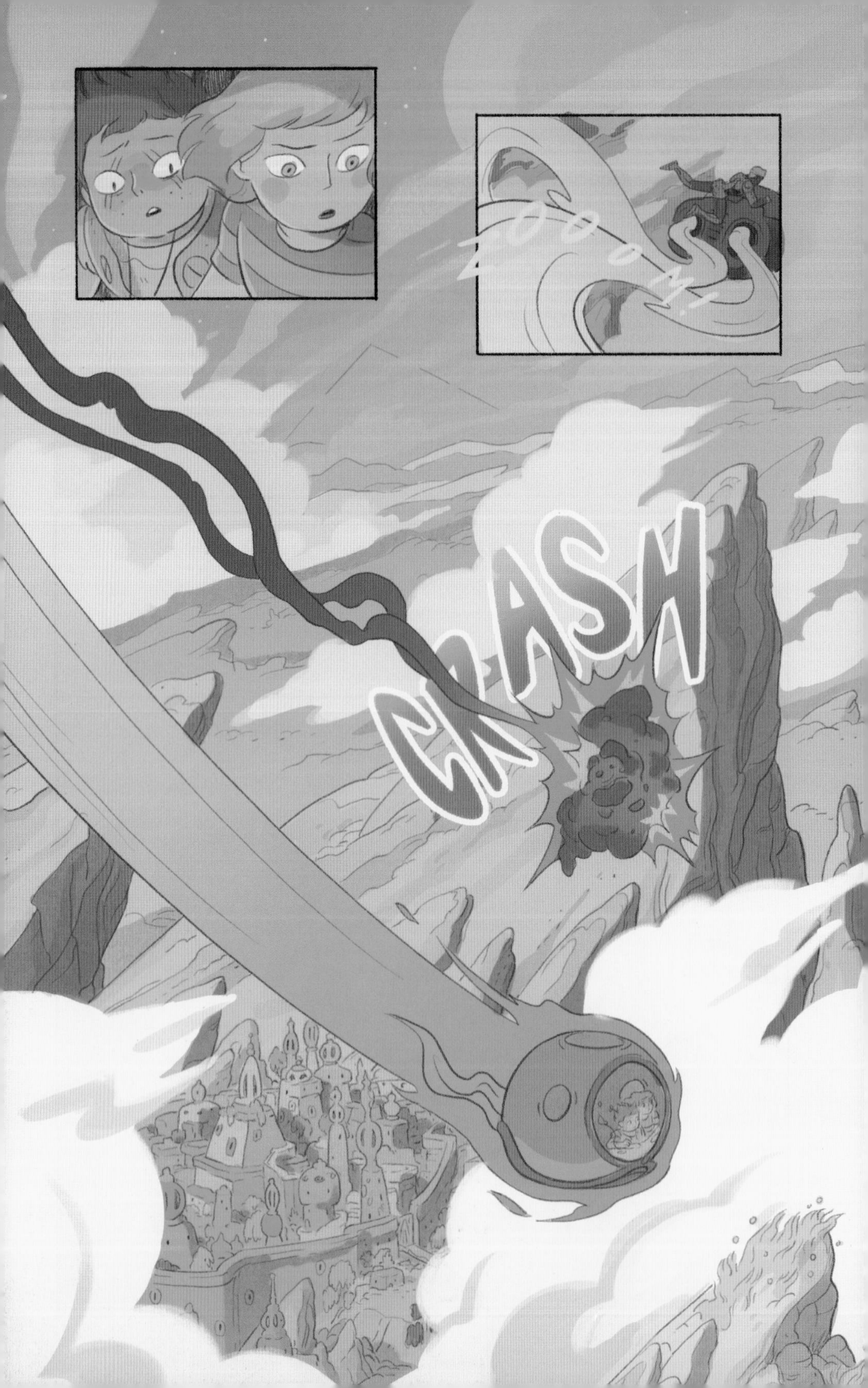

ZOOOOM!!
CRASH

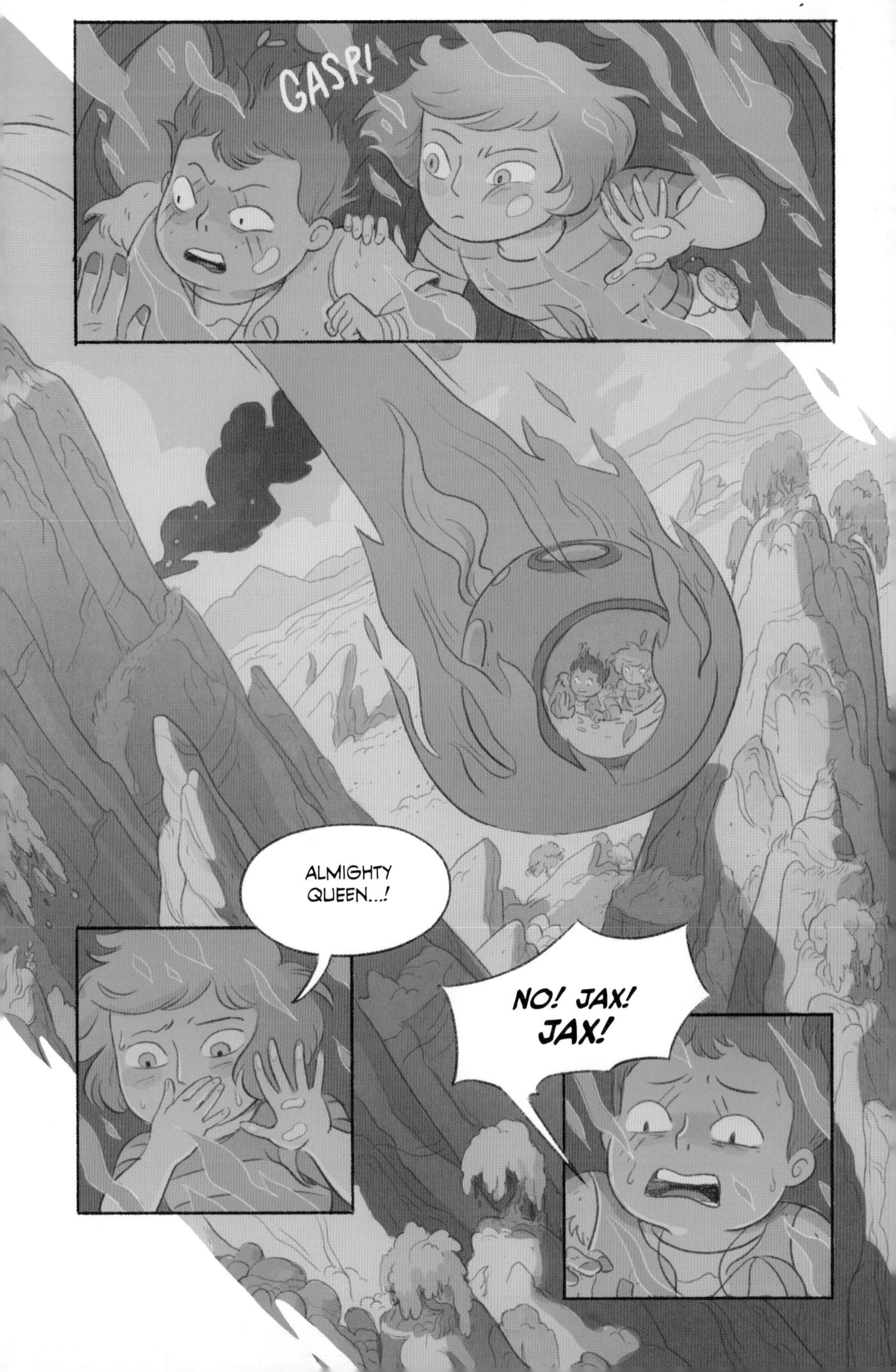
GASP!
ALMIGHTY QUEEN...!
NO! JAX! JAX!

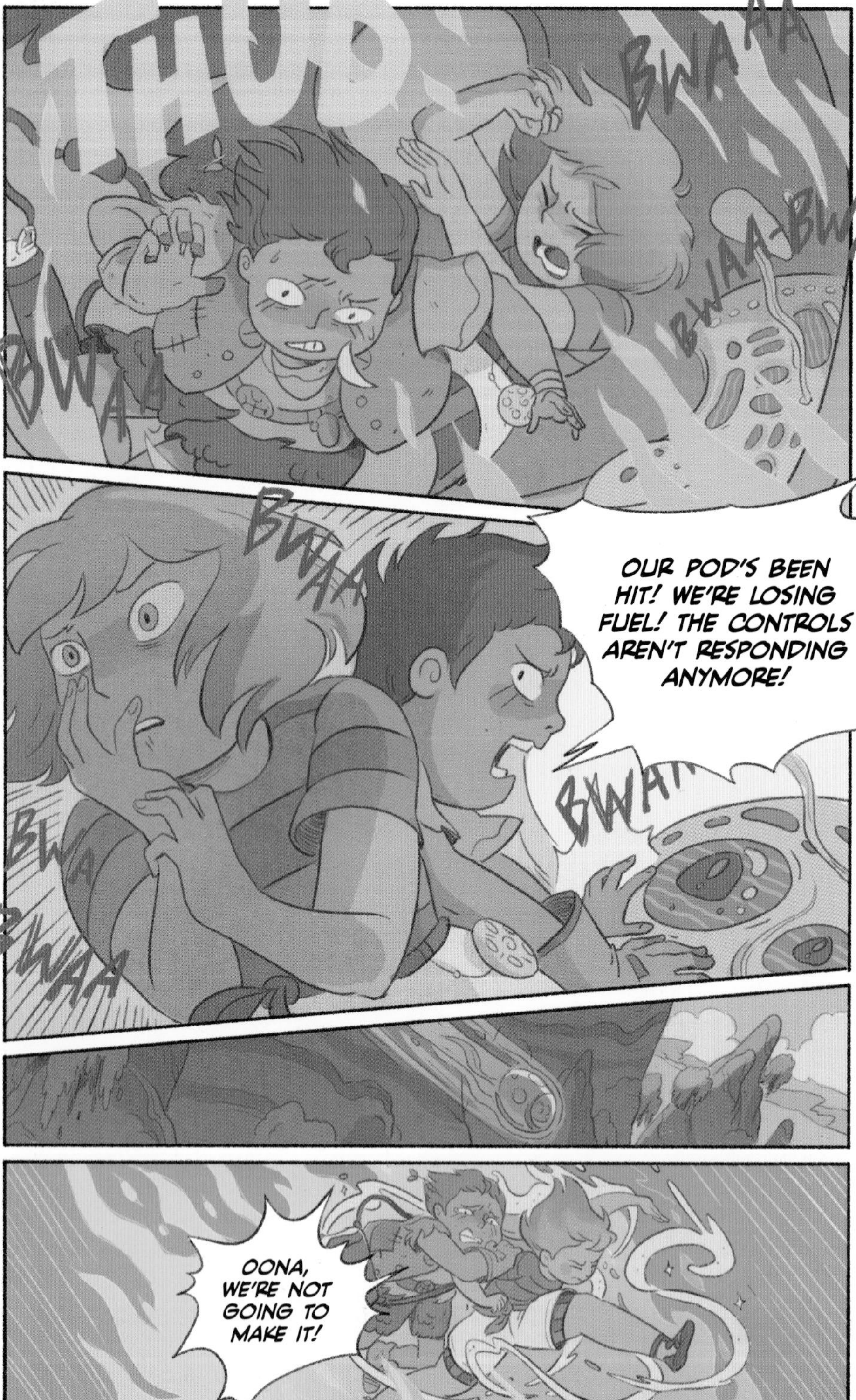
THUD
BWAAAA
BWAA-BWAA
BWAA
BWAA
OUR POD'S BEEN HIT! WE'RE LOSING FUEL! THE CONTROLS AREN'T RESPONDING ANYMORE!
BWAA
BWA
BWAA
OONA, WE'RE NOT GOING TO MAKE IT!
SSHHFF

Chapter 3

THE SACRED OIL

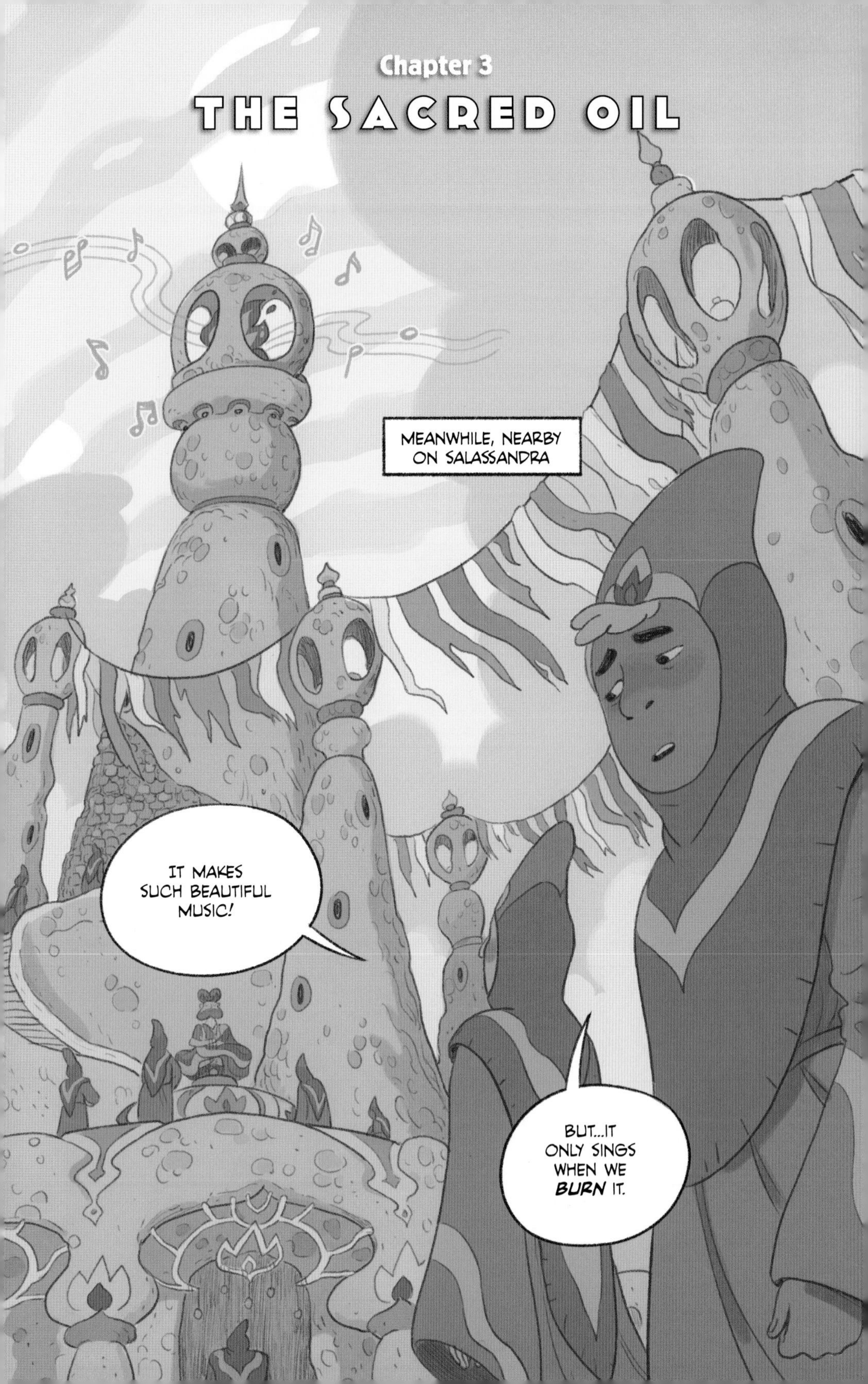
MEANWHILE, NEARBY ON SALASSANDRA
IT MAKES SUCH BEAUTIFUL MUSIC!
BUT...IT ONLY SINGS WHEN WE *BURN* IT.

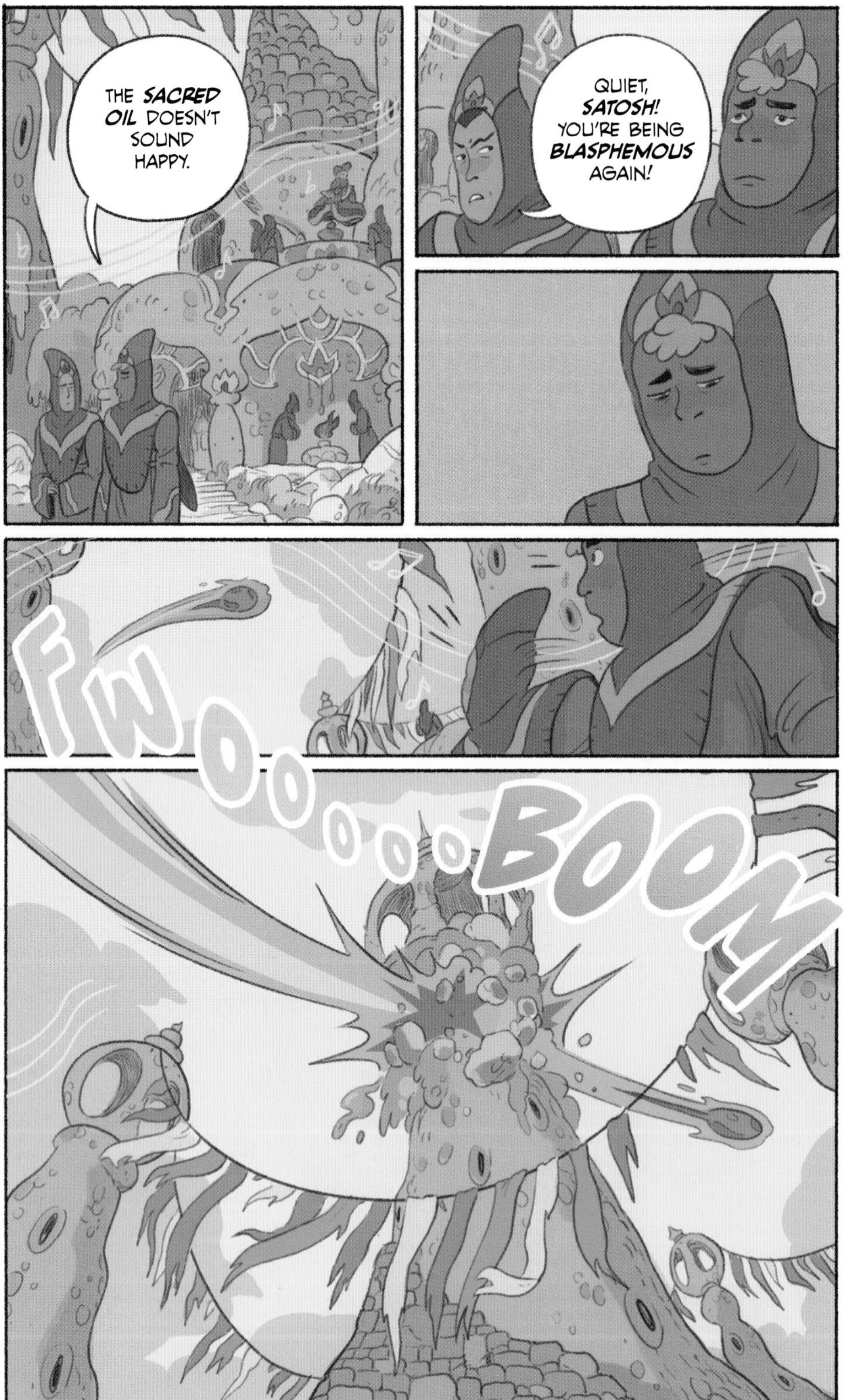
THE **SACRED OIL** DOESN'T SOUND HAPPY.
QUIET, **SATOSH!** YOU'RE BEING **BLASPHEMOUS** AGAIN!
FWOOOO...BOOM

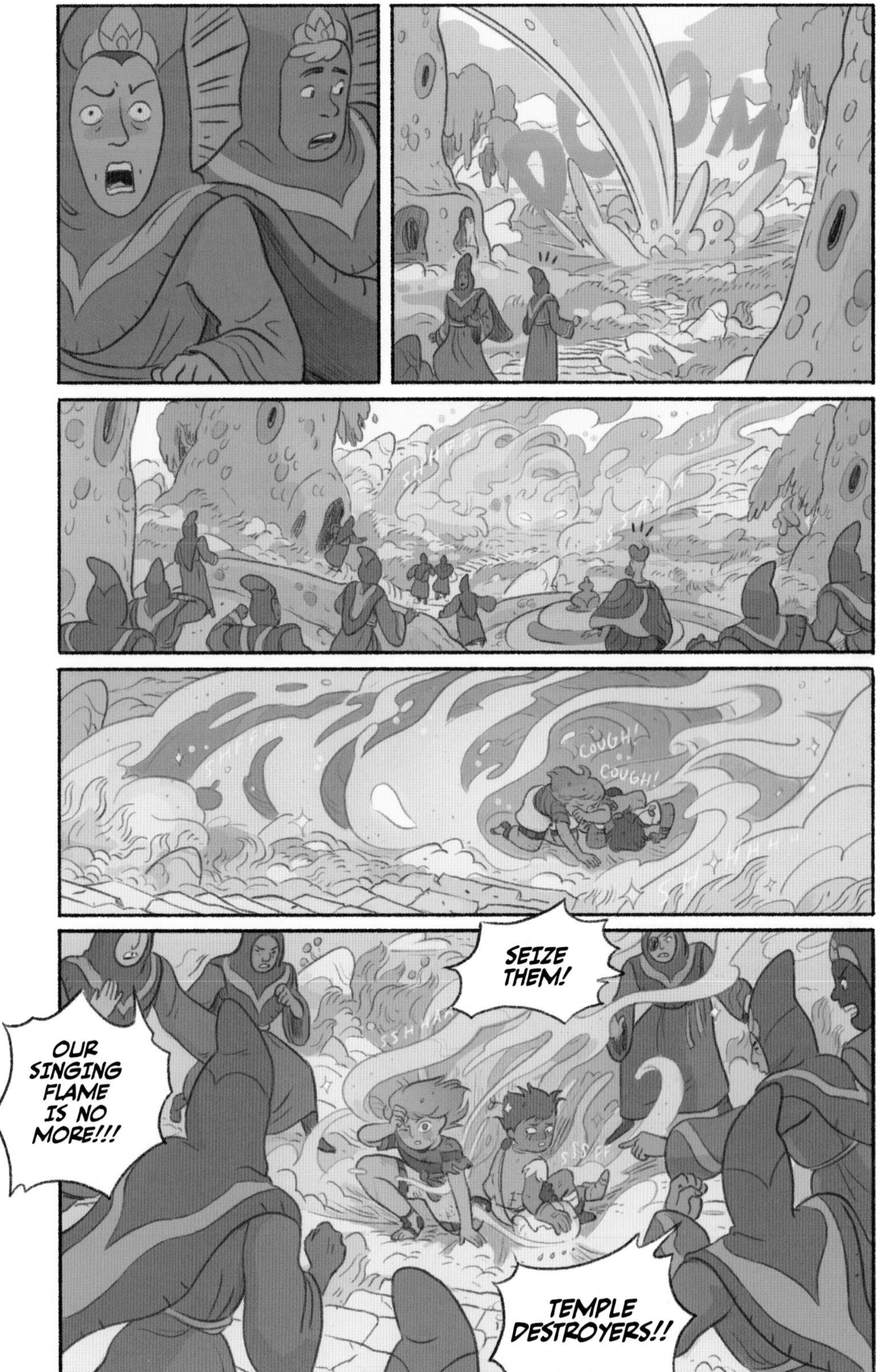
DOOM
COUGH!
COUGH!
OUR SINGING FLAME IS NO MORE!!!
SEIZE THEM!
TEMPLE DESTROYERS!!

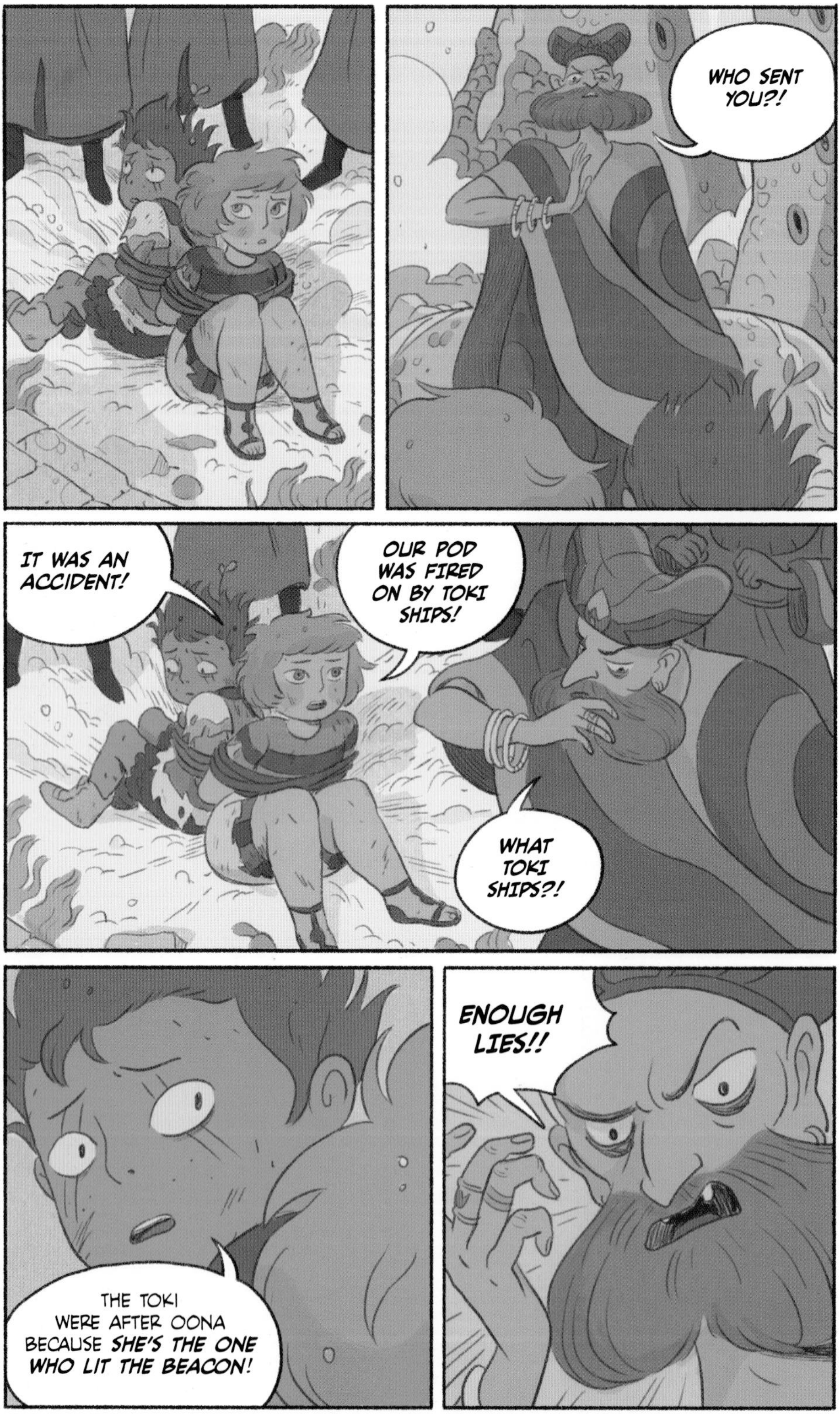
WHO SENT YOU?!
IT WAS AN ACCIDENT!
OUR POD WAS FIRED ON BY TOKI SHIPS!
WHAT TOKI SHIPS?!
ENOUGH LIES!!
THE TOKI WERE AFTER OONA BECAUSE SHE'S THE ONE WHO LIT THE BEACON!

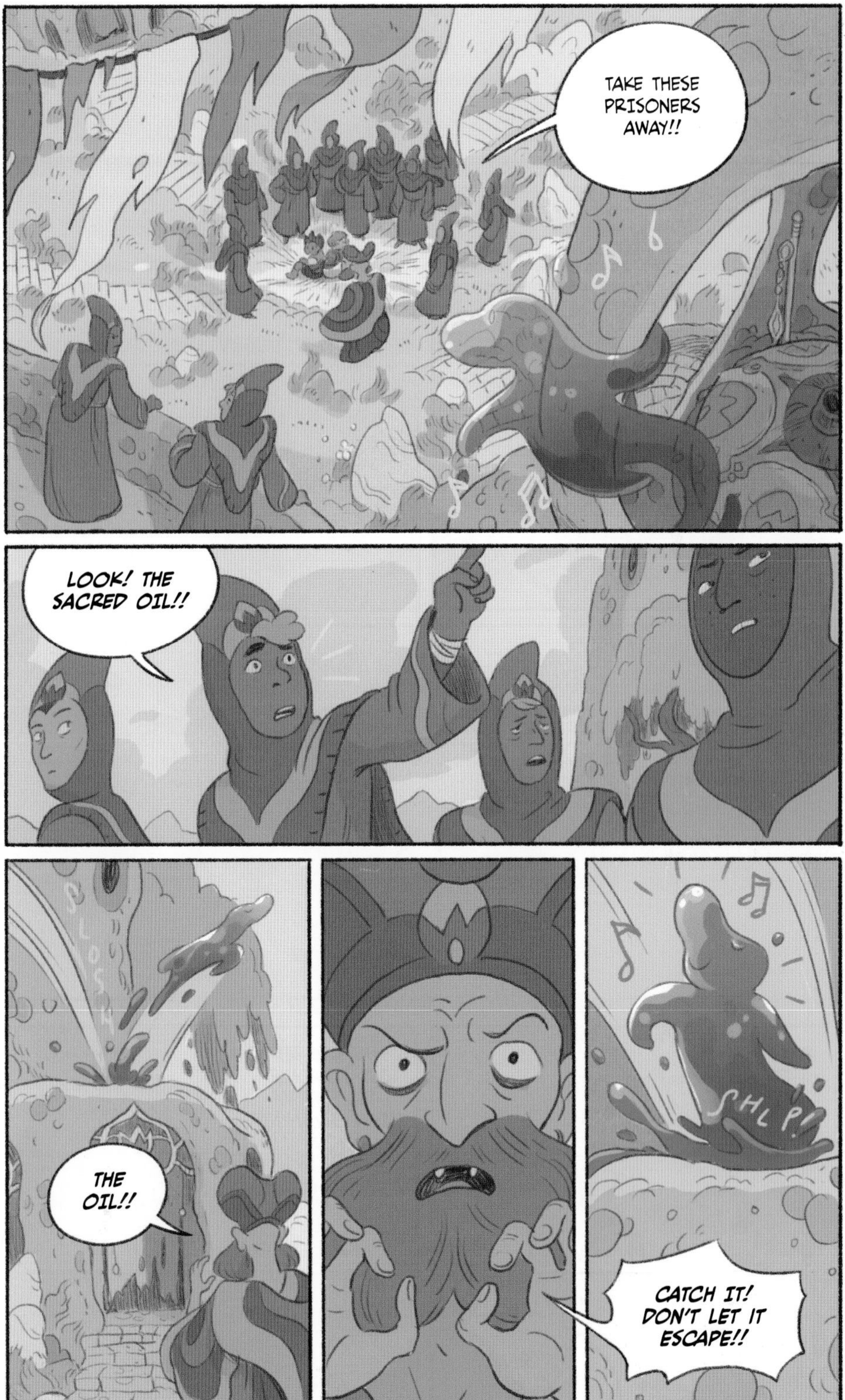
TAKE THESE PRISONERS AWAY!!
LOOK! THE SACRED OIL!!
SLOSH
THE OIL!!
CATCH IT! DON'T LET IT ESCAPE!!
SHLP!

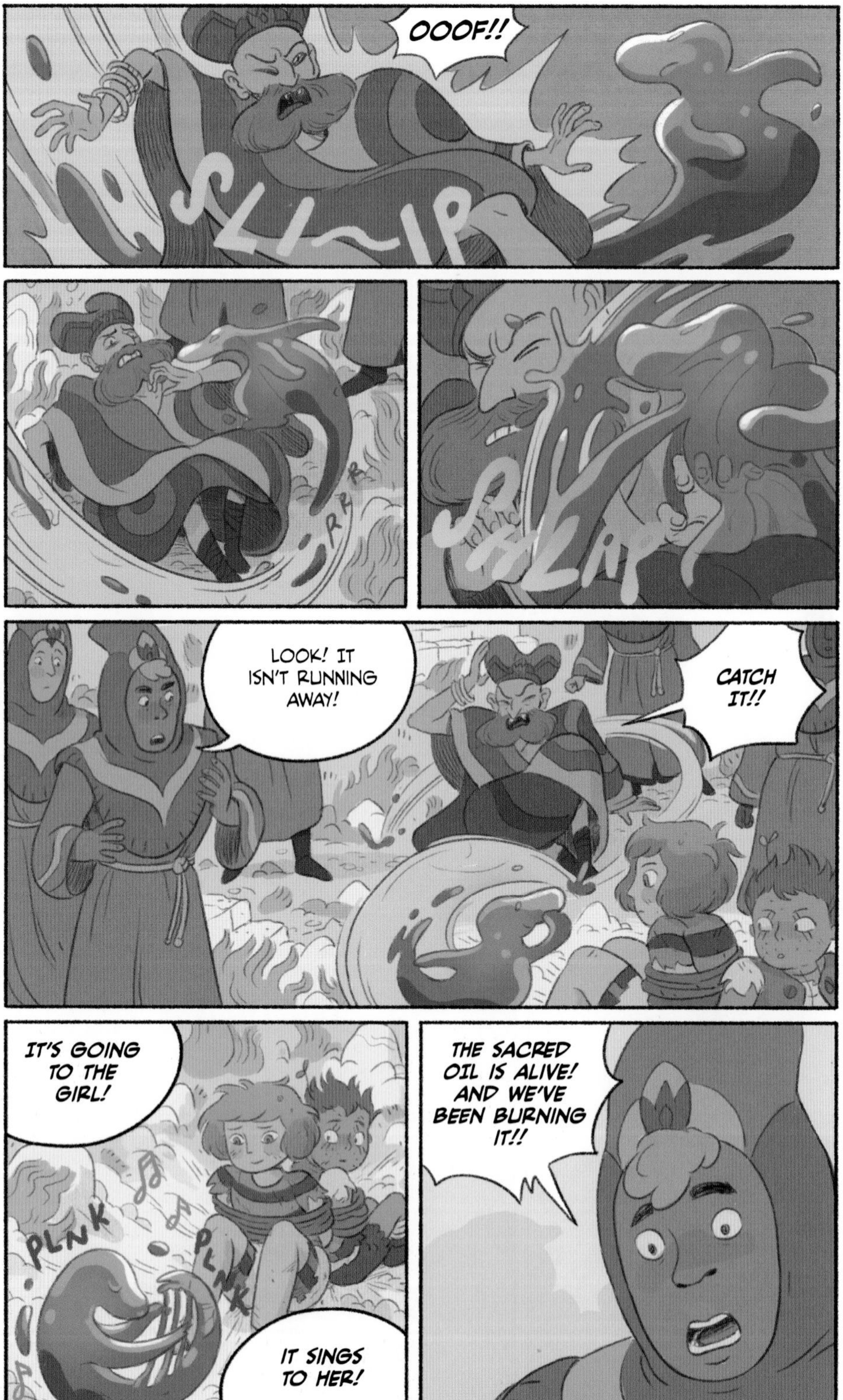
OOOF!!
SLI~IP
SHLIP
LOOK! IT ISN'T RUNNING AWAY!
CATCH IT!!
IT'S GOING TO THE GIRL!
PLNK
PLNK
IT SINGS TO HER!
THE SACRED OIL IS ALIVE! AND WE'VE BEEN BURNING IT!!

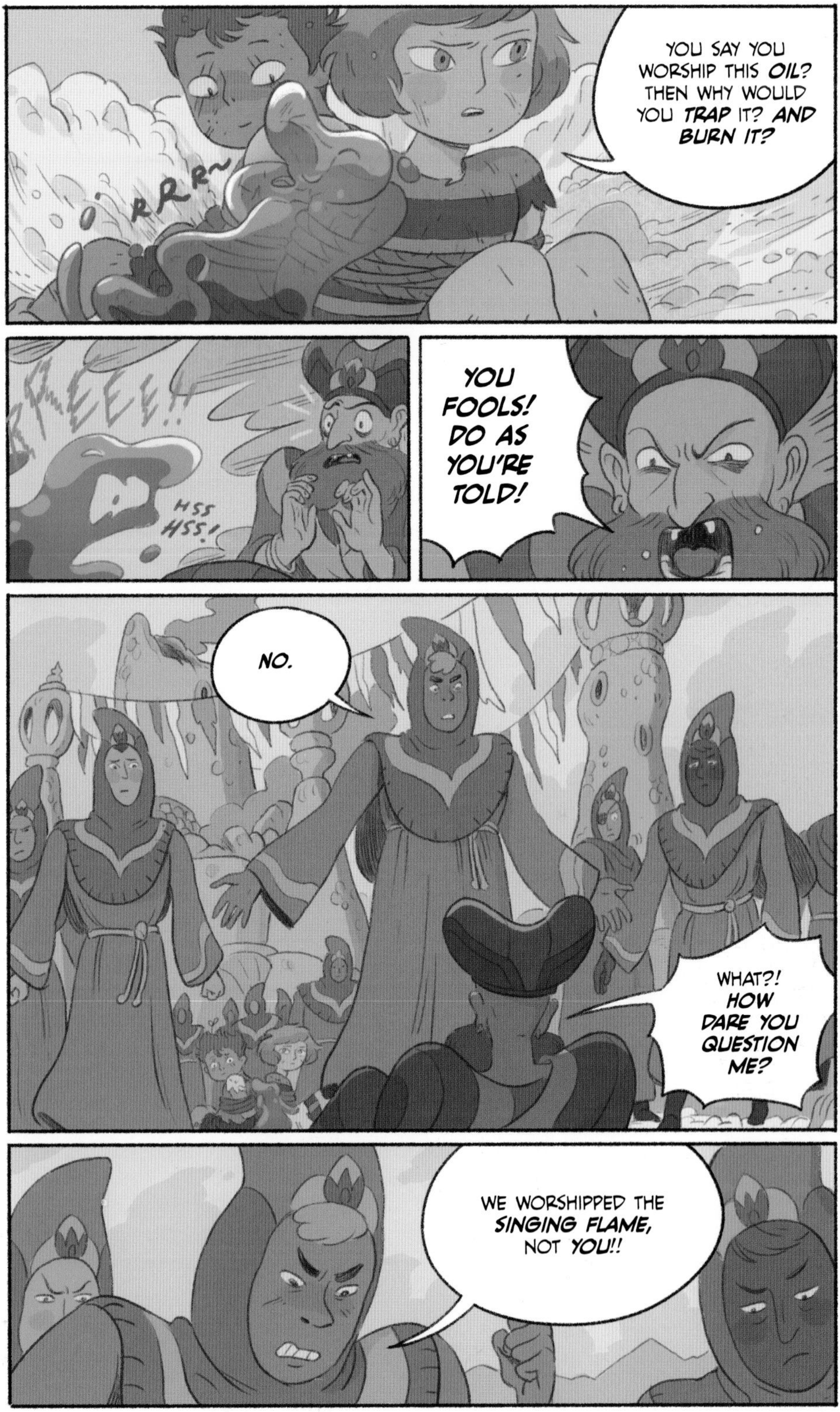
RRR~
YOU SAY YOU WORSHIP THIS OIL? THEN WHY WOULD YOU TRAP IT? AND BURN IT?
HSS HSS!
YOU FOOLS! DO AS YOU'RE TOLD!
NO.
WHAT?! HOW DARE YOU QUESTION ME?
WE WORSHIPPED THE SINGING FLAME, NOT YOU!!

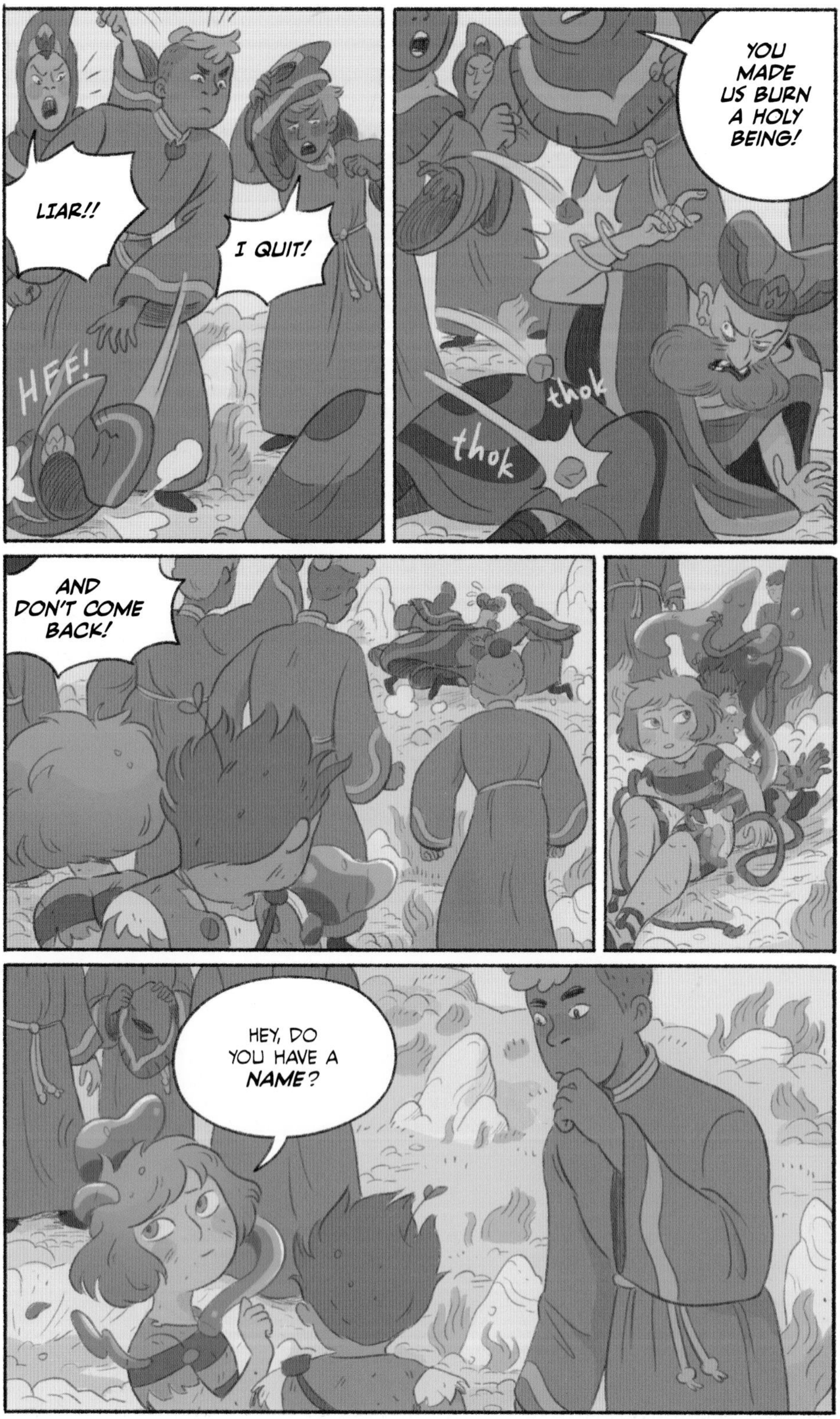
LIAR!!
I QUIT!
HFF!
YOU MADE US BURN A HOLY BEING!
thok
thok
AND DON'T COME BACK!
HEY, DO YOU HAVE A NAME?

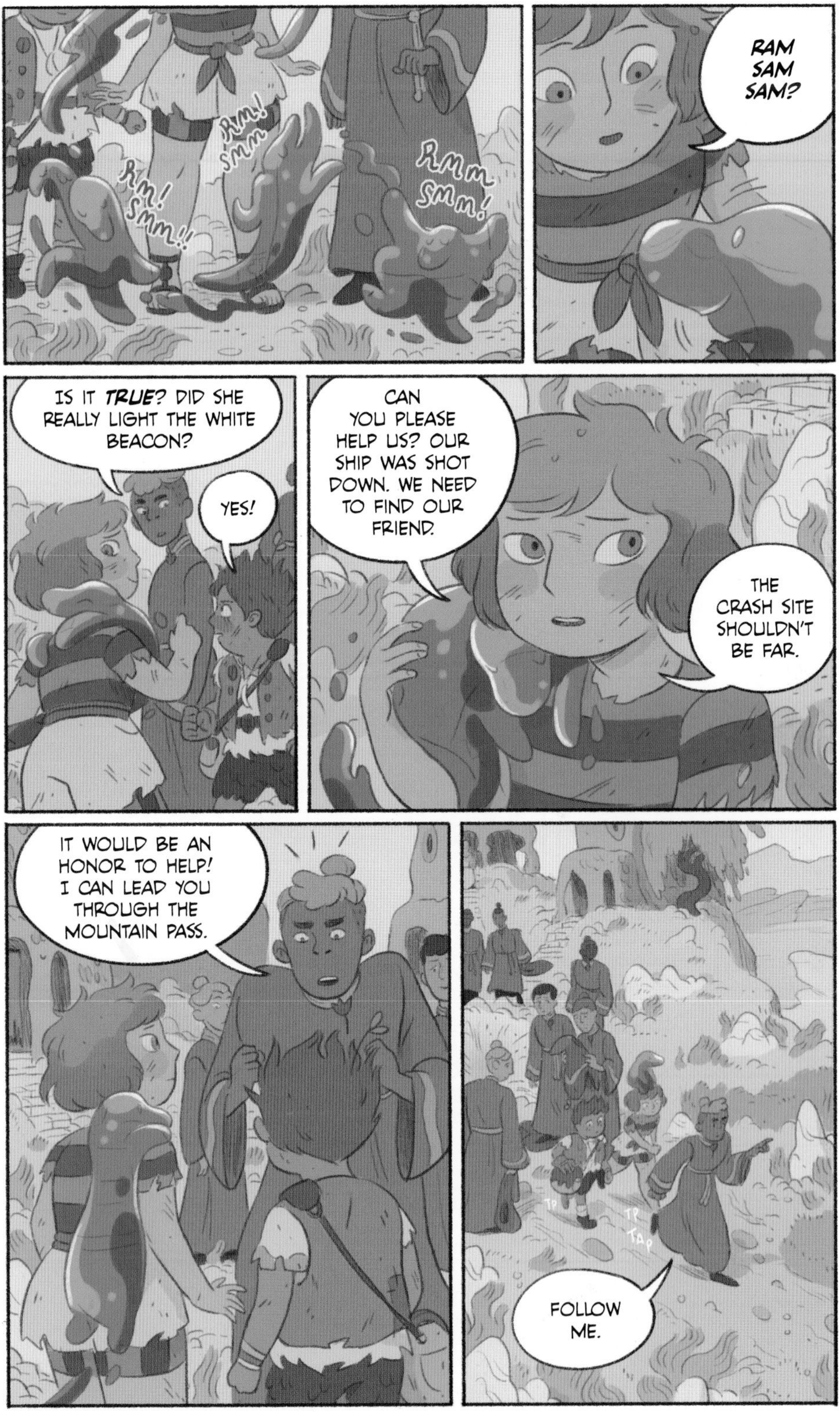
Rm! Smm!!
Rm! Smm
Rmm Smm!
RAM SAM SAM?
IS IT TRUE? DID SHE REALLY LIGHT THE WHITE BEACON?
YES!
CAN YOU PLEASE HELP US? OUR SHIP WAS SHOT DOWN. WE NEED TO FIND OUR FRIEND.
THE CRASH SITE SHOULDN'T BE FAR.
IT WOULD BE AN HONOR TO HELP! I CAN LEAD YOU THROUGH THE MOUNTAIN PASS.
TP
TP TAP
FOLLOW ME.

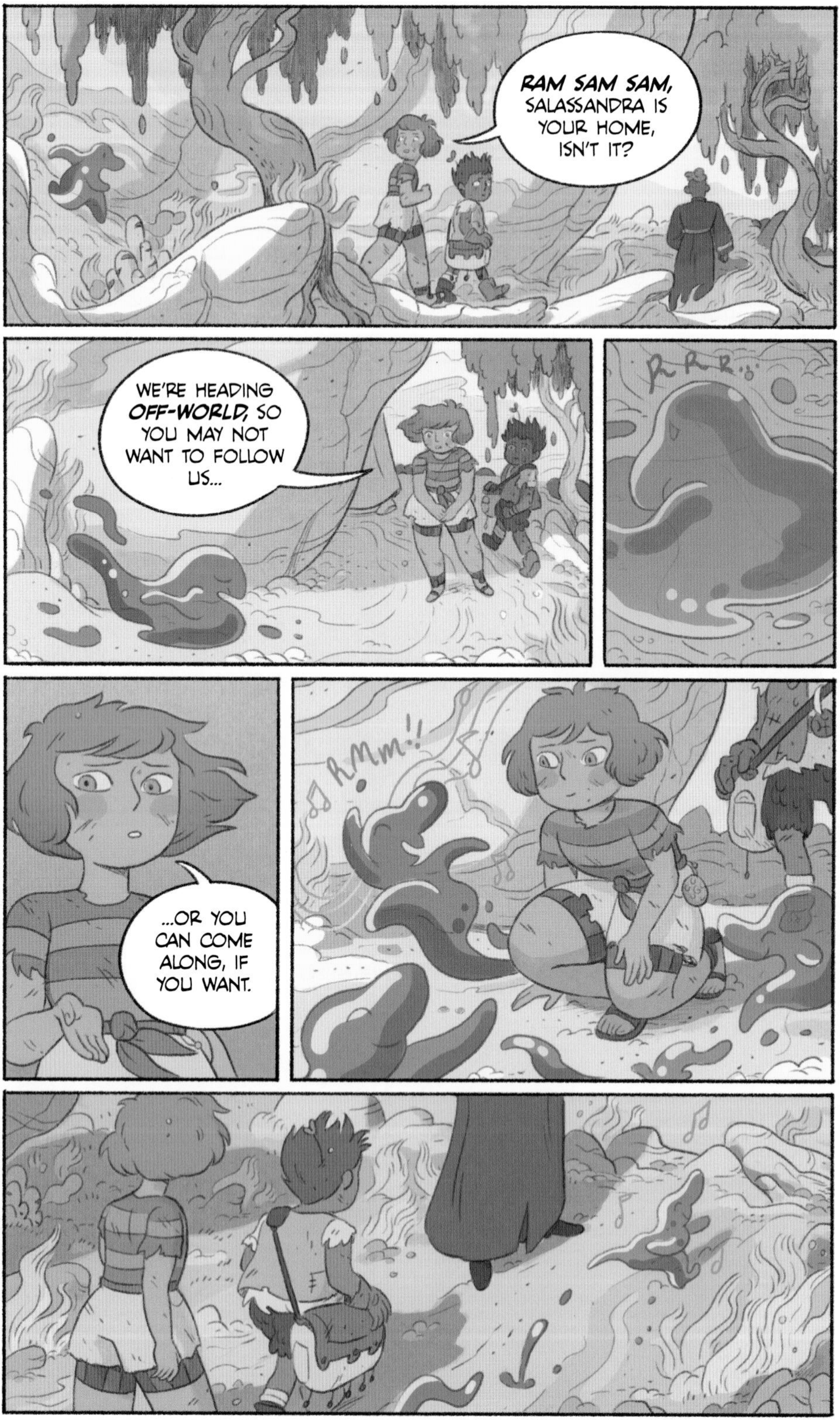
RAM SAM SAM, SALASSANDRA IS YOUR HOME, ISN'T IT?
WE'RE HEADING OFF-WORLD, SO YOU MAY NOT WANT TO FOLLOW US...
...OR YOU CAN COME ALONG, IF YOU WANT.

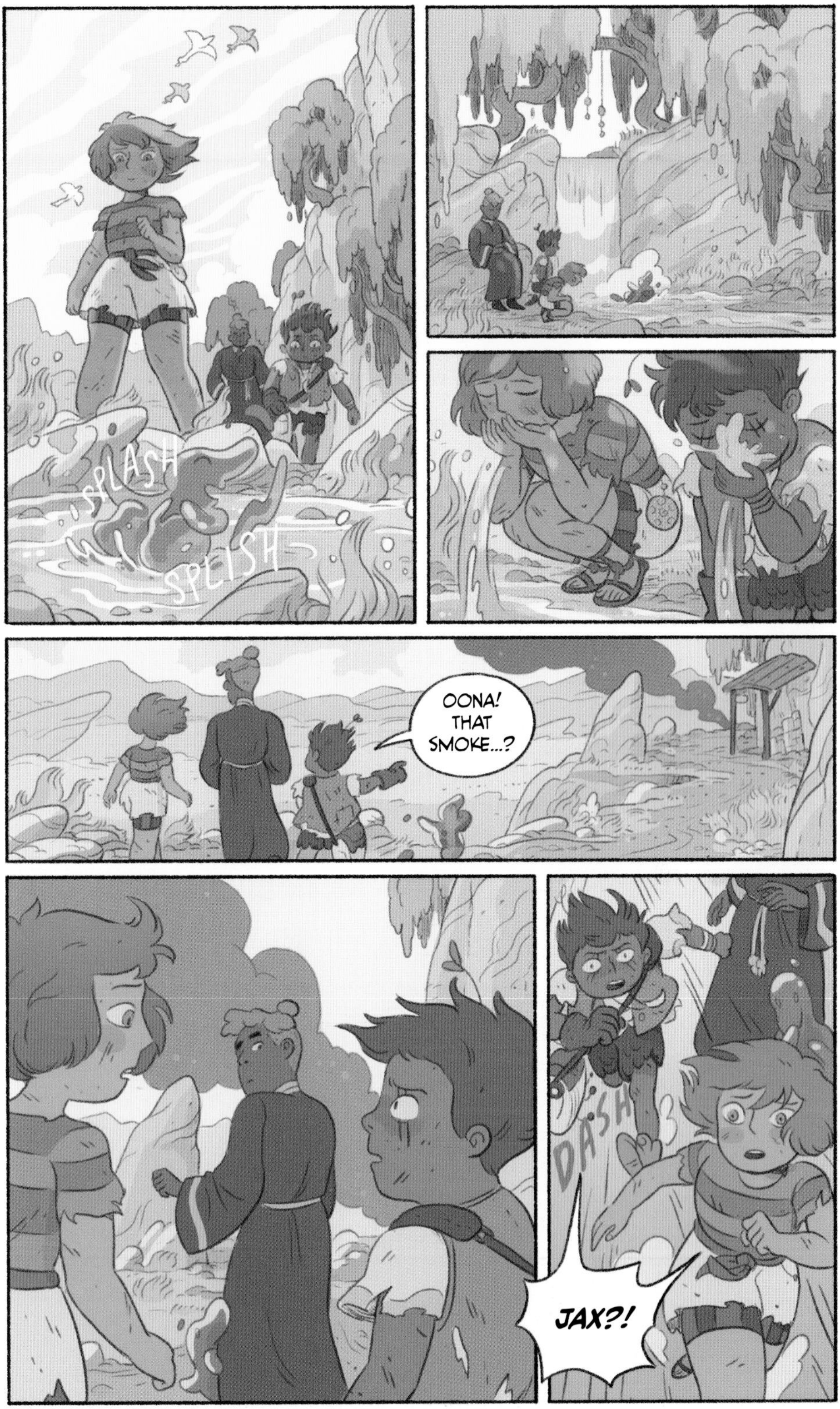
SPLASH
SPLISH
OONA! THAT SMOKE...?
DASH
JAX?!

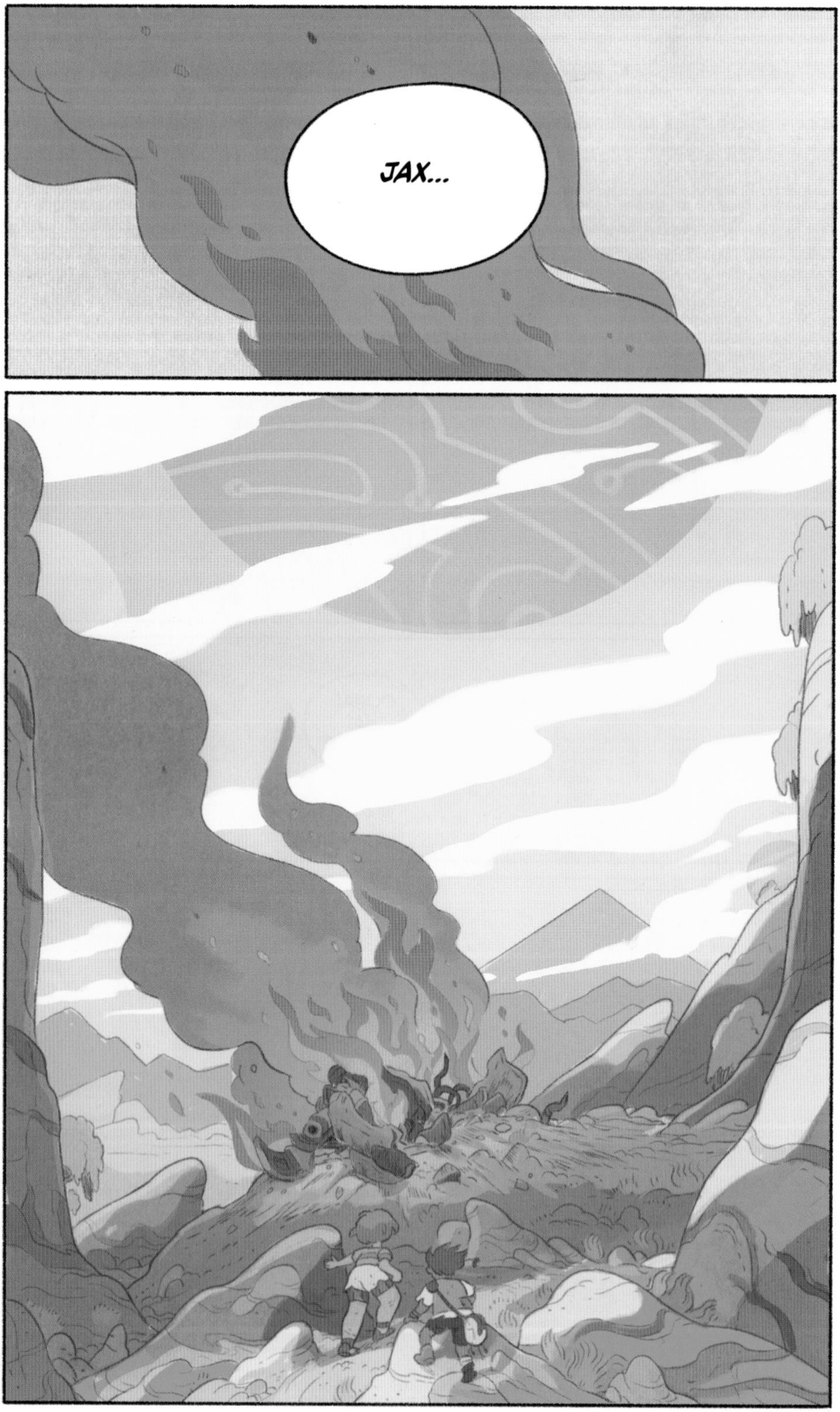
JAX...

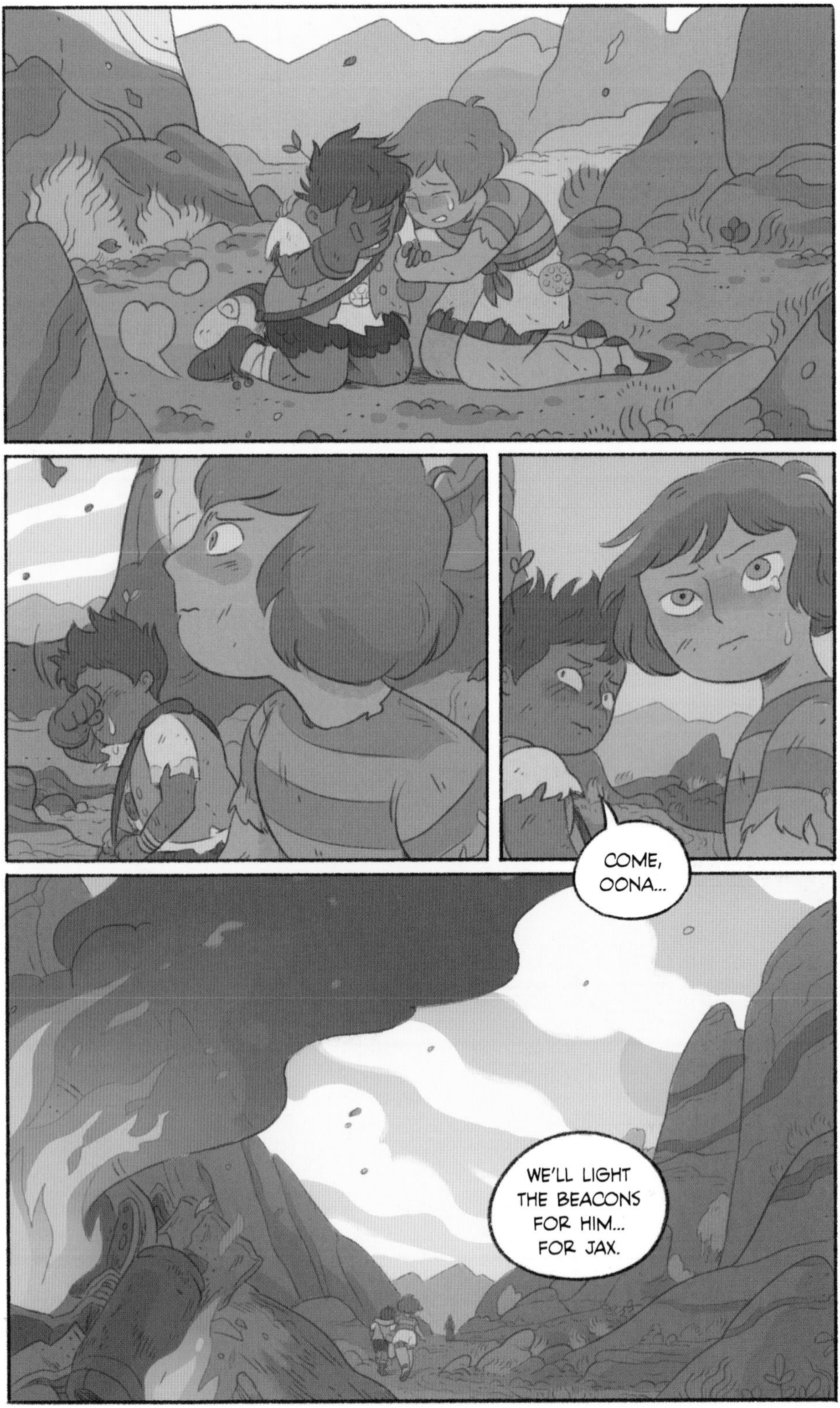
COME, OONA...
WE'LL LIGHT THE BEACONS FOR HIM... FOR JAX.

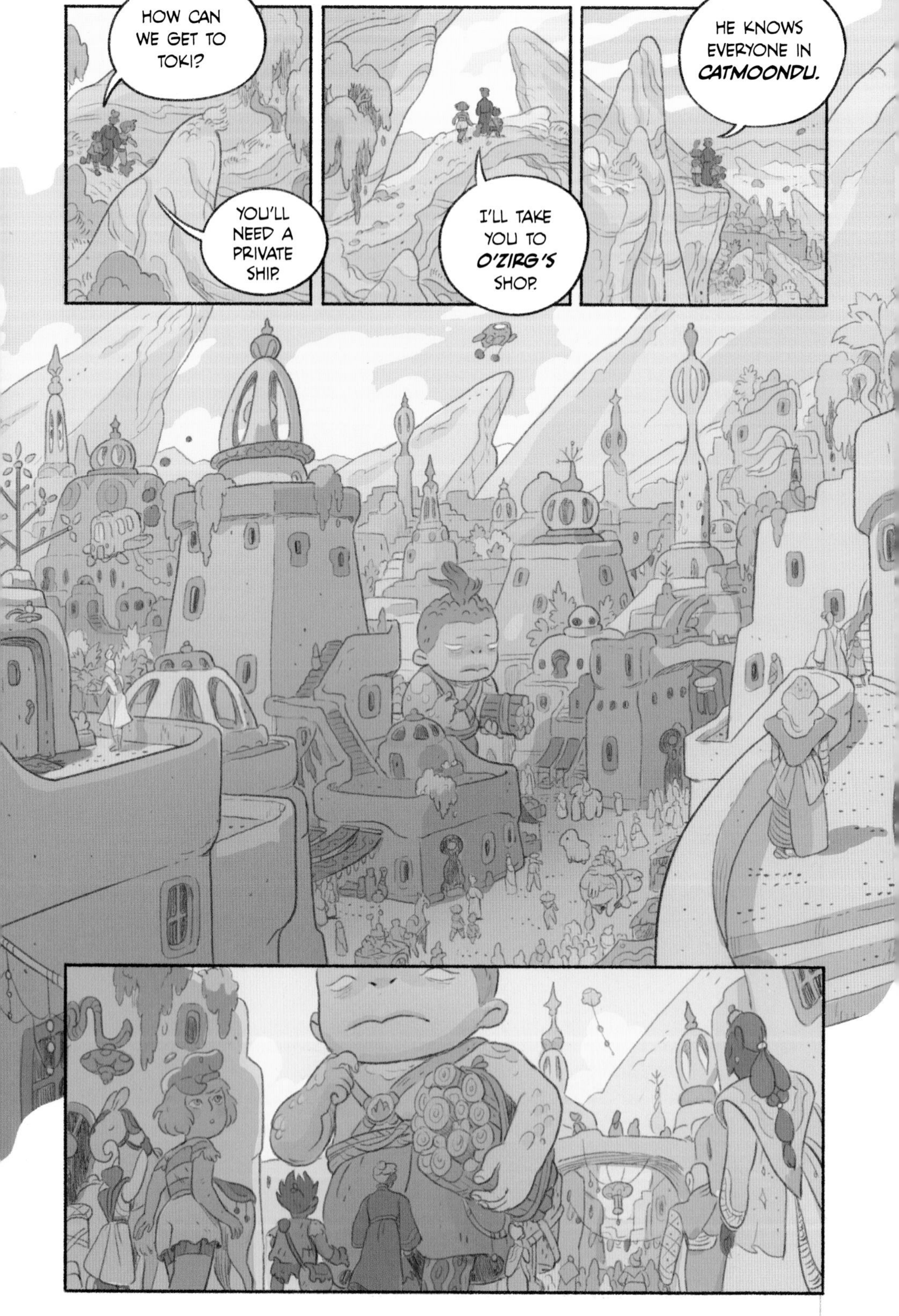
HOW CAN WE GET TO TOKI?
YOU'LL NEED A PRIVATE SHIP.
I'LL TAKE YOU TO O'ZIRG'S SHOP.
HE KNOWS EVERYONE IN CATMOONDU.

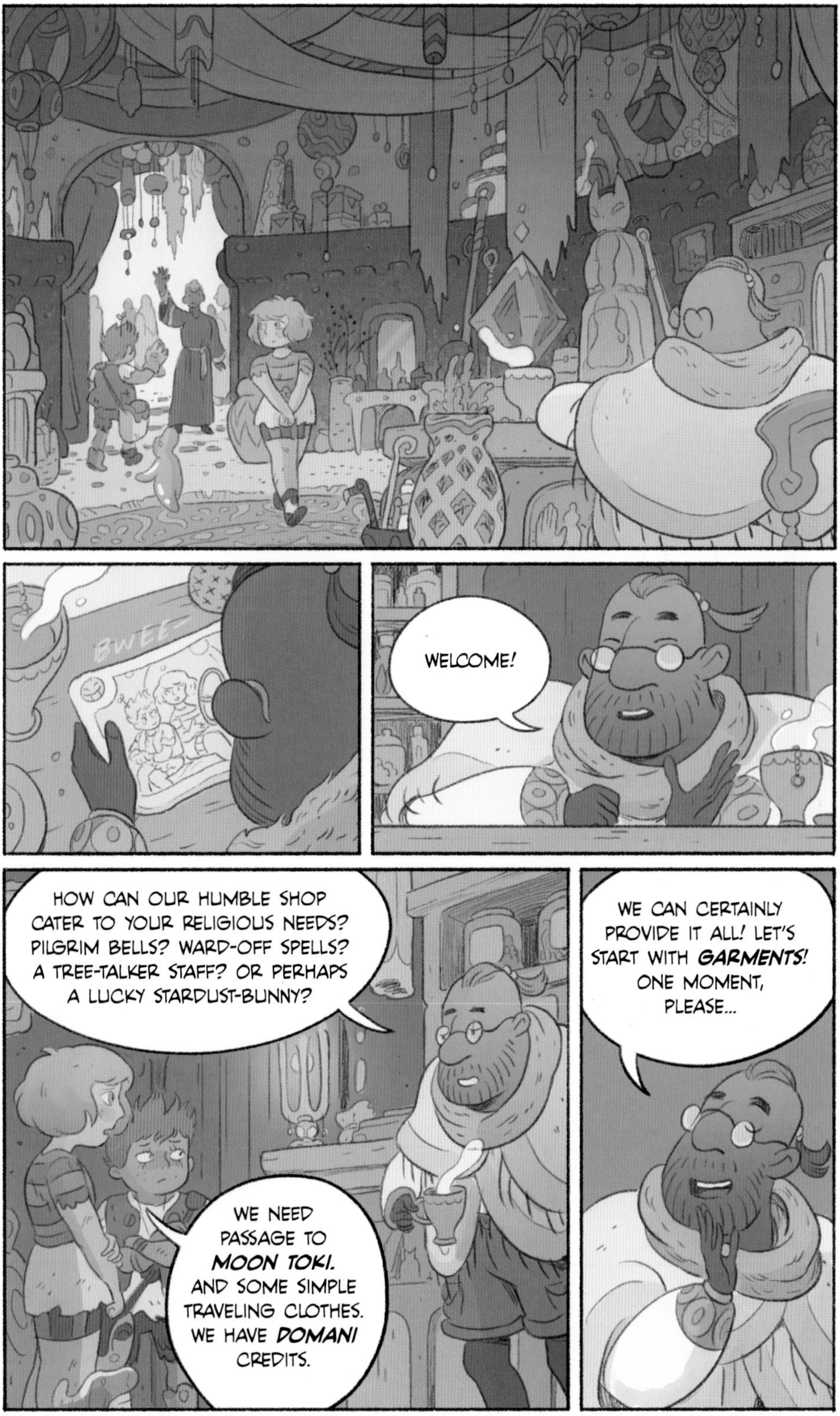
BWEE-
WELCOME!
HOW CAN OUR HUMBLE SHOP CATER TO YOUR RELIGIOUS NEEDS? PILGRIM BELLS? WARD-OFF SPELLS? A TREE-TALKER STAFF? OR PERHAPS A LUCKY STARDUST-BUNNY?
WE NEED PASSAGE TO MOON TOKI. AND SOME SIMPLE TRAVELING CLOTHES. WE HAVE DOMANI CREDITS.
WE CAN CERTAINLY PROVIDE IT ALL! LET'S START WITH GARMENTS! ONE MOMENT, PLEASE...

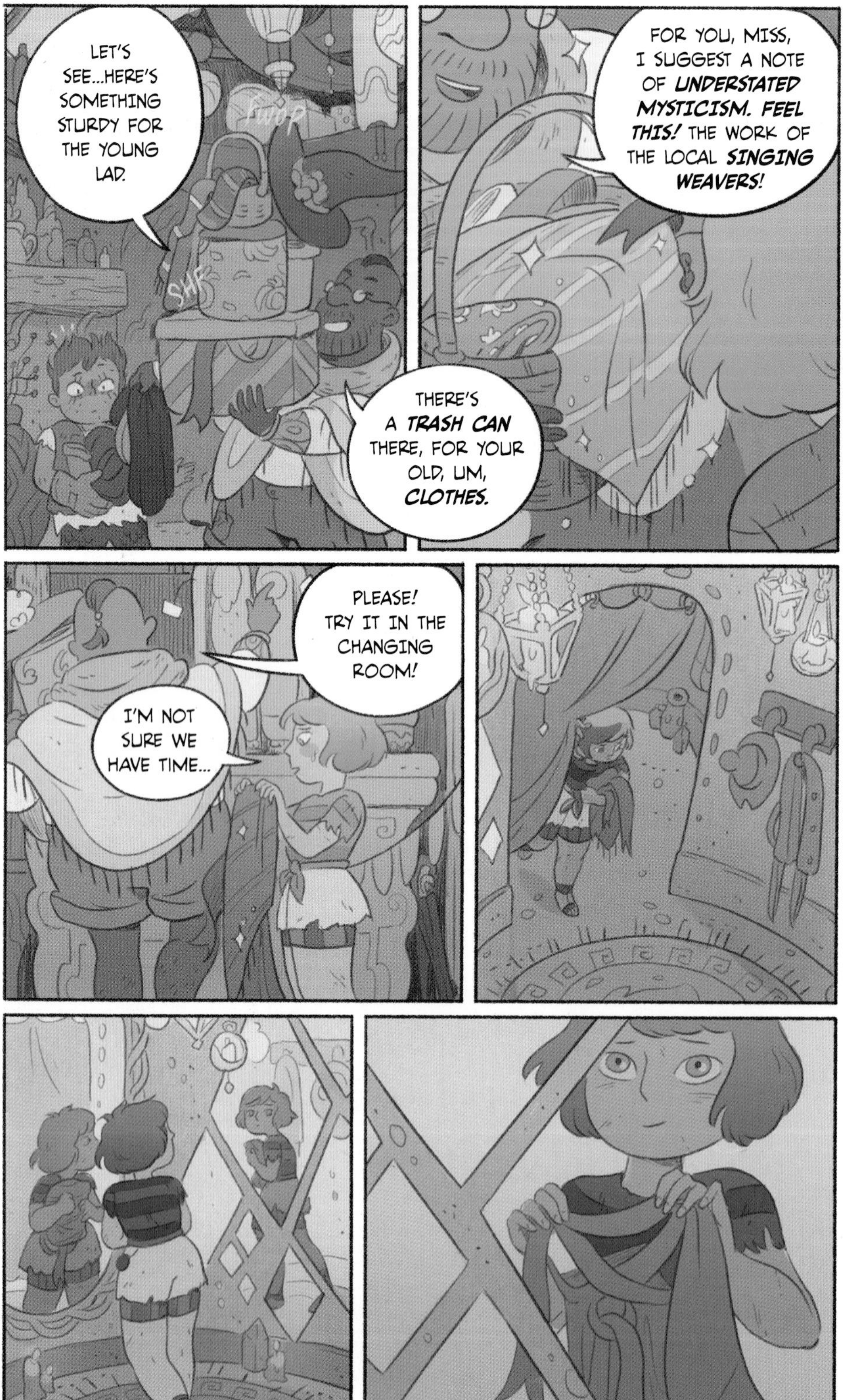
LET'S SEE...HERE'S SOMETHING STURDY FOR THE YOUNG LAD.
FWOP
SHF
THERE'S A TRASH CAN THERE, FOR YOUR OLD, UM, CLOTHES.
FOR YOU, MISS, I SUGGEST A NOTE OF UNDERSTATED MYSTICISM. FEEL THIS! THE WORK OF THE LOCAL SINGING WEAVERS!
PLEASE! TRY IT IN THE CHANGING ROOM!
I'M NOT SURE WE HAVE TIME...

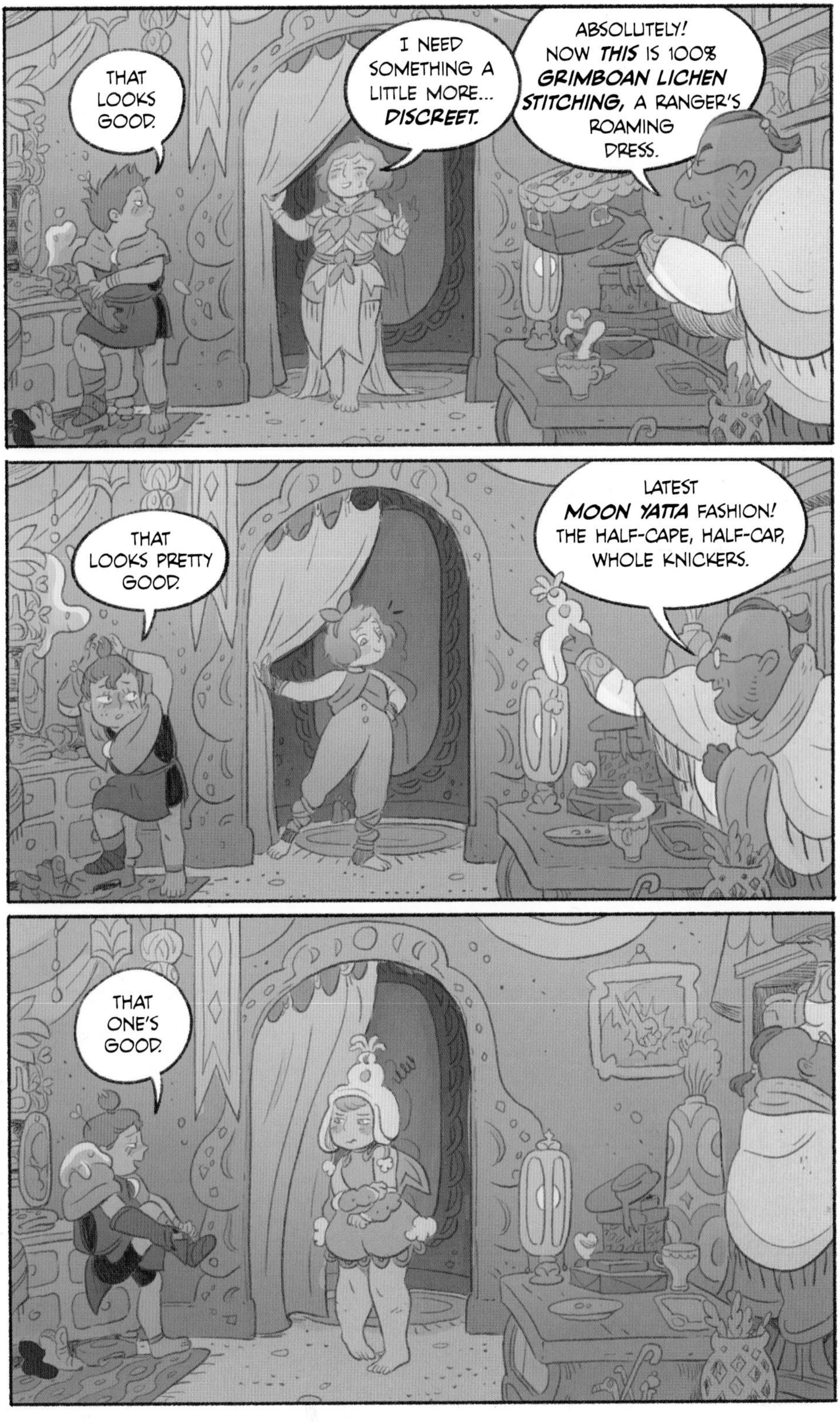
THAT LOOKS GOOD.
I NEED SOMETHING A LITTLE MORE... ***DISCREET.***
ABSOLUTELY! NOW ***THIS*** IS 100% ***GRIMBOAN LICHEN STITCHING,*** A RANGER'S ROAMING DRESS.
THAT LOOKS PRETTY GOOD.
LATEST ***MOON YATTA*** FASHION! THE HALF-CAPE, HALF-CAP, WHOLE KNICKERS.
THAT ONE'S GOOD.

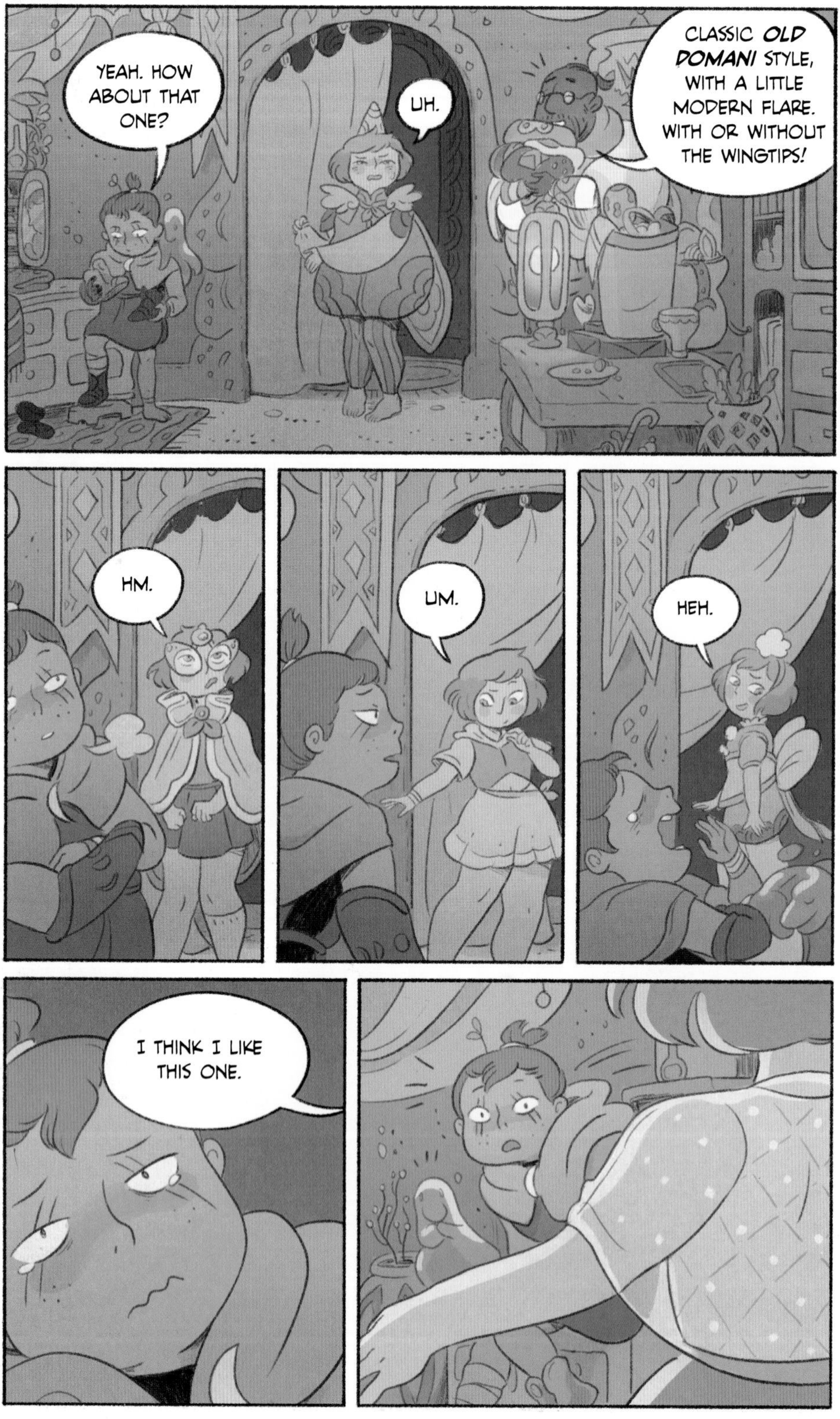
YEAH. HOW ABOUT THAT ONE?
UH.
CLASSIC OLD DOMANI STYLE, WITH A LITTLE MODERN FLARE. WITH OR WITHOUT THE WINGTIPS!
HM.
UM.
HEH.
I THINK I LIKE THIS ONE.

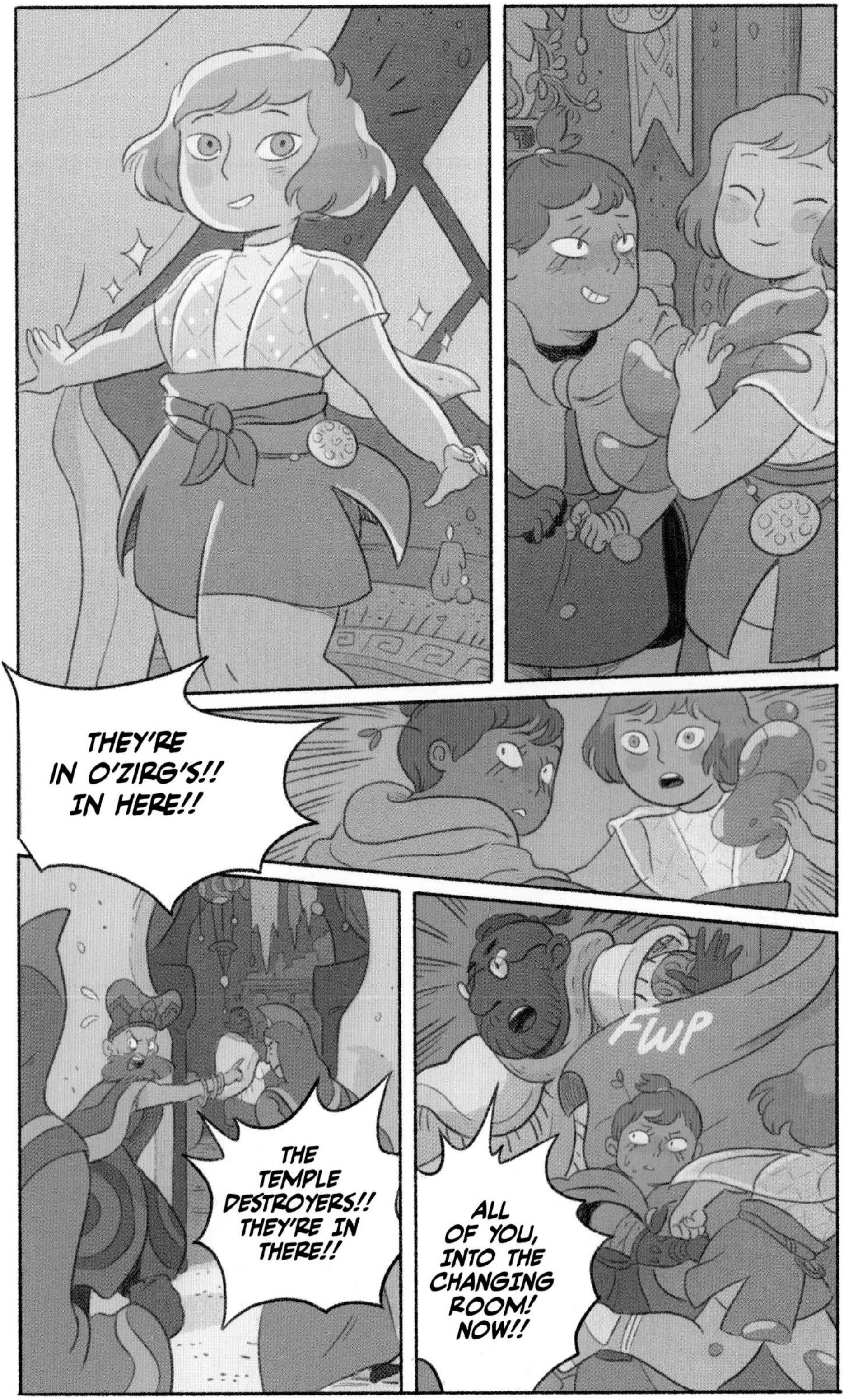
THEY'RE IN O'ZIRG'S!! IN HERE!!
THE TEMPLE DESTROYERS!! THEY'RE IN THERE!!
FWP
ALL OF YOU, INTO THE CHANGING ROOM! NOW!!

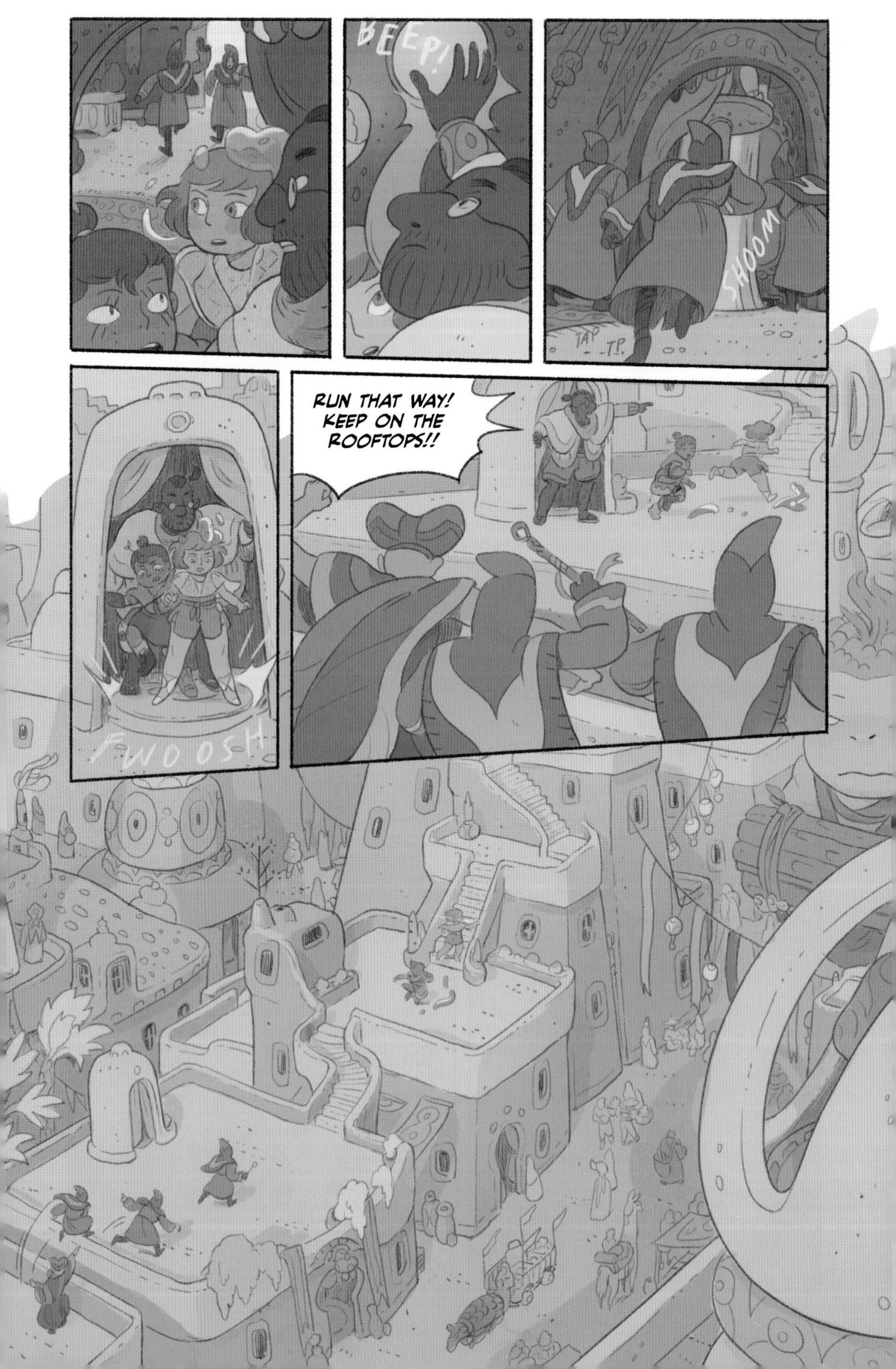
BEEP!
SHOOM
TAP
TP
FWOOSH
RUN THAT WAY! KEEP ON THE ROOFTOPS!!

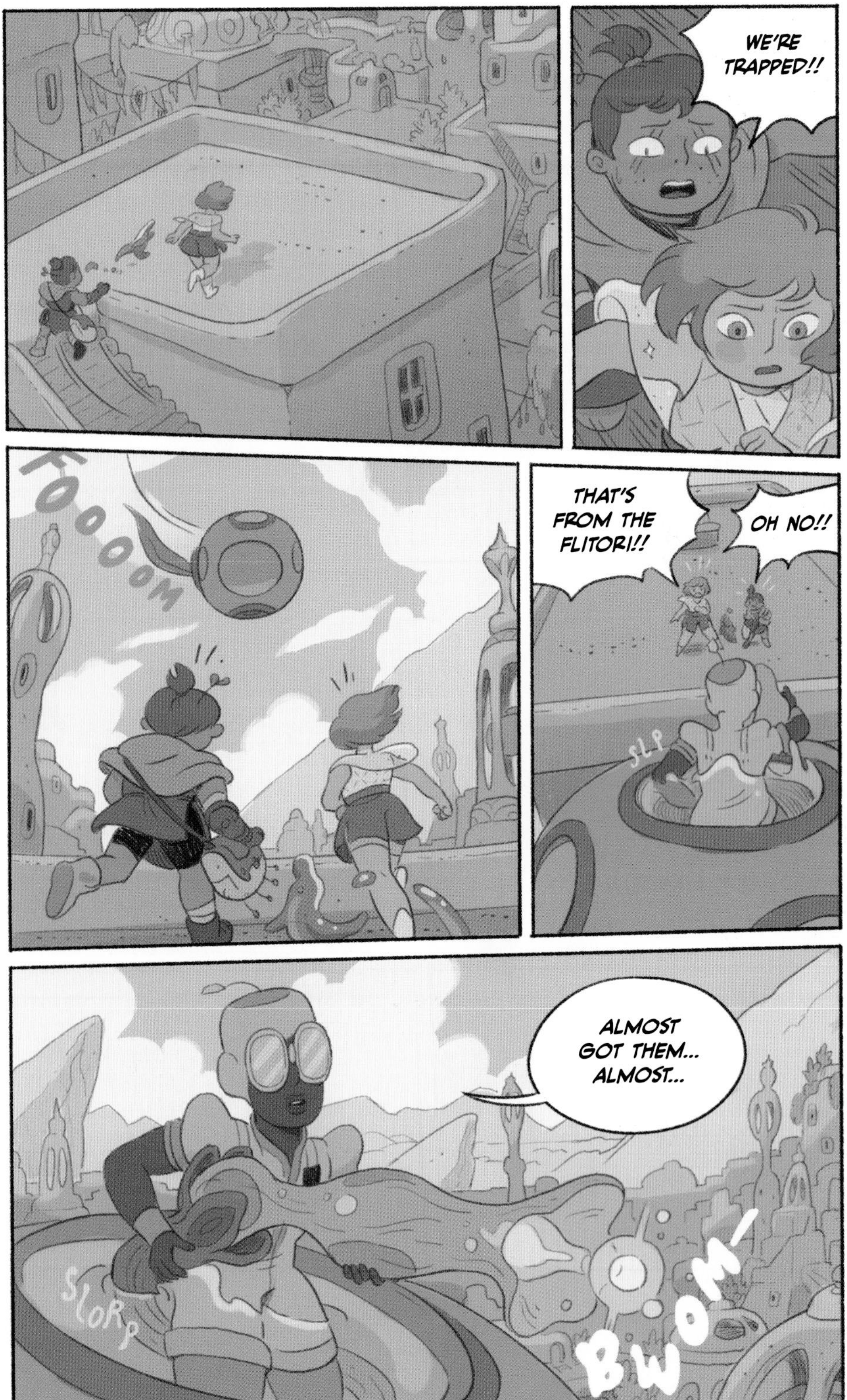
WE'RE TRAPPED!!
FOOOOM
THAT'S FROM THE FLITORI!!
OH NO!!
SLP
ALMOST GOT THEM... ALMOST...
SLORP
BWOM!

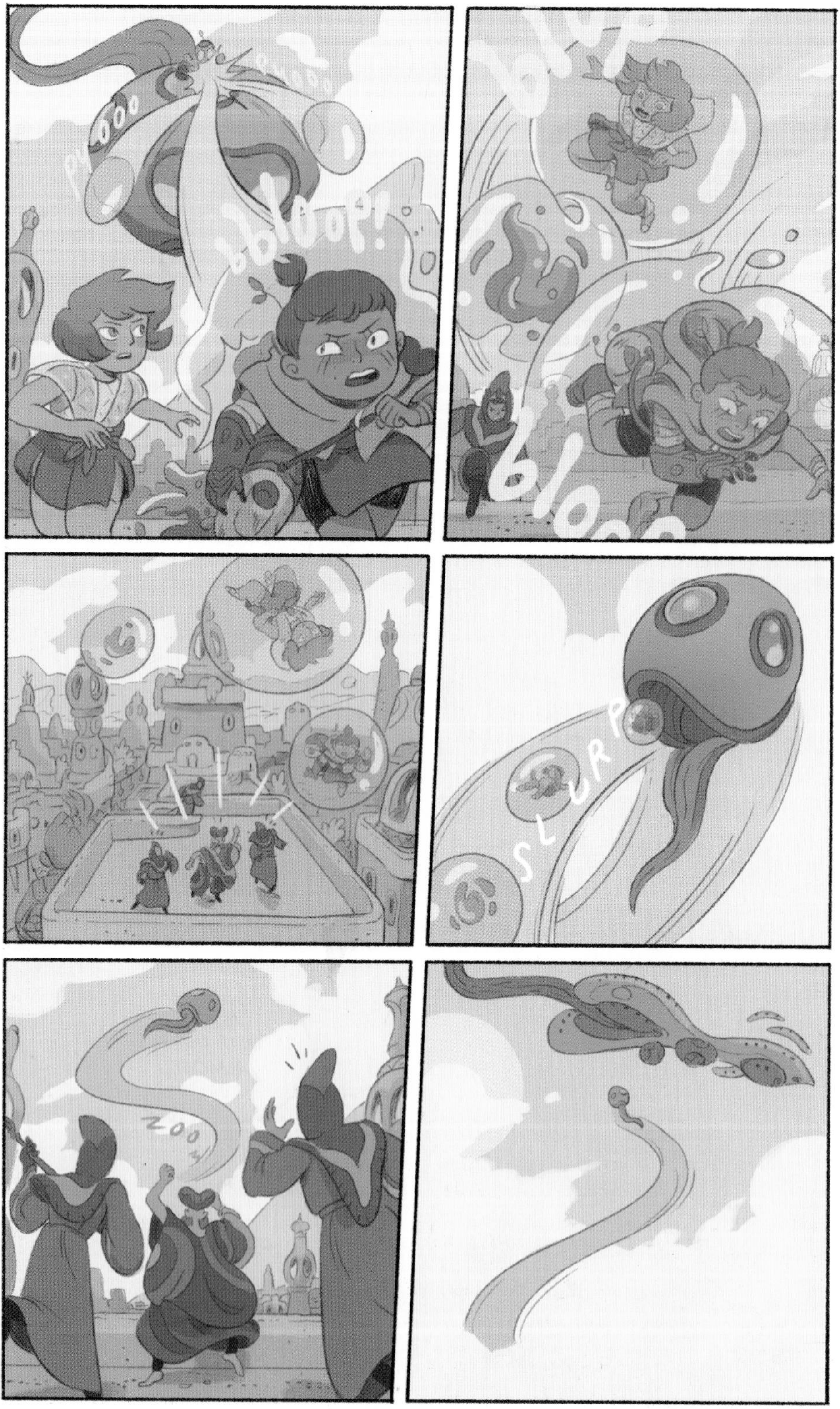
PYOOO
PYOOOO
BLOOP!
BLOP
SLURP
ZOOM

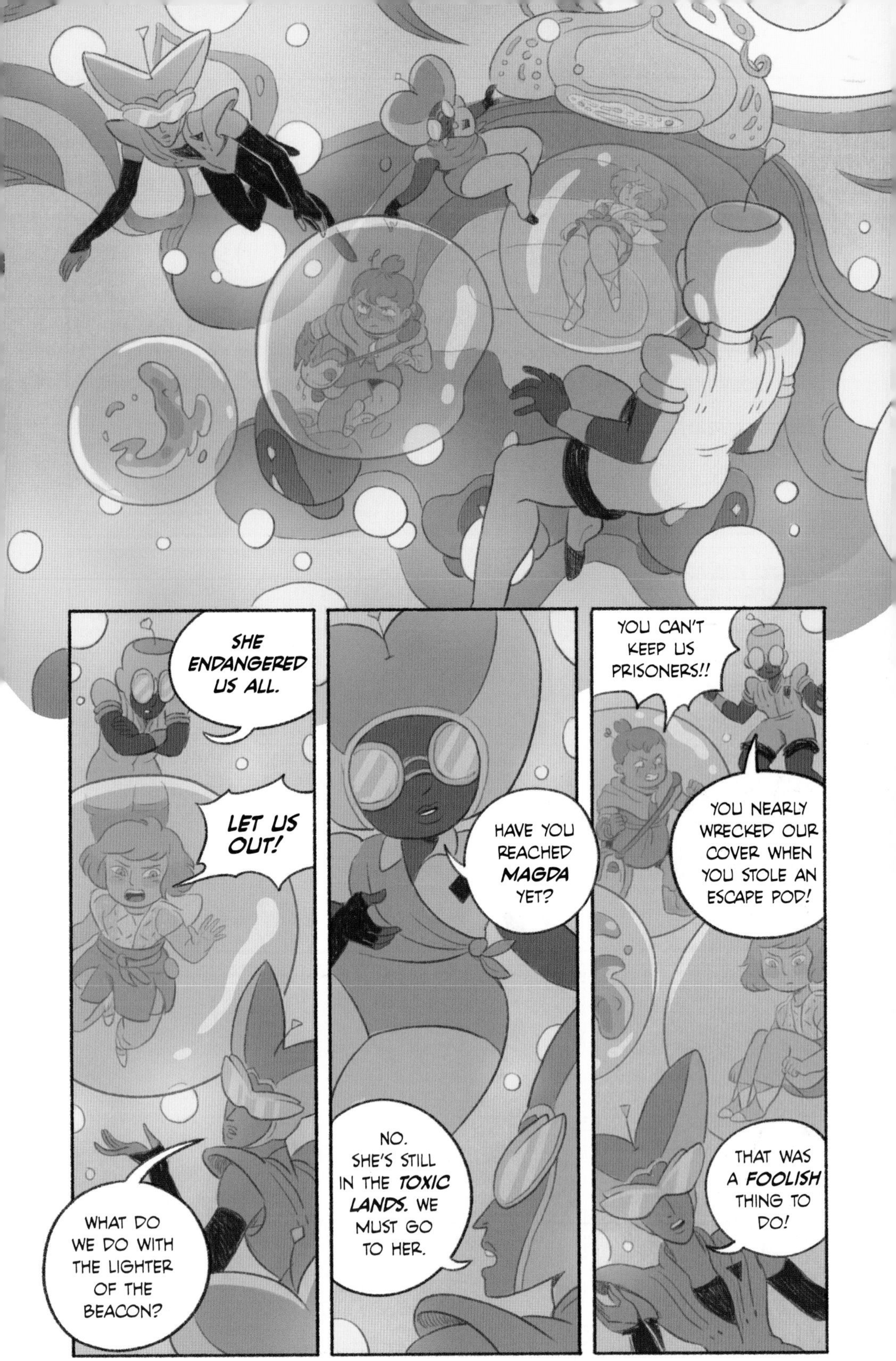
SHE ENDANGERED US ALL.
LET US OUT!
WHAT DO WE DO WITH THE LIGHTER OF THE BEACON?
HAVE YOU REACHED MAGDA YET?
NO. SHE'S STILL IN THE TOXIC LANDS. WE MUST GO TO HER.
YOU CAN'T KEEP US PRISONERS!!
YOU NEARLY WRECKED OUR COVER WHEN YOU STOLE AN ESCAPE POD!
THAT WAS A FOOLISH THING TO DO!

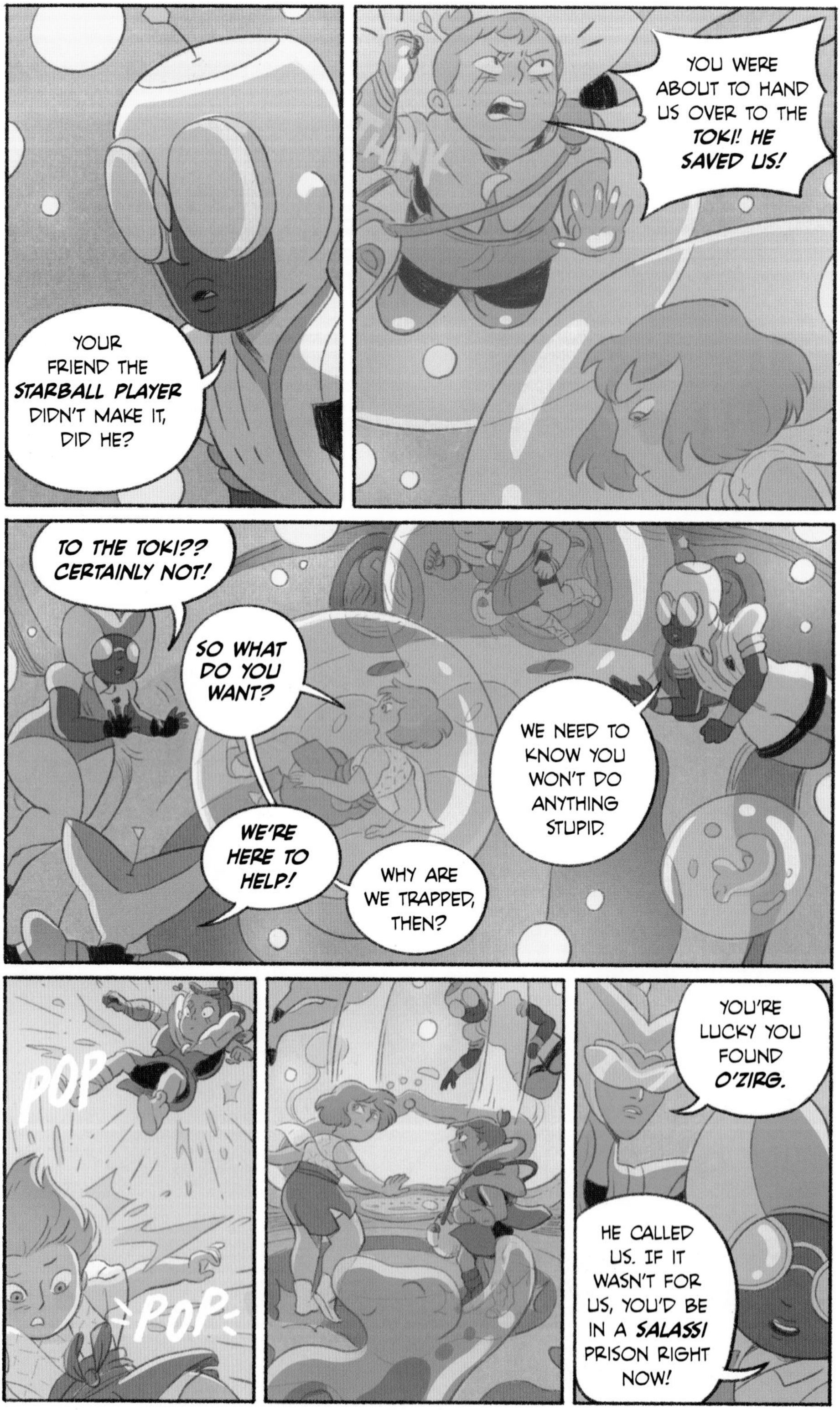
YOUR FRIEND THE STARBALL PLAYER DIDN'T MAKE IT, DID HE?
YOU WERE ABOUT TO HAND US OVER TO THE TOKI! HE SAVED US!
TO THE TOKI?? CERTAINLY NOT!
SO WHAT DO YOU WANT?
WE'RE HERE TO HELP!
WHY ARE WE TRAPPED, THEN?
WE NEED TO KNOW YOU WON'T DO ANYTHING STUPID.
POP
POP
YOU'RE LUCKY YOU FOUND O'ZIRG.
HE CALLED US. IF IT WASN'T FOR US, YOU'D BE IN A SALASSI PRISON RIGHT NOW!

LIKE O'ZIRG, WE BELONG TO *THE ORDER OF THE QUEEN'S ARM.*

AS IN *THE GREAT QUEEN'S* ARM?

THE ARM THAT HOLDS DOWN *THE MIMIC'S HEART?*

YES.

THE ORDER HAS BEEN FIGHTING THE MIMIC FOR CENTURIES.

WE MONITOR ITS ACTIVITY IN ALL THE WORLDS.

WHERE IS IT?

BOOP!

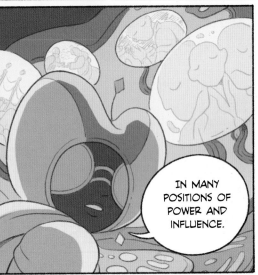

IN MANY POSITIONS OF POWER AND INFLUENCE.

HUH?! *HOW MANY* MIMICS ARE THERE?!

WE BELIEVE THERE'S *A CENTRAL ENTITY...*

...BUT IT *MULTIPLIES* THROUGH THE PEOPLE WHO OFFER IT A GOOD *HOME.*

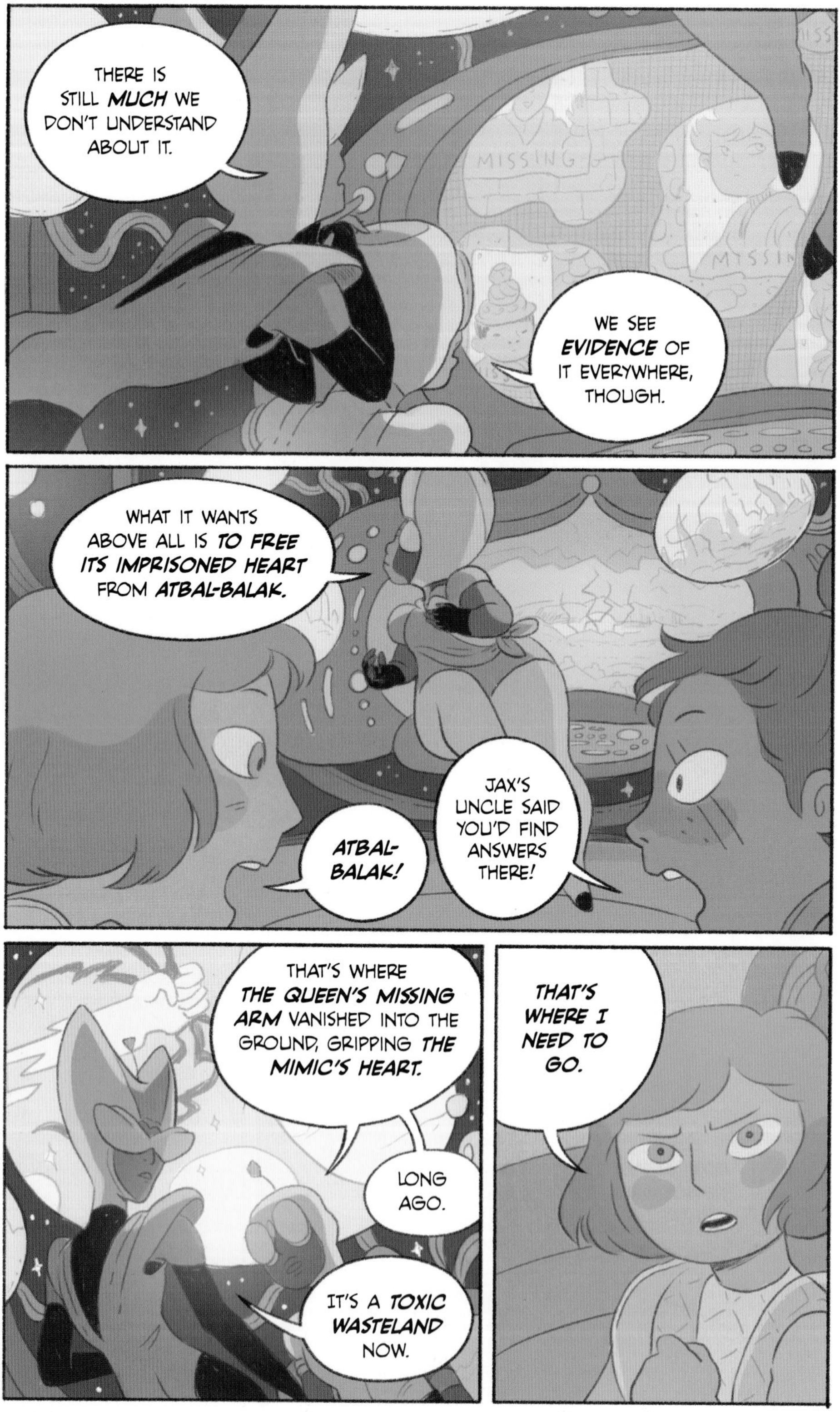
THERE IS STILL MUCH WE DON'T UNDERSTAND ABOUT IT.
MISSING
WE SEE EVIDENCE OF IT EVERYWHERE, THOUGH.
WHAT IT WANTS ABOVE ALL IS TO FREE ITS IMPRISONED HEART FROM ATBAL-BALAK.
ATBAL-BALAK!
JAX'S UNCLE SAID YOU'D FIND ANSWERS THERE!
THAT'S WHERE THE QUEEN'S MISSING ARM VANISHED INTO THE GROUND, GRIPPING THE MIMIC'S HEART.
LONG AGO.
IT'S A TOXIC WASTELAND NOW.
THAT'S WHERE I NEED TO GO.

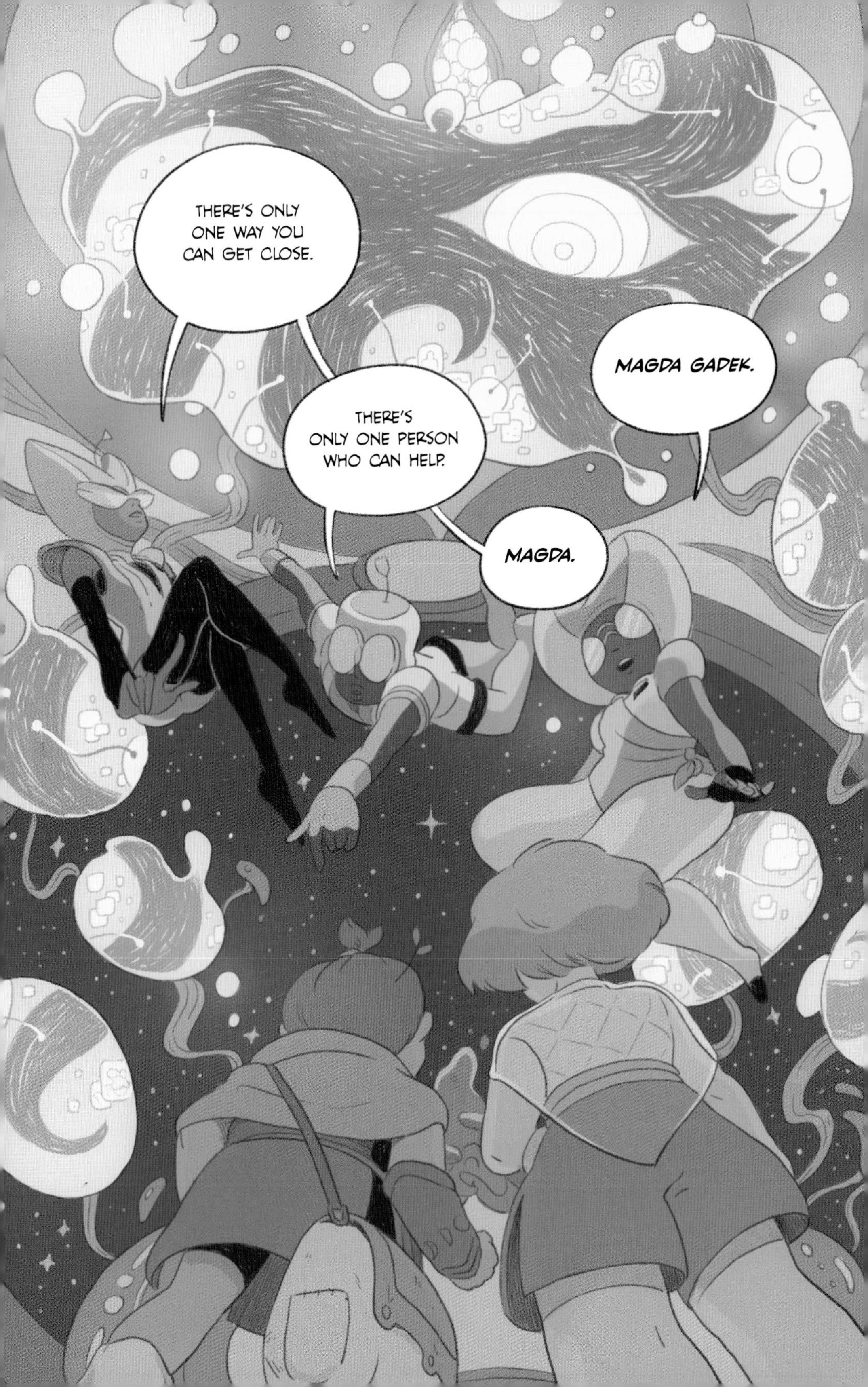
THERE'S ONLY ONE WAY YOU CAN GET CLOSE.
THERE'S ONLY ONE PERSON WHO CAN HELP.
MAGDA GADEK.
MAGDA.

Chapter 4

SHADOWS OF ATBAL-BALAK

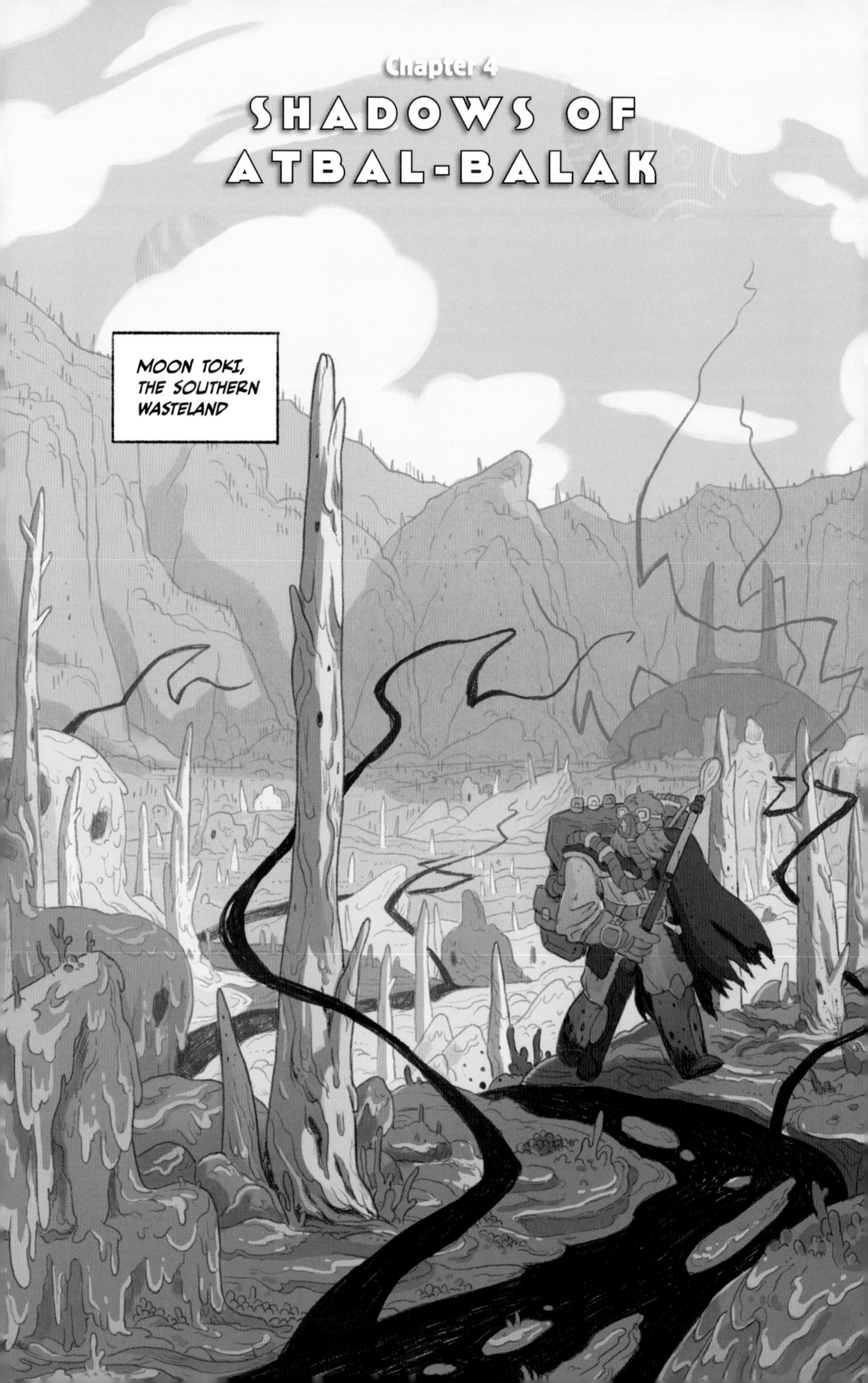
MOON TOKI, THE SOUTHERN WASTELAND

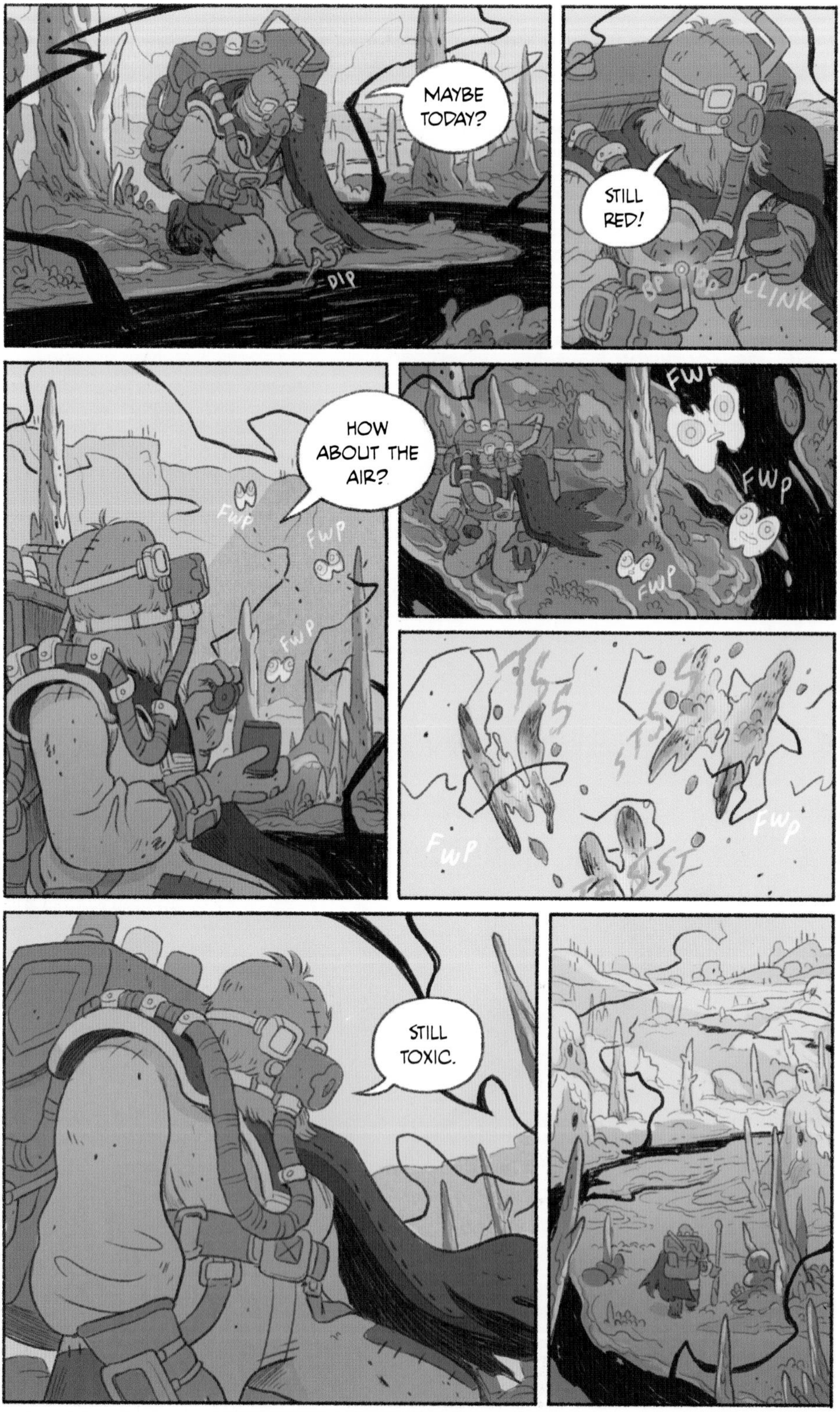
MAYBE TODAY?
DIP
STILL RED!
BP
BP
CLINK
HOW ABOUT THE AIR?
FWP
FWP
FWP
FWP
FWP
FWP
FWP
FWP
FWP
STILL TOXIC.

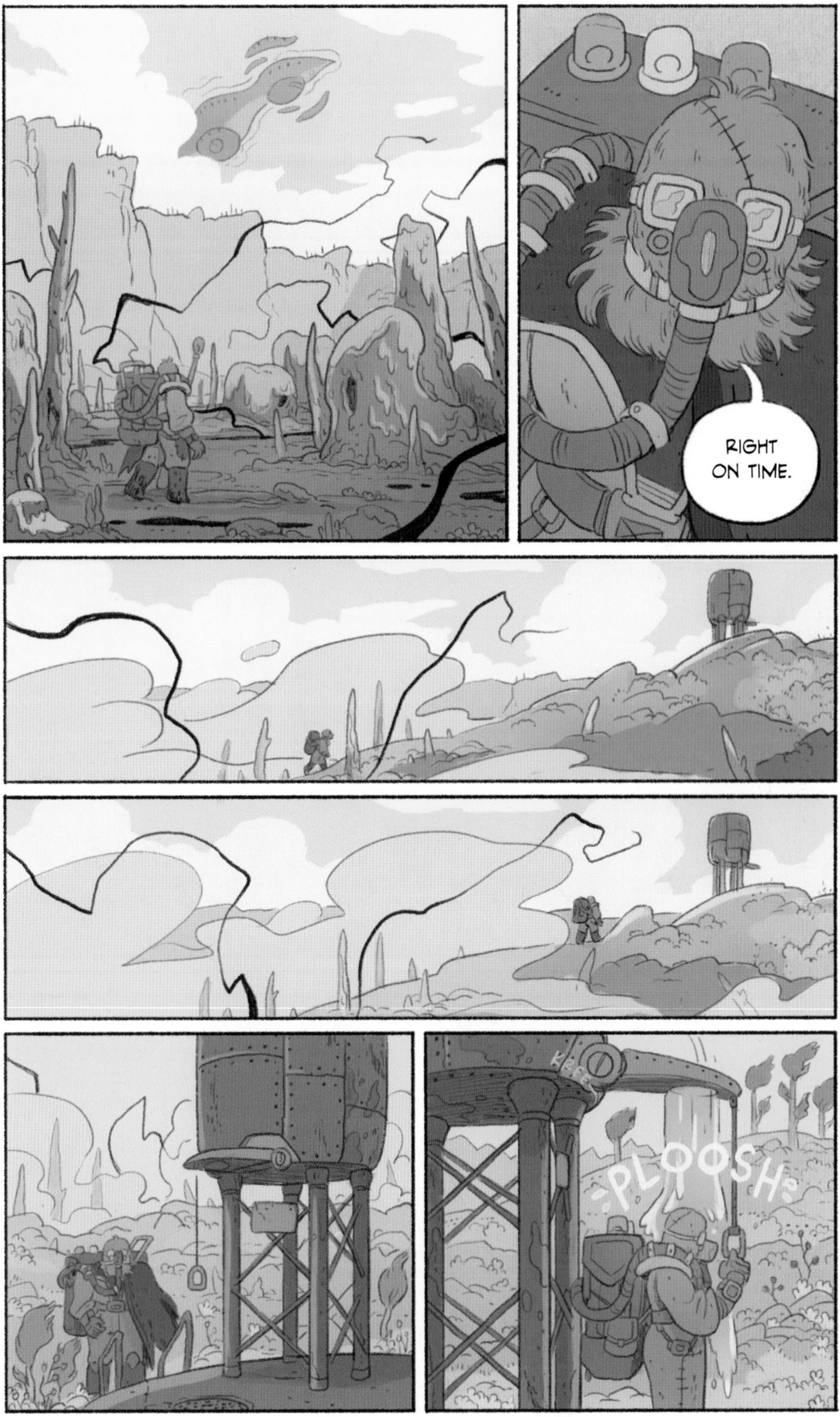
RIGHT ON TIME.
PLOOSH

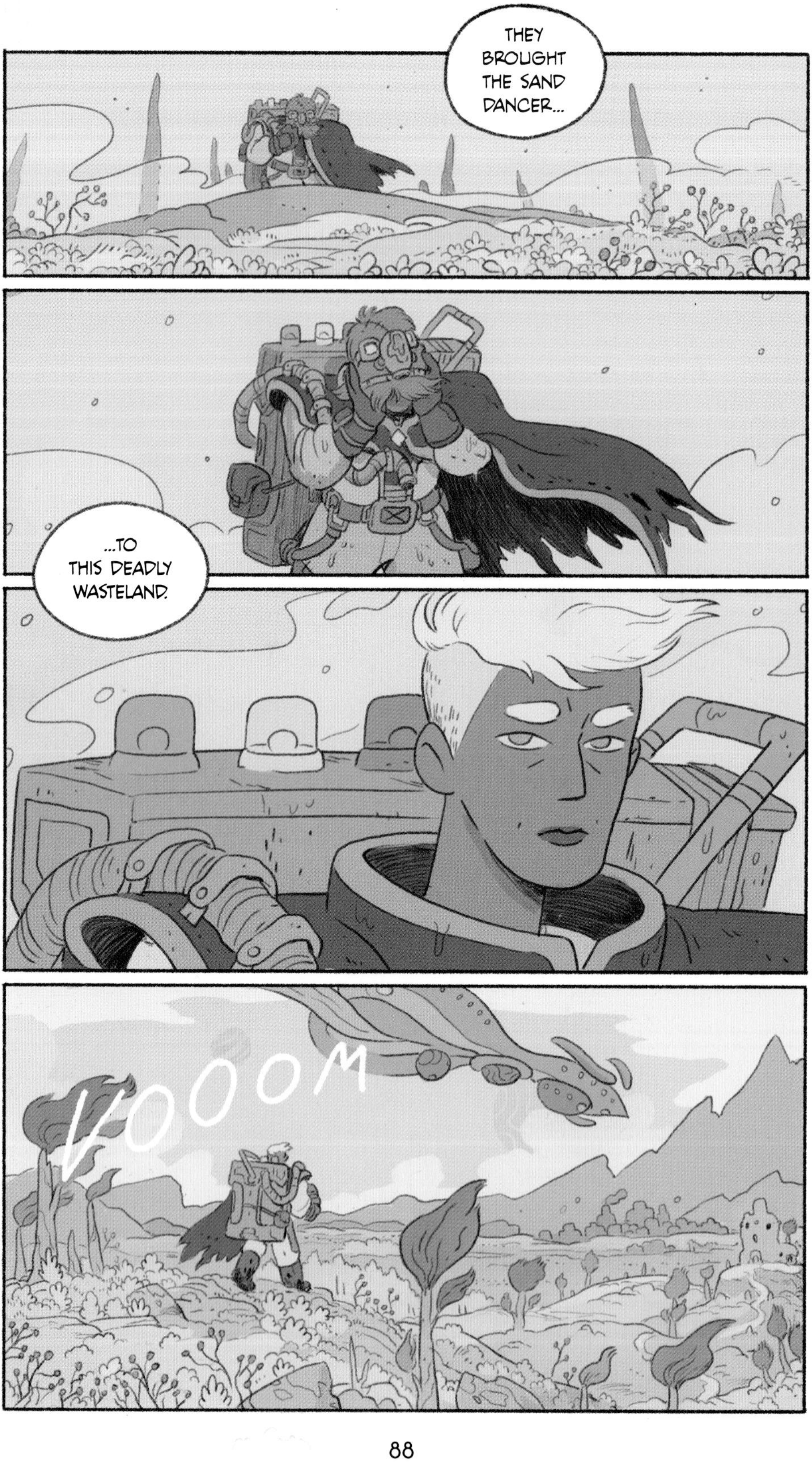
THEY BROUGHT THE SAND DANCER...
...TO THIS DEADLY WASTELAND.
VOOOM

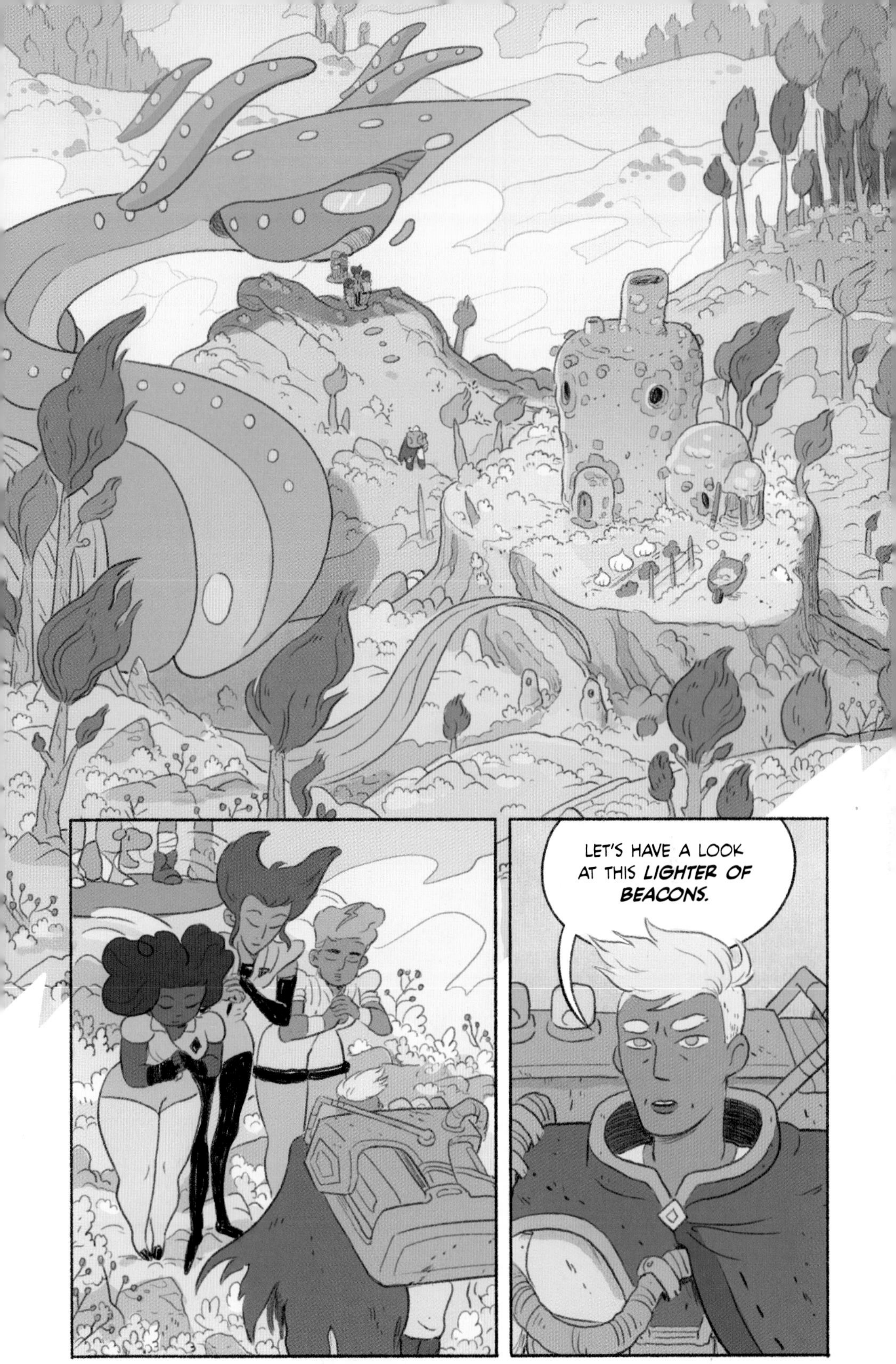
LET'S HAVE A LOOK AT THIS LIGHTER OF BEACONS.

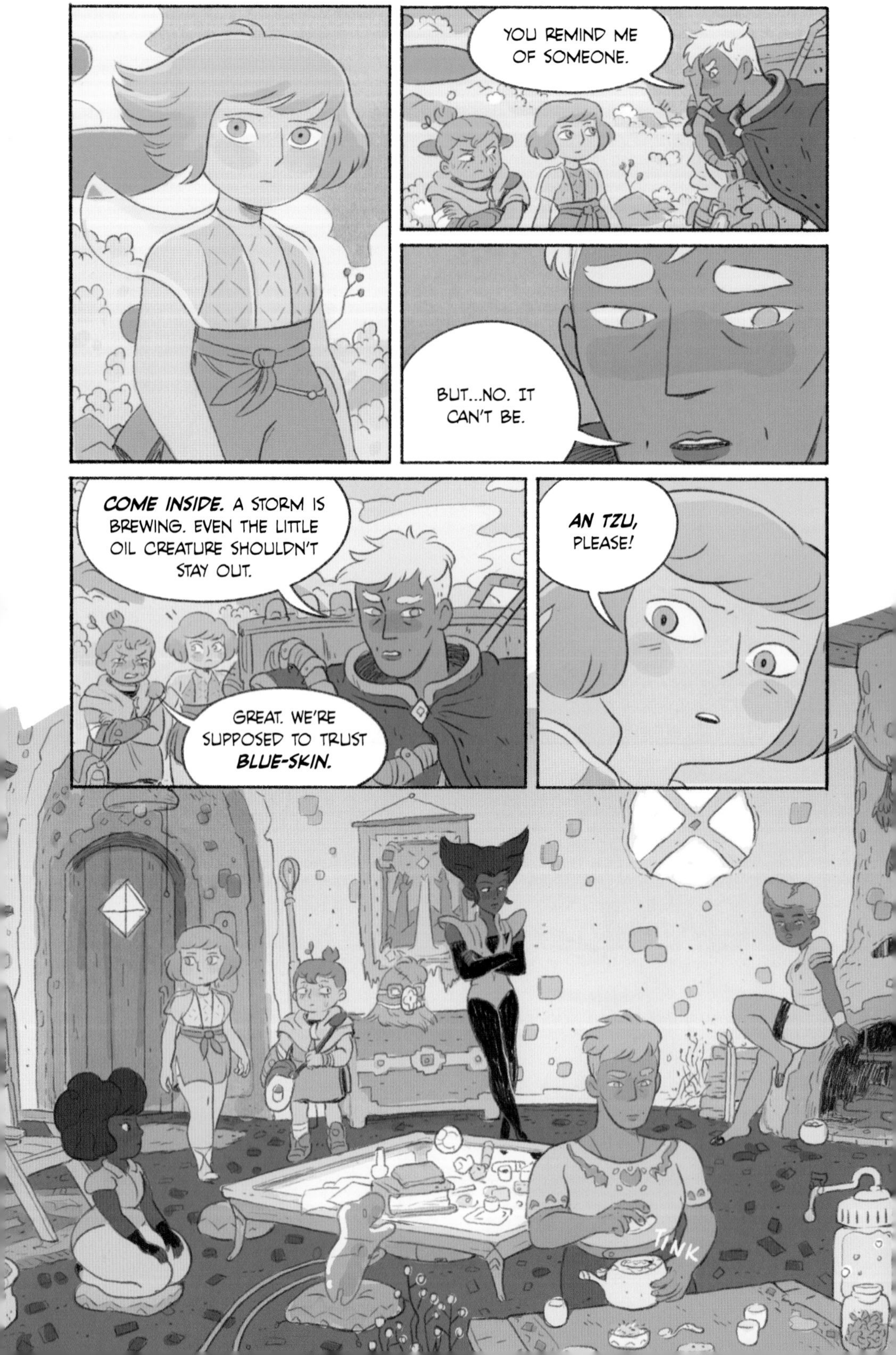
YOU REMIND ME OF SOMEONE.
BUT...NO. IT CAN'T BE.
COME INSIDE. A STORM IS BREWING. EVEN THE LITTLE OIL CREATURE SHOULDN'T STAY OUT.
GREAT. WE'RE SUPPOSED TO TRUST BLUE-SKIN.
AN TZU, PLEASE!
TINK

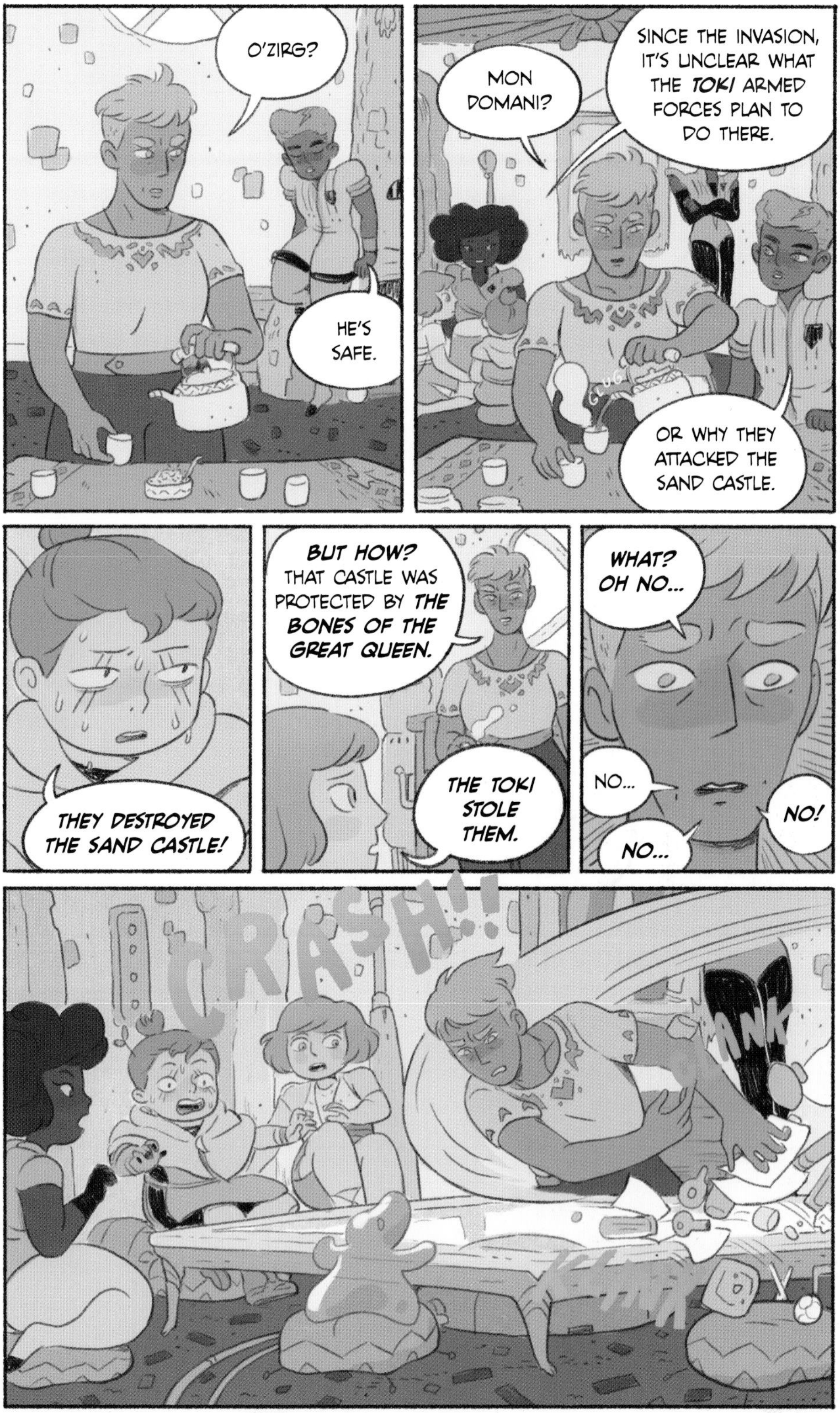
O'ZIRG?
HE'S SAFE.
MON DOMANI?
SINCE THE INVASION, IT'S UNCLEAR WHAT THE *TOKI* ARMED FORCES PLAN TO DO THERE.
GLUG
OR WHY THEY ATTACKED THE SAND CASTLE.
THEY DESTROYED THE SAND CASTLE!
BUT HOW? THAT CASTLE WAS PROTECTED BY *THE BONES OF THE GREAT QUEEN.*
THE TOKI STOLE THEM.
WHAT? OH NO...
NO...
NO...
NO!
CRASH!!

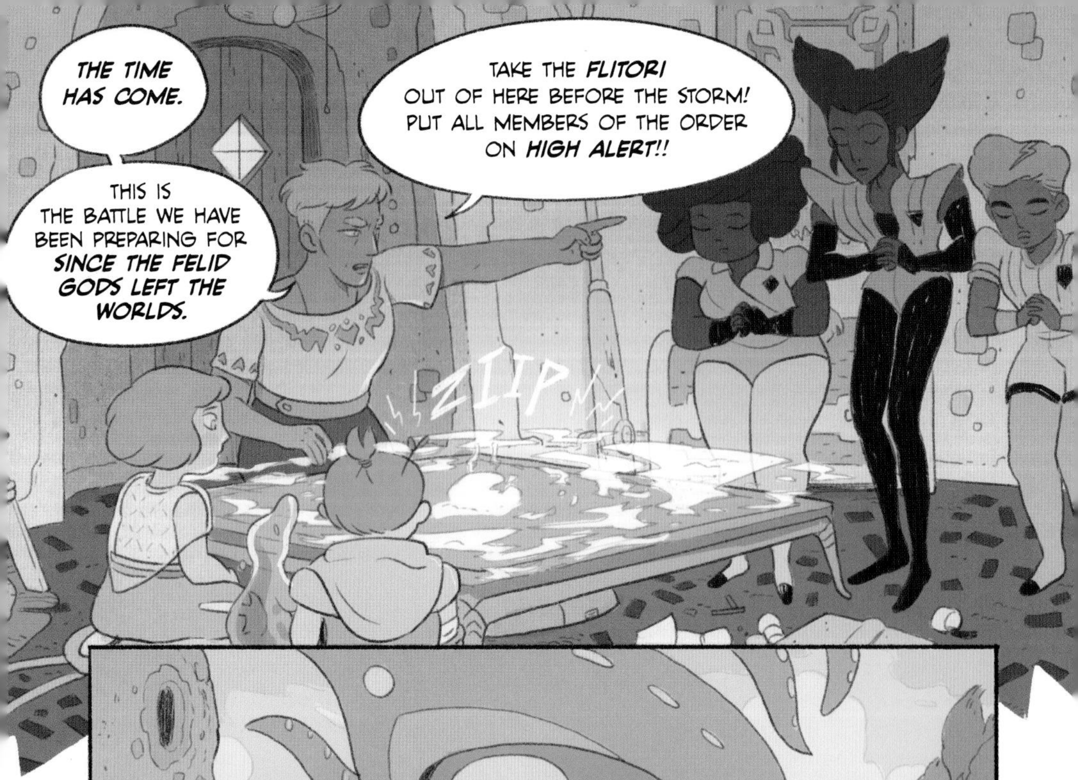
THE TIME HAS COME.
THIS IS THE BATTLE WE HAVE BEEN PREPARING FOR SINCE THE FELID GODS LEFT THE WORLDS.
TAKE THE FLITORI OUT OF HERE BEFORE THE STORM! PUT ALL MEMBERS OF THE ORDER ON HIGH ALERT!!
ZIIP

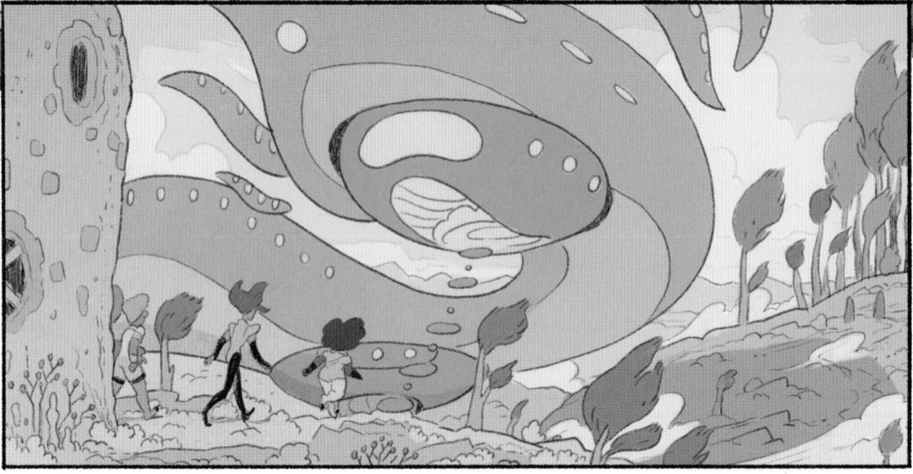

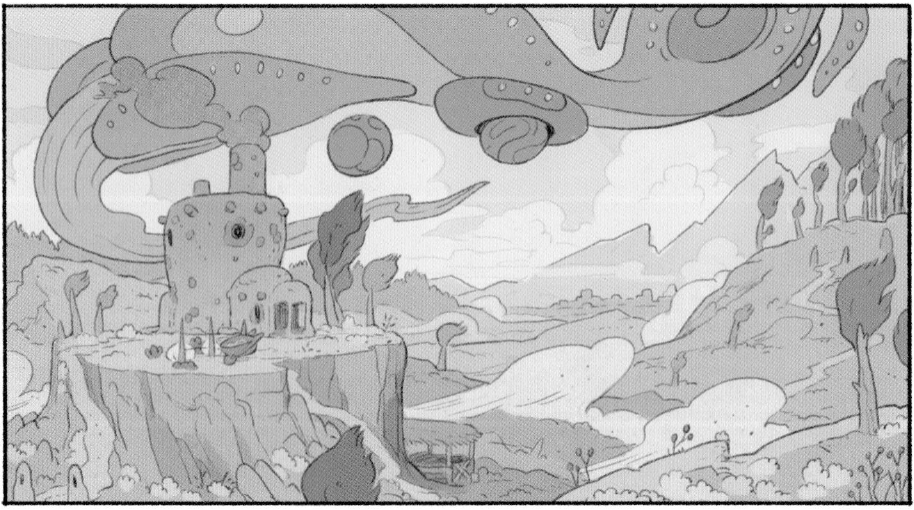

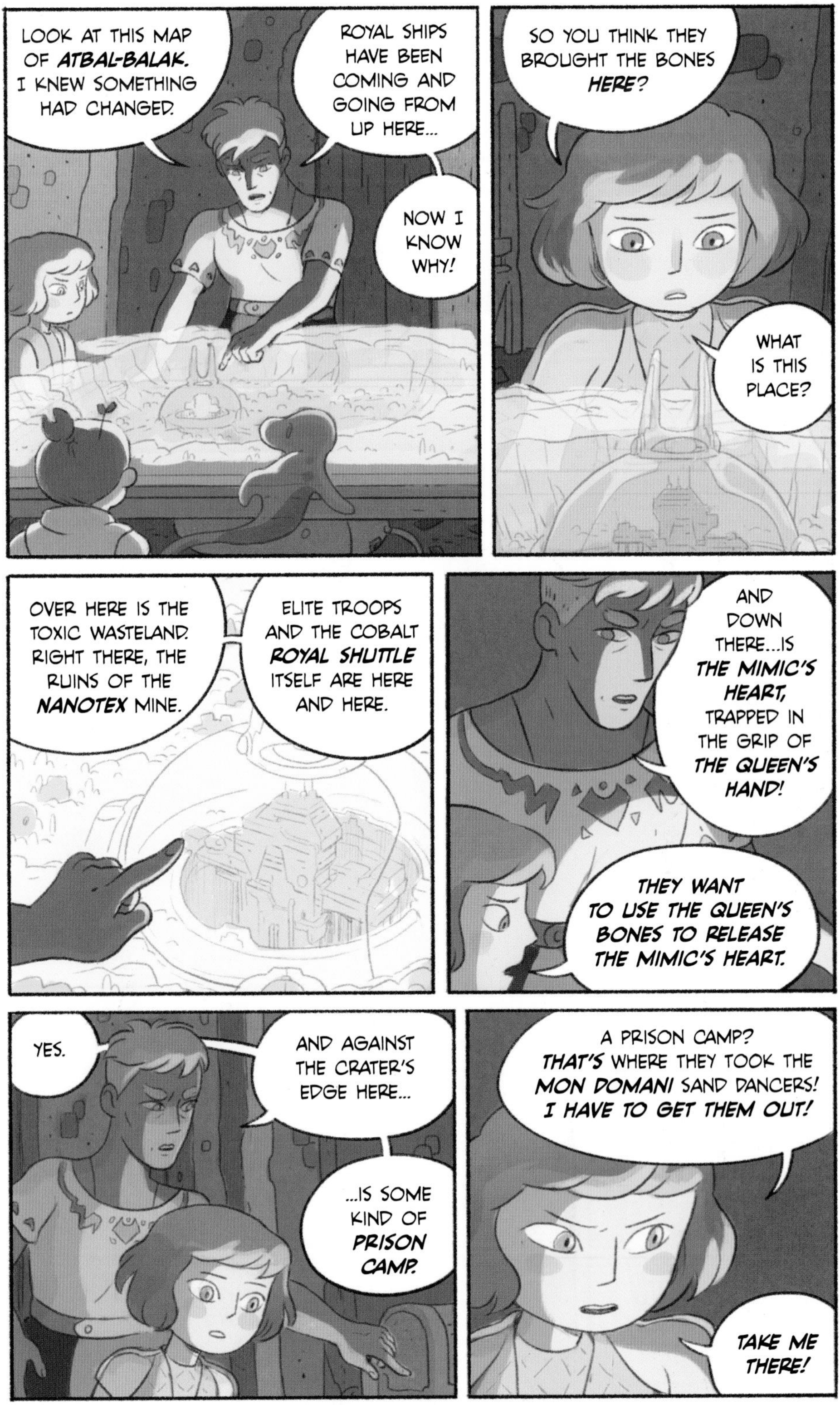
LOOK AT THIS MAP OF ATBAL-BALAK. I KNEW SOMETHING HAD CHANGED.
ROYAL SHIPS HAVE BEEN COMING AND GOING FROM UP HERE...
NOW I KNOW WHY!
SO YOU THINK THEY BROUGHT THE BONES HERE?
WHAT IS THIS PLACE?
OVER HERE IS THE TOXIC WASTELAND. RIGHT THERE, THE RUINS OF THE NANOTEX MINE.
ELITE TROOPS AND THE COBALT ROYAL SHUTTLE ITSELF ARE HERE AND HERE.
AND DOWN THERE...IS THE MIMIC'S HEART, TRAPPED IN THE GRIP OF THE QUEEN'S HAND!
THEY WANT TO USE THE QUEEN'S BONES TO RELEASE THE MIMIC'S HEART.
YES.
AND AGAINST THE CRATER'S EDGE HERE...
...IS SOME KIND OF PRISON CAMP.
A PRISON CAMP? THAT'S WHERE THEY TOOK THE MON DOMANI SAND DANCERS! I HAVE TO GET THEM OUT!
TAKE ME THERE!

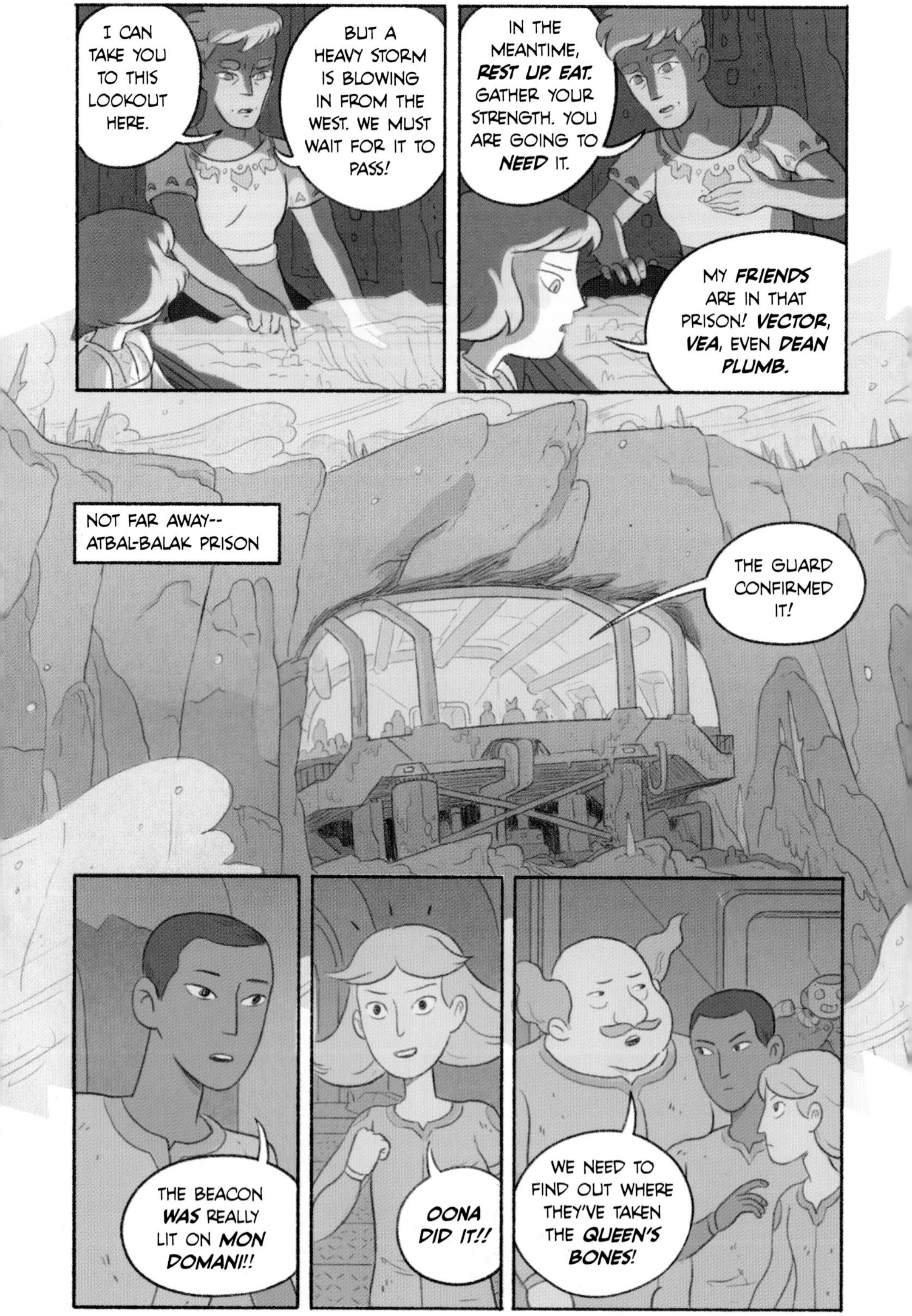
I CAN TAKE YOU TO THIS LOOKOUT HERE.
BUT A HEAVY STORM IS BLOWING IN FROM THE WEST. WE MUST WAIT FOR IT TO PASS!
IN THE MEANTIME, REST UP. EAT. GATHER YOUR STRENGTH. YOU ARE GOING TO NEED IT.
MY FRIENDS ARE IN THAT PRISON! VECTOR, VEA, EVEN DEAN PLUMB.
NOT FAR AWAY-- ATBAL-BALAK PRISON
THE GUARD CONFIRMED IT!
THE BEACON WAS REALLY LIT ON MON DOMANI!!
OONA DID IT!!
WE NEED TO FIND OUT WHERE THEY'VE TAKEN THE QUEEN'S BONES!

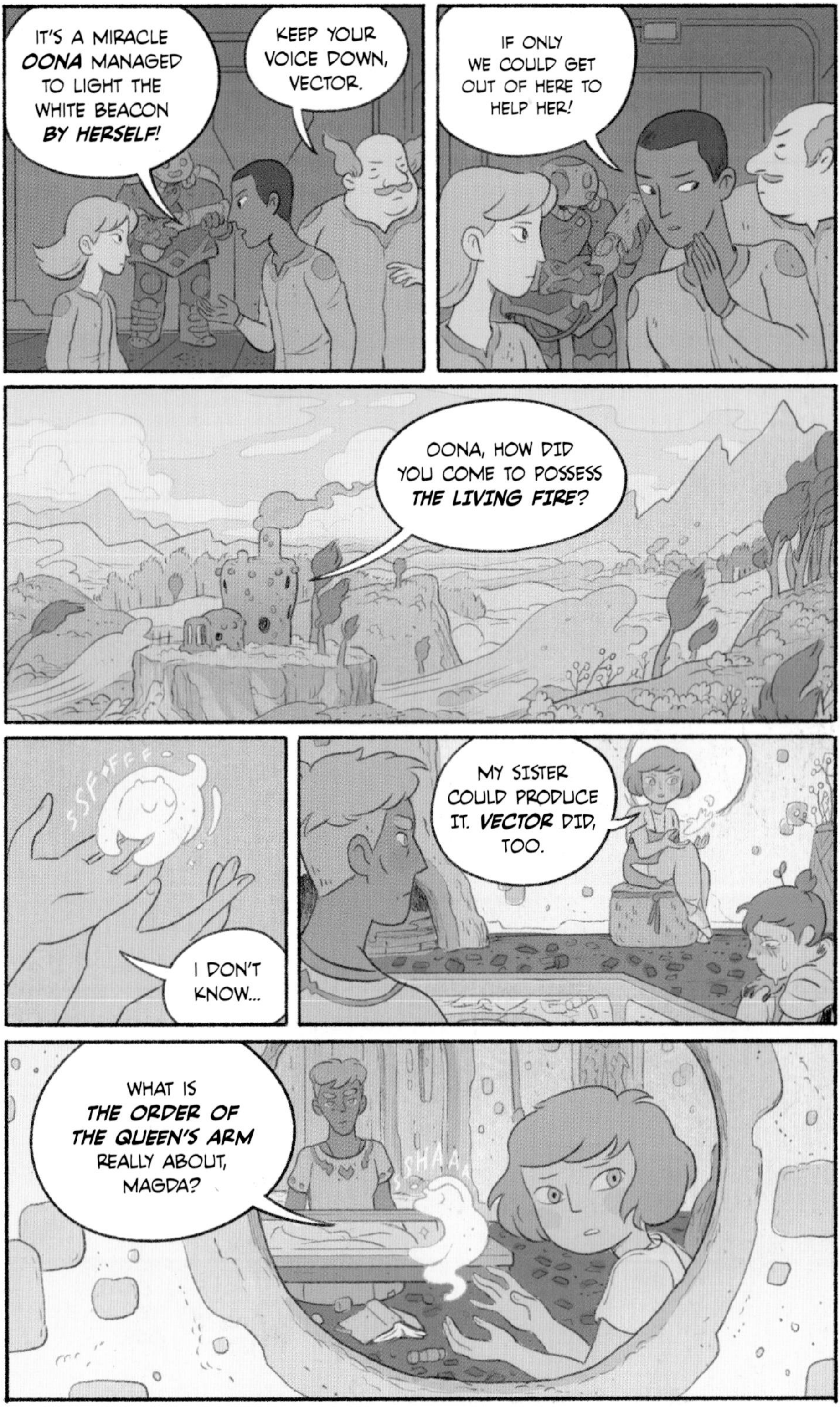
IT'S A MIRACLE OONA MANAGED TO LIGHT THE WHITE BEACON BY HERSELF!
KEEP YOUR VOICE DOWN, VECTOR.
IF ONLY WE COULD GET OUT OF HERE TO HELP HER!
OONA, HOW DID YOU COME TO POSSESS THE LIVING FIRE?
SSFFFF
I DON'T KNOW...
MY SISTER COULD PRODUCE IT. VECTOR DID, TOO.
WHAT IS THE ORDER OF THE QUEEN'S ARM REALLY ABOUT, MAGDA?
SHAAA

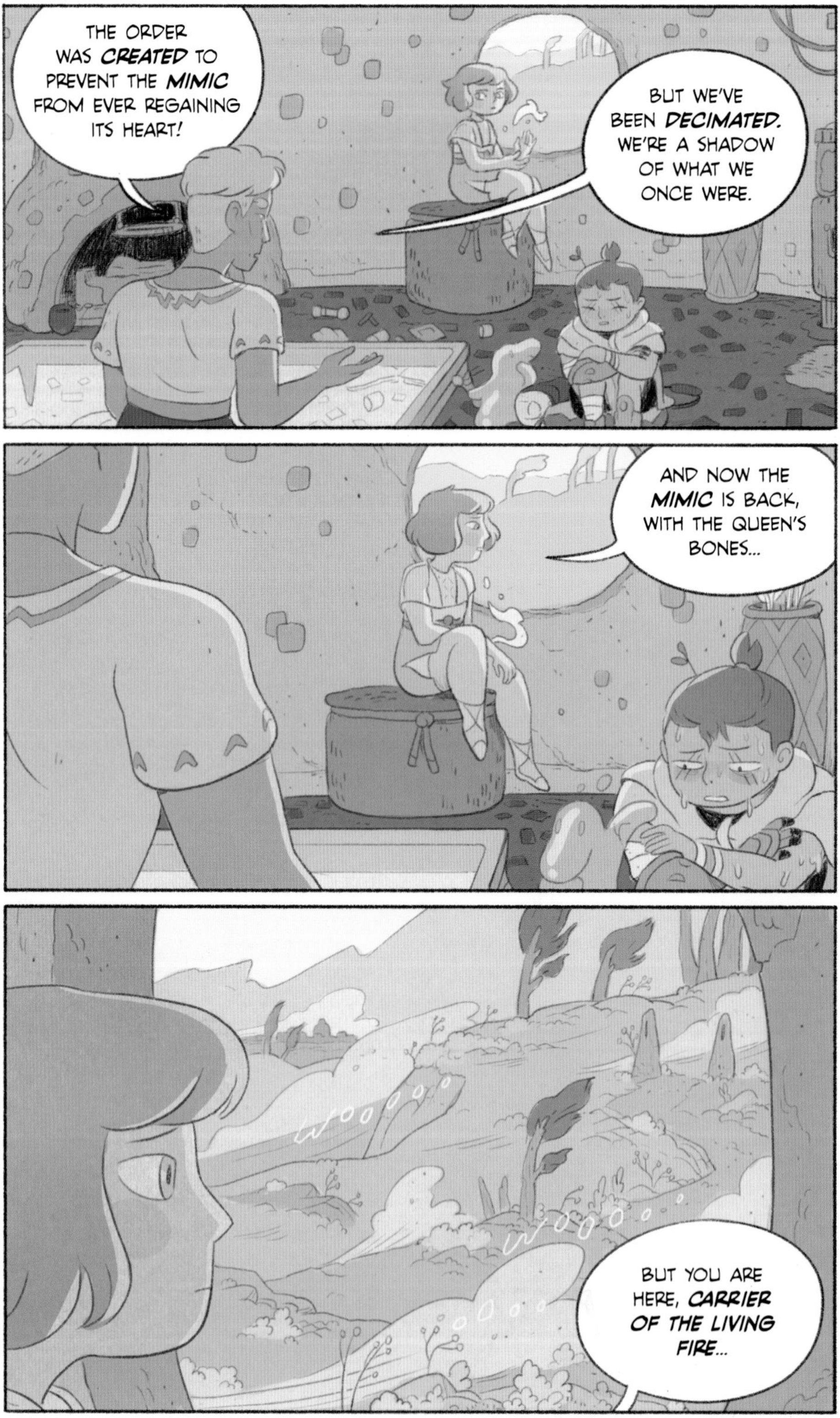
THE ORDER WAS CREATED TO PREVENT THE MIMIC FROM EVER REGAINING ITS HEART!
BUT WE'VE BEEN DECIMATED. WE'RE A SHADOW OF WHAT WE ONCE WERE.
AND NOW THE MIMIC IS BACK, WITH THE QUEEN'S BONES...
WOOOOOO
WOOOOO
BUT YOU ARE HERE, CARRIER OF THE LIVING FIRE...

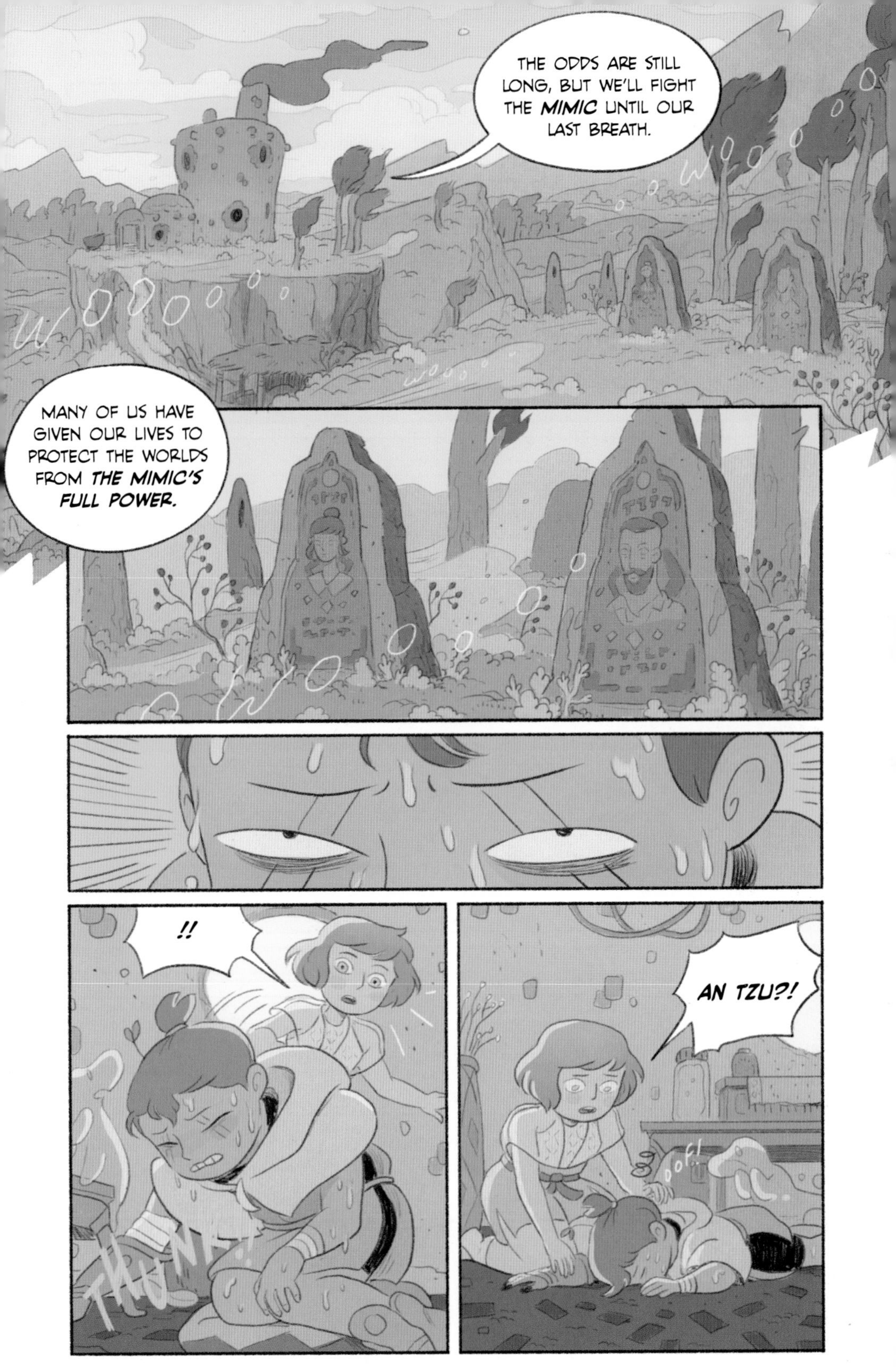
THE ODDS ARE STILL LONG, BUT WE'LL FIGHT THE MIMIC UNTIL OUR LAST BREATH.
WOOOOoo
WOOOOooo
MANY OF US HAVE GIVEN OUR LIVES TO PROTECT THE WORLDS FROM THE MIMIC'S FULL POWER.
!!
THUNK!
AN TZU?!
OOF!

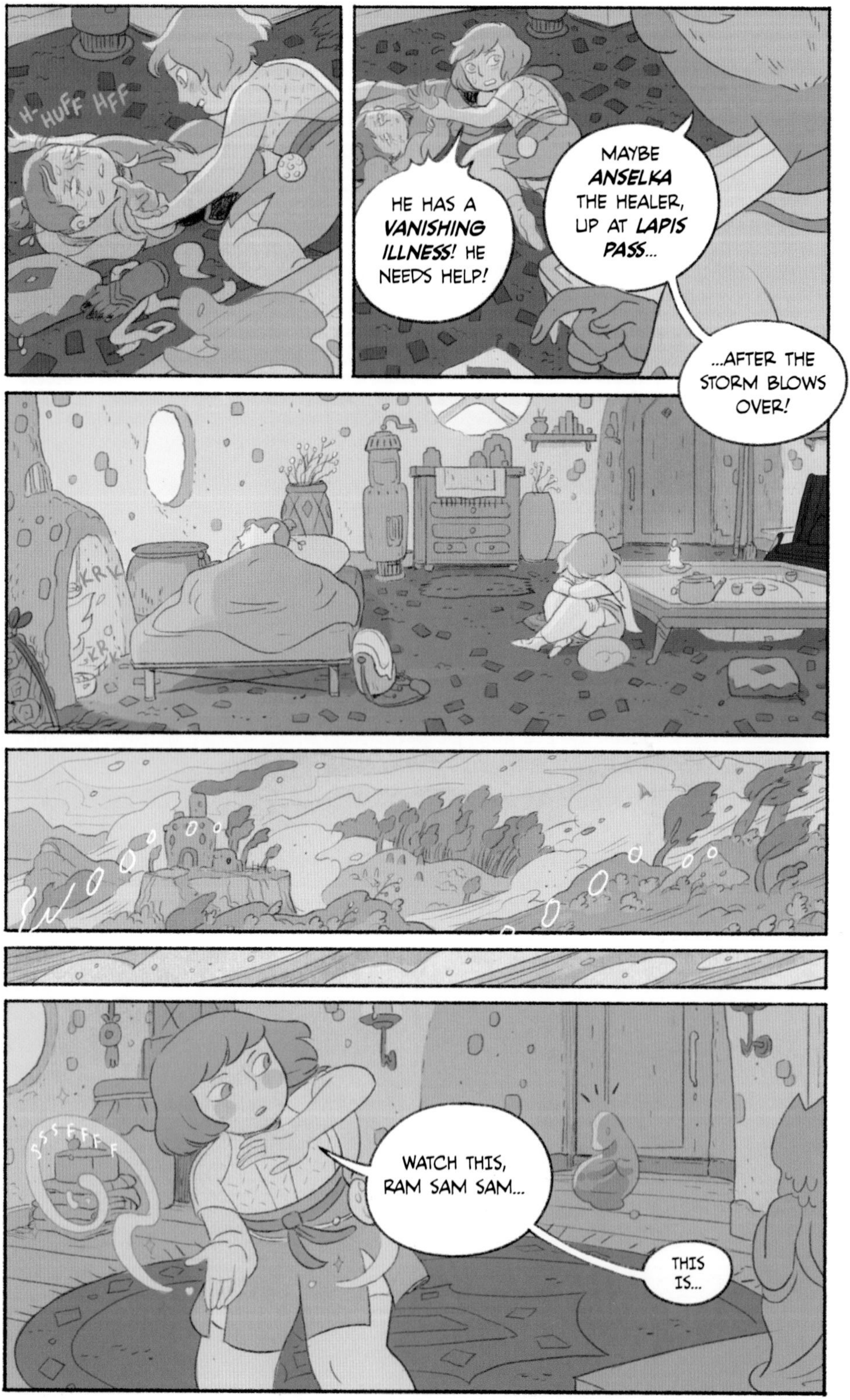
H-HUFF HFF
HE HAS A VANISHING ILLNESS! HE NEEDS HELP!
MAYBE ANSELKA THE HEALER, UP AT LAPIS PASS...
...AFTER THE STORM BLOWS OVER!
KRK
KR TK
SSSFFFF
WATCH THIS, RAM SAM SAM...
THIS IS...

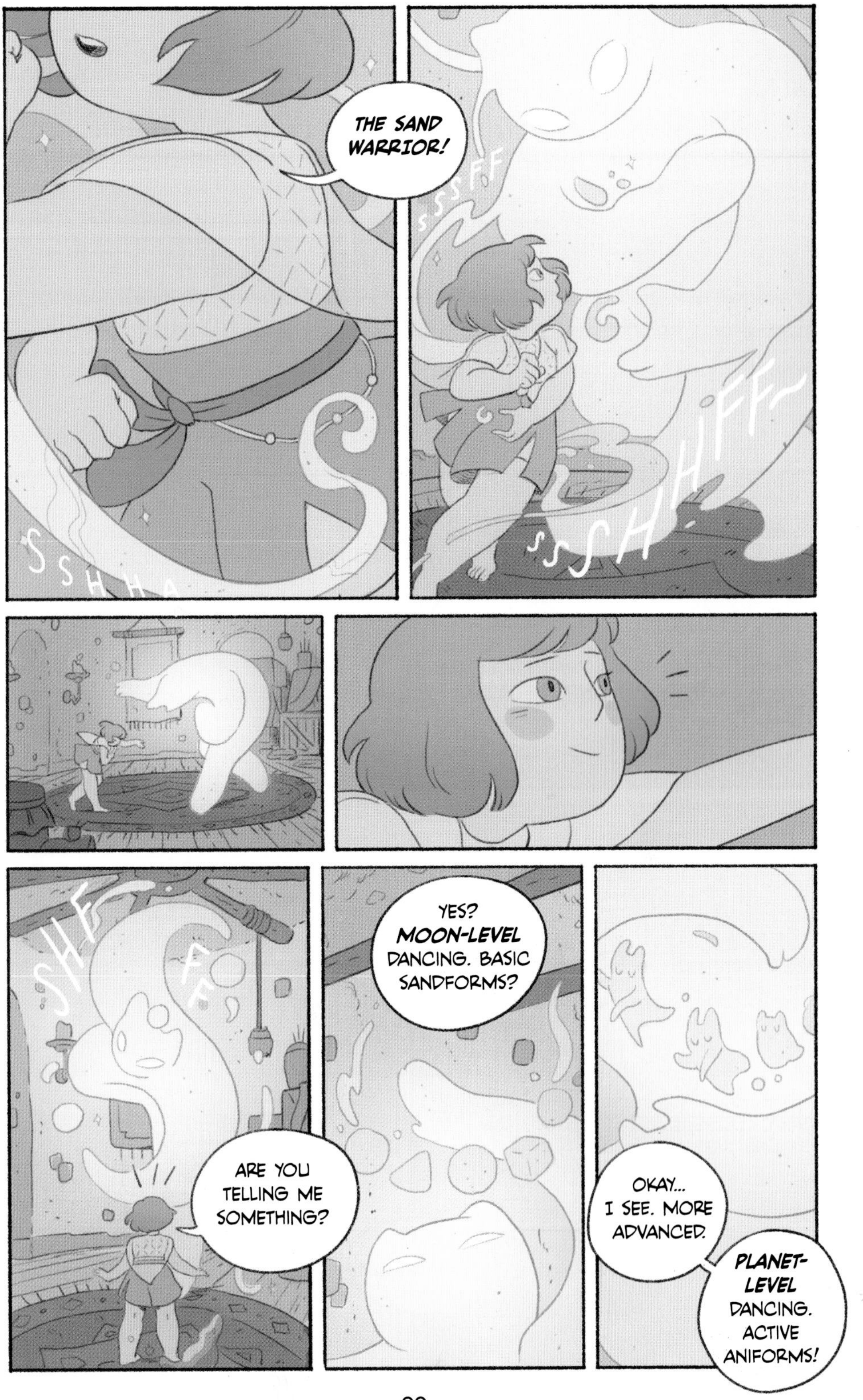
THE SAND WARRIOR!
SSHHA
SSSFF
SSHHFF~
SHFF
ARE YOU TELLING ME SOMETHING?
YES? MOON-LEVEL DANCING. BASIC SANDFORMS?
OKAY... I SEE. MORE ADVANCED.
PLANET-LEVEL DANCING. ACTIVE ANIFORMS!

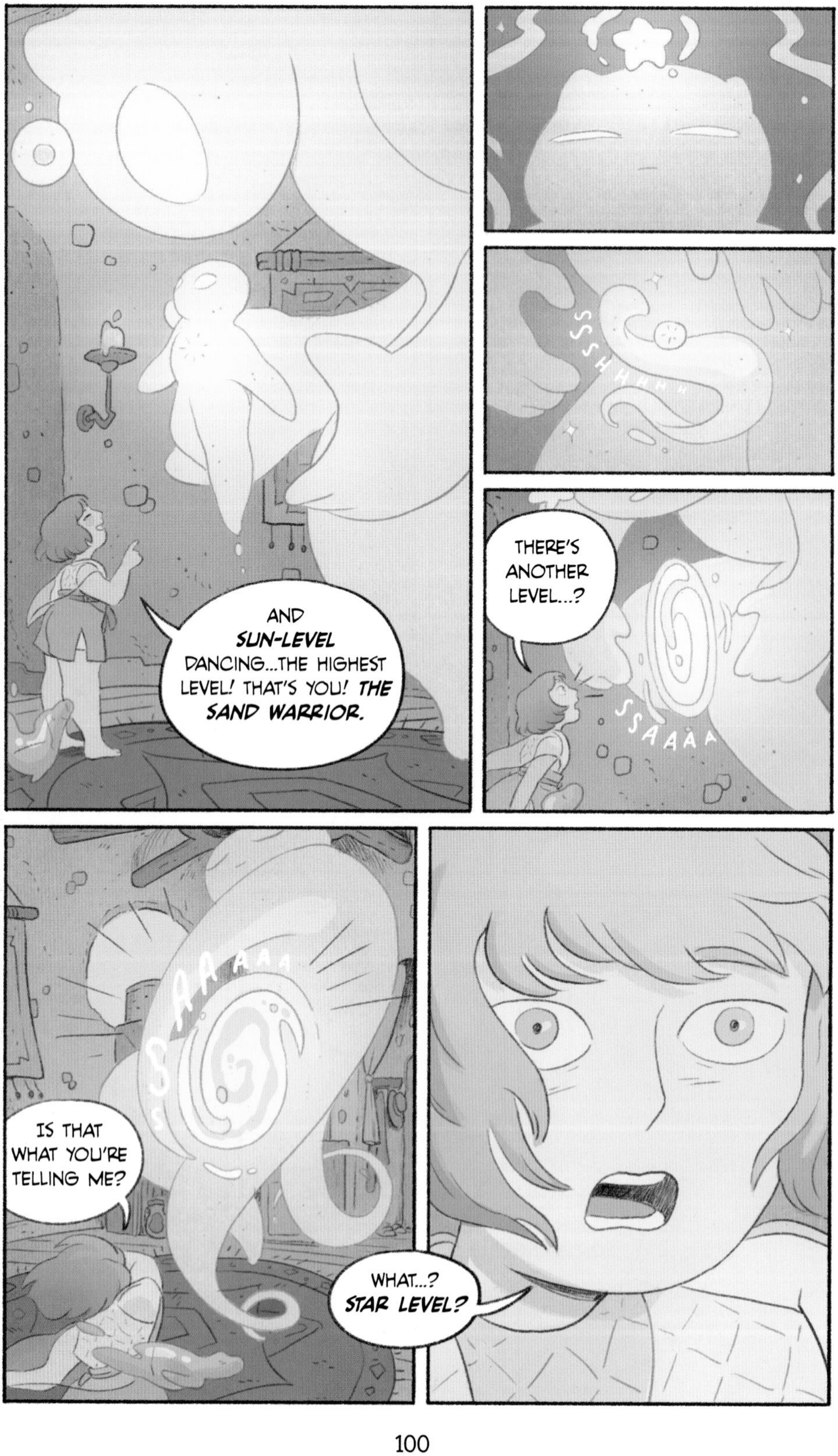
AND SUN-LEVEL DANCING...THE HIGHEST LEVEL! THAT'S YOU! THE SAND WARRIOR.
SSSHHHHH
THERE'S ANOTHER LEVEL...?
SSAAAA
SSAAAAA
IS THAT WHAT YOU'RE TELLING ME?
WHAT...? STAR LEVEL?

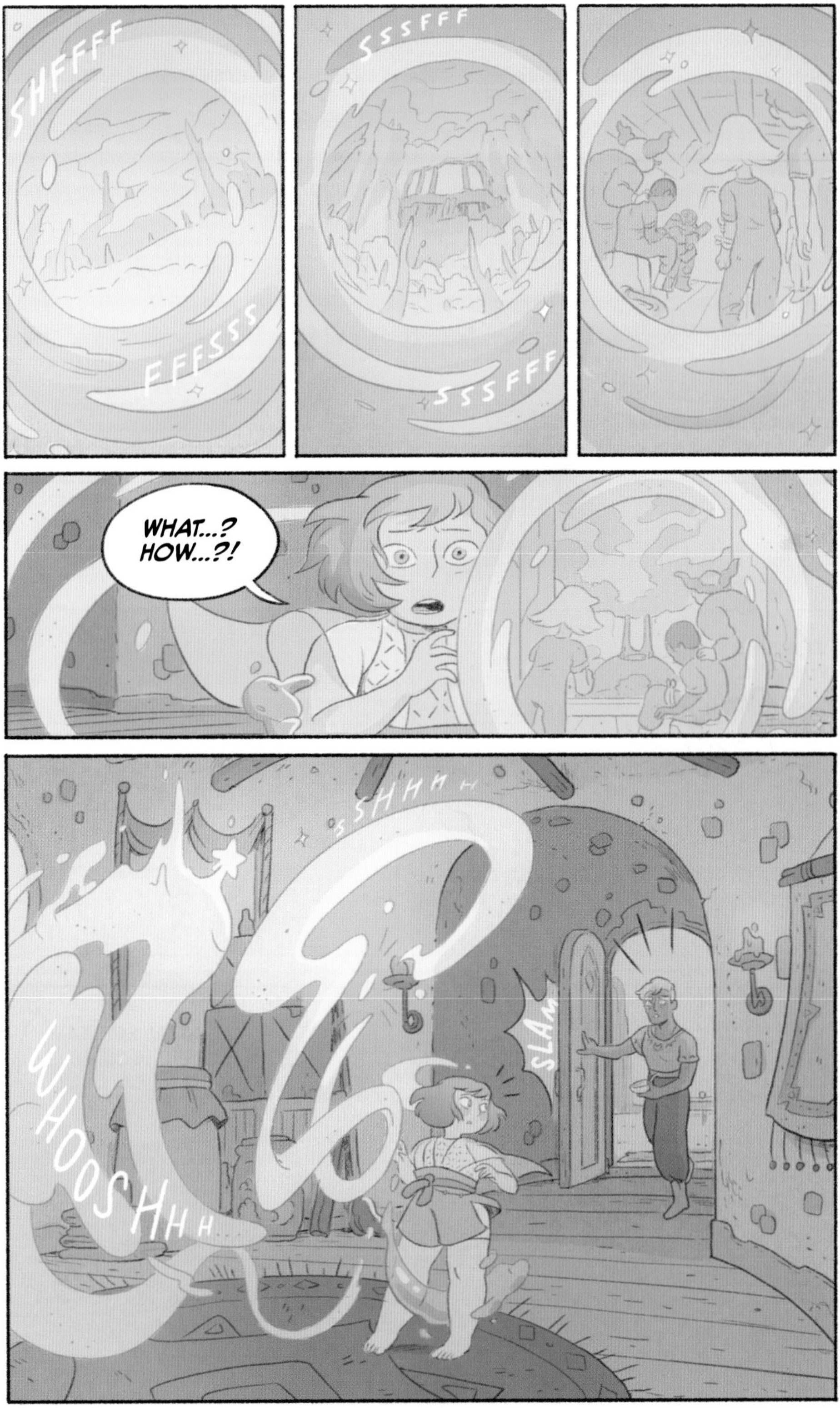
SHFFFF
FFFSSS
SSSFFF
SSSFFF
WHAT...? HOW...?!
SSHHHH
SLAM
WHOOSHHHH

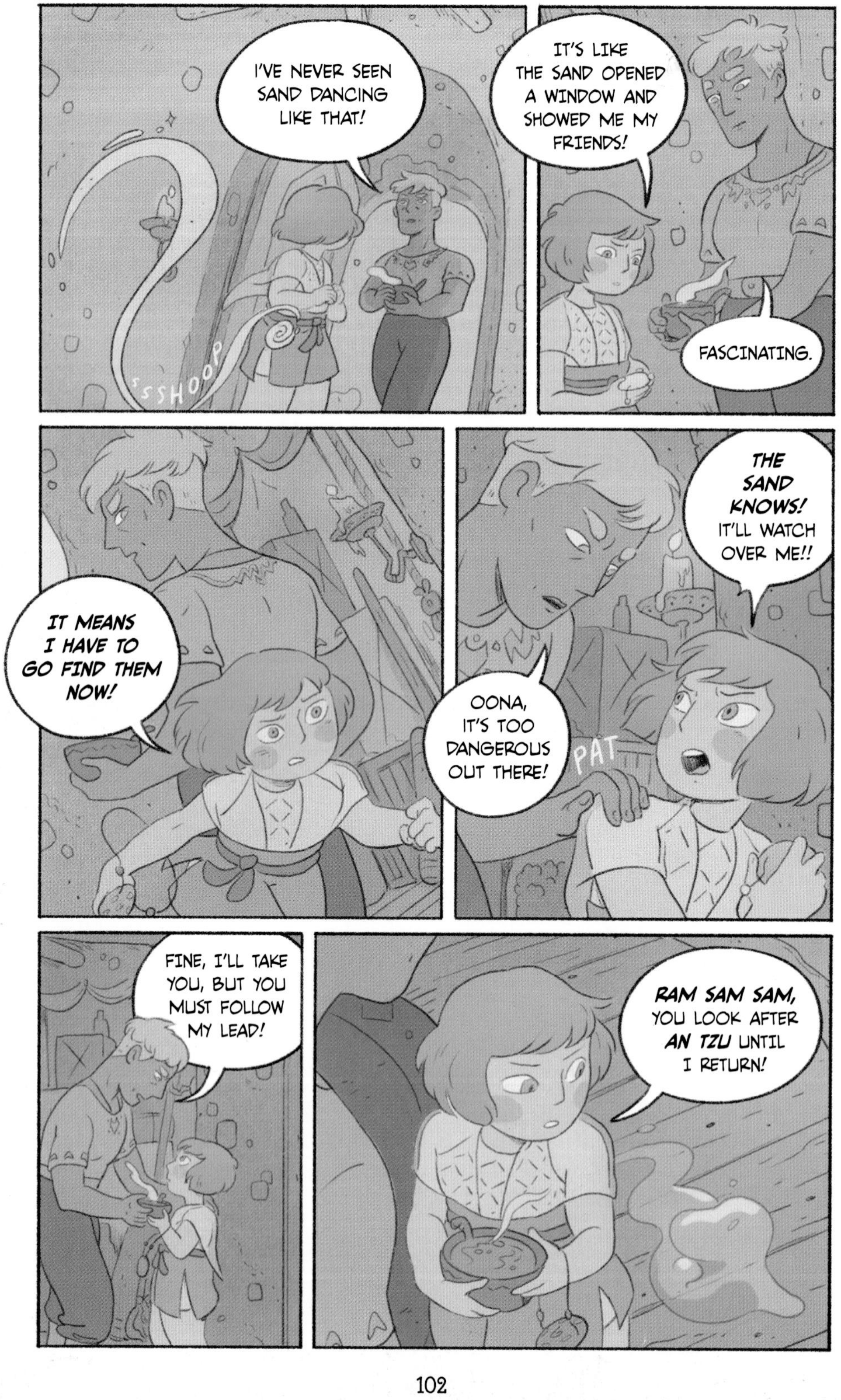
I'VE NEVER SEEN SAND DANCING LIKE THAT!
SSSHOOP
IT'S LIKE THE SAND OPENED A WINDOW AND SHOWED ME MY FRIENDS!
FASCINATING.
IT MEANS I HAVE TO GO FIND THEM NOW!
THE SAND KNOWS! IT'LL WATCH OVER ME!!
OONA, IT'S TOO DANGEROUS OUT THERE!
PAT
FINE, I'LL TAKE YOU, BUT YOU MUST FOLLOW MY LEAD!
RAM SAM SAM, YOU LOOK AFTER AN TZU UNTIL I RETURN!

Chapter 5
CAUGHT IN A STORM

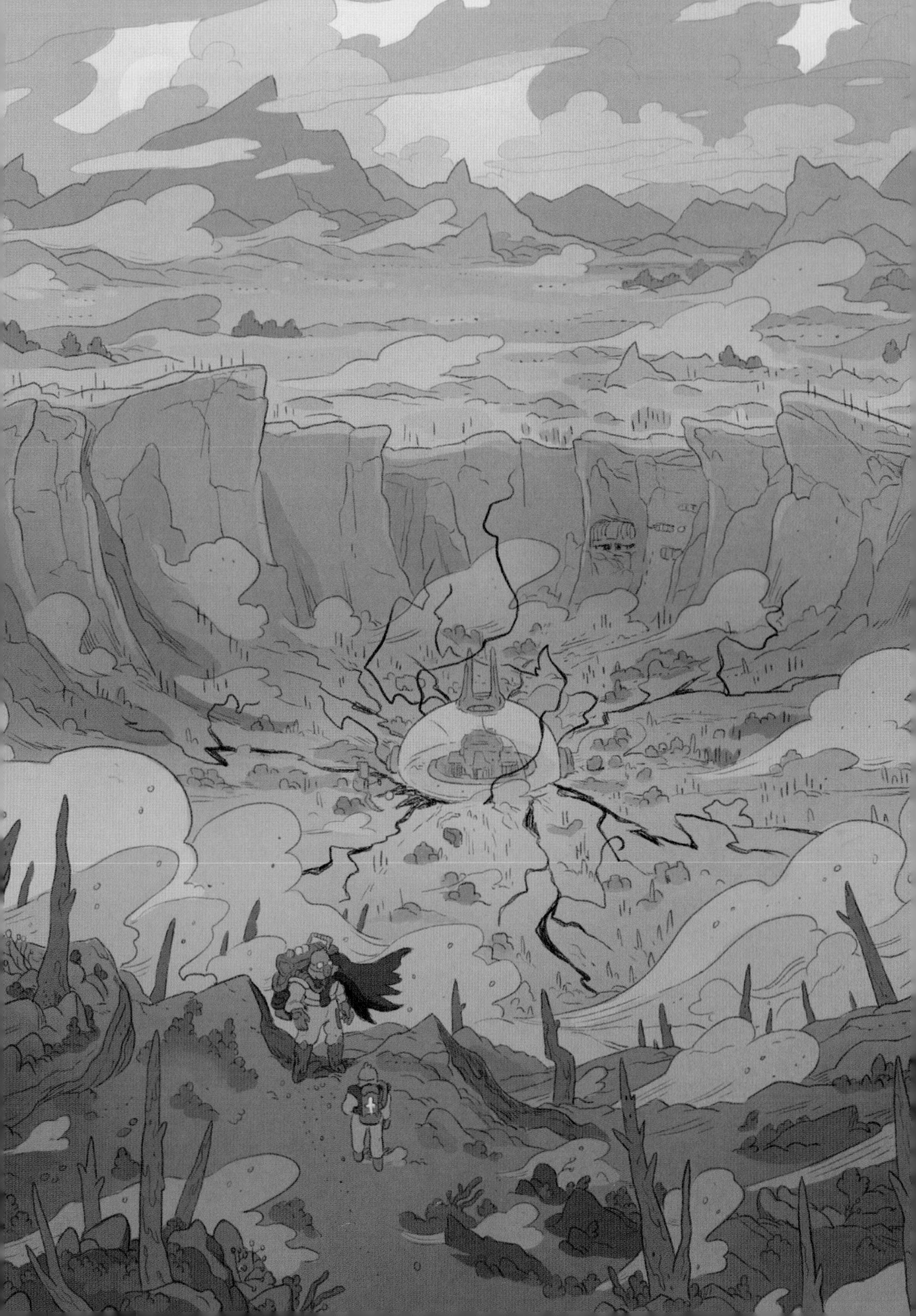

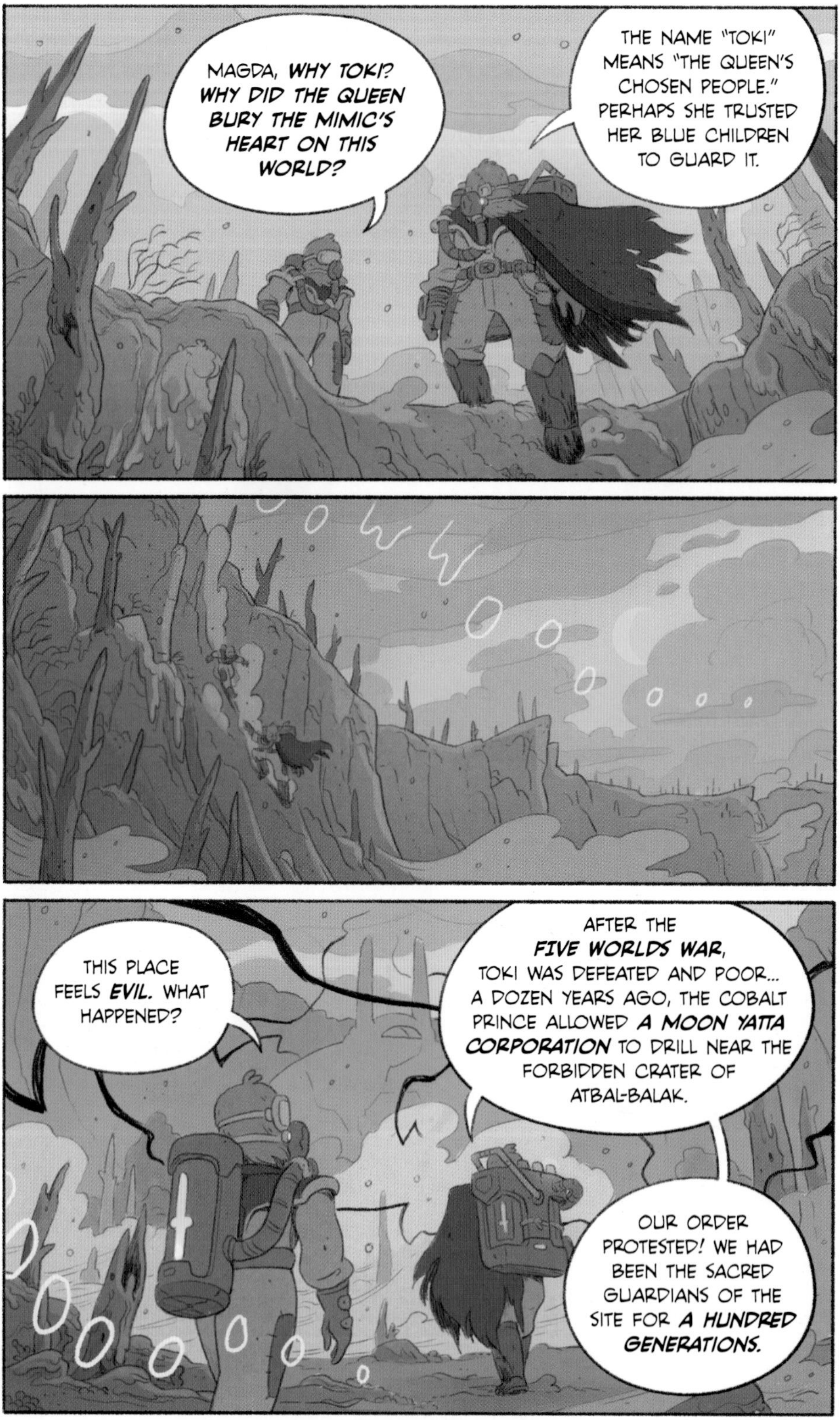
MAGDA, WHY TOKI? WHY DID THE QUEEN BURY THE MIMIC'S HEART ON THIS WORLD?
THE NAME "TOKI" MEANS "THE QUEEN'S CHOSEN PEOPLE." PERHAPS SHE TRUSTED HER BLUE CHILDREN TO GUARD IT.
OOWWOOOOoo
THIS PLACE FEELS EVIL. WHAT HAPPENED?
AFTER THE FIVE WORLDS WAR, TOKI WAS DEFEATED AND POOR... A DOZEN YEARS AGO, THE COBALT PRINCE ALLOWED A MOON YATTA CORPORATION TO DRILL NEAR THE FORBIDDEN CRATER OF ATBAL-BALAK.
OUR ORDER PROTESTED! WE HAD BEEN THE SACRED GUARDIANS OF THE SITE FOR A HUNDRED GENERATIONS.

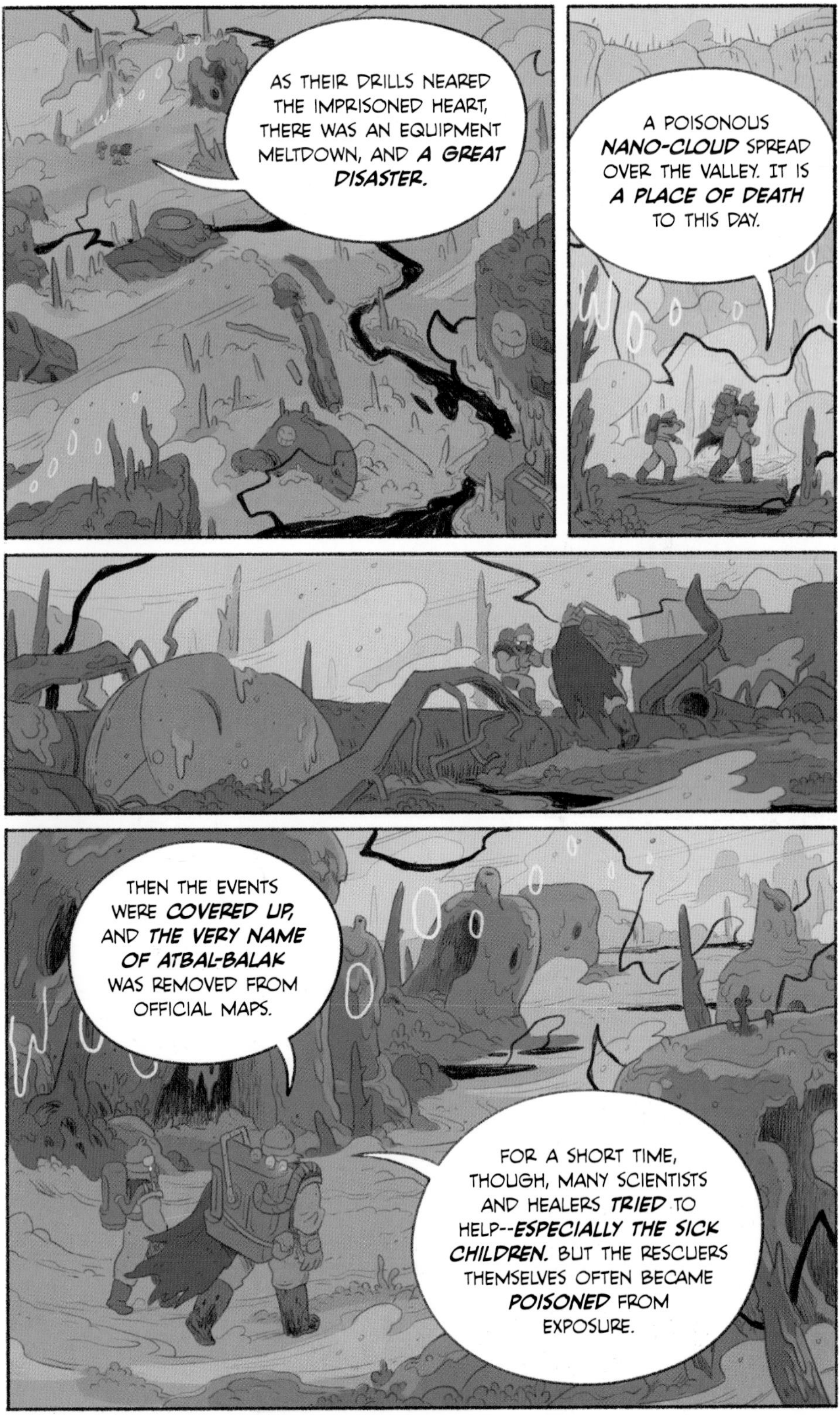
AS THEIR DRILLS NEARED THE IMPRISONED HEART, THERE WAS AN EQUIPMENT MELTDOWN, AND ***A GREAT DISASTER.***
A POISONOUS ***NANO-CLOUD*** SPREAD OVER THE VALLEY. IT IS ***A PLACE OF DEATH*** TO THIS DAY.
THEN THE EVENTS WERE ***COVERED UP,*** AND ***THE VERY NAME OF ATBAL-BALAK*** WAS REMOVED FROM OFFICIAL MAPS.
FOR A SHORT TIME, THOUGH, MANY SCIENTISTS AND HEALERS ***TRIED*** TO HELP--***ESPECIALLY THE SICK CHILDREN.*** BUT THE RESCUERS THEMSELVES OFTEN BECAME ***POISONED*** FROM EXPOSURE.

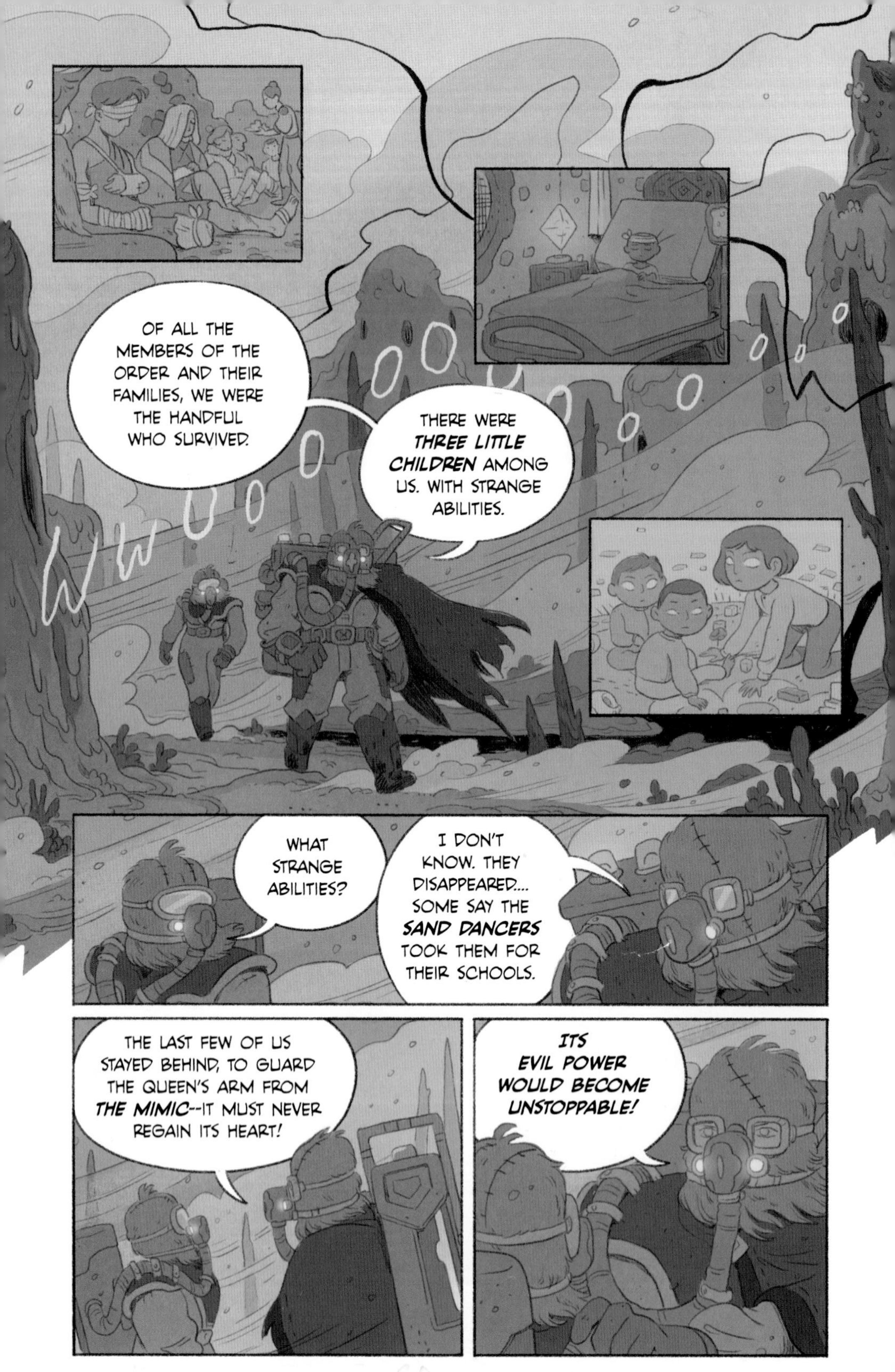
OF ALL THE MEMBERS OF THE ORDER AND THEIR FAMILIES, WE WERE THE HANDFUL WHO SURVIVED.
THERE WERE THREE LITTLE CHILDREN AMONG US. WITH STRANGE ABILITIES.
WWOOOOOOOOOOOOO
WHAT STRANGE ABILITIES?
I DON'T KNOW. THEY DISAPPEARED.... SOME SAY THE SAND DANCERS TOOK THEM FOR THEIR SCHOOLS.
THE LAST FEW OF US STAYED BEHIND, TO GUARD THE QUEEN'S ARM FROM THE MIMIC--IT MUST NEVER REGAIN ITS HEART!
ITS EVIL POWER WOULD BECOME UNSTOPPABLE!

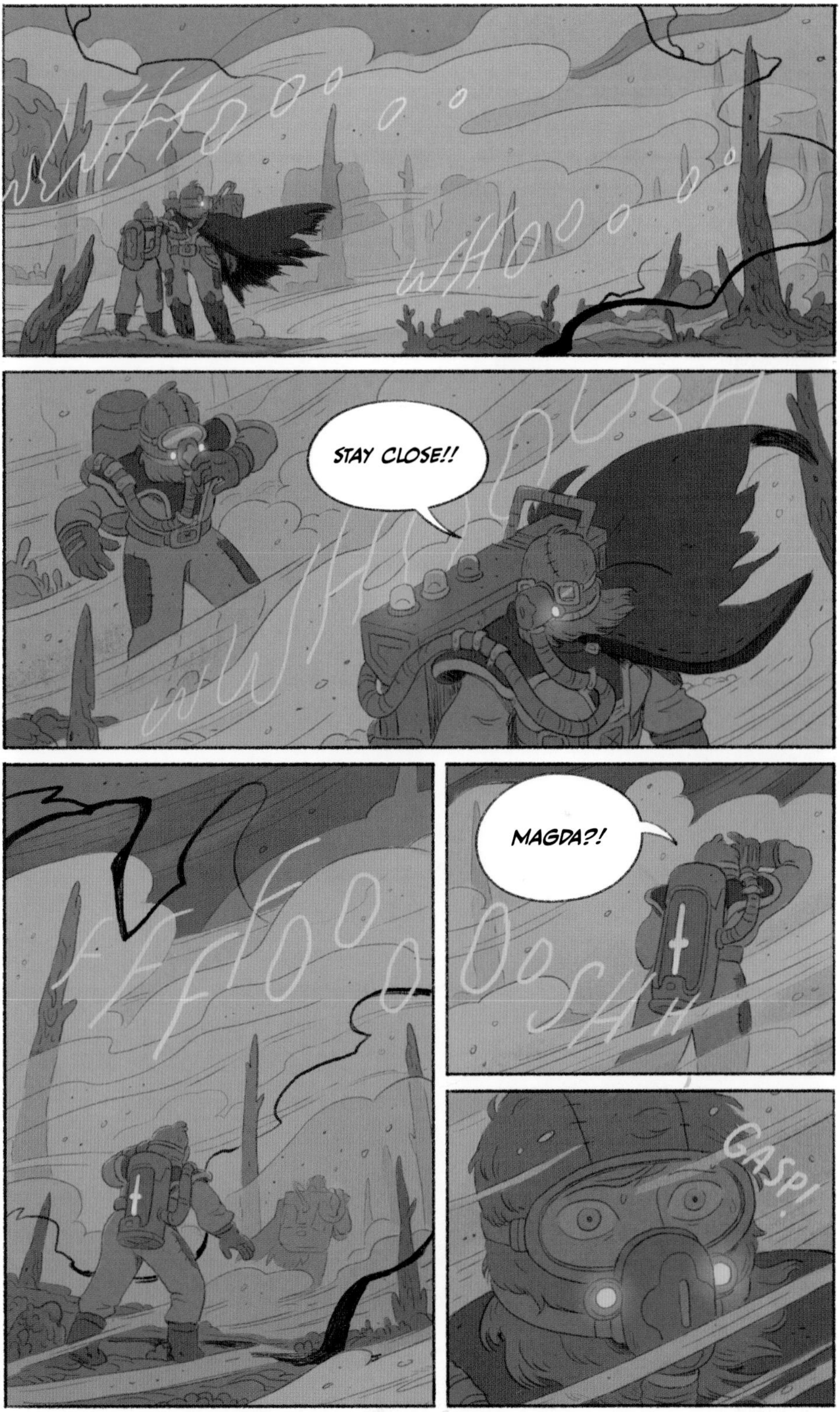
WHHOOooo
WHOOOooo
STAY CLOSE!!
WWHHOOOOSH
FFFOOOOOOSHH
MAGDA?!
GASP!

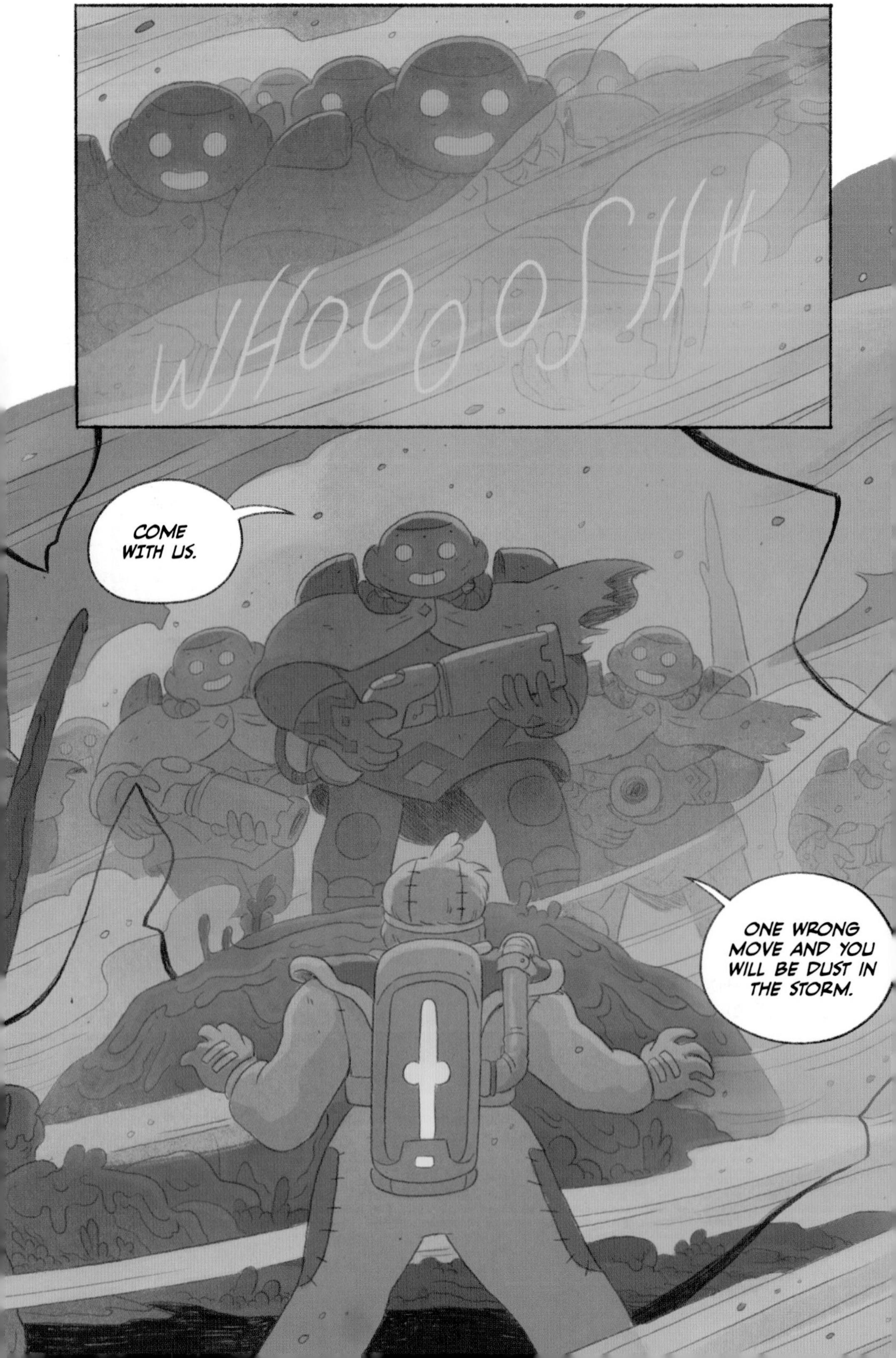
WHOOOOSHH
COME WITH US.
ONE WRONG MOVE AND YOU WILL BE DUST IN THE STORM.

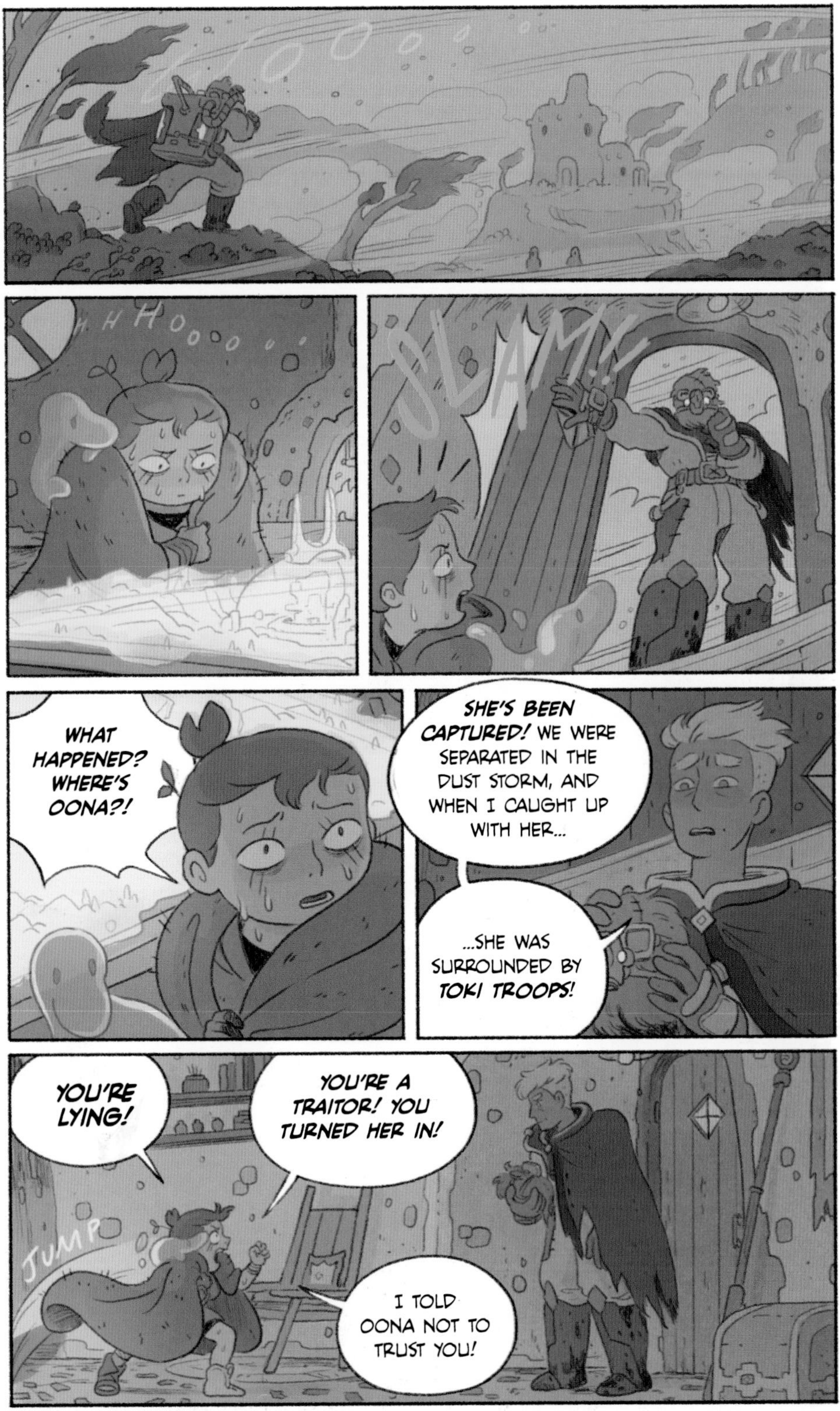
HHHOooo
SLAM!!
WHAT HAPPENED? WHERE'S OONA?!
SHE'S BEEN CAPTURED! WE WERE SEPARATED IN THE DUST STORM, AND WHEN I CAUGHT UP WITH HER...
...SHE WAS SURROUNDED BY TOKI TROOPS!
YOU'RE LYING!
YOU'RE A TRAITOR! YOU TURNED HER IN!
JUMP
I TOLD OONA NOT TO TRUST YOU!

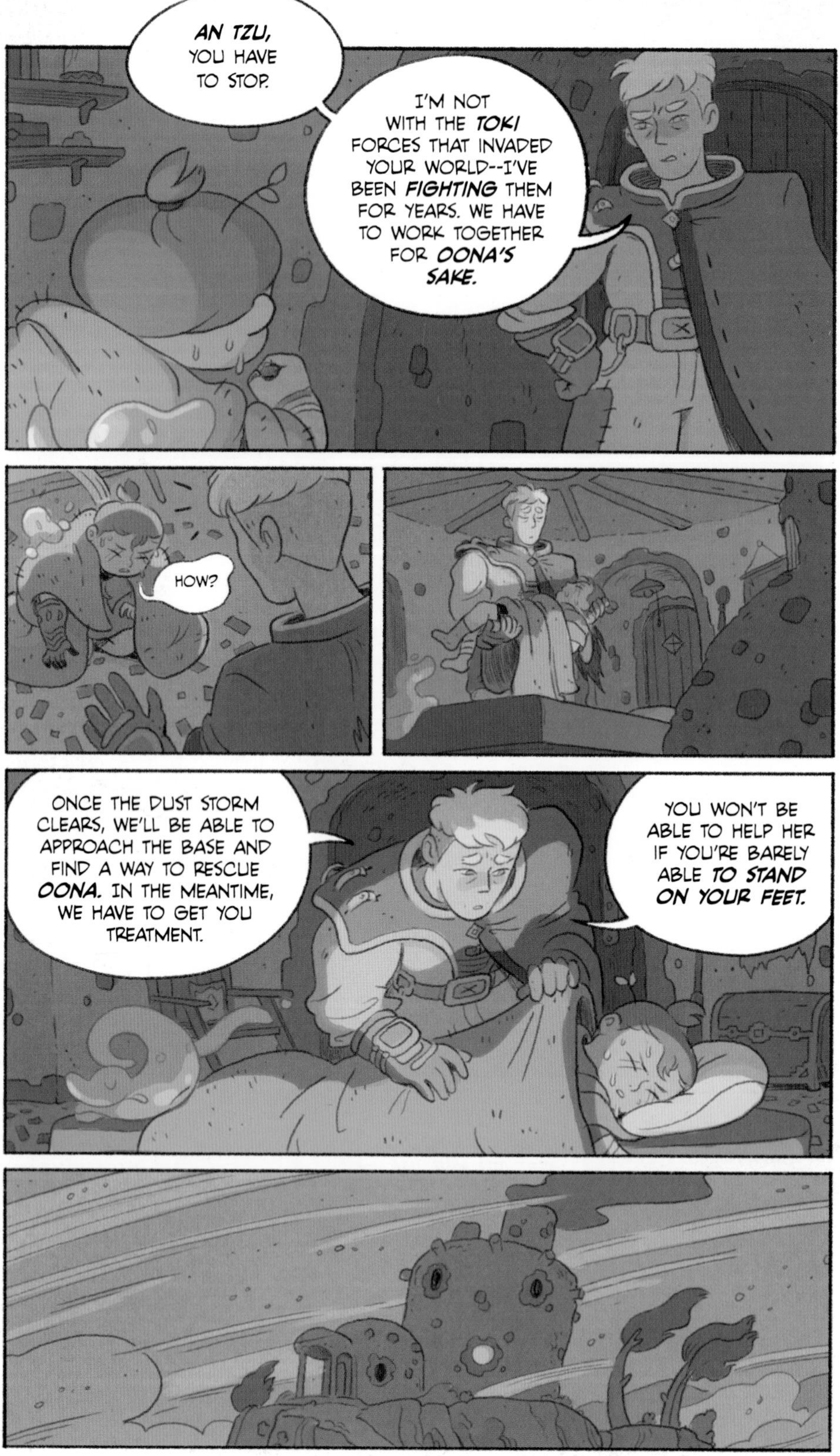
AN TZU, YOU HAVE TO STOP.
I'M NOT WITH THE TOKI FORCES THAT INVADED YOUR WORLD--I'VE BEEN FIGHTING THEM FOR YEARS. WE HAVE TO WORK TOGETHER FOR OONA'S SAKE.
HOW?
ONCE THE DUST STORM CLEARS, WE'LL BE ABLE TO APPROACH THE BASE AND FIND A WAY TO RESCUE OONA. IN THE MEANTIME, WE HAVE TO GET YOU TREATMENT.
YOU WON'T BE ABLE TO HELP HER IF YOU'RE BARELY ABLE TO STAND ON YOUR FEET.

Chapter 6
THE PRINCE'S OFFER

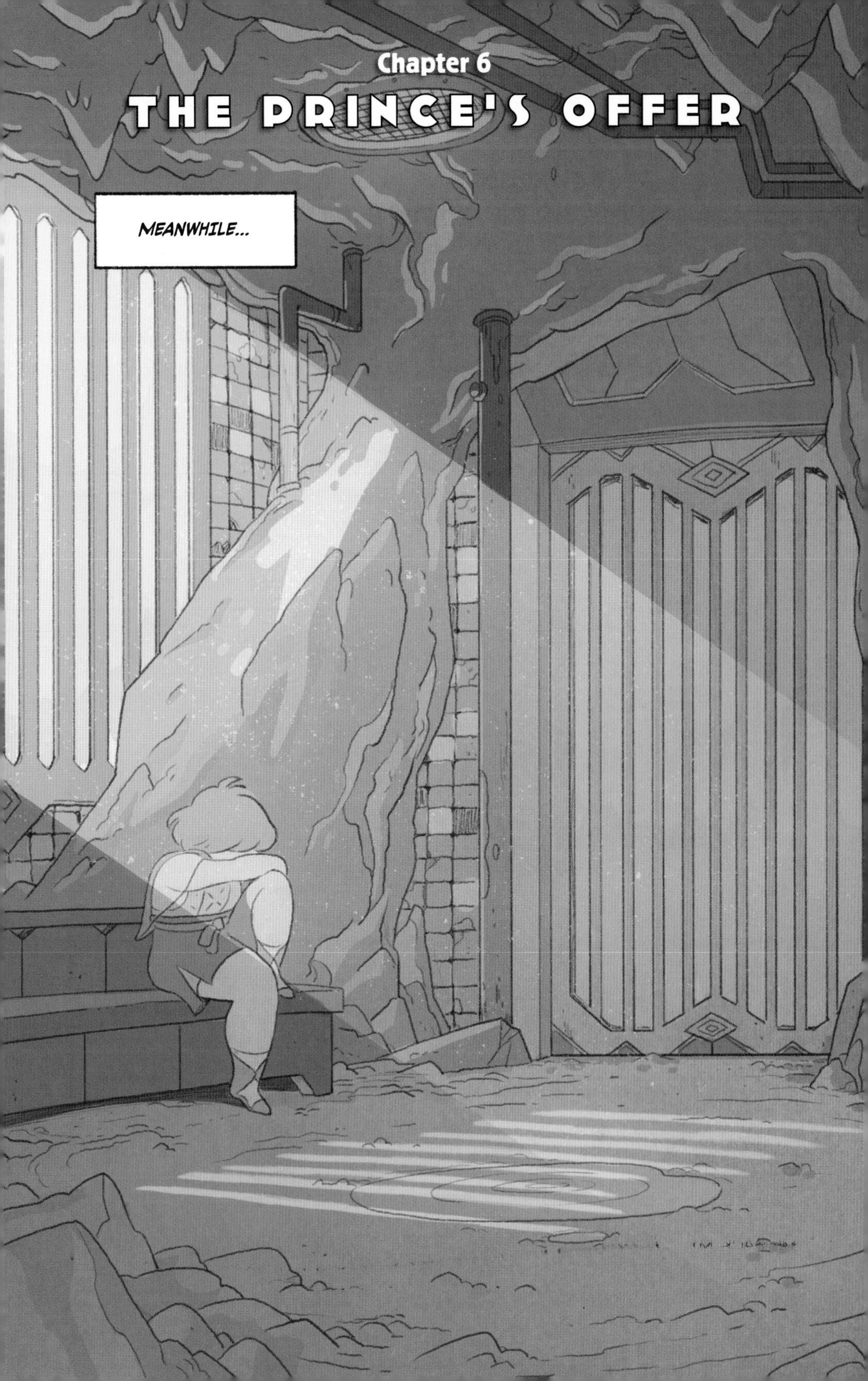
MEANWHILE...

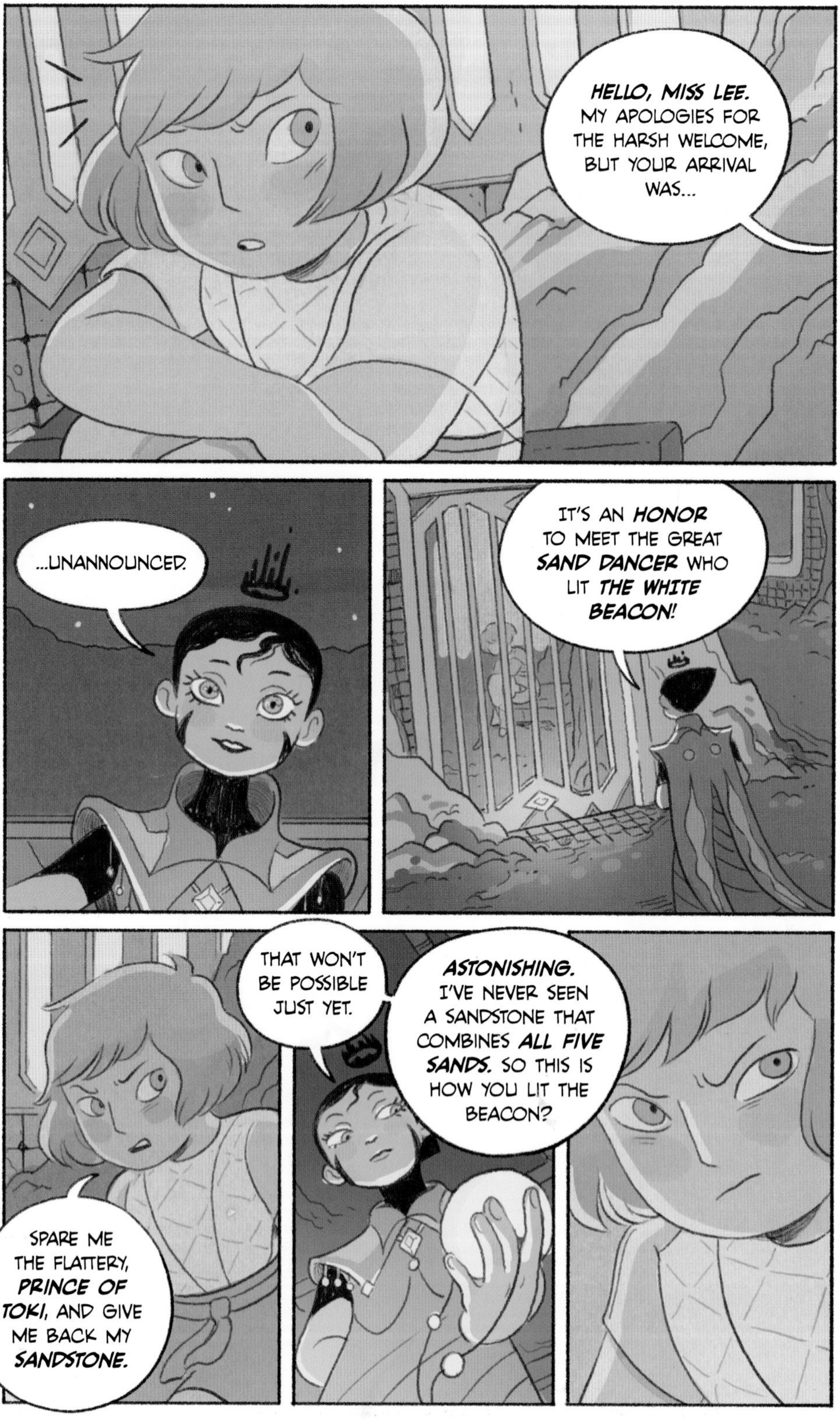
HELLO, MISS LEE. MY APOLOGIES FOR THE HARSH WELCOME, BUT YOUR ARRIVAL WAS...
...UNANNOUNCED.
IT'S AN HONOR TO MEET THE GREAT SAND DANCER WHO LIT THE WHITE BEACON!
SPARE ME THE FLATTERY, PRINCE OF TOKI, AND GIVE ME BACK MY SANDSTONE.
THAT WON'T BE POSSIBLE JUST YET.
ASTONISHING. I'VE NEVER SEEN A SANDSTONE THAT COMBINES ALL FIVE SANDS. SO THIS IS HOW YOU LIT THE BEACON?

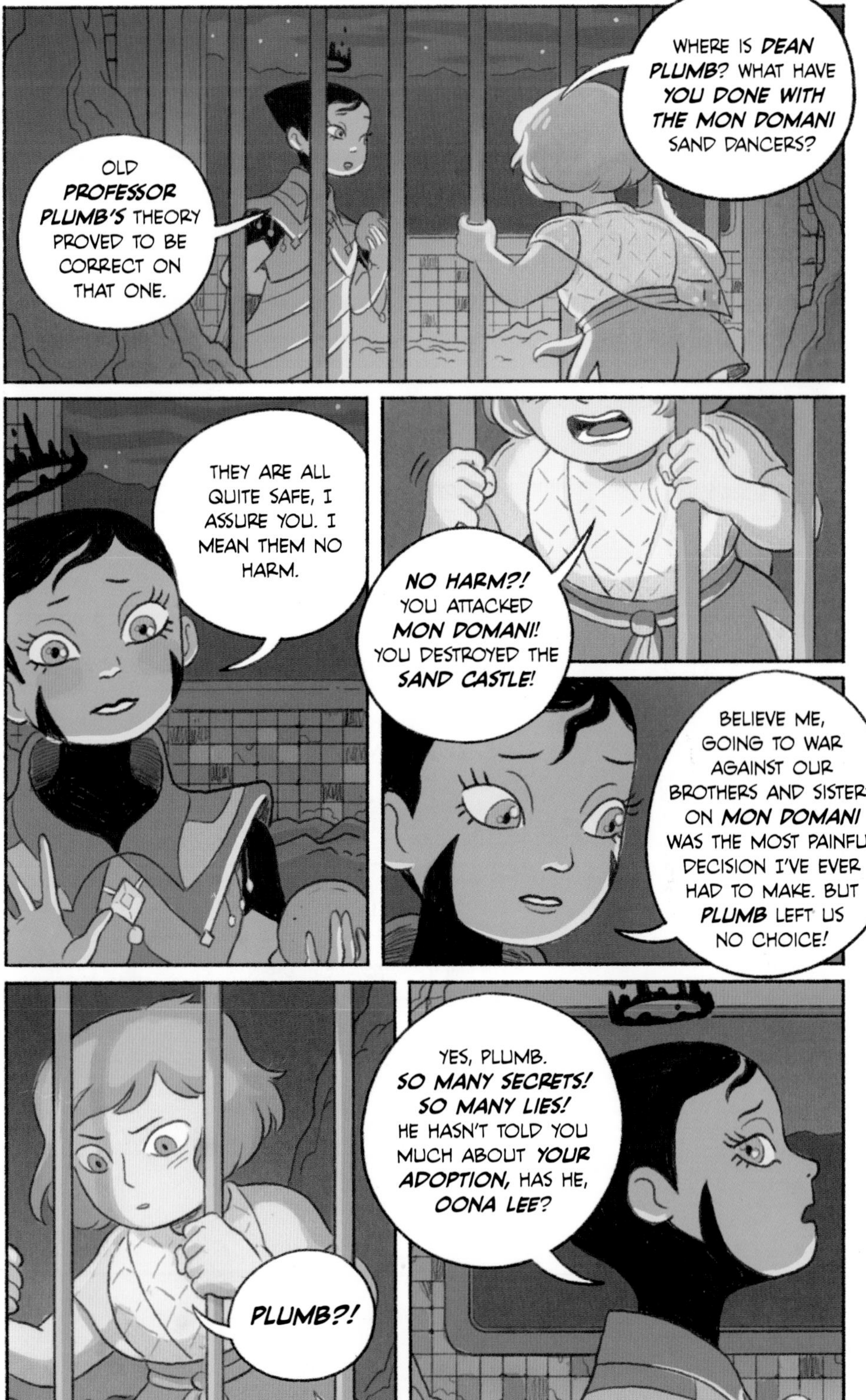
WHERE IS DEAN PLUMB? WHAT HAVE YOU DONE WITH THE MON DOMANI SAND DANCERS?
OLD PROFESSOR PLUMB'S THEORY PROVED TO BE CORRECT ON THAT ONE.
THEY ARE ALL QUITE SAFE, I ASSURE YOU. I MEAN THEM NO HARM.
NO HARM?! YOU ATTACKED MON DOMANI! YOU DESTROYED THE SAND CASTLE!
BELIEVE ME, GOING TO WAR AGAINST OUR BROTHERS AND SISTERS ON MON DOMANI WAS THE MOST PAINFUL DECISION I'VE EVER HAD TO MAKE. BUT PLUMB LEFT US NO CHOICE!
PLUMB?!
YES, PLUMB. SO MANY SECRETS! SO MANY LIES! HE HASN'T TOLD YOU MUCH ABOUT YOUR ADOPTION, HAS HE, OONA LEE?

WHAT? WHAT DOES MY *ADOPTION* HAVE TO DO WITH--?

DID *PLUMB* EVER MENTION *ATBAL-BALAK?*

NO...

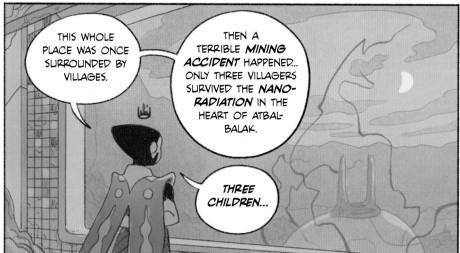

THIS WHOLE PLACE WAS ONCE SURROUNDED BY VILLAGES.

THEN A TERRIBLE *MINING ACCIDENT* HAPPENED... ONLY THREE VILLAGERS SURVIVED THE *NANO-RADIATION* IN THE HEART OF ATBAL-BALAK.

THREE CHILDREN...

THREE CHILDREN?

THREE LITTLE *TOKI* CHILDREN. THEY HAD STRANGE ABILITIES.

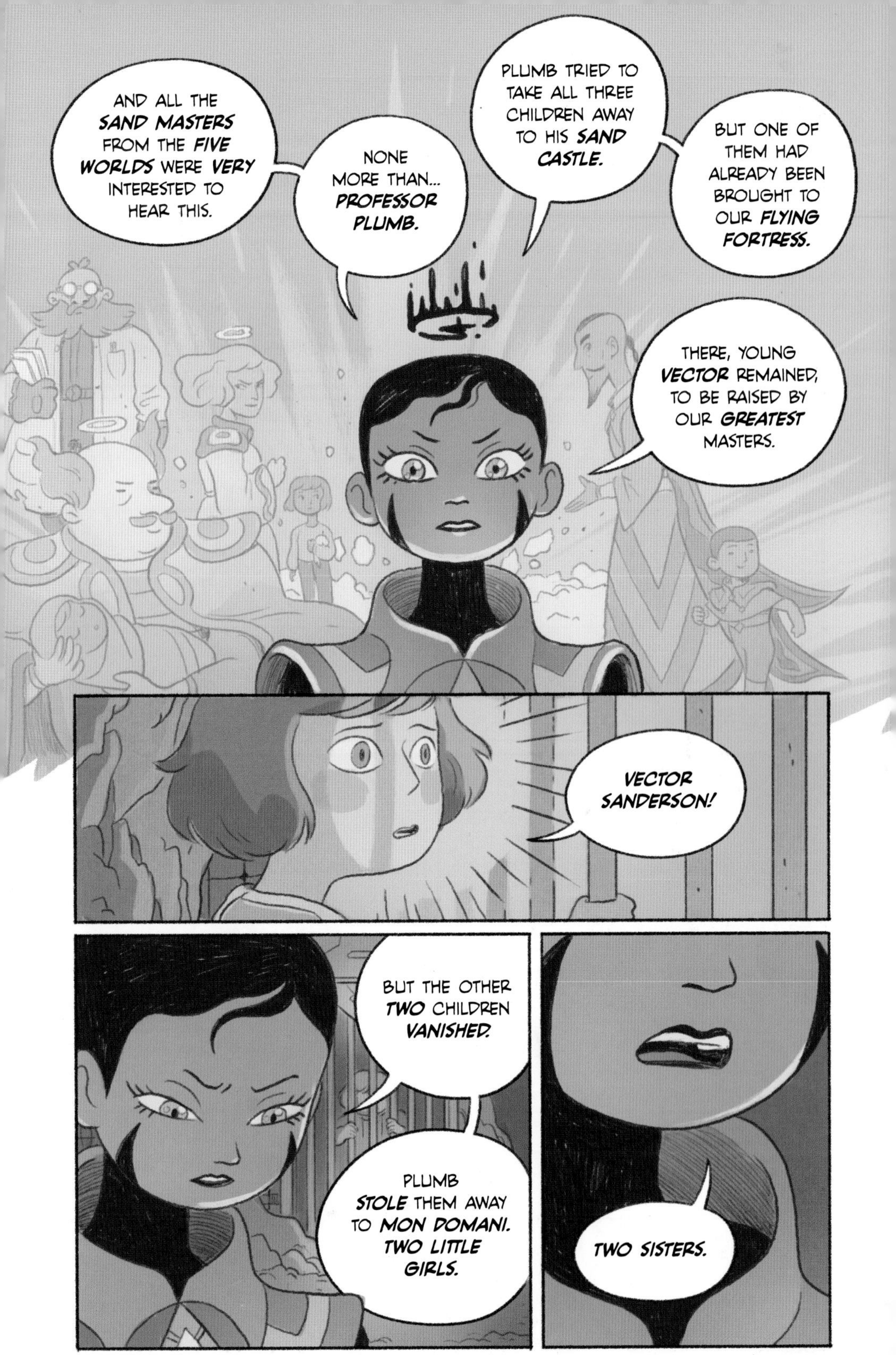
AND ALL THE SAND MASTERS FROM THE FIVE WORLDS WERE VERY INTERESTED TO HEAR THIS.
NONE MORE THAN... PROFESSOR PLUMB.
PLUMB TRIED TO TAKE ALL THREE CHILDREN AWAY TO HIS SAND CASTLE.
BUT ONE OF THEM HAD ALREADY BEEN BROUGHT TO OUR FLYING FORTRESS.
THERE, YOUNG VECTOR REMAINED, TO BE RAISED BY OUR GREATEST MASTERS.
VECTOR SANDERSON!
BUT THE OTHER TWO CHILDREN VANISHED.
PLUMB STOLE THEM AWAY TO MON DOMANI. TWO LITTLE GIRLS.
TWO SISTERS.

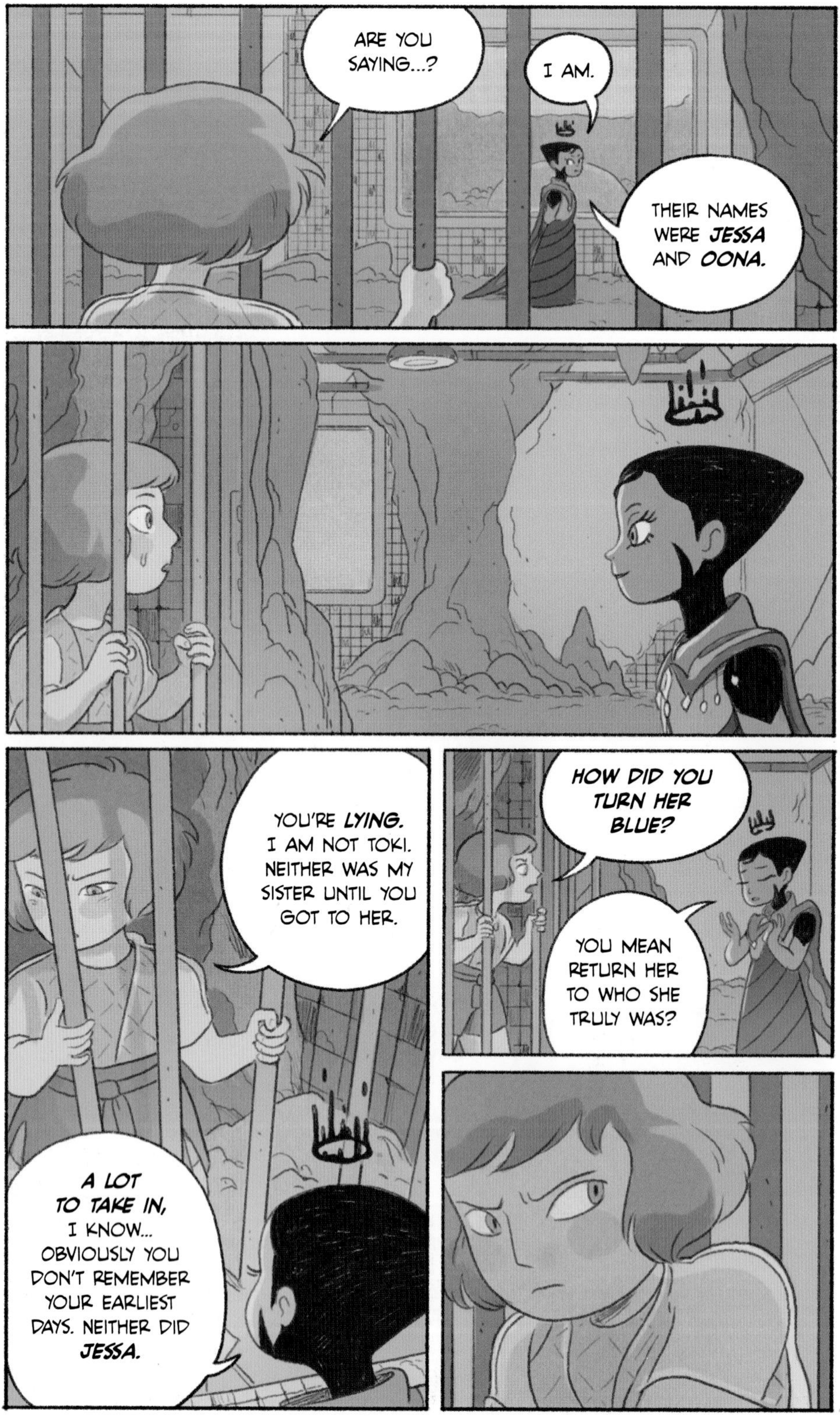
ARE YOU SAYING...?
I AM.
THEIR NAMES WERE JESSA AND OONA.
YOU'RE LYING. I AM NOT TOKI. NEITHER WAS MY SISTER UNTIL YOU GOT TO HER.
A LOT TO TAKE IN, I KNOW... OBVIOUSLY YOU DON'T REMEMBER YOUR EARLIEST DAYS. NEITHER DID JESSA.
HOW DID YOU TURN HER BLUE?
YOU MEAN RETURN HER TO WHO SHE TRULY WAS?

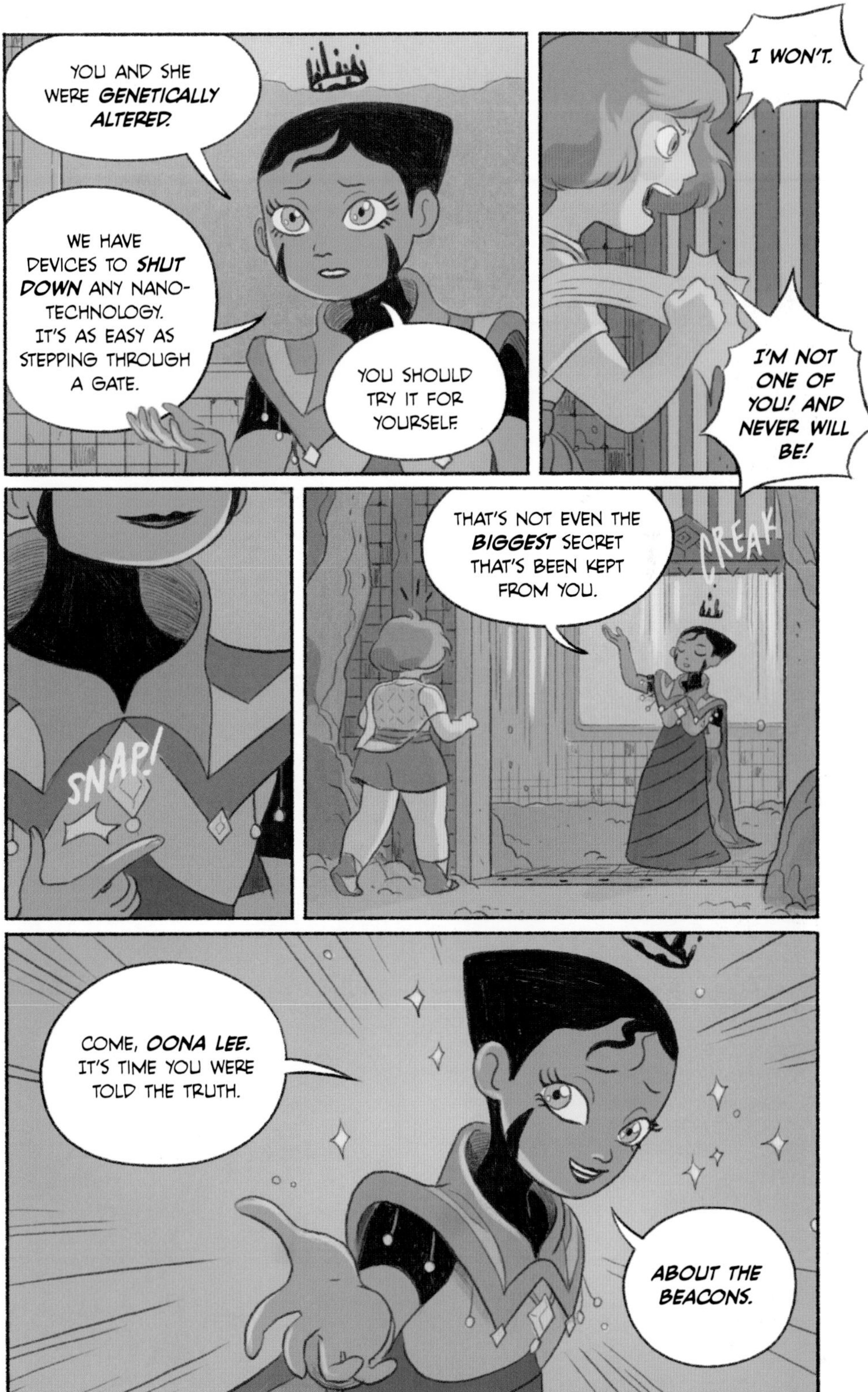
YOU AND SHE WERE GENETICALLY ALTERED.
WE HAVE DEVICES TO SHUT DOWN ANY NANO-TECHNOLOGY. IT'S AS EASY AS STEPPING THROUGH A GATE.
YOU SHOULD TRY IT FOR YOURSELF.
I WON'T.
I'M NOT ONE OF YOU! AND NEVER WILL BE!
SNAP!
THAT'S NOT EVEN THE BIGGEST SECRET THAT'S BEEN KEPT FROM YOU.
CREAK
COME, OONA LEE. IT'S TIME YOU WERE TOLD THE TRUTH.
ABOUT THE BEACONS.

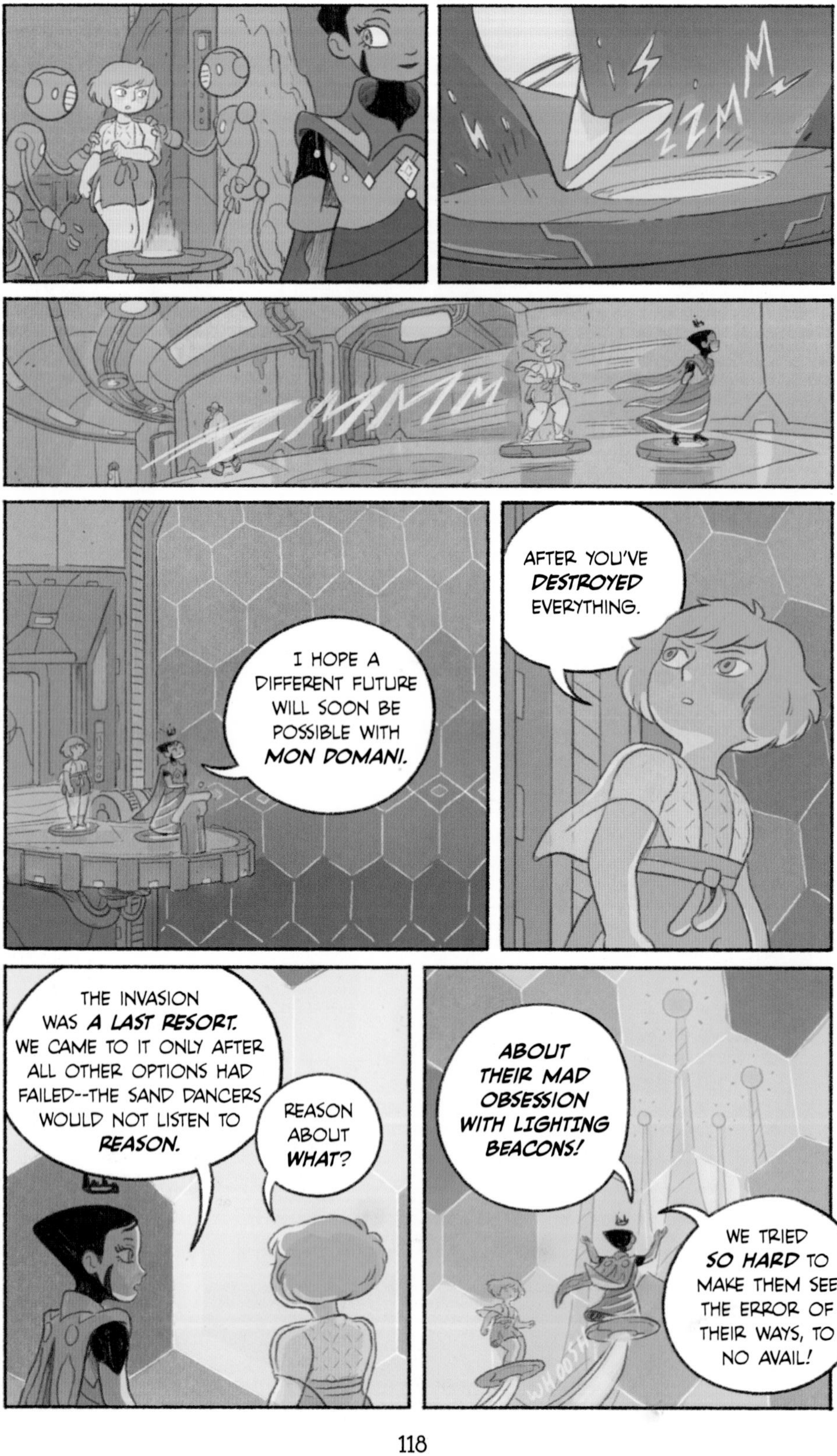
ZZMM
ZMMM
I HOPE A DIFFERENT FUTURE WILL SOON BE POSSIBLE WITH MON DOMANI.
AFTER YOU'VE DESTROYED EVERYTHING.
THE INVASION WAS A LAST RESORT. WE CAME TO IT ONLY AFTER ALL OTHER OPTIONS HAD FAILED--THE SAND DANCERS WOULD NOT LISTEN TO REASON.
REASON ABOUT WHAT?
ABOUT THEIR MAD OBSESSION WITH LIGHTING BEACONS!
WE TRIED SO HARD TO MAKE THEM SEE THE ERROR OF THEIR WAYS, TO NO AVAIL!

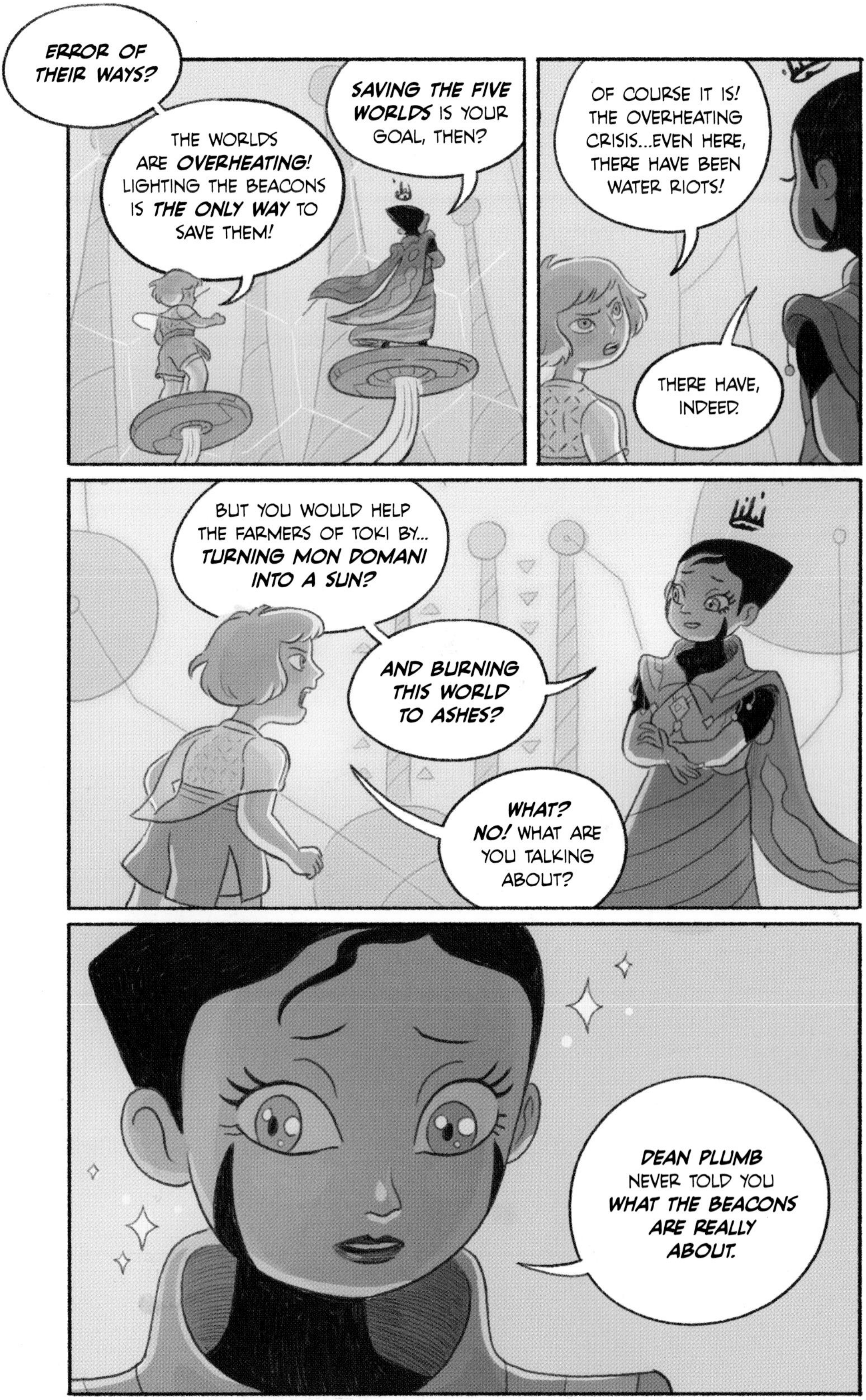
ERROR OF THEIR WAYS?
THE WORLDS ARE OVERHEATING! LIGHTING THE BEACONS IS THE ONLY WAY TO SAVE THEM!
SAVING THE FIVE WORLDS IS YOUR GOAL, THEN?
OF COURSE IT IS! THE OVERHEATING CRISIS...EVEN HERE, THERE HAVE BEEN WATER RIOTS!
THERE HAVE, INDEED.
BUT YOU WOULD HELP THE FARMERS OF TOKI BY... TURNING MON DOMANI INTO A SUN?
AND BURNING THIS WORLD TO ASHES?
WHAT? NO! WHAT ARE YOU TALKING ABOUT?
DEAN PLUMB NEVER TOLD YOU WHAT THE BEACONS ARE REALLY ABOUT.

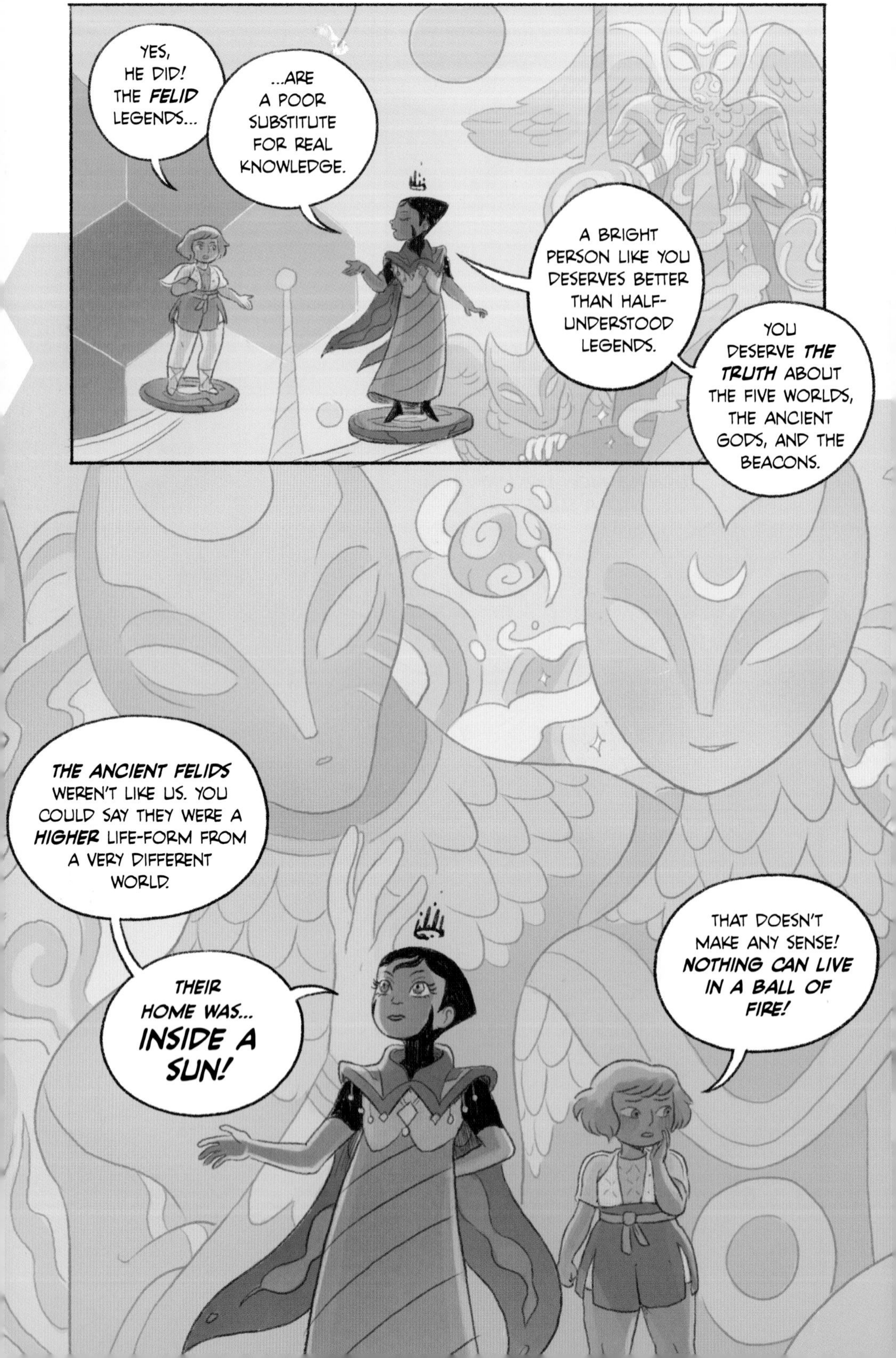
YES, HE DID! THE FELID LEGENDS...
...ARE A POOR SUBSTITUTE FOR REAL KNOWLEDGE.
A BRIGHT PERSON LIKE YOU DESERVES BETTER THAN HALF-UNDERSTOOD LEGENDS.
YOU DESERVE THE TRUTH ABOUT THE FIVE WORLDS, THE ANCIENT GODS, AND THE BEACONS.
THE ANCIENT FELIDS WEREN'T LIKE US. YOU COULD SAY THEY WERE A HIGHER LIFE-FORM FROM A VERY DIFFERENT WORLD.
THEIR HOME WAS... INSIDE A SUN!
THAT DOESN'T MAKE ANY SENSE! NOTHING CAN LIVE IN A BALL OF FIRE!

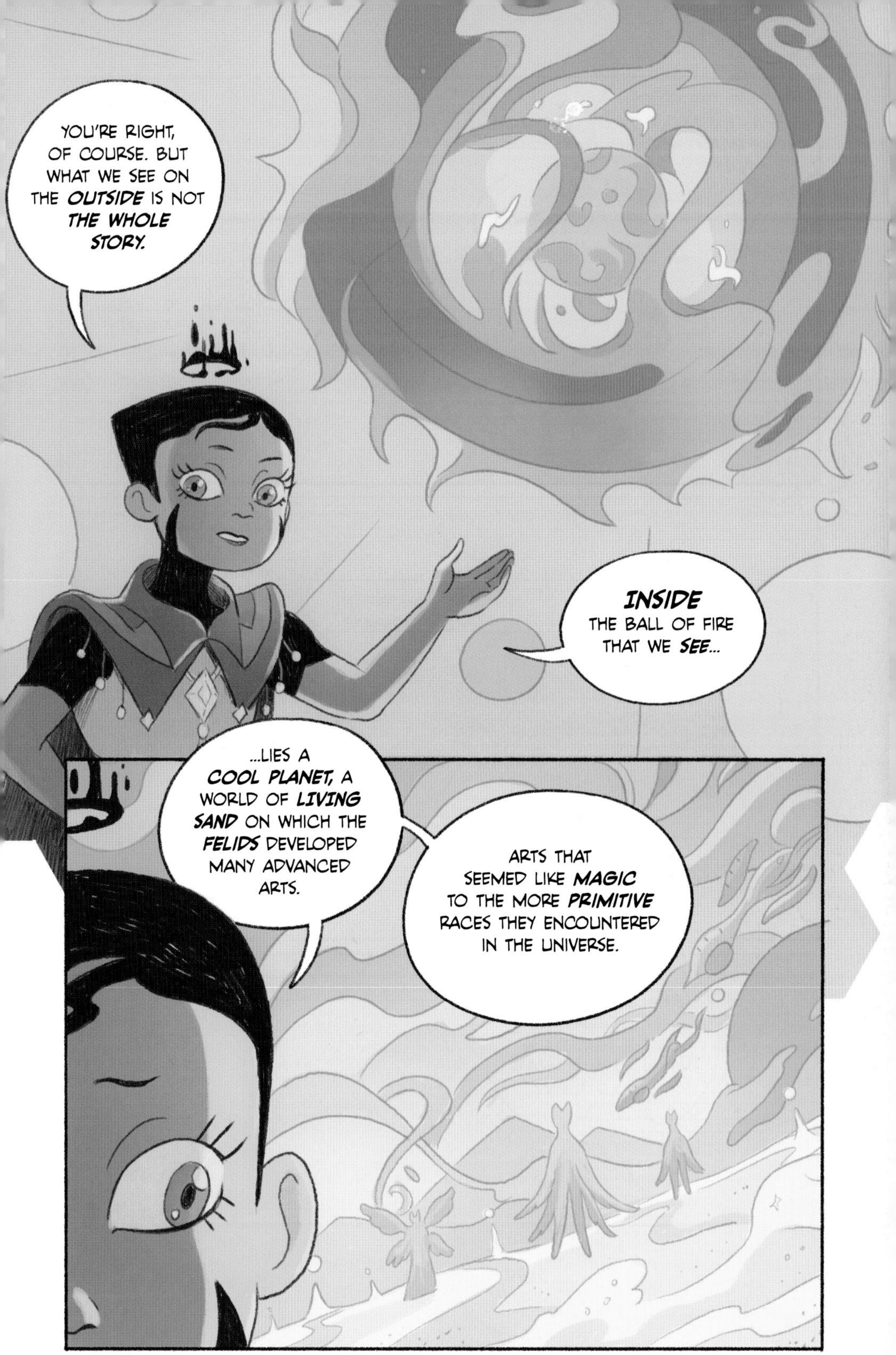
YOU'RE RIGHT, OF COURSE. BUT WHAT WE SEE ON THE OUTSIDE IS NOT THE WHOLE STORY.
INSIDE THE BALL OF FIRE THAT WE SEE...
...LIES A COOL PLANET, A WORLD OF LIVING SAND ON WHICH THE FELIDS DEVELOPED MANY ADVANCED ARTS.
ARTS THAT SEEMED LIKE MAGIC TO THE MORE PRIMITIVE RACES THEY ENCOUNTERED IN THE UNIVERSE.

YOU SEE, THE FELIDS KNEW THAT MOONS CAN EVOLVE INTO PLANETS...
AND PLANETS CAN TURN INTO SUNS.
BUT RATHER THAN WAIT MILLIONS OF YEARS FOR THAT TO HAPPEN, THEY HAD TOOLS TO SPEED THINGS UP.
THEY FIRST LANDED ON MON DOMANI.
AND TRANSFORMED HER FOUR MOONS-- INTO QUASI-PLANETS.
THE GIANT BEACONS WERE SET UP IN PREPARATION FOR THE NEXT STAGE-- WHEN MON DOMANI WOULD TURN INTO...
...SUN DOMANI!

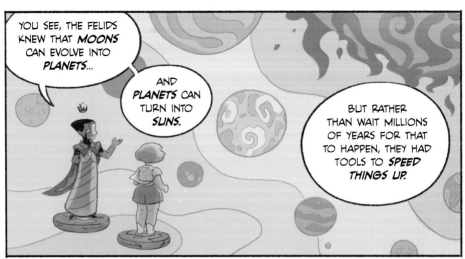

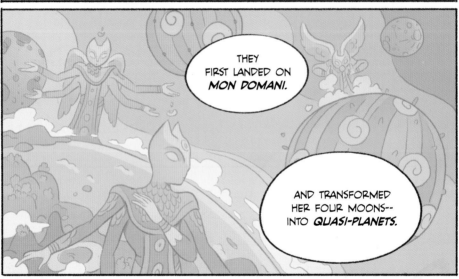

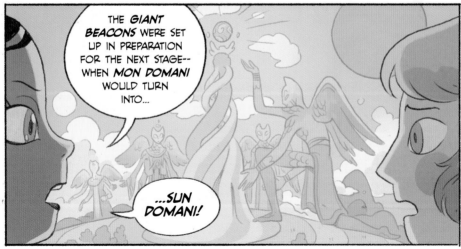

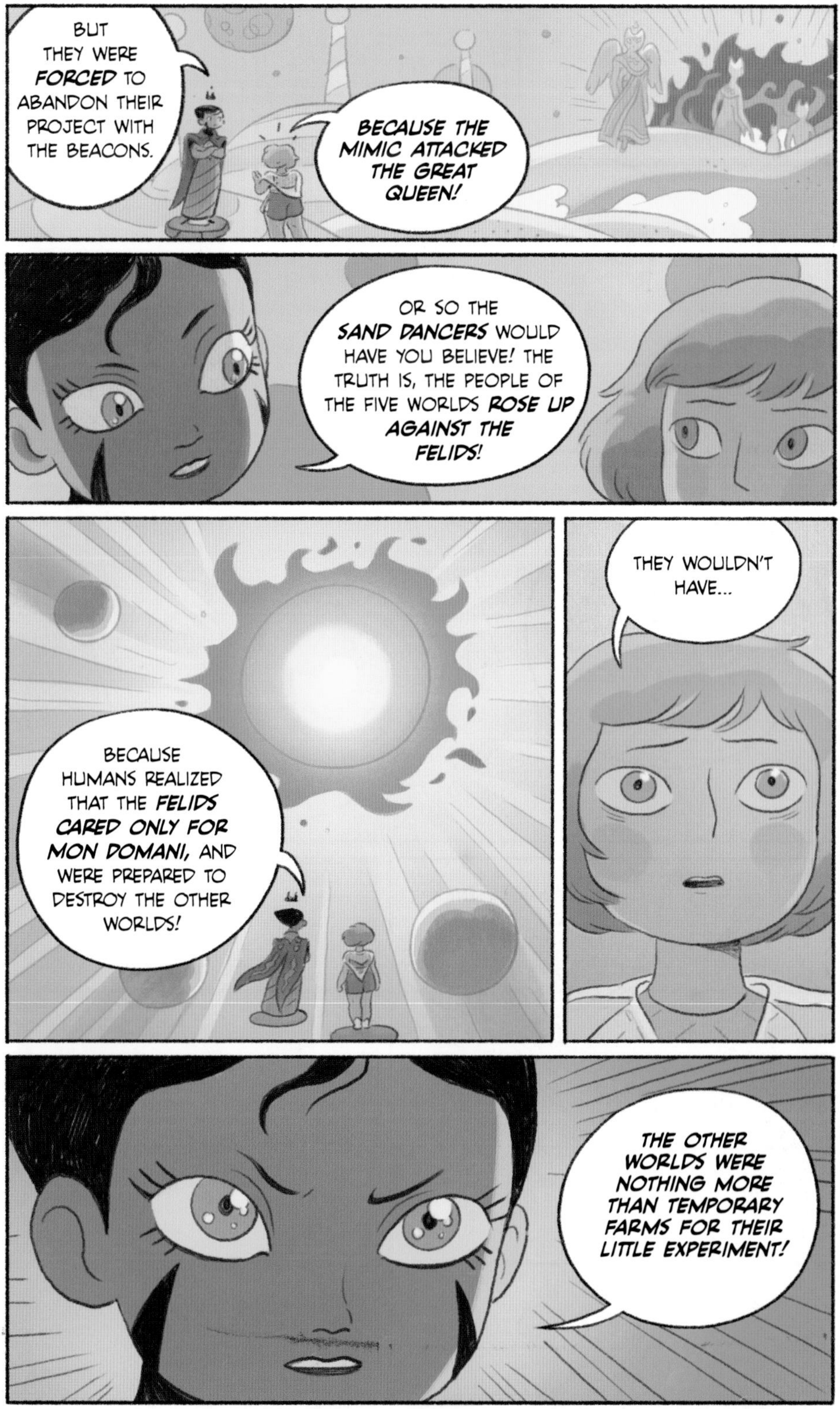
BUT THEY WERE FORCED TO ABANDON THEIR PROJECT WITH THE BEACONS.
BECAUSE THE MIMIC ATTACKED THE GREAT QUEEN!
OR SO THE SAND DANCERS WOULD HAVE YOU BELIEVE! THE TRUTH IS, THE PEOPLE OF THE FIVE WORLDS ROSE UP AGAINST THE FELIDS!
BECAUSE HUMANS REALIZED THAT THE FELIDS CARED ONLY FOR MON DOMANI, AND WERE PREPARED TO DESTROY THE OTHER WORLDS!
THEY WOULDN'T HAVE...
THE OTHER WORLDS WERE NOTHING MORE THAN TEMPORARY FARMS FOR THEIR LITTLE EXPERIMENT!

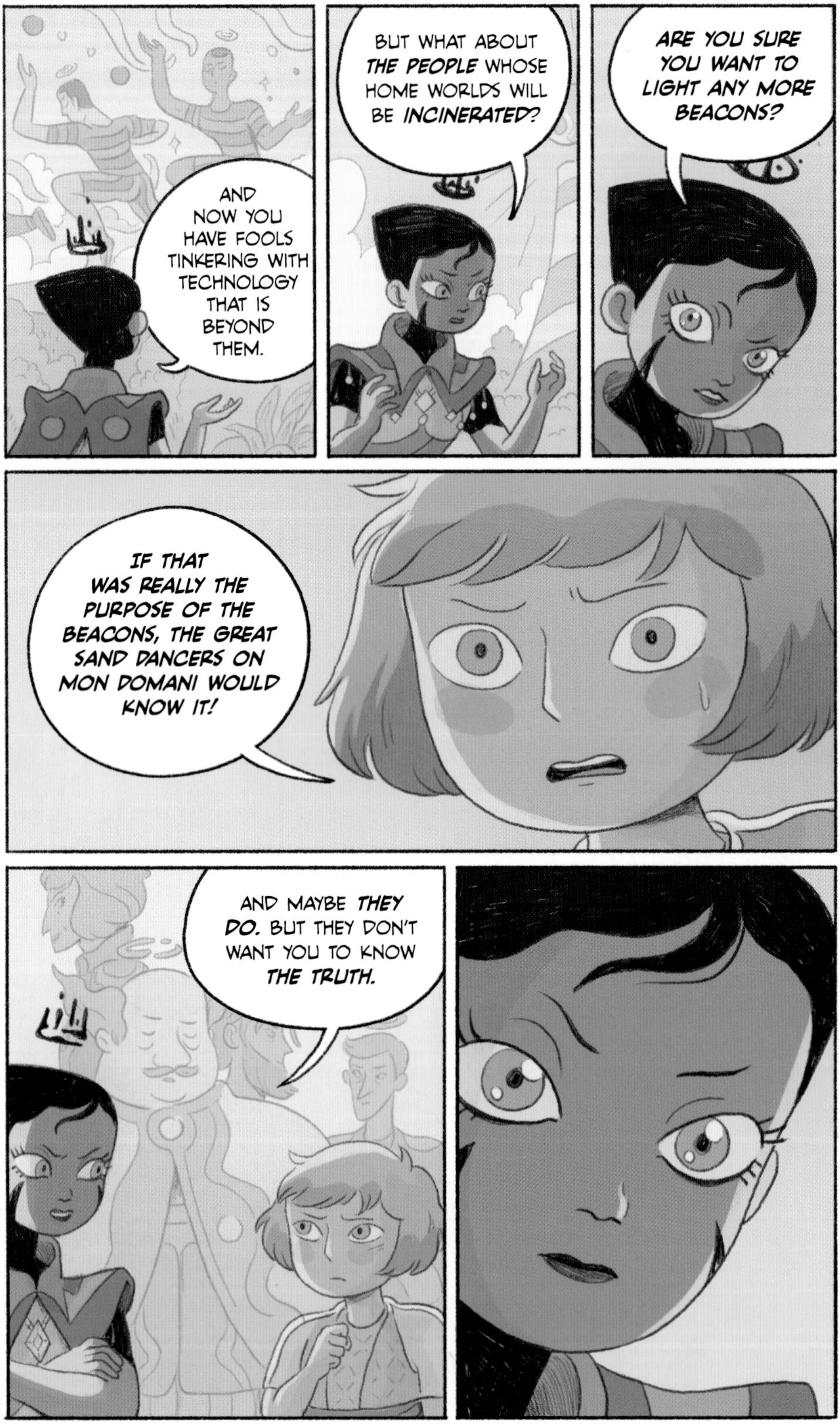
AND NOW YOU HAVE FOOLS TINKERING WITH TECHNOLOGY THAT IS BEYOND THEM.
BUT WHAT ABOUT THE PEOPLE WHOSE HOME WORLDS WILL BE INCINERATED?
ARE YOU SURE YOU WANT TO LIGHT ANY MORE BEACONS?
IF THAT WAS REALLY THE PURPOSE OF THE BEACONS, THE GREAT SAND DANCERS ON MON DOMANI WOULD KNOW IT!
AND MAYBE THEY DO. BUT THEY DON'T WANT YOU TO KNOW THE TRUTH.

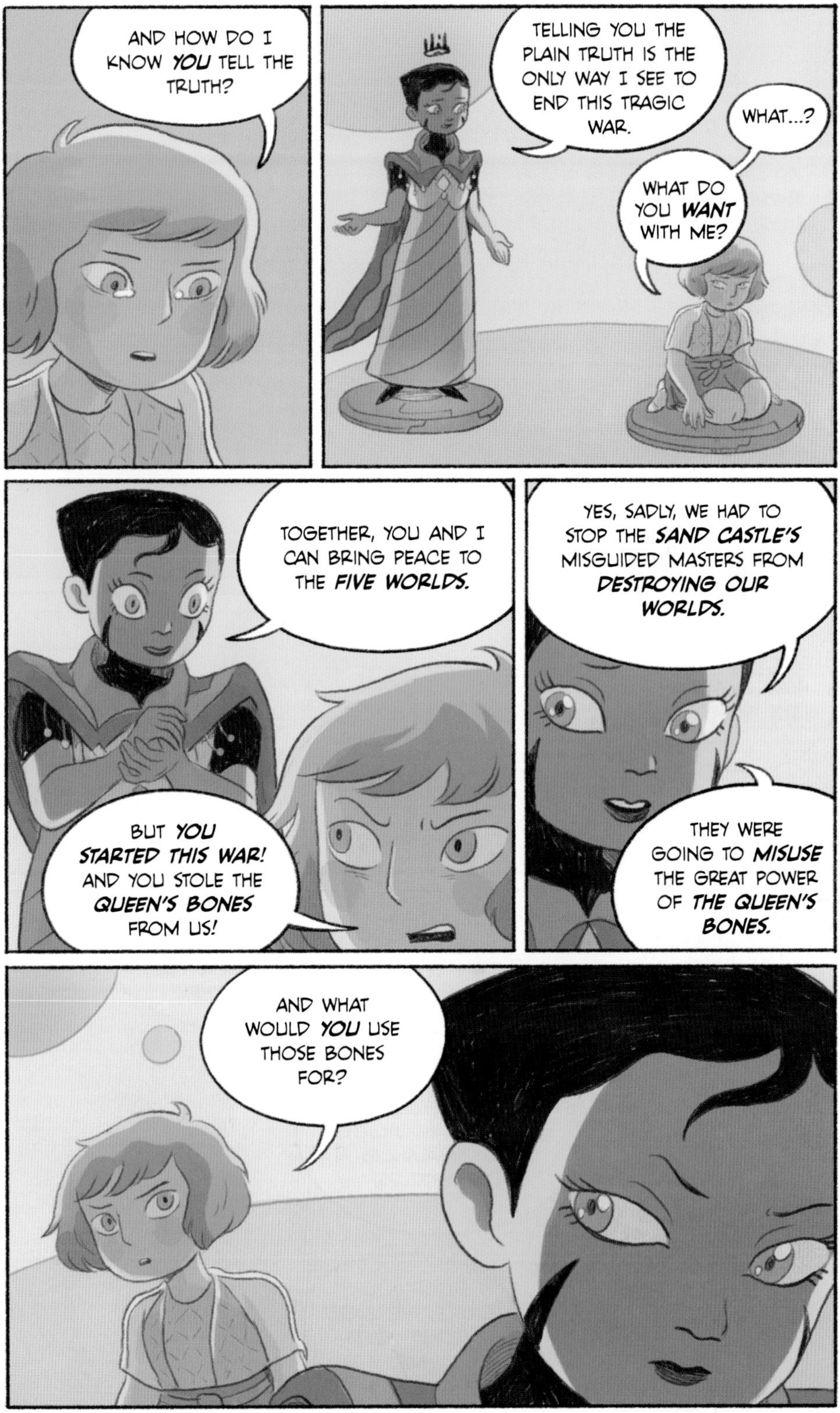
AND HOW DO I KNOW YOU TELL THE TRUTH?
TELLING YOU THE PLAIN TRUTH IS THE ONLY WAY I SEE TO END THIS TRAGIC WAR.
WHAT...?
WHAT DO YOU WANT WITH ME?
TOGETHER, YOU AND I CAN BRING PEACE TO THE FIVE WORLDS.
BUT YOU STARTED THIS WAR! AND YOU STOLE THE QUEEN'S BONES FROM US!
YES, SADLY, WE HAD TO STOP THE SAND CASTLE'S MISGUIDED MASTERS FROM DESTROYING OUR WORLDS.
THEY WERE GOING TO MISUSE THE GREAT POWER OF THE QUEEN'S BONES.
AND WHAT WOULD YOU USE THOSE BONES FOR?

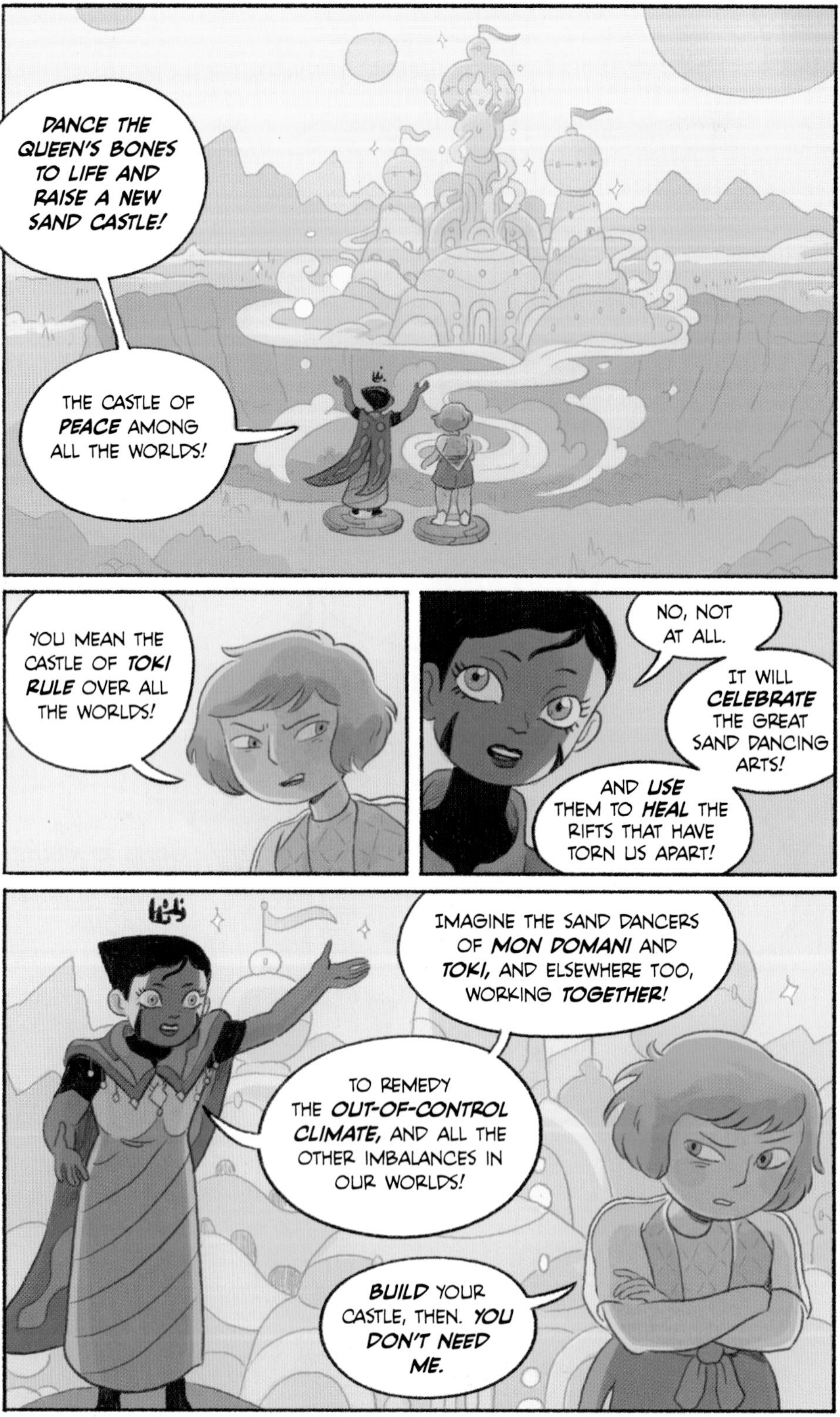
DANCE THE QUEEN'S BONES TO LIFE AND RAISE A NEW SAND CASTLE!
THE CASTLE OF PEACE AMONG ALL THE WORLDS!
YOU MEAN THE CASTLE OF TOKI RULE OVER ALL THE WORLDS!
NO, NOT AT ALL.
IT WILL CELEBRATE THE GREAT SAND DANCING ARTS!
AND USE THEM TO HEAL THE RIFTS THAT HAVE TORN US APART!
IMAGINE THE SAND DANCERS OF MON DOMANI AND TOKI, AND ELSEWHERE TOO, WORKING TOGETHER!
TO REMEDY THE OUT-OF-CONTROL CLIMATE, AND ALL THE OTHER IMBALANCES IN OUR WORLDS!
BUILD YOUR CASTLE, THEN. YOU DON'T NEED ME.

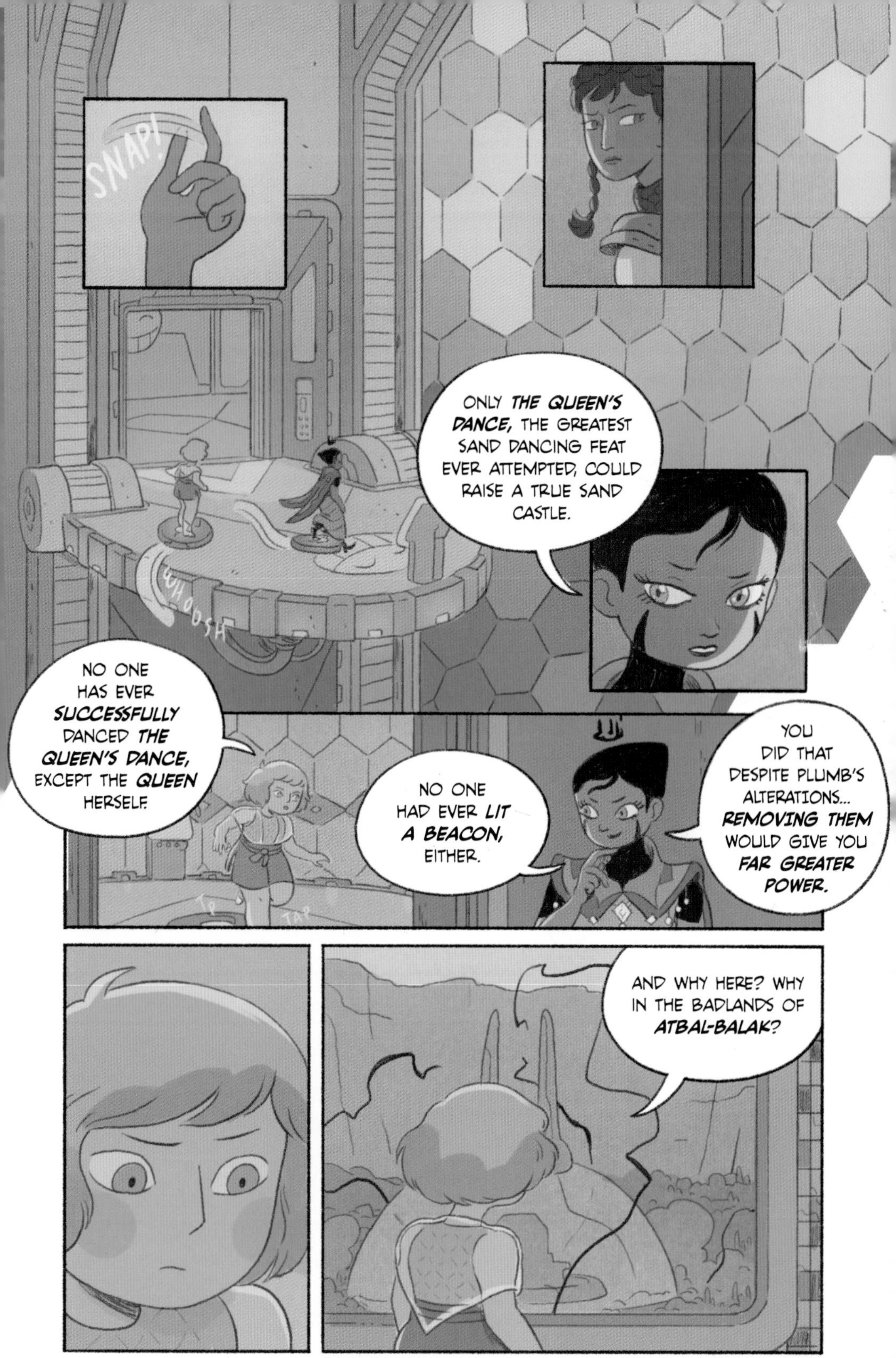
SNAP!
ONLY THE QUEEN'S DANCE, THE GREATEST SAND DANCING FEAT EVER ATTEMPTED, COULD RAISE A TRUE SAND CASTLE.
WHOOSH
NO ONE HAS EVER SUCCESSFULLY DANCED THE QUEEN'S DANCE, EXCEPT THE QUEEN HERSELF.
NO ONE HAD EVER LIT A BEACON, EITHER.
YOU DID THAT DESPITE PLUMB'S ALTERATIONS... REMOVING THEM WOULD GIVE YOU FAR GREATER POWER.
TAP
AND WHY HERE? WHY IN THE BADLANDS OF ATBAL-BALAK?

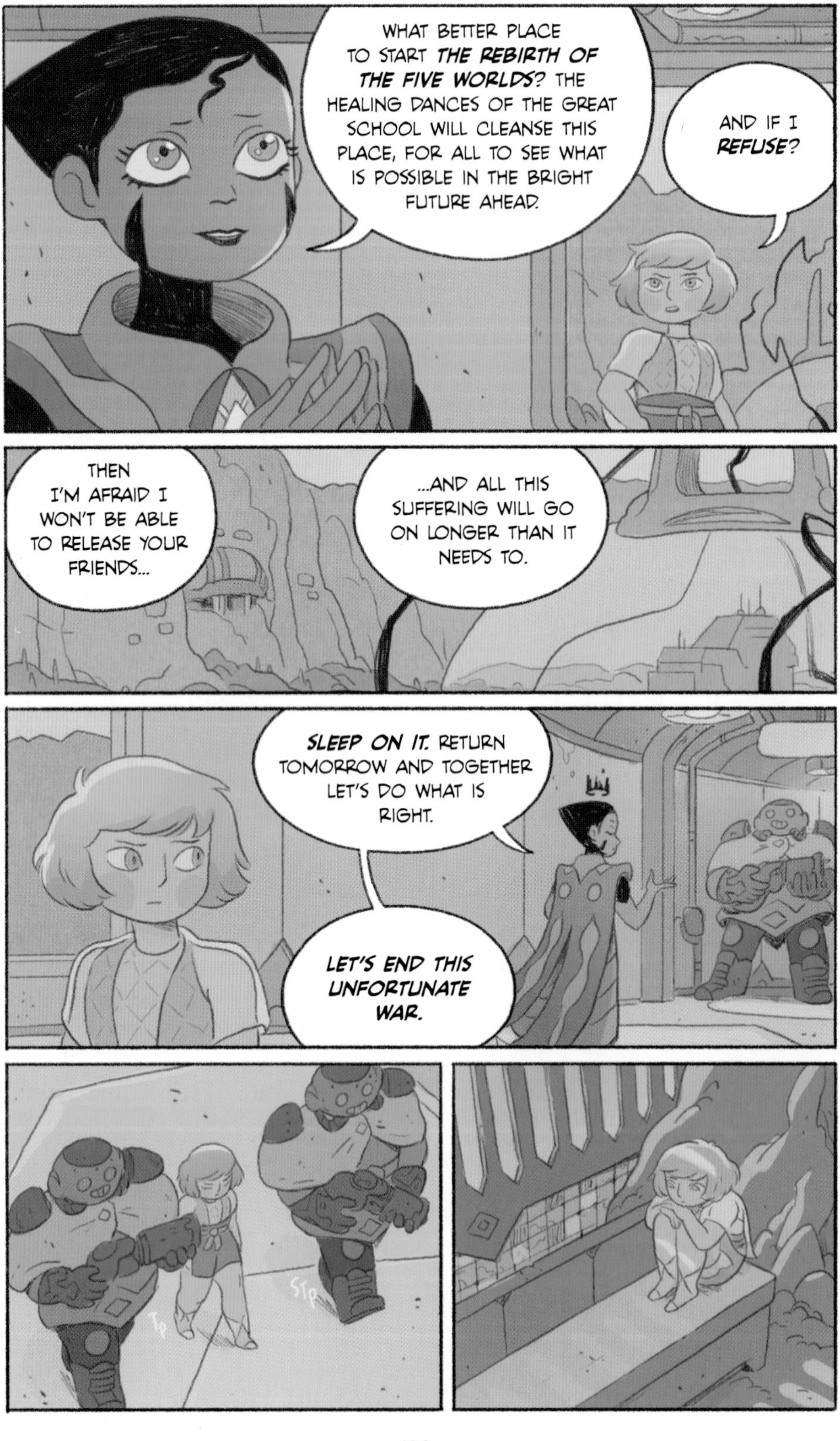
WHAT BETTER PLACE TO START *THE REBIRTH OF THE FIVE WORLDS*? THE HEALING DANCES OF THE GREAT SCHOOL WILL CLEANSE THIS PLACE, FOR ALL TO SEE WHAT IS POSSIBLE IN THE BRIGHT FUTURE AHEAD.
AND IF I *REFUSE*?
THEN I'M AFRAID I WON'T BE ABLE TO RELEASE YOUR FRIENDS...
...AND ALL THIS SUFFERING WILL GO ON LONGER THAN IT NEEDS TO.
SLEEP ON IT. RETURN TOMORROW AND TOGETHER LET'S DO WHAT IS RIGHT.
LET'S END THIS UNFORTUNATE WAR.

WHAT SAY YOU, *ZAYD?* WILL SHE JOIN OUR CAUSE?

YES, YOUR HIGHNESS. MY *SISTER* WILL COME AROUND. I WILL SEE HER TONIGHT. *AND MAKE SURE OF IT.*

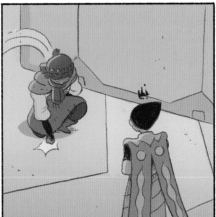

Chapter 7

THE SECRET OF THE BLUE BEACON

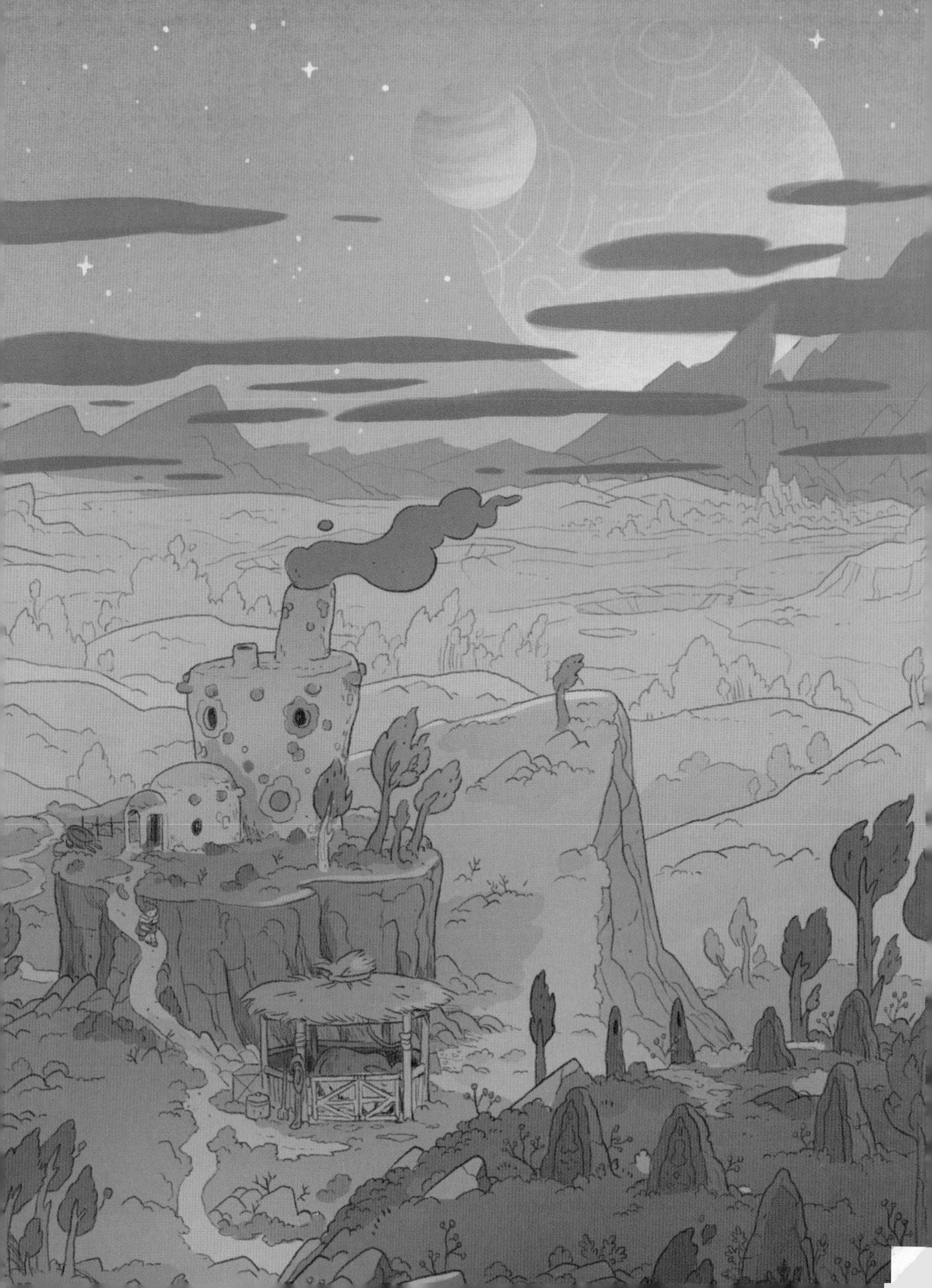

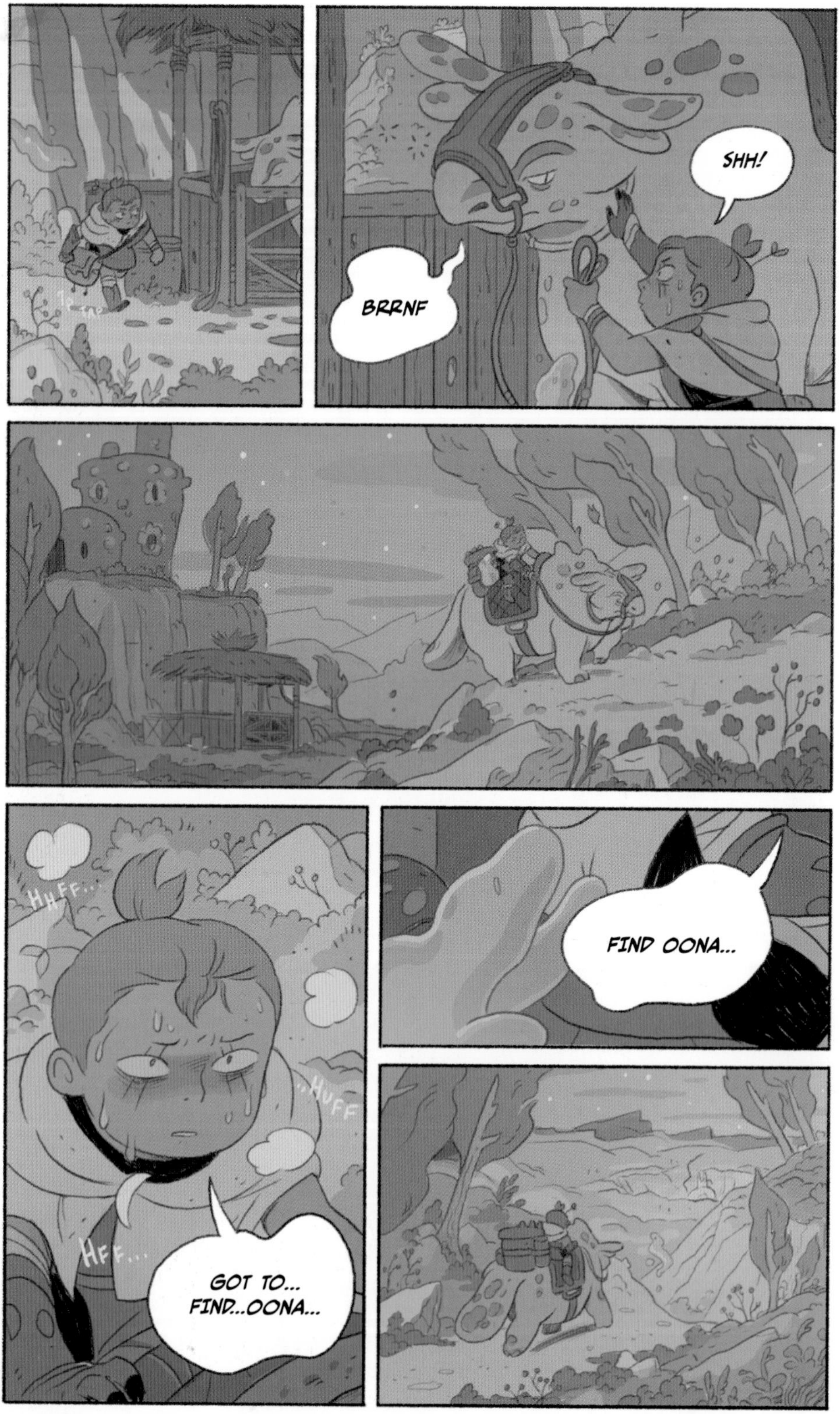
SHH!
BRRNF
HUFF...
...HUFF
HFF...
GOT TO... FIND...OONA...
FIND OONA...

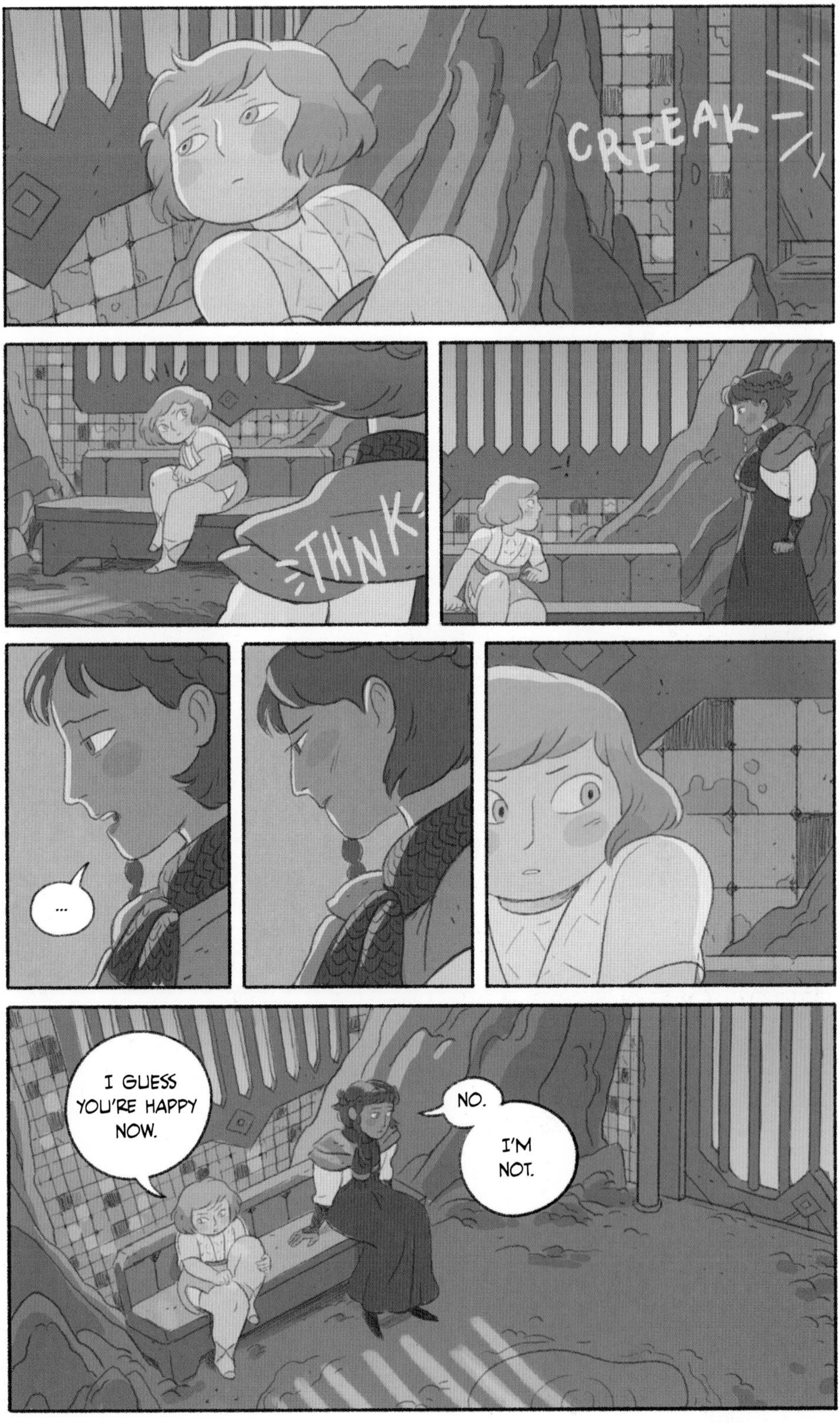
CREEAK
THNK
...
I GUESS YOU'RE HAPPY NOW.
NO.
I'M NOT.

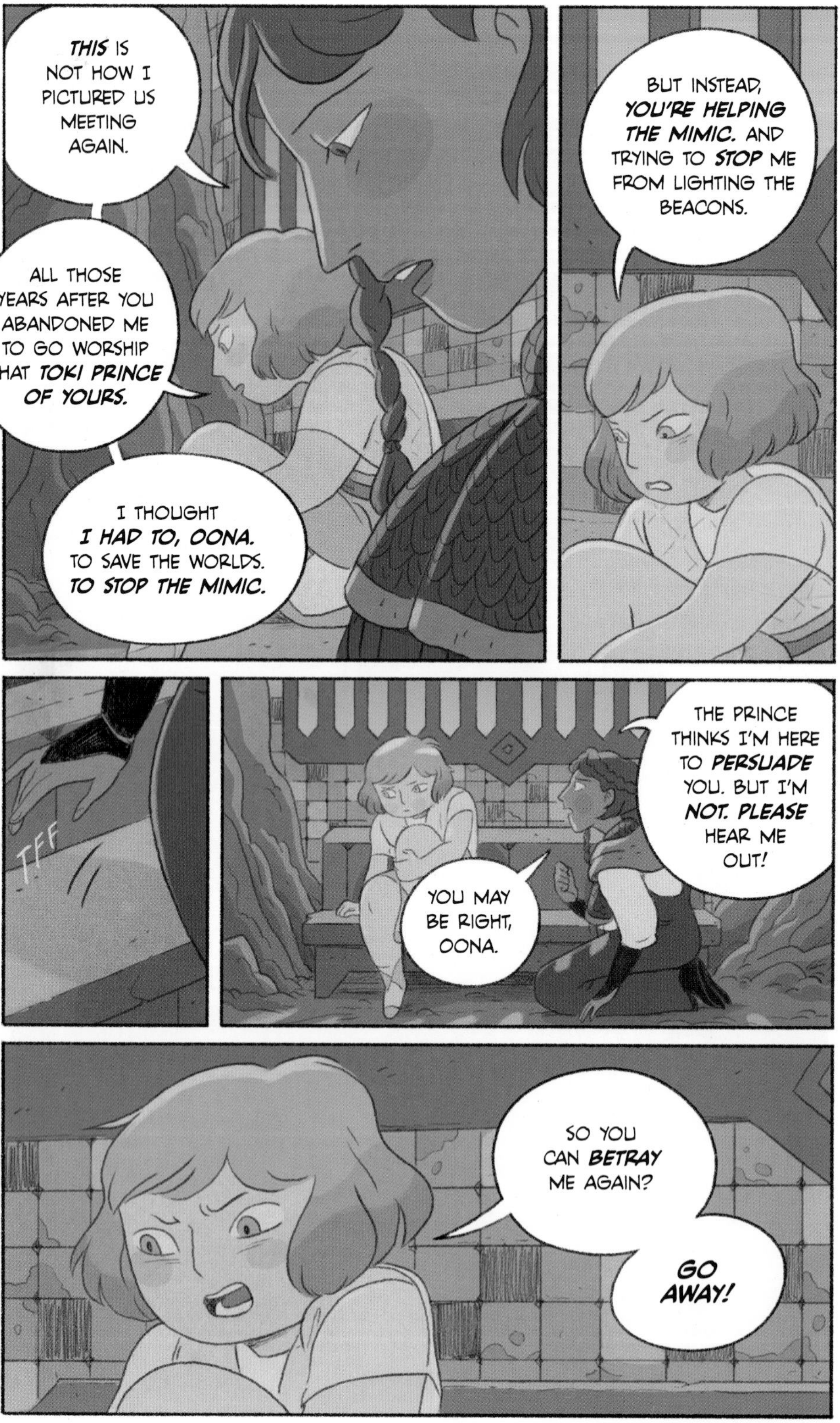
THIS IS NOT HOW I PICTURED US MEETING AGAIN.
ALL THOSE YEARS AFTER YOU ABANDONED ME TO GO WORSHIP THAT TOKI PRINCE OF YOURS.
I THOUGHT I HAD TO, OONA. TO SAVE THE WORLDS. TO STOP THE MIMIC.
BUT INSTEAD, YOU'RE HELPING THE MIMIC. AND TRYING TO STOP ME FROM LIGHTING THE BEACONS.
TFF
THE PRINCE THINKS I'M HERE TO PERSUADE YOU. BUT I'M NOT. PLEASE HEAR ME OUT!
YOU MAY BE RIGHT, OONA.
SO YOU CAN BETRAY ME AGAIN?
GO AWAY!

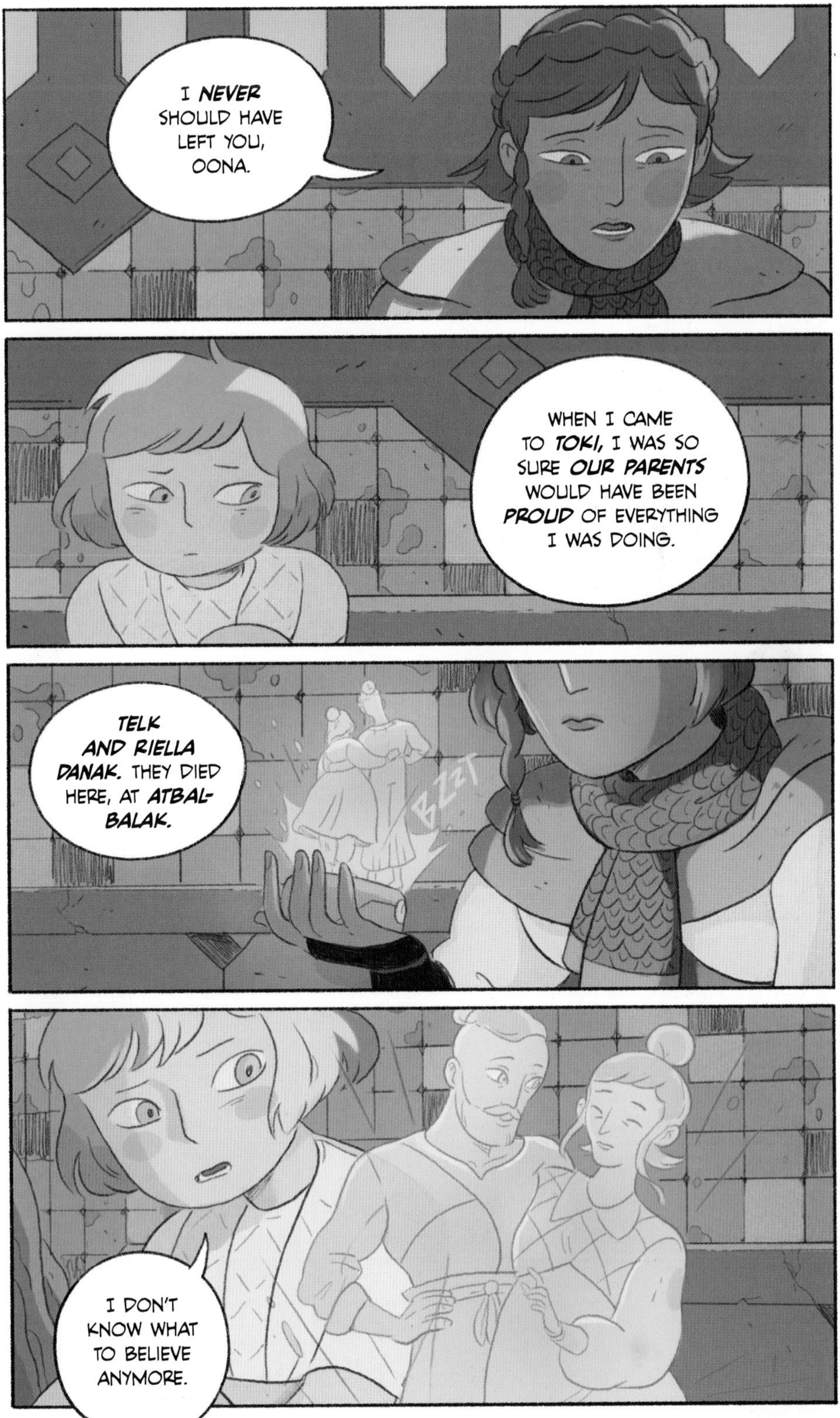
I **NEVER** SHOULD HAVE LEFT YOU, OONA.
WHEN I CAME TO **TOKI,** I WAS SO SURE **OUR PARENTS** WOULD HAVE BEEN **PROUD** OF EVERYTHING I WAS DOING.
TELK AND RIELLA DANAK. THEY DIED HERE, AT **ATBAL-BALAK.**
BZZT
I DON'T KNOW WHAT TO BELIEVE ANYMORE.

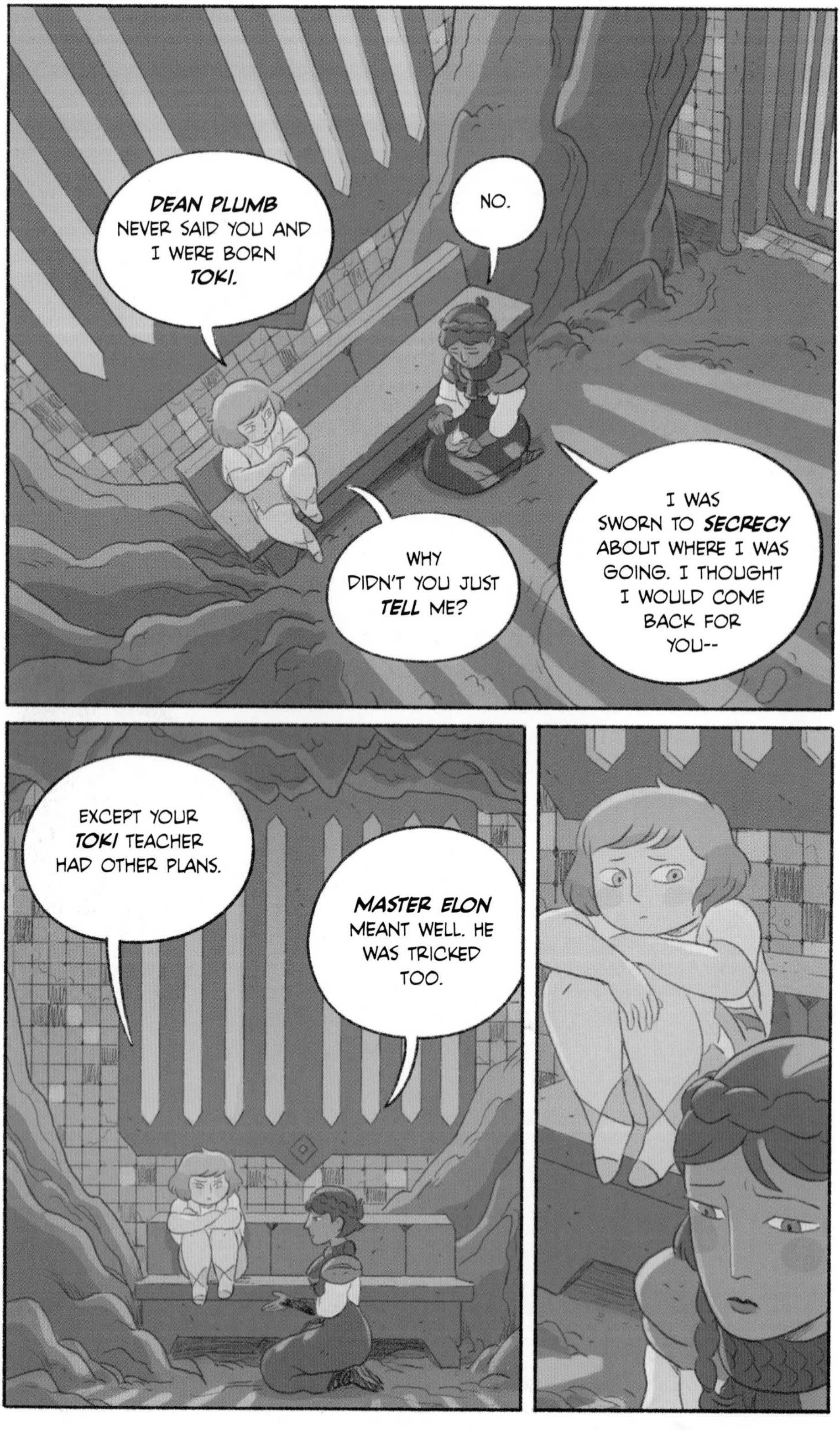
DEAN PLUMB NEVER SAID YOU AND I WERE BORN TOKI.
NO.
WHY DIDN'T YOU JUST TELL ME?
I WAS SWORN TO SECRECY ABOUT WHERE I WAS GOING. I THOUGHT I WOULD COME BACK FOR YOU--
EXCEPT YOUR TOKI TEACHER HAD OTHER PLANS.
MASTER ELON MEANT WELL. HE WAS TRICKED TOO.

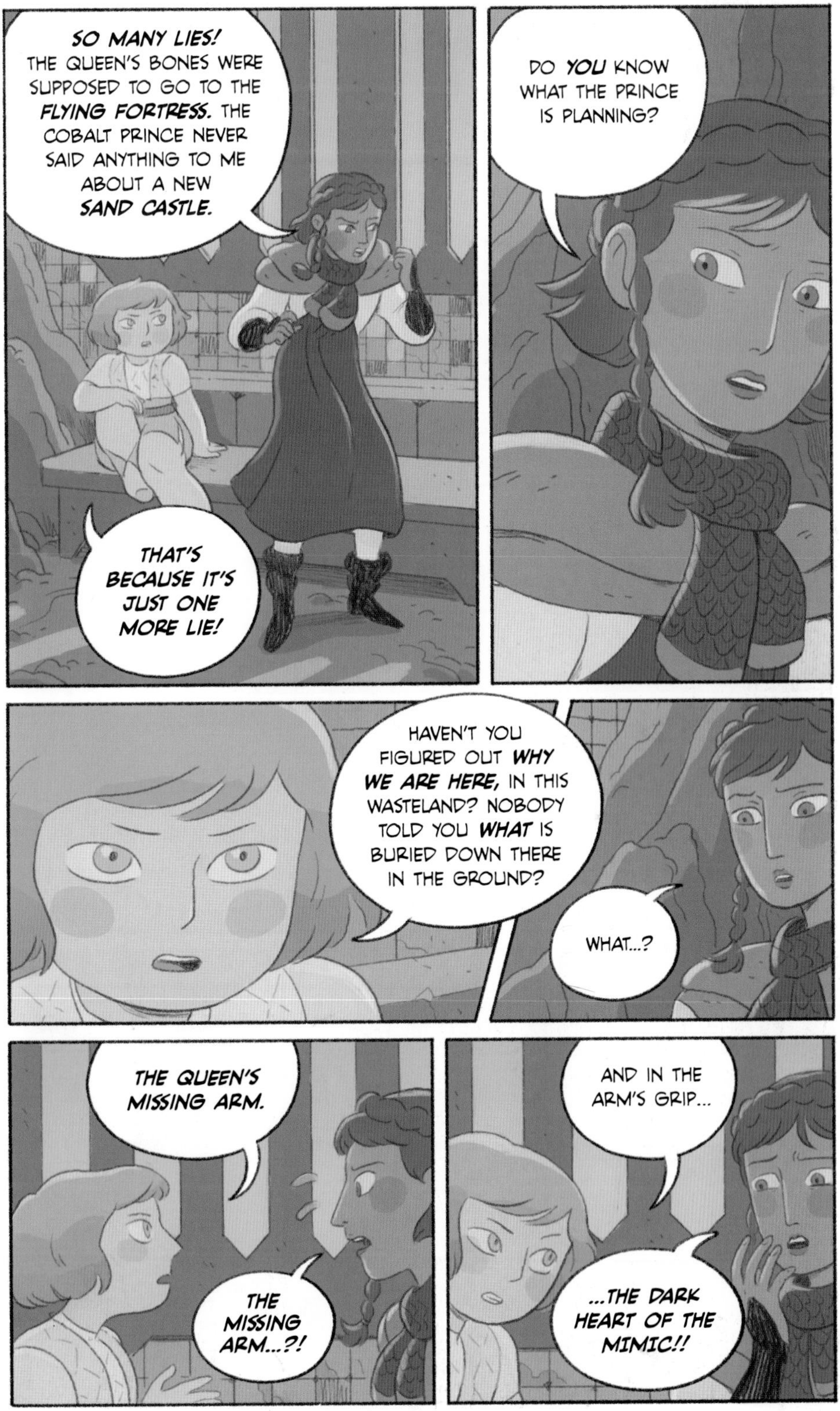

SO MANY LIES! THE QUEEN'S BONES WERE SUPPOSED TO GO TO THE FLYING FORTRESS. THE COBALT PRINCE NEVER SAID ANYTHING TO ME ABOUT A NEW SAND CASTLE.
THAT'S BECAUSE IT'S JUST ONE MORE LIE!
DO YOU KNOW WHAT THE PRINCE IS PLANNING?
HAVEN'T YOU FIGURED OUT WHY WE ARE HERE, IN THIS WASTELAND? NOBODY TOLD YOU WHAT IS BURIED DOWN THERE IN THE GROUND?
WHAT...?
THE QUEEN'S MISSING ARM.
THE MISSING ARM...?!
AND IN THE ARM'S GRIP...
...THE DARK HEART OF THE MIMIC!!

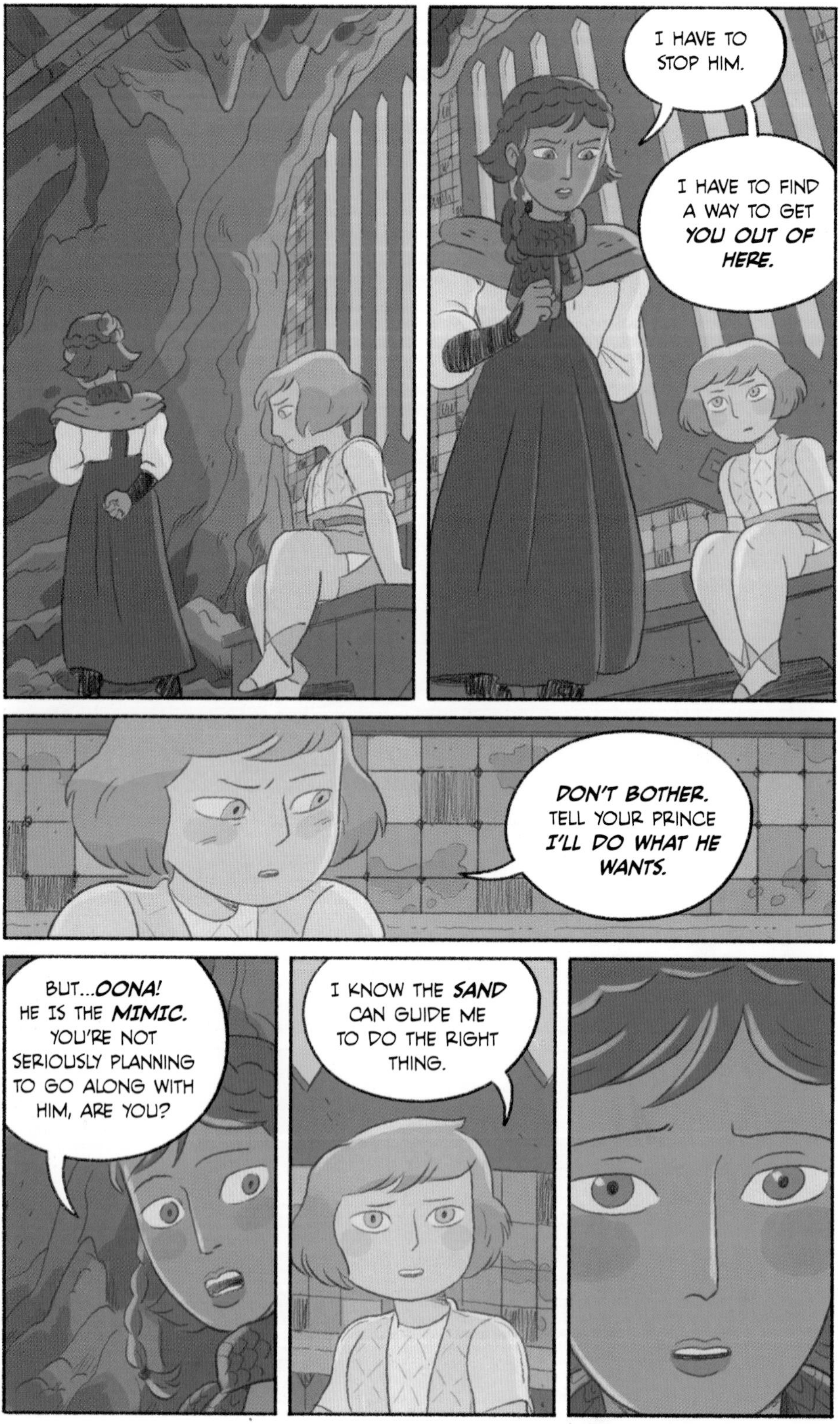
I HAVE TO STOP HIM.
I HAVE TO FIND A WAY TO GET *YOU OUT OF HERE.*
DON'T BOTHER. TELL YOUR PRINCE *I'LL DO WHAT HE WANTS.*
BUT...*OONA!* HE IS THE *MIMIC.* YOU'RE NOT SERIOUSLY PLANNING TO GO ALONG WITH HIM, ARE YOU?
I KNOW THE *SAND* CAN GUIDE ME TO DO THE RIGHT THING.

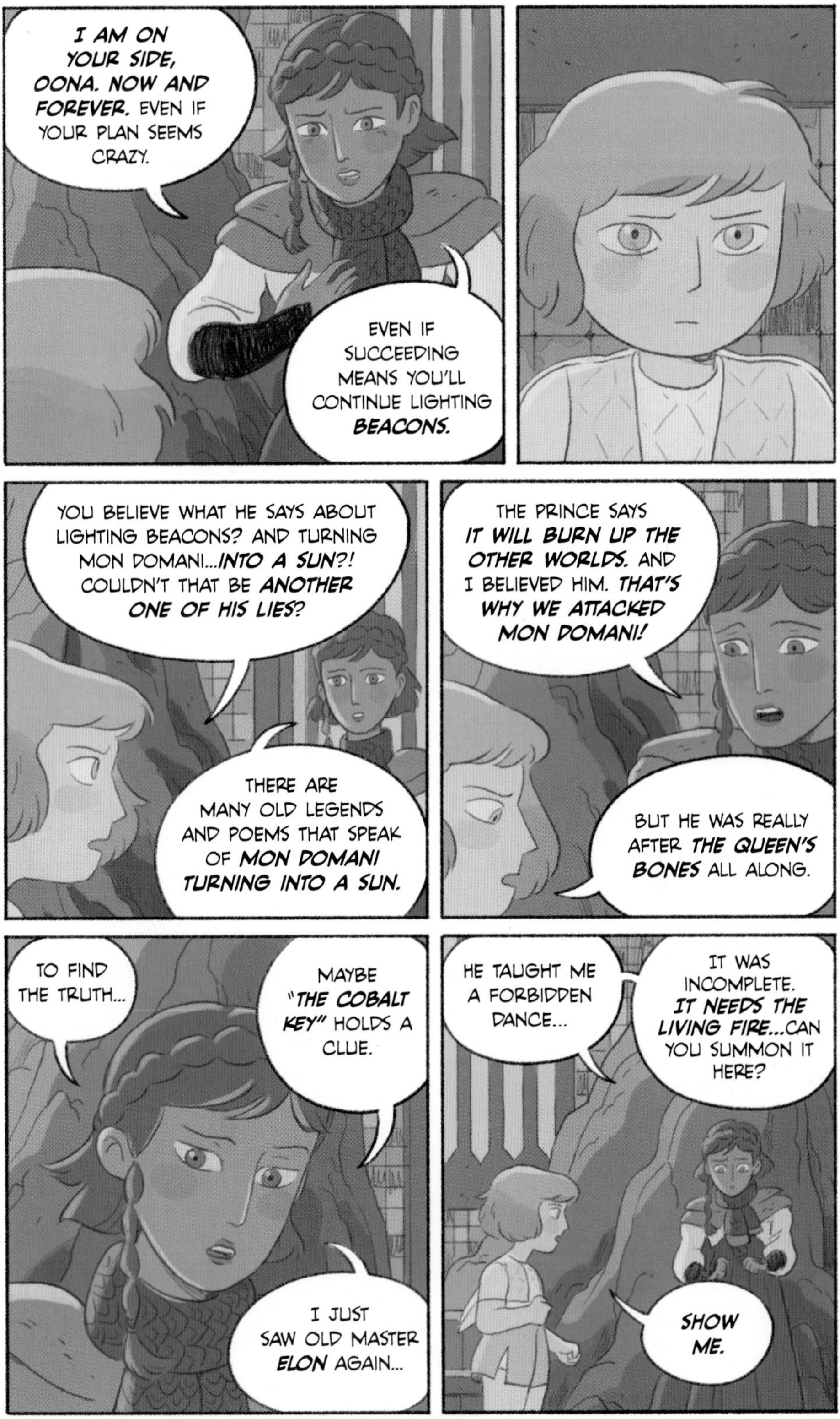
I AM ON YOUR SIDE, OONA. NOW AND FOREVER. EVEN IF YOUR PLAN SEEMS CRAZY.
EVEN IF SUCCEEDING MEANS YOU'LL CONTINUE LIGHTING BEACONS.
YOU BELIEVE WHAT HE SAYS ABOUT LIGHTING BEACONS? AND TURNING MON DOMANI...INTO A SUN?! COULDN'T THAT BE ANOTHER ONE OF HIS LIES?
THERE ARE MANY OLD LEGENDS AND POEMS THAT SPEAK OF MON DOMANI TURNING INTO A SUN.
THE PRINCE SAYS IT WILL BURN UP THE OTHER WORLDS. AND I BELIEVED HIM. THAT'S WHY WE ATTACKED MON DOMANI!
BUT HE WAS REALLY AFTER THE QUEEN'S BONES ALL ALONG.
TO FIND THE TRUTH...
MAYBE "THE COBALT KEY" HOLDS A CLUE.
I JUST SAW OLD MASTER ELON AGAIN...
HE TAUGHT ME A FORBIDDEN DANCE...
IT WAS INCOMPLETE. IT NEEDS THE LIVING FIRE...CAN YOU SUMMON IT HERE?
SHOW ME.

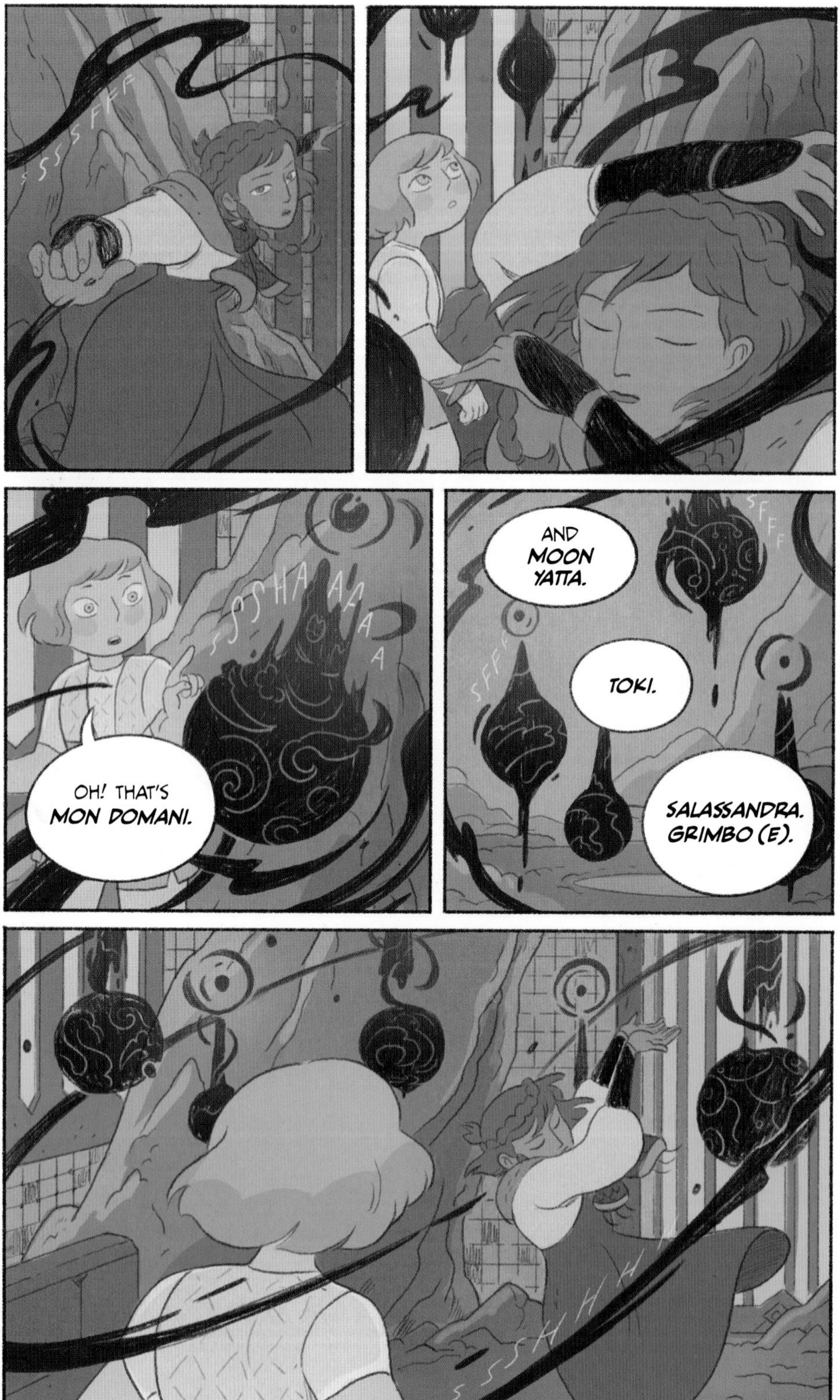
OH! THAT'S MON DOMANI.
AND MOON YATTA.
TOKI.
SALASSANDRA. GRIMBO (E).

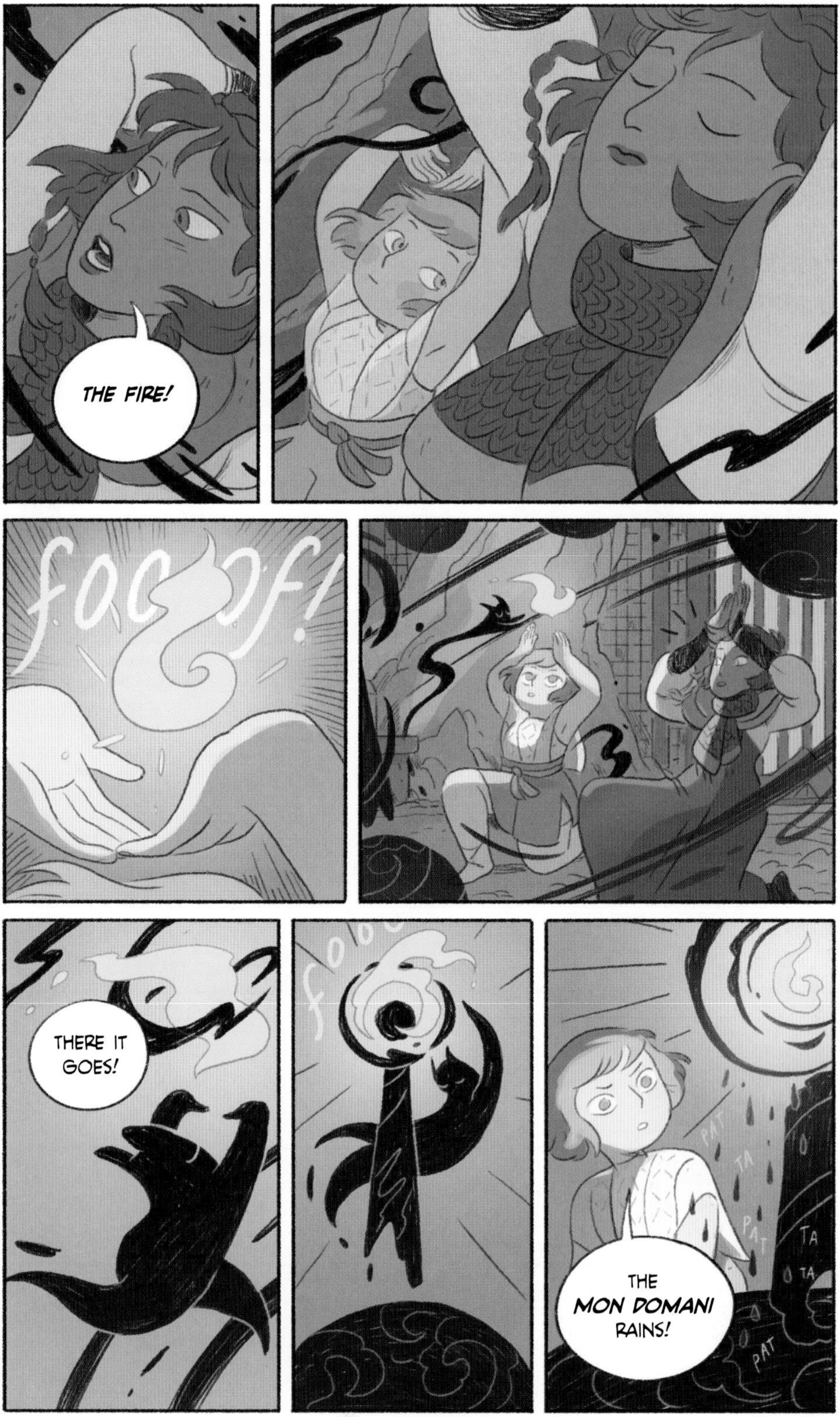
THE FIRE!
FOOOF!
THERE IT GOES!
FOOO
THE MON DOMANI RAINS!
PAT
TA
PAT
TA
TA
PAT

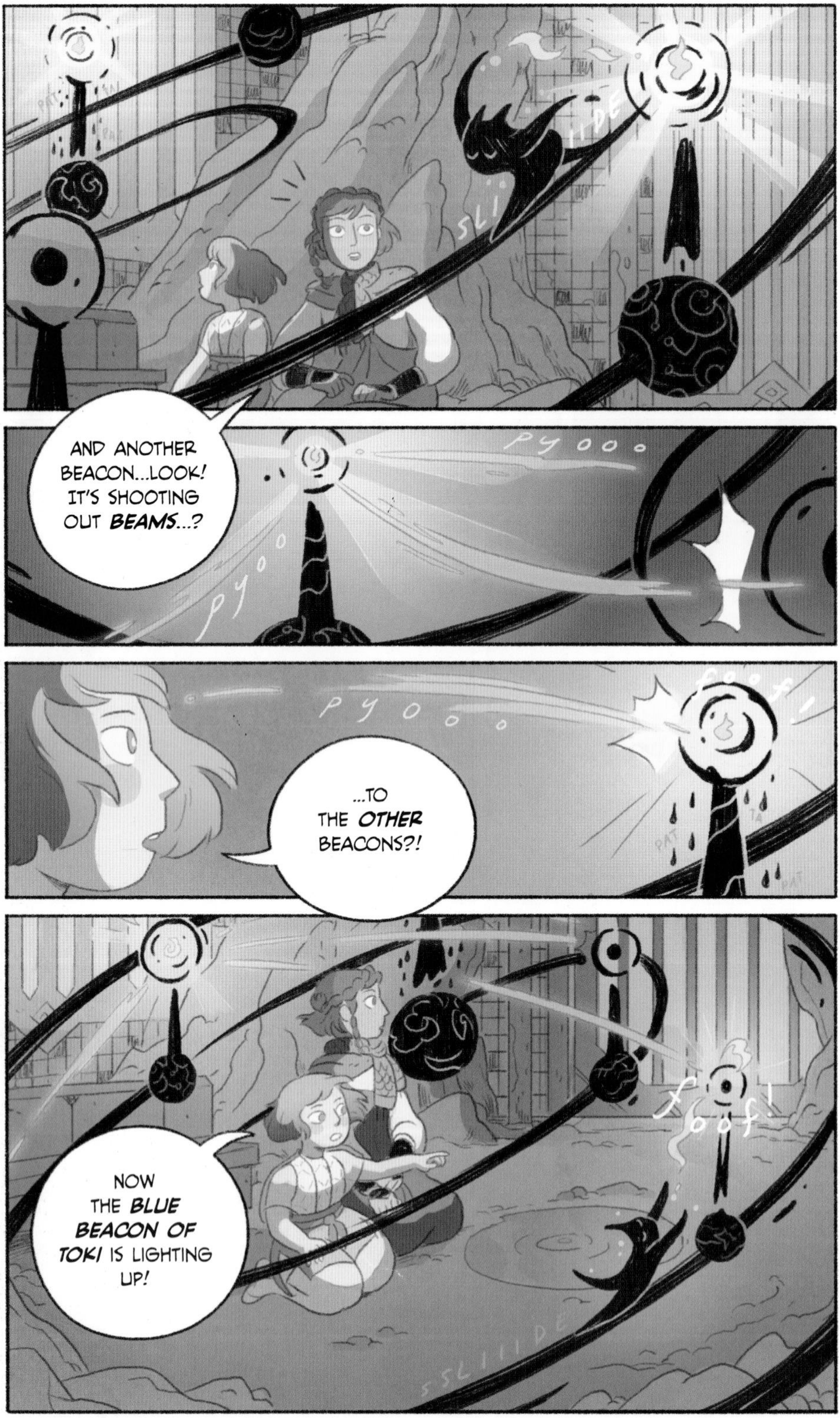
PAT
PAT
PAT
SLI
IIDE
AND ANOTHER BEACON...LOOK! IT'S SHOOTING OUT BEAMS...?
PYOOO
PYOO
PYOOO
FOOF!
...TO THE OTHER BEACONS?!
PAT
TA
PAT
PAT
NOW THE BLUE BEACON OF TOKI IS LIGHTING UP!
FOOF!
SSLIIIDE

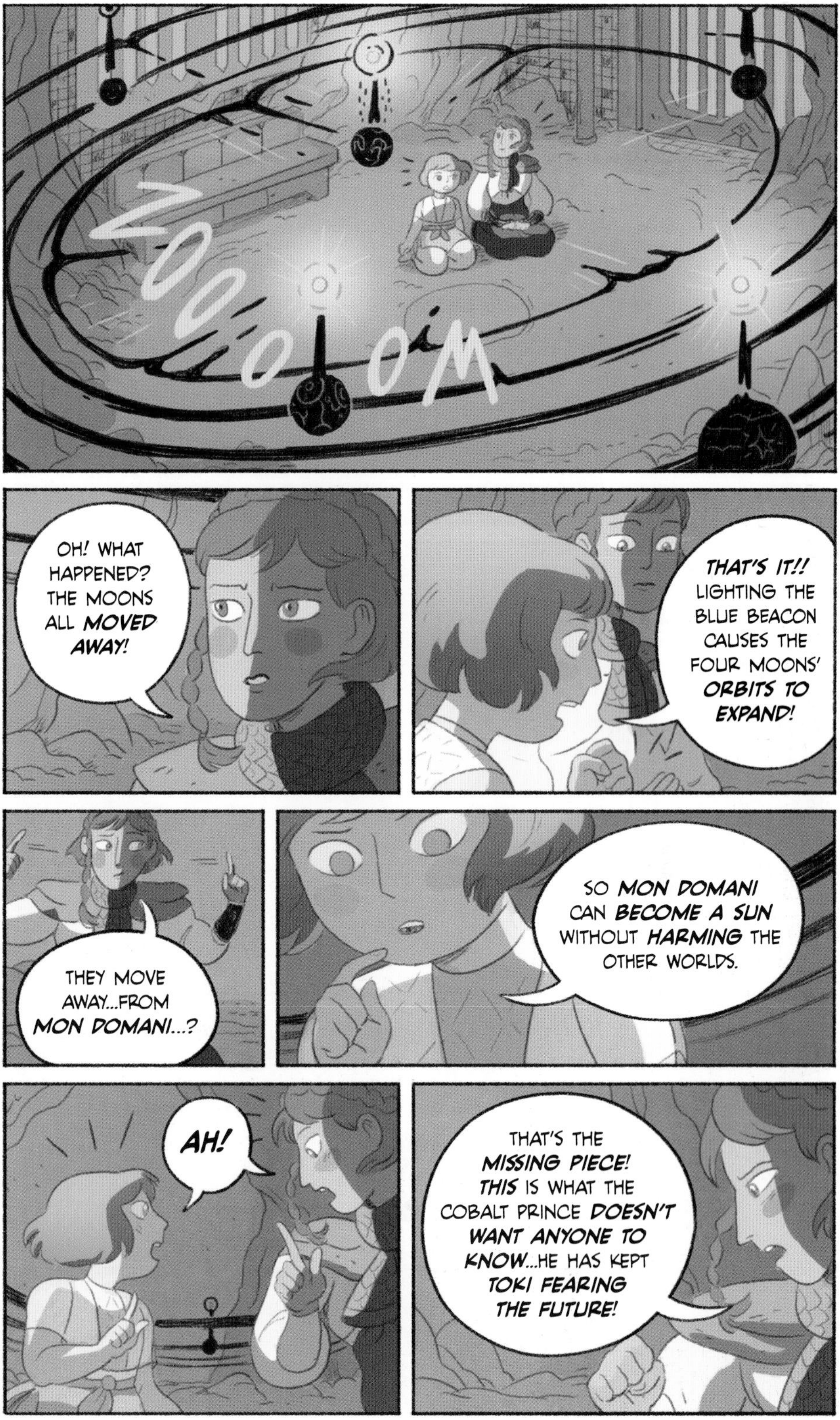

ZOOOOOM
OH! WHAT HAPPENED? THE MOONS ALL MOVED AWAY!
THAT'S IT!! LIGHTING THE BLUE BEACON CAUSES THE FOUR MOONS' ORBITS TO EXPAND!
THEY MOVE AWAY...FROM MON DOMANI...?
SO MON DOMANI CAN BECOME A SUN WITHOUT HARMING THE OTHER WORLDS.
AH!
THAT'S THE MISSING PIECE! THIS IS WHAT THE COBALT PRINCE DOESN'T WANT ANYONE TO KNOW...HE HAS KEPT TOKI FEARING THE FUTURE!

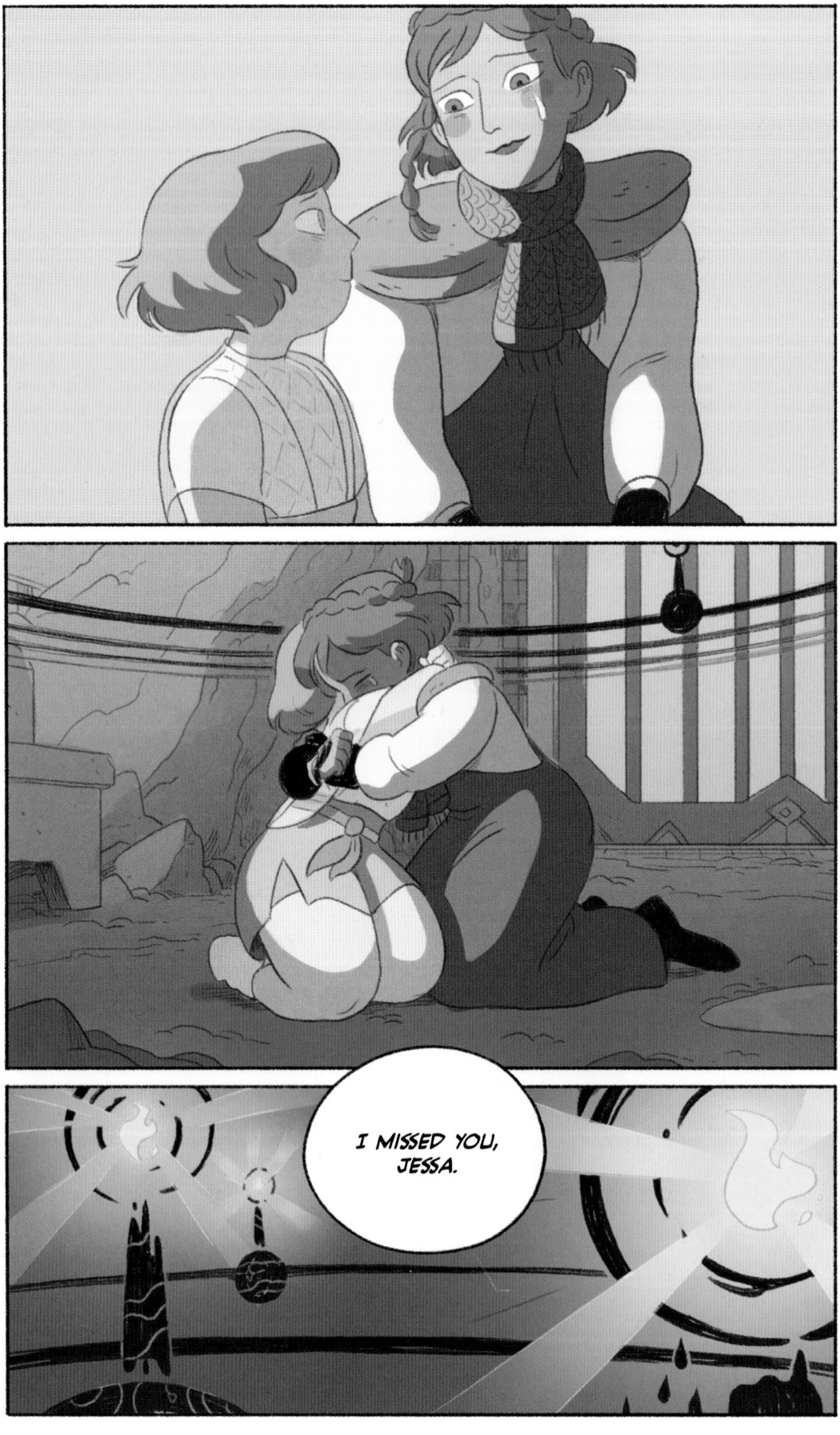
I MISSED YOU, JESSA.

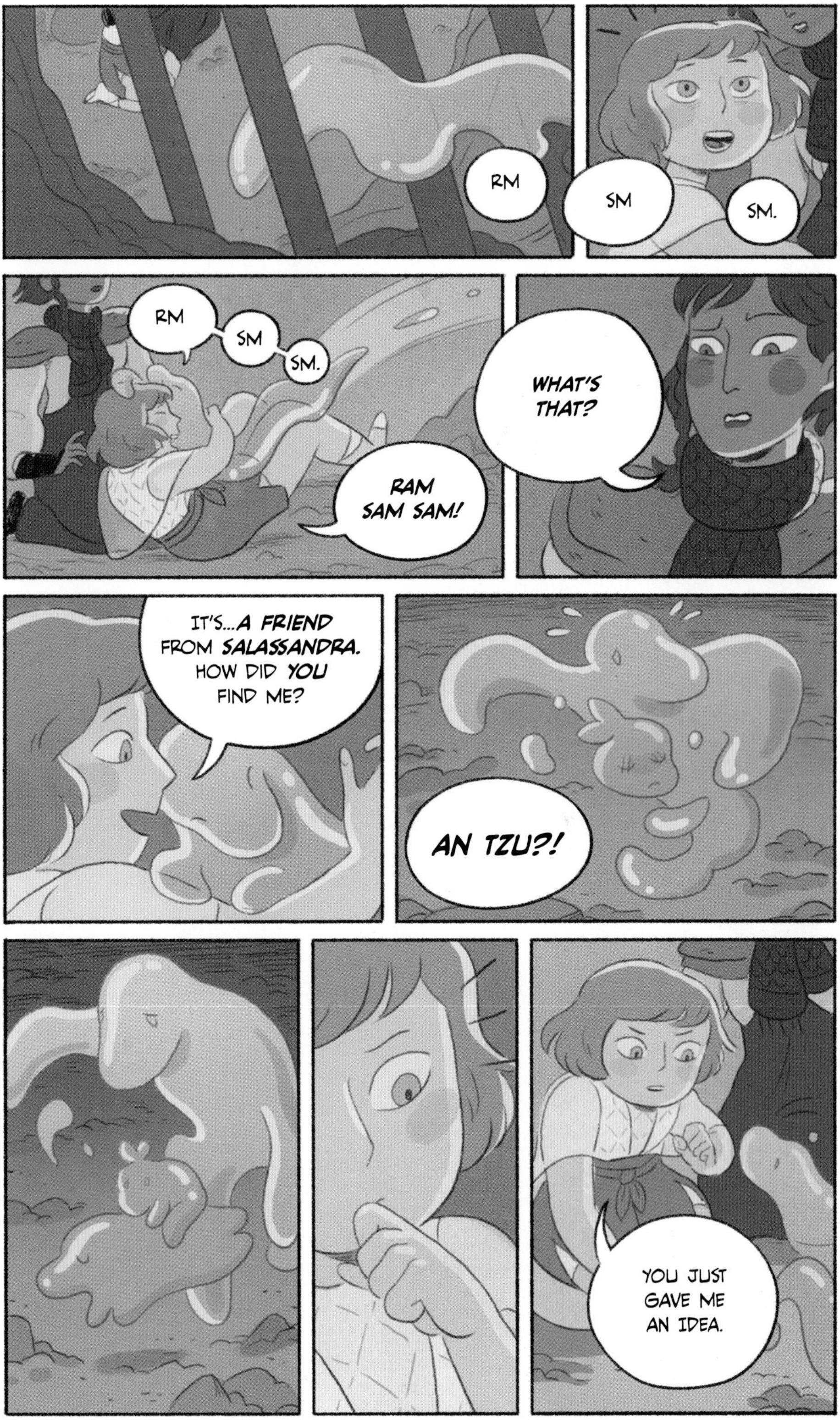
RM
SM
SM.
RM
SM
SM.
RAM SAM SAM!
WHAT'S THAT?
IT'S...A FRIEND FROM SALASSANDRA. HOW DID YOU FIND ME?
AN TZU?!
YOU JUST GAVE ME AN IDEA.

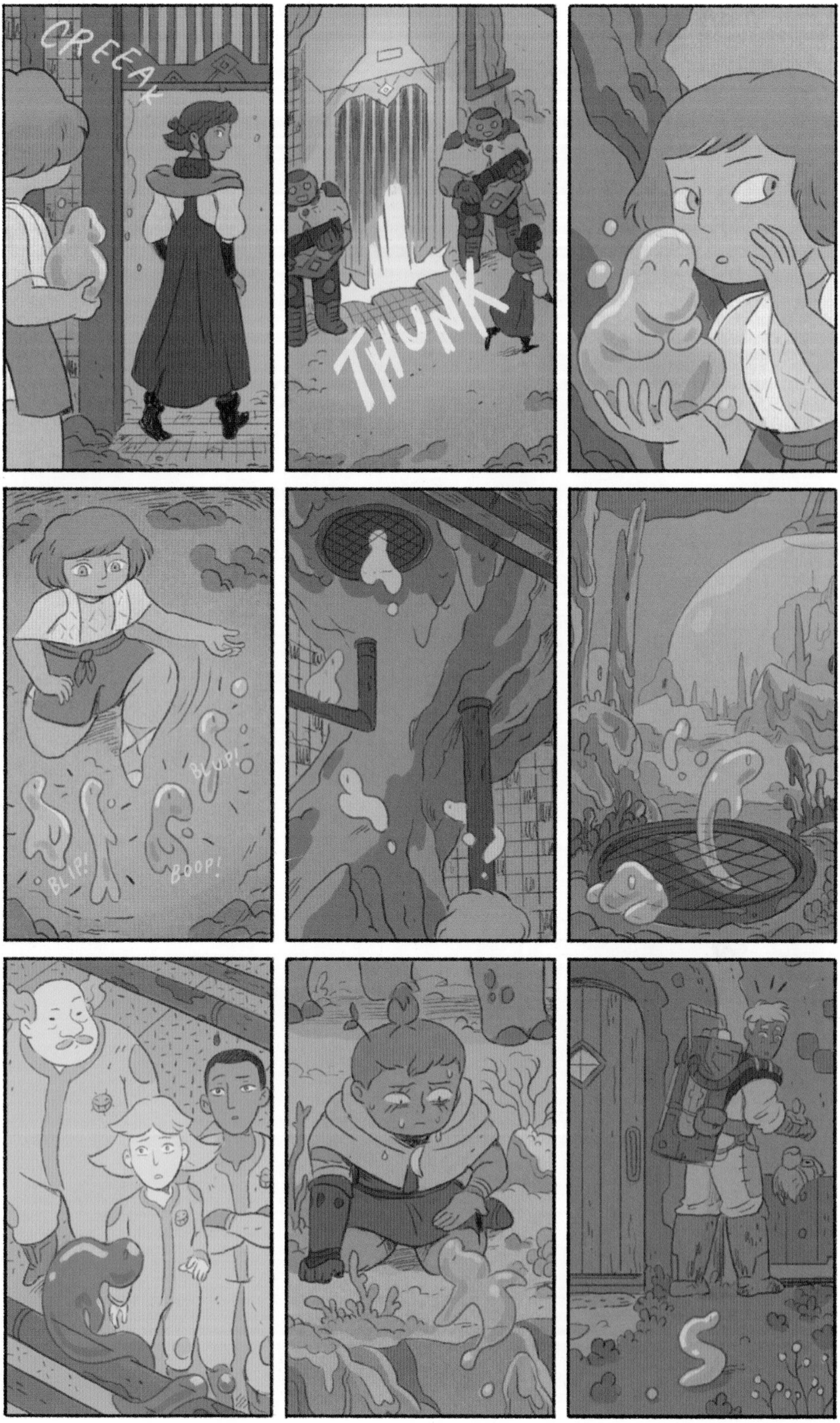
CREEAK
THUNK
BLUP!
BLIP!
BOOP!

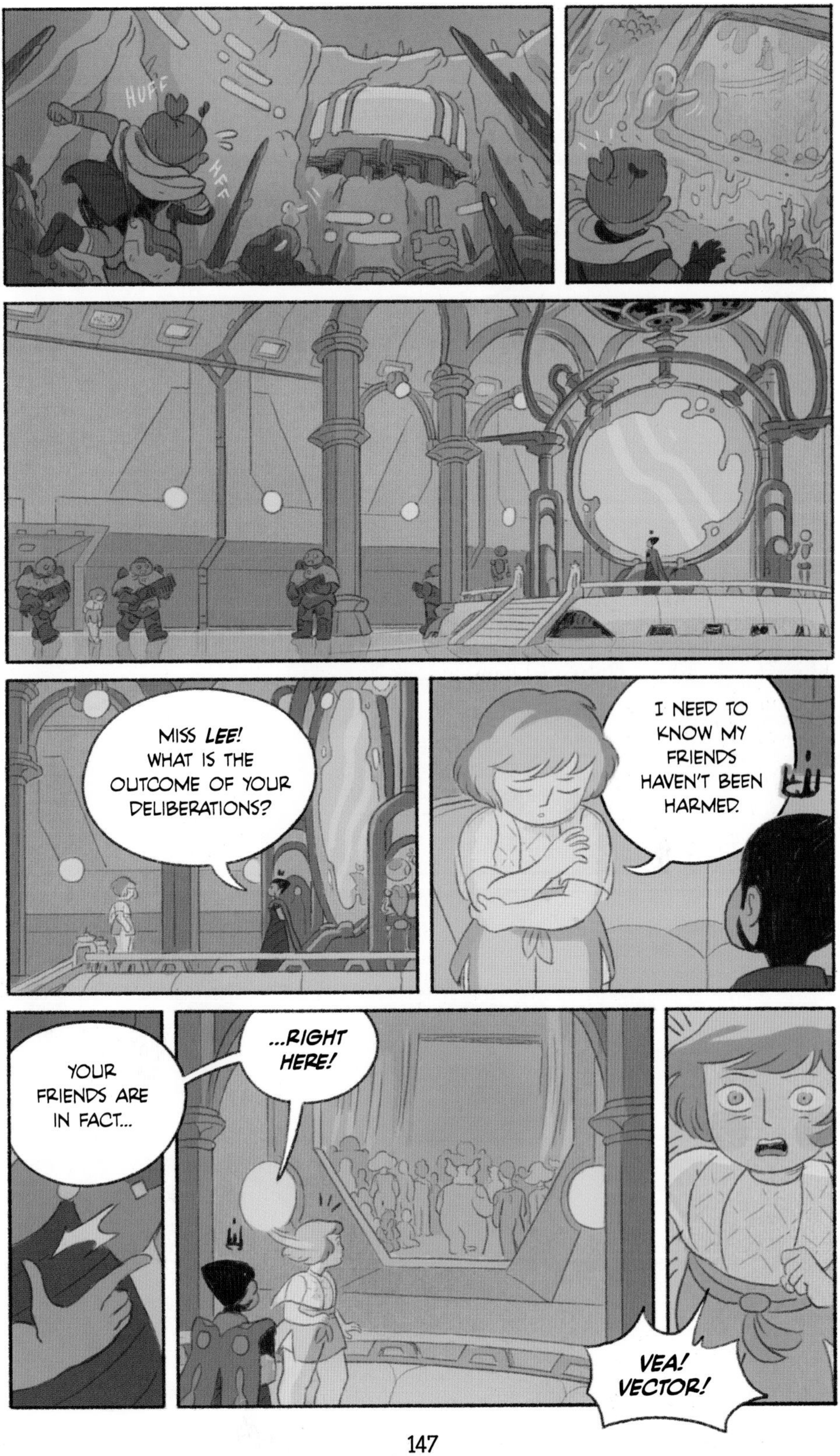
HUFF
HFF
MISS LEE! WHAT IS THE OUTCOME OF YOUR DELIBERATIONS?
I NEED TO KNOW MY FRIENDS HAVEN'T BEEN HARMED.
YOUR FRIENDS ARE IN FACT...
...RIGHT HERE!
VEA! VECTOR!

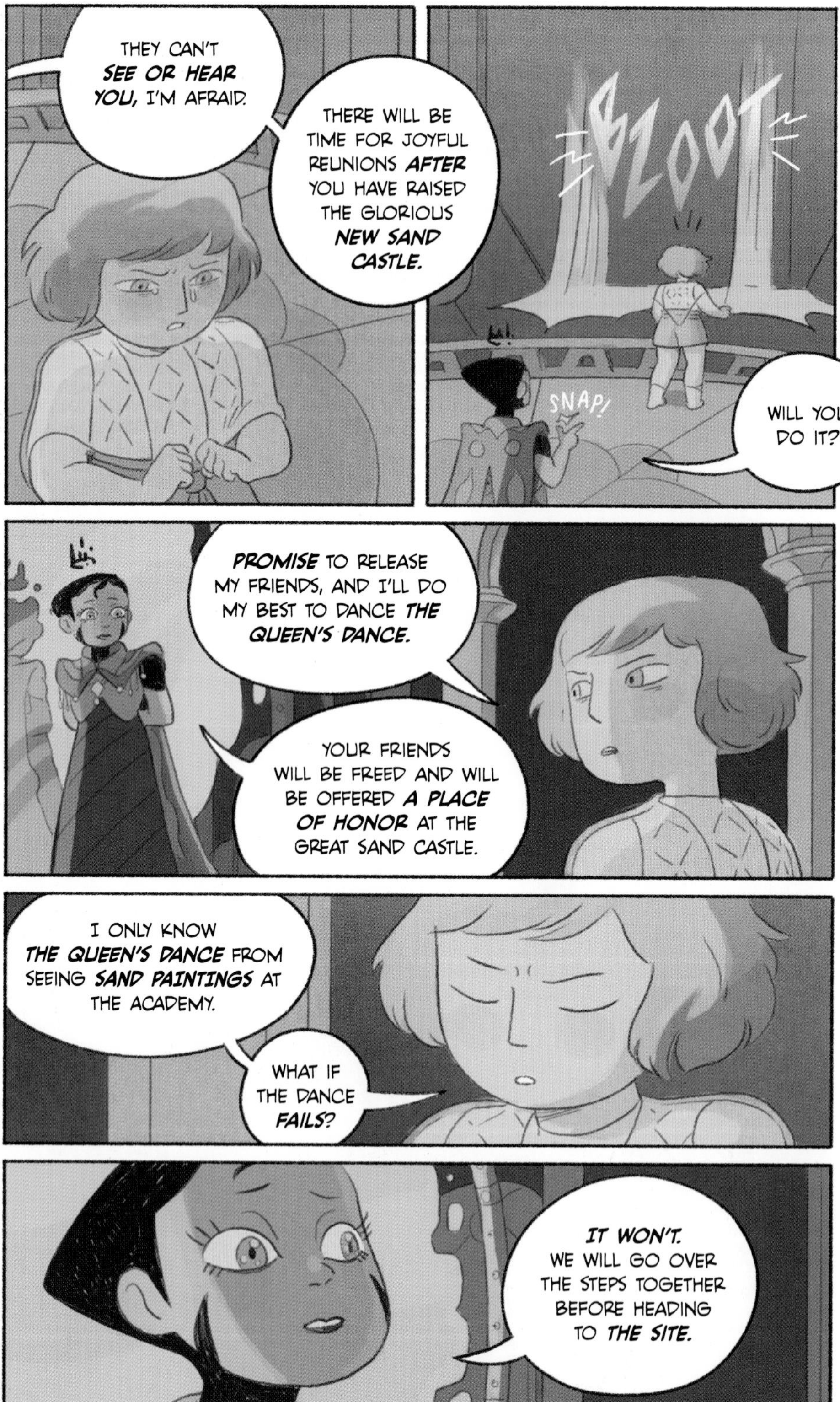
THEY CAN'T SEE OR HEAR YOU, I'M AFRAID.
THERE WILL BE TIME FOR JOYFUL REUNIONS AFTER YOU HAVE RAISED THE GLORIOUS NEW SAND CASTLE.
BZOOT
SNAP!
WILL YOU DO IT?
PROMISE TO RELEASE MY FRIENDS, AND I'LL DO MY BEST TO DANCE THE QUEEN'S DANCE.
YOUR FRIENDS WILL BE FREED AND WILL BE OFFERED A PLACE OF HONOR AT THE GREAT SAND CASTLE.
I ONLY KNOW THE QUEEN'S DANCE FROM SEEING SAND PAINTINGS AT THE ACADEMY.
WHAT IF THE DANCE FAILS?
IT WON'T. WE WILL GO OVER THE STEPS TOGETHER BEFORE HEADING TO THE SITE.

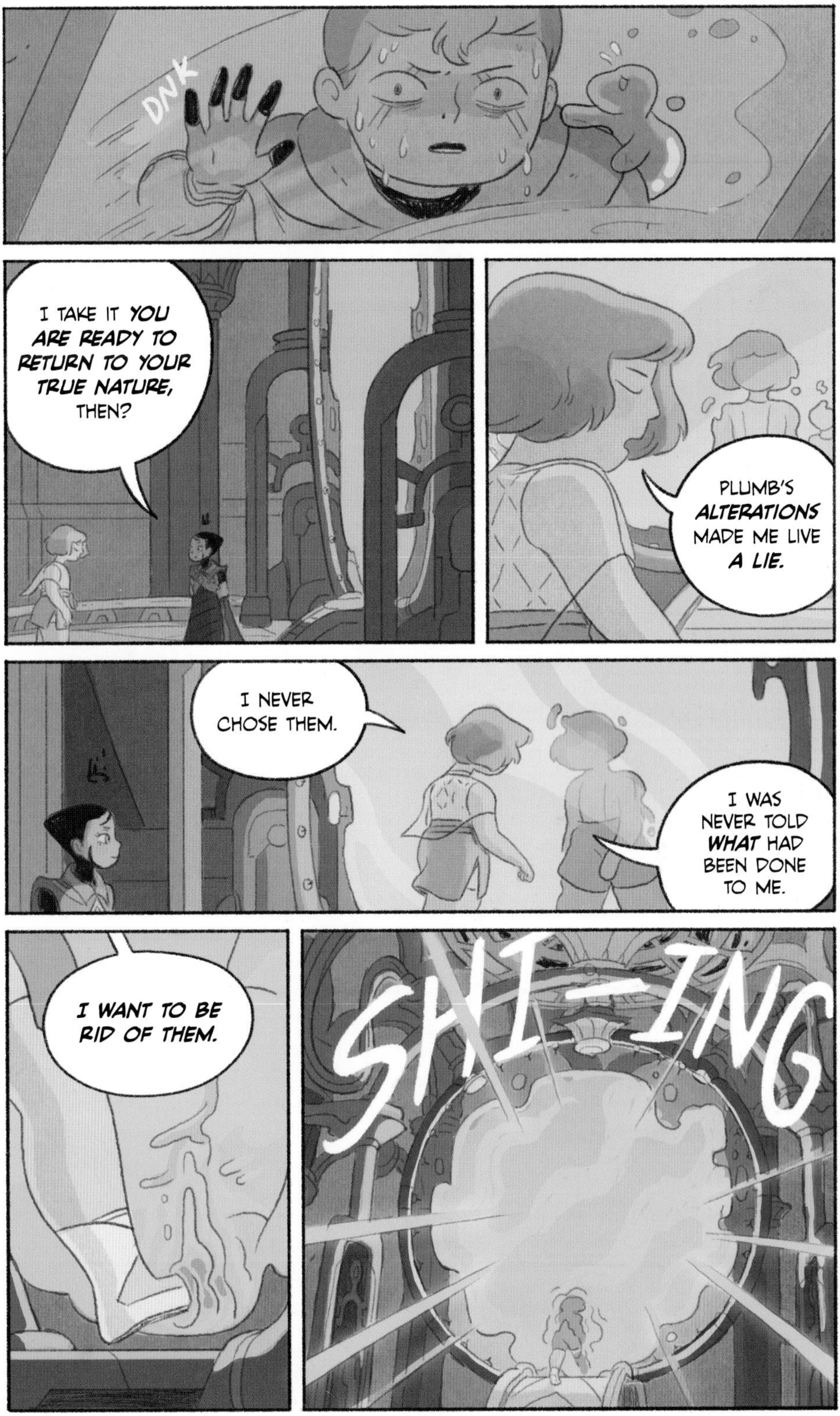
DNK
I TAKE IT YOU ARE READY TO RETURN TO YOUR TRUE NATURE, THEN?
PLUMB'S ALTERATIONS MADE ME LIVE A LIE.
I NEVER CHOSE THEM.
I WAS NEVER TOLD WHAT HAD BEEN DONE TO ME.
I WANT TO BE RID OF THEM.
SHI-ING

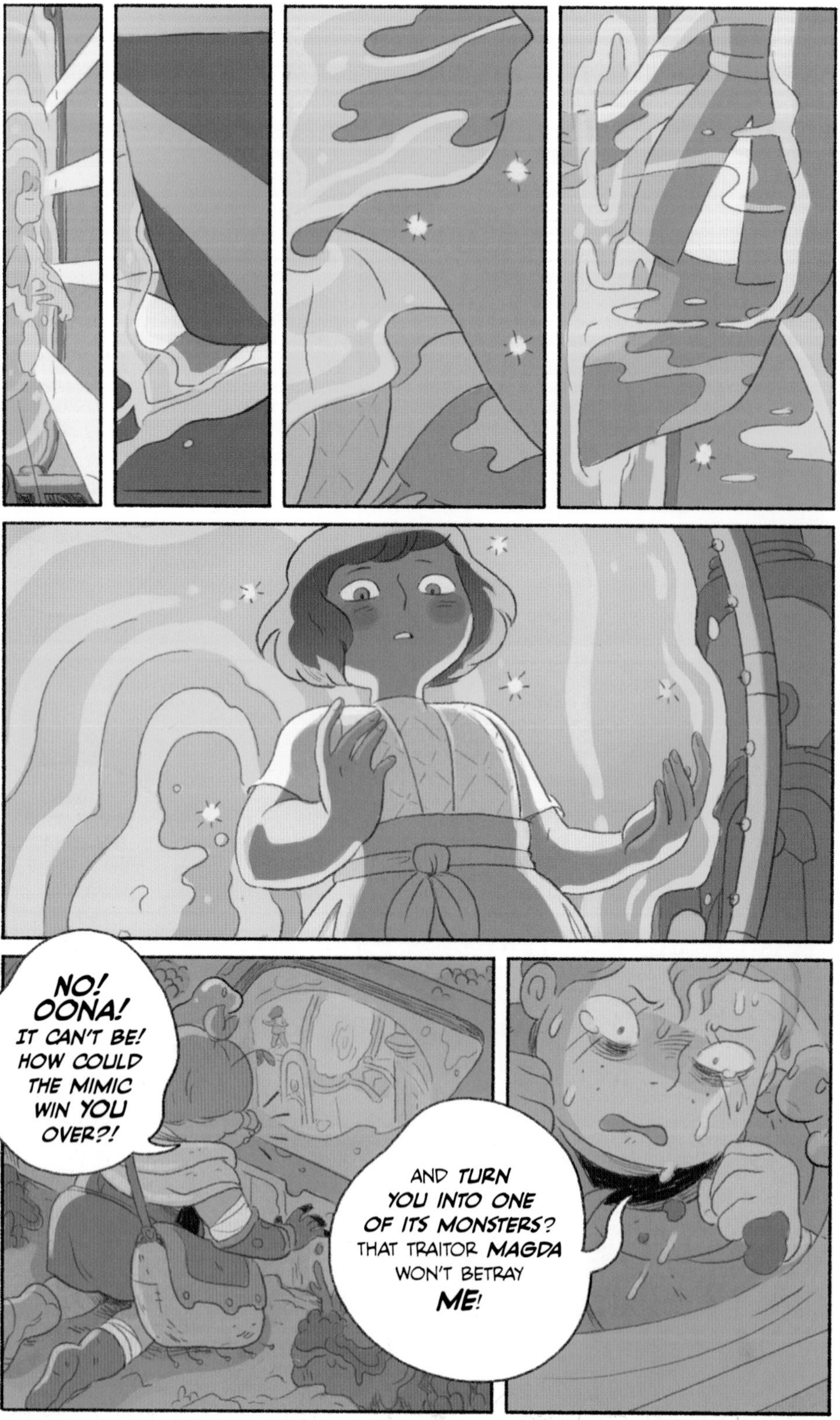
NO! OONA! IT CAN'T BE! HOW COULD THE MIMIC WIN YOU OVER?!
AND TURN YOU INTO ONE OF ITS MONSTERS? THAT TRAITOR MAGDA WON'T BETRAY ME!

Chapter 8

DREAMING OF THE GODS

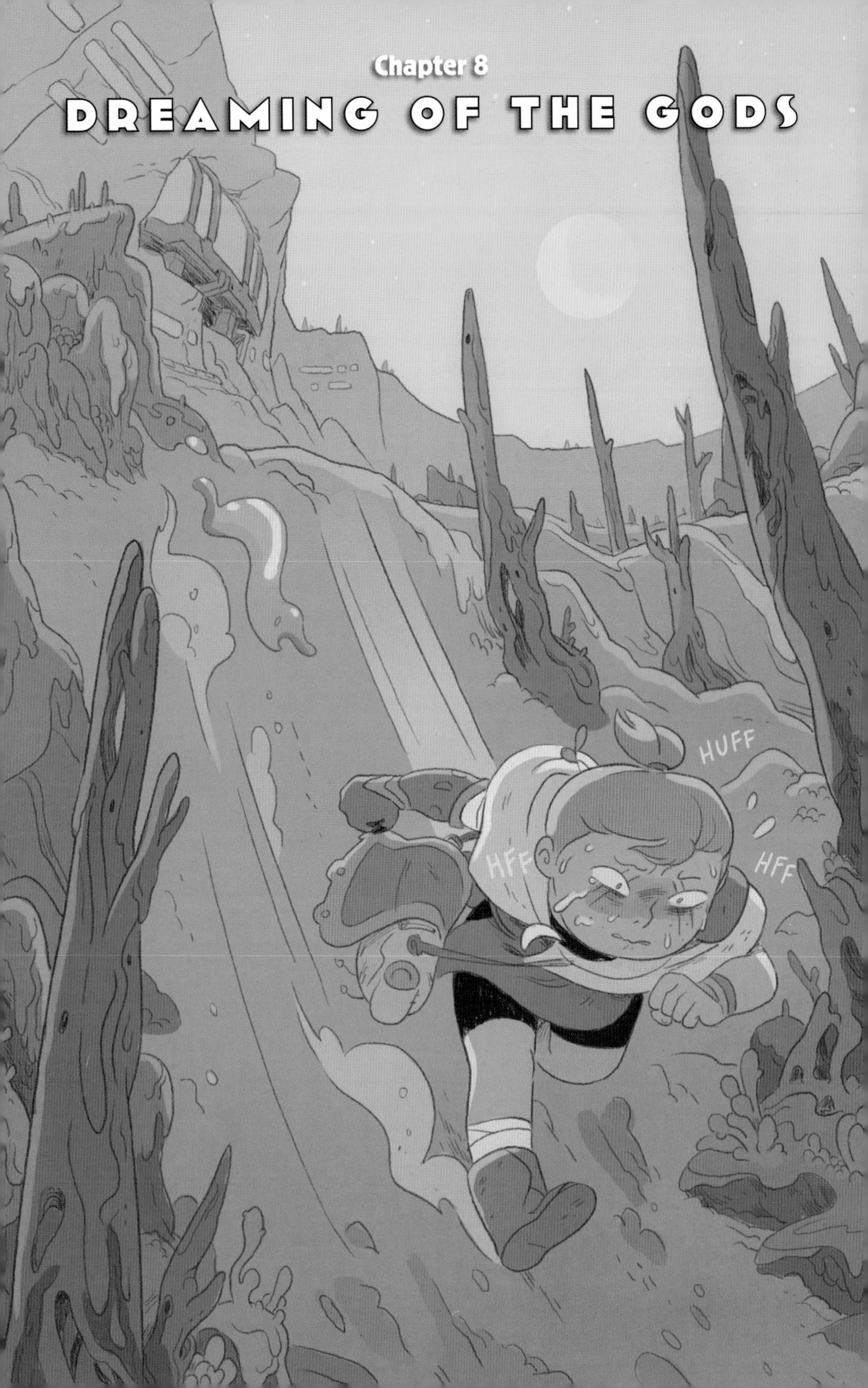

HUFF
HFF
HFF

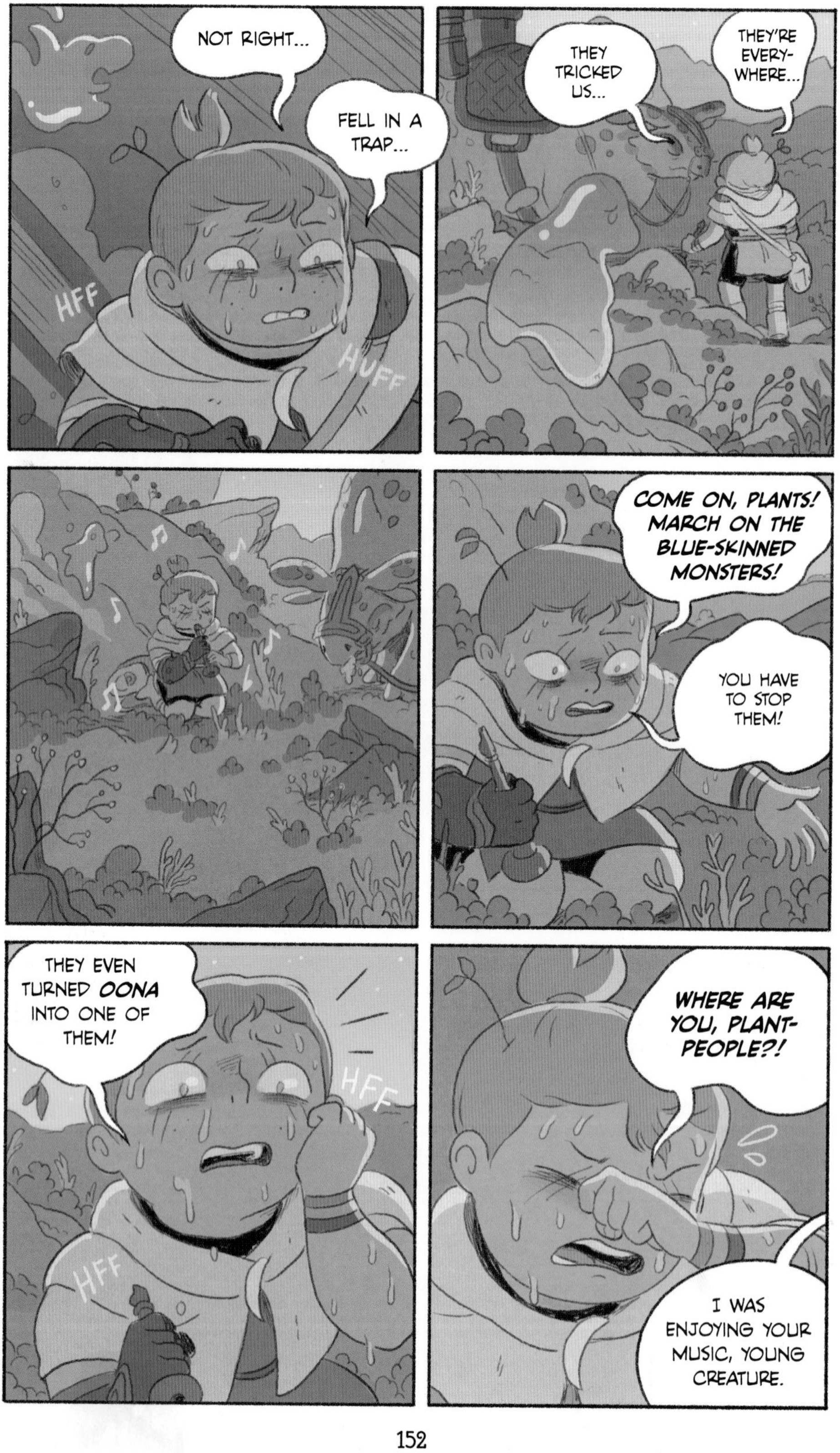
NOT RIGHT...
FELL IN A TRAP...
HFF
HUFF
THEY TRICKED US...
THEY'RE EVERY-WHERE...
COME ON, PLANTS! MARCH ON THE BLUE-SKINNED MONSTERS!
YOU HAVE TO STOP THEM!
THEY EVEN TURNED OONA INTO ONE OF THEM!
HFF
HFF
WHERE ARE YOU, PLANT-PEOPLE?!
I WAS ENJOYING YOUR MUSIC, YOUNG CREATURE.

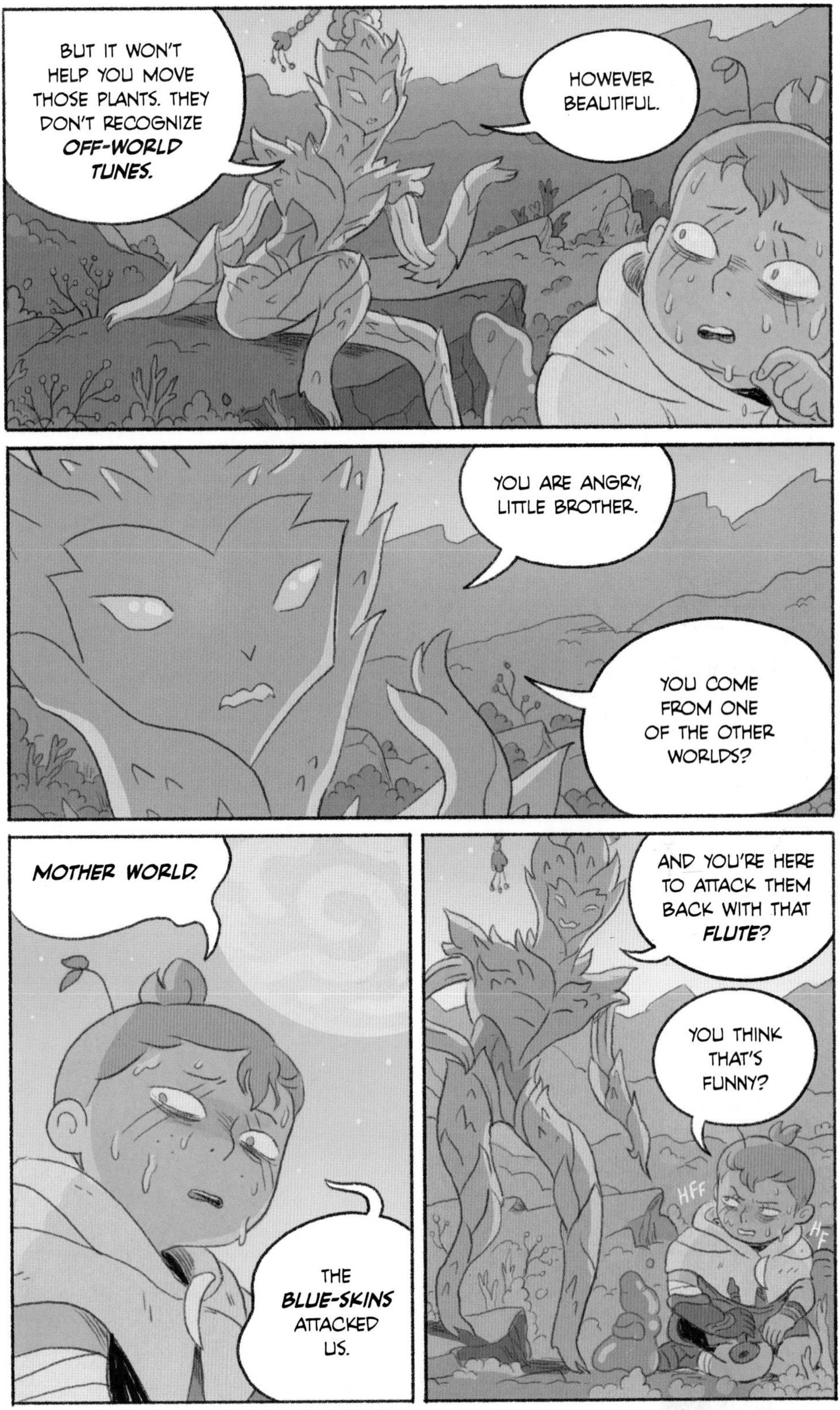
BUT IT WON'T HELP YOU MOVE THOSE PLANTS. THEY DON'T RECOGNIZE OFF-WORLD TUNES.
HOWEVER BEAUTIFUL.
YOU ARE ANGRY, LITTLE BROTHER.
YOU COME FROM ONE OF THE OTHER WORLDS?
MOTHER WORLD.
THE BLUE-SKINS ATTACKED US.
AND YOU'RE HERE TO ATTACK THEM BACK WITH THAT FLUTE?
YOU THINK THAT'S FUNNY?
HFF
HF

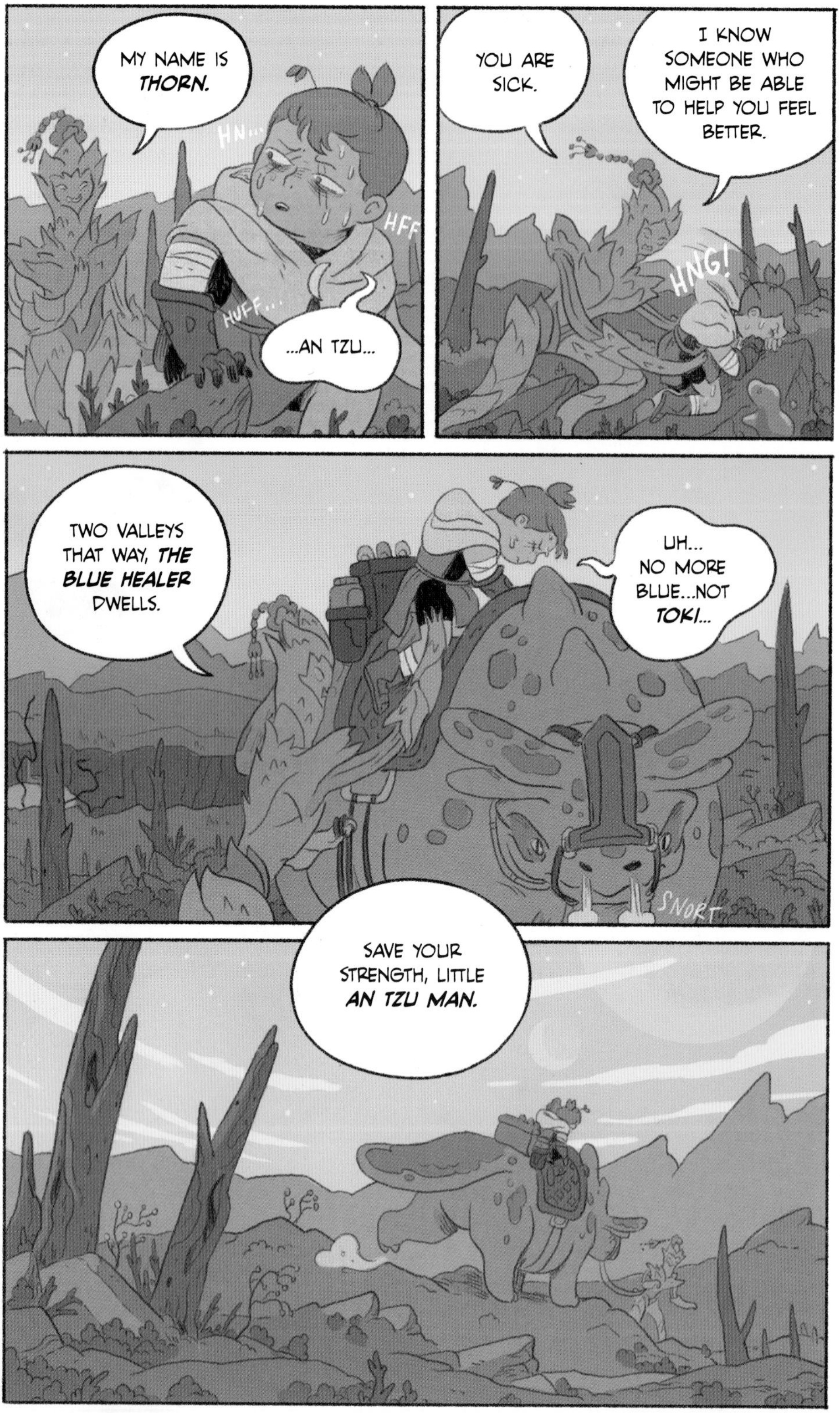
MY NAME IS THORN.
HN...
HFF
HUFF...
...AN TZU...
YOU ARE SICK.
I KNOW SOMEONE WHO MIGHT BE ABLE TO HELP YOU FEEL BETTER.
HNG!
TWO VALLEYS THAT WAY, THE BLUE HEALER DWELLS.
UH... NO MORE BLUE...NOT TOKI...
SNORT
SAVE YOUR STRENGTH, LITTLE AN TZU MAN.

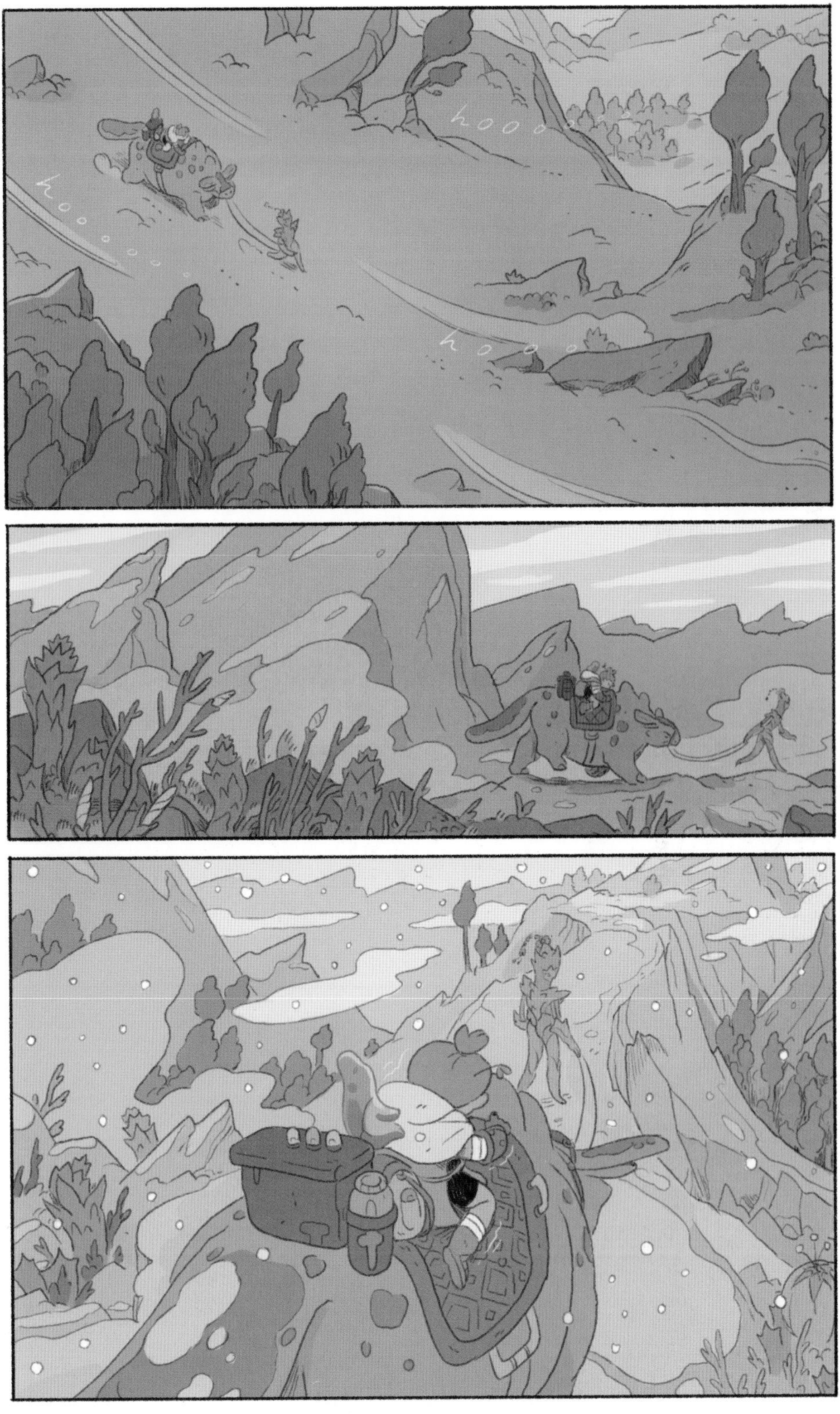
hoooooo
hoooo
hoooo

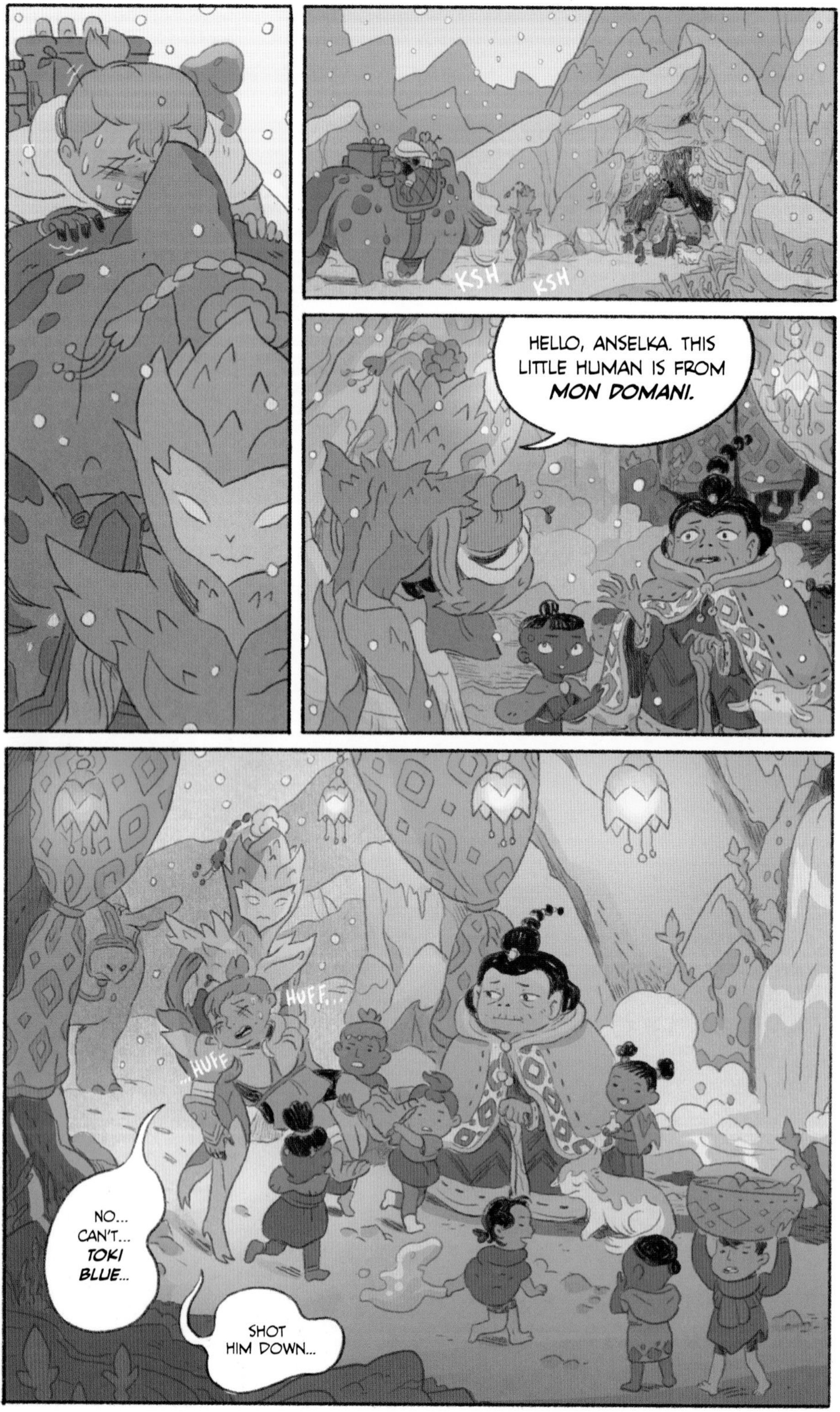
KSH KSH
HELLO, ANSELKA. THIS LITTLE HUMAN IS FROM MON DOMANI.
HUFF...
...HUFF
NO... CAN'T... TOKI BLUE...
SHOT HIM DOWN...

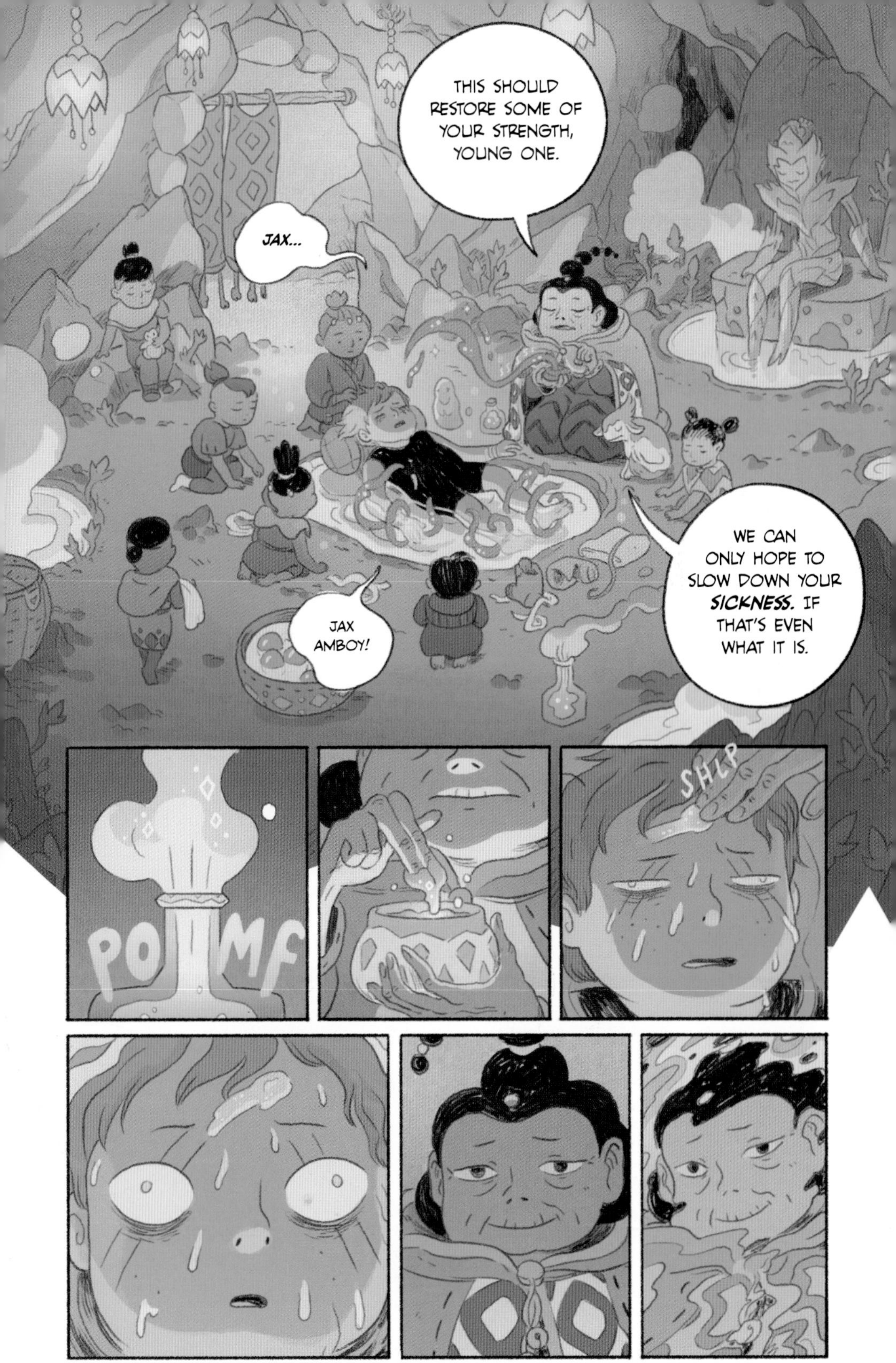
THIS SHOULD RESTORE SOME OF YOUR STRENGTH, YOUNG ONE.
JAX...
WE CAN ONLY HOPE TO SLOW DOWN YOUR *SICKNESS.* IF THAT'S EVEN WHAT IT IS.
JAX AMBOY!
POMF
SHLP

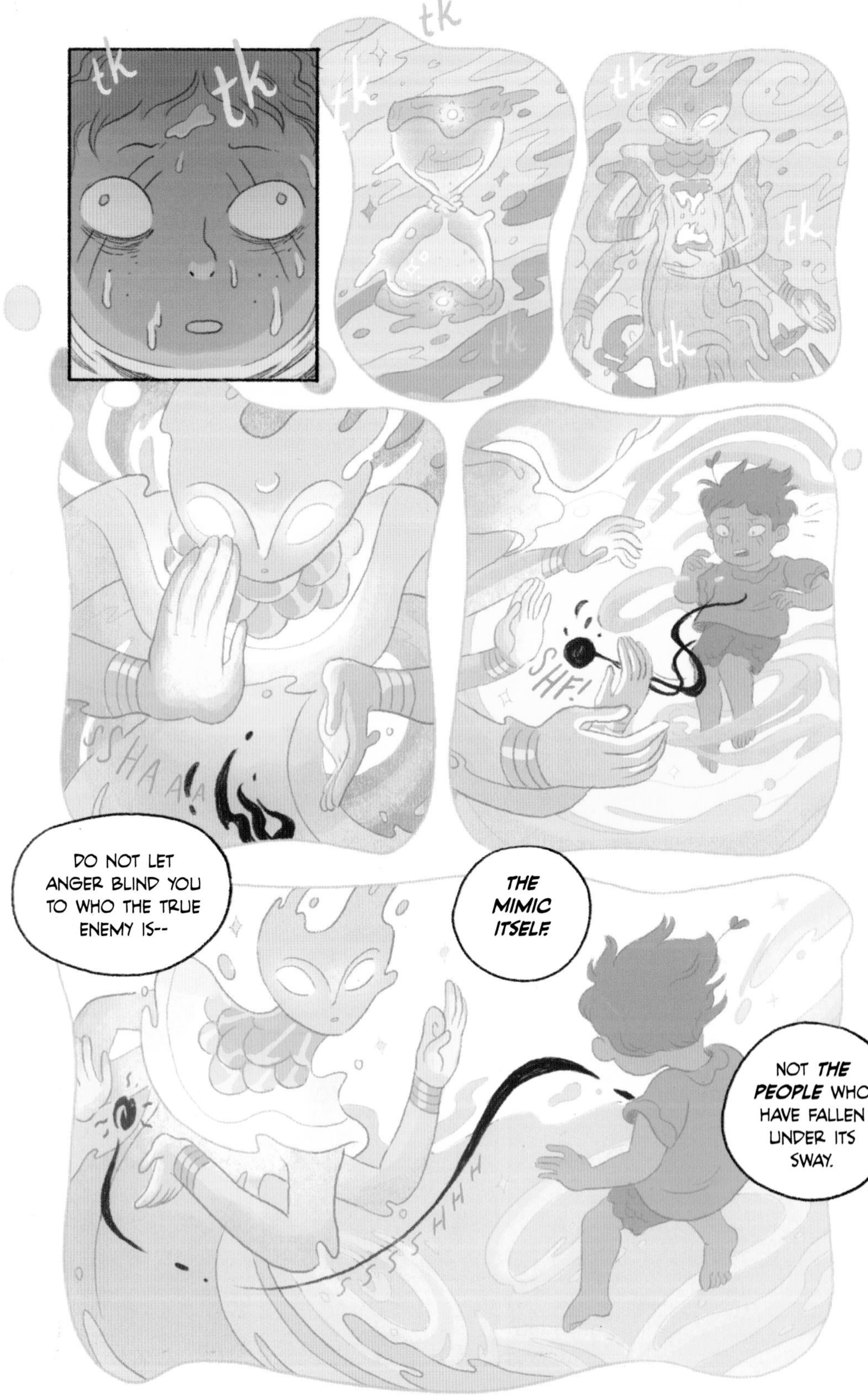
tk
tk
tk
tk
tk
tk
tk
tk
SSHAAA
SHF!
DO NOT LET ANGER BLIND YOU TO WHO THE TRUE ENEMY IS--
THE MIMIC ITSELF.
NOT THE PEOPLE WHO HAVE FALLEN UNDER ITS SWAY.
SSSSSHHHH

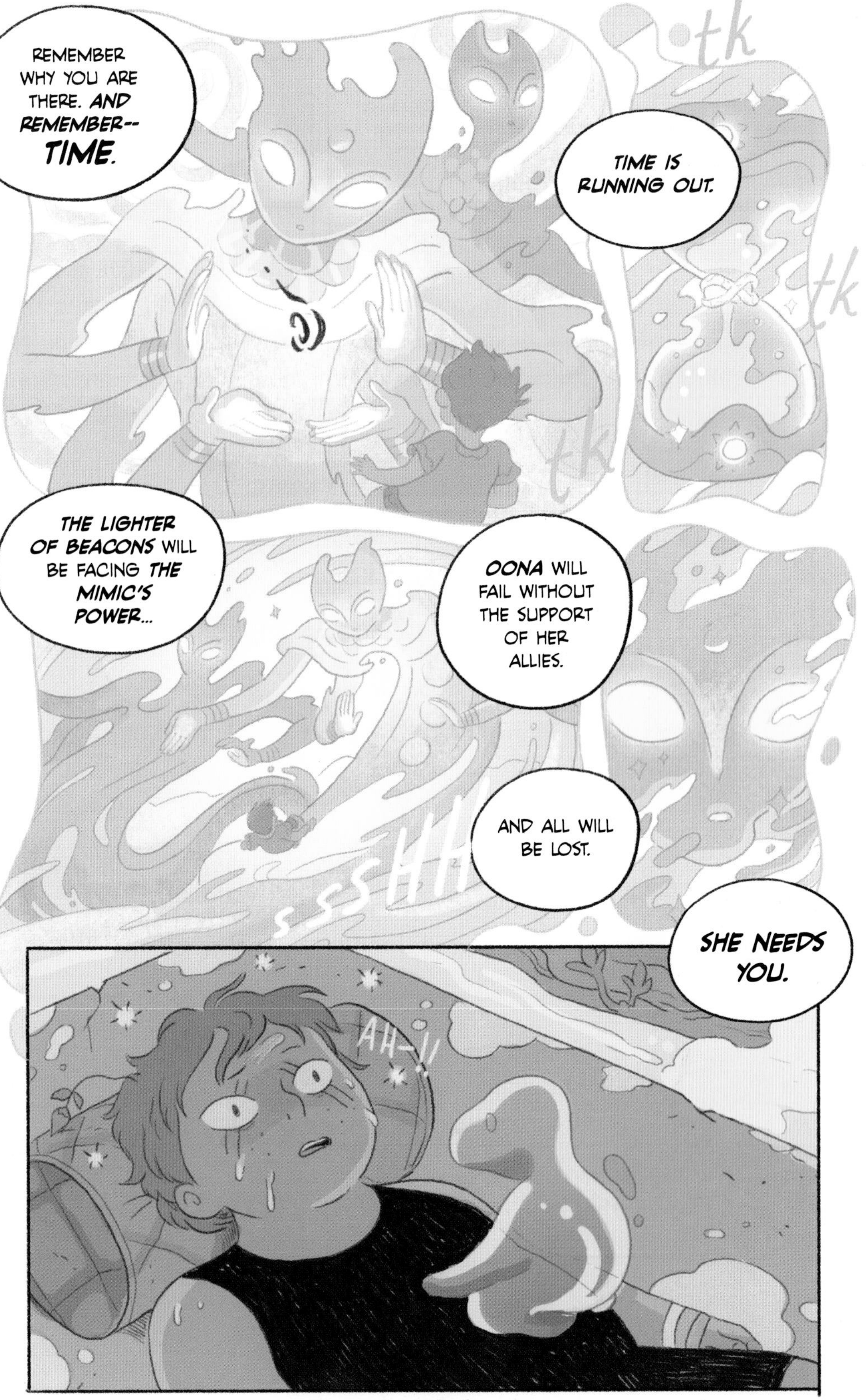

REMEMBER WHY YOU ARE THERE. AND REMEMBER-- TIME.
tk
TIME IS RUNNING OUT.
tk
tk
THE LIGHTER OF BEACONS WILL BE FACING THE MIMIC'S POWER...
OONA WILL FAIL WITHOUT THE SUPPORT OF HER ALLIES.
AND ALL WILL BE LOST.
SSSHH
SHE NEEDS YOU.
AH-!!

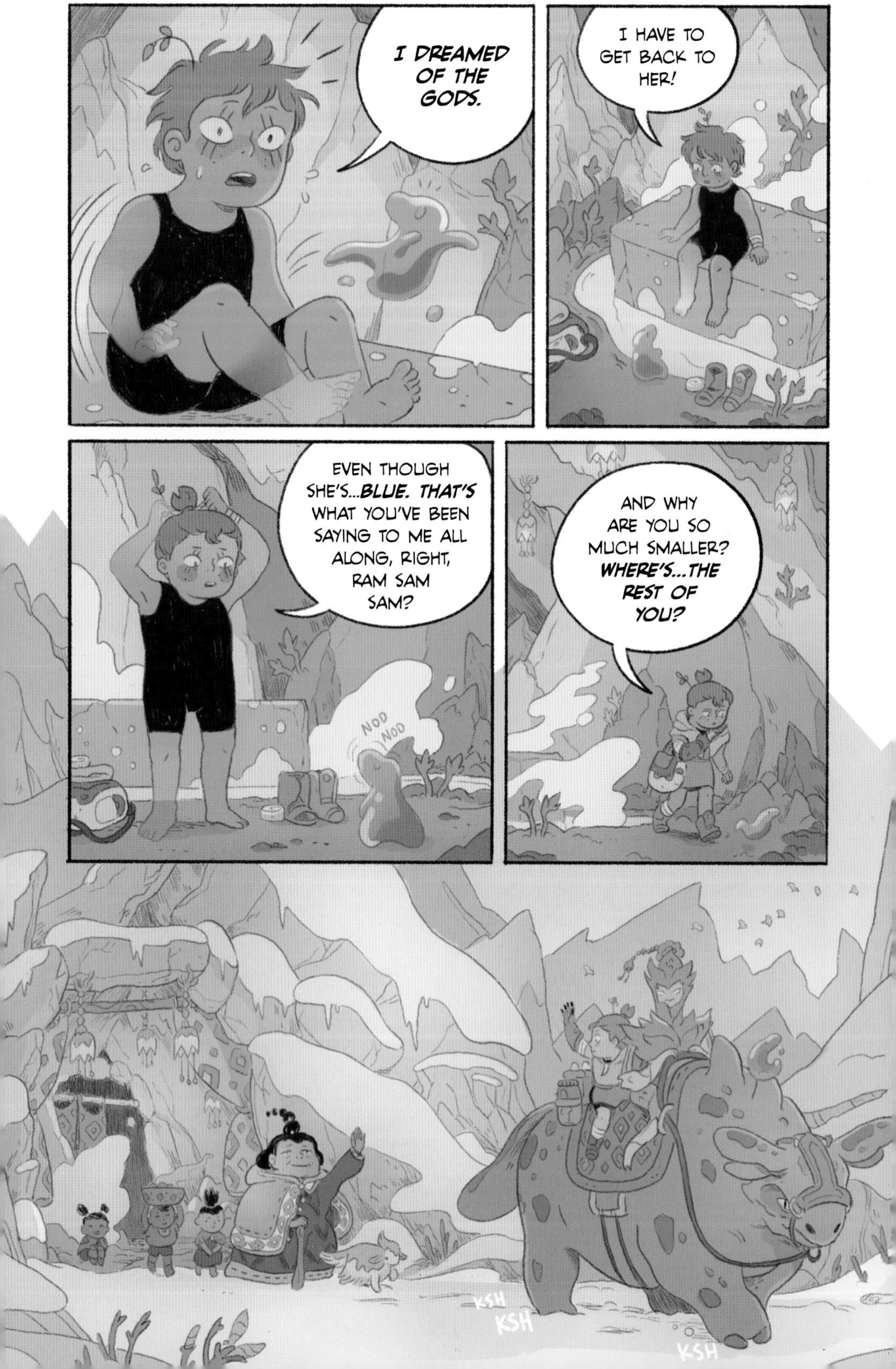

I DREAMED OF THE GODS.
I HAVE TO GET BACK TO HER!
EVEN THOUGH SHE'S...BLUE. THAT'S WHAT YOU'VE BEEN SAYING TO ME ALL ALONG, RIGHT, RAM SAM SAM?
NOD NOD
AND WHY ARE YOU SO MUCH SMALLER? WHERE'S...THE REST OF YOU?
KSH KSH
KSH

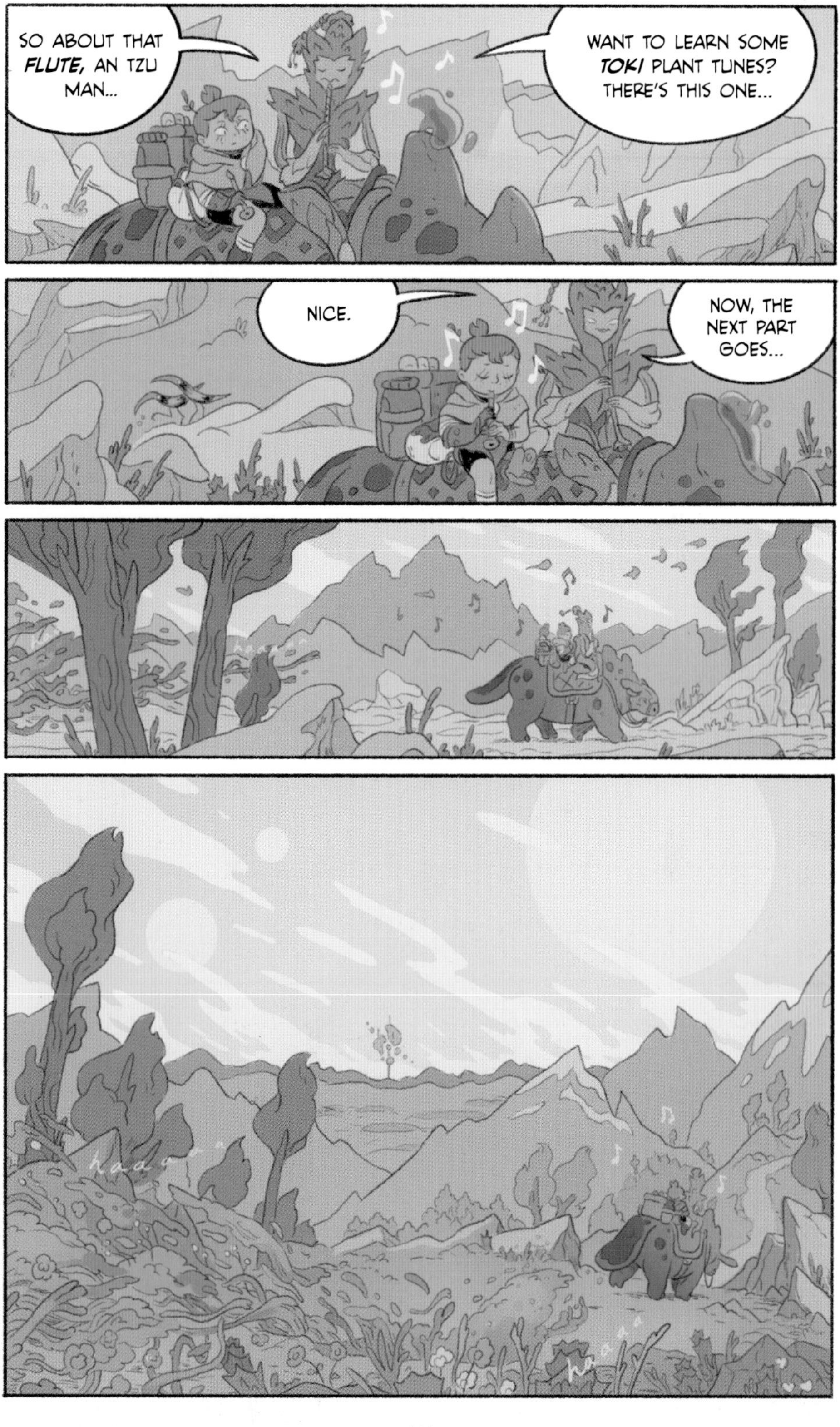
SO ABOUT THAT FLUTE, AN TZU MAN...
WANT TO LEARN SOME TOKI PLANT TUNES? THERE'S THIS ONE...
NICE.
NOW, THE NEXT PART GOES...

Chapter 9

THE QUEEN'S BONES

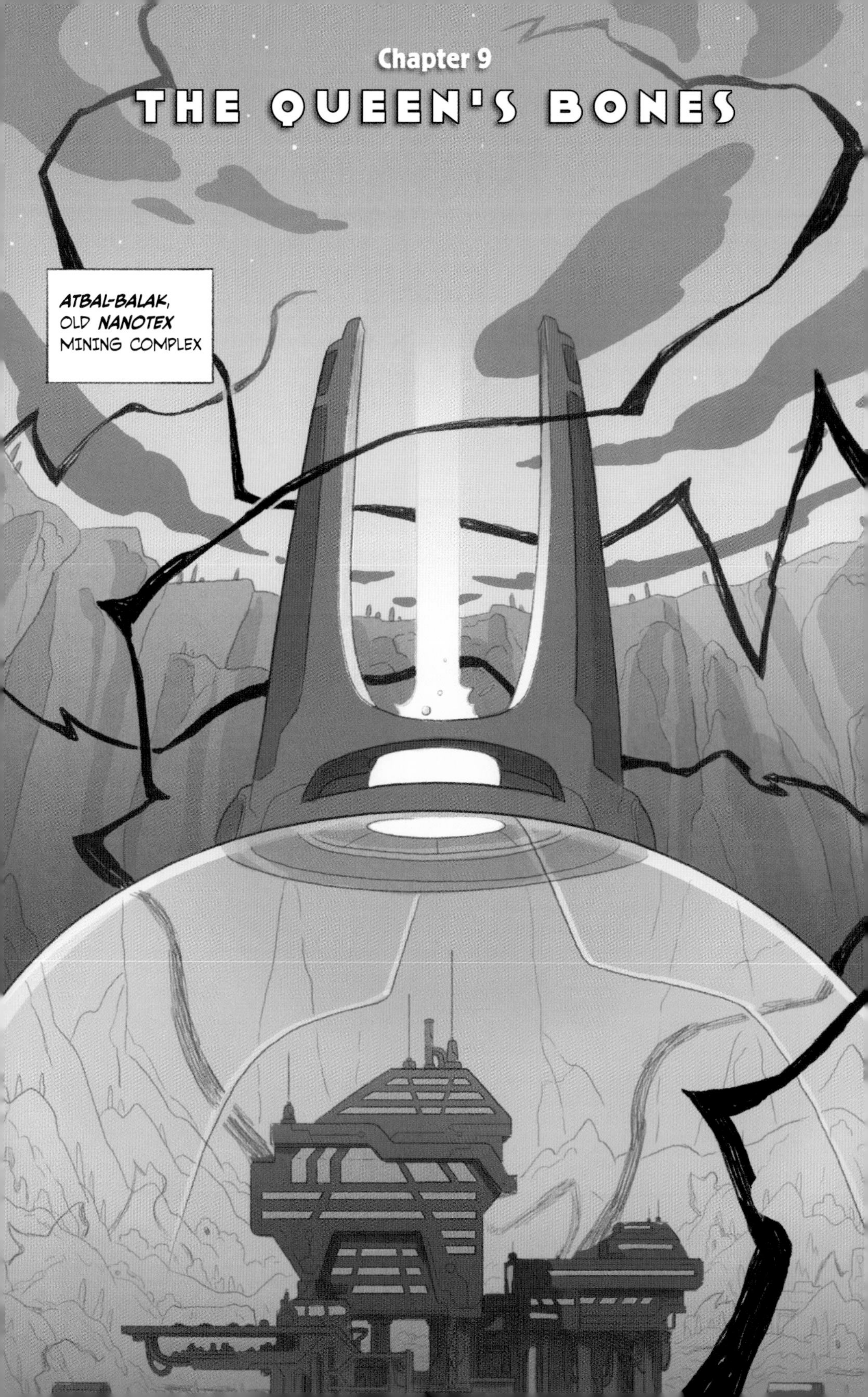
ATBAL-BALAK, OLD NANOTEX MINING COMPLEX

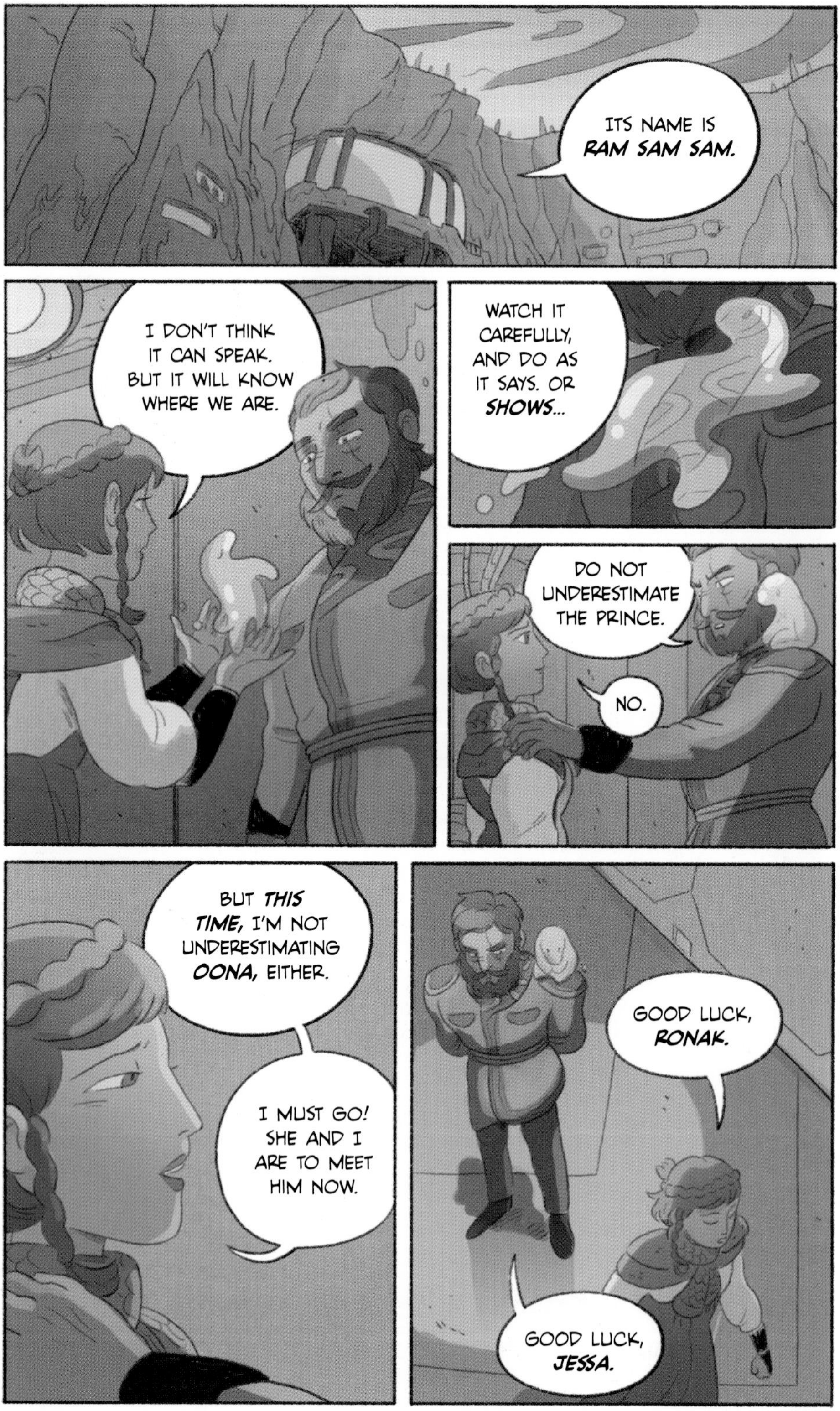
ITS NAME IS *RAM SAM SAM.*
I DON'T THINK IT CAN SPEAK. BUT IT WILL KNOW WHERE WE ARE.
WATCH IT CAREFULLY, AND DO AS IT SAYS. OR *SHOWS*...
DO NOT UNDERESTIMATE THE PRINCE.
NO.
BUT *THIS TIME,* I'M NOT UNDERESTIMATING *OONA,* EITHER.
I MUST GO! SHE AND I ARE TO MEET HIM NOW.
GOOD LUCK, *RONAK.*
GOOD LUCK, *JESSA.*

AND HERE IS *JESSA.* THE SISTERS REUNITED!

ON WE GO, NOW, TO THE HEART OF *ATBAL-BALAK!* LET'S NOT KEEP THE GREAT QUEEN WAITING, SHALL WE?

HER *BONES* ARE THERE ALREADY.

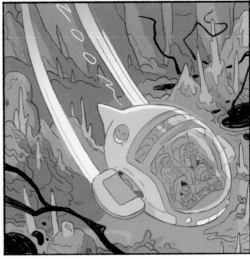

ZOOM

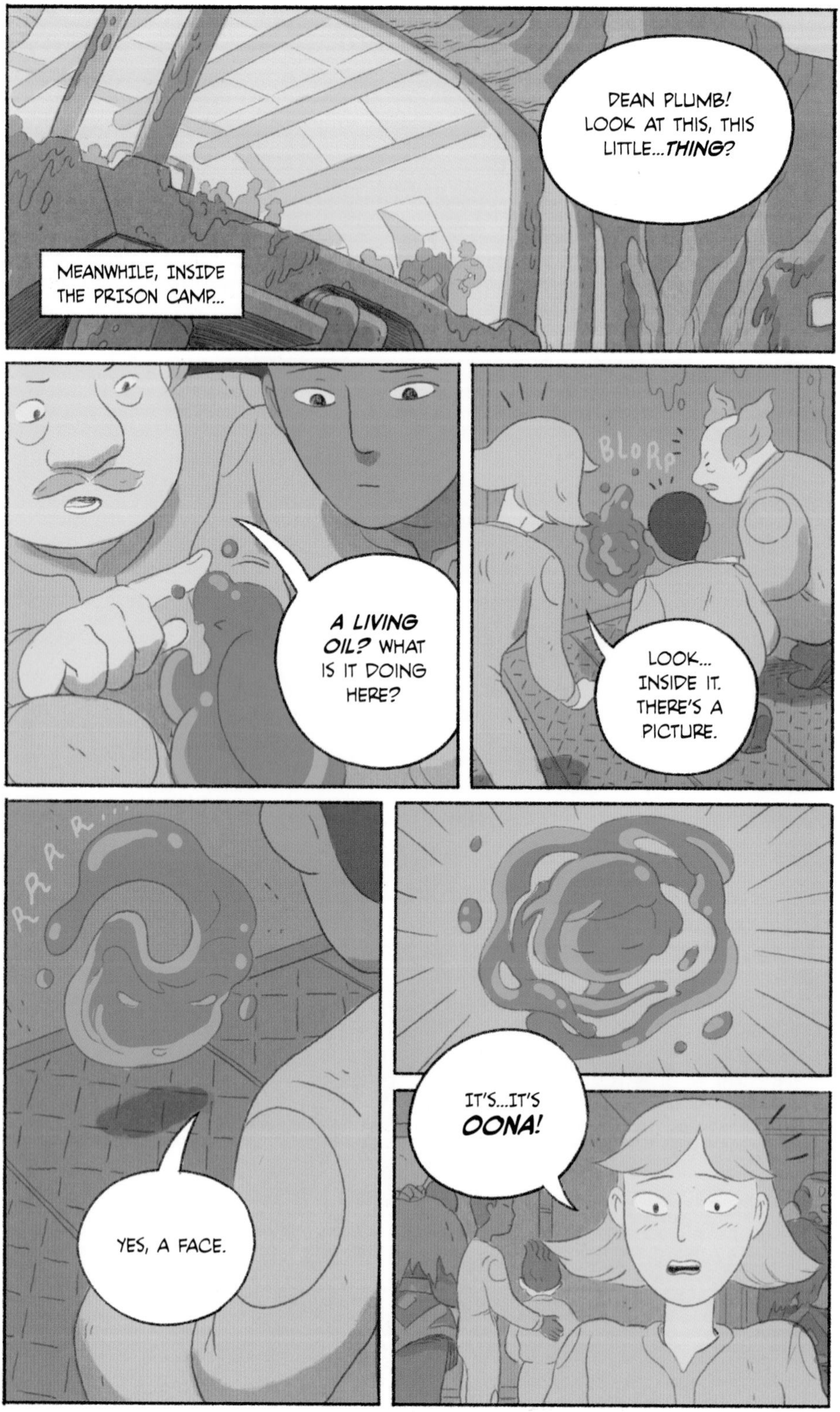
DEAN PLUMB! LOOK AT THIS, THIS LITTLE...THING?
MEANWHILE, INSIDE THE PRISON CAMP...
A LIVING OIL? WHAT IS IT DOING HERE?
BLORP
LOOK... INSIDE IT. THERE'S A PICTURE.
RRRR...
YES, A FACE.
IT'S...IT'S OONA!

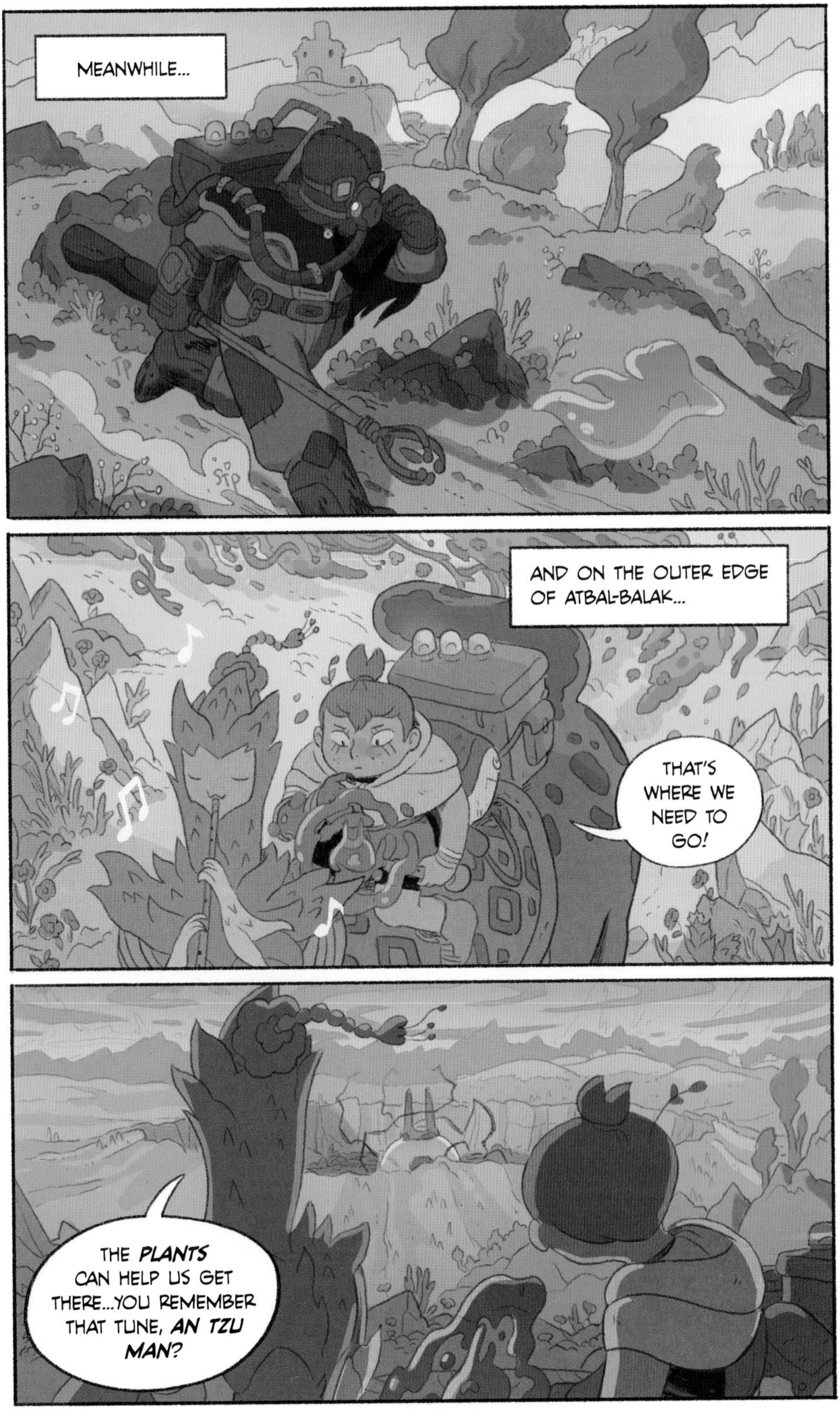
MEANWHILE...
AND ON THE OUTER EDGE OF ATBAL-BALAK...
THAT'S WHERE WE NEED TO GO!
THE *PLANTS* CAN HELP US GET THERE...YOU REMEMBER THAT TUNE, *AN TZU MAN*?

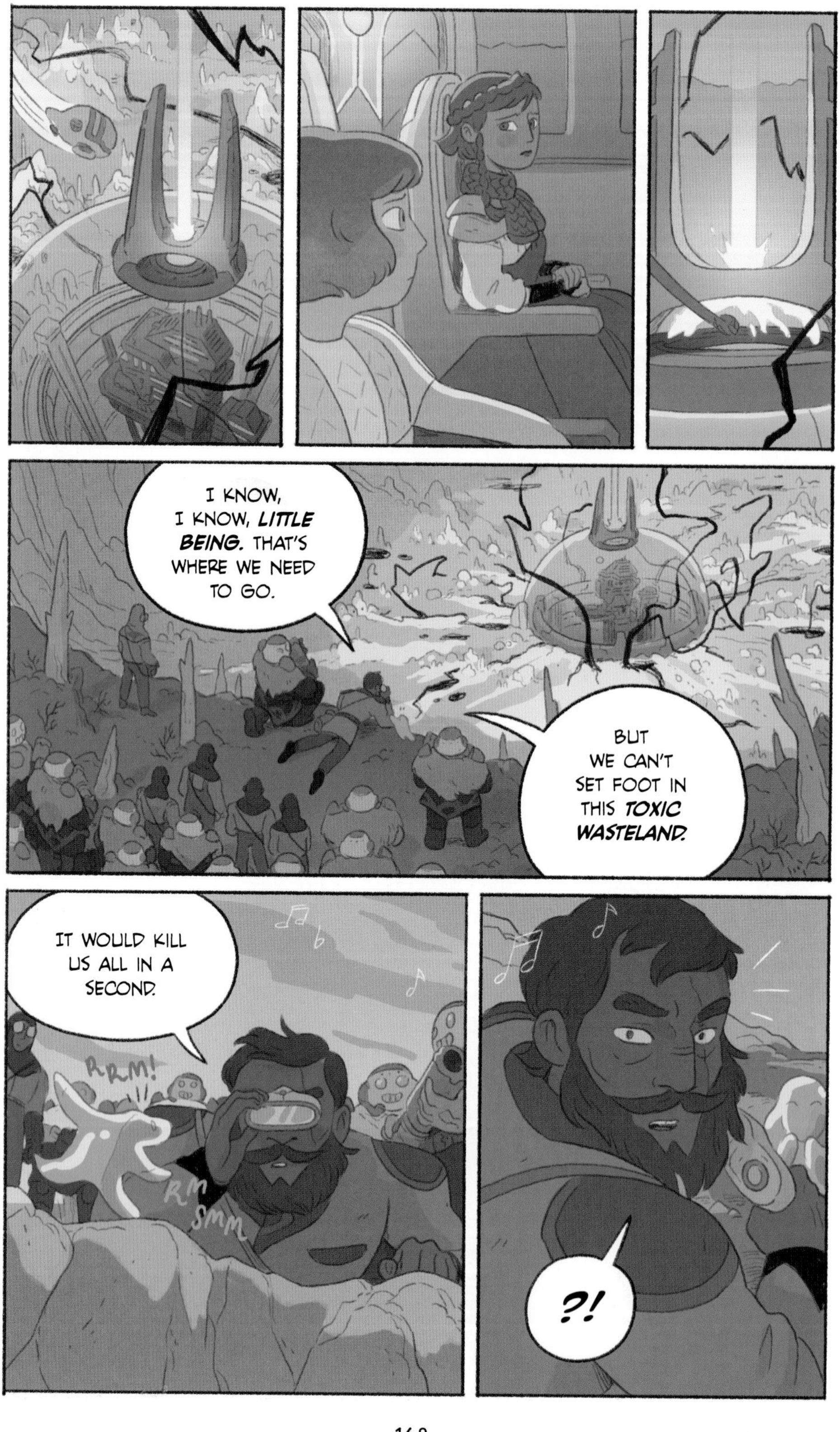

I KNOW, I KNOW, LITTLE BEING. THAT'S WHERE WE NEED TO GO.
BUT WE CAN'T SET FOOT IN THIS TOXIC WASTELAND.
IT WOULD KILL US ALL IN A SECOND.
RRM!
?!

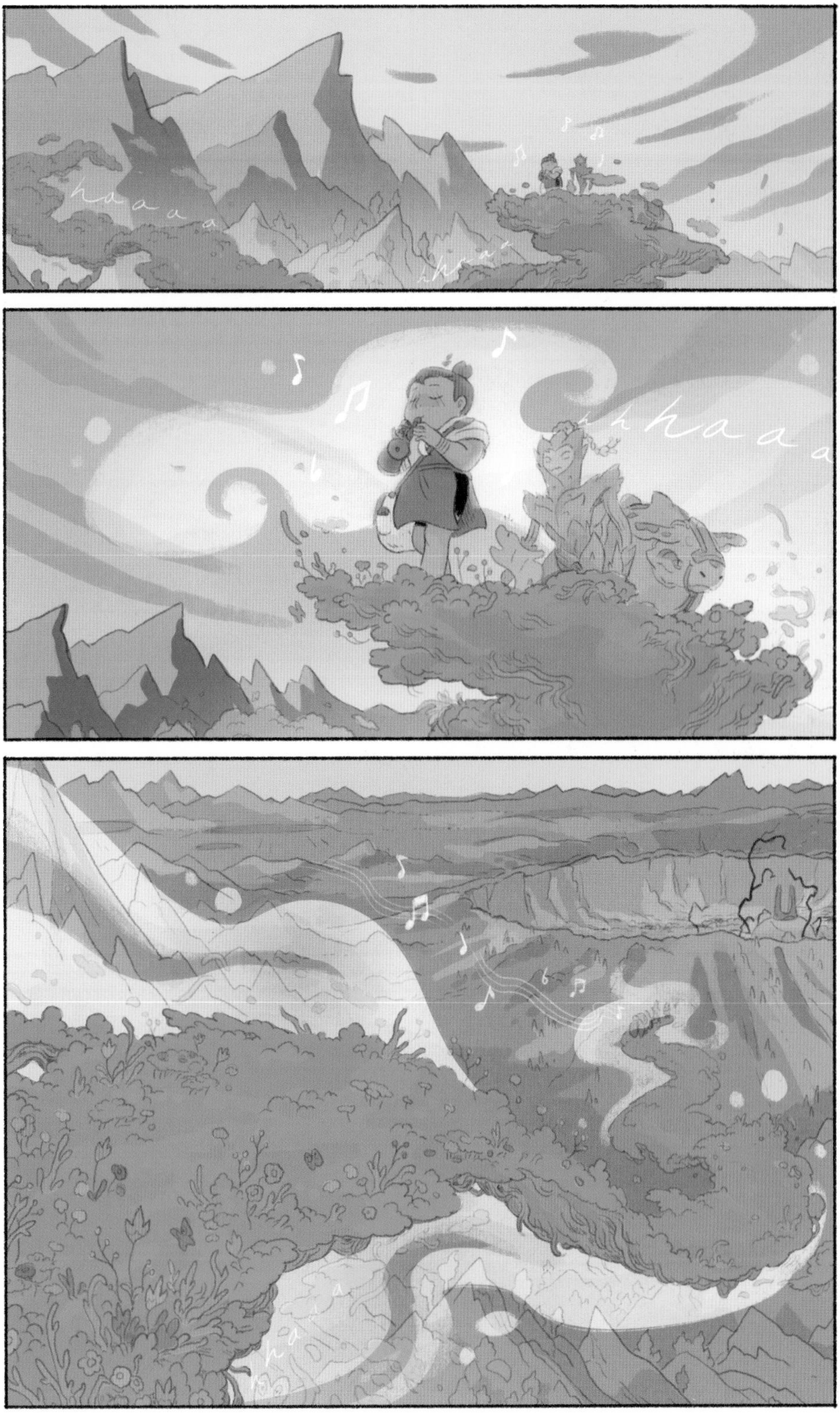

haaaa
hhaaa

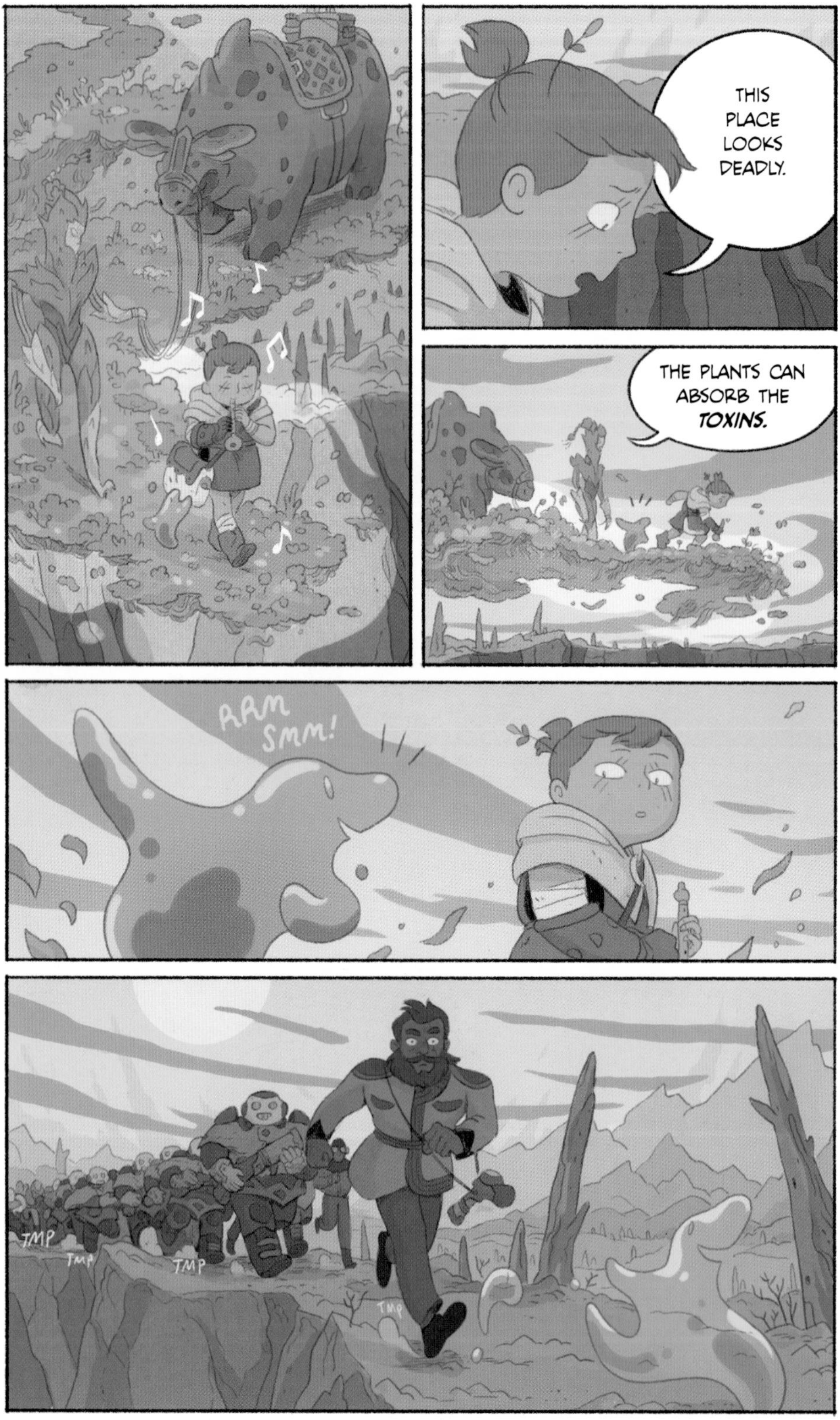
THIS PLACE LOOKS DEADLY.
THE PLANTS CAN ABSORB THE *TOXINS.*
RRM SMM!
TMP
TMP
TMP
TMP

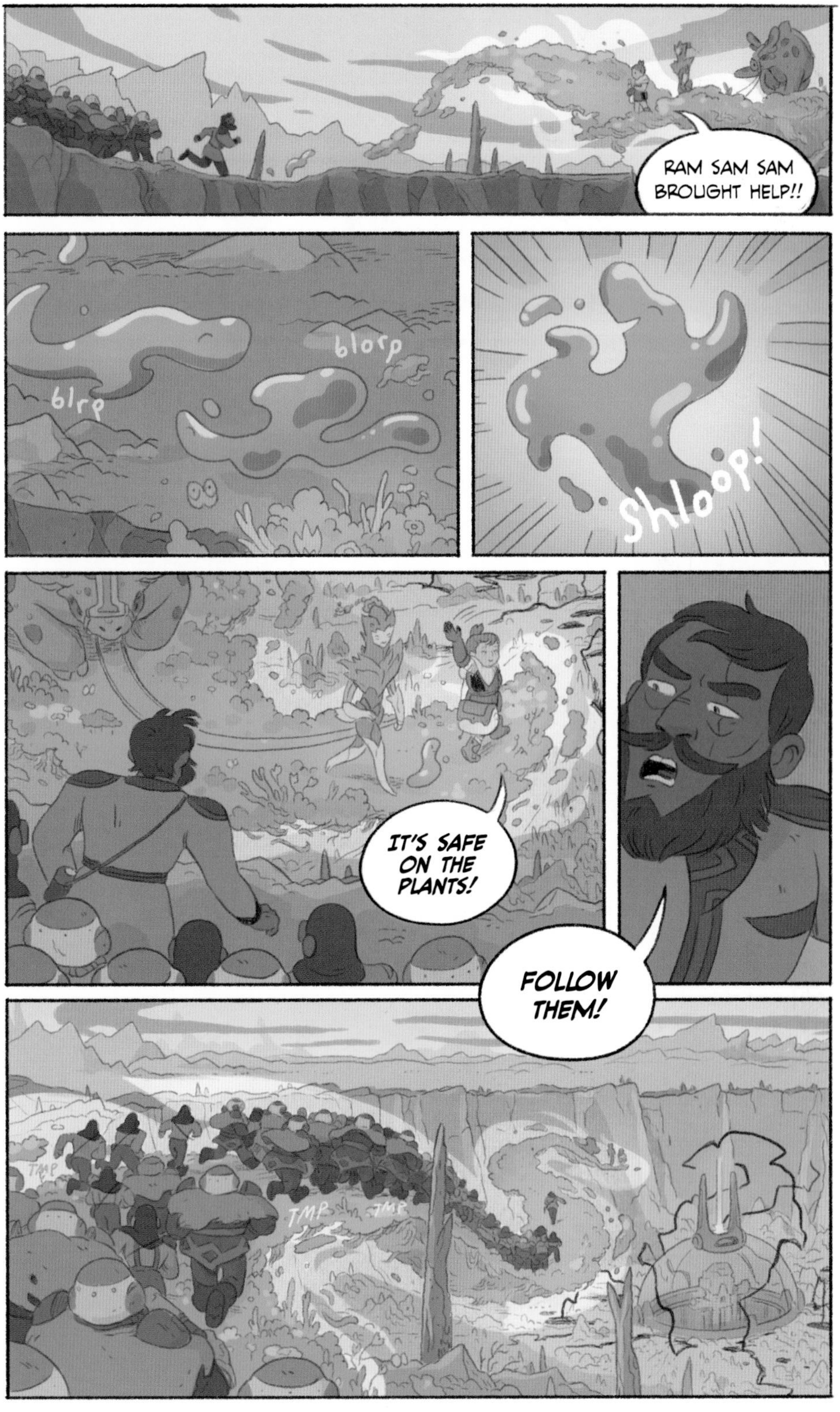
RAM SAM SAM BROUGHT HELP!!
blorp
blrp
Shloop!
IT'S SAFE ON THE PLANTS!
FOLLOW THEM!
TMP
TMP TMP

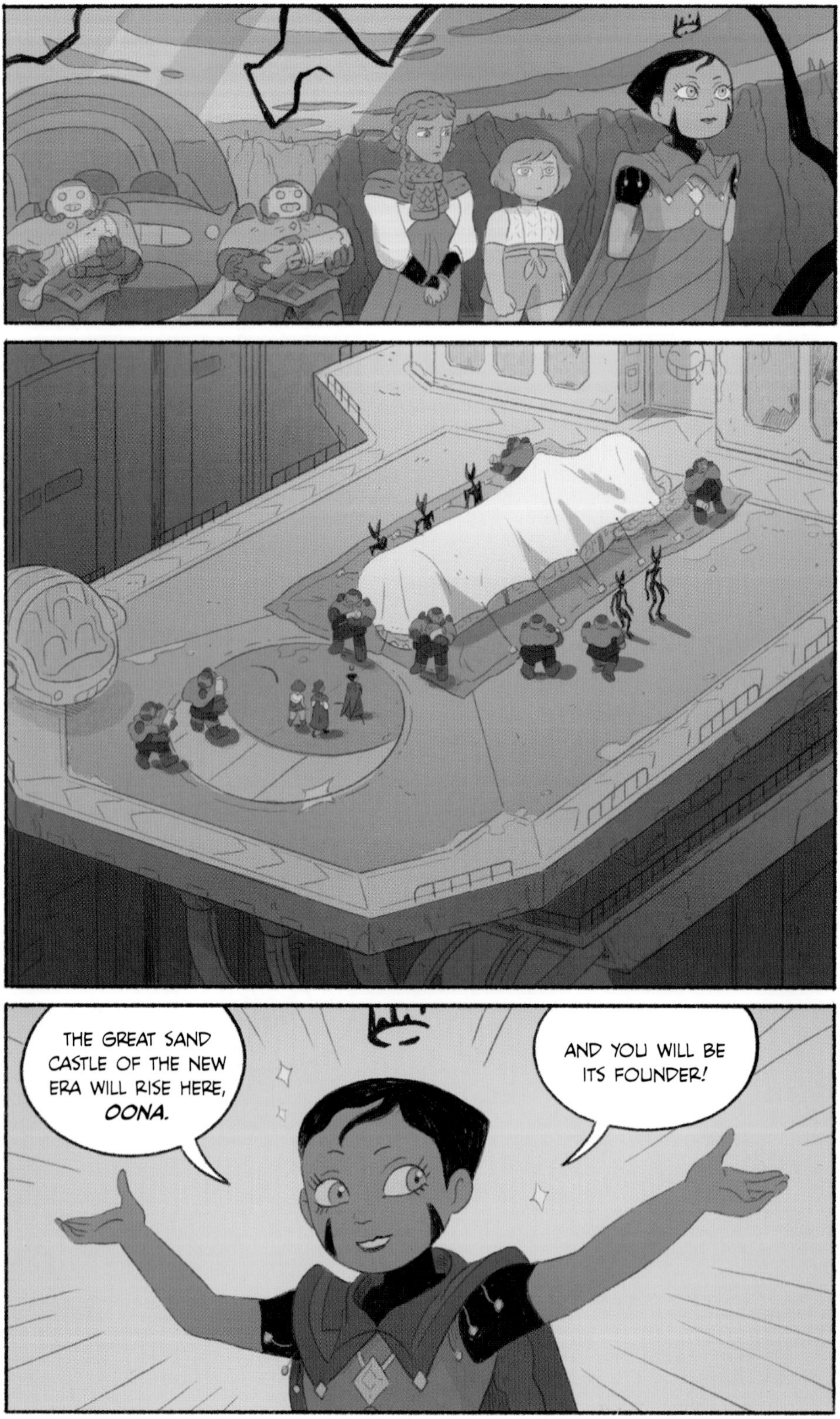
THE GREAT SAND CASTLE OF THE NEW ERA WILL RISE HERE, OONA.
AND YOU WILL BE ITS FOUNDER!

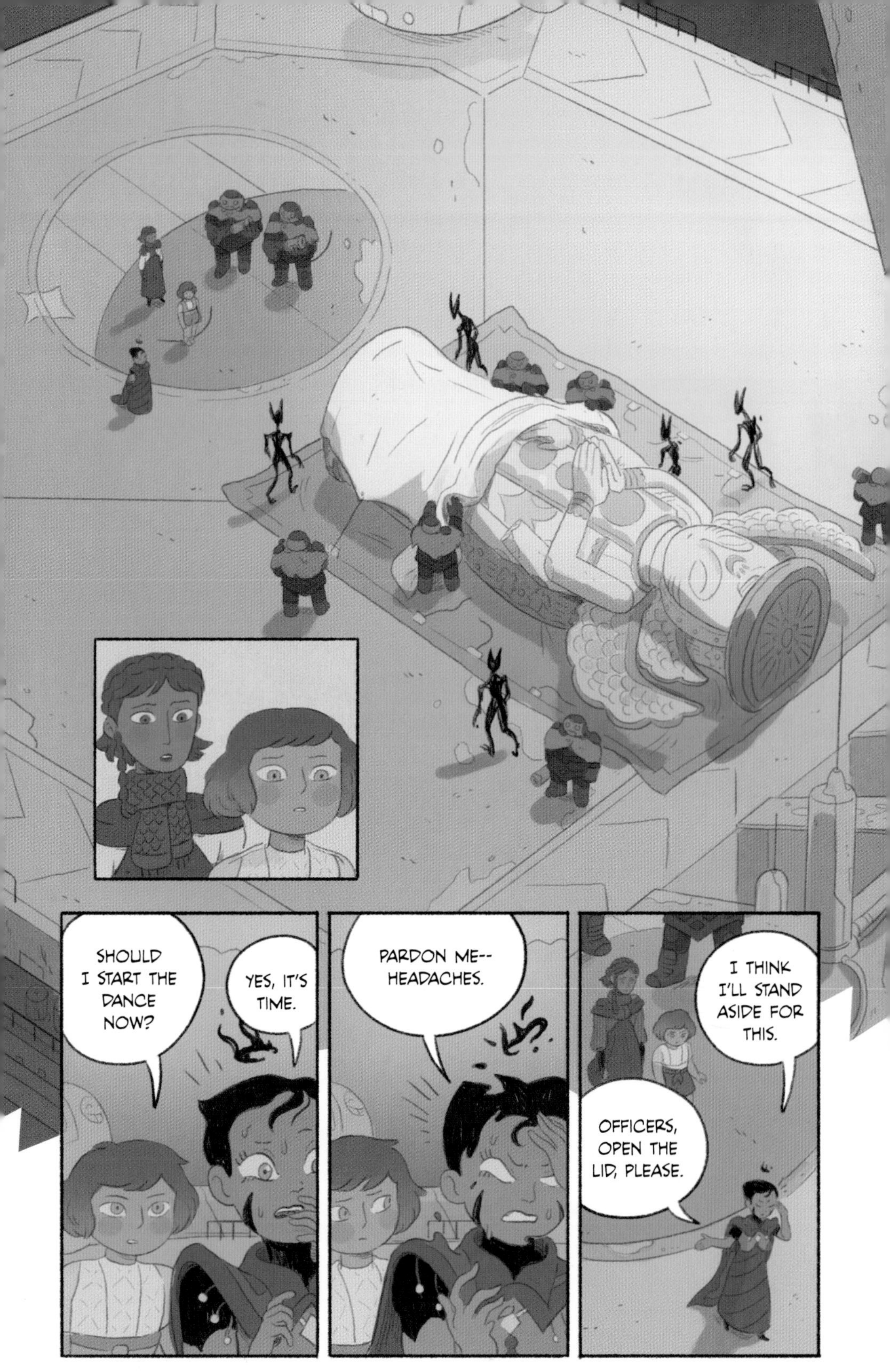
SHOULD I START THE DANCE NOW?
YES, IT'S TIME.
PARDON ME-- HEADACHES.
I THINK I'LL STAND ASIDE FOR THIS.
OFFICERS, OPEN THE LID, PLEASE.

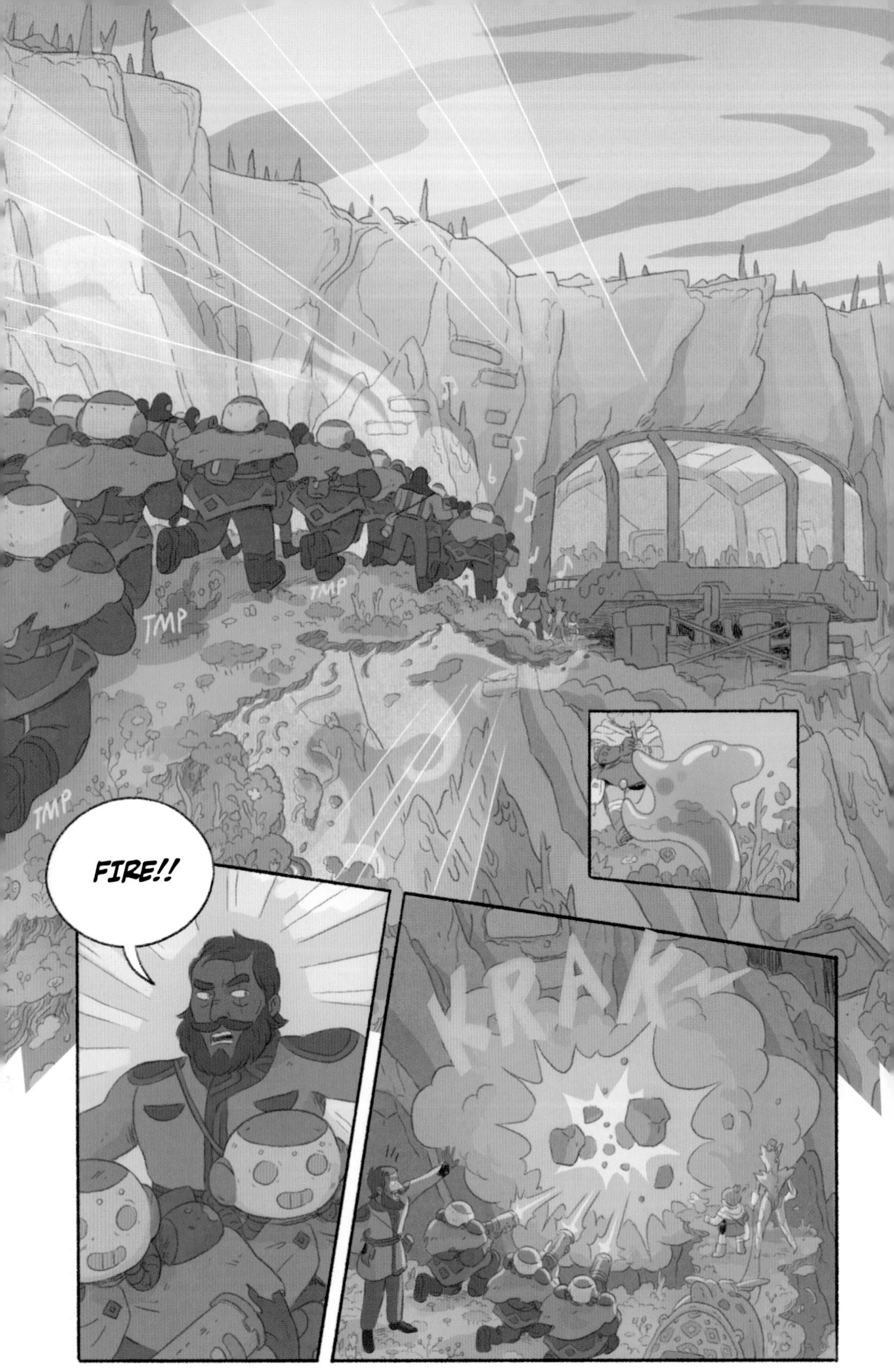
TMP
TMP
TMP
FIRE!!
KRAK

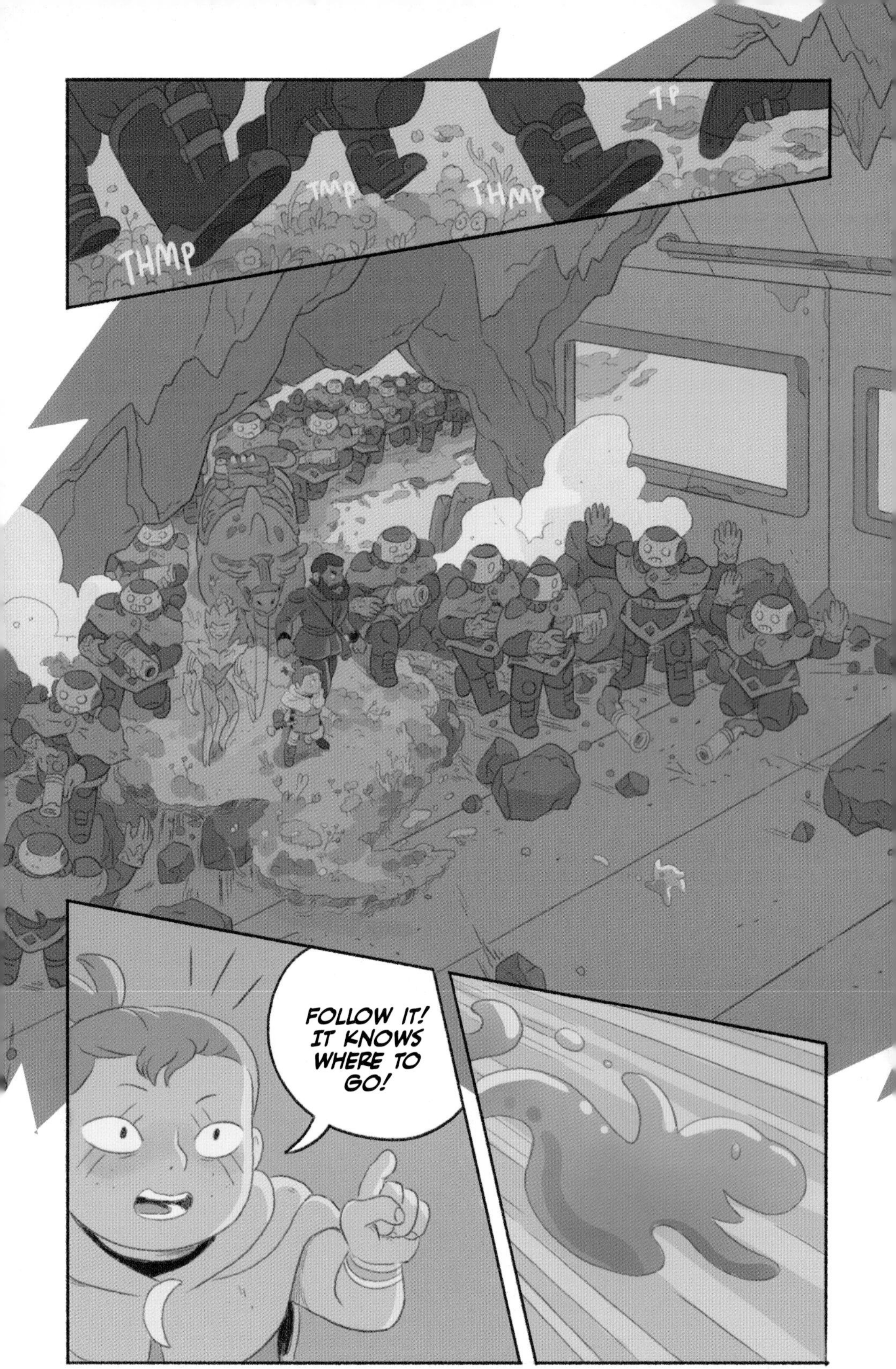
THMP
TMP
THMP
TP
FOLLOW IT! IT KNOWS WHERE TO GO!

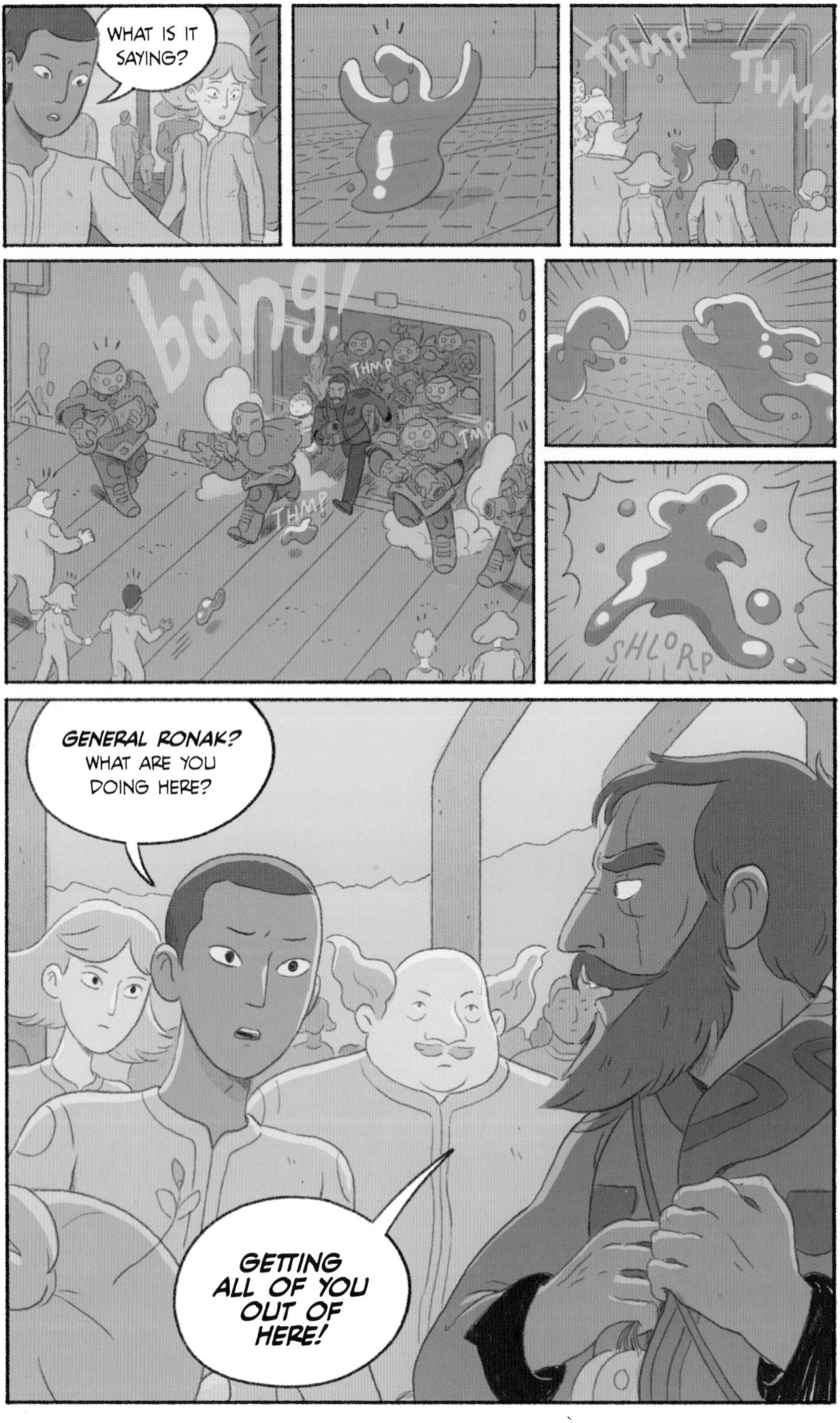
WHAT IS IT SAYING?
THMP THMP
bang!
THMP
TMP
THMP
SHLORP
GENERAL RONAK? WHAT ARE YOU DOING HERE?
GETTING ALL OF YOU OUT OF HERE!

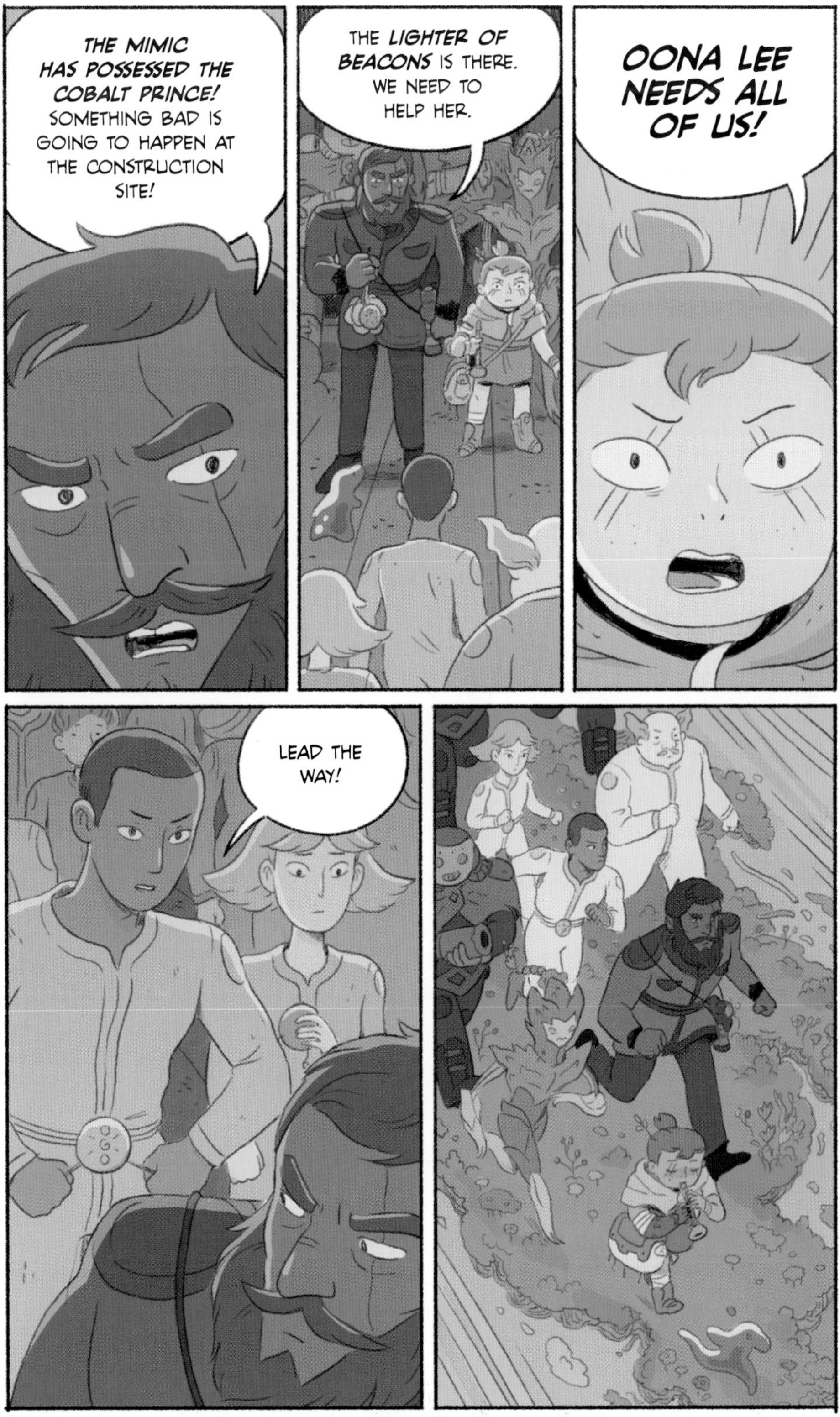
THE MIMIC HAS POSSESSED THE COBALT PRINCE! SOMETHING BAD IS GOING TO HAPPEN AT THE CONSTRUCTION SITE!
THE LIGHTER OF BEACONS IS THERE. WE NEED TO HELP HER.
OONA LEE NEEDS ALL OF US!
LEAD THE WAY!

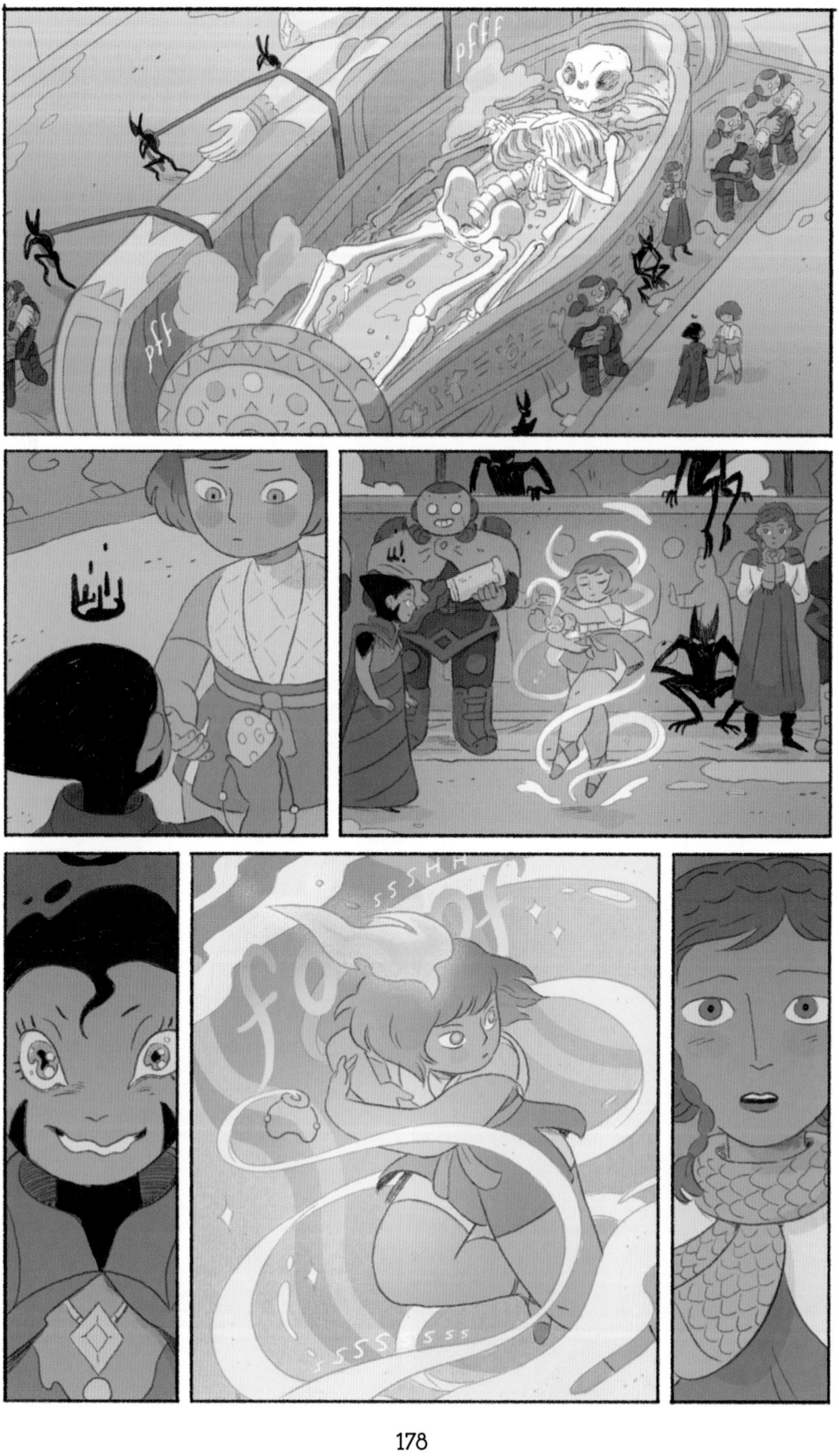
pfff
pff

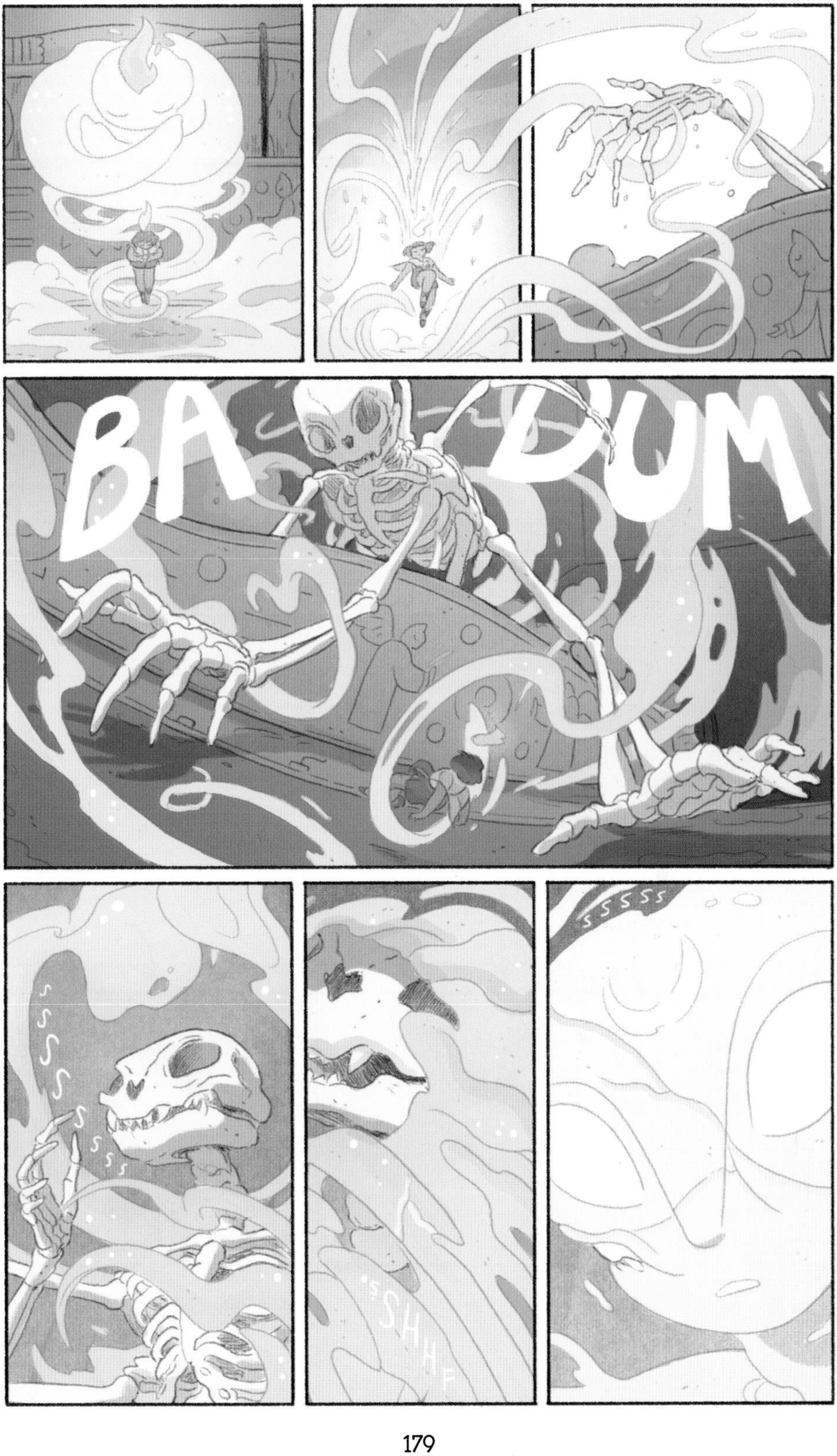
BA DUM
ssSSSSssss
sSHHF
ssssss

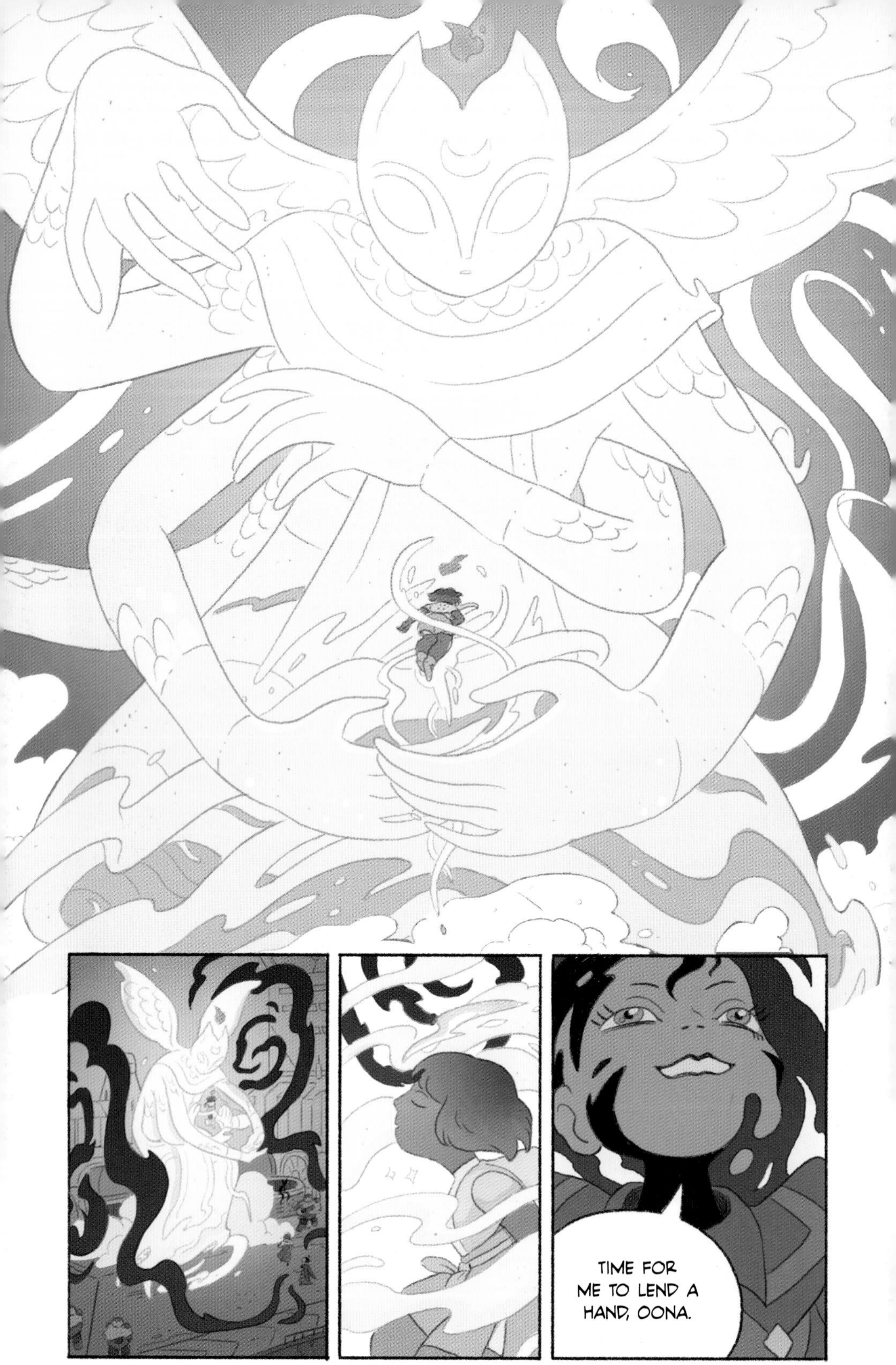
TIME FOR
ME TO LEND A
HAND, OONA.

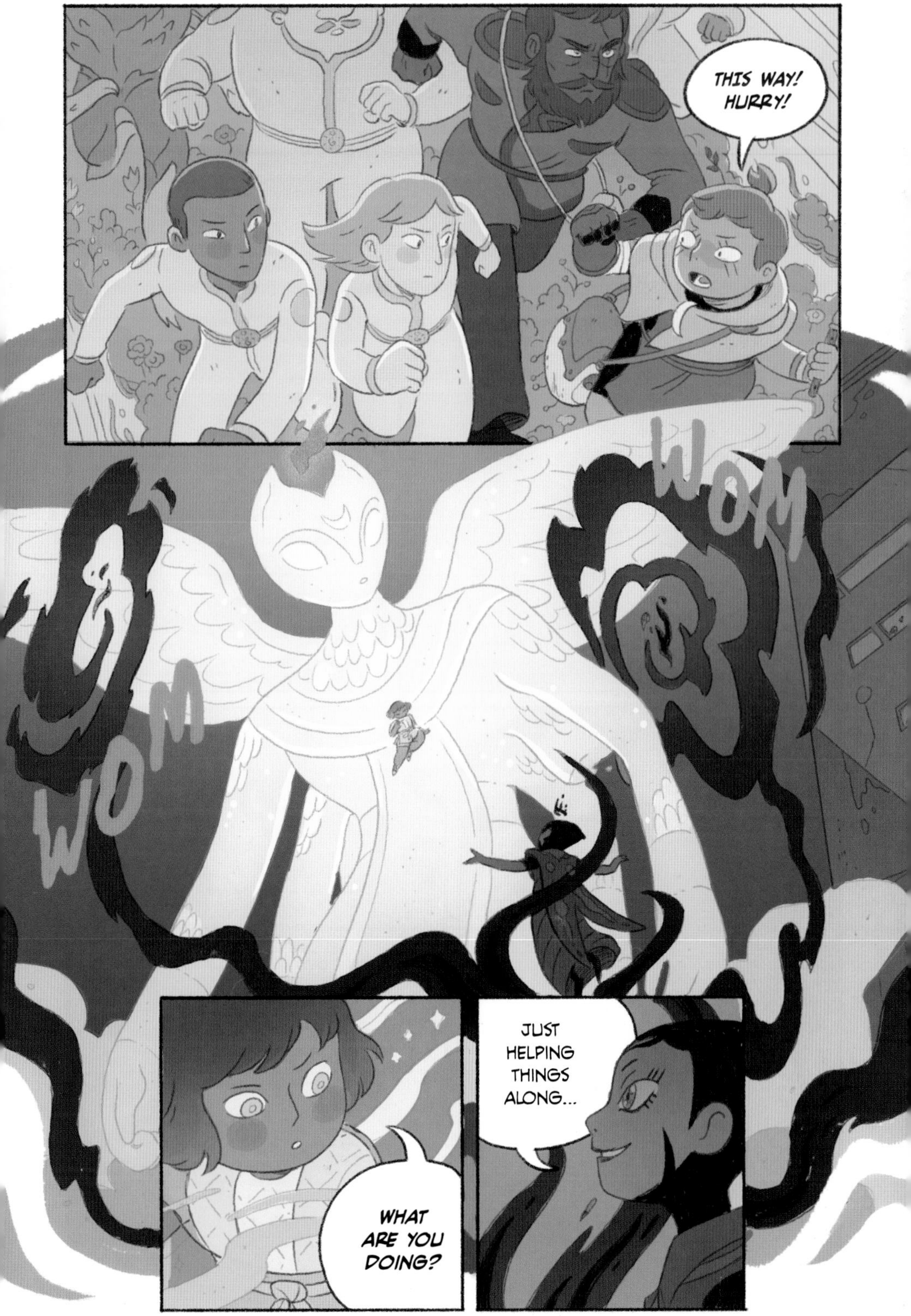
THIS WAY! HURRY!
WOM
WOM
WHAT ARE YOU DOING?
JUST HELPING THINGS ALONG...

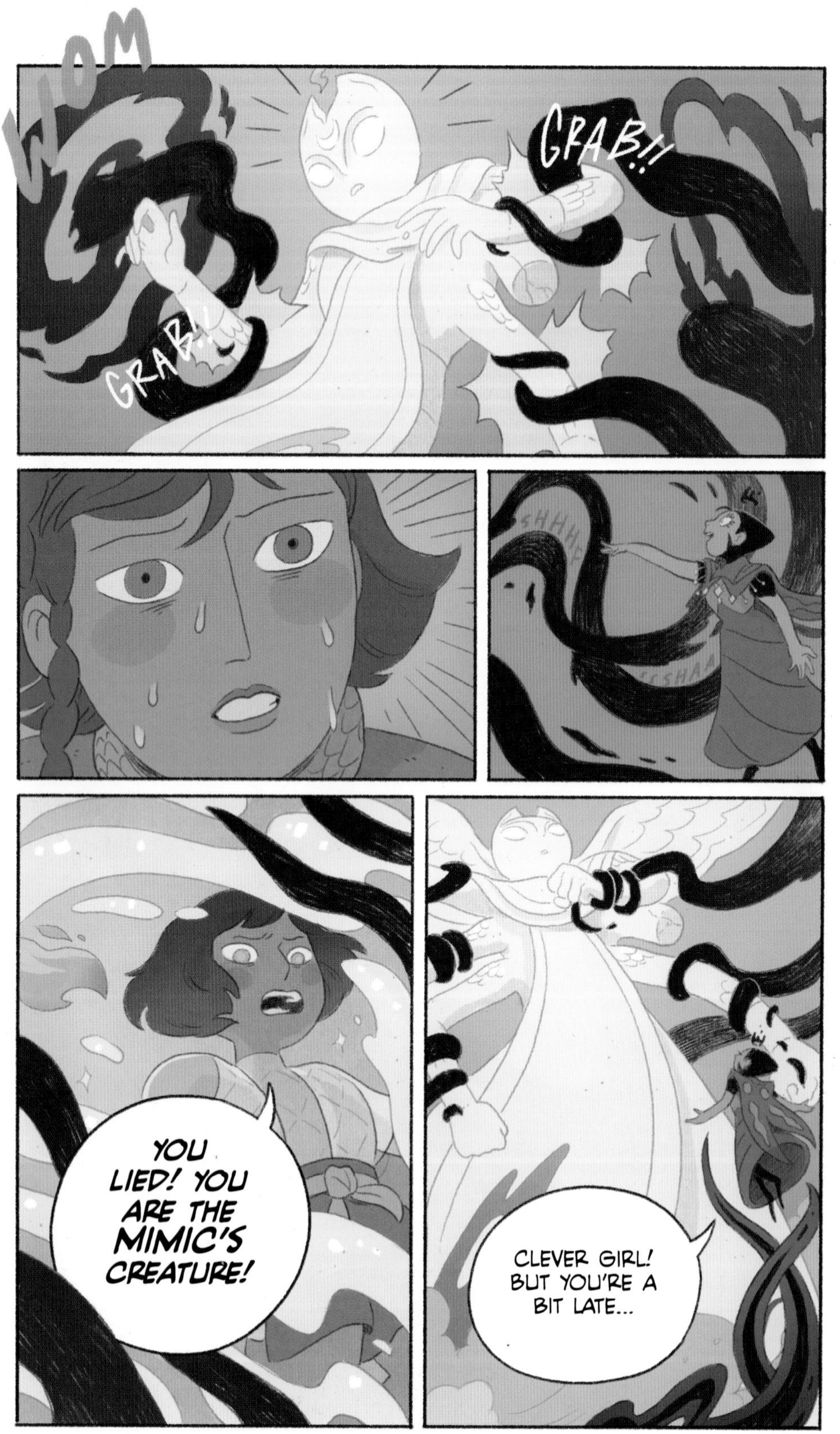
WOM
GRAB!!
GRAB!!
YOU LIED! YOU ARE THE MIMIC'S CREATURE!
CLEVER GIRL! BUT YOU'RE A BIT LATE...

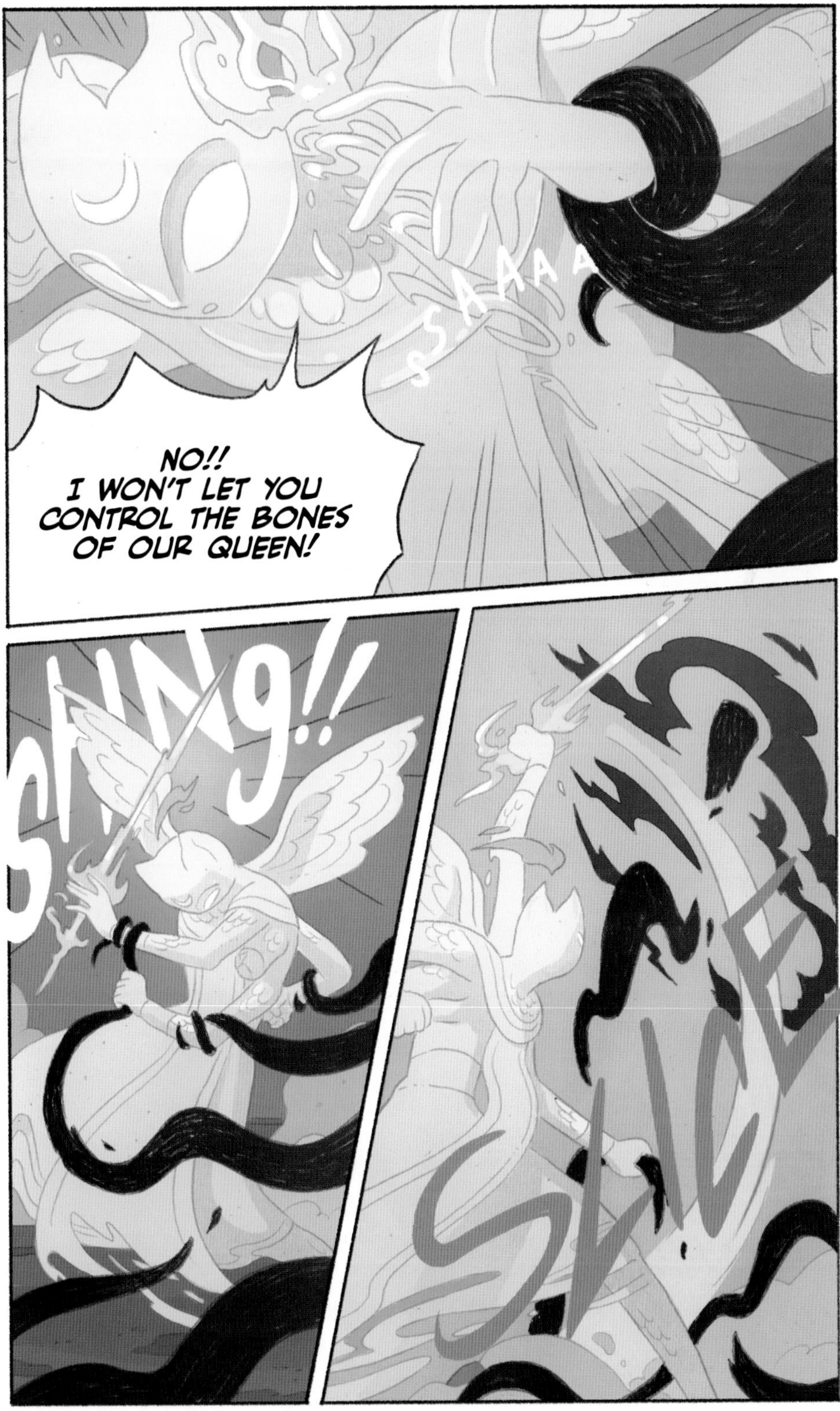
SSAAAA
NO!! I WON'T LET YOU CONTROL THE BONES OF OUR QUEEN!
SHING!!
SLICE

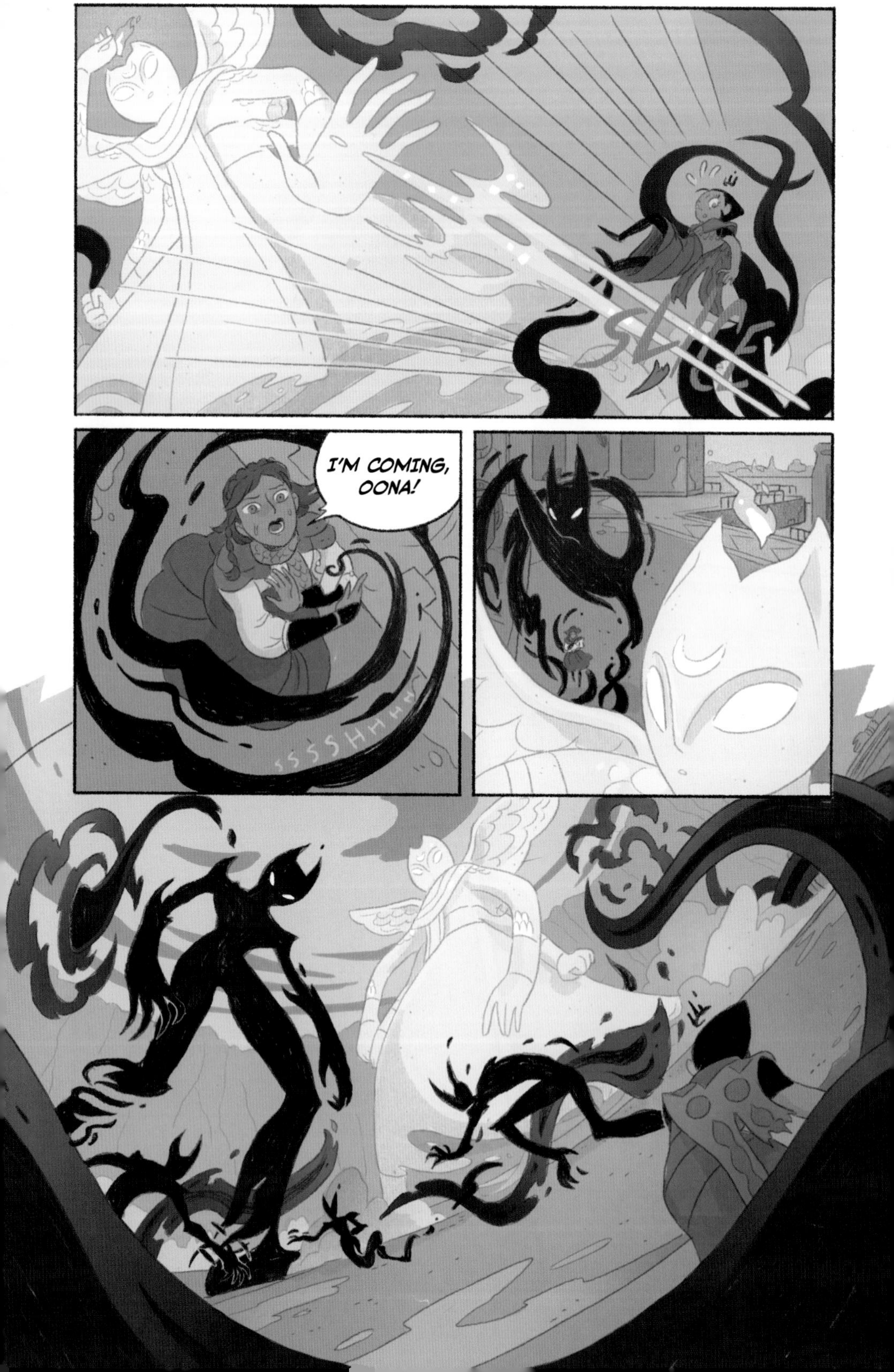
SLICE
I'M COMING, OONA!
SSSSHHHHH

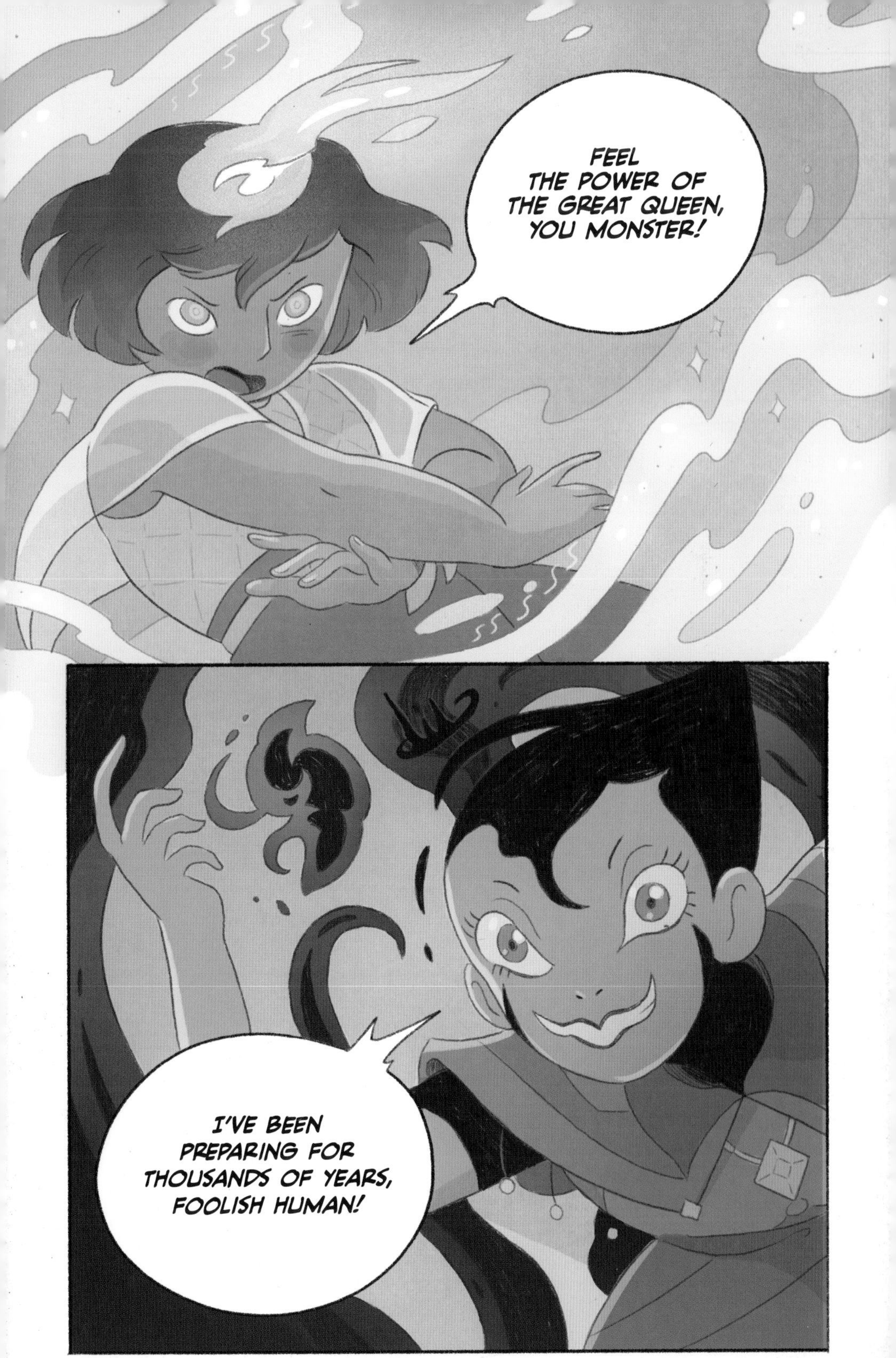
FEEL THE POWER OF THE GREAT QUEEN, YOU MONSTER!
I'VE BEEN PREPARING FOR THOUSANDS OF YEARS, FOOLISH HUMAN!

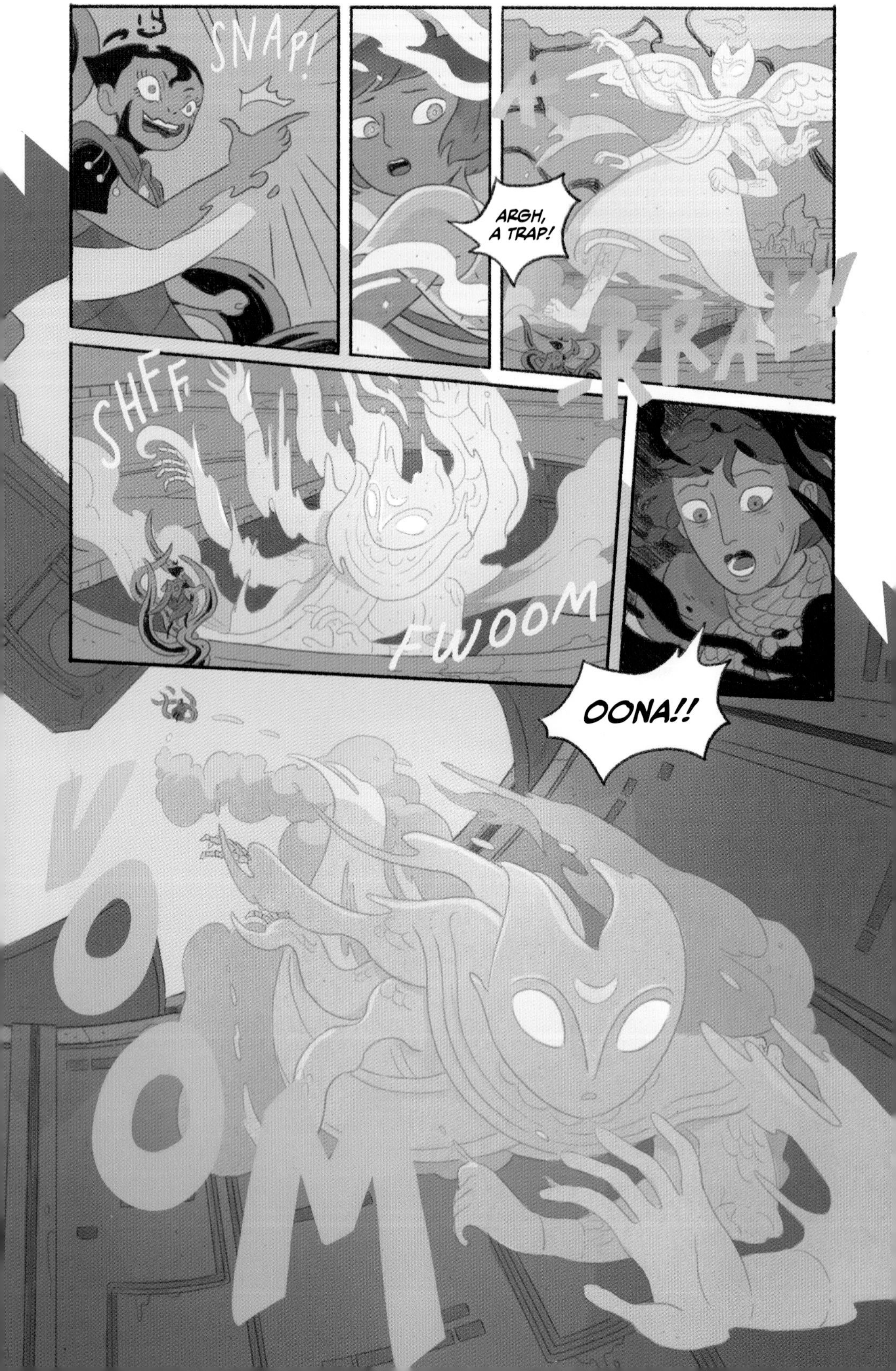
SNAP!
ARGH, A TRAP!
KRAK!
SHFF
FWOOM
OONA!!
VOOM

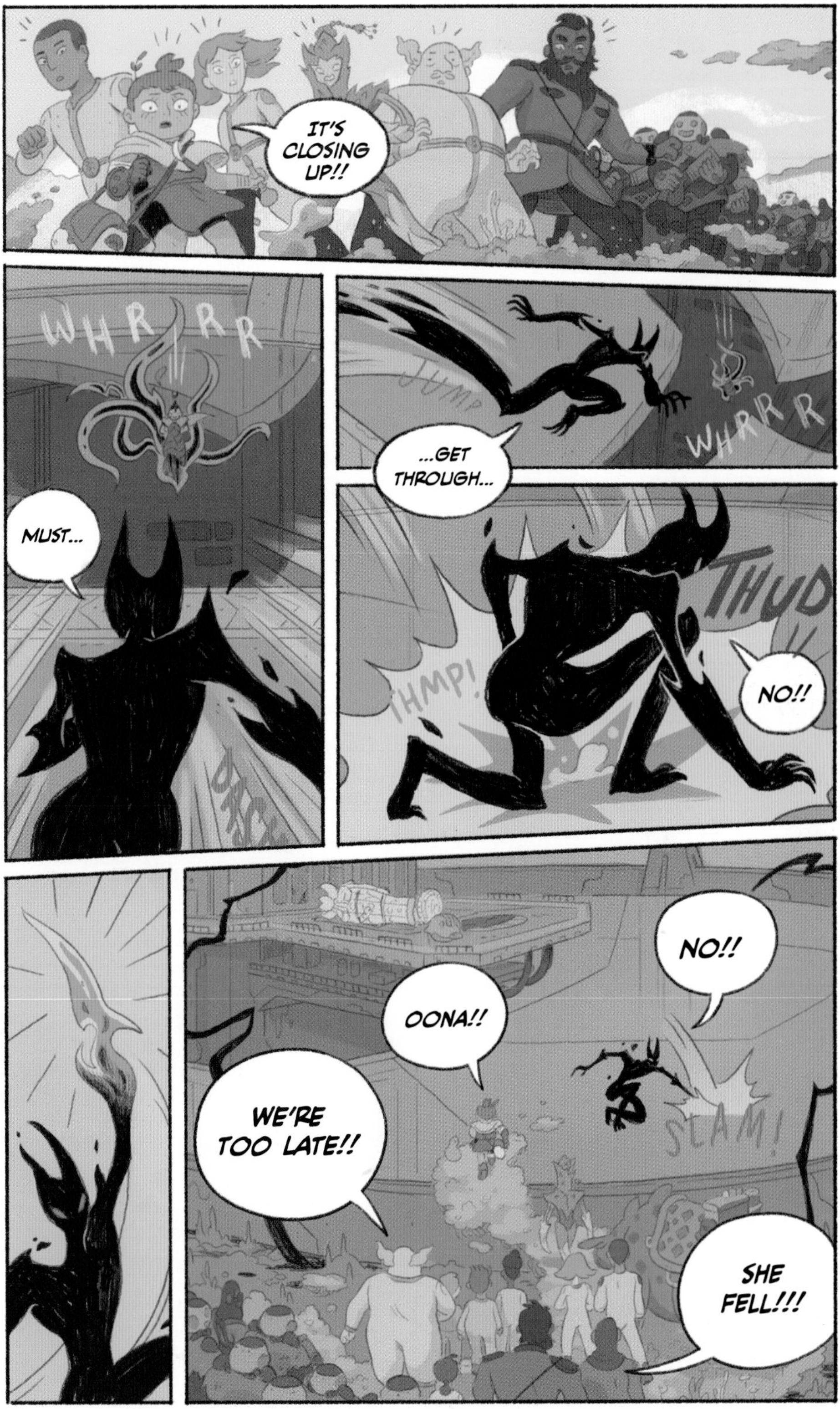
IT'S CLOSING UP!!
WHRRRR
JUMP
WHRRR
MUST...
...GET THROUGH...
THUD
THMP!
NO!!
NO!!
OONA!!
WE'RE TOO LATE!!
SLAM!
SHE FELL!!!

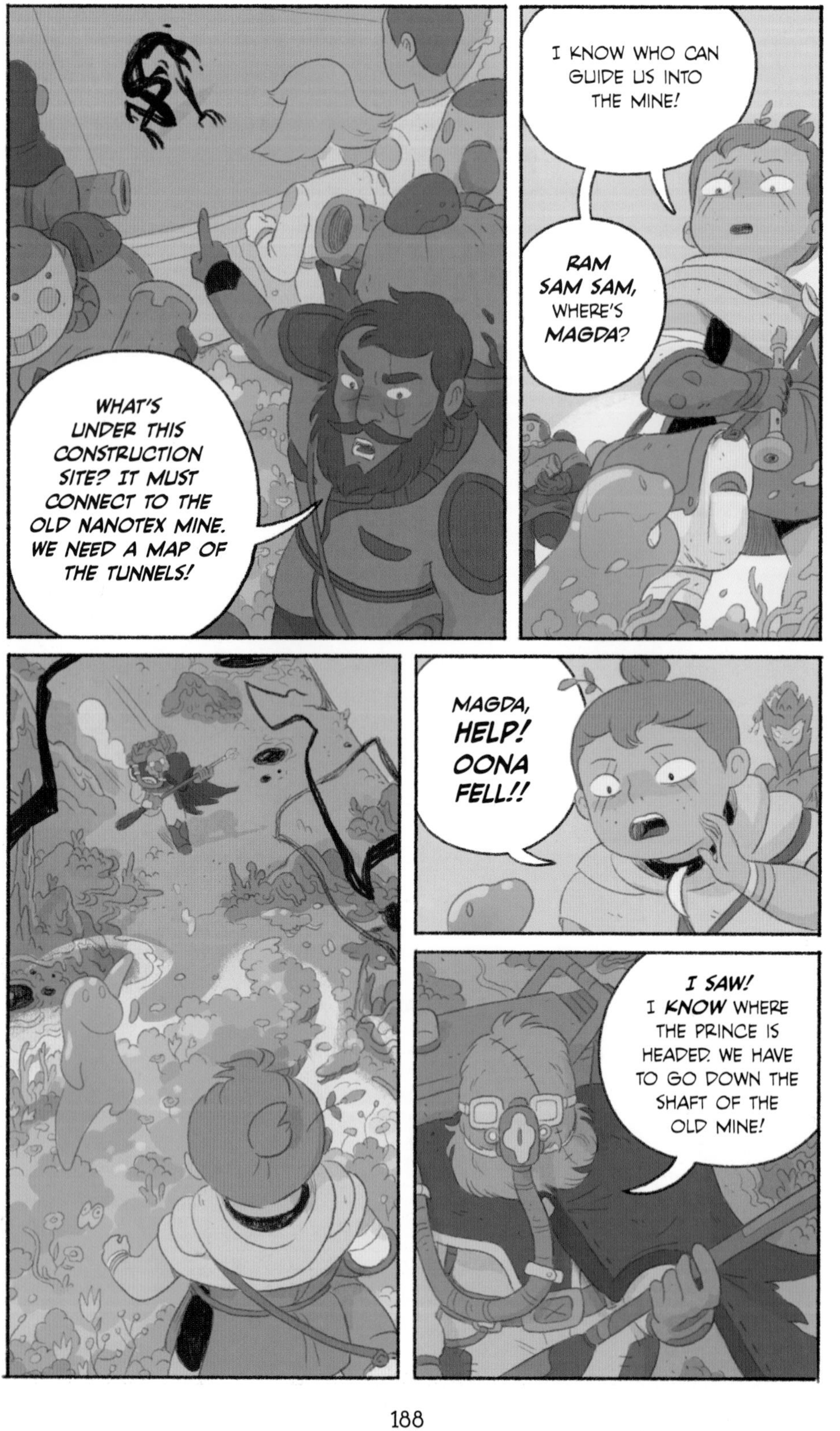
WHAT'S UNDER THIS CONSTRUCTION SITE? IT MUST CONNECT TO THE OLD NANOTEX MINE. WE NEED A MAP OF THE TUNNELS!
I KNOW WHO CAN GUIDE US INTO THE MINE!
RAM SAM SAM, WHERE'S MAGDA?
MAGDA, HELP! OONA FELL!!
I SAW! I KNOW WHERE THE PRINCE IS HEADED. WE HAVE TO GO DOWN THE SHAFT OF THE OLD MINE!

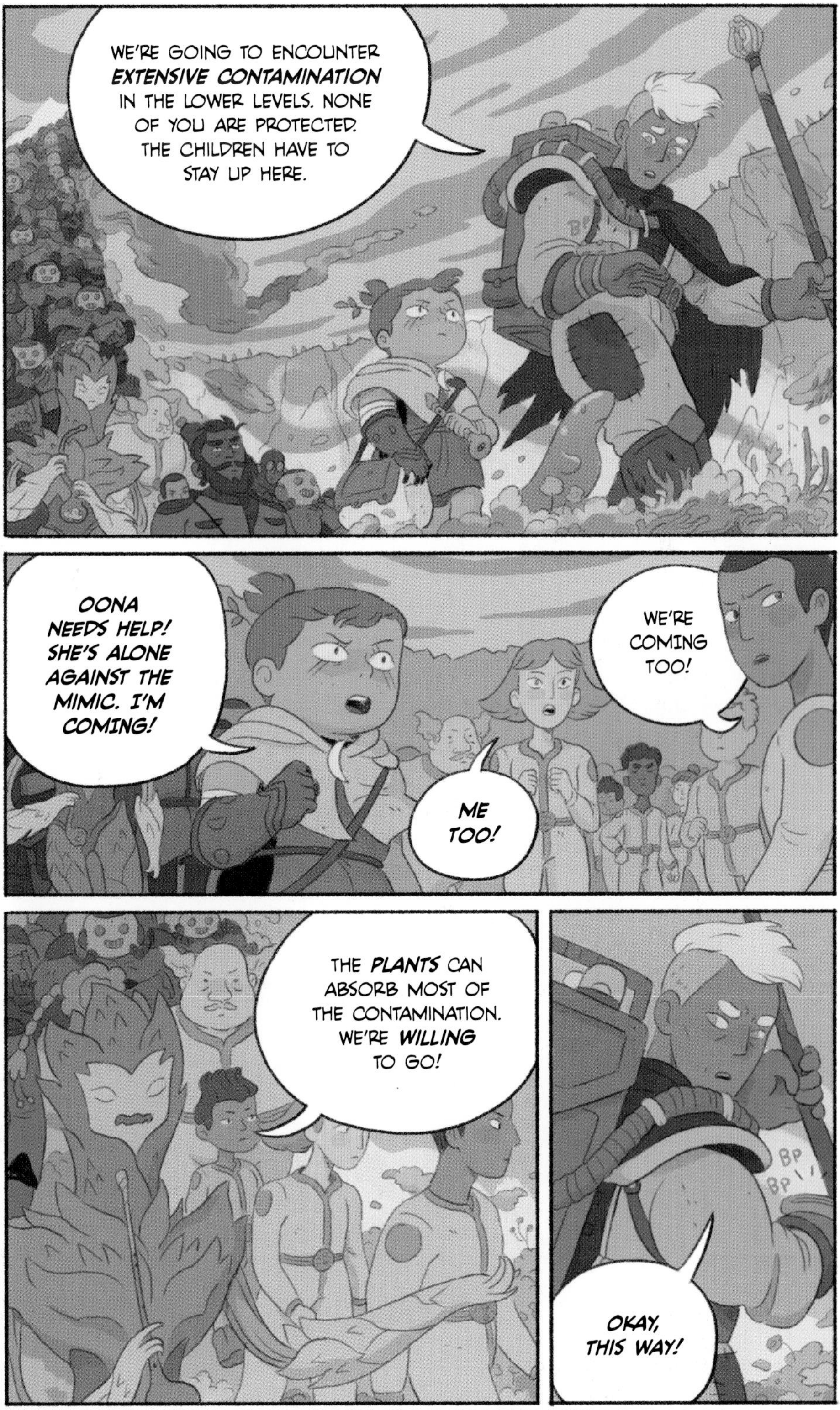
WE'RE GOING TO ENCOUNTER ***EXTENSIVE CONTAMINATION*** IN THE LOWER LEVELS. NONE OF YOU ARE PROTECTED. THE CHILDREN HAVE TO STAY UP HERE.
OONA NEEDS HELP! SHE'S ALONE AGAINST THE MIMIC. I'M COMING!
WE'RE COMING TOO!
ME TOO!
THE ***PLANTS*** CAN ABSORB MOST OF THE CONTAMINATION. WE'RE ***WILLING*** TO GO!
OKAY, THIS WAY!
BP BP

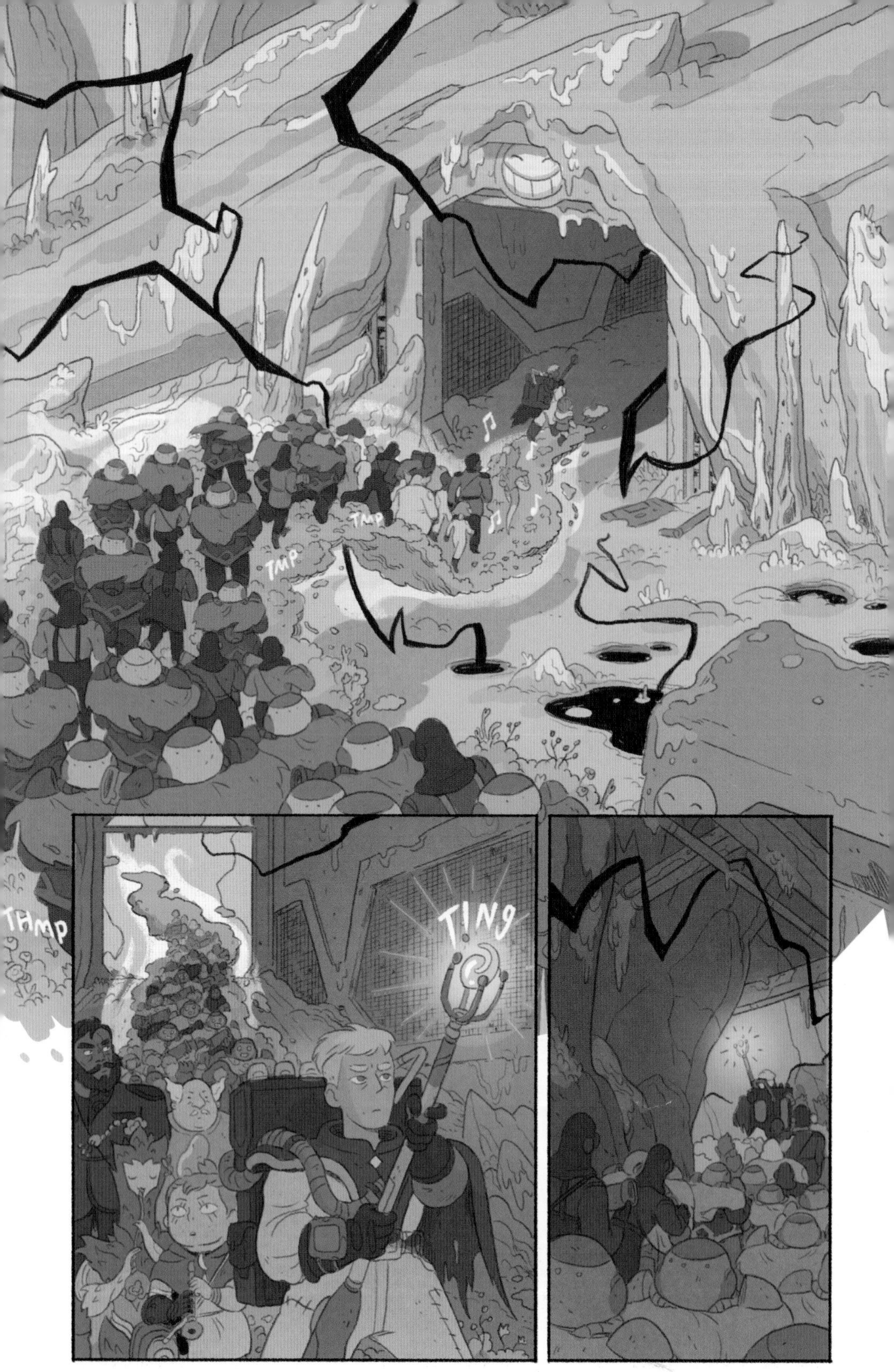
TMP
TMP
THMP
TING

MEANWHILE...

THERE MUST BE A FASTER WAY DOWN! *WE'VE GOT TO REACH OONA!!*

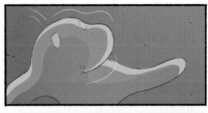

SSSHHAA

HUP!

BZZT

CH-DUNK

CH-DUNK

CH-DU

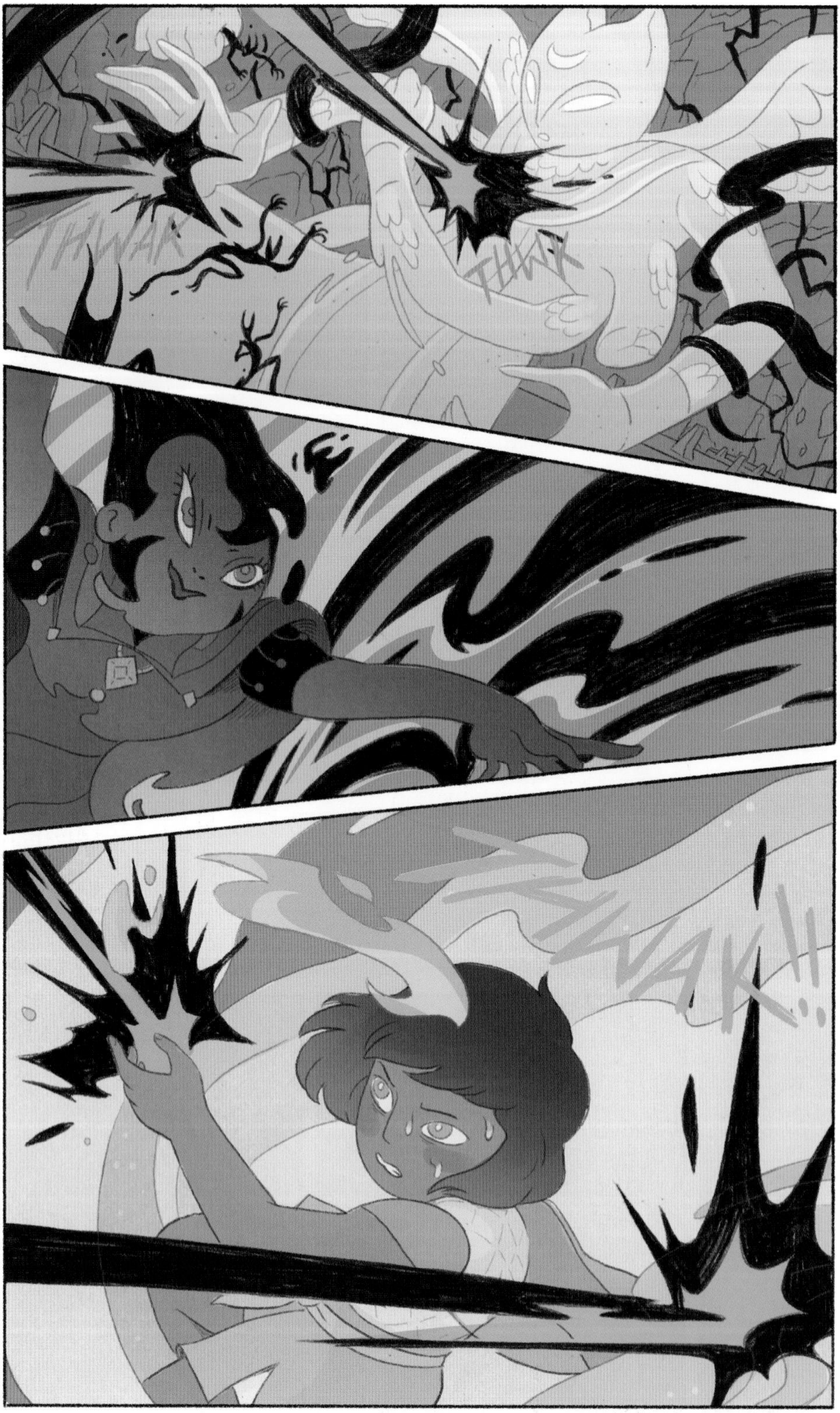
THWAK
THWK
THWAK!!

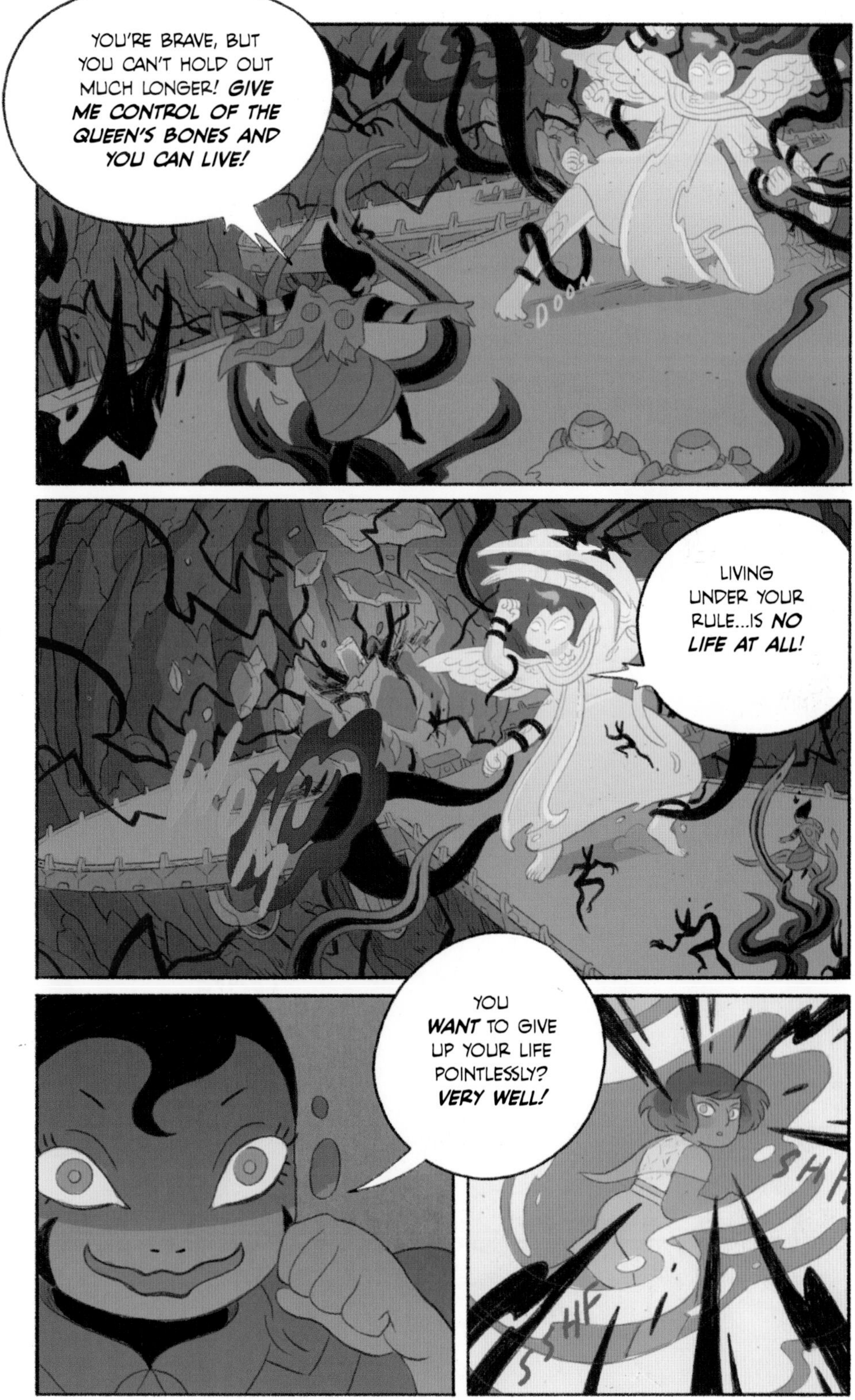
YOU'RE BRAVE, BUT YOU CAN'T HOLD OUT MUCH LONGER! **GIVE ME CONTROL OF THE QUEEN'S BONES AND YOU CAN LIVE!**
DOOM
LIVING UNDER YOUR RULE...IS **NO LIFE AT ALL!**
YOU **WANT** TO GIVE UP YOUR LIFE POINTLESSLY? **VERY WELL!**

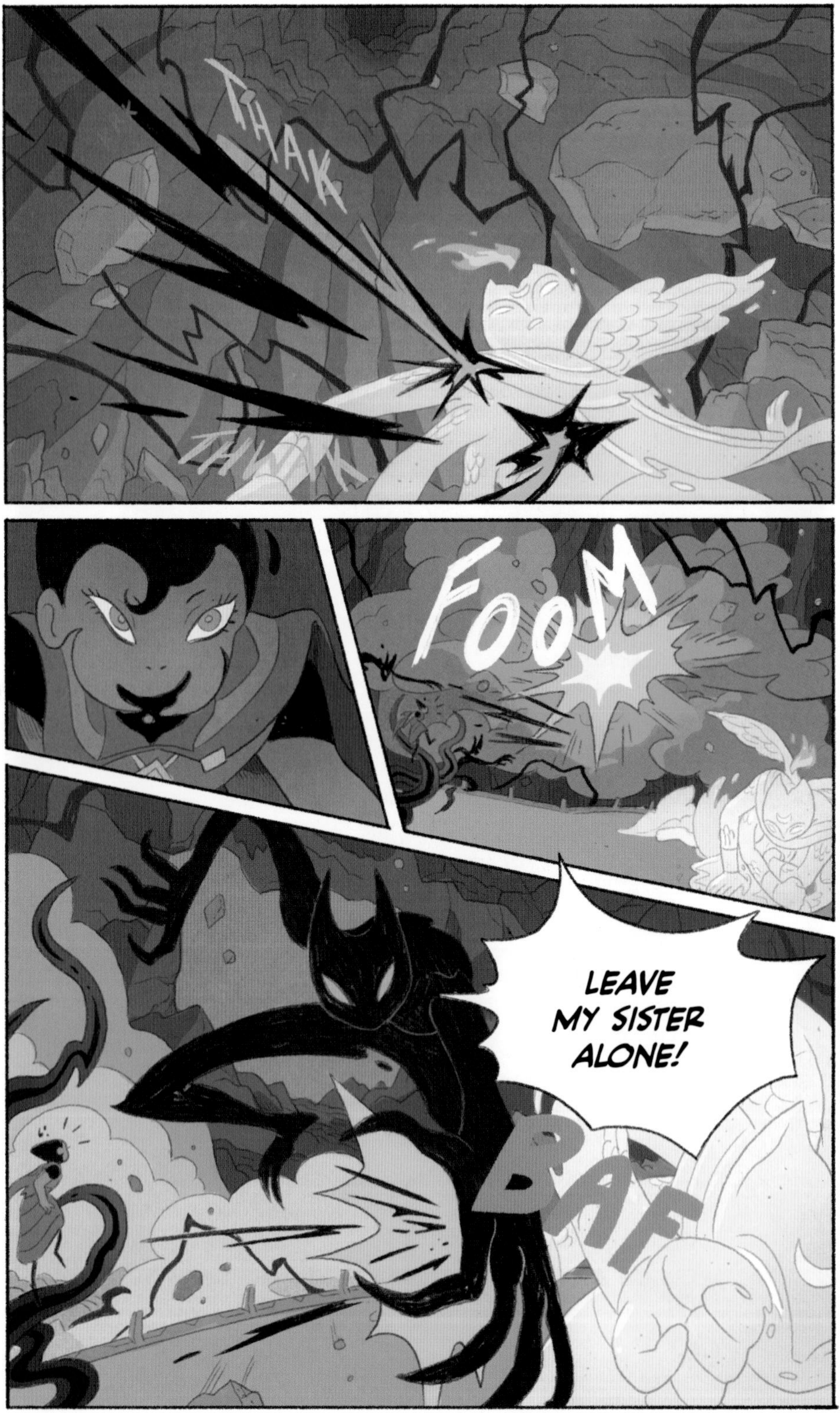
THAK
THWAK
FOOM
LEAVE MY SISTER ALONE!
BAF

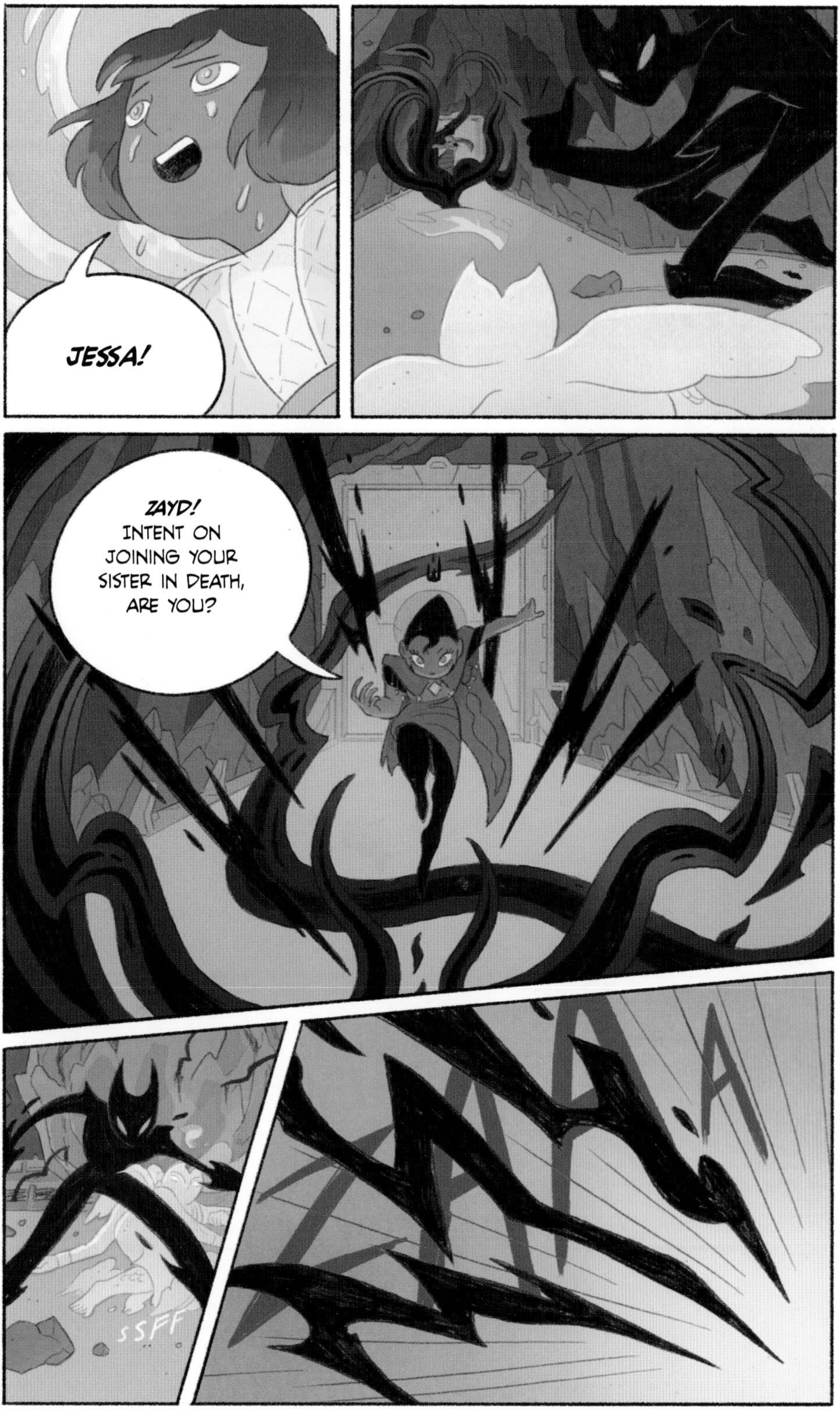
JESSA!
ZAYD! INTENT ON JOINING YOUR SISTER IN DEATH, ARE YOU?
SSFF

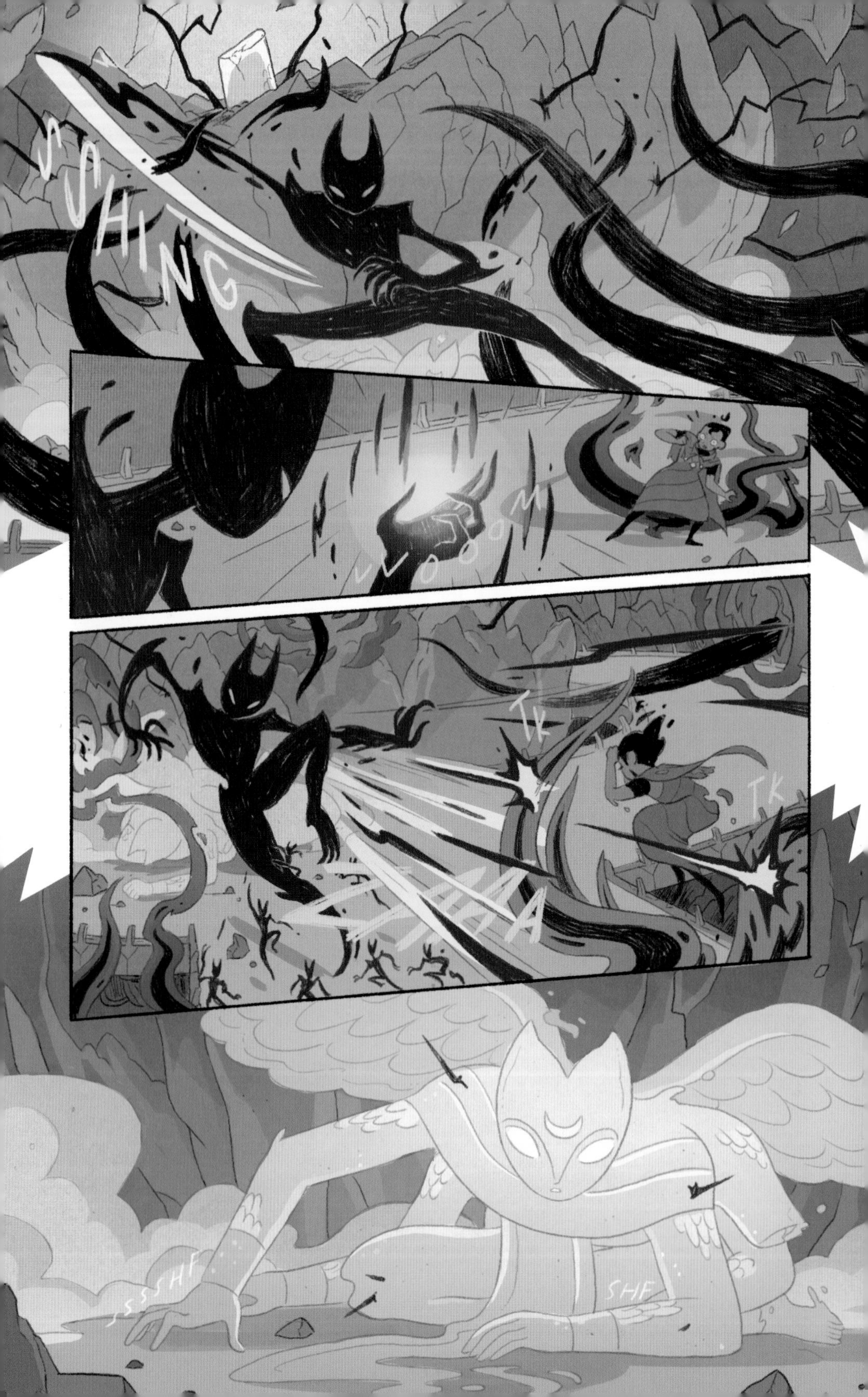
SHING
VVOOOOM
TK
TK
AAAA
SSSSHF
SHF

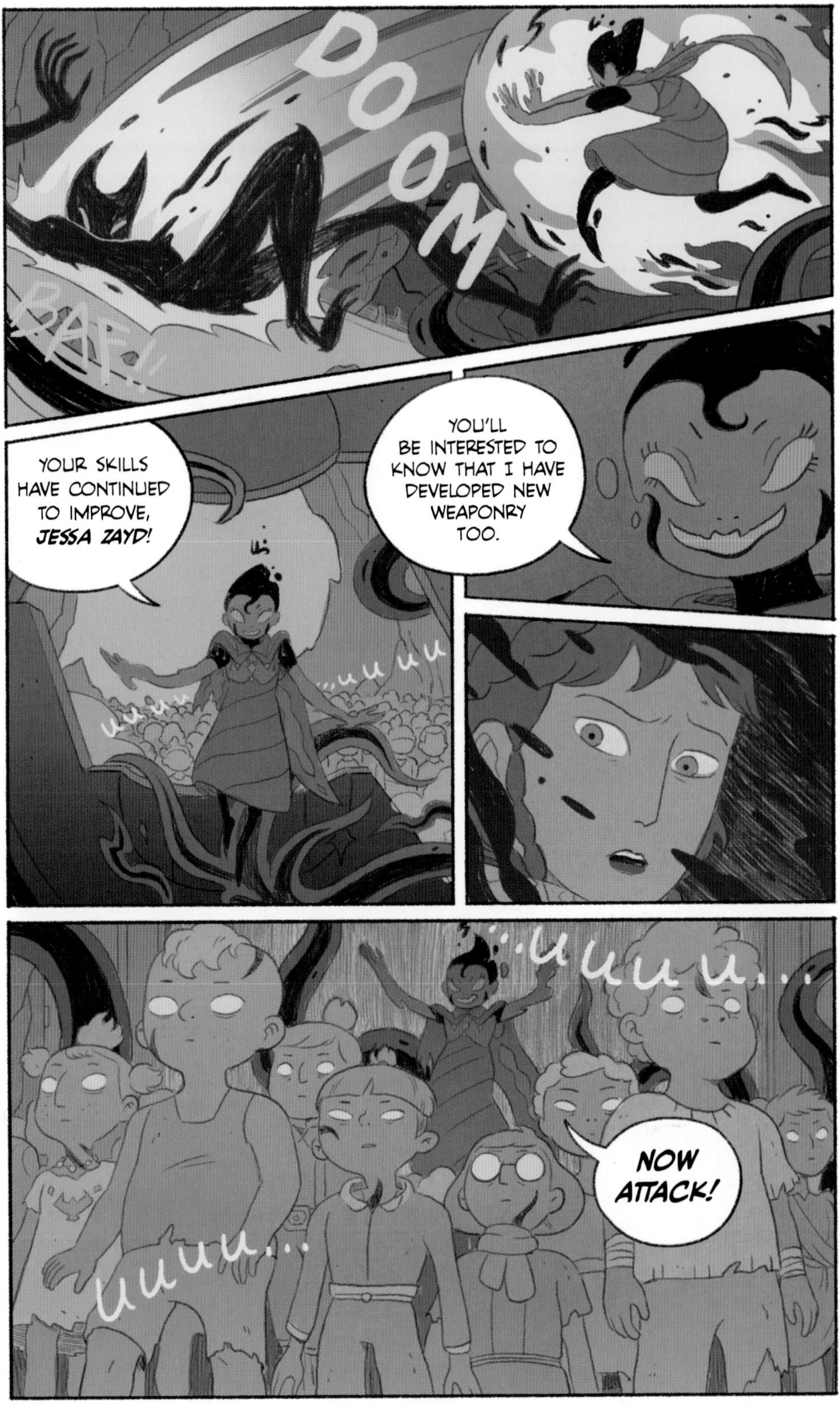
DOOM
BAF!!
YOUR SKILLS HAVE CONTINUED TO IMPROVE, JESSA ZAYD!
YOU'LL BE INTERESTED TO KNOW THAT I HAVE DEVELOPED NEW WEAPONRY TOO.
...uuuu uuu
uuuu
...uuuu...
NOW ATTACK!
uuuu...

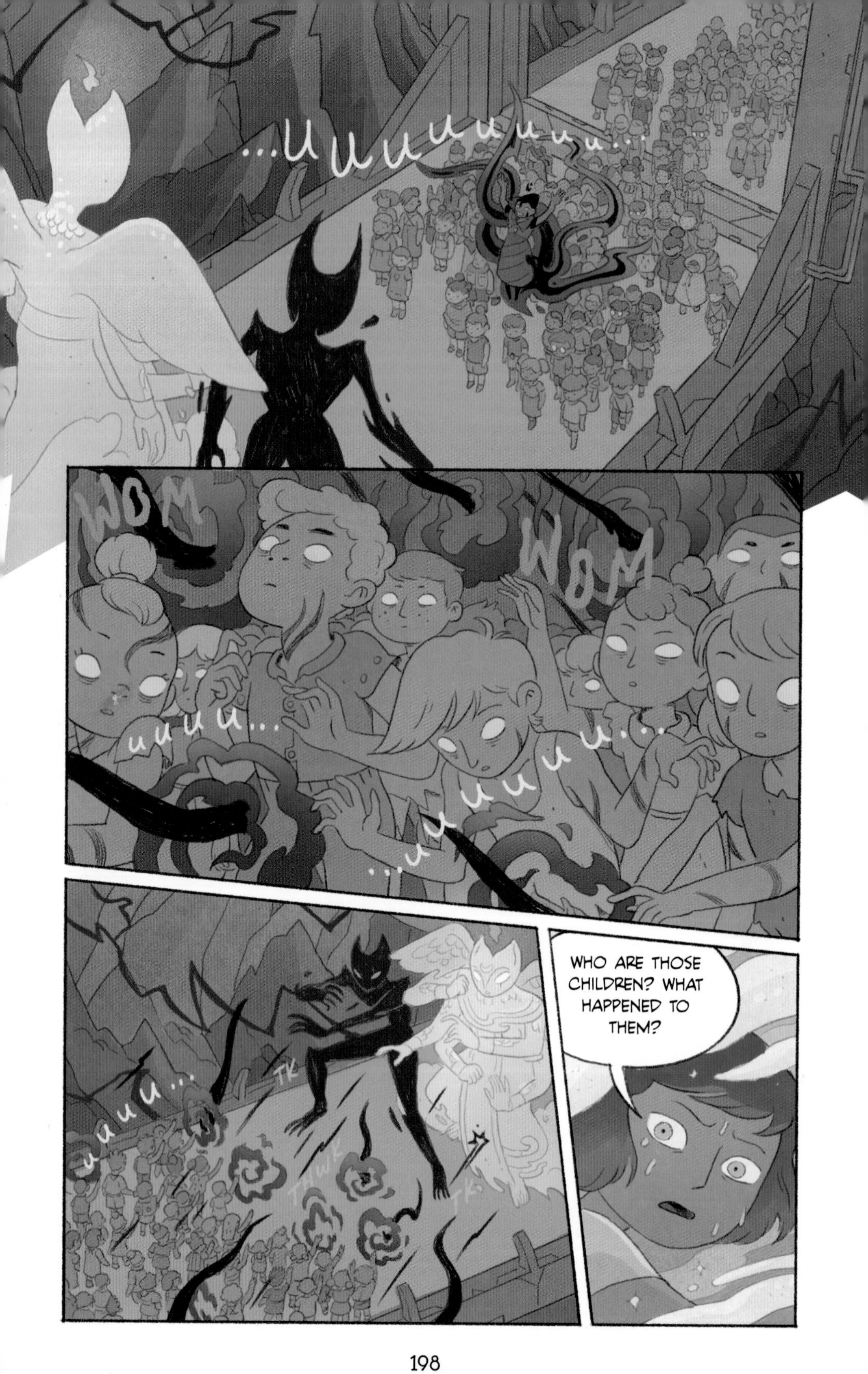

...UUUUUUUUU...
WOM
WOM
UUUU...
UUUUUUU...
...UU
UUUU...
TK
THWK
TK
WHO ARE THOSE CHILDREN? WHAT HAPPENED TO THEM?

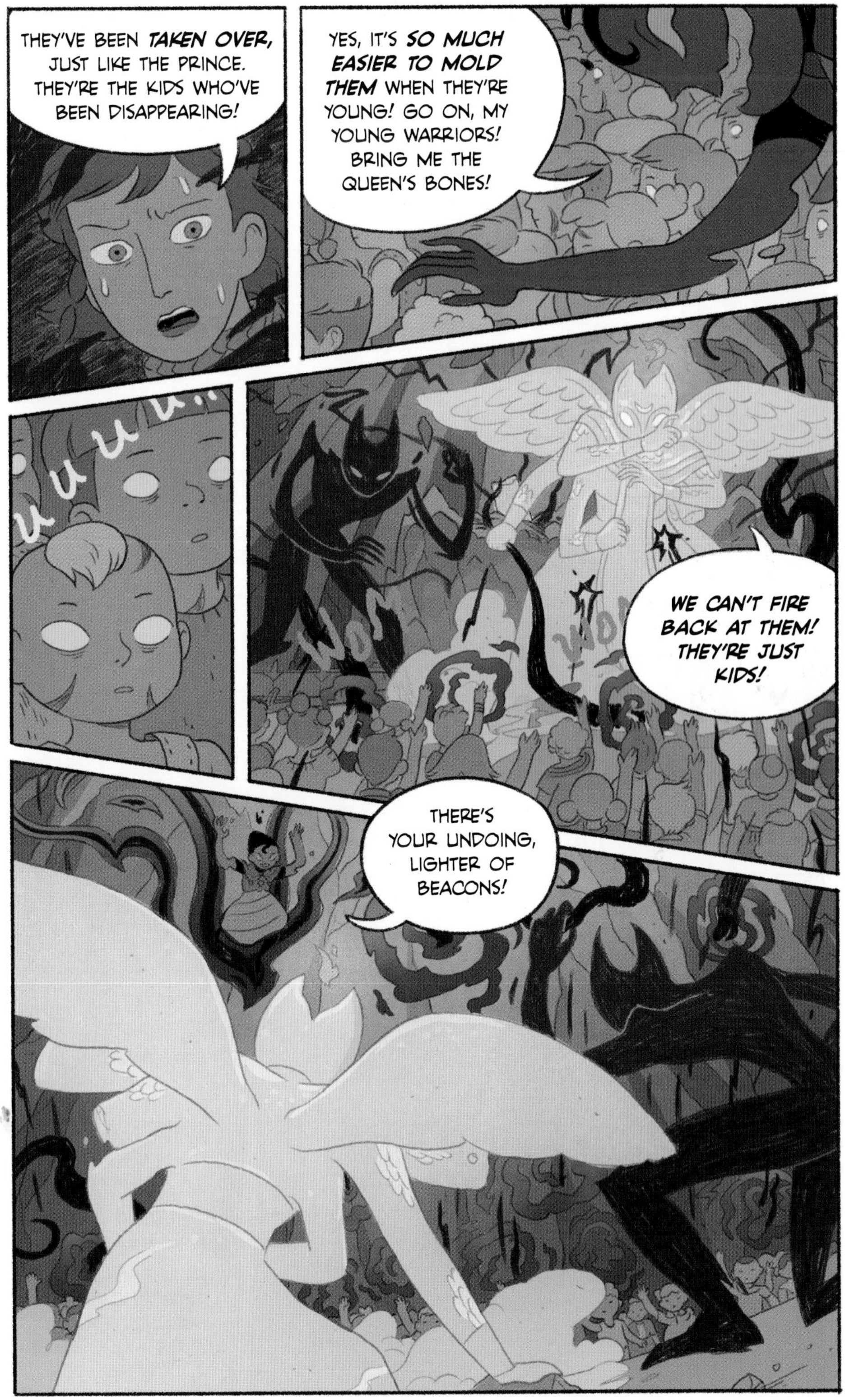
THEY'VE BEEN **TAKEN OVER,** JUST LIKE THE PRINCE. THEY'RE THE KIDS WHO'VE BEEN DISAPPEARING!
YES, IT'S **SO MUCH EASIER TO MOLD THEM** WHEN THEY'RE YOUNG! GO ON, MY YOUNG WARRIORS! BRING ME THE QUEEN'S BONES!
UUUUU...
WE CAN'T FIRE BACK AT THEM! THEY'RE JUST KIDS!
THERE'S YOUR UNDOING, LIGHTER OF BEACONS!

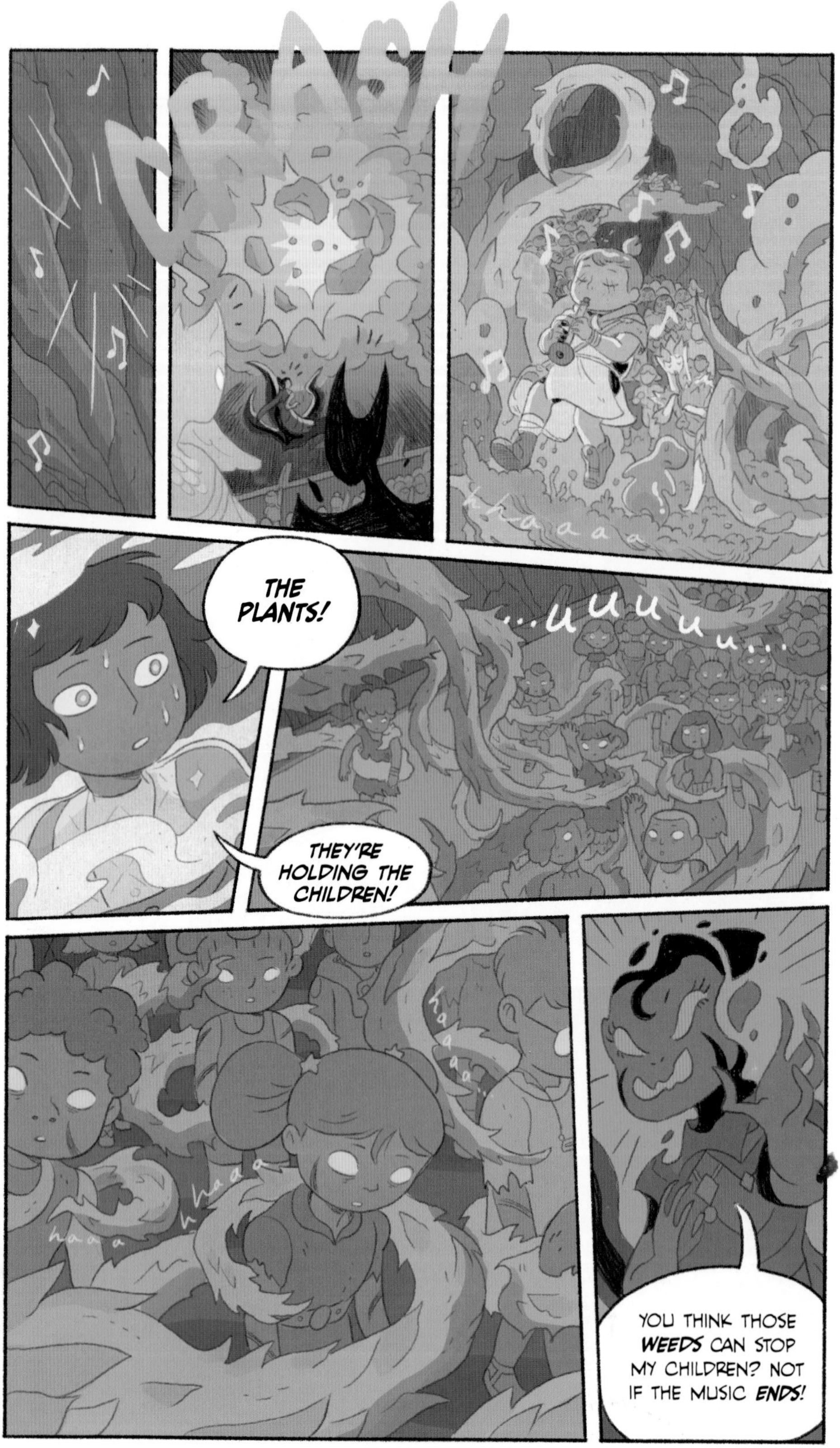
CRASH
hhaaaaaa
THE PLANTS!
...uuuuuuu...
THEY'RE HOLDING THE CHILDREN!
haaaa...
hhaaa
haaa
YOU THINK THOSE **WEEDS** CAN STOP MY CHILDREN? NOT IF THE MUSIC **ENDS!**

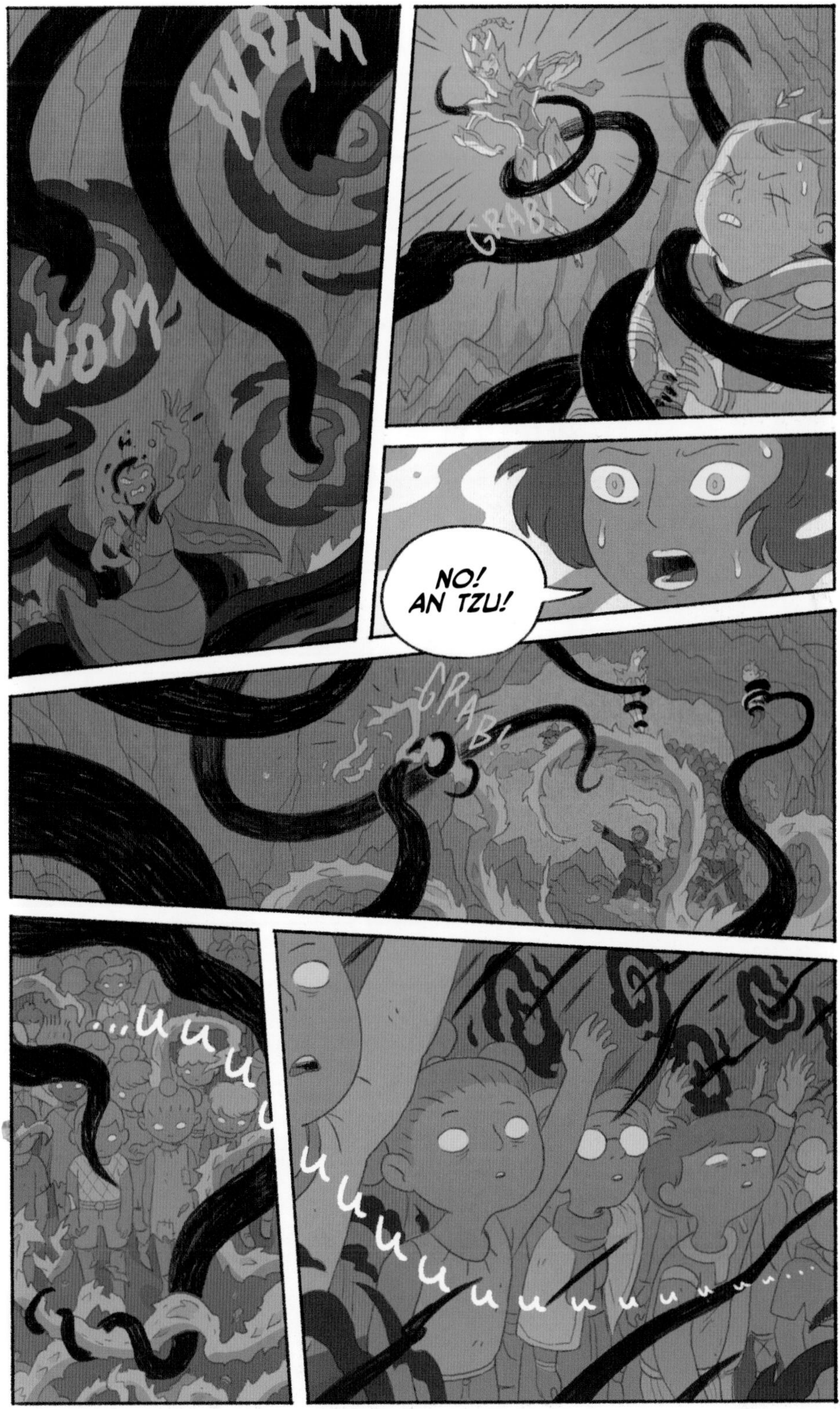
WOM
WOM
GRAB!
NO! AN TZU!
GRAB!
...uuuuuuuuuuuuuuuuuuuuuu...

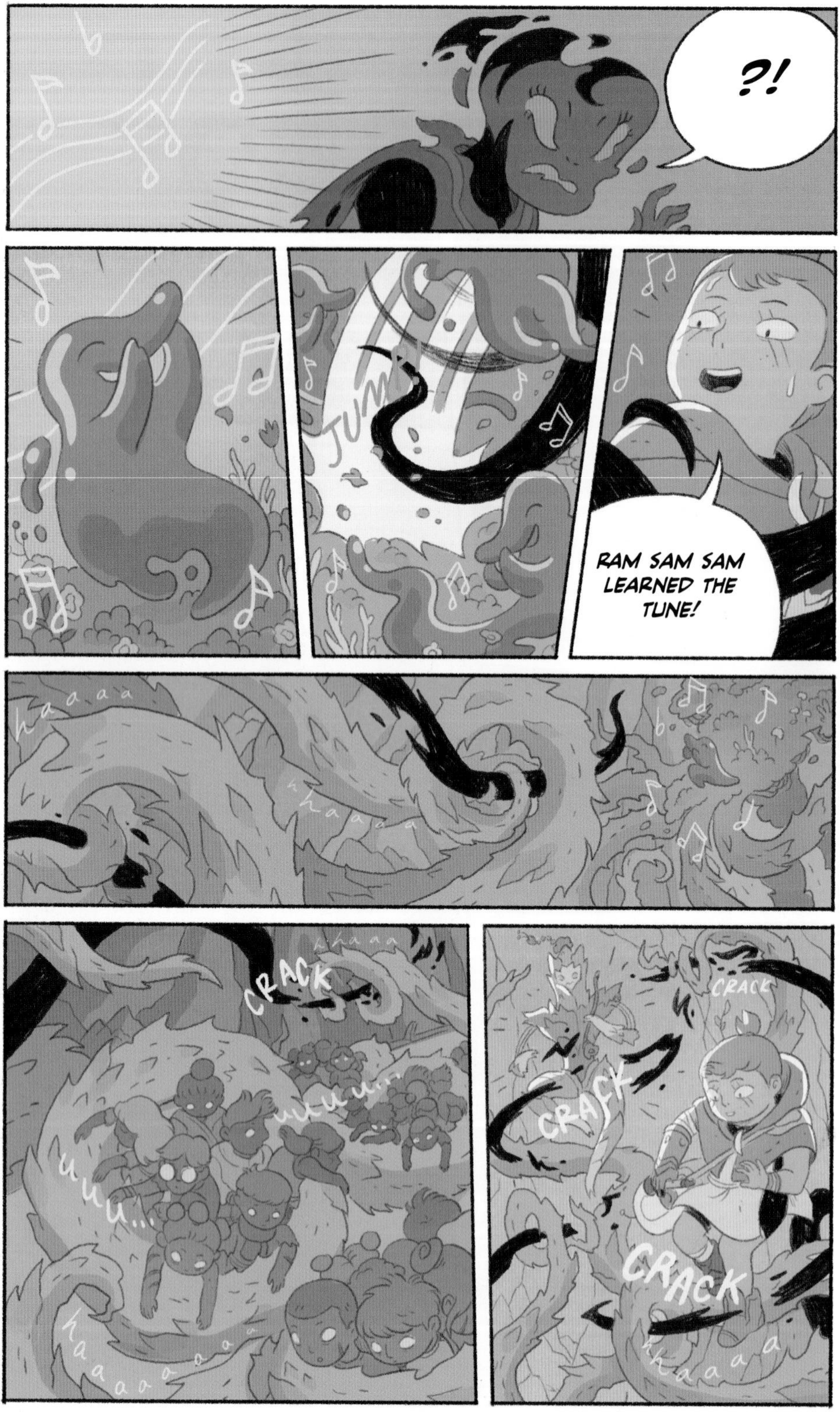
?!
RAM SAM SAM LEARNED THE TUNE!
haaaa
CRACK
uuuu...
uuu...
haaaaaaaaa
CRACK
CRACK
CRACK
haaaaa

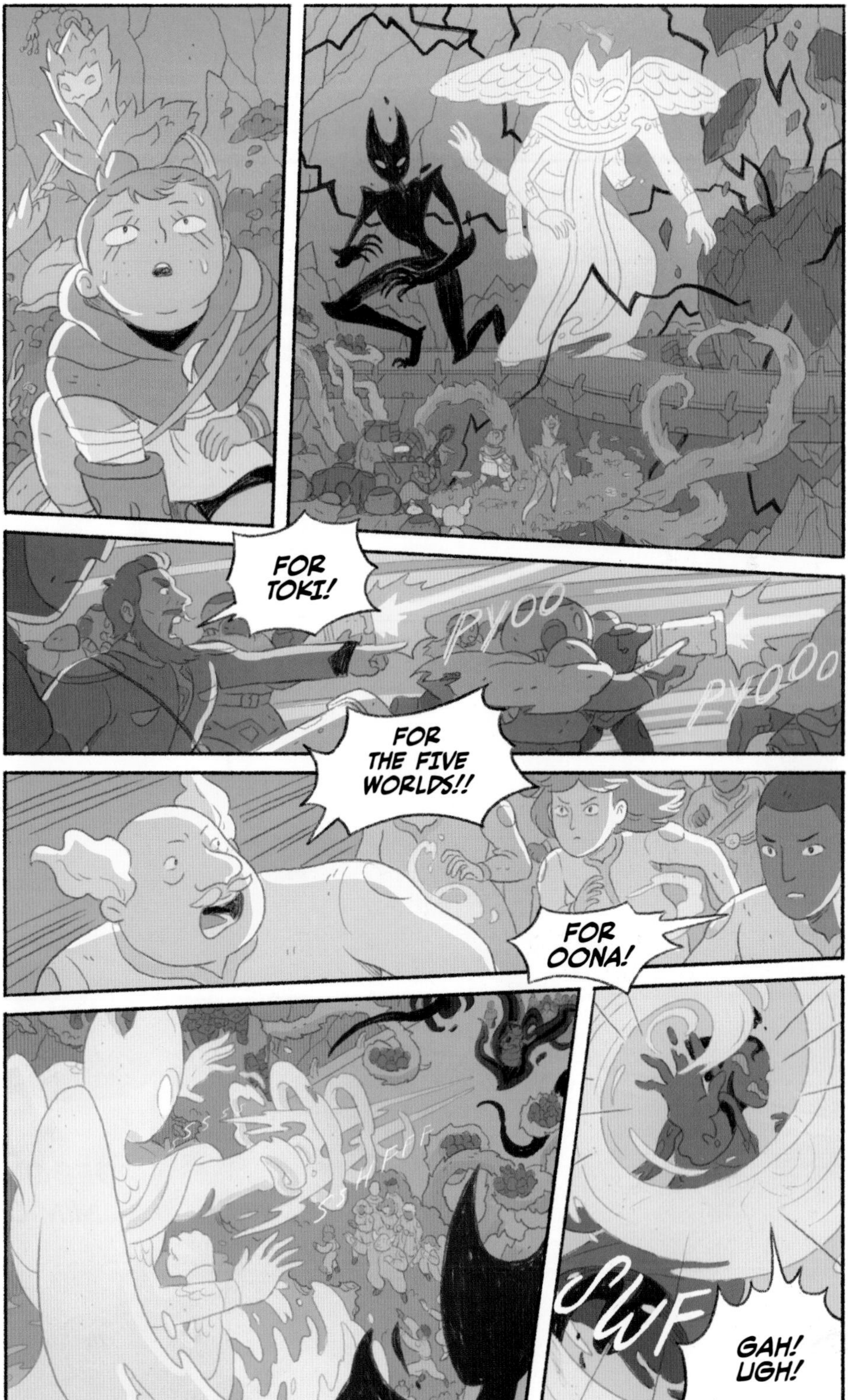
FOR TOKI!
PYOO
PYOOOO
FOR THE FIVE WORLDS!!
FOR OONA!
SSS
SSHFFF
SWF
GAH! UGH!

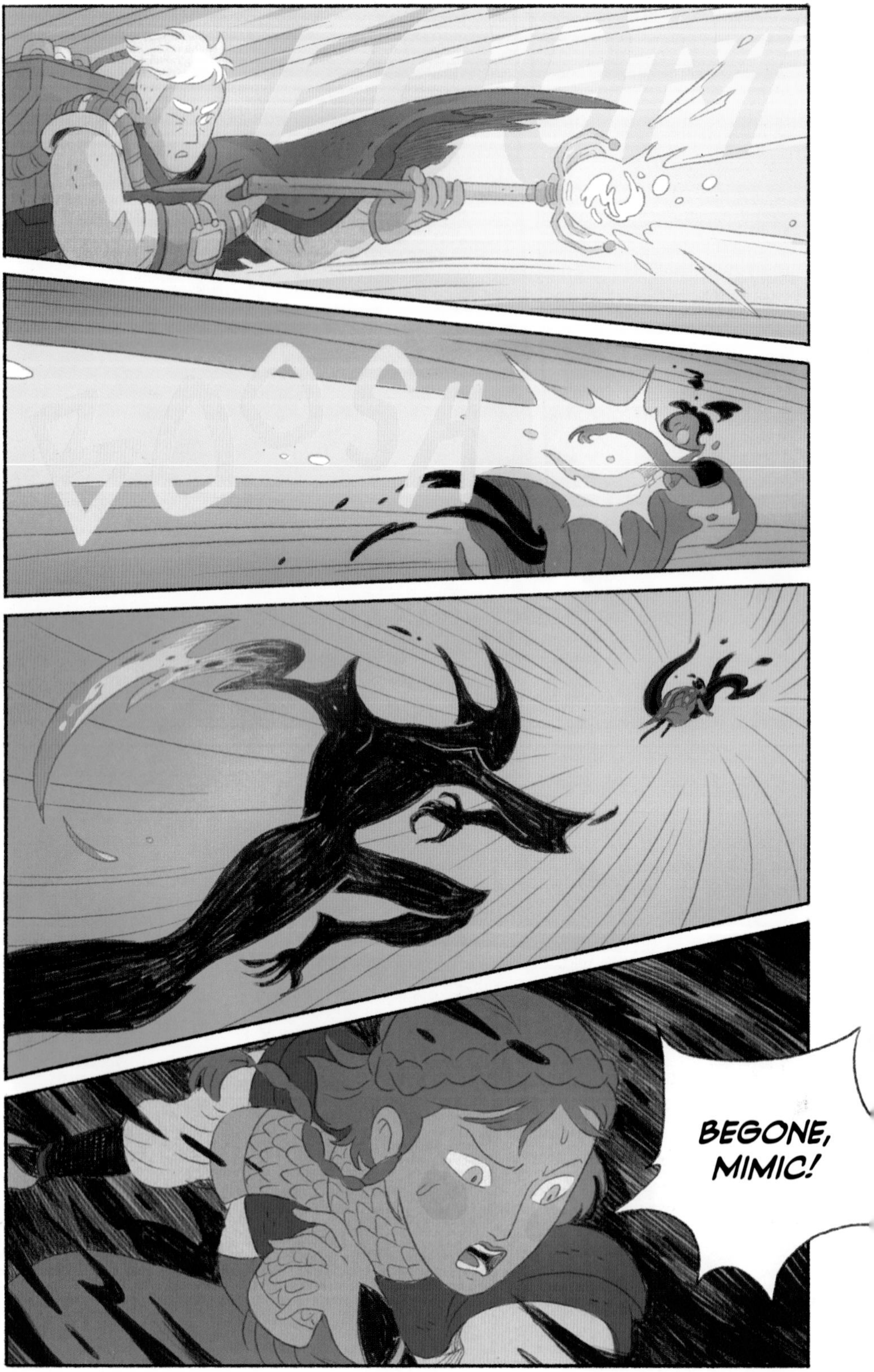
BEGONE, MIMIC!

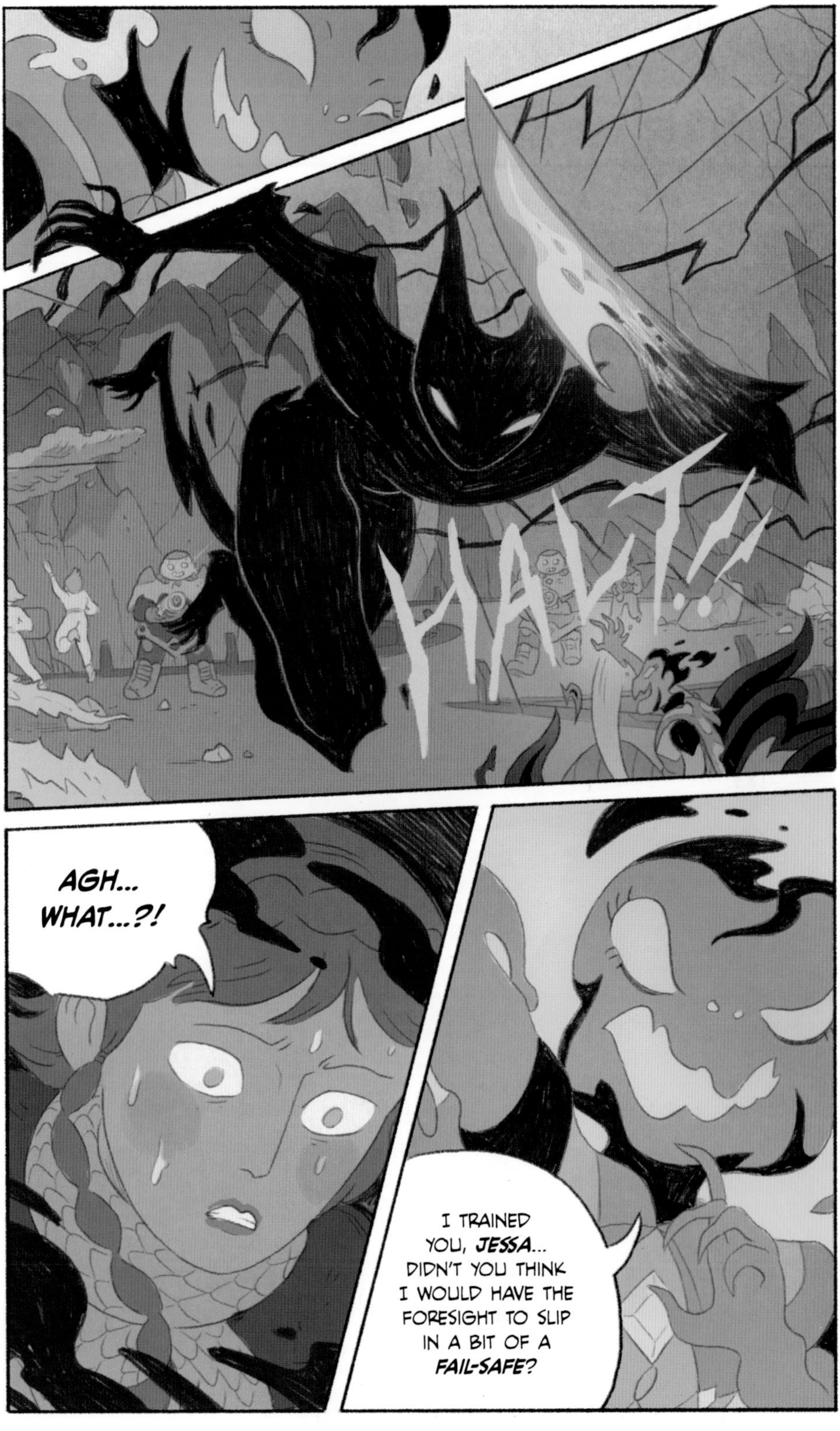
HALT!!
AGH... WHAT...?!
I TRAINED YOU, JESSA... DIDN'T YOU THINK I WOULD HAVE THE FORESIGHT TO SLIP IN A BIT OF A FAIL-SAFE?

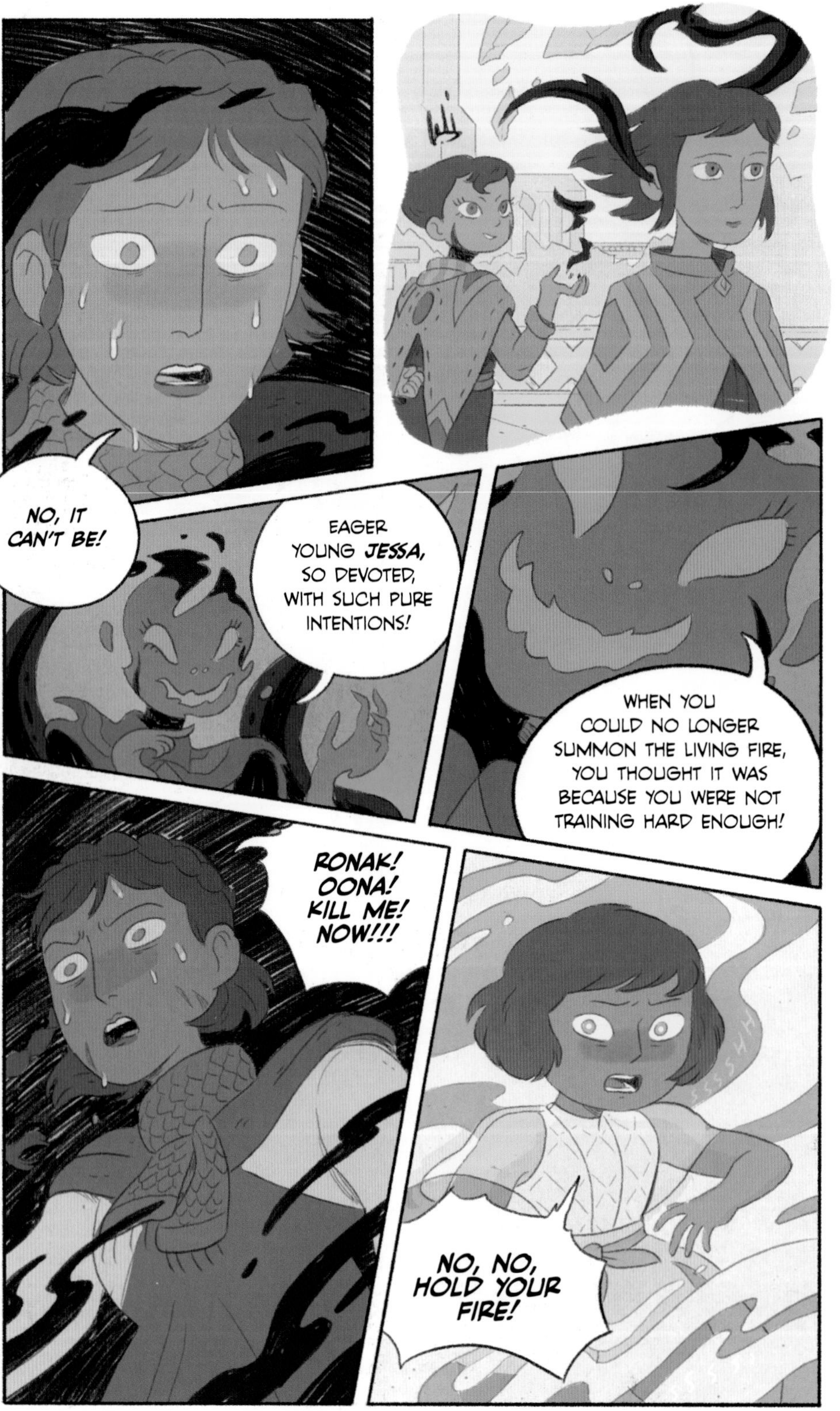
NO, IT CAN'T BE!
EAGER YOUNG JESSA, SO DEVOTED, WITH SUCH PURE INTENTIONS!
WHEN YOU COULD NO LONGER SUMMON THE LIVING FIRE, YOU THOUGHT IT WAS BECAUSE YOU WERE NOT TRAINING HARD ENOUGH!
RONAK! OONA! KILL ME! NOW!!!
NO, NO, HOLD YOUR FIRE!

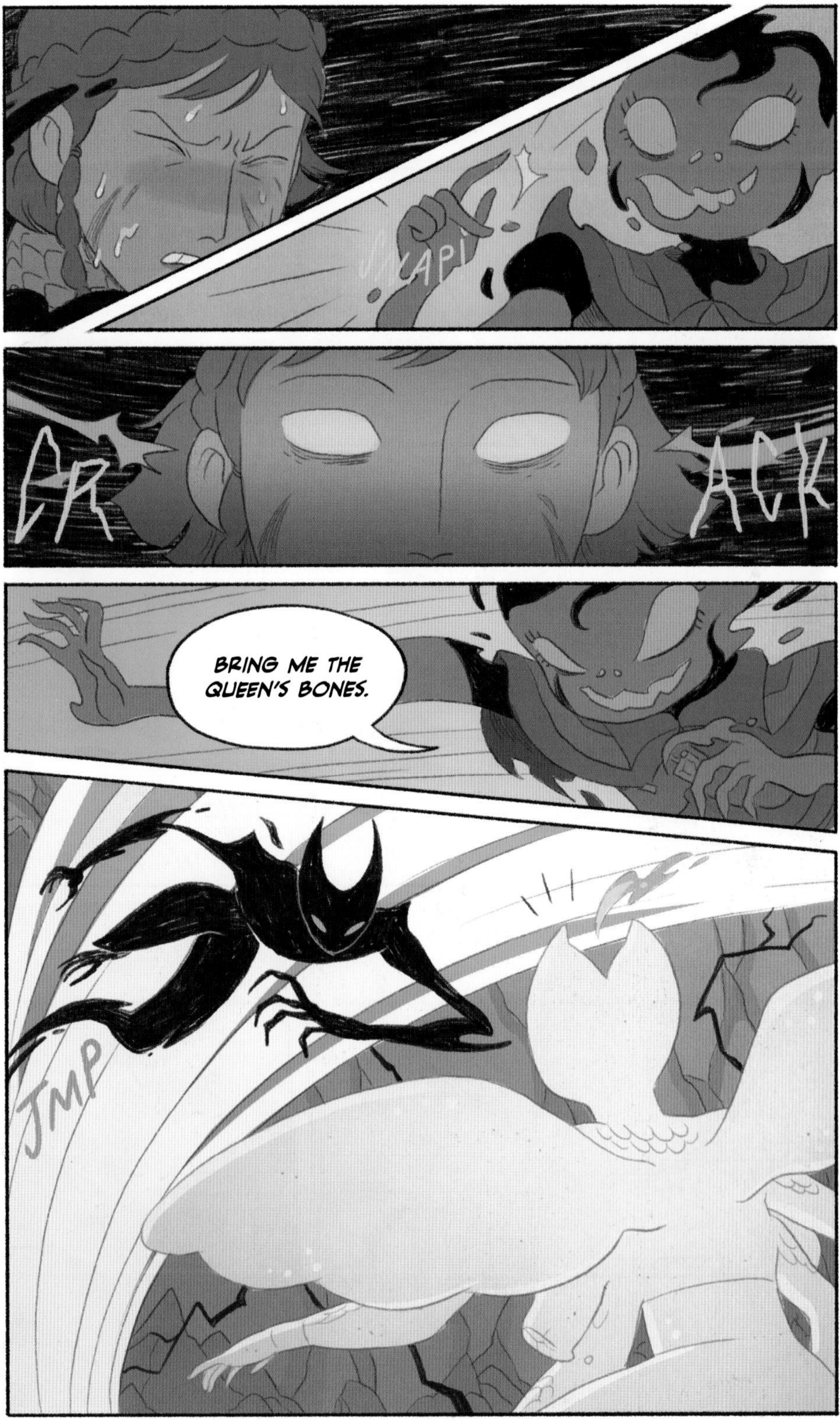
CRACK
BRING ME THE QUEEN'S BONES.
JMP

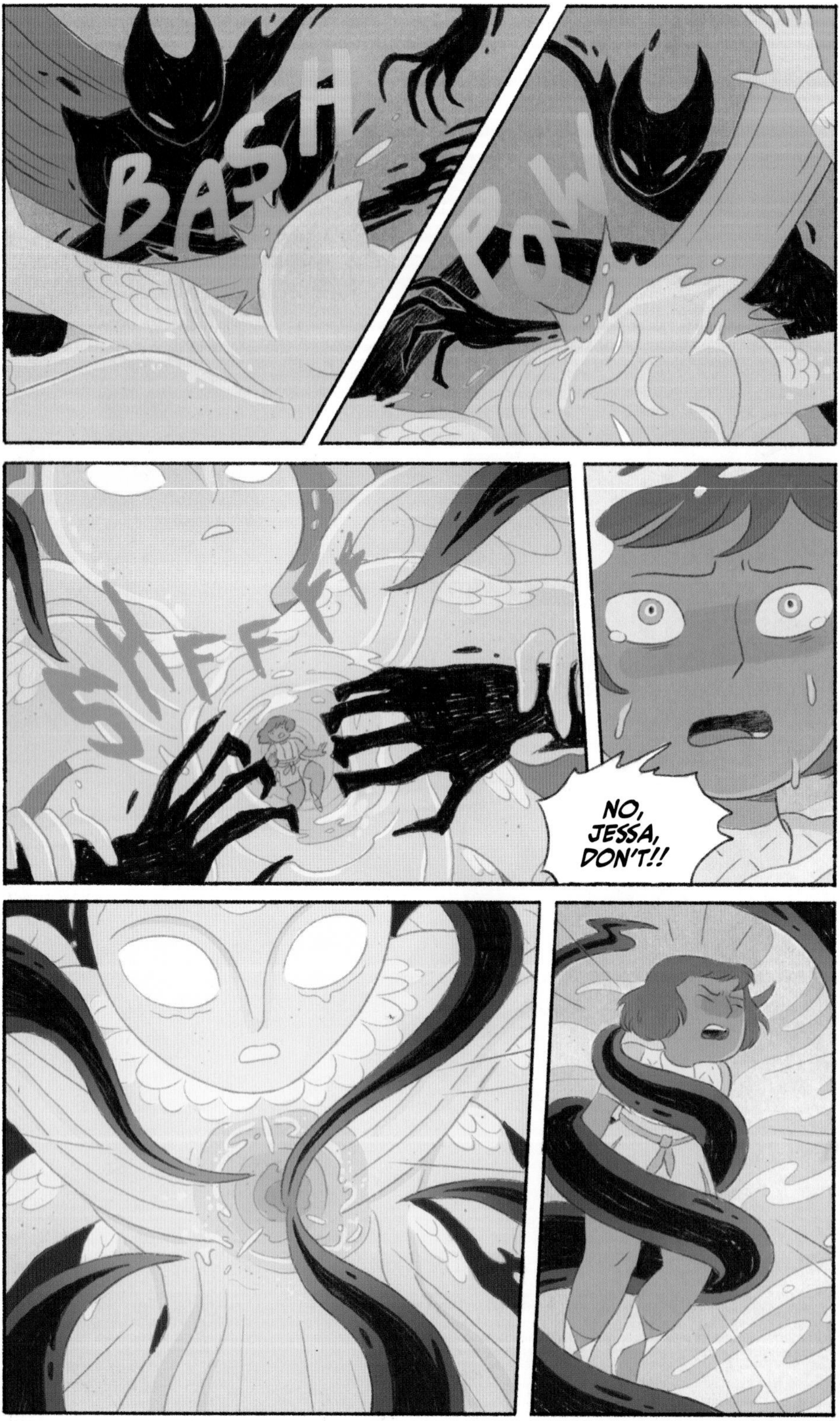
BASH
POW
SHFFFF
NO, JESSA, DON'T!!

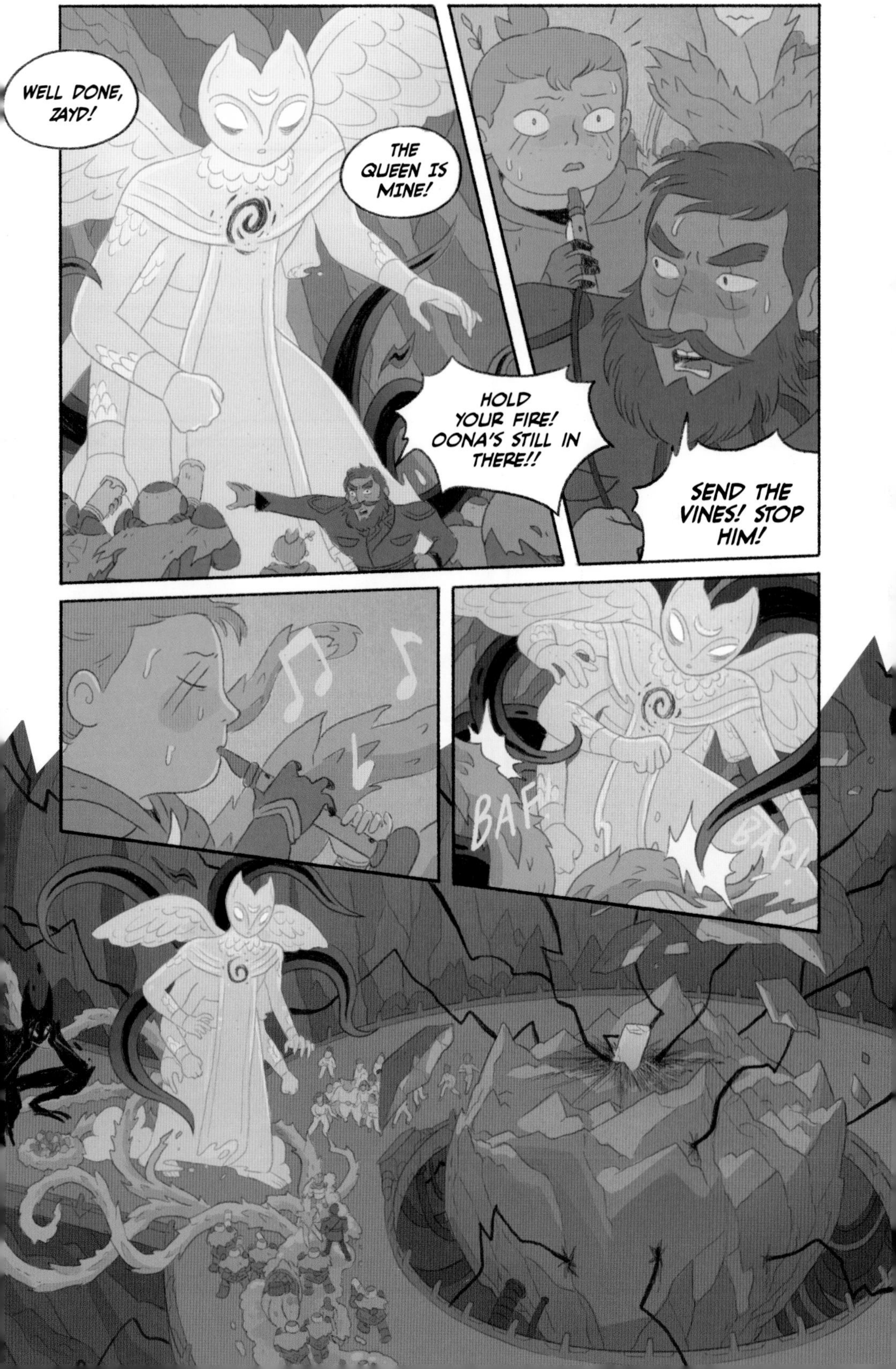
WELL DONE, ZAYD!
THE QUEEN IS MINE!
HOLD YOUR FIRE! OONA'S STILL IN THERE!!
SEND THE VINES! STOP HIM!
BAF!
BAF!

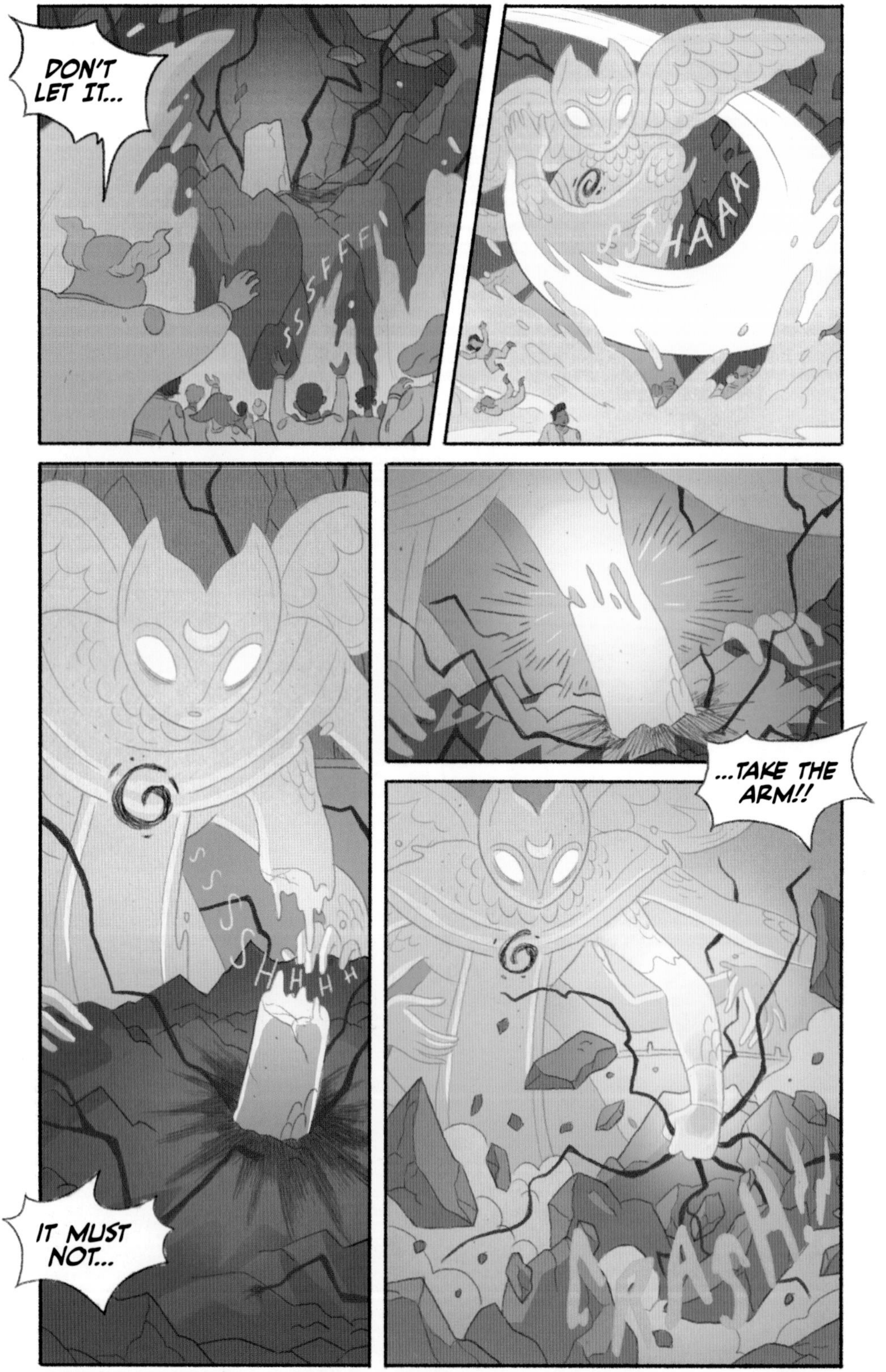
DON'T LET IT...
SSSFFF
SSHAAA
...TAKE THE ARM!!
SSSSHHHHH
IT MUST NOT...
CRASH!!

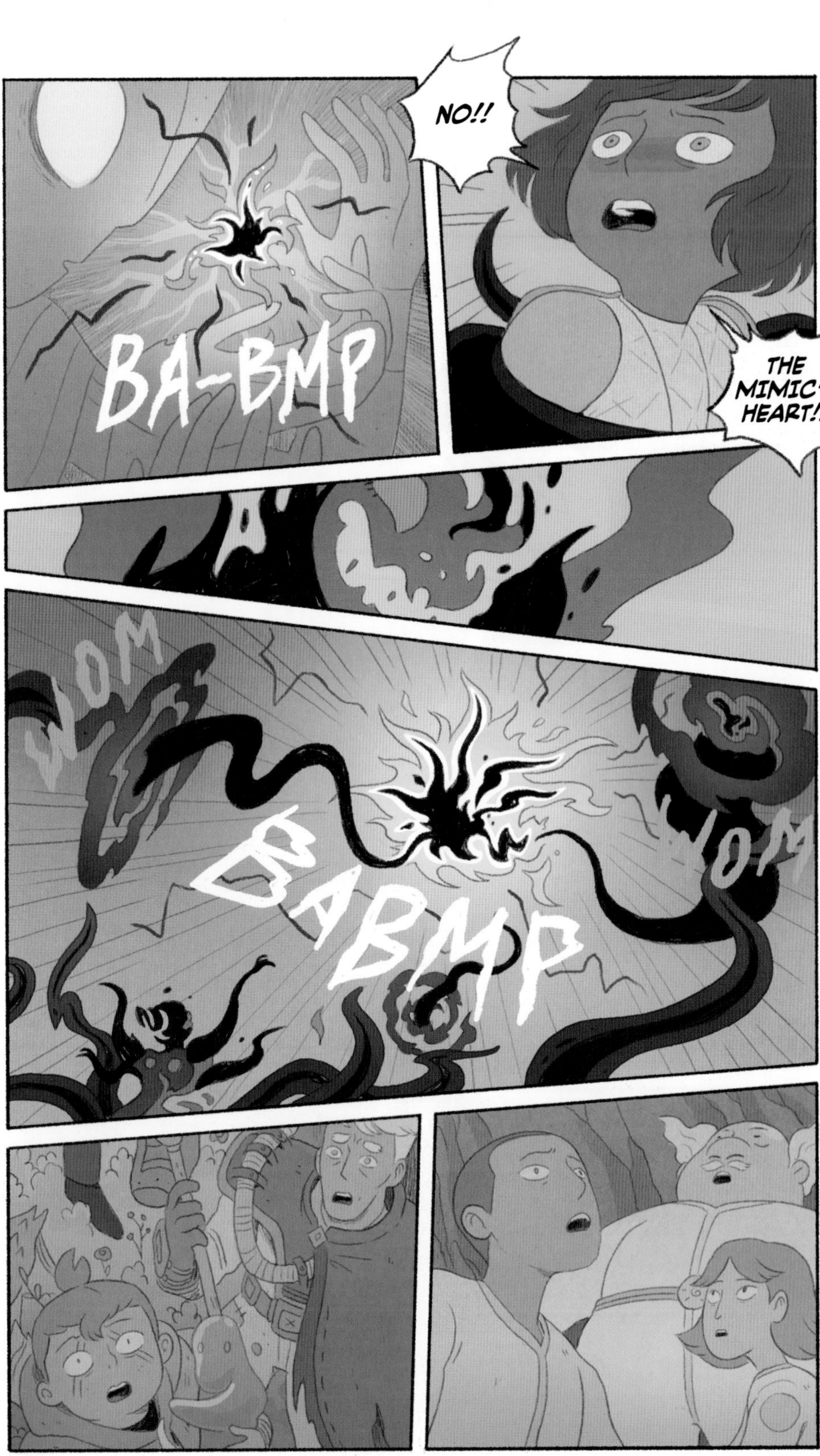
BA-BMP
NO!!
THE MIMIC'S HEART!!
WOM
BABMP
WOM

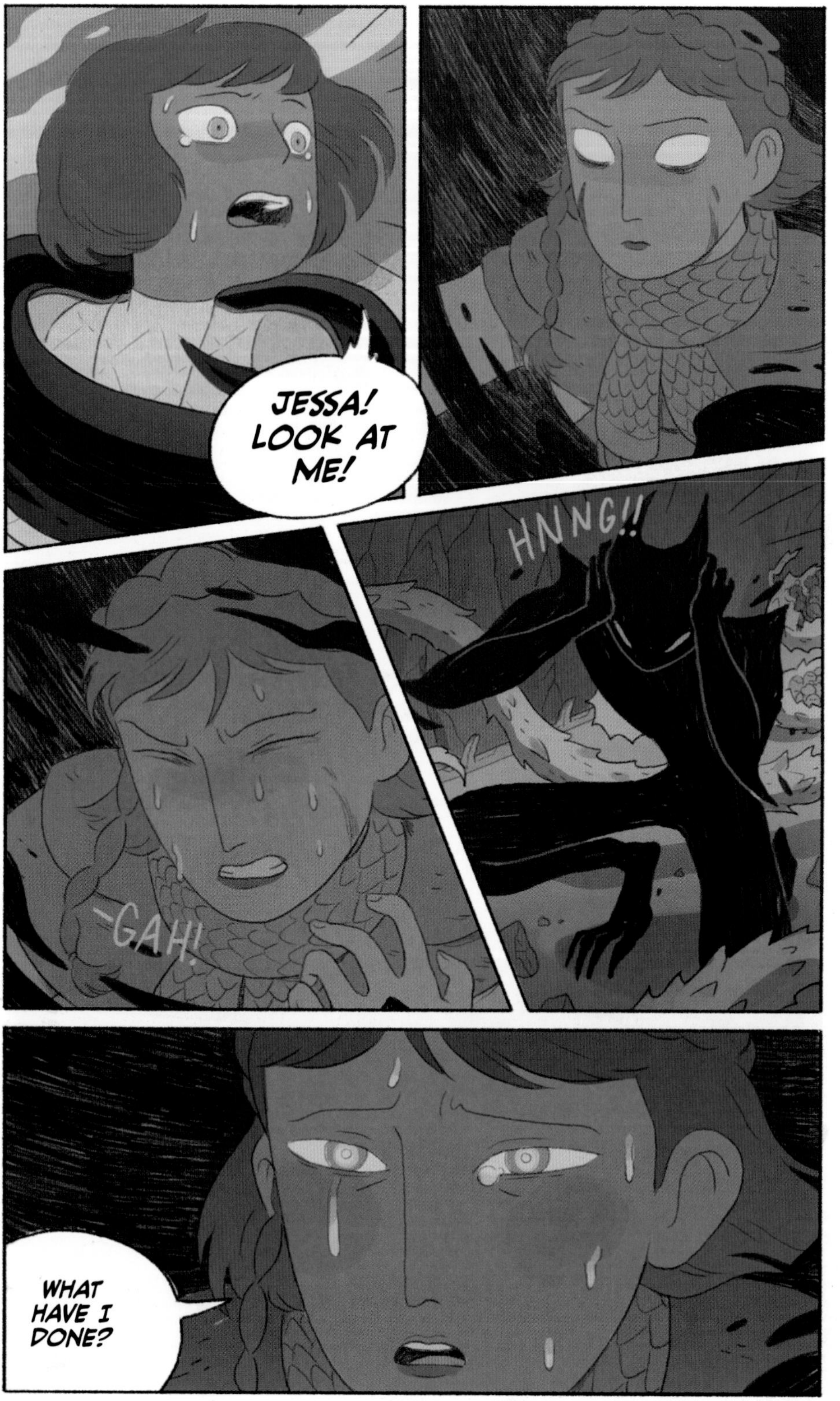
JESSA! LOOK AT ME!
HNNG!!
-GAH!
WHAT HAVE I DONE?

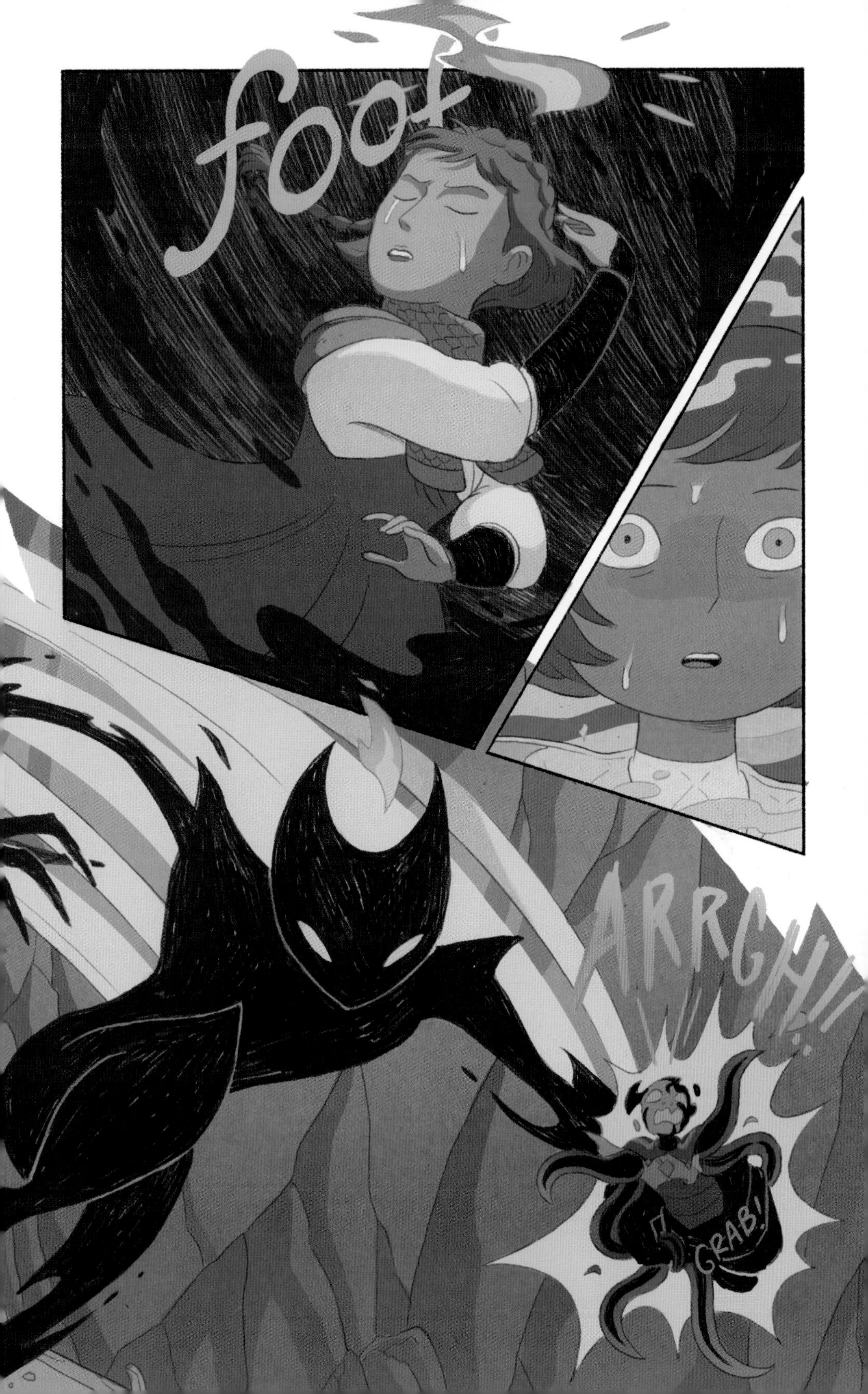
foof
ARRGH!!!
GRAB!

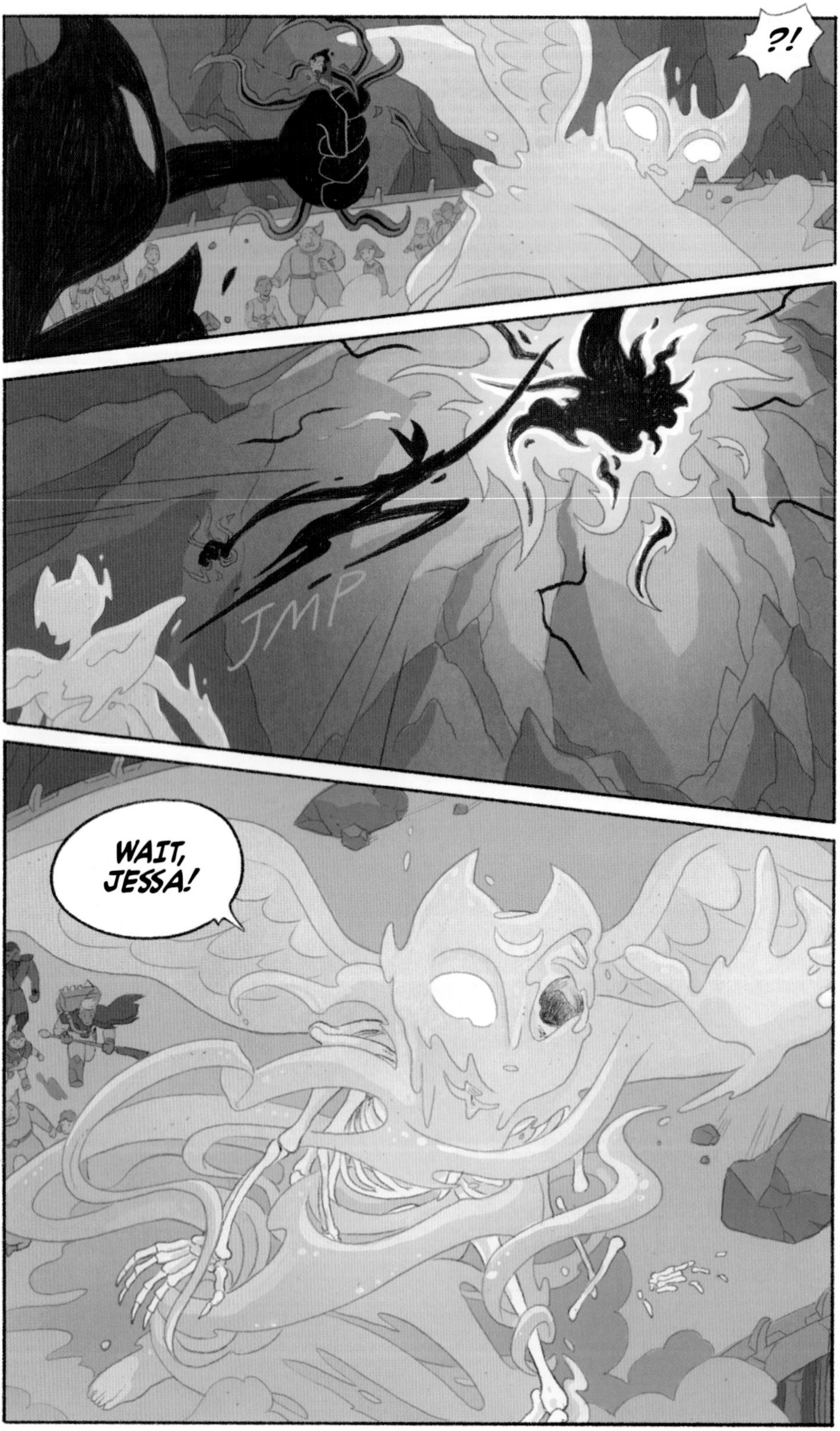
?!
JMP
WAIT, JESSA!

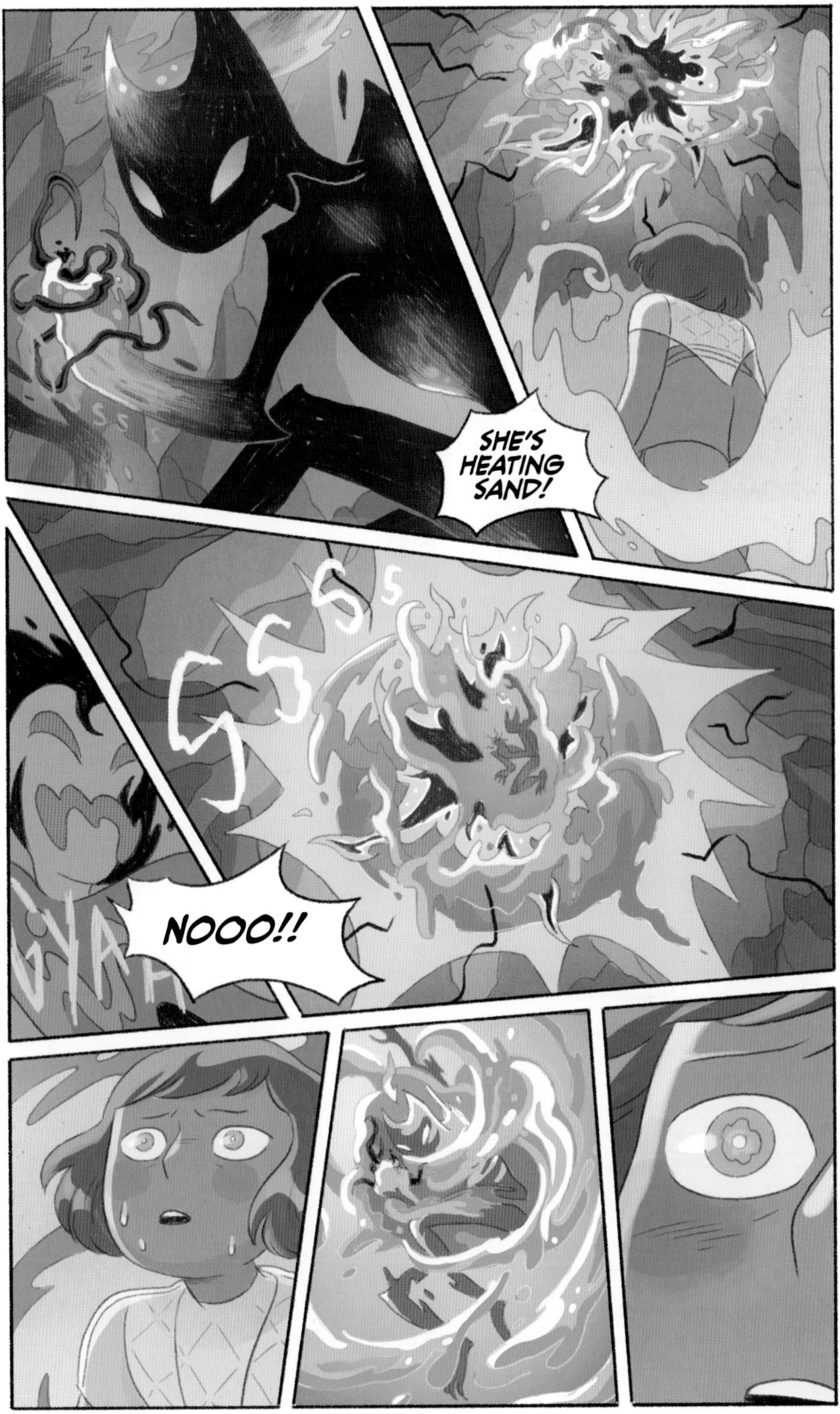
SSS
SHE'S HEATING SAND!
SSSSS
GYAH
NOOO!!

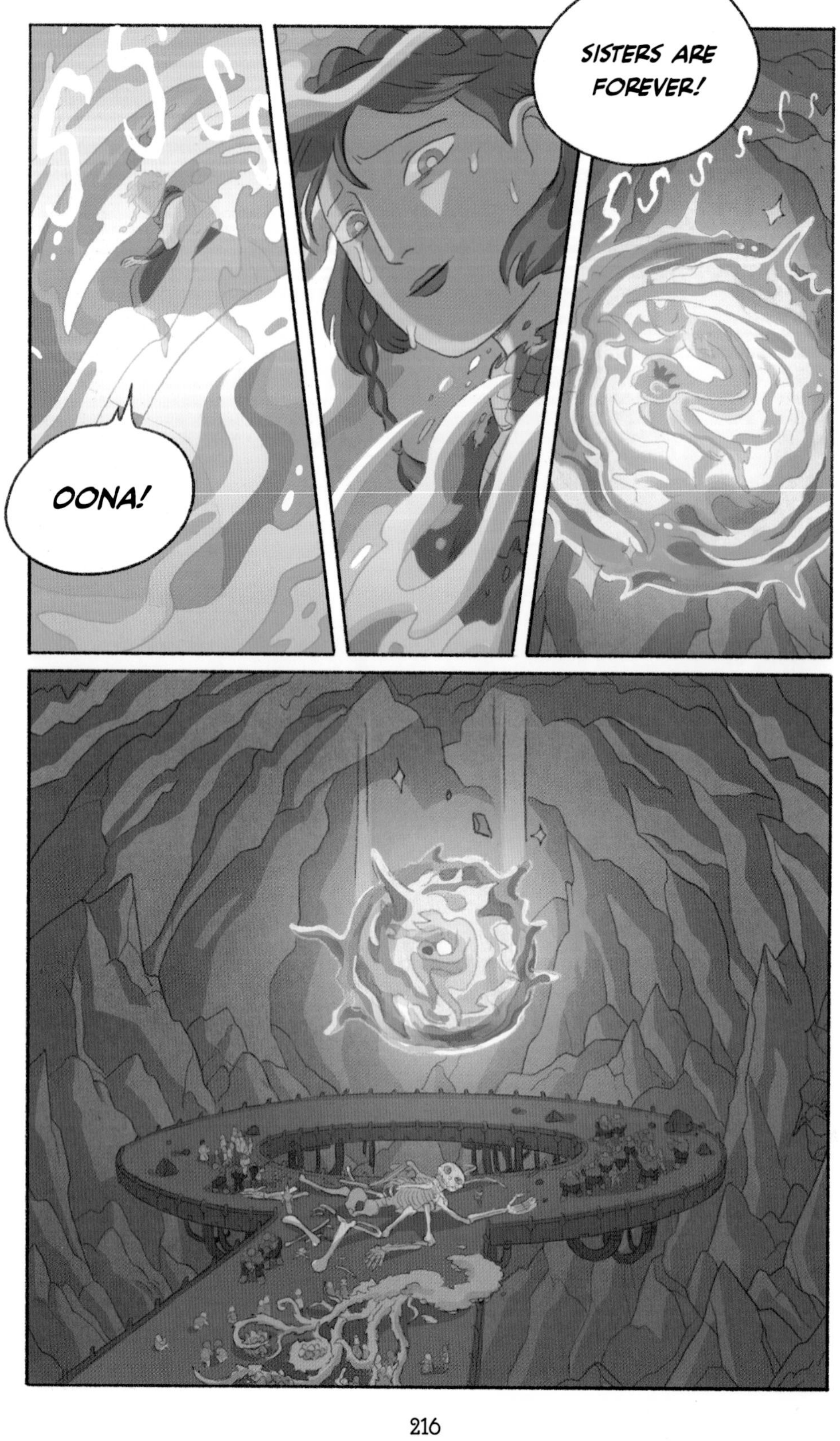
OONA!
SISTERS ARE FOREVER!

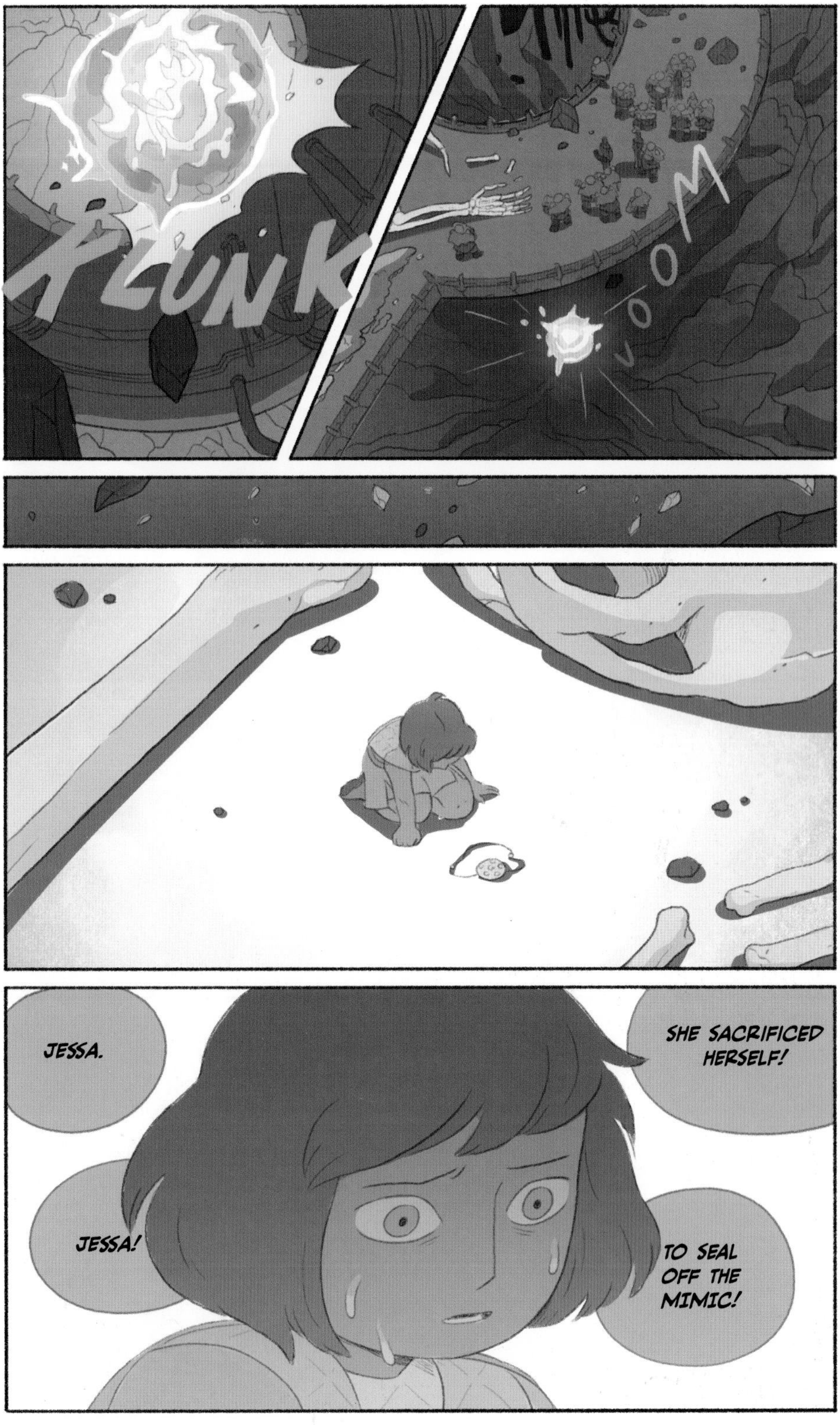
KLUNK
VOOOM
JESSA.
SHE SACRIFICED HERSELF!
JESSA!
TO SEAL OFF THE MIMIC!

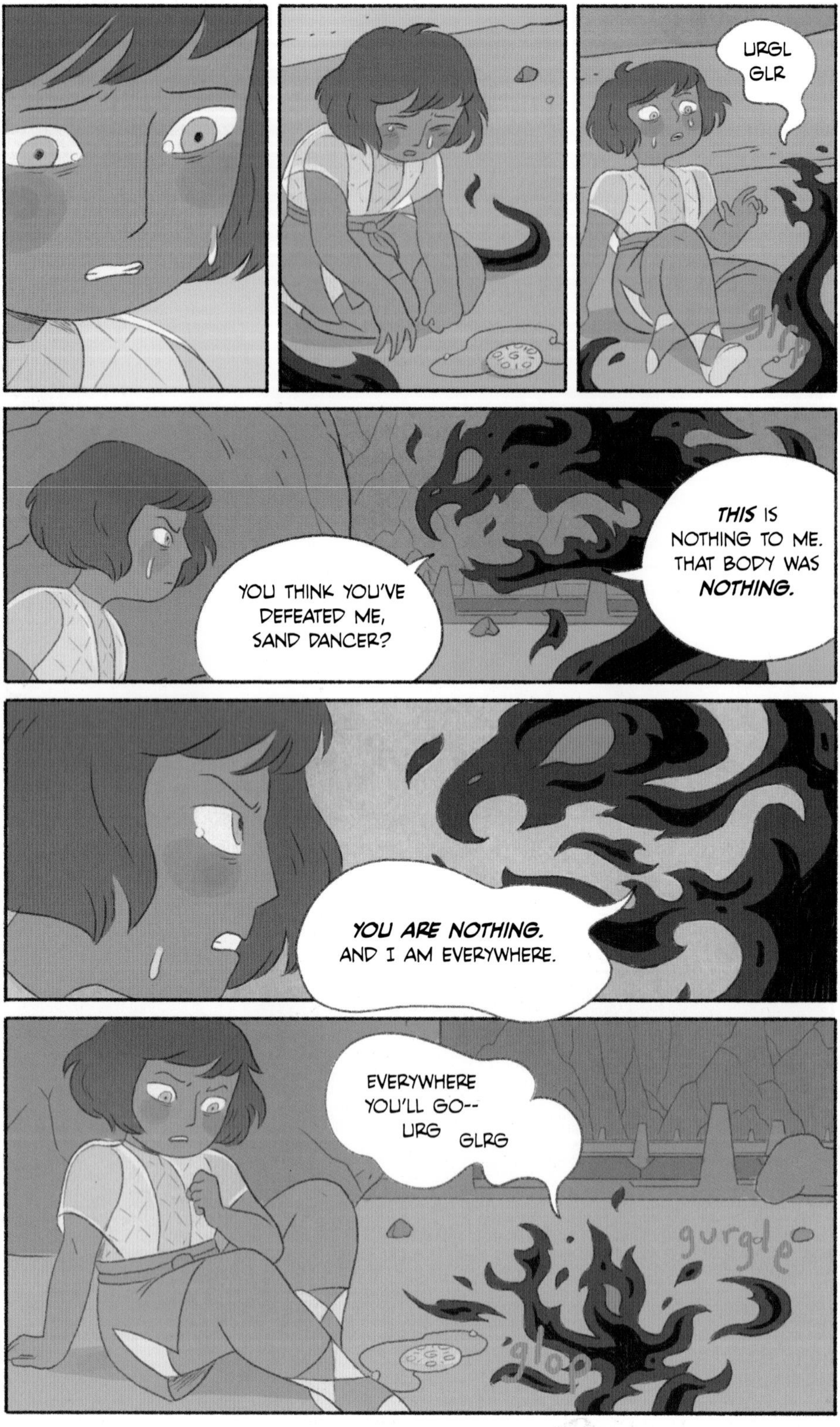
URGL GLR
glrp
YOU THINK YOU'VE DEFEATED ME, SAND DANCER?
THIS IS NOTHING TO ME. THAT BODY WAS NOTHING.
YOU ARE NOTHING. AND I AM EVERYWHERE.
EVERYWHERE YOU'LL GO-- URG GLRG
gurgle
glop

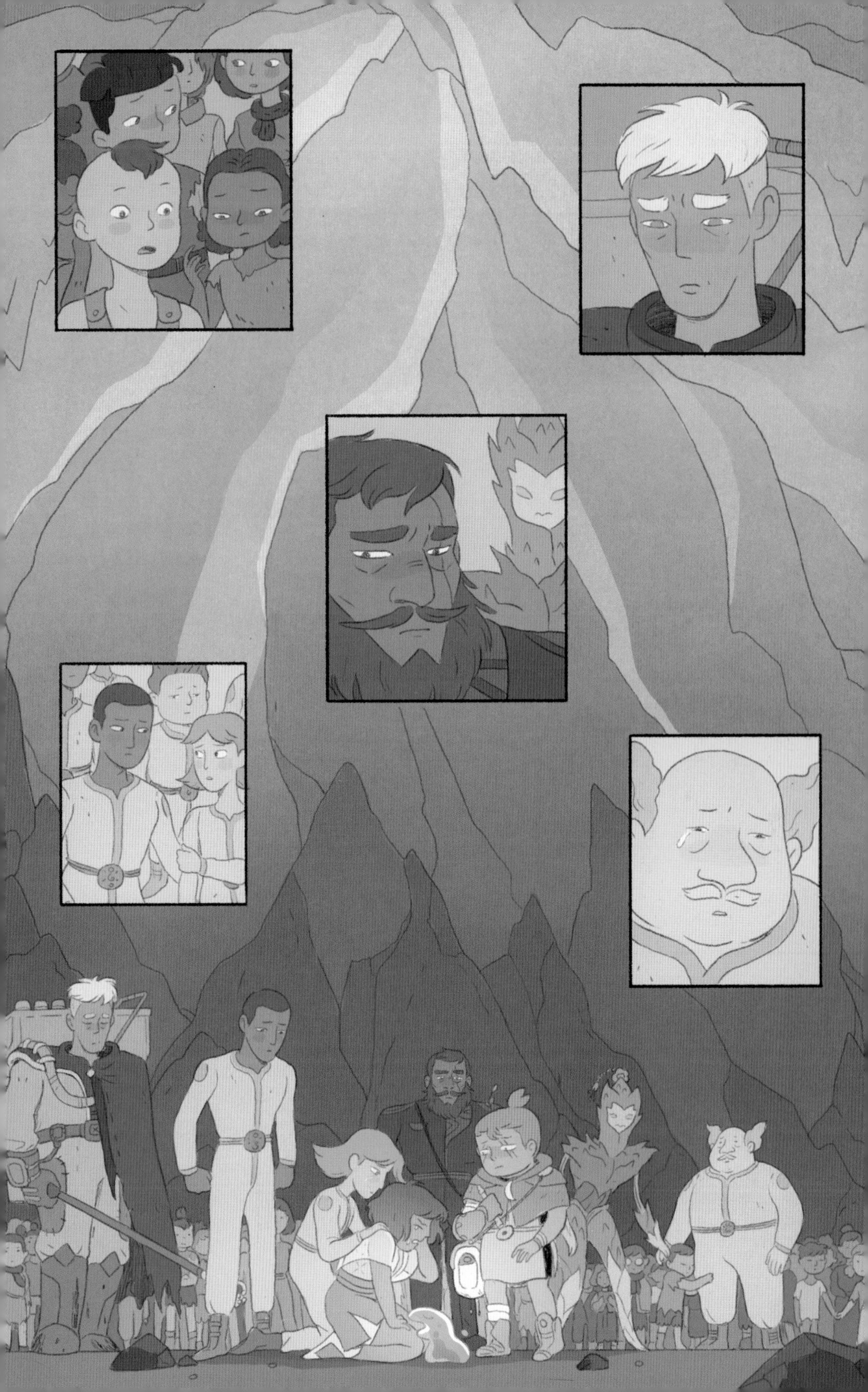

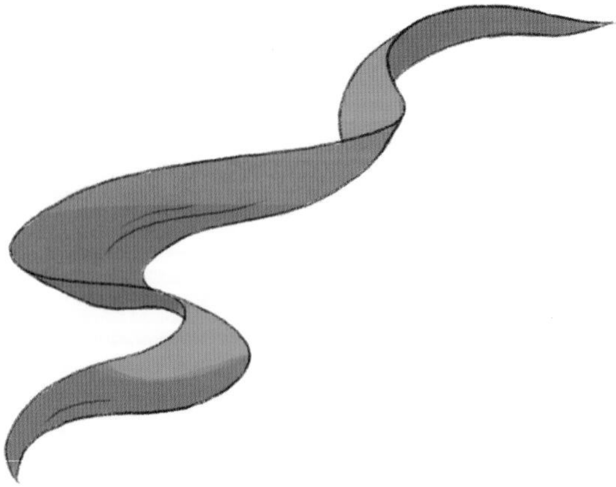

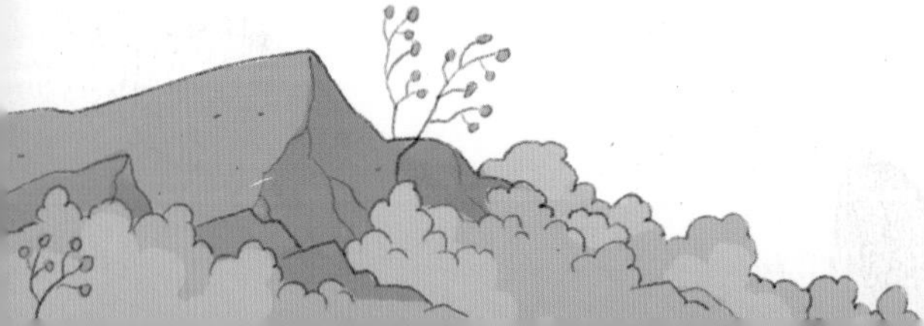

EPILOGUE

A FAREWELL AND A GREETING

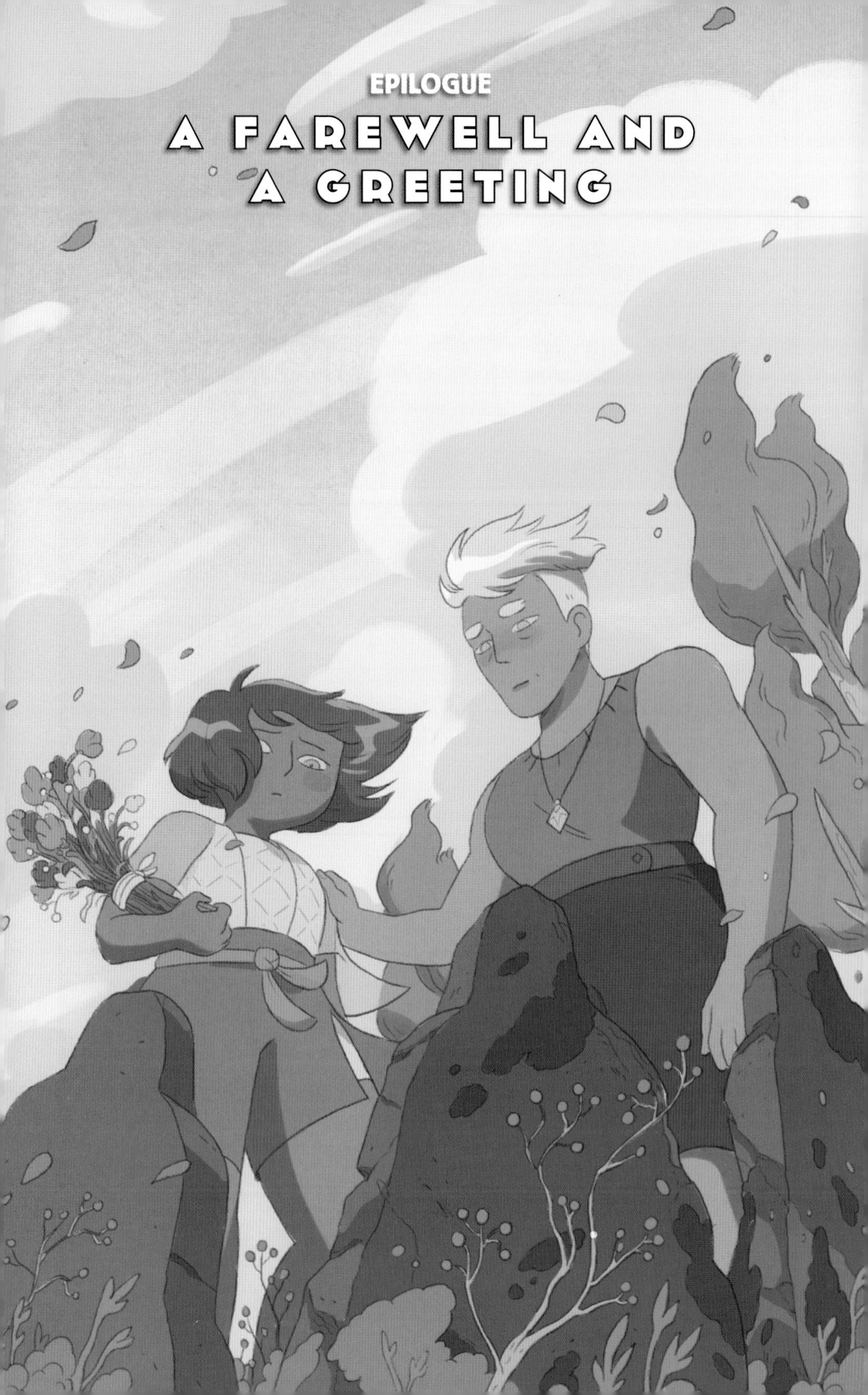

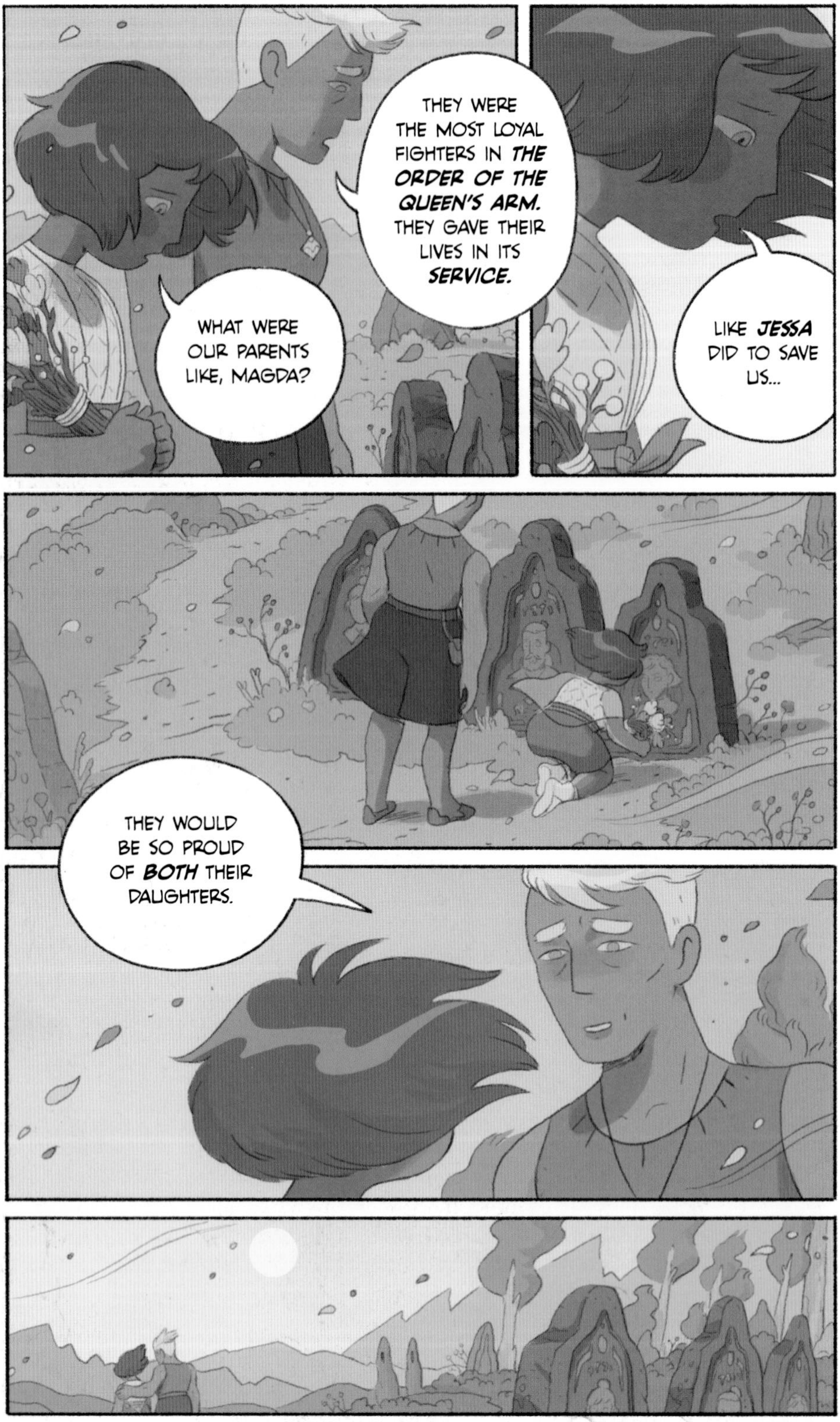
WHAT WERE OUR PARENTS LIKE, MAGDA?
THEY WERE THE MOST LOYAL FIGHTERS IN **THE ORDER OF THE QUEEN'S ARM.** THEY GAVE THEIR LIVES IN ITS **SERVICE.**
LIKE **JESSA** DID TO SAVE US...
THEY WOULD BE SO PROUD OF **BOTH** THEIR DAUGHTERS.

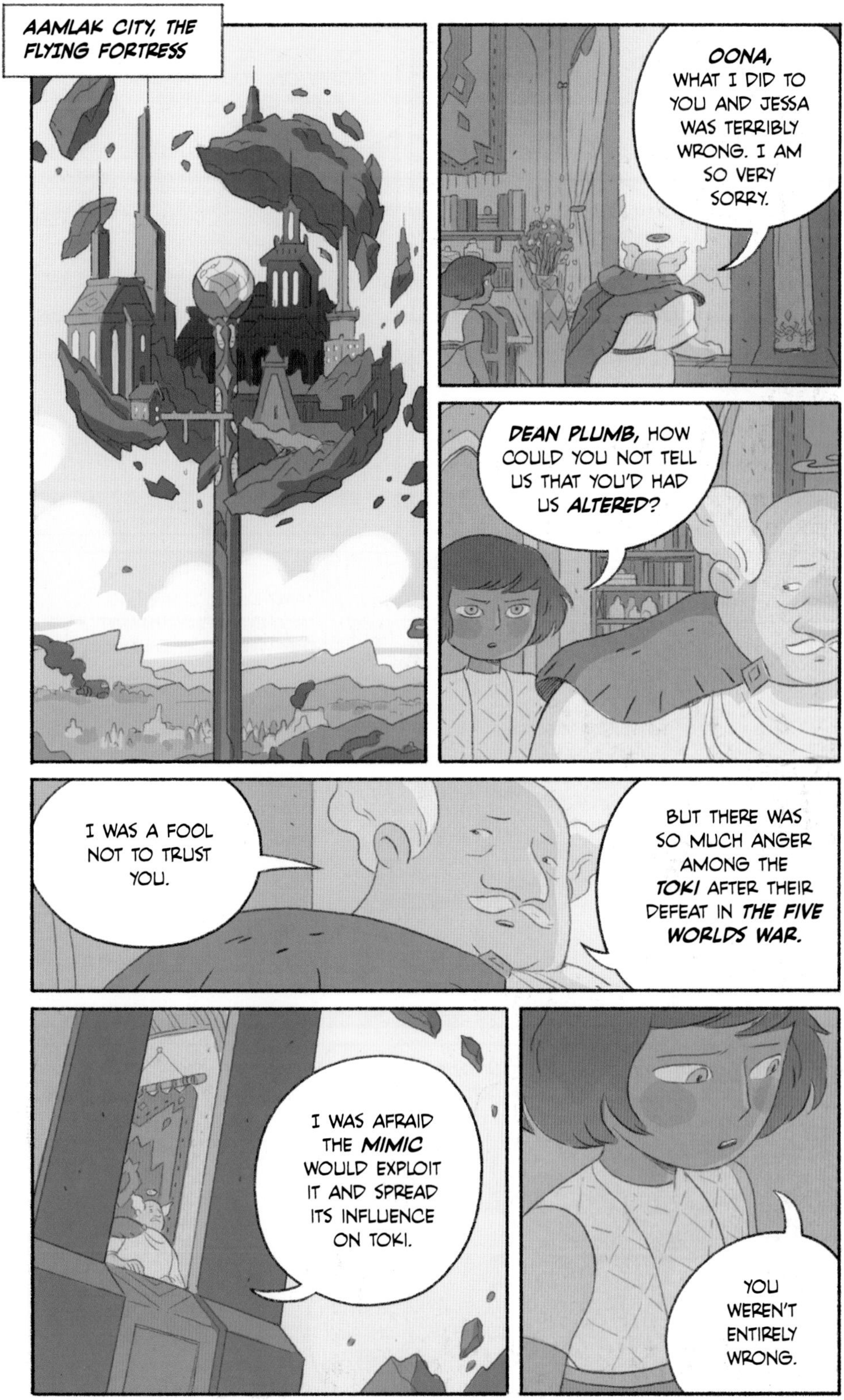
AAMLAK CITY, THE FLYING FORTRESS
OONA, WHAT I DID TO YOU AND JESSA WAS TERRIBLY WRONG. I AM SO VERY SORRY.
DEAN PLUMB, HOW COULD YOU NOT TELL US THAT YOU'D HAD US ALTERED?
I WAS A FOOL NOT TO TRUST YOU.
BUT THERE WAS SO MUCH ANGER AMONG THE TOKI AFTER THEIR DEFEAT IN THE FIVE WORLDS WAR.
I WAS AFRAID THE MIMIC WOULD EXPLOIT IT AND SPREAD ITS INFLUENCE ON TOKI.
YOU WEREN'T ENTIRELY WRONG.

SO WHEN I HEARD THAT THREE YOUNG KIDS AT *ATBAL-BALAK* HAD MANIFESTED *THE LIVING FIRE*...

...I THOUGHT THOSE POWERS SHOULD SERVE *THE SAND CASTLE,* RATHER THAN *TOKI* UNDER THE MIMIC'S SWAY.

YOU DID THAT THROUGH *DECEPTION.* YOU CHANGED *EVERY CELL* IN OUR BODIES.

YOU WIPED OUR MEMORIES OF BEING BLUE!

WHAT I DID WAS UNFORGIVABLE.

YOU AND JESSA SHOULD HAVE GROWN UP AS YOUR OWN BEAUTIFUL *TOKI* SELVES, LIKE *VECTOR.* THAT IS WHAT I PLAN TO TELL THE NEW TOKI AUTHORITIES...

AND I WILL SUBMIT TO WHATEVER *PUNISHMENT* THEY SEE FIT TO GIVE ME FOR MY CRIME.

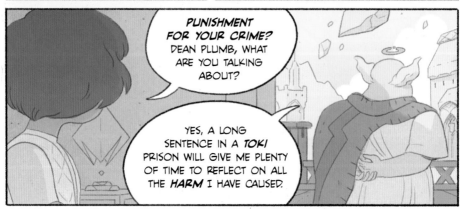

PUNISHMENT FOR YOUR CRIME? DEAN PLUMB, WHAT ARE YOU TALKING ABOUT?

YES, A LONG SENTENCE IN A *TOKI* PRISON WILL GIVE ME PLENTY OF TIME TO REFLECT ON ALL THE *HARM* I HAVE CAUSED.

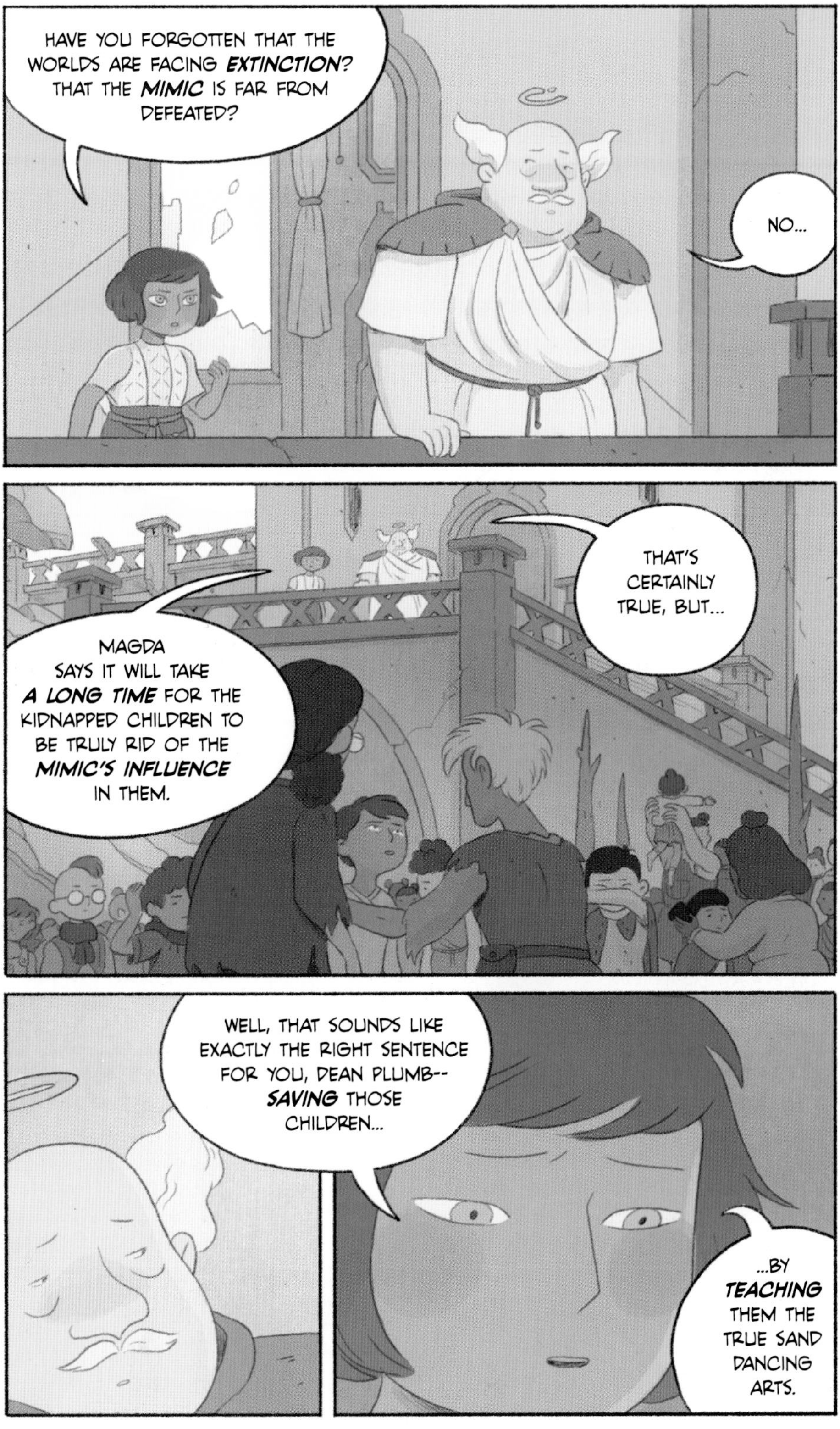
HAVE YOU FORGOTTEN THAT THE WORLDS ARE FACING EXTINCTION? THAT THE MIMIC IS FAR FROM DEFEATED?
NO...
THAT'S CERTAINLY TRUE, BUT...
MAGDA SAYS IT WILL TAKE A LONG TIME FOR THE KIDNAPPED CHILDREN TO BE TRULY RID OF THE MIMIC'S INFLUENCE IN THEM.
WELL, THAT SOUNDS LIKE EXACTLY THE RIGHT SENTENCE FOR YOU, DEAN PLUMB-- SAVING THOSE CHILDREN...
...BY TEACHING THEM THE TRUE SAND DANCING ARTS.

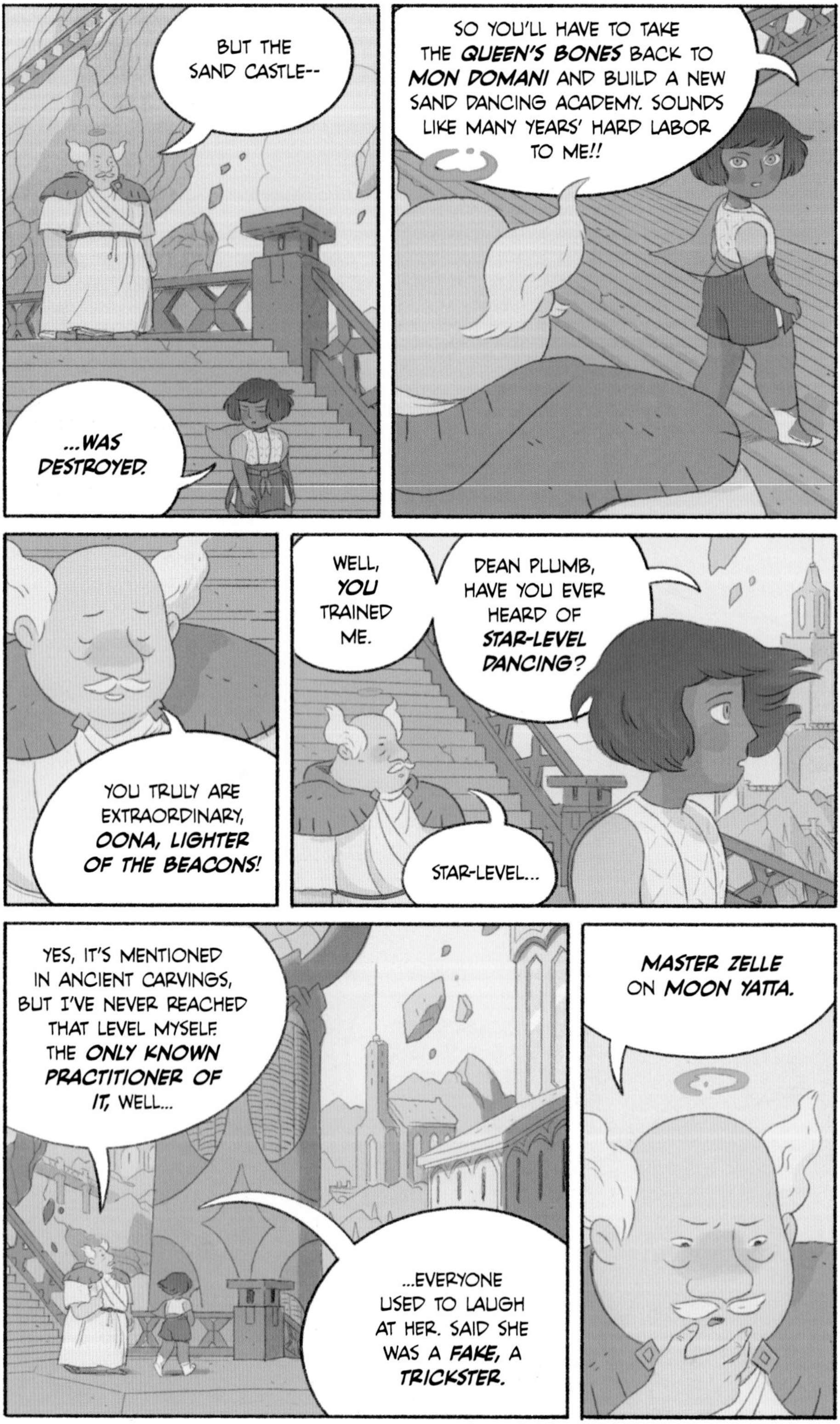
BUT THE SAND CASTLE--
...WAS DESTROYED.
SO YOU'LL HAVE TO TAKE THE QUEEN'S BONES BACK TO MON DOMANI AND BUILD A NEW SAND DANCING ACADEMY. SOUNDS LIKE MANY YEARS' HARD LABOR TO ME!!
YOU TRULY ARE EXTRAORDINARY, OONA, LIGHTER OF THE BEACONS!
WELL, YOU TRAINED ME.
DEAN PLUMB, HAVE YOU EVER HEARD OF STAR-LEVEL DANCING?
STAR-LEVEL...
YES, IT'S MENTIONED IN ANCIENT CARVINGS, BUT I'VE NEVER REACHED THAT LEVEL MYSELF. THE ONLY KNOWN PRACTITIONER OF IT, WELL...
...EVERYONE USED TO LAUGH AT HER. SAID SHE WAS A FAKE, A TRICKSTER.
MASTER ZELLE ON MOON YATTA.

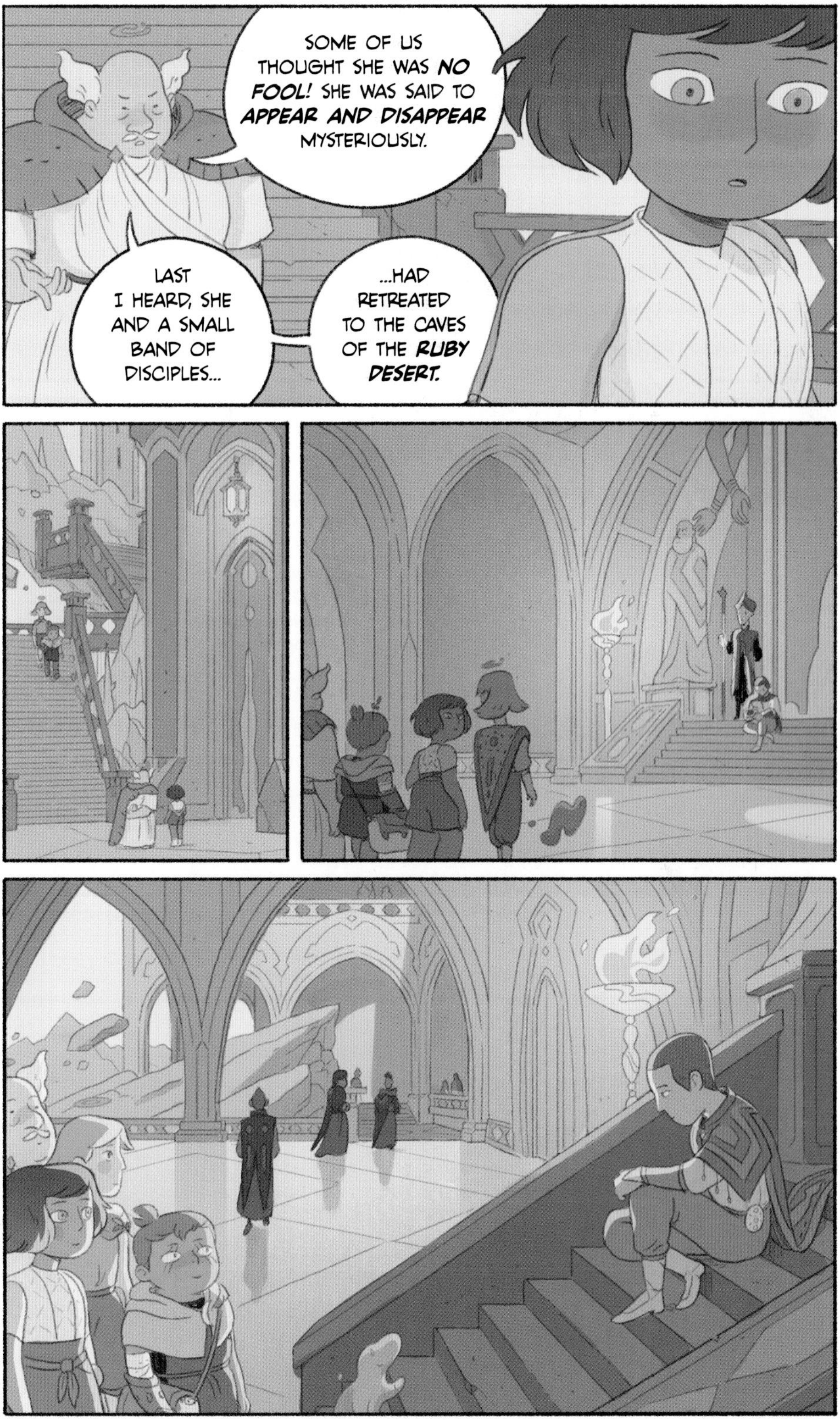
SOME OF US THOUGHT SHE WAS NO FOOL! SHE WAS SAID TO APPEAR AND DISAPPEAR MYSTERIOUSLY.
LAST I HEARD, SHE AND A SMALL BAND OF DISCIPLES...
...HAD RETREATED TO THE CAVES OF THE RUBY DESERT.

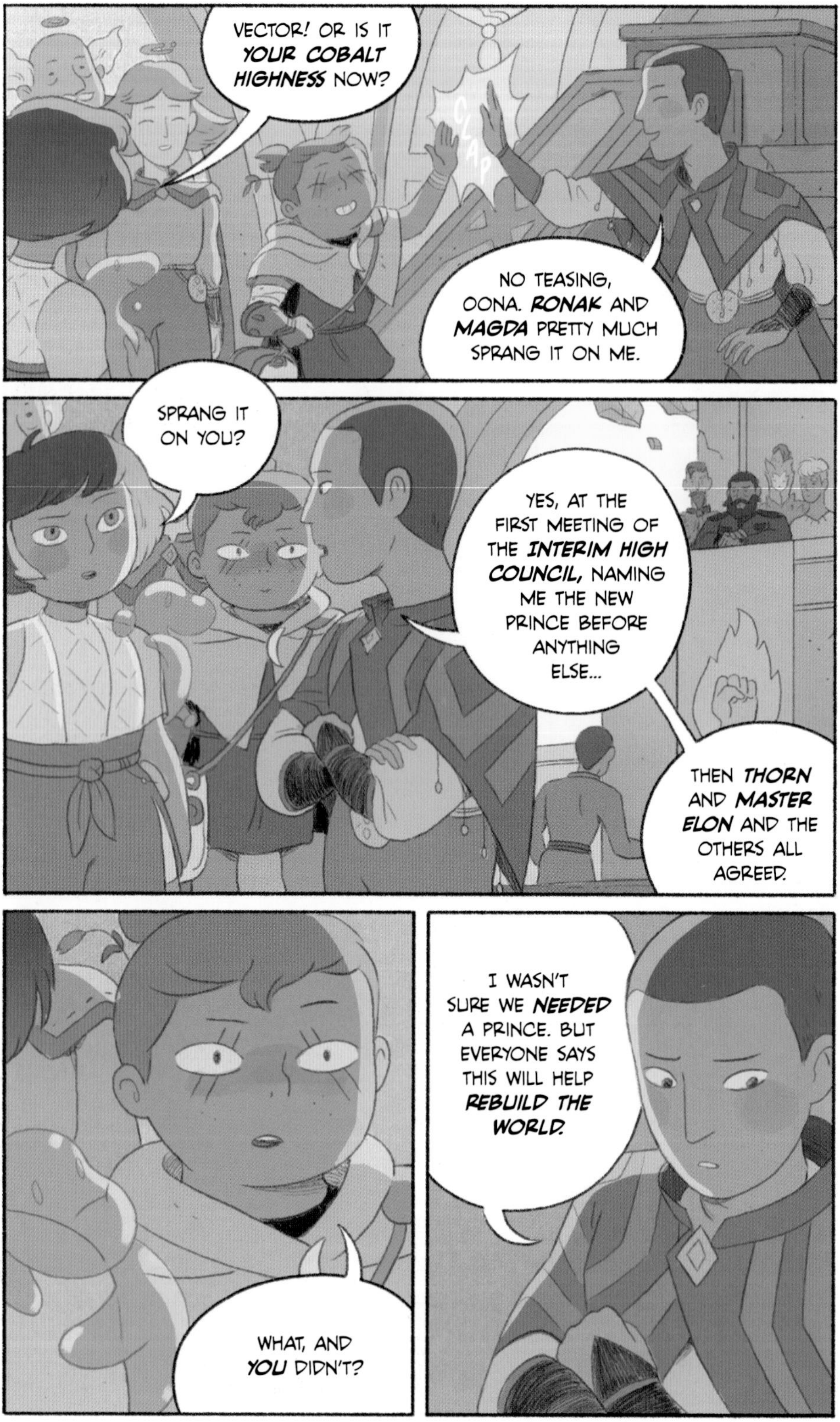
VECTOR! OR IS IT YOUR COBALT HIGHNESS NOW?
CLAP
NO TEASING, OONA. RONAK AND MAGDA PRETTY MUCH SPRANG IT ON ME.
SPRANG IT ON YOU?
YES, AT THE FIRST MEETING OF THE INTERIM HIGH COUNCIL, NAMING ME THE NEW PRINCE BEFORE ANYTHING ELSE...
THEN THORN AND MASTER ELON AND THE OTHERS ALL AGREED.
WHAT, AND YOU DIDN'T?
I WASN'T SURE WE NEEDED A PRINCE. BUT EVERYONE SAYS THIS WILL HELP REBUILD THE WORLD.

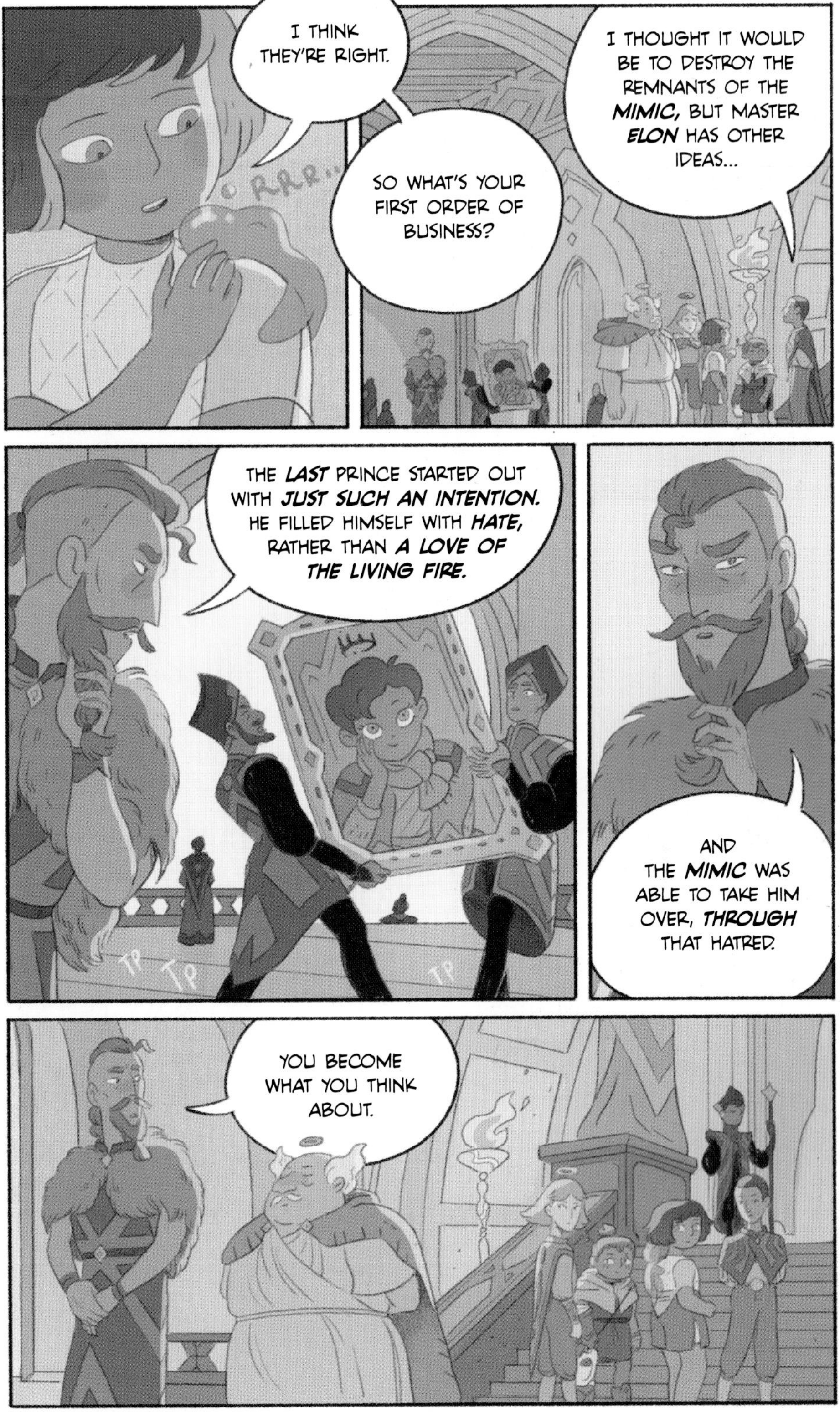
I THINK THEY'RE RIGHT.
RRR...
SO WHAT'S YOUR FIRST ORDER OF BUSINESS?
I THOUGHT IT WOULD BE TO DESTROY THE REMNANTS OF THE MIMIC, BUT MASTER ELON HAS OTHER IDEAS...
THE LAST PRINCE STARTED OUT WITH JUST SUCH AN INTENTION. HE FILLED HIMSELF WITH HATE, RATHER THAN A LOVE OF THE LIVING FIRE.
TP TP TP
AND THE MIMIC WAS ABLE TO TAKE HIM OVER, THROUGH THAT HATRED.
YOU BECOME WHAT YOU THINK ABOUT.

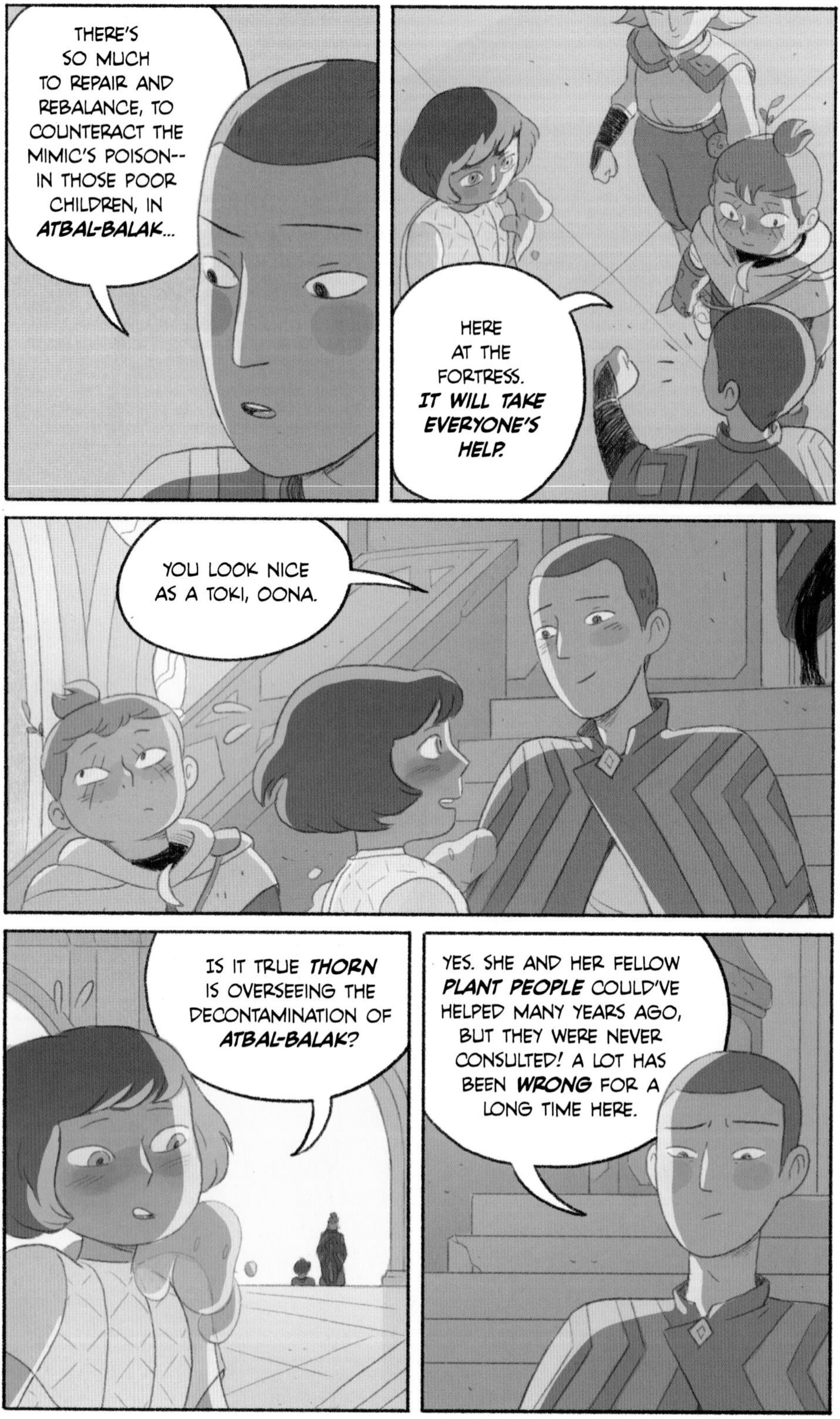
THERE'S SO MUCH TO REPAIR AND REBALANCE, TO COUNTERACT THE MIMIC'S POISON-- IN THOSE POOR CHILDREN, IN ATBAL-BALAK...
HERE AT THE FORTRESS. IT WILL TAKE EVERYONE'S HELP.
YOU LOOK NICE AS A TOKI, OONA.
IS IT TRUE THORN IS OVERSEEING THE DECONTAMINATION OF ATBAL-BALAK?
YES. SHE AND HER FELLOW PLANT PEOPLE COULD'VE HELPED MANY YEARS AGO, BUT THEY WERE NEVER CONSULTED! A LOT HAS BEEN WRONG FOR A LONG TIME HERE.

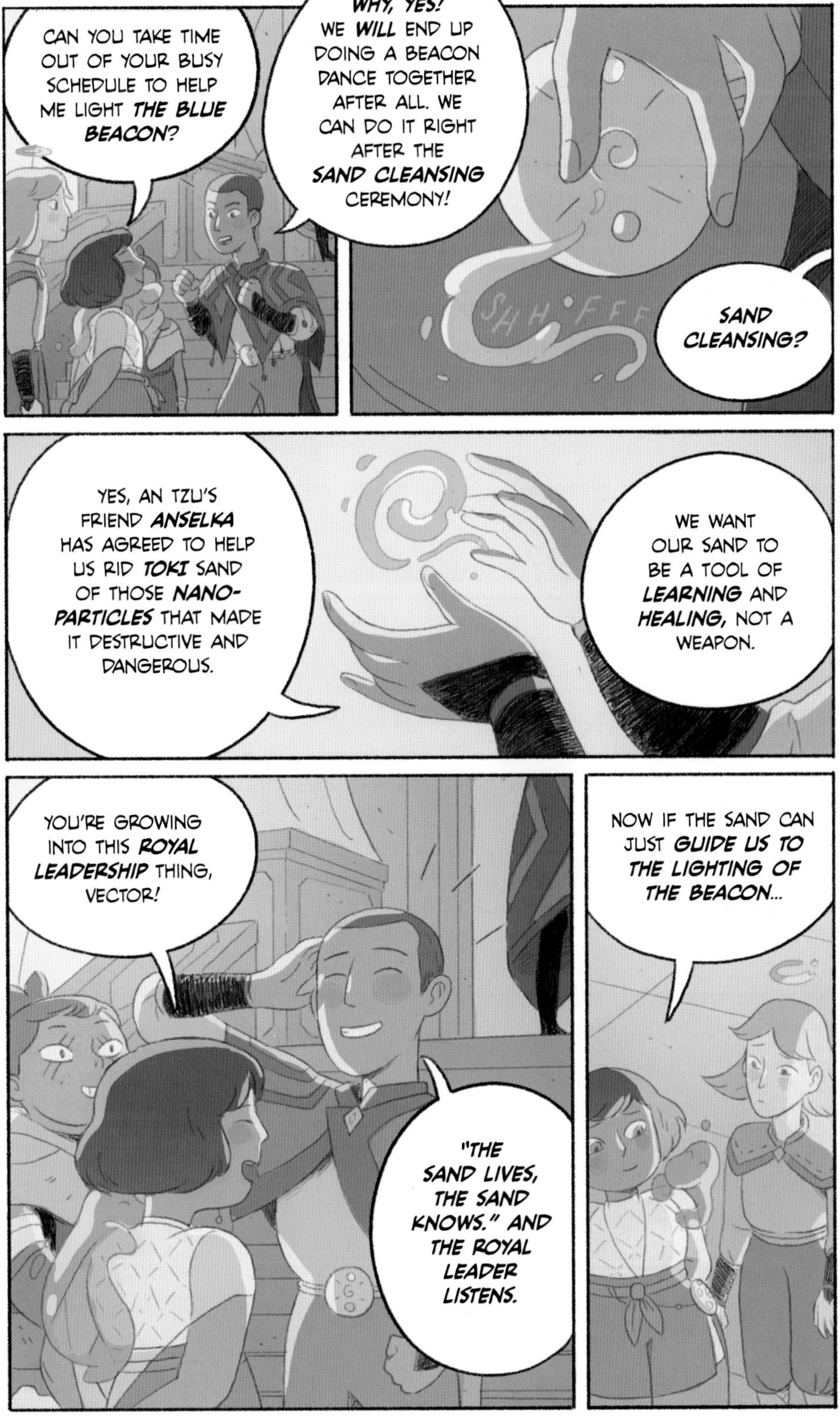

CAN YOU TAKE TIME OUT OF YOUR BUSY SCHEDULE TO HELP ME LIGHT THE BLUE BEACON?
WHY, YES! WE WILL END UP DOING A BEACON DANCE TOGETHER AFTER ALL. WE CAN DO IT RIGHT AFTER THE SAND CLEANSING CEREMONY!
SHHFFF
SAND CLEANSING?
YES, AN TZU'S FRIEND ANSELKA HAS AGREED TO HELP US RID TOKI SAND OF THOSE NANO-PARTICLES THAT MADE IT DESTRUCTIVE AND DANGEROUS.
WE WANT OUR SAND TO BE A TOOL OF LEARNING AND HEALING, NOT A WEAPON.
YOU'RE GROWING INTO THIS ROYAL LEADERSHIP THING, VECTOR!
"THE SAND LIVES, THE SAND KNOWS." AND THE ROYAL LEADER LISTENS.
NOW IF THE SAND CAN JUST GUIDE US TO THE LIGHTING OF THE BEACON...

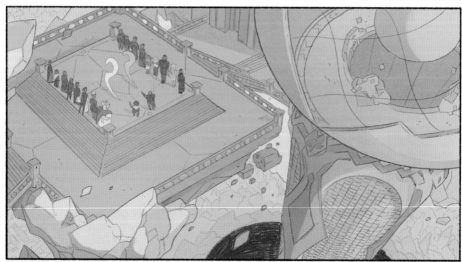

THE NEW PRINCE IS YOUNG. HE WILL MAKE MISTAKES.

AND WHEN HE DOES, WE WILL BE READY.

THE CROWDS ARE CHEERING HIM TODAY.

BUT *OUR POWERFUL FRIENDS* ON *MOON YATTA* WILL SUPPORT US WHEN THE TIME COMES.

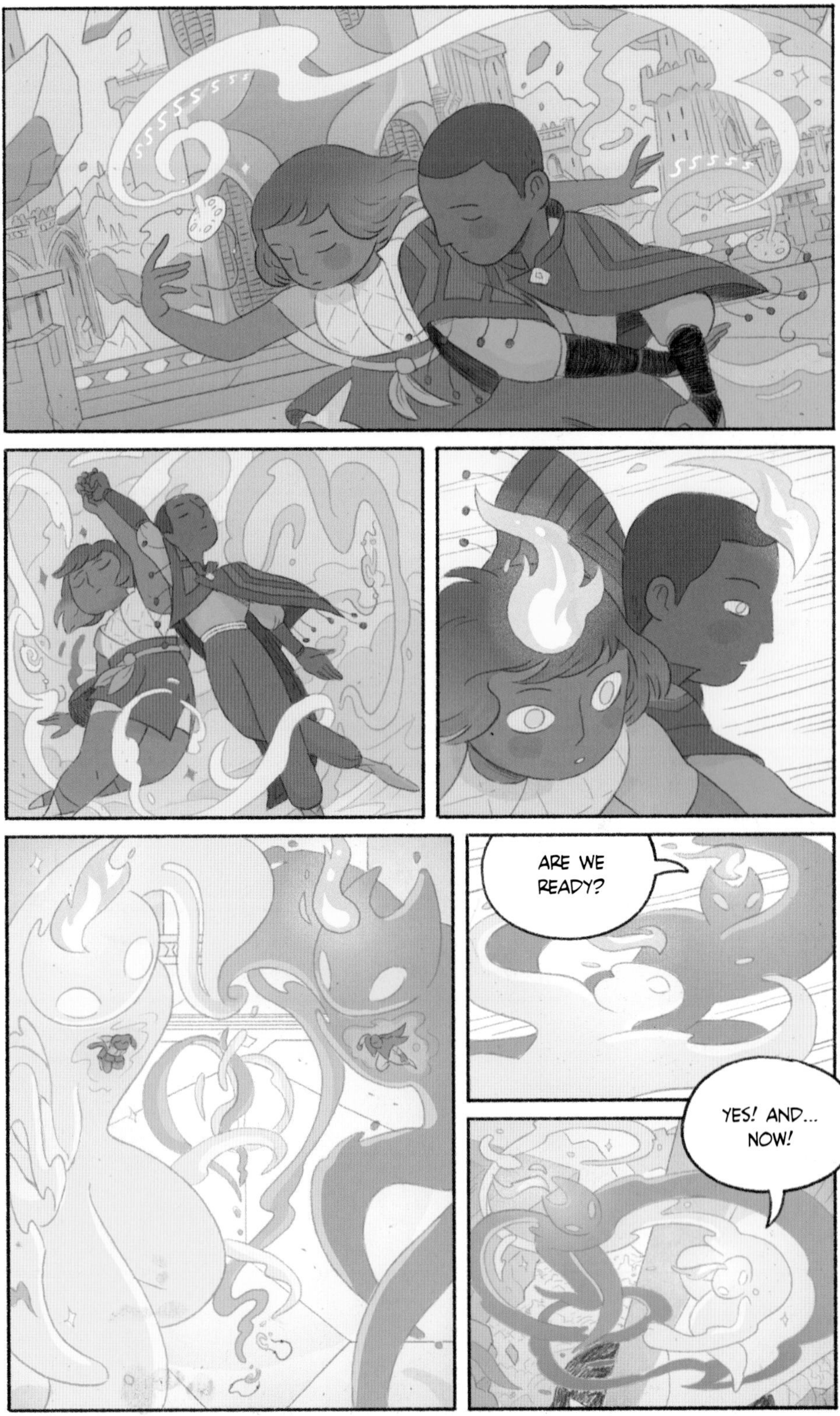
SSSSSSSS
SSSSS
ARE WE READY?
YES! AND... NOW!

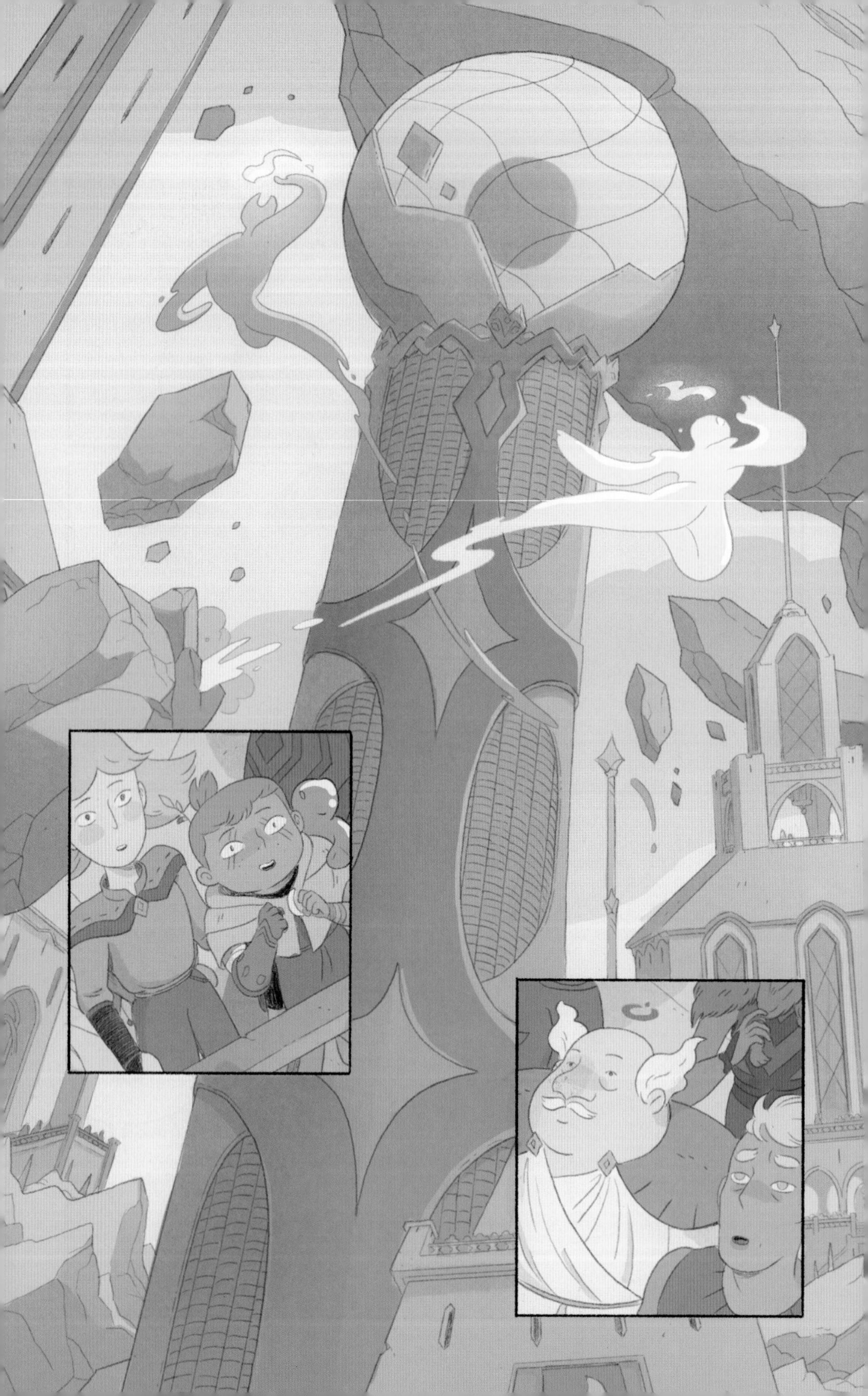

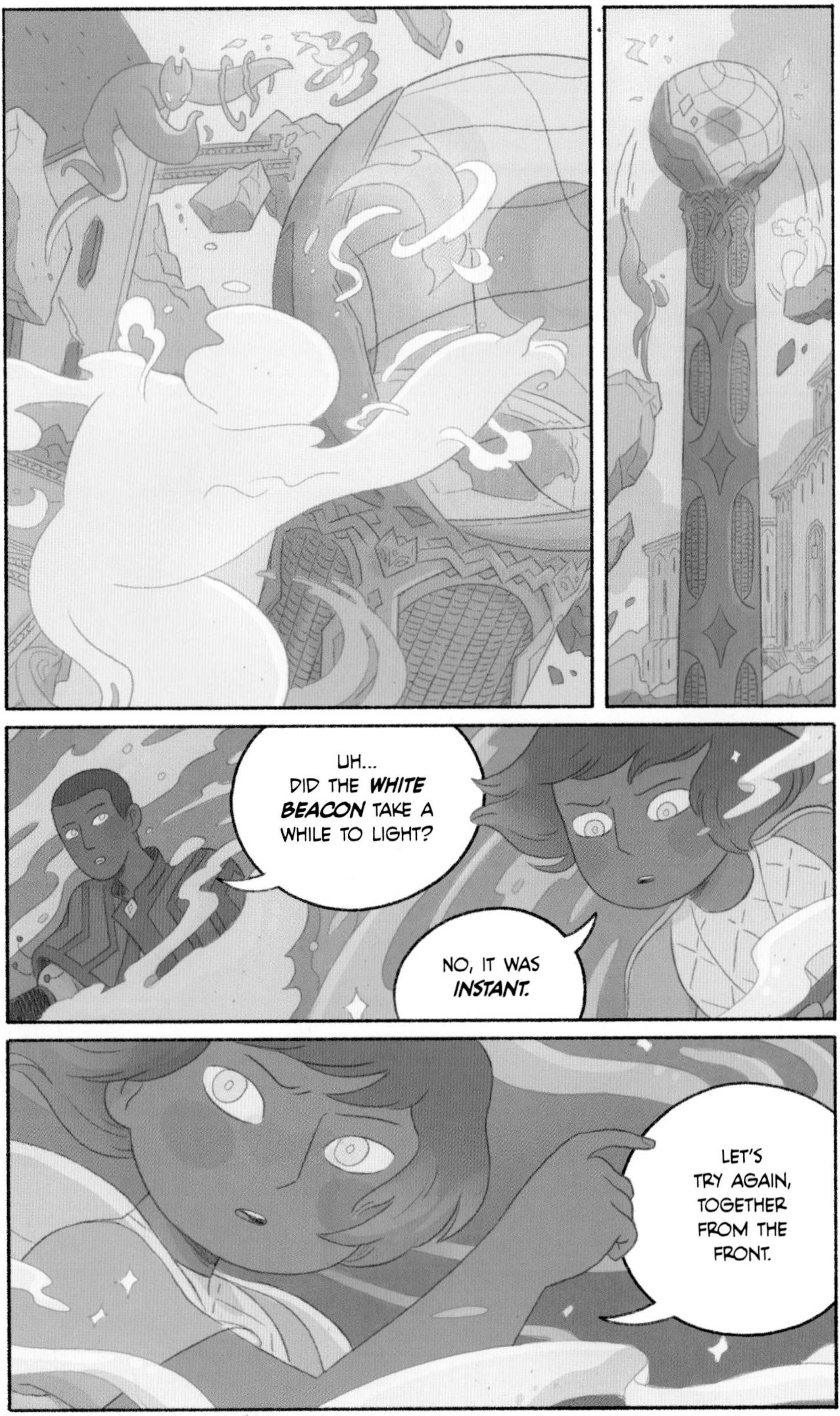
UH... DID THE ***WHITE BEACON*** TAKE A WHILE TO LIGHT?
NO, IT WAS ***INSTANT.***
LET'S TRY AGAIN, TOGETHER FROM THE FRONT.

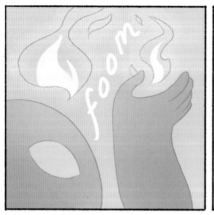

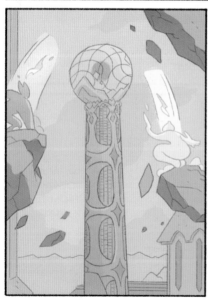

WHY WON'T IT LIGHT?! ONCE MORE!

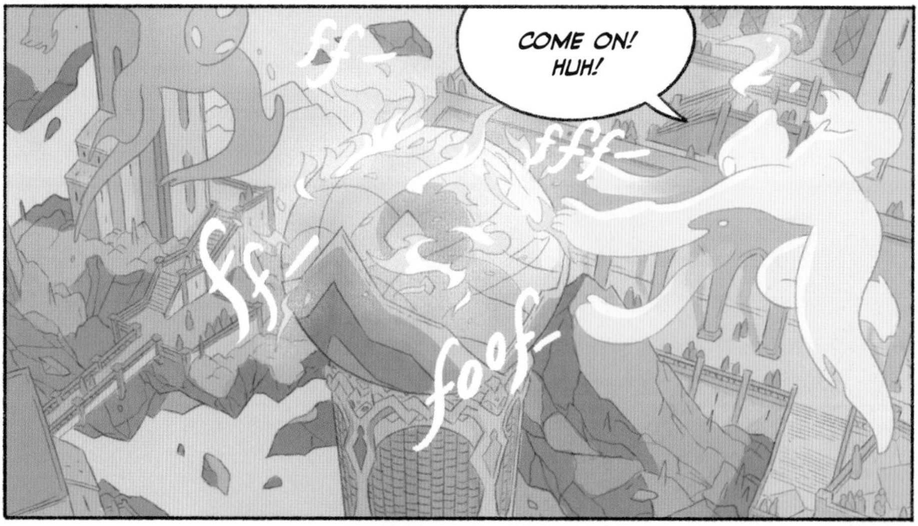
ff-
COME ON!
HUH!
fff-
ff-
foof-

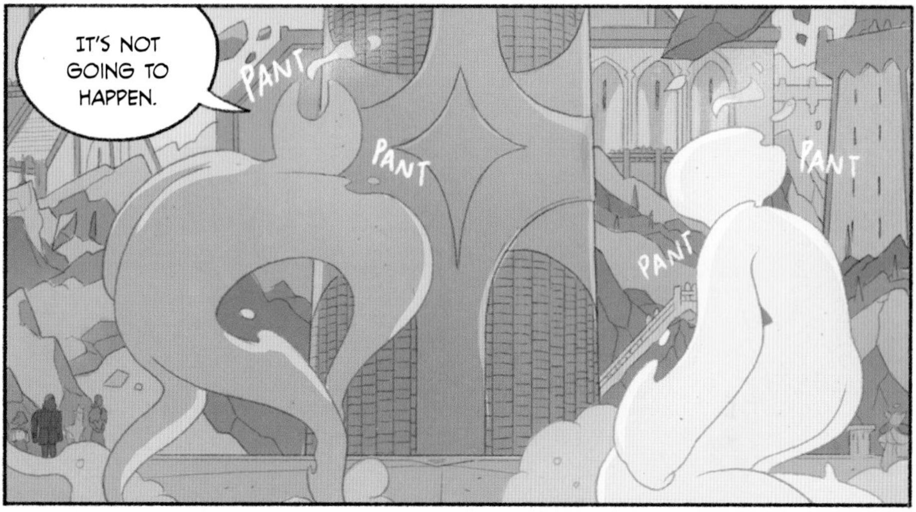
IT'S NOT GOING TO HAPPEN.
PANT
PANT
PANT
PANT

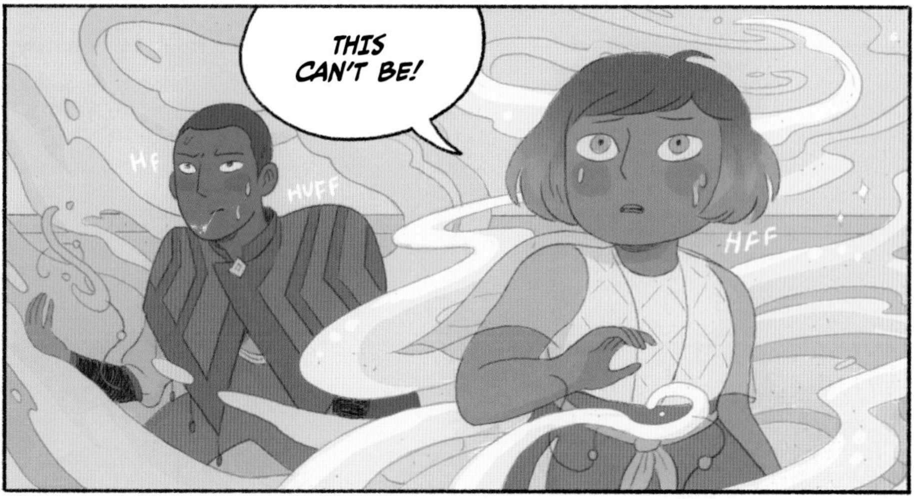
THIS CAN'T BE!
HF
HUFF
HFF

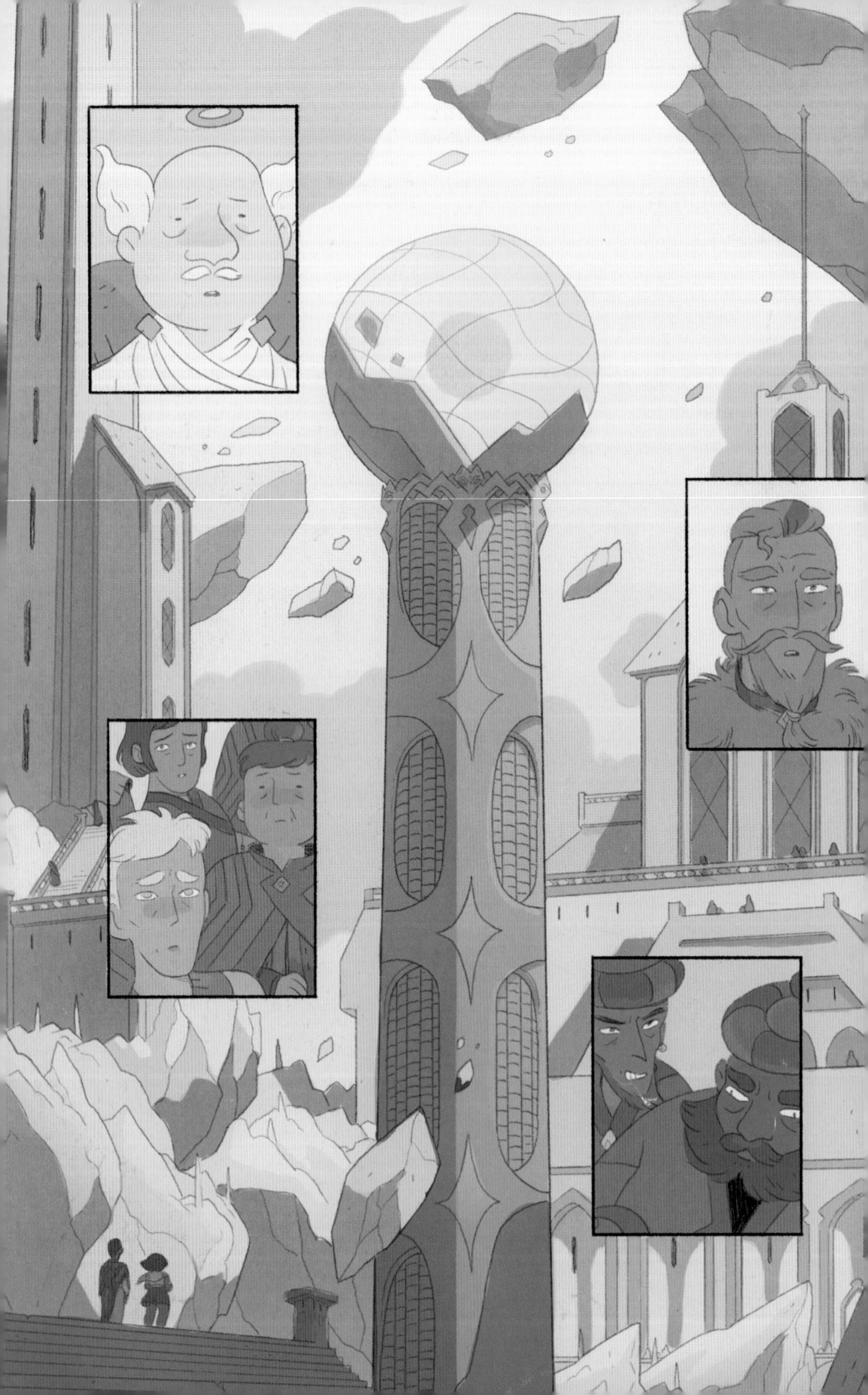

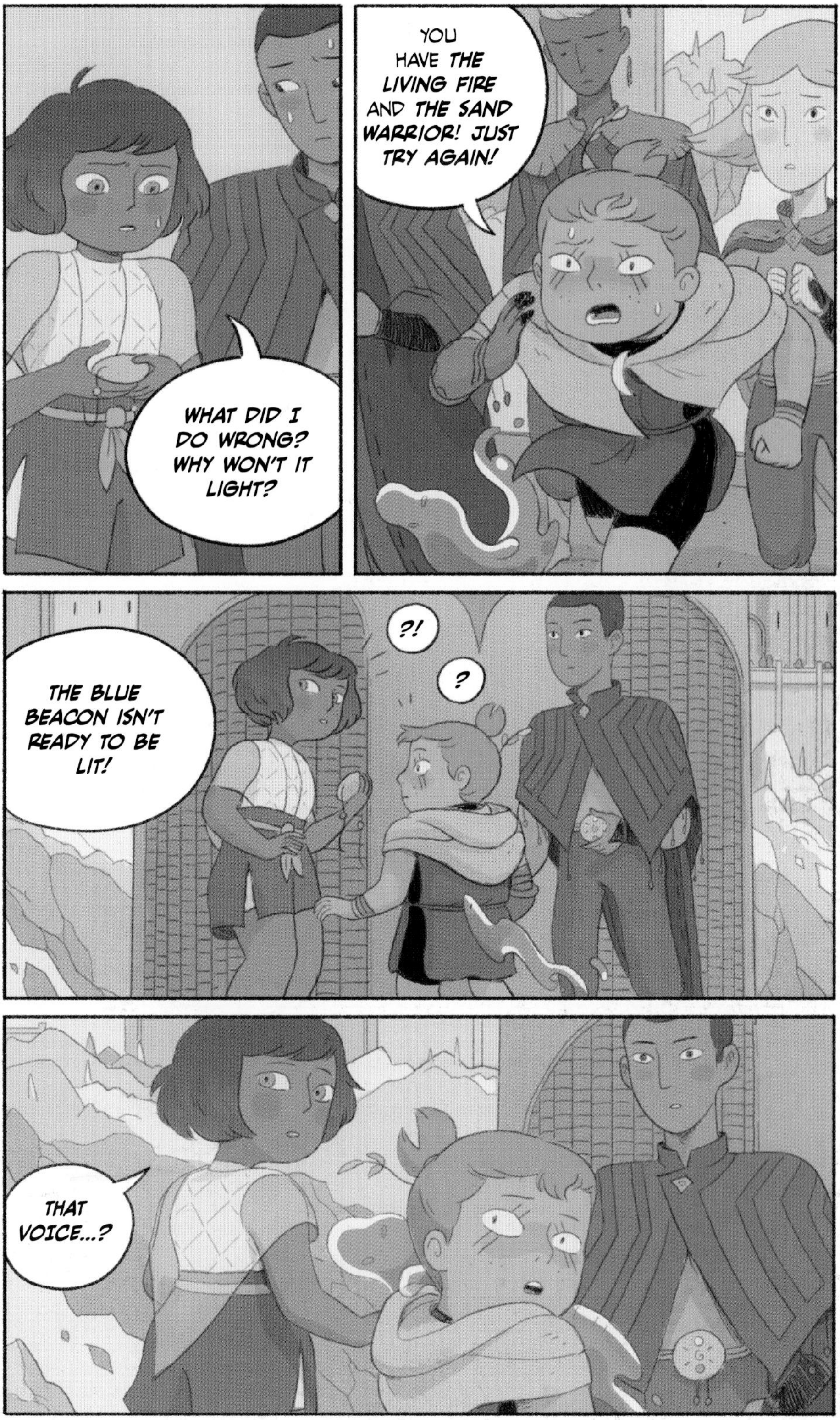
WHAT DID I DO WRONG? WHY WON'T IT LIGHT?
YOU HAVE THE LIVING FIRE AND THE SAND WARRIOR! JUST TRY AGAIN!
THE BLUE BEACON ISN'T READY TO BE LIT!
?!
?
THAT VOICE...?

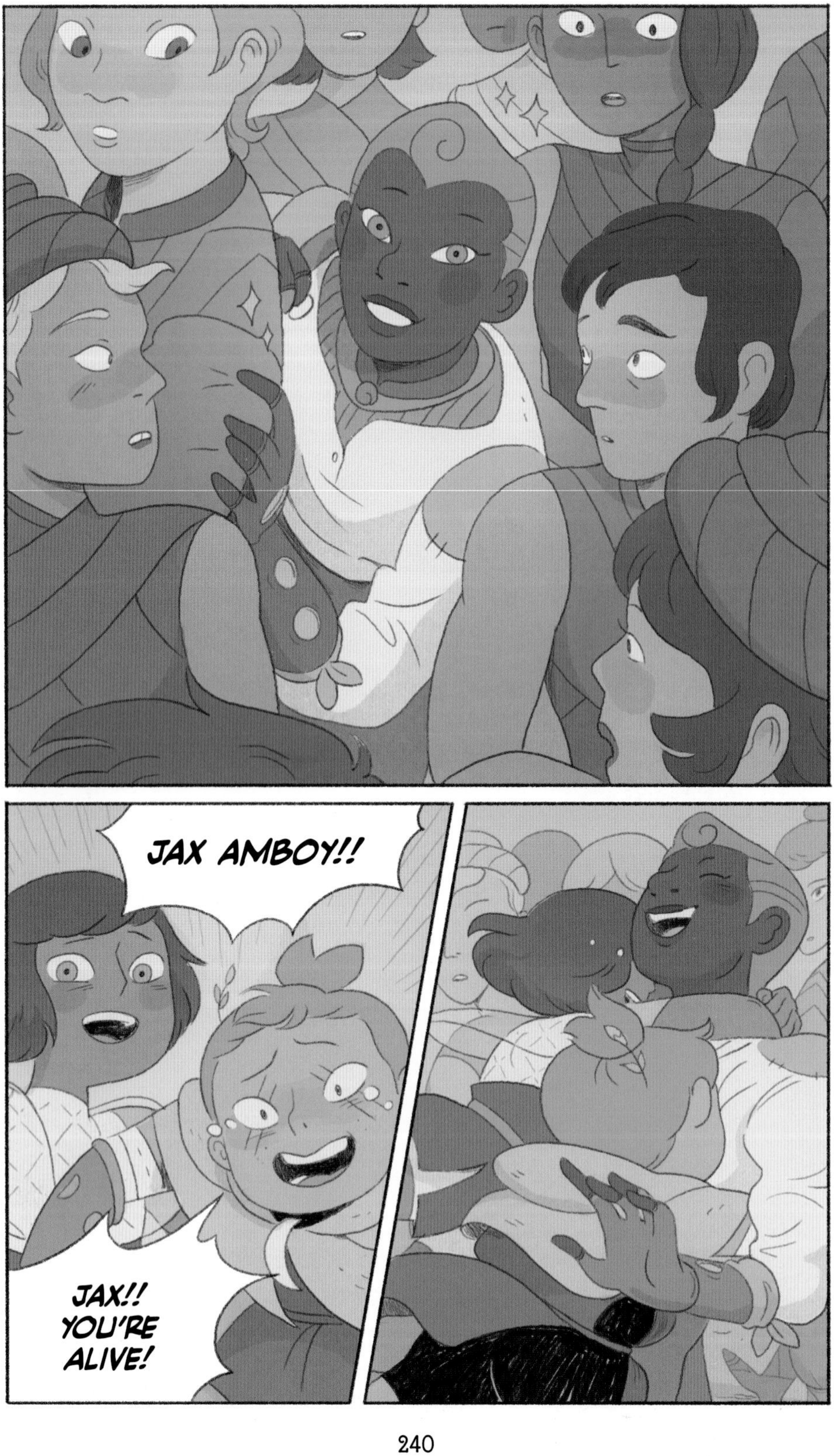
JAX AMBOY!!
JAX!! YOU'RE ALIVE!

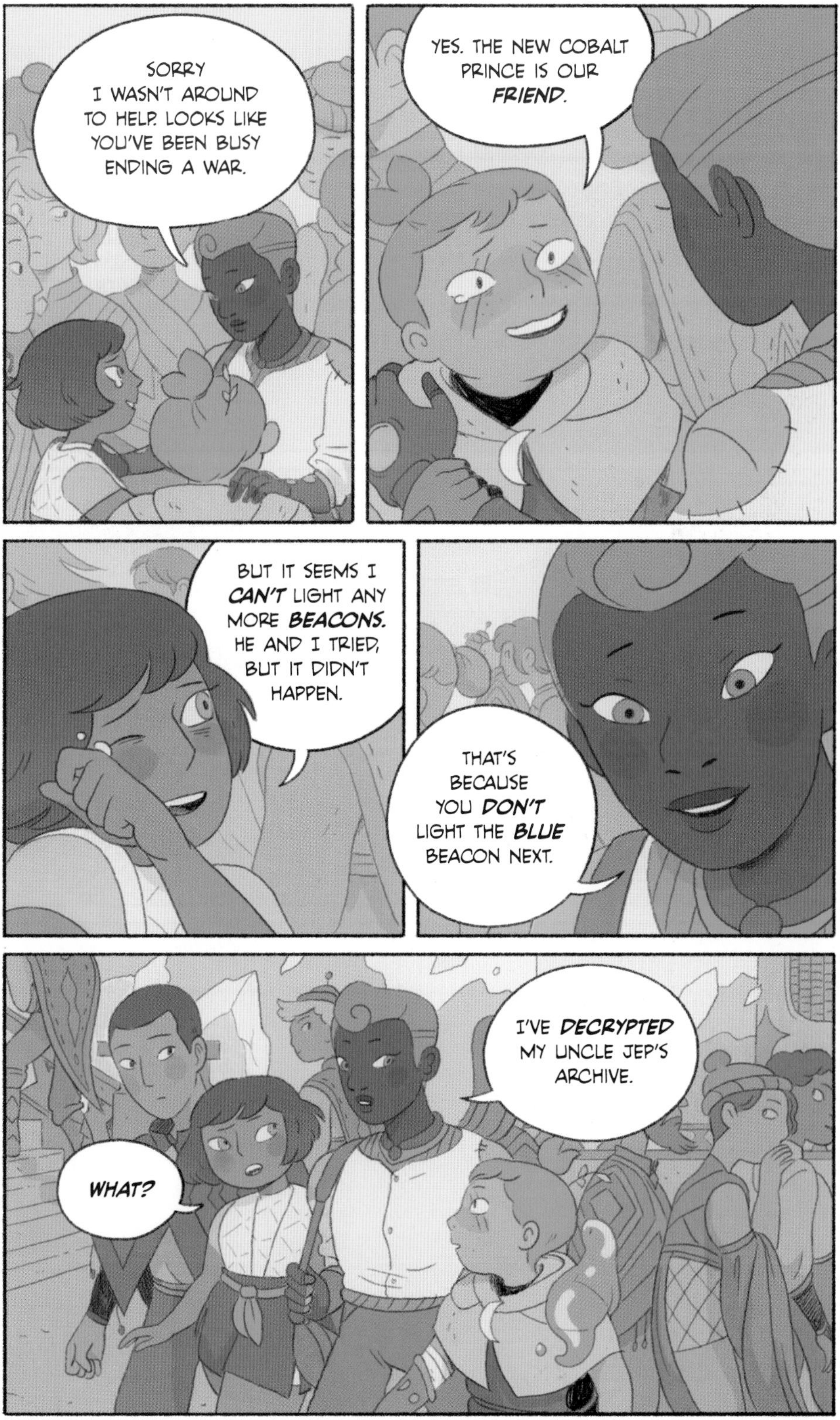
SORRY I WASN'T AROUND TO HELP. LOOKS LIKE YOU'VE BEEN BUSY ENDING A WAR.
YES. THE NEW COBALT PRINCE IS OUR **FRIEND.**
BUT IT SEEMS I **CAN'T** LIGHT ANY MORE **BEACONS.** HE AND I TRIED, BUT IT DIDN'T HAPPEN.
THAT'S BECAUSE YOU **DON'T** LIGHT THE **BLUE** BEACON NEXT.
I'VE **DECRYPTED** MY UNCLE JEP'S ARCHIVE.
WHAT?

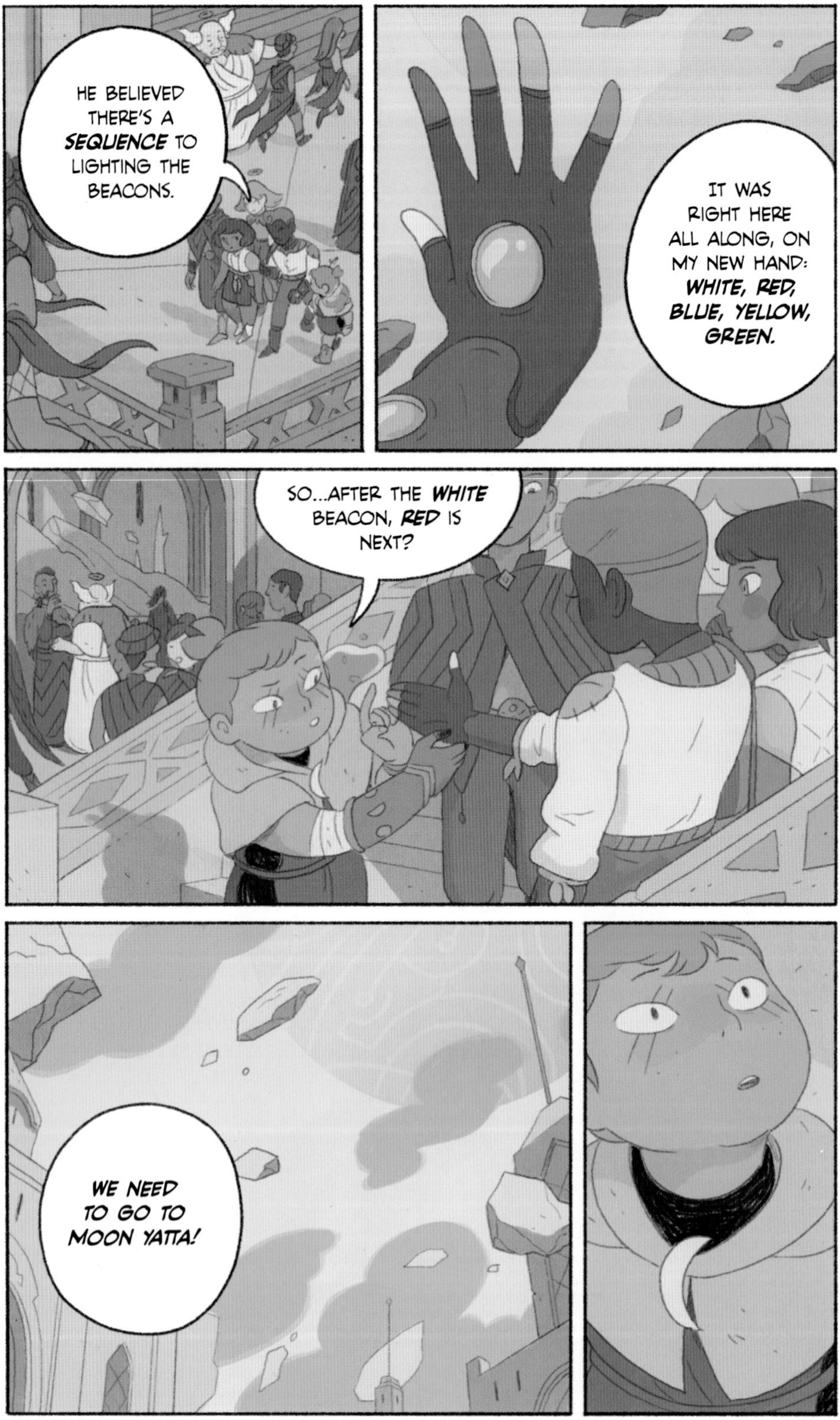
HE BELIEVED THERE'S A SEQUENCE TO LIGHTING THE BEACONS.
IT WAS RIGHT HERE ALL ALONG, ON MY NEW HAND: WHITE, RED, BLUE, YELLOW, GREEN.
SO...AFTER THE WHITE BEACON, RED IS NEXT?
WE NEED TO GO TO MOON YATTA!

THE THREE CAPTAINS OF THE *FLITORI* WILL BE GLAD TO SEE YOU AGAIN!

OFF YOU GO, THEN, *LIGHTER OF BEACONS!*

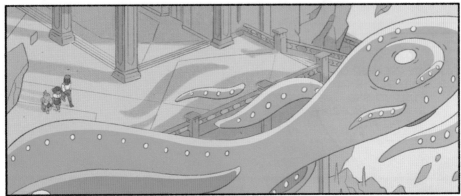

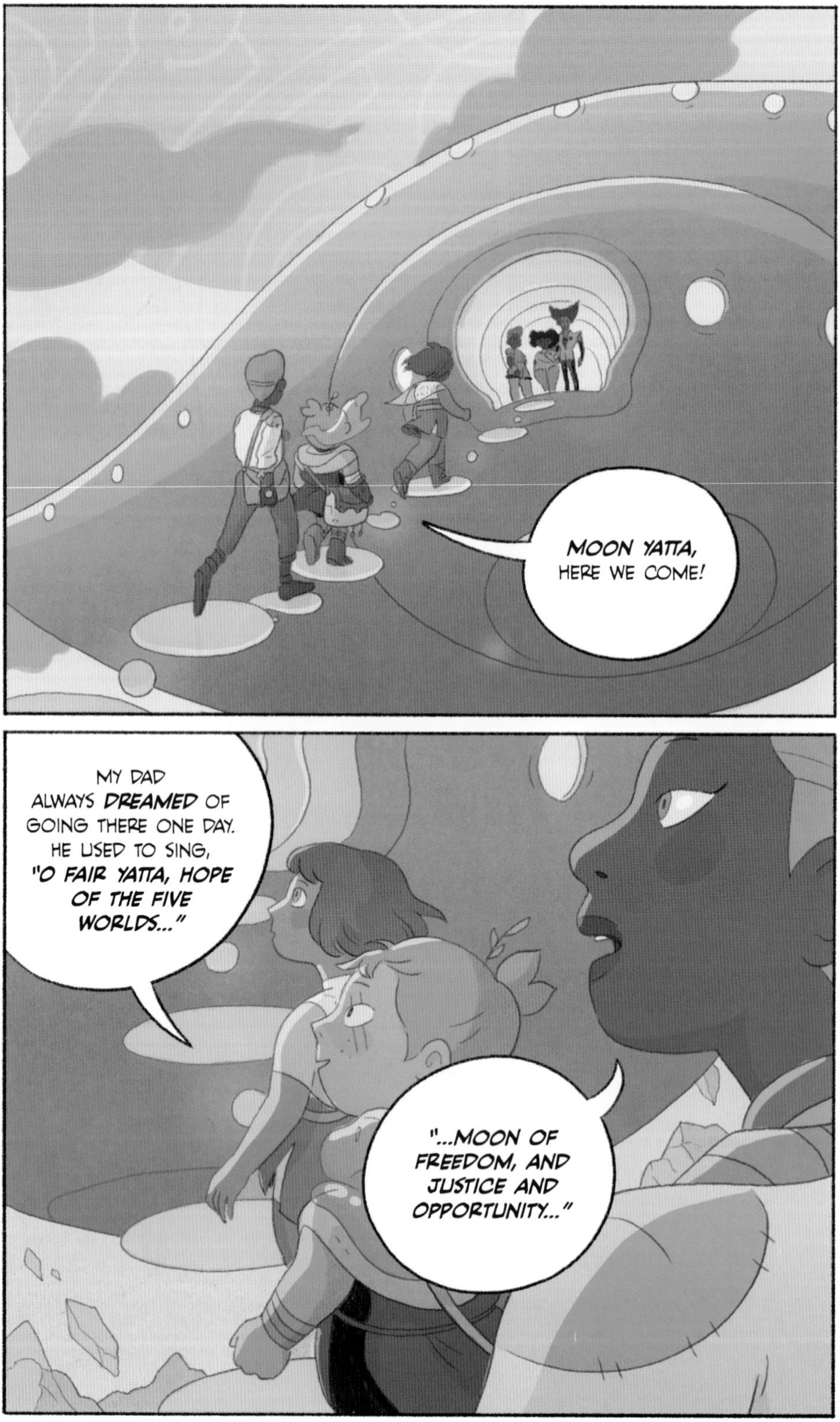
MOON YATTA, HERE WE COME!
MY DAD ALWAYS DREAMED OF GOING THERE ONE DAY. HE USED TO SING, "O FAIR YATTA, HOPE OF THE FIVE WORLDS..."
"...MOON OF FREEDOM, AND JUSTICE AND OPPORTUNITY..."

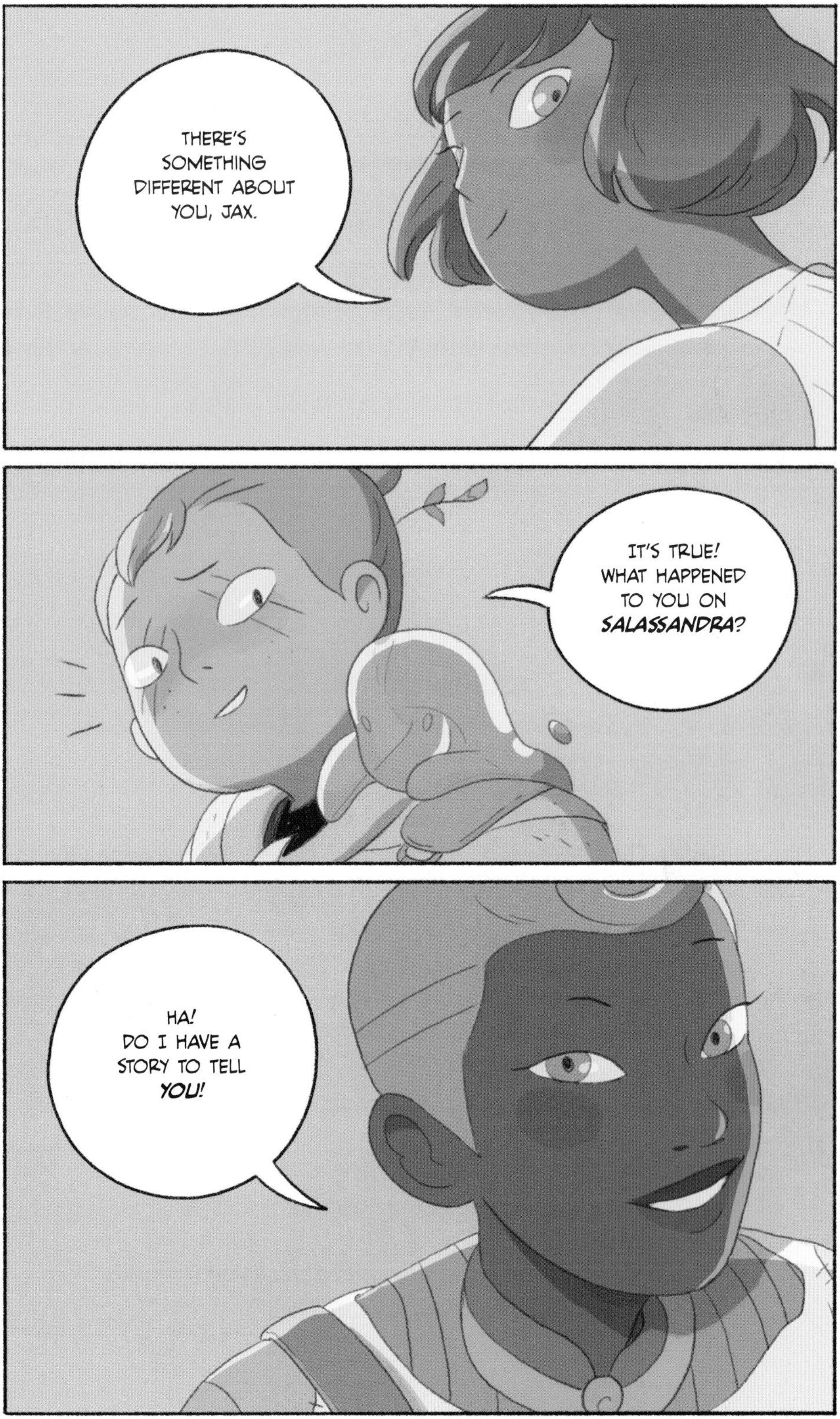
THERE'S SOMETHING DIFFERENT ABOUT YOU, JAX.
IT'S TRUE! WHAT HAPPENED TO YOU ON *SALASSANDRA*?
HA! DO I HAVE A STORY TO TELL *YOU!*

TO BE CONTINUED IN 5W3: ***THE RED MAZE***

To Milo—MS

To Harvey and Milo—AS

To Adeetje—XB

To Gram—MR

To the Macfarlane family—BS

ACKNOWLEDGMENTS

Tanya McKinnon, always

Our amazing Random House team:
Michelle Nagler, Chelsea Eberly, Elizabeth Tardiff, Kelly McGauley, Aisha Cloud,
Joshua Redlich, Kim Lauber, Alison Kolani, Dominique Cimina, Lisa Nadel,
Adrienne Waintraub, Laura Antonacci, John Adamo, Jocelyn Lange, Joe English,
Mallory Loehr, Barbara Marcus

+ Special thanks for added help, friendship & magic:
Siena Siegel, Sonia Siegel, Shudan Yeh, Felix Siegel, Julien & Clio Siegel,
Julie Sandfort, Viviana Simon, Hilde McKinnon, Sam Dutter, Cynthia Cheng

And Lisa Yee, Kazu Kibuishi, Noelle Stevenson, Gene Luen Yang,
Vera Brosgol, Lee Wade, Sam Bosma, Kali Ciesemier

And for lighting the way to beloved new worlds:
Ursula K. LeGuin, Hayao Miyazaki, Neil Gaiman

Copyright © 2018 by Antzu Pantzu, LLC

All rights reserved. Published in the United States by Random House Children's Books,
a division of Penguin Random House LLC, New York.

Random House and the colophon are registered trademarks of
Penguin Random House LLC.

Visit us on the Web! rhcbooks.com

Educators and librarians, for a variety of teaching tools, visit us at RHTeachersLibrarians.com

Library of Congress Cataloging-in-Publication Data
Names: Siegel, Mark, 1967– , author. | Siegel, Alexis, author. | Bouma, Xanthe, illustrator. |
Rockefeller, Matt, illustrator. | Sun, Boya, illustrator.
Title: The cobalt prince / Mark Siegel, Alexis Siegel ;
illustrated by Xanthe Bouma, Matt Rockefeller, and Boya Sun.
Description: First edition. | New York : Random House, [2018] | Series: 5 worlds ; book 2 |
Summary: Sisters Jessa and Oona, and new friend Ram Sam Sam, try to stop the Cobalt Prince
from Toki, who orders a strike on Mon Domani, starting a new worlds war.
Identifiers: LCCN 2017026243 | ISBN 978-1-101-93589-7 (hardcover) | ISBN 978-1-101-93591-0 (pbk.) |
ISBN 978-1-101-93605-4 (ebook) | ISBN 978-1-101-93590-3 (lib. bdg.)
Subjects: LCSH: Graphic novels. | CYAC: Graphic novels. | Heroes—Fiction. | Adventure and adventurers—
Fiction. | Science fiction.
Classification: LCC PZ7.7.S4825 Cob 2018 | DDC 741.5/973—dc23

MANUFACTURED IN CHINA

10 9 8 7 6 5 4 3 2 1

First Edition

Where has Jax been? What adventures are in store? Find out in

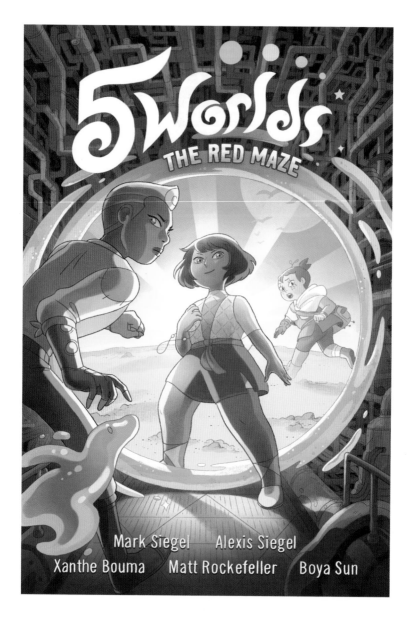

5Worlds
THE RED MAZE

Mark Siegel   Alexis Siegel

Xanthe Bouma   Matt Rockefeller   Boya Sun

5W3:
THE RED MAZE

MARK SIEGEL has written and illustrated several award-winning picture books and graphic novels, including the *New York Times* bestseller **Sailor Twain** and **Oskar and the Eight Blessings.** He is also the editorial and creative director of First Second Books. He lives with his family in New York.

ALEXIS SIEGEL is a writer and translator based in Switzerland. He has translated a number of bestselling graphic novels, including Joann Sfar's **The Rabbi's Cat** and Pénélope Bagieu's **Exquisite Corpse** into English and Gene Luen Yang's **American Born Chinese** into French.

XANTHE BOUMA is an illustrator based in Southern California. When not working on picture books such as **Little Sid,** fashion illustration, and comics, Xanthe enjoys soaking up the beachside sun.

MATT ROCKEFELLER is an illustrator and comic artist from Tucson, Arizona. His work has appeared in a variety of formats, including book covers, animation, and picture books such as **Train, Rocket,** and **Pop!** He also illustrates the middle-grade series **The Explorers.**

BOYA SUN is an illustrator and coauthor of the graphic novel **Chasma Knights.** Originally from China, Boya has traveled from Canada to the United States and now lives in Northern California.

A Sneak Peek at the Making of 5W2

Character Development

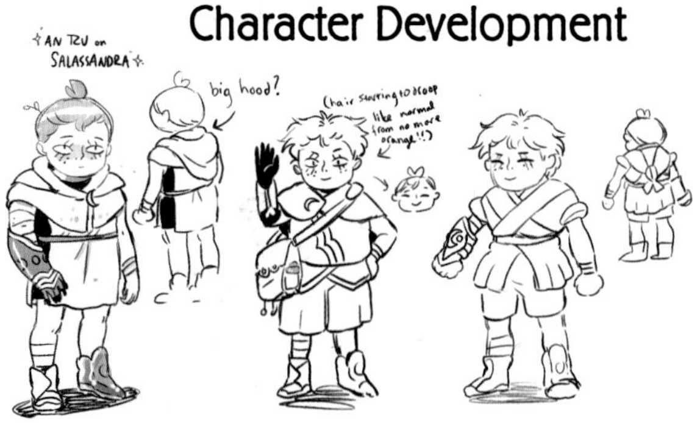
AN TZU on SALASSANDRA
big hood?
(hair starting to droop like normal from no more orange!!)
An Tzu (Xanthe)

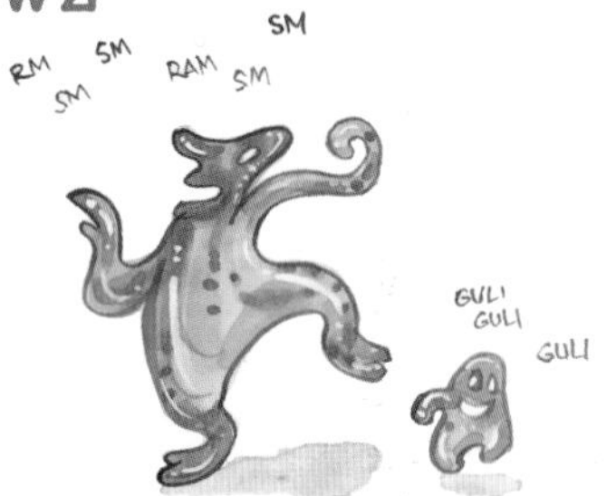
RAM SM SM RAM SM SM
GULI GULI GULI
Early Ram Sam Sam (Mark)

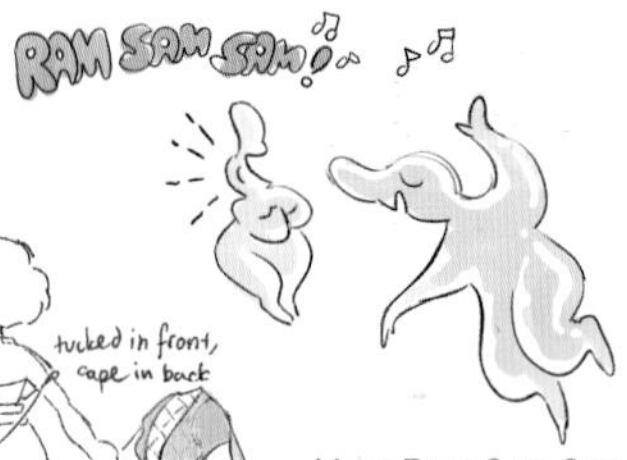
RAM SAM SAM!
More Ram Sam Sam (Xanthe)

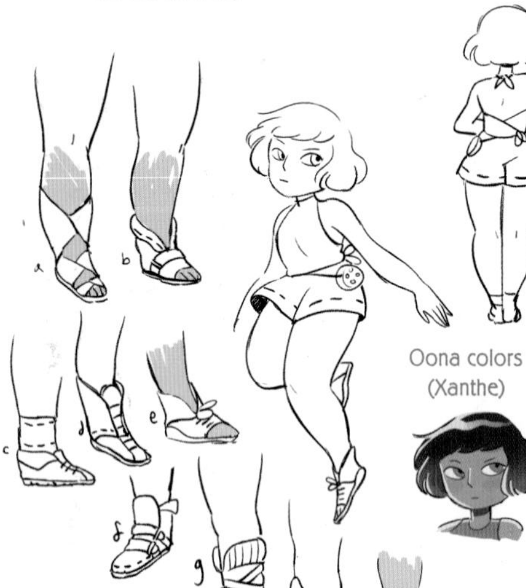
a
b
c
d
e
f
g
h
i

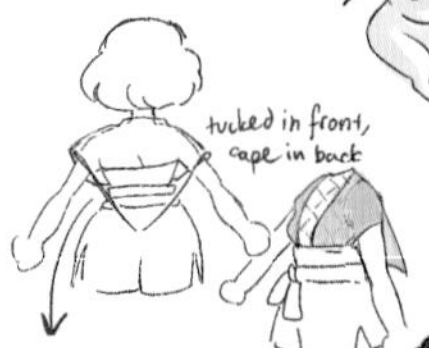
tucked in front, cape in back

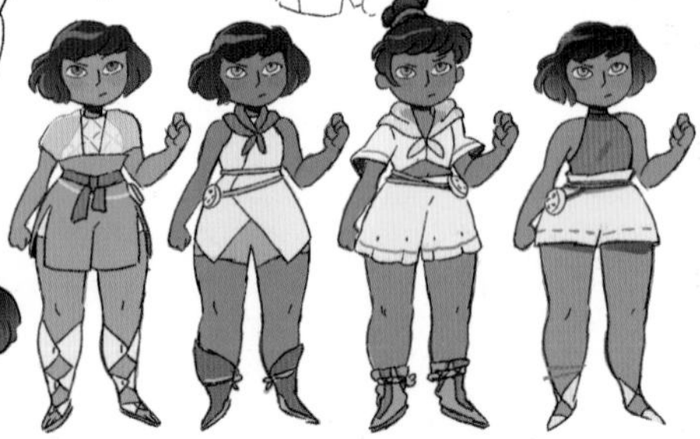
Oona colors (Xanthe)

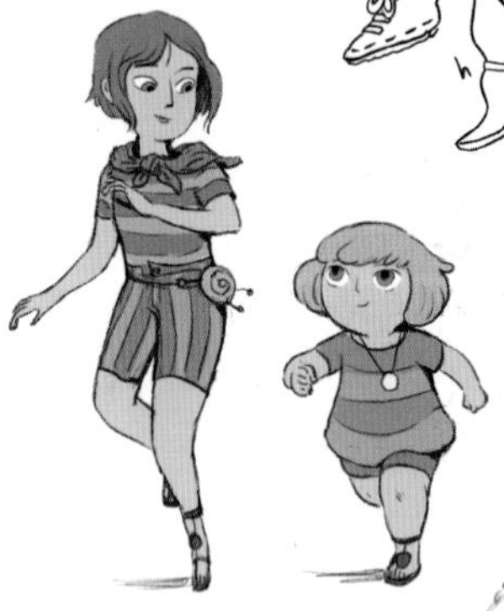
Young Jessa and Oona (Boya)

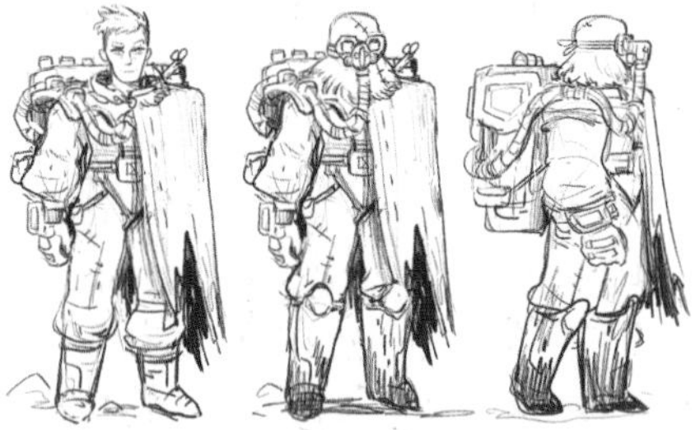
Magda Gadek (Matt)

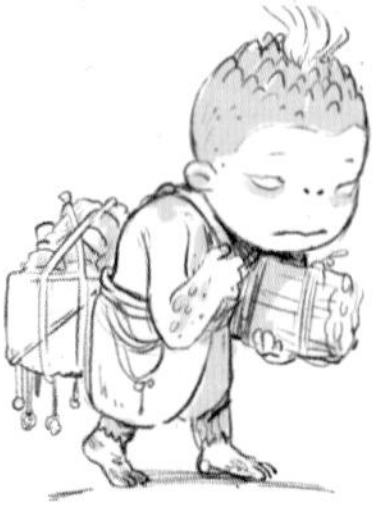
Giant Chibi (Matt)

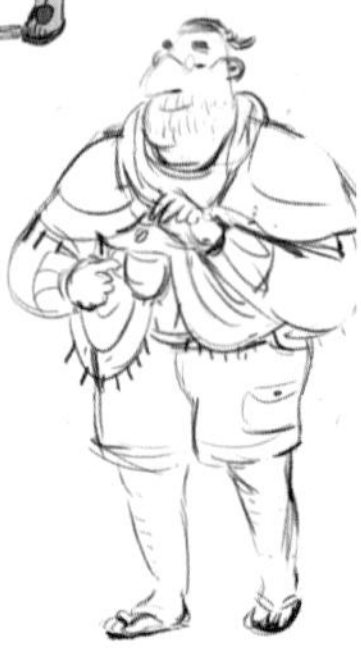
O'Zirg (Boya)

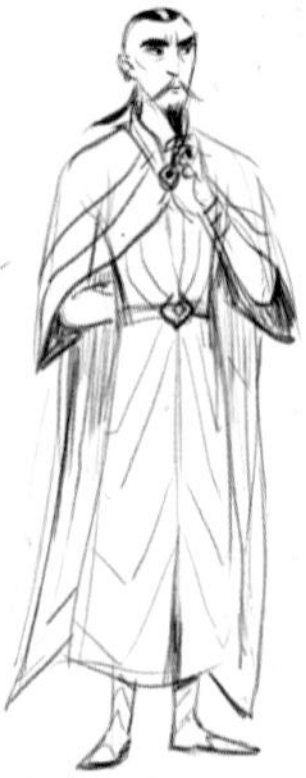
Master Elon (Boya)

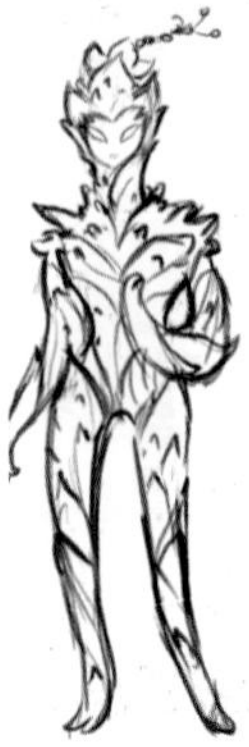
Thorn (Boya)

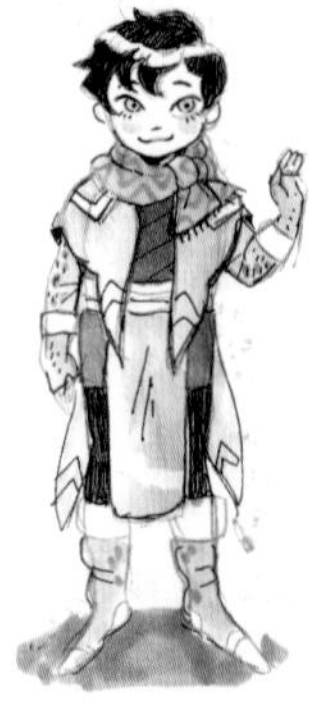
Prince before Mimic (Xanthe)

World Building

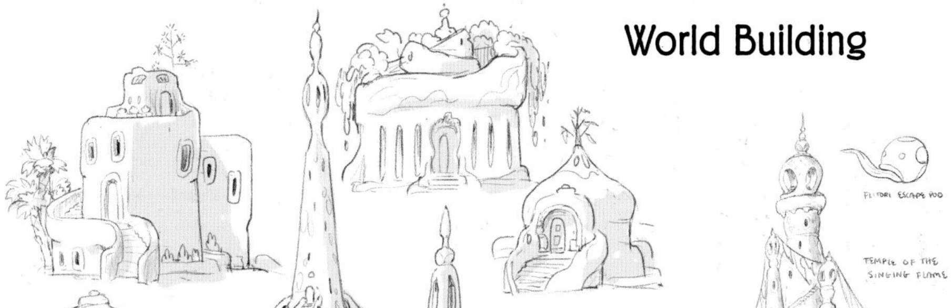
FLITORI ESCAPE POD
TEMPLE OF THE SINGING FLAME

Salassandra studies (Matt)

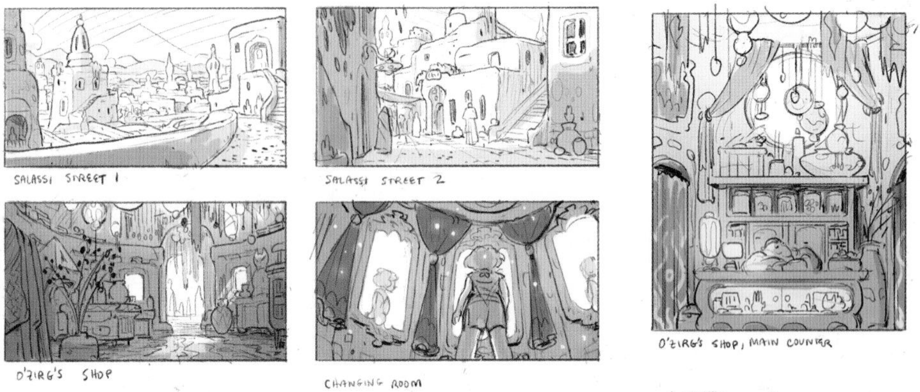
SALASSI STREET 1
SALASSI STREET 2
O'ZIRG'S SHOP, MAIN COUNTER
O'ZIRG'S SHOP
CHANGING ROOM

Toki studies (Matt)

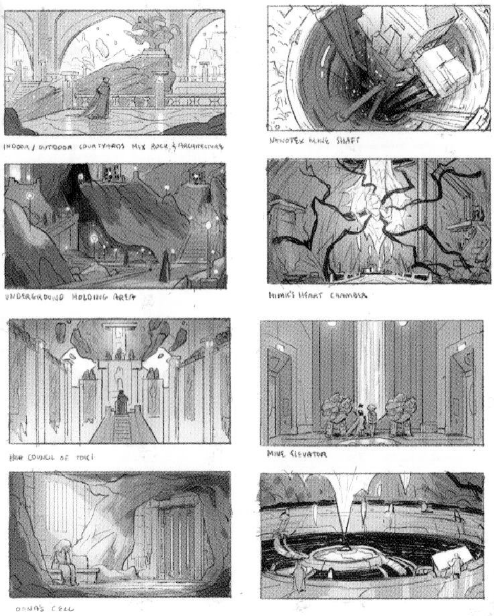
INDOOR / OUTDOOR COURTYARDS MIX ROCK & ARCHITECTURE
NANOTEX MINE SHAFT
UNDERGROUND HOLDING AREA
NIMA'S HEART CHAMBER
HIGH COUNCIL OF TOKI
MINE ELEVATOR
OONA'S CELL

Mapping out the battle of Atbal-Balak (Matt)

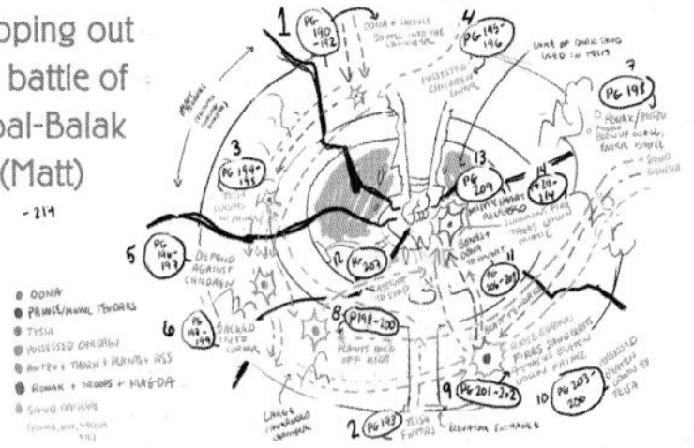

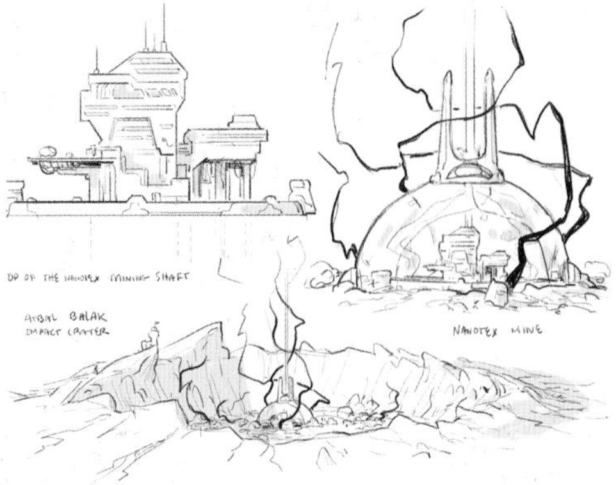
TOP OF THE NANOTEX MINING SHAFT
ATBAL BALAK IMPACT CRATER
NANOTEX MINE

...and many sketchbooks more!

Discover more 5W online!

@5WorldsTeam

POST YOUR **COSPLAY** PHOTOS
AND SHARE YOUR BEST **FAN ART**
WITH OTHER 5-WORLDERS!

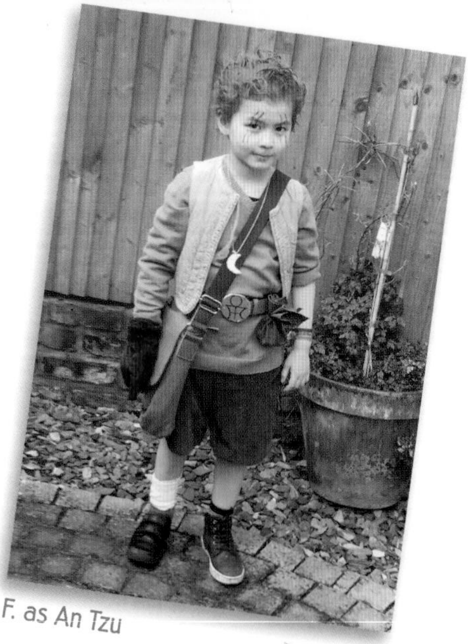

F. as An Tzu

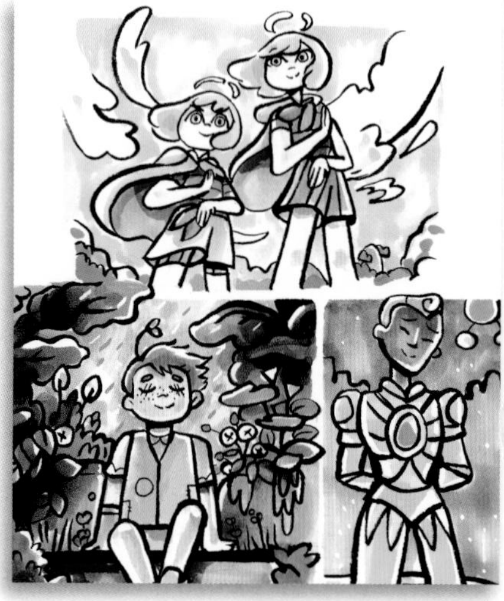

Olivia Huynh

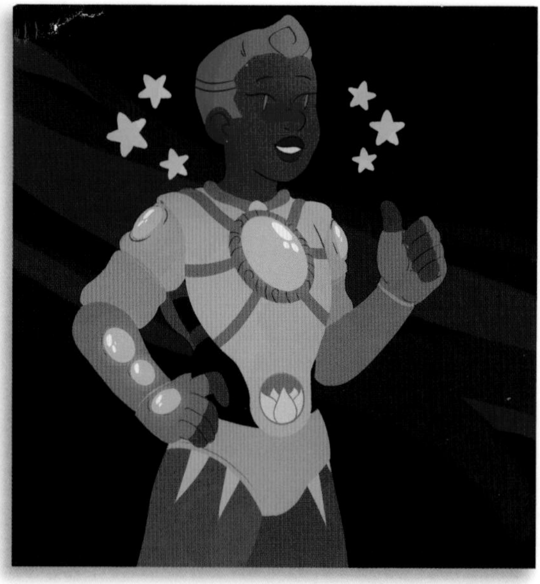

Summer Ramos

AND STAY TUNED
FOR CONTESTS
AND SPECIAL EVENTS
ON A PLANET NEAR YOU!

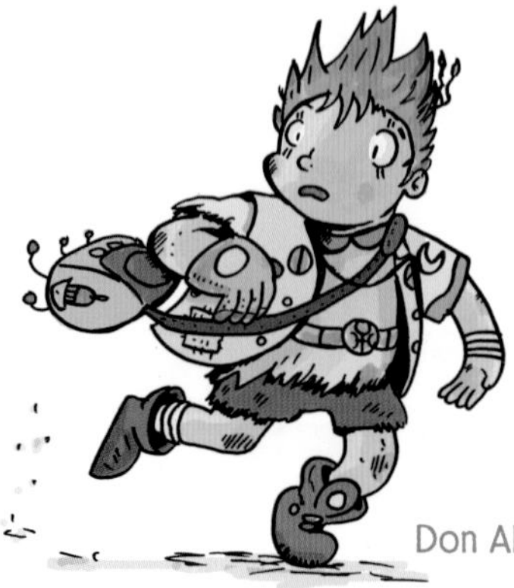

Don Ahé

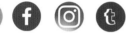

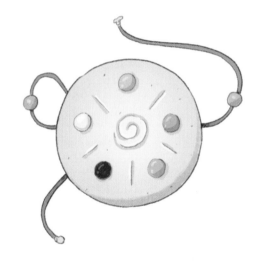

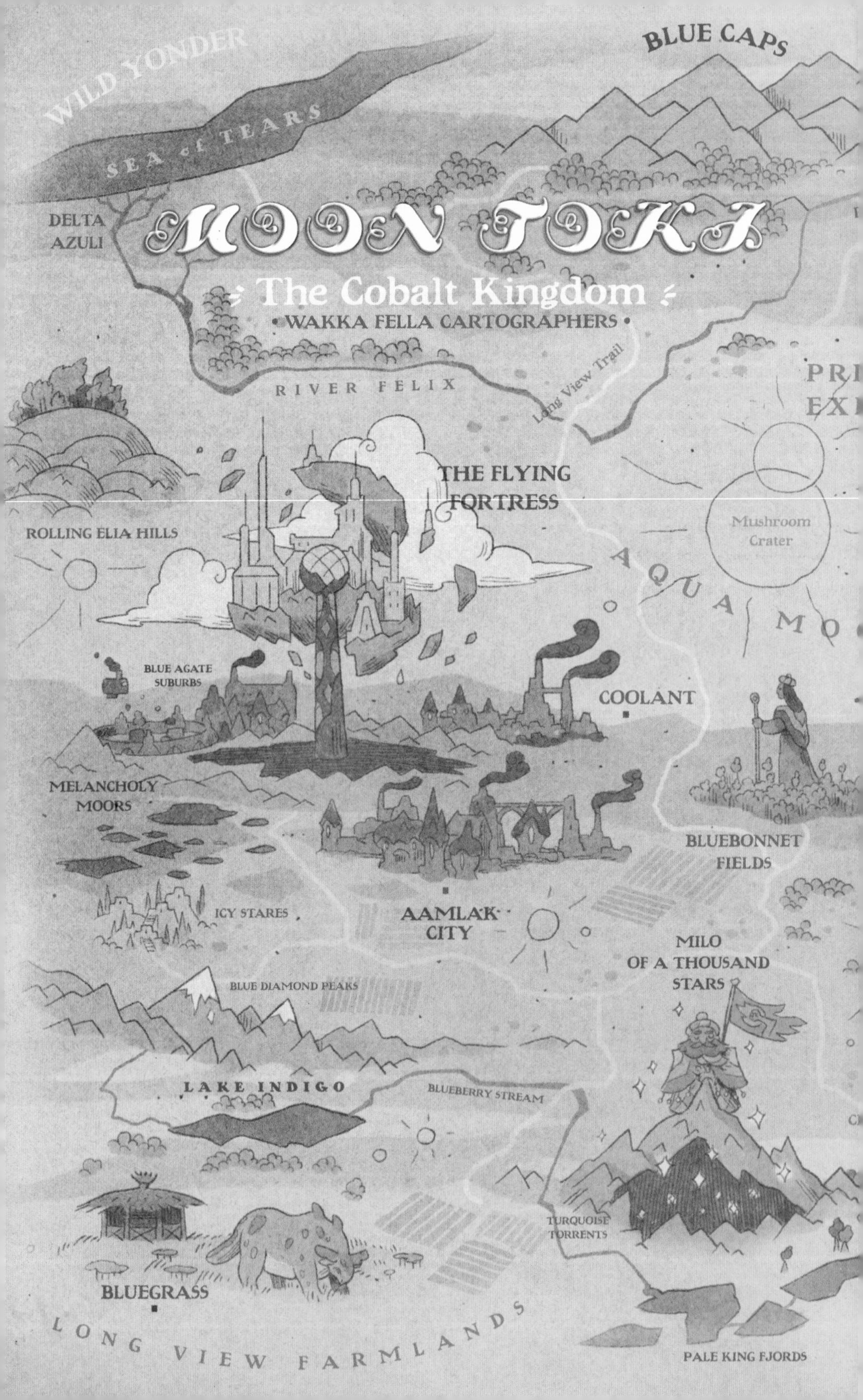
MOON TOKI
The Cobalt Kingdom
• WAKKA FELLA CARTOGRAPHERS •
WILD YONDER
SEA of TEARS
BLUE CAPS
DELTA
AZULI
RIVER FELIX
Long View Trail
THE FLYING
FORTRESS
Mushroom
Crater
ROLLING ELIA HILLS
AQUA MO
BLUE AGATE
SUBURBS
COOLANT
MELANCHOLY
MOORS
BLUEBONNET
FIELDS
ICY STARES
AAMLAK
CITY
MILO
OF A THOUSAND
STARS
BLUE DIAMOND PEAKS
LAKE INDIGO
BLUEBERRY STREAM
TURQUOISE
TORRENTS
BLUEGRASS
LONG VIEW FARMLANDS
PALE KING FJORDS